The
MX Book
of
New
Sherlock
Holmes
Stories

Part XLIV
2024 Annual
(1889-1897)

THE MX BOOK OF NEW SHERLOCK HOLMES STORIES

PART XLIV
2024 ANNUAL
(1889-1897)

SOUTHAMPTON STREET

359

EDITED
By
David
Marcum

OFFICES

TRADITIONAL HOLMES
ADVENTURES
COMPILED FOR THE
BENEFIT OF THE
RESTORATION OF
UNDERSHAW

ISBN Hardback 978-1-80424-482-1
ISBN Paperback 978-1-80424-483-8
AUK ePub ISBN 978-1-80424-484-5
AUK PDF ISBN 978-1-80424-485-2

Published in the UK by
MX Publishing
335 Princess Park Manor, Royal Drive,
London, N11 3GX
www.mxpublishing.co.uk

David Marcum can be reached at:
thepapersofsherlockholmes@gmail.com

Cover design by Brian Belanger
www.belangerbooks.com and *www.redbubble.com/people/zhahadun*

Internal Illustrations by Sidney Paget

CONTENTS

Forewords

Editor's Foreword: *"A fake, is it? Well, strike me!"*   1
     by David Marcum

Foreword   9
     by Daniel Stashower

A Letter From Scotland Yard   11
     by Roger Johnson

An Ongoing Legacy for Sherlock Holmes   15
     by Steve Emecz

A Word from Undershaw   17
     by Emma West

Moriarty (*A Poem*)   33
     by Kevin Patrick McCann

Adventures

The Disputed Debutante   35
     by I.A. Watson

The Deaths on the Edge of Standish Woods   69
     by Stephen Herczeg

The Disappeared Doctor   86
     by Paula Hammond

The Adventure of Heirloom Necklace   99
     by Tracy J. Revels

(Continued on the next page . . .)

The Case of the Ignoble Cuckold 117
    by Tom Turley

The Midsummer Murders 144
    by Paul A. Freeman

The Adventure of the Absentee Officer 162
    by Daniel Lenois

A Bucket's Worth of Help 176
    by David Marcum

Magic Squares 201
    by Marcia Wilson

The Adventure of the Moving Pictures 228
    by Shane Simmons

Death of a Mudlark 244
    by David MacGregor

The Adventure of the Serpent's Head 260
    by Arthur Hall

The Adventure of the Aged Actor 287
    by Tracy J. Revels

The Stratford Street Lodgers 303
    by Naching T. Kassa

The Other Woman 318
    by Susan Knight

The Adventure of the Surrey Revenant 340
    by Alan Dimes

(Continued on the next page . . .)

A Generous Helping of Deceit   355
    by DJ Tyrer

Hollingbourne Grange   370
    by Mike Chinn

The Professor's Assistant   389
    by Chris Chan

The Mysterious Death of the Russian Anarchist   407
    by Jonathan Schneer

A Matter of ABC   420
    by Susan Knight

The Taverne Emerald   450
    by Alan Dimes

About the Contributors   467

These additional adventures are contained in
Part XLIII: 2024 Annual
(1874-1888)

Devil's Milk – Marcia Wilson
The Mystery of the Extraneous Cadaver – Mike Adamson
The Adventure of the Doubtful Conviction – Arthur Hall
The Case at the Turkish Bath – Brenda Seabrooke
The Silent Prisoner – Ember Pepper
The Predilections of a Pious Poisoner – Mike Adamson
The Devil's Snare – Paula Hammond
Umbrella Trouble – Robert Stapleton
The Adventure of the Siren's Tower – Tracy J. Revels
Lightning Strikes Once – Kevin P. Thornton
The Missing Calabash – P.C. Shumway
The Burning Heart – MJH Simmonds
The Curious Case of the Transmuting Tome – Daniel Lenois
The Adventure of the Restless Knight – Will Murray
The Six-Thirteen from Fairfield Junction – Denis O. Smith
The Most Terrible Murderer – Alan Dimes
Boxing Day, Brother Mine – Gretchen Altabef
The Case of Colonel Warburton's Madness – Jane Rubino
The Exploited Assassins – David Marcum
The Case of the Missing Docker – Jonathan Schneer

Part XLV: 2024 Annual
(1898-1917)

The Adventure of the Awakened Mummy – Tracy J. Revels
The Adventure of the Unknown Traitor – Arthur Hall
The Yorkshire Chieftain – Robert Stapleton
The Little White Lie – Jeffrey A. Lockwood
The Riddle of Parsons Lodge – Mark Mower
The Arthritic Beneficiary – Dan Rowley and Don Baxter

(Continued on the next page . . . .)

The Bell-Ringer's Requiem – Daniel Lenois
The Gemini Pearl Necklace – Roger Riccard
The Conk-Singleton Forgery – Alan Dimes
The Case of the Misbegotten Missives – Daniel D. Victor
The Missing Mathematical Timber – Ian Ableson
The Adventure of the Elfrincham Maze – Alan Dimes
The Bewildering Bicycle Business – Craig Stephen Copland
Death at the Diogenes Club – Tim Newton Anderson
Gruner's Diary – David Marcum
The Tsushima Legacy – Mike Adamson
The Problem of the Locked Room – Daniel D. Victor
The Beast of Birling Gap – Paul Hiscock
The Worker – Marcia Wilson
The Lambeth Twin – Martin Daley
"Now Comes the Mystery – Brett Fawcett

These additional Sherlock Holmes adventures
can be found in the previous volumes of
The MX Book of New Sherlock Holmes Stories

PART I: 1881-1889
Foreword – Leslie S. Klinger
Foreword – Roger Johnson
Foreword – David Marcum
Sherlock Holmes of London (A Verse in Four Fits) – Michael Kurland
The Adventure of the Slipshod Charlady – John Hall
The Case of the Lichfield Murder – Hugh Ashton
The Kingdom of the Blind – Adrian Middleton
The Adventure of the Pawnbroker's Daughter – David Marcum
The Adventure of the Defenestrated Princess – Jayantika Ganguly
The Adventure of the Inn on the Marsh – Denis O. Smith
The Adventure of the Traveling Orchestra – Amy Thomas
The Haunting of Sherlock Holmes – Kevin David Barratt
Sherlock Holmes and the Allegro Mystery – Luke Benjamen Kuhns
The Deadly Soldier – Summer Perkins
The Case of the Vanishing Stars – Deanna Baran
The Song of the Mudlark – Shane Simmons
The Tale of the Forty Thieves – C.H. Dye
The Strange Missive of Germaine Wilkes – Mark Mower
The Case of the Vanished Killer – Derrick Belanger
The Adventure of the Aspen Papers – Daniel D. Victor
The Ululation of Wolves – Steve Mountain
The Case of the Vanishing Inn – Stephen Wade
The King of Diamonds – John Heywood
The Adventure of Urquhart Manse – Will Thomas
The Adventure of the Seventh Stain – Daniel McGachey
The Two Umbrellas – Martin Rosenstock
The Adventure of the Fateful Malady – Craig Janacek

PART II: 1890-1895
Foreword – Catherine Cooke
Foreword – Roger Johnson
Foreword – David Marcum
The Bachelor of Baker Street Muses on Irene Adler (A Poem) – Carole Nelson Douglas
The Affair of Miss Finney – Ann Margaret Lewis
The Adventure of the Bookshop Owner – Vincent W. Wright
The Case of the Unrepentant Husband – William Patrick Maynard
The Verse of Death – Matthew Booth
Lord Garnett's Skulls – J.R. Campbell
Larceny in the Sky with Diamonds – Robert V. Stapleton
The Glennon Falls – Sam Wiebe
The Adventure of *The Sleeping Cardinal* – Jeremy Branton Holstein

(Continued on the next page . . . .)

The Case of the Anarchist's Bomb – Bill Crider
The Riddle of the Rideau Rifles – Peter Calamai
The Adventure of the Willow Basket – Lyndsay Faye
The Onion Vendor's Secret – Marcia Wilson
The Adventure of the Murderous Numismatist – Jack Grochot
The Saviour of Cripplegate Square – Bert Coules
A Study in Abstruse Detail – Wendy C. Fries
The Adventure of the St. Nicholas the Elephant – Christopher Redmond
The Lady on the Bridge – Mike Hogan
The Adventure of the Poison Tea Epidemic – Carl L. Heifetz
The Man on Westminster Bridge – Dick Gillman

PART III: 1896-1929
Foreword – David Stuart Davies
Foreword – Roger Johnson
Foreword – David Marcum
Two Sonnets (Poems) – Bonnie MacBird
Harbinger of Death – Geri Schear
The Adventure of the Regular Passenger – Paul D. Gilbert
The Perfect Spy – Stuart Douglas
A Mistress – Missing – Lyn McConchie
Two Plus Two – Phil Growick
The Adventure of the Coptic Patriarch – Séamus Duffy
The Royal Arsenal Affair – Leslie F.E. Coombs
The Adventure of the Sunken Parsley – Mark Alberstat
The Strange Case of the Violin Savant – GC Rosenquist
The Hopkins Brothers Affair – Iain McLaughlin and Claire Bartlett
The Disembodied Assassin – Andrew Lane
The Adventure of the Dark Tower – Peter K. Andersson
The Adventure of the Reluctant Corpse – Matthew J. Elliott
The Inspector of Graves – Jim French
The Adventure of the Parson's Son – Bob Byrne
The Adventure of the Botanist's Glove – James Lovegrove
A Most Diabolical Plot – Tim Symonds
The Opera Thief – Larry Millett
Blood Brothers – Kim Krisco
The Adventure of *The White Bird* – C. Edward Davis
The Adventure of the Avaricious Bookkeeper – Joel and Carolyn Senter

PART IV – 2016 Annual
Foreword – Steven Rothman
Foreword – Richard Doyle
Foreword – Roger Johnson
Foreword – Melissa Farnham
Foreword – Steve Emecz
Foreword – David Marcum
Toast to Mrs. Hudson (A Poem) – Arlene Mantin Levy
The Tale of the First Adventure – Derrick Belanger

(Continued on the next page . . . .)

The Adventure of the Turkish Cipher – Deanna Baran
The Adventure of the Missing Necklace – Daniel D. Victor
The Case of the Rondel Dagger – Mark Mower
The Adventure of the Double-Edged Hoard – Craig Janacek
The Adventure of the Impossible Murders – Jayantika Ganguly
The Watcher in the Woods – Denis O. Smith
The Wargrave Resurrection – Matthew Booth
Relating To One of My Old Cases – J.R. Campbell
The Adventure at the Beau Soleil – Bonnie MacBird
The Adventure of the Phantom Coachman – Arthur Hall
The Adventure of the Arsenic Dumplings – Bob Byrne
The Disappearing Anarchist Trick – Andrew Lane
The Adventure of the Grace Chalice – Roger Johnson
The Adventure of John Vincent Harden – Hugh Ashton
Murder at Tragere House – David Stuart Davies
The Adventure of *The Green Lady* – Vincent W. Wright
The Adventure of the Fellow Traveller – Daniel McGachey
The Adventure of the Highgate Financier – Nicholas Utechin
A Game of Illusion – Jeremy Holstein
The London Wheel – David Marcum
The Adventure of the Half-Melted Wolf – Marcia Wilson

PART V – Christmas Adventures

Foreword – Jonathan Kellerman
Foreword – Roger Johnson
Foreword – David Marcum
The Ballad of the Carbuncle (A Poem) – Ashley D. Polasek
The Case of the Ruby Necklace – Bob Byrne
The Jet Brooch – Denis O. Smith
The Adventure of the Missing Irregular – Amy Thomas
The Adventure of the Knighted Watchmaker – Derrick Belanger
The Stolen Relic – David Marcum
A Christmas Goose – C.H. Dye
The Adventure of the Long-Lost Enemy – Marcia Wilson
The Queen's Writing Table – Julie McKuras
The Blue Carbuncle – Sir Arthur Conan Doyle (Dramatised by Bert Coules)
The Case of the Christmas Cracker – John Hall
The Man Who Believed in Nothing – Jim French
The Case of the Christmas Star – S.F. Bennett
The Christmas Card Mystery – Narrelle M. Harris
The Question of the Death Bed Conversion – William Patrick Maynard
The Adventure of the Christmas Surprise – Vincent W. Wright
A Bauble in Scandinavia – James Lovegrove
The Adventure of Marcus Davery – Arthur Hall
The Adventure of the Purple Poet – Nicholas Utechin

(Continued on the next page . . . .)

The Adventure of the Vanishing Man – Mike Chinn
The Adventure of the Empty Manger – Tracy J. Revels
A Perpetrator in a Pear Tree – Roger Riccard
The Case of the Christmas Trifle – Wendy C. Fries
The Adventure of the Christmas Stocking – Paul D. Gilbert
The Adventure of the Golden Hunter – Jan Edwards
The Curious Case of the Well-Connected Criminal – Molly Carr
The Case of the Reformed Sinner – S. Subramanian
The Adventure of the Improbable Intruder – Peter K. Andersson
The Adventure of the Handsome Ogre – Matthew J. Elliott
The Adventure of the Deceased Doctor – Hugh Ashton
The Mile End Mynah Bird – Mark Mower

PART VI – 2017 Annual

Foreword – Colin Jeavons
Foreword – Nicholas Utechin
Foreword – Roger Johnson
Foreword – David Marcum
Sweet Violin (A Poem) – Bonnie MacBird
The Adventure of the Murdered Spinster – Bob Byrne
The Irregular – Julie McKuras
The Coffee Trader's Dilemma – Derrick Belanger
The Two Patricks – Robert Perret
The Adventure at St. Catherine's – Deanna Baran
The Adventure of a Thousand Stings – GC Rosenquist
The Adventure of the Returned Captain – Hugh Ashton
The Adventure of the Wonderful Toy – David Timson
The Adventure of the Cat's Claws – Shane Simmons
The Grave Message – Stephen Wade
The Radicant Munificent Society – Mark Mower
The Adventure of the Apologetic Assassin – David Friend
The Adventure of the Traveling Corpse – Nick Cardillo
The Adventure of the Apothecary's Prescription – Roger Riccard
The Case of the Bereaved Author – S. Subramanian
The Tetanus Epidemic – Carl L. Heifetz
The Bubble Reputation – Geri Schear
The Case of the Vanishing Venus – S.F. Bennett
The Adventure of the Vanishing Apprentice – Jennifer Copping
The Adventure of the Apothecary Shop – Jim French
The Case of the Plummeting Painter – Carla Coupe
The Case of the Temperamental Terrier – Narrelle M. Harris
The Adventure of the Frightened Architect – Arthur Hall
The Adventure of the Sunken Indiaman – Craig Janacek
The Exorcism of the Haunted Stick – Marcia Wilson
The Adventure of the Queen's Teardrop – Tracy Revels
The Curious Case of the Charwoman's Brooch – Molly Carr

(Continued on the next page . . . .)

The Unwelcome Client – Keith Hann
The Tempest of Lyme – David Ruffle
The Problem of the Holy Oil – David Marcum
A Scandal in Serbia – Thomas A. Turley
The Curious Case of Mr. Marconi – Jan Edwards
Mr. Holmes and Dr. Watson Learn to Fly – C. Edward Davis
Die Weisse Frau – Tim Symonds
A Case of Mistaken Identity – Daniel D. Victor

PART VII – Eliminate the Impossible: 1880-1891

Foreword – Lee Child
Foreword – Rand B. Lee
Foreword – Michael Cox
Foreword – Roger Johnson
Foreword – Melissa Farnham
Foreword – David Marcum
No Ghosts Need Apply (A Poem) – Jacquelynn Morris
The Melancholy Methodist – Mark Mower
The Curious Case of the Sweated Horse – Jan Edwards
The Adventure of the Second William Wilson – Daniel D. Victor
The Adventure of the Marchindale Stiletto – James Lovegrove
The Case of the Cursed Clock – Gayle Lange Puhl
The Tranquility of the Morning – Mike Hogan
A Ghost from Christmas Past – Thomas A. Turley
The Blank Photograph – James Moffett
The Adventure of A Rat. – Adrian Middleton
The Adventure of Vanaprastha – Hugh Ashton
The Ghost of Lincoln – Geri Schear
The Manor House Ghost – S. Subramanian
The Case of the Unquiet Grave – John Hall
The Adventure of the Mortal Combat – Jayantika Ganguly
The Last Encore of Quentin Carol – S.F. Bennett
The Case of the Petty Curses – Steven Philip Jones
The Tuttman Gallery – Jim French
The Second Life of Jabez Salt – John Linwood Grant
The Mystery of the Scarab Earrings – Thomas Fortenberry
The Adventure of the Haunted Room – Mike Chinn
The Pharaoh's Curse – Robert V. Stapleton
The Vampire of the Lyceum – Charles Veley and Anna Elliott
The Adventure of the Mind's Eye – Shane Simmons

PART VIII – Eliminate the Impossible: 1892-1905

Foreword – Lee Child
Foreword – Rand B. Lee
Foreword – Michael Cox
Foreword – Roger Johnson
Foreword – Melissa Farnham

(Continued on the next page . . . .)

Foreword – David Marcum
Sherlock Holmes in the Lavender field (A Poem) – Christopher James
The Adventure of the Lama's Dream – Deanna Baran
The Ghost of Dorset House – Tim Symonds
The Peculiar Persecution of John Vincent Harden – Sandor Jay Sonnen
The Case of the Biblical Colours – Ben Cardall
The Inexplicable Death of Matthew Arnatt – Andrew Lane
The Adventure of the Highgate Spectre – Michael Mallory
The Case of the Corpse Flower – Wendy C. Fries
The Problem of the Five Razors – Aaron Smith
The Adventure of the Moonlit Shadow – Arthur Hall
The Ghost of Otis Maunder – David Friend
The Adventure of the Pharaoh's Tablet – Robert Perret
The Haunting of Hamilton Gardens – Nick Cardillo
The Adventure of the Risen Corpse – Paul D. Gilbert
The Mysterious Mourner – Cindy Dye
The Adventure of the Hungry Ghost – Tracy Revels
In the Realm of the Wretched King – Derrick Belanger
The Case of the Little Washerwoman – William Meikle
The Catacomb Saint Affair – Marcia Wilson
The Curious Case of Charlotte Musgrave – Roger Riccard
The Adventure of the Awakened Spirit – Craig Janacek
The Adventure of the Theatre Ghost – Jeremy Branton Holstein
The Adventure of the Glassy Ghost – Will Murray
The Affair of the Grange Haunting – David Ruffle
The Adventure of the Pallid Mask – Daniel McGachey
The Two Different Women – David Marcum

Part IX – 2018 Annual (1879-1895)

Foreword – Nicholas Meyer
Foreword – Roger Johnson
Foreword – Melissa Farnham
Foreword – Steve Emecz
Foreword – David Marcum
Violet Smith (A Poem) – Amy Thomas
The Adventure of the Temperance Society – Deanna Baran
The Adventure of the Fool and His Money – Roger Riccard
The Helverton Inheritance – David Marcum
The Adventure of the Faithful Servant – Tracy Revels
The Adventure of the Parisian Butcher – Nick Cardillo
The Missing Empress – Robert Stapleton
The Resplendent Plane Tree – Kevin P. Thornton
The Strange Adventure of the Doomed Sextette – Leslie Charteris and Denis Green
        (Introduction by Ian Dickerson)
The Adventure of the Old Boys' Club – Shane Simmons
The Case of the Golden Trail – James Moffett
The Detective Who Cried Wolf – C.H. Dye

(Continued on the next page . . . .)

The Lambeth Poisoner Case – Stephen Gaspar
The Confession of Anna Jarrow – S. F. Bennett
The Adventure of the Disappearing Dictionary – Sonia Fetherston
The Fairy Hills Horror – Geri Schear
A Loathsome and Remarkable Adventure – Marcia Wilson
The Adventure of the Multiple Moriartys – David Friend
The Influence Machine – Mark Mower

Part X – 2018 Annual (1896-1916)
Foreword – Nicholas Meyer
Foreword – Roger Johnson
Foreword – Melissa Farnham
Foreword – Steve Emecz
Foreword – David Marcum
A Man of Twice Exceptions (A Poem) – Derrick Belanger
The Horned God – Kelvin Jones
The Coughing Man – Jim French
The Adventure of Canal Reach – Arthur Hall
A Simple Case of Abduction – Mike Hogan
A Case of Embezzlement – Steven Ehrman
The Adventure of the Vanishing Diplomat – Greg Hatcher
The Adventure of the Perfidious Partner – Jayantika Ganguly
A Brush With Death – Dick Gillman
A Revenge Served Cold – Maurice Barkley
The Case of the Anonymous Client – Paul A. Freeman
Capitol Murder – Daniel D. Victor
The Case of the Dead Detective – Martin Rosenstock
The Musician Who Spoke From the Grave – Peter Coe Verbica
The Adventure of the Future Funeral – Hugh Ashton
The Problem of the Bruised Tongues – Will Murray
The Mystery of the Change of Art – Robert Perret
The Parsimonious Peacekeeper – Thaddeus Tuffentsamer
The Case of the Dirty Hand – G.L. Schulze
The Mystery of the Missing Artefacts – Tim Symonds

Part XI: Some Untold Cases (1880-1891)
Foreword – Lyndsay Faye
Foreword – Roger Johnson
Foreword – Melissa Grigsby
Foreword – Steve Emecz
Foreword – David Marcum
Unrecorded Holmes Cases (A Sonnet) – Arlene Mantin Levy and Mark Levy
The Most Repellant Man – Jayantika Ganguly
The Singular Adventure of the Extinguished Wicks – Will Murray
Mrs. Forrester's Complication – Roger Riccard
The Adventure of Vittoria, the Circus Belle – Tracy Revels

(Continued on the next page . . . .)

The Adventure of the Silver Skull – Hugh Ashton
The Pimlico Poisoner – Matthew Simmonds
The Grosvenor Square Furniture Van – David Ruffle
The Adventure of the Paradol Chamber – Paul W. Nash
The Bishopgate Jewel Case – Mike Hogan
The Singular Tragedy of the Atkinson Brothers of Trincomalee – Craig Stephen Copland
Colonel Warburton's Madness – Gayle Lange Puhl
The Adventure at Bellingbeck Park – Deanna Baran
The Giant Rat of Sumatra – Leslie Charteris and Denis Green
       (Introduction by Ian Dickerson)
The Vatican Cameos – Kevin P. Thornton
The Case of the Gila Monster – Stephen Herczeg
The Bogus Laundry Affair – Robert Perret
Inspector Lestrade and the Molesey Mystery – M.A. Wilson and Richard Dean Starr

Part XII: Some Untold Cases (1894-1902)
Foreword – Lyndsay Faye
Foreword – Roger Johnson
Foreword – Melissa Grigsby
Foreword – Steve Emecz
Foreword – David Marcum
It's Always Time (*A Poem*) – "Anon."
The Shanghaied Surgeon – C.H. Dye
The Trusted Advisor – David Marcum
A Shame Harder Than Death – Thomas Fortenberry
The Adventure of the Smith-Mortimer Succession – Daniel D. Victor
A Repulsive Story and a Terrible Death – Nik Morton
The Adventure of the Dishonourable Discharge – Craig Janacek
The Adventure of the Admirable Patriot – S. Subramanian
The Abernetty Transactions – Jim French
Dr. Agar and the Dinosaur – Robert Stapleton
The Giant Rat of Sumatra – Nick Cardillo
The Adventure of the Black Plague – Paul D. Gilbert
Vigor, the Hammersmith Wonder – Mike Hogan
A Correspondence Concerning Mr. James Phillimore – Derrick Belanger
The Curious Case of the Two Coptic Patriarchs – John Linwood Grant
The Conk-Singleton Forgery Case – Mark Mower
Another Case of Identity – Jane Rubino
The Adventure of the Exalted Victim – Arthur Hall

PART XIII: 2019 Annual (1881-1890)
Foreword – Will Thomas
Foreword – Roger Johnson
Foreword – Melissa Grigsby
Foreword – Steve Emecz
Foreword – David Marcum
Inscrutable (*A Poem*) – Jacquelynn Morris

(Continued on the next page . . . .)

The Folly of Age – Derrick Belanger
The Fashionably-Dressed Girl – Mark Mower
The Odour of Neroli – Brenda Seabrooke
The Coffee House Girl – David Marcum
The Mystery of the Green Room – Robert Stapleton
The Case of the Enthusiastic Amateur – S.F. Bennett
The Adventure of the Missing Cousin – Edwin A. Enstrom
The Roses of Highclough House – MJH Simmonds
The Shackled Man – Andrew Bryant
The Yellow Star of Cairo – Tim Gambrell
The Adventure of the Winterhall Monster – Tracy Revels
The Grosvenor Square Furniture Van – Hugh Ashton
The Voyage of *Albion's Thistle* – Sean M. Wright
Bootless in Chippenham – Marino C. Alvarez
The Clerkenwell Shadow – Paul Hiscock
The Adventure of the Worried Banker – Arthur Hall
The Recovery of the Ashes – Kevin P. Thornton
The Mystery of the Patient Fisherman – Jim French
Sherlock Holmes in Bedlam – David Friend
The Adventure of the Ambulatory Cadaver – Shane Simmons
The Dutch Impostors – Peter Coe Verbica
The Missing Adam Tiler – Mark Wardecker

PART XIV: 2019 Annual (1891 -1897)

Foreword – Will Thomas
Foreword – Roger Johnson
Foreword – Melissa Grigsby
Foreword – Steve Emecz
Foreword – David Marcum
Skein of Tales (*A Poem*) – Jacquelynn Morris
The Adventure of the Royal Albert Hall – Charles Veley and Anna Elliott
The Tower of Fear – Mark Sohn
The Carroun Document – David Marcum
The Threadneedle Street Murder – S. Subramanian
The Collegiate Leprechaun – Roger Riccard
A Malversation of Mummies – Marcia Wilson
The Adventure of the Silent Witness – Tracy J. Revels
The Second Whitechapel Murderer – Arthur Hall
The Adventure of the Jeweled Falcon – GC Rosenquist
The Adventure of the Crossbow – Edwin A. Enstrom
The Adventure of the Delusional Wife – Jayantika Ganguly
Child's Play – C.H. Dye
The Lancelot Connection – Matthew Booth
The Adventure of the Modern Guy Fawkes – Stephen Herczeg
Mr. Clever, Baker Street – Geri Schear
The Adventure of the Scarlet Rosebud – Liz Hedgecock

(Continued on the next page . . . .)

The Poisoned Regiment – Carl Heifetz
The Case of the Persecuted Poacher – Gayle Lange Puhl
It's Time – Harry DeMaio
The Case of the Fourpenny Coffin – I.A. Watson
The Horror in King Street – Thomas A. Burns, Jr.

PART XV: 2019 Annual (1898-1917)

Foreword – Will Thomas
Foreword – Roger Johnson
Foreword – Melissa Grigsby
Foreword – Steve Emecz
Foreword – David Marcum
Two Poems – Christopher James
The Whitechapel Butcher – Mark Mower
The Incomparable Miss Incognita – Thomas Fortenberry
The Adventure of the Twofold Purpose – Robert Perret
The Adventure of the Green Gifts – Tracy J. Revels
The Turk's Head – Robert Stapleton
A Ghost in the Mirror – Peter Coe Verbica
The Mysterious Mr. Rim – Maurice Barkley
The Adventure of the Fatal Jewel-Box – Edwin A. Enstrom
Mass Murder – William Todd
The Notable Musician – Roger Riccard
The Devil's Painting – Kelvin I. Jones
The Adventure of the Silent Sister – Arthur Hall
A Skeleton's Sorry Story – Jack Grochot
An Actor and a Rare One – David Marcum
The Silver Bullet – Dick Gillman
The Adventure at Throne of Gilt – Will Murray
"The Boy Who Would Be King – Dick Gillman
The Case of the Seventeenth Monk – Tim Symonds
Alas, Poor Will – Mike Hogan
The Case of the Haunted Chateau – Leslie Charteris and Denis Green
        (Introduction by Ian Dickerson)
The Adventure of the Weeping Stone – Nick Cardillo
The Adventure of the Three Telegrams – Darryl Webber

Part XVI – Whatever Remains . . . Must Be the Truth (1881-1890)

Foreword – Kareem Abdul-Jabbar
Foreword – Roger Johnson
Foreword – Steve Emecz
Foreword – David Marcum
The Hound of the Baskervilles (Retold) (*A Poem*) – Josh Pachter
The Wylington Lake Monster – Derrick Belanger
The *Juju* Men of Richmond – Mark Sohn

(Continued on the next page . . . .)

The Adventure of the Headless Lady – Tracy J. Revels
Angelus Domini Nuntiavit – Kevin P. Thornton
The Blue Lady of Dunraven – Andrew Bryant
The Adventure of the Ghoulish Grenadier – Josh Anderson and David Friend
The Curse of Barcombe Keep – Brenda Seabrooke
The Affair of the Regressive Man – David Marcum
The Adventure of the Giant's Wife – I.A. Watson
The Adventure of Miss Anna Truegrace – Arthur Hall
The Haunting of Bottomly's Grandmother – Tim Gambrell
The Adventure of the Intrusive Spirit – Shane Simmons
The Paddington Poltergeist – Bob Bishop
The Spectral Pterosaur – Mark Mower
The Weird of Caxton – Kelvin Jones
The Adventure of the Obsessive Ghost – Jayantika Ganguly

Part XVII – Whatever Remains . . . Must Be the Truth (1891-1898)

Foreword – Kareem Abdul-Jabbar
Foreword – Roger Johnson
Foreword – Steve Emecz
Foreword – David Marcum
The Violin Thief (*A Poem*) – Christopher James
The Spectre of Scarborough Castle – Charles Veley and Anna Elliott
The Case for Which the World is Not Yet Prepared – Steven Philip Jones
The Adventure of the Returning Spirit – Arthur Hall
The Adventure of the Bewitched Tenant – Michael Mallory
The Misadventures of the Bonnie Boy – Will Murray
The Adventure of the *Danse Macabre* – Paul D. Gilbert
The Strange Persecution of John Vincent Harden – S. Subramanian
The Dead Quiet Library – Roger Riccard
The Adventure of the Sugar Merchant – Stephen Herczeg
The Adventure of the Undertaker's Fetch – Tracy J. Revels
The Holloway Ghosts – Hugh Ashton
The Diogenes Club Poltergeist – Chris Chan
The Madness of Colonel Warburton – Bert Coules
The Return of the Noble Bachelor – Jane Rubino
The Reappearance of Mr. James Phillimore – David Marcum
The Miracle Worker – Geri Schear
The Hand of Mesmer – Dick Gillman

Part XVIII – Whatever Remains . . . Must Be the Truth (1899-1925)

Foreword – Kareem Abdul-Jabbar
Foreword – Roger Johnson
Foreword – Steve Emecz
Foreword – David Marcum
The Adventure of the Lighthouse on the Moor (*A Poem*) – Christopher James
The Witch of Ellenby – Thomas A. Burns, Jr.

(Continued on the next page . . . .)

The Tollington Ghost – Roger Silverwood
You Only Live Thrice – Robert Stapleton
The Adventure of the Fair Lad – Craig Janacek
The Adventure of the Voodoo Curse – Gareth Tilley
The Cassandra of Providence Place – Paul Hiscock
The Adventure of the House Abandoned – Arthur Hall
The Winterbourne Phantom – M.J. Elliott
The Murderous Mercedes – Harry DeMaio
The Solitary Violinist – Tom Turley
The Cunning Man – Kelvin I. Jones
The Adventure of Khamaat's Curse – Tracy J. Revels
The Adventure of the Weeping Mary – Matthew White
The Unnerved Estate Agent – David Marcum
Death in The House of the Black Madonna – Nick Cardillo
The Case of the Ivy-Covered Tomb – S.F. Bennett

Part XIX: 2020 Annual (1882-1890)

Foreword – John Lescroart
Foreword – Roger Johnson
Foreword – Lizzy Butler
Foreword – Steve Emecz
Foreword – David Marcum
Holmes's Prayer (*A Poem*) – Christopher James
A Case of Paternity – Matthew White
The Raspberry Tart – Roger Riccard
The Mystery of the Elusive Bard – Kevin P. Thornton
The Man in the Maroon Suit – Chris Chan
The Scholar of Silchester Court – Nick Cardillo
The Adventure of the Changed Man – MJH. Simmonds
The Adventure of the Tea-Stained Diamonds – Craig Stephen Copland
The Indigo Impossibility – Will Murray
The Case of the Emerald Knife-Throwers – Ian Ableson
A Game of Skittles – Thomas A. Turley
The Gordon Square Discovery – David Marcum
The Tattooed Rose – Dick Gillman
The Problem at Pentonville Prison – David Friend
The Nautch Night Case – Brenda Seabrooke
The Disappearing Prisoner – Arthur Hall
The Case of the Missing Pipe – James Moffett
The Whitehaven Ransom – Robert Stapleton
The Enlightenment of Newton – Dick Gillman
The Impaled Man – Andrew Bryant
The Mystery of the Elusive Li Shen – Will Murray
The Mahmudabad Result – Andrew Bryant

(Continued on the next page . . . .)

The Adventure of the Matched Set – Peter Coe Verbica
When the Prince First Dined at the Diogenes Club – Sean M. Wright
The Sweetenbury Safe Affair – Tim Gambrell

Part XX: 2020 Annual (1891-1897)
Foreword – John Lescroart
Foreword – Roger Johnson
Foreword – Lizzy Butler
Foreword – Steve Emecz
Foreword – David Marcum
The Sibling (*A Poem*) – Jacquelynn Morris
Blood and Gunpowder – Thomas A. Burns, Jr.
The Atelier of Death – Harry DeMaio
The Adventure of the Beauty Trap – Tracy Revels
A Case of Unfinished Business – Steven Philip Jones
The Case of the S.S. Bokhara – Mark Mower
The Adventure of the American Opera Singer – Deanna Baran
The Keadby Cross – David Marcum
The Adventure at Dead Man's Hole – Stephen Herczeg
The Elusive Mr. Chester – Arthur Hall
The Adventure of Old Black Duffel – Will Murray
The Blood-Spattered Bridge – Gayle Lange Puhl
The Tomorrow Man – S.F. Bennett
The Sweet Science of Bruising – Kevin P. Thornton
The Mystery of Sherlock Holmes – Christopher Todd
The Elusive Mr. Phillimore – Matthew J. Elliott
The Murders in the Maharajah's Railway Carriage – Charles Veley and Anna Elliott
The Ransomed Miracle – I.A. Watson
The Adventure of the Unkind Turn – Robert Perret
The Perplexing X'ing – Sonia Fetherston
The Case of the Short-Sighted Clown – Susan Knight

Part XXI: 2020 Annual (1898-1923)
Foreword – John Lescroart
Foreword – Roger Johnson
Foreword – Lizzy Butler
Foreword – Steve Emecz
Foreword – David Marcum
The Case of the Missing Rhyme (*A Poem*) – Joseph W. Svec III
The Problem of the St. Francis Parish Robbery – R.K. Radek
The Adventure of the Grand Vizier – Arthur Hall
The Mummy's Curse – DJ Tyrer
The Fractured Freemason of Fitzrovia – David L. Leal
The Bleeding Heart – Paula Hammond
The Secret Admirer – Jayantika Ganguly

(Continued on the next page . . . .)

The Deceased Priest – Peter Coe Verbica
The Case of the Rewrapped Presents – Bob Byrne
The Invisible Assassin – Geri Shear
The Adventure of the Chocolate Pot – Hugh Ashton
The Adventure of the Incessant Workers – Arthur Hall
When Best Served Cold – Stephen Mason
The Cat's Meat Lady of Cavendish Square – David Marcum
The Unveiled Lodger – Mark Mower
The League of Unhappy Orphans – Leslie Charteris and Denis Green
        (Introduction by Ian Dickerson)
The Adventure of the Three Fables – Jane Rubino
The Cobbler's Treasure – Dick Gillman
The Adventure of the Wells Beach Ruffians – Derrick Belanger
The Adventure of the Doctor's Hand – Michael Mallory
The Case of the Purloined Talisman – John Lawrence

Part XXII: Some More Untold Cases (1877-1887)

Foreword – Otto Penzler
Foreword – Roger Johnson
Foreword – Steve Emecz
Foreword – Jacqueline Silver
Foreword – David Marcum
The Philosophy of Holmes (*A Poem*) – Christopher James
The Terror of the Tankerville – S.F. Bennett
The Singular Affair of the Aluminium Crutch – William Todd
The Trifling Matter of Mortimer Maberley – Geri Schear
Abracadaver – Susan Knight
The Secret in Lowndes Court – David Marcum
Vittoria, the Circus Bell – Bob Bishop
The Adventure of the Vanished Husband – Tracy J. Revels
Merridew of Abominable Memory – Chris Chan
The Substitute Thief – Richard Paolinelli
The Whole Story Concerning the Politician, the Lighthouse, and the Trained Cormorant –
        Derrick Belanger
A Child's Reward – Stephen Mason
The Case of the Elusive Umbrella – Leslie Charteris and Denis Green
        (Introduction by Ian Dickerson)
The Strange Death of an Art Dealer – Tim Symonds
Watch Him Fall – Liese Sherwood-Fabre
The Adventure of the Transatlantic Gila – Ian Ableson
Intruders at Baker Street – Chris Chan
The Paradol Chamber – Mark Mower
Wolf Island – Robert Stapleton
The Etherage Escapade – Roger Riccard

(Continued on the next page . . . .)

The Dundas Separation Case – Kevin P. Thornton
The Broken Glass – Denis O. Smith

Part XXIII: Some More Untold Cases (1888-1894)
Foreword – Otto Penzler
Foreword – Roger Johnson
Foreword – Steve Emecz
Foreword – Jacqueline Silver
Foreword – David Marcum
The Housekeeper (*A Poem*) – John Linwood Grant
The Uncanny Adventure of the Hammersmith Wonder – Will Murray
Mrs. Forrester's Domestic Complication– Tim Gambrell
The Adventure of the Abducted Bard – I.A. Watson
The Adventure of the Loring Riddle – Craig Janacek
To the Manor Bound – Jane Rubino
The Crimes of John Clay – Paul Hiscock
The Adventure of the Nonpareil Club – Hugh Ashton
The Adventure of the Singular Worm – Mike Chinn
The Adventure of the Forgotten Brolly – Shane Simmons
The Adventure of the Tired Captain – Dacre Stoker and Leverett Butts
The Rhayader Legacy – David Marcum
The Adventure of the Tired Captain – Matthew J. Elliott
The Secret of Colonel Warburton's Insanity – Paul D. Gilbert
The Adventure of Merridew of Abominable Memory – Tracy J. Revels
The Affair of the Hellingstone Rubies – Margaret Walsh
The Adventure of the Drewhampton Poisoner – Arthur Hall
The Incident of the Dual Intrusions – Barry Clay
The Case of the Un-Paralleled Adventures – Steven Philip Jones
The Affair of the Friesland – Jan van Koningsveld
The Forgetful Detective – Marcia Wilson
The Smith-Mortimer Succession – Tim Gambrell
The Repulsive Matter of the Bloodless Banker – Will Murray

Part XXIV: Some More Untold Cases (1895-1903)
Foreword – Otto Penzler
Foreword – Roger Johnson
Foreword – Steve Emecz
Foreword – Jacqueline Silver
Foreword – David Marcum
Sherlock Holmes and the Return of the Missing Rhyme (*A Poem*) – Joseph W. Svec III
The Comet Wine's Funeral – Marcia Wilson
The Case of the Accused Cook – Brenda Seabrooke
The Case of Vanderbilt and the Yeggman – Stephen Herczeg

(Continued on the next page . . . .)

The Tragedy of Woodman's Lee – Tracy J. Revels
The Murdered Millionaire – Kevin P. Thornton
Another Case of Identity – Thomas A. Burns, Jr.
The Case of Indelible Evidence – Dick Gillman
The Adventure of Parsley and Butter – Jayantika Ganguly
The Adventure of the Nile Traveler – John Davis
The Curious Case of the Crusader's Cross – DJ Tyrer
An Act of Faith – Harry DeMaio
The Adventure of the Conk-Singleton Forgery – Arthur Hall
A Simple Matter – Susan Knight
The Hammerford Will Business – David Marcum
The Adventure of Mr. Fairdale Hobbs – Arthur Hall
The Adventure of the Abergavenny Murder – Craig Stephen Copland
The Chinese Puzzle Box – Gayle Lange Puhl
The Adventure of the Refused Knighthood – Craig Stephen Copland
The Case of the Consulting Physician – John Lawrence
The Man from Deptford – John Linwood Grant
The Case of the Impossible Assassin – Paula Hammond

Part XXV: 2021 Annual (1881-1888)

Foreword – Peter Lovesey
Foreword – Roger Johnson
Foreword – Steve Emecz
Foreword – Jacqueline Silver
Foreword – David Marcum
Baskerville Hall (*A Poem*) – Kelvin I. Jones
The Persian Slipper – Brenda Seabrooke
The Adventure of the Doll Maker's Daughter – Matthew White
The Flinders Case – Kevin McCann
The Sunderland Tragedies – David Marcum
The Tin Soldiers – Paul Hiscock
The Shattered Man – MJH Simmonds
The Hungarian Doctor – Denis O. Smith
The Black Hole of Berlin – Robert Stapleton
The Thirteenth Step – Keith Hann
The Missing Murderer – Marcia Wilson
Dial Square – Martin Daley
The Adventure of the Deadly Tradition – Matthew J. Elliott
The Adventure of the Fabricated Vision – Craig Janacek
The Adventure of the Murdered Maharajah – Hugh Ashton
The God of War – Hal Glatzer
The Atkinson Brothers of Trincomalee – Stephen Gaspar

(Continued on the next page . . . .)

The Switched String – Chris Chan
The Case of the Secret Samaritan – Jane Rubino
The Bishopsgate Jewel Case – Stephen Gaspar

Part XXVI: 2021 Annual (1889-1897)
Foreword – Peter Lovesey
Foreword – Roger Johnson
Foreword – Steve Emecz
Foreword – Jacqueline Silver
Foreword – David Marcum
221b Baker Street (*A Poem*) – Kevin Patrick McCann
The Burglary Season – Marcia Wilson
The Lamplighter at Rosebery Avenue – James Moffett
The Disfigured Hand – Peter Coe Verbica
The Adventure of the Bloody Duck – Margaret Walsh
The Tragedy at Longpool – James Gelter
The Case of the Viscount's Daughter – Naching T. Kassa
The Key in the Snuffbox – DJ Tyrer
The Race for the Gleghorn Estate – Ian Ableson
The Isa Bird Befuddlement – Kevin P. Thornton
The Cliddesden Questions – David Marcum
Death in Verbier – Adrian Middleton
The King's Cross Road Somnambulist – Dick Gillman
The Magic Bullet – Peter Coe Verbica
The Petulant Patient – Geri Schear
The Mystery of the Groaning Stone – Mark Mower
The Strange Case of the Pale Boy – Susan Knight
The Adventure of the Zande Dagger – Frank Schildiner
The Adventure of the Vengeful Daughter – Arthur Hall
Do the Needful – Harry DeMaio
The Count, the Banker, the Thief, and the Seven Half-sovereigns – Mike Hogan
The Adventure of the Unsprung Mousetrap – Anthony Gurney
The Confectioner's Captives – I.A. Watson

Part XXVII: 2021 Annual (1898-1928)
Foreword – Peter Lovesey
Foreword – Roger Johnson
Foreword – Steve Emecz
Foreword – Jacqueline Silver
Foreword – David Marcum
Sherlock Holmes Returns: The Missing Rhyme (*A Poem*) – Joseph W. Svec, III
The Adventure of the Hero's Heir – Tracy J. Revels
The Curious Case of the Soldier's Letter – John Davis
The Case of the Norwegian Daredevil – John Lawrence
The Case of the Borneo Tribesman – Stephen Herczeg
The Adventure of the White Roses – Tracy J. Revels

(Continued on the next page . . . .)

Mrs. Crichton's Ledger – Tim Gambrell
The Adventure of the Not-Very-Merry Widows – Craig Stephen Copland
The Son of God – Jeremy Branton Holstein
The Adventure of the Disgraced Captain – Thomas A. Turley
The Woman Who Returned From the Dead – Arthur Hall
The Farraway Street Lodger – David Marcum
The Mystery of Foxglove Lodge – S.C. Toft
The Strange Adventure of Murder by Remote Control – Leslie Charteris and Denis Green
        (Introduction by Ian Dickerson)
The Case of The Blue Parrot – Roger Riccard
The Adventure of the Expelled Master – Will Murray
The Case of the Suicidal Suffragist – John Lawrence
The Welbeck Abbey Shooting Party – Thomas A. Turley
Case No. 358 – Marcia Wilson

Part XXVIII: More Christmas Adventures (1869-1888)

Foreword – Nancy Holder
Foreword – Roger Johnson
Foreword – Steve Emecz
Foreword – Emma West
Foreword – David Marcum
A Sherlockian Christmas (A Poem) – Joseph W. Svec III
No Malice Intended – Deanna Baran
The Yuletide Heist – Mark Mower
A Yuletide Tragedy – Thomas A. Turley
The Adventure of the Christmas Lesson – Will Murray
The Christmas Card Case – Brenda Seabrooke
The Chatterton-Smythe Affair – Tim Gambrell
Christmas at the Red Lion – Thomas A. Burns, Jr.
A Study in Murder – Amy Thomas
The Christmas Ghost of Crailloch Taigh – David Marcum
The Six-Fingered Scoundrel – Jeffrey A. Lockwood
The Case of the Duplicitous Suitor – John Lawrence
The Sebastopol Clasp – Martin Daley
The Silent Brotherhood – Dick Gillman
The Case of the Christmas Pudding – Liz Hedgecock
The St. Stephen's Day Mystery – Paul Hiscock
A Fine Kettle of Fish – Mike Hogan
The Case of the Left Foot – Stephen Herczeg
The Case of the Golden Grail – Roger Riccard

(Continued on the next page . . . .)

Part XXIX: More Christmas Adventures (1889-1896)

Foreword – Nancy Holder
Foreword – Roger Johnson
Foreword – Steve Emecz
Foreword – Emma West
Foreword – David Marcum
Baskerville Hall in Winter (A Poem) – Christopher James
The Sword in the Spruce – Ian Ableson
The Adventure of the Serpentine Body – Wayne Anderson
The Adventure of the Fugitive Irregular – Gordon Linzner
The Father Christmas Brigade – David Marcum
The Incident of the Stolen Christmas Present – Barry Clay
The Man of Miracles – Derrick Belanger
Absent Friends – Wayne Anderson
The Incident in Regent Street – Harry DeMaio
The Baffling Adventure of the Baby Jesus – Craig Stephen Copland
The Adventure of the Second Sister – Matthew White
The Twelve Days – I.A. Watson
The Dilemma of Mr. Henry Baker – Paul D. Gilbert
The Adventure of the Injured Man – Arthur Hall
The Krampus Who Came to Call – Marcia Wilson
The Adventure of the Christmas Wish – Margaret Walsh
The Adventure of the Viking Ghost – Frank Schildiner
The Adventure of the Secret Manuscript – Dan Rowley
The Adventure of the Christmas Suitors – Tracy J. Revels

Part XXX: More Christmas Adventures (1897-1928)

Foreword – Nancy Holder
Foreword – Roger Johnson
Foreword – Steve Emecz
Foreword – Emma West
Foreword – David Marcum
Baker Street in Snow (1890) (A Poem) – Christopher James
The Purloined Present – DJ Tyrer
The Case of the Cursory Curse – Andrew Bryant
The St. Giles Child Murders – Tim Gambrell
A Featureless Crime – Geri Schear
The Case of the Earnest Young Man – Paula Hammond
The Adventure of the Dextrous Doctor – Jayantika Ganguly
The Mystery of Maple Tree Lodge – Susan Knight
The Adventure of the Maligned Mineralogist – Arthur Hall
Christmas Magic – Kevin Thornton
The Adventure of the Christmas Threat – Arthur Hall
The Adventure of the Stolen Christmas Gift – Michael Mallory
The Colourful Skein of Life – Julie McKuras

(Continued on the next page . . . .)

The Adventure of the Chained Phantom – J.S. Rowlinson
Santa's Little Elves – Kevin Thornton
The Case of the Holly-Sprig Pudding – Naching T. Kassa
The Canterbury Manifesto – David Marcum
The Case of the Disappearing Beaune – J. Lawrence Matthews
A Price Above Rubies – Jane Rubino
The Intrigue of the Red Christmas – Shane Simmons
The Bitter Gravestones – Chris Chan
The Midnight Mass Murder – Paul Hiscock

Part XXXI: 2022 Annual (1875-1887)

Foreword – Jeffrey Hatcher
Foreword – Roger Johnson
Foreword – Steve Emecz
Foreword – Emma West
Foreword – David Marcum
The Nemesis of Sherlock Holmes (A Poem) – Kelvin I. Jones
The Unsettling Incident of the History Professor's Wife – Sean M. Wright
The Princess Alice Tragedy – John Lawrence
The Adventure of the Amorous Balloonist – I.A. Watson
The Pilkington Case – Kevin Patrick McCann
The Adventure of the Disappointed Lover – Arthur Hall
The Case of the Impressionist Painting – Tim Symonds
The Adventure of the Old Explorer – Tracy J. Revels
Dr. Watson's Dilemma – Susan Knight
The Colonial Exhibition – Hal Glatzer
The Adventure of the Drunken Teetotaler – Thomas A. Burns, Jr.
The Curse of Hollyhock House – Geri Schear
The Sethian Messiah – David Marcum
Dead Man's Hand – Robert Stapleton
The Case of the Wary Maid – Gordon Linzner
The Adventure of the Alexandrian Scroll – David MacGregor
The Case of the Woman at Margate – Terry Golledge
A Question of Innocence – DJ Tyrer
The Grosvenor Square Furniture Van – Terry Golledge
The Adventure of the Veiled Man – Tracy J. Revels
The Disappearance of Dr. Markey – Stephen Herczeg
The Case of the Irish Demonstration – Dan Rowley

Part XXXII: 2022 Annual (1888-1895)

Foreword – Jeffrey Hatcher
Foreword – Roger Johnson
Foreword – Steve Emecz

(Continued on the next page . . . .)

Foreword – Emma West
Foreword – David Marcum
The Hound (A Poem) – Kevin Patrick McCann
The Adventure of the Merryman and His Maid – Hal Glatzer
The Four Door-Handles – Arianna Fox
The Merton Friends – Terry Golledge
The Distasteful Affair of the Minatory Messages – David Marcum
The Adventure of the Tired Captain – Craig Janacek
The Grey Man – James Gelter
The Hyde Park Mystery – Mike Hogan
The Adventure of the Troubled Wife – Arthur Hall
The Horror of Forrest Farm – Tracy J. Revels
The Addleton Tragedy – Terry Golledge
The Adventure of the Doss House Ramble – Will Murray
The Black Beast of the Hurlers Stones – Roger Riccard
The Torso at Highgate Cemetery – Tim Symonds
The Disappearance of the Highgate Flowers – Tracy J. Revels
The Adventure of the New York Professor – Wayne Anderson
The Adventure of the Remarkable Worm – Alan Dimes
The Stone of Ill Omen – Mike Chinn
The Commotion at the Diogenes Club – Paul Hiscock
The Case of the Reappearing Wineskin – Ian Ableson

Part XXXIII: 2022 Annual (1896-1919)

Foreword – Jeffrey Hatcher
Foreword – Roger Johnson
Foreword – Steve Emecz
Foreword – Emma West
Foreword – David Marcum
Of Law and Justice (A Poem) – Alisha Shea
The Crown of Light – Terry Golledge
The Case of the Unknown Skull – Naching T. Kassa
The Strange Case of the Man from Edinburgh – Susan Knight
The Adventure of the Silk Scarf – Terry Golledge
Barstobrick House – Martin Daley
The Case of the Abstemious Burglar – Dan Rowley
The Blackfenn Marsh Monster – Marcia Wilson
The Disappearance of Little Charlie – Tracy J. Revels
The Adventure of the Impudent Impostor – Josh Cerefice
The Fatal Adventure of the French Onion Soup – Craig Stephen Copland
The Adventure of the Subversive Student – Jeffrey A Lockwood
The Adventure of the Spinster's Courtship – Tracy J. Revels
The Politician, the Lighthouse, and the Trained Cormorant – Mark Wardecker
The Gillette Play's the Thing! – David Marcum
The Derisible Dirigible Mystery – Kevin P. Thornton

(Continued on the next page . . . .)

The Ambassador's Skating Competition – Tim Symonds
What Came Before – Thomas A. Turley
The Adventure of the Art Exhibit – Dan Rowley
The Adventure of Peter the Painter – David MacGregor
The Valley of Tears – Andrew Bryant
The Adventure of the Tinker's Arms – Arthur Hall
The Adventure of the Murdered Medium – Hugh Ashton

Part XXXIV: "However Improbable . . . ." (1878-1888)

Foreword – Nicholas Rowe
Foreword – Roger Johnson
Foreword Steve Emecz
Foreword – Emma West
Foreword – David Marcum
However Improbable (A Poem) – Joseph W. Svec III
The Monster's Mop and Pail – Marcia Wilson
The Wordless Widow – Gordon Linzner
The Mystery of the Spectral Shelter – Will Murray
The Adventure of the Dead Heir – Dan Rowley
The Body in Question – Tim Newton Anderson
The Adventure of the False Confessions – Arthur Hall
His Own Hangman – Thomas A. Burns, Jr.
The Mediobogdum Sword – David Marcum
The Adventure of The Sisters McClelland – James Gelter
The Mystery of the Vengeful Bride – DJ Tyrer
A Fatal Illusion – Paul Hiscock
The Adventure of the Newmarket Killings – Leslie Charteris and Denis Green
        (Introduction by Ian Dickerson)
The Possession of Miranda Beasmore – Stephen Herczeg
The Adventure of the Haunted Portrait – Tracy J. Revels
The Crisis of Count de Vermilion – Roger Riccard
The Adventure of Three-Card Monte – Anisha Jagdeep
The Adventure of the Armchair Detective – John McNabb

Part XXXV: "However Improbable . . . ." (1889-1896)

Foreword – Nicholas Rowe
Foreword – Roger Johnson
Foreword Steve Emecz
Foreword – Emma West
Foreword – David Marcum
The Widow of Neptune (A Poem) – Christopher James
The Devil of Dickon's Dike Farm – Margaret Walsh
The Christmas *Doppelgänger* – M.J. Elliott
The Terror of Asgard Tower – Paul D. Gilbert
The Well-Lit Séance – David Marcum
The Adventure of the Deadly Illness – Dan Rowley and Don Baxter

(Continued on the next page . . . .)

Doctor Watson's Baffled Colleague – Sean M. Wright and DeForeest B. Wright, III
The Case of the Deity's Disappearance – Jane Rubino
The Tragedy of Mr. Ernest Bidmead – Arthur Hall
The Adventure of the Buried Bride – Tracy J. Revels
The Adventure of James Edward Phillimore – Alan Dimes
Soldier of Fortune – Geri Schear
The Mystery of the Murderous Ghost – Susan Knight
Mycroft's Ghost – The Davies Brothers
The Terror of Trowbridge Wood – Josh Cerefice
The Fantastical Vision of Randolph Sitwell – Mark Mower
The Adventure of the Paternal Ghost – Arthur Hall
Pit of Death – Robert Stapleton
The Jade Swan – Charles Veley and Anna Elliott
The Devil Went Down to Surrey – Naching T. Kassa
The Dowager Lady Isobel Frobisher – Martin Daley
The Confounding Confessional Confrontation – Kevin P. Thornton
The Adventure of the Long-Distance Bullet – I.A. Watson

Part XXXVI: "However Improbable . . . ." (1897-1919)

Foreword – Nicholas Rowe
Foreword – Roger Johnson
Foreword Steve Emecz
Foreword – Emma West
Foreword – David Marcum
The Mythological Holmes (A Poem) – Alisha Shea
The Adventure of the Murderous Ghost – Tracy J. Revels
The High Table Hallucination – David L. Leal
The Checkmate Murder – Josh Cerefice
When Spaghetti was Served at the Diogenes Club – John Farrell
Holmes Run – Amanda J.A. Knight
The Adventure of the Murderous Gentleman – Arthur Hall
The Puzzle Master – William Todd
The Curse of Kisin – Liese Sherwood-Fabre
The Case of the Blood-Stained Leek – Margaret Walsh
The Bookseller's Donkey – Hal Glatzer
The Adventure of the Black Perambulator – Tracy J. Revels
The Adventure of the Surrey Inn – Leslie Charteris and Denis Green
          (Introduction by Ian Dickerson)   )
The Adventure of the Traveller in Time – Arthur Hall
The Adventure of the Restless Dead – Craig Janacek
The Vodou Drum – David Marcum
The Burglary at Undershaw – Tim Symonds

(Continued on the next page . . . .)

The Case of the Missing Minute – Dan Rowley
The Peacock Arrow – Chris Chan
The Spy on the Western Front – Tim Symonds

Part XXXVII: 2023 Annual (1875-1889)
Foreword – Michael Sims
Foreword – Roger Johnson
Foreword Steve Emecz
Foreword – Emma West
Foreword – David Marcum
The Adventure of the Improbable American – Will Murray
The Return of Springheeled Jack – Brenda Seagrove
The Incident of the Pointless Abduction – Arthur Hall
The Adventure of the Absent Crossing Sweeper – Steven Philip Jones
The Adventure of the Disappearing – Dan Rowley and Don Baxter
The Abridge Disappearance – David Marcum
The Adventure of the Green Horse – Hugh Ashton
The Adventure of Woodgate Manor – Sonya Kudei
The Incident of the Mangled Rose Buses – Barry Clay
The Sandwich Murder – DJ Tyrer
The Adventure of the Wandering Stones – Mark Wardecker
The Charity Collection – Paul Hiscock
The Catastrophic Cyclist – Tom Turley
The Adventure of the Sketched Bride – James Gelter
The Adventure of the Downing Street Demise – Brett Fawcett
The Continental Conspiracy – Martin Daley
The Belmore Street Museum Affair – Bob Byrne
The Adventure of the Furniture Collector – Tracy J. Revels
The Serpent's Tooth – Matthew White

Part XXXVIII: 2023 Annual (1889-1896)
Foreword – Michael Sims
Foreword – Roger Johnson
Foreword Steve Emecz
Foreword – Emma West
Foreword – David Marcum
The Muddled Monologue – Ian Ableson
Bad Timing – Gordon Linzner
The Adventure of the Living Terror – Craig Janacek
The Adventure of the Predatory Philanthropist – I.A. Watson
The Affair of the Addleton Giant – Margaret Walsh
The Adventure of the Faithful Wolfhound – Tracy J. Revels
The Texas Legation Business – David Marcum
Death at Simpsons – David MacGregor
The Adventure of the Reluctant Executioner – Arthur Hall

(Continued on the next page . . . .)

The Norwegian Shipping Agent – Sonya Kudei
Lucky Star – Jen Matteis
A Matter of Convenience – Geri Schear
The Spectral Centurion – Charles Veley and Anna Elliott
The Hyde Park Blackmailer – Peter Coe Verbica
The Adventure of the Counterfeit Uncle – Michael Mallory
The Adventure of the Seven Sins – Tracy J. Revels
The Adventure of the Fourth Key – Carlos Orsi
The Adventure of the Deathstalker – Susan Knight
The Keeper of the Eddystone Light – Tim Newton Anderson

Part XXXIX: 2023 Annual (1897-1923)

Foreword – Michael Sims
Foreword – Roger Johnson
Foreword Steve Emecz
Foreword – Emma West
Foreword – David Marcum
The Case of the Curative Cruise – Dan Rowley and Don Baxter
The Totten Wood Mystery – William Todd
The Case of the Hesitant Client – Naching T. Kassa
A Study in Eldritch – Naching T. Kassa
The Stanhope Orphan – Ember Pepper
The Adventure of the Rainsford Inheritance – Alan Dimes
The Adventure of the Terrified Urchin – Arthur Hall
The King of Spades – Peter Coe Verbica
A Touch of the Dramatic – Jane Rubino
Two Goodly Gentlemen – Paula Hammond
The Adventure of the Folded Overcoat – Tracy J. Revels
The Third Baroness – Kevin Thornton
The Adventure of the Elusive Assassin – Arthur Hall
The Adventure of the Lost Alliance – Tom Turley
The Adventure of the Substitute Murder – Arthur Hall
The Case of the Lighthouse, the Trained Cormorant, and the Frightened Politician –
    Leslie Charteris and Denis Green *(Introduction by Ian Dickerson)*
The Curious Circumstances of the Imitation Ripper – David Marcum
The Adventure of the Petulant Queen – Shane Simmons
The Sketchy Blackmailer – Roger Riccard
The Green Honey – Chris Chan
The Case of the Disfigured Lieutenant – John Lawrence

Part XL: Further Untold Cases (1879-1886)

Foreword – Tom Mead
Foreword – Roger Johnson
Foreword Steve Emecz
Foreword – Emma West
Foreword – David Marcum

(Continued on the next page . . . .)

The Case of the Cases of Vamberry Burgundy – Roger Riccard
The Adventure of the Aluminium Crutch – Tracy J. Revels
The Most Winning Woman – Liese Sherwood-Fabre
Mrs. Farintosh's Opal Tiara – Brenda Seabrooke
A Case of Duplicity – Gordon Linzner
The Adventure of the Fraudulent Benefactor – Mike Adamson
The Adventure of the Dead Rats – Hugh Ashton
The Laodicean Letters – David Marcum
A Case of Exceptional Brilliants – Jane Rubino
The True Account of the Dorrington Ruby Affair – Brett Fawcett
The Adventure of the Old Russian Woman – Susan Knight
The Adventure of the Silver Snail – Alan Dimes
The Adventure of the Invisible Weapon – Arthur Hall
The Backwater Affair – Paula Hammond
The Adventure of the Opening Eyes – Tracy J. Revels
The Man in the Rain with a Dog – Brenda Seabrooke
The Problem of the Grosvenor Square Moving Van – Tim Newton Anderson
The Dark Tavern – Robert Stapleton

Part XLI: Further Untold Cases (1877-1892)

Foreword – Tom Mead
Foreword – Roger Johnson
Foreword Steve Emecz
Foreword – Emma West
Foreword – David Marcum
The Case of the Trepoff Murder – Stephen Herczeg
The Strange Case of the Disappearing Factor – Margaret Walsh
The Mystery of the Three Mendicants – Paul D. Gilbert
The Difficult Ordeal of the Paradol Chamber – Will Murray
The Amateur Mendicant Society – David MacGregor
The Amnesiac's Peril – Barry Clay
The Mystery of the Unstolen Document – Mike Chinn
The Adventure of the Infernal Philanthropist – Tim Newton Anderson
The Adventure of the Murdered Mistress – Ember Pepper
The Rouen Scandal – Martin Daley
The Adventure of the Cheerful Prisoner – Arthur Hall
The Adventure of the Tired Captain – Naching T. Kassa
A Dreadful Record of Sin – David Marcum
Mathews of Charing Cross – Ember Pepper
The Grey Lama – Adrian Middleton

Part XLII: Further Untold Cases (1894-1922)

Foreword – Tom Mead
Foreword – Roger Johnson
Foreword Steve Emecz
Foreword – Emma West
Foreword – David Marcum

(Continued on the next page . . . .)

The Addleton Tragedy – Arthur Hall
The Book of Lucifer – Alan Dimes
The Adventure of the Curious Mother – Tracy J. Revels
The Mulberry Frock Coat Mystery – DJ Tyrer
The Tracking and Arrest of a Cold-Blooded Scoundrel – David Marcum
A Sudden Death at the Savoy – Dan Rowley
The Adventure of the Cardinal's Notebook – Deanna Baran
Death in the Workhouse – Thomas A. Burns, Jr
The Crimson Trail – Brenda Seabrooke
The Three Archers – Alan Dimes
The Three Maids – I.A. Watson
The Adventure of the African Prospector – Arthur Hall
The Unlikely Assassin – Tim Newton Anderson
The Two-Line Note – Chris Chan
The Stolen Brougham – Dan Rowley
The Theft at the Wallace Collection – Barry Clay
The St. Pancras Puzzle – Susan Knight
The Impossible Adventure of the Vanishing Murderer – Barry Clay
Mr. Phillimore's Umbrella – Paul Hiscock
Trouble at Emberly – Kevin P. Thornton

The following contributors appear in these companion volumes:
Part XLIII – 2024 Annual (1874-1888)
Part XLV – 2024 Annual (1898-1917)

Editor's Foreword:
"A fake, is it? Well, strike me!"
by David Marcum

Once upon a time, in long-ago days that are receding inexorably away from us into the misty past, the opportunities for admirers of Mr. Sherlock Holmes to enjoy his adventures were quite thin on the ground. For the first six years between late 1887 and late 1893, there were only twenty-six published Holmes narratives – *Twenty-six!* – with the last of those telling of Holmes's supposed death at the Reichenbach Falls. Then there was nothing – officially and Canonically, that is – until *The Hound of the Baskervilles* was serially released in 1901-1902. The next thirty-three Canonical tales appeared over the following twenty-five years, with more than one-third of those appearing as *The Return of Sherlock Holmes* (1903-1904), while publication of the others were sometimes separated from one another by years.

And then, the well might have dried up. At the end of the 1920's, both Watson and then the First Literary Agent had died, and Holmes was long removed to Sussex. He wasn't exactly retired from detection, but the majority of his time was then more involved in his apiaristic studies, and also working on his *magnum opus*, *The Whole Art of Detection*. For the admirers of Mr. Sherlock Holmes, there was a vast Holmesian vacuum.

Of course, there were other detectives who had filled the void when Holmes left Baker Street, although their arrivals didn't occur overnight. Dr. John Thorndyke was accepting clients at 5A King's Bench Walk in the late 1890's, so he overlapped Holmes's London practice by a few years. Solar Pons went into private practice in 1907 – possibly at 7B Praed Street, or perhaps somewhere else in those early days before moving so close to Paddington Station. Sometime after arriving in England as a war refugee in 1916, Hercule Poirot made his way to London and set up a consulting practice at No. 14 Farraway Street. The 1920's welcomed Lord Peter Wimsey to 110A Piccadilly Street and Albert Campion at 17A Bottle Street, with plenty of work for both. Their various biographers and literary agents provided information when news of Holmes was lacking, but what was needed – then and now and always – were more of Holmes's cases. *Lots more.*

In the early days, there were many Holmes parodies, but they're bogus and forgettable wastes of time. Seeing the supposedly "clever" and "humorous" ways that Holmes and Watson's names were misspelled and distorted is now quite painful. Why go down those dead-end rabbit holes if stories about the True Holmes can be obtained?

The earliest extra-Canonical adventure was William Gillette's 1899 play (and later film and radio show) *Sherlock Holmes*. It had some painful inaccuracies – that bizarre romance that Gillette awkwardly jammed onto the conclusion, and ignorantly naming Professor Moriarty *Robert* instead of *James* – but it helped to fill the chasm. Then, decades later, Edith Meiser brilliantly realized that Holmes's adventures would be perfect when dramatized for the young radio medium. After multiple broadcasts of many of the pitifully few sixty Canonical stories, she brought forth additional previously unrevealed adventures – "The Hindoo in the Wicker Basket", "The Haunted Clock", and possibly the first explanation behind the events of "The Giant Rat of Sumatra". After Meiser's association with the radio show ended, other chroniclers – like Denis Green, Leslie Charteris, and Anthony Boucher – carried on her important work.

Although many details of these early extra-Canonical adventures ended up being incorrect, courtesy of script writers adding their own poorly informed touches to Watson's notes, it was still good news when a number of new stories also appeared in the 1930's and 1940's by way of films starring Clive Brook, Arthur Wontner, and Basil Rathbone. In the 1950's, Adrian Conan Doyle, son of the First Literary Agent, and John Dickson Carr revealed *The Exploits of Sherlock Holmes*. While Adrian, along with his brother Denis, had made many enemies within the Sherlockian community that resulted in attacks on this particular Holmesian volume, it's actually an excellent collection of stories about the *True Holmes* – set in the correct period, and with no non-Sherlockian aspects and agendas awkwardly grafted on.

1959's Hammer version of *The Hound* was notable for several reasons: The first time Holmes was excellently acted by Peter Cushing. The first Holmes film in color. But also because it had a vastly altered and fictional ending. (This wasn't the first time that *The Hound* had been violated. Several German versions leapt in entirely absurd directions, and even Rathbone's version added a séance and left out Lestrade.)

The 1960's gave us, in addition to the Canonical offerings of Peter Cushing and Douglas Wilmer, the first film encounter between Holmes and Jack the Ripper, *A Study in Terror* (1965 – although the first print encounter Ripper Was Caught] in 1907). The book version of *A Study in Terror* contains extended alternating chapters of both Holmes's investigation and Ellery Queen's contemporary follow-up as he's reading Watson's account – and along the way, it happily provides another book in the Queen Canon.

The parodies had continued all along, of course. All sorts of films over the years indirectly referenced Holmes when they placed characters in deerstalkers – Laurel and Hardy, The Three Stooges, The Marx Brothers, Abbott and Costello, and even The Little Rascals (a.k.a. Our Gang, depending on your generation). 1956 brought the brilliant *Deduce, You Say,* starring Daffy Duck and Porky Pig as Dorlock Homes and Dr. Watkins. Throughout, no one ever said that Daffy Duck or Harpo Marx or Lou Costello had actually *played* Sherlock Holmes. People had enough sense to realize that Holmes was *Holmes* – separate from these completely different characters displaying Sherlockian aspects. But in 1971, the shift between harmless Holmesian parody and more detrimental Holmesian replacement began to occur with *They Might Be Giants* starring George C. Scott. He portrayed a modern-day judge, Justin Playfair, who slides into mental illness after the death of his wife. He believes he's Holmes, and those around him seem to believe it, but there is never any question – Scott is playing *Justin Playfair,* a man with a debilitating delusion, and he is *not* ever actually *Sherlock Holmes.*

And yet . . . when people now make lists of Holmes on screen, they list George C. Scott as Holmes – *although he never actually played Sherlock Holmes!*

This terrible trend of slapping Holmes's name on any character and then asserting that this *was* Holmes, as if Holmes was some body-and-time hopping Time Lord, began to gain traction. In *The Return of the World's Greatest Detective*, Larry Hagman plays *Sherman* Holmes, a modern-day policeman whose motorcycle falls on him – and he wakes up believing that's he's *Sherlock* Holmes – and now some people think that Larry Hagman played Holmes. 1984's *The Return of Sherlock Holmes* was a new twist – Sherlock Holmes had been frozen in the 1890's and was thawed out in the 1980's. The same sad gimmick was repeated in *1994: Baker Street.* In neither case did the actors actually play Holmes, as Holmes was *not* frozen and thawed out in the latter Twentieth Century – but people still credit these as actual Holmes films, and indicate that these actors played Holmes – which they did not. These films eroded the actual facts about Holmes in people's minds, wherein they forget or willfully ignore that Holmes was a man born in 1854, and not a thawed-out Holmesicle in modern times. Nor was he a mentally ill judge or brain-damaged motorcycle cop.

In between these two frozen films, Michael Caine played Reginald Kincaid – and not Sherlock Holmes – in *Without a Clue* (1988). This is another parody Holmes film, and not a legitimate post-Canonical work – and yet, lists and artwork regularly include Caine as "Sherlock Holmes", despite the fact that he never played him.

3

Meanwhile, the idea of using Holmes in non-Holmes ways continued to grow as well. There have been more versions of Sherlock Holmes-versus-Dracula than I care to list here, and sadly, in almost every case the authors forget Holmes's dictum of "No ghosts [*or vampires*] need apply,", and they essentially and simply re-tell Bram Stoker's *Dracula* with Holmes replacing Van Helsing. This opened the door to all kinds of other Holmes-as-Van Helsing encounters with Frankenstein, the Wolfman, demons and devils (including Satan himself), mummies, Lovecraftian Gods, steam-punk monstrosities, dinosaurs, sea monsters, space aliens, brain-eating spoors, brain-eating space-alien spoors, and just about any other supernatural critter imaginable. *No ghosts need apply? Pfui!* In these cases, no normal client need apply, because Holmes is too busy looking for his cross and his garlic and his holy water and his silver bullets for the next monster encounter.

And as *Fake Holmes* became even more un-moored from *True Holmes*, it was easier to graft on various other aspects – taking him from the person described in the Canon to a various levels of dysfunctional brokenness, to the point that certain television shows presented him as a full-on sociopathic murderer or a tattooed New York drug addict paying off a prostitute at the exact moment he meets his new Watson (and that we, the viewer, first meet him too).

But thankfully, the *True Holmes* has *not* been lost in this red tide of Holmes-in-name-only.

In 1974, Nicholas Meyer inaugurated the new (and still ongoing) Sherlockian Golden Age with his discovery of *The Seven-Per-Cent Solution.* The story is flawed, of course – the parts about Moriarty being a victim, for instance, and that the Great Hiatus never occurred, were apparently grafted onto the manuscript by Moriarty's heirs in an effort to rehabilitate his reputation. Still, the world was electrified when this book was released, for it became apparent that there were unknown Watsonian manuscripts out there in the world, waiting to be discovered – in scattered Tin Dispatch Boxes (for there were apparently more than one of those,) and hidden in people's attics and buried in their grandparent's papers. In 1975, *The Seven-Per-Cent Solution* became a major film, further pouring gas on the previously smoldering *True Holmes* fire. Stories began to trickle forth from authors like Sean Wright and Nick Utechin and Daniel Stashower – slowly at first, and then more and more and more. That particular genie, thank God, was out of the bottle for good.

But imagine a world where Nicholas Meyer and the rest *didn't* discover Watson's manuscripts – first *The Seven-Per-Cent Solution*, and then others. Would the misdirection taken by George C. Scott's *They Might Be Giants* have become more influential? Would the parodies and subversive versions of *Fake Holmes* have become even more established with no Sherlockian Golden Age to hold them in check? Would Holmes as Van Helsing become the new norm, replacing in people's mind the Canonical Holmes, and making the latter original adventures no more than footnotes or a jumping-off place? Or would Holmes have irrevocably become the poster child for murderous sociopaths, as almost became the case in the early 2000's after the frantic and urgent efforts of that television show's producers to permanently hijack him that way?

In 2015, *The MX Book of New Sherlock Holmes Stories* was specifically created to remind people of the *True Holmes* – a hero and not a villain. A consulting detective, and not a monster hunter. Someone to be admired and taken seriously, and not a subject of comedy and ridicule. A champion born in 1854 and set in a specific era, and not a Doctor Who wanna-be who can be dropped into any timeline.

Now, nearly ten years later, with 45 volumes (and more in preparation) and over 920 stories, more weight has been added to the scales on the side of the *True Holmes*. But *Fake Holmes* is still sitting over there, grinning and gibbering on the other side of the see-saw, and the work isn't done.

We can but try.

* * * * *

"Of course, I could only stammer out my thanks."
– *The unhappy John Hector McFarlane,* "The Norwood Builder"

As always when one of these collections is finished, I want to thank with all my heart my incredible, patient, brilliant, kind, and beautiful wife of nearly thirty-six years, Rebecca – Every day I count my blessings and realize how lucky I am, for she is the finest and fairest of them all!!! – and our amazing, funny, creative, talented, and wonderful son, and my friend, Dan. I love you both, and you are everything to me!

With each new set of the MX anthologies, some things get easier, and there are also new challenges. For several years, the stresses of real life have been much greater than when this series started. Through all of this, the amazing contributors have once again pulled some amazing works from The Tin Dispatch Box. I'm more grateful than I can express to every contributor who has donated both time and royalties to this ongoing project – both for the current set, and also the 200+ contributors from around the world since the beginning. It's amazing what we've accomplished – as just mentioned, over 920 new Holmes adventures in 45 volumes (so far), and over $120,000 raised for the Undershaw school for special needs children!

I also want to give special recognition to the multiple contributors of this set: Arthur Hall, Tracy Revels, Marcia Wilson, Daniel D. Victor, Susan Knight, Alan Dimes, Paula Hammond, Mike Adamson, Jonathan Schneer, and Daniel Lenois.

Additionally, I cannot express how thankful I am to all of those who keep buying these books and making them the largest and most popular Sherlockian anthology ever.

I'm so glad to have gotten to know so many of you through this process – both contributors and readers. It's an undeniable fact that Sherlock Holmes people are the *best* people!

I wish especially thank the following:

- *Daniel Stashower* – I first became aware of Mr. Stashower in 1985, when his Holmes adventure *The Adventure of the Ectoplasmic Man* was first published. That was during those dark days when only one or two good traditional Canonical Holmes pastiches were published per year – and that's if it was a good year! I was halfway through college, and bought it and devoured it, impressed at the meeting between Holmes and Watson and Houdini, and also learning a lot more about Houdini than I'd previously known.

  From there, Mr. Stashower went on to write and edit a number of other works, including several volumes about the First Literary Agent (*Teller of Tales: The Life of Arthur Conan Doyle* and *Arthur Conan Doyle: A Life in Letters*, both multiple winners of the Agatha, the Edgar, and the Anthony awards, and *Dangerous Work: Diary of an Arctic Adventure*) and co-editing four Holmes anthologies (with Martin H. Greenberg): *Murder in Baker Street, Murder, My Dear Watson, Ghosts in Baker Street*, and *Sherlock Holmes in America.*

  I was thrilled to finally meet him in 2020 when I attended the Sherlock Holmes Birthday Weekend in New York, when he signed for me another volume he'd co-edited, *The Worst Man in London* (containing the facsimile manuscript of "Charles Augustus Milverton", along with a number of related essays). His work has been important and impressive, but personally I'm most grateful for what he's done to bring more Holmes adventures to light. Having admired his Sherlockian work for nearly forty years, I'm thrilled that he's a part of these books.

6

- *Steve Emecz* – From my first association with MX in 2013, I observed that MX (under Steve Emecz's leadership) was *the* fast-rising superstar of the Sherlockian publishing world – and more than ten years later, that has not changed. Connecting with MX and Steve Emecz was personally an amazing life-changing event for me, as it has been for countless other Sherlockian authors. It has led me to write many more stories, and then to edit books, along with unexpected additional Holmes Pilgrimages to England – none of which might have happened otherwise. By way of my first email with Steve, I've had the chance to make some incredible Sherlockian friends and play in the Holmesian Sandbox in ways that I would have never dreamed possible.

  MX has become *the* powerhouse premiere Sherlockian Publisher, providing new stories for those (like me) who need them, and writing and editing opportunities for those (like me) who might not otherwise have had the chance.

  Through it all, Steve has been one of the most positive and supportive people that I've ever known.

  From the beginning, Steve has let me explore various Sherlockian projects and open up my own personal possibilities in ways that otherwise would have never happened. Thank you, Steve, for every opportunity!

- *Roger Johnson* – From his immediate support at the time of the first volumes in this series to the present, I can't imagine Roger not being part of these books, and once again he has heeded the call. His Sherlockian knowledge is exceptional, as is the work that he does to further the cause of The Master. But even more than that, both Roger and his wife, Jean Upton, are simply the finest and best of people, and I'm very lucky to know both of them. Many many thanks for being part of this.

- *Brian Belanger* – I initially became acquainted with Brian when he took over the duties of creating the covers for MX Books, and I found him to be a great collaborator, and wonderfully creative too. I've worked with him on many projects with MX and Belanger Books, which he co-founded with his brother Derrick Belanger, also a good friend. Along with MX Publishing, Derrick and Brian have absolutely locked up the Sherlockian publishing field with a vast amount of amazing material. It's very gratifying to see the old

7

dinosaurs trembling with every new and worthy Sherlockian project, one after another after another, that these two companies create. Luckily MX and Belanger Books work closely with one another, and I'm thrilled to be associated with both of them. Many thanks to Brian for all he does for both publishers, and for all he's done for me personally.

And finally, last but certainly *not* least, thanks to **Sir Arthur Conan Doyle**: Author, doctor, adventurer, and the Founder of the Sherlockian Feast. Honored, and present in spirit.

As I always note when putting together an anthology of Holmes stories, the effort has been a labor of love. These adventures are just more tiny threads woven into the ongoing Great Holmes Tapestry, continuing to grow and grow, for there can *never* be enough stories about the man whom Watson described as *"the best and wisest . . . whom I have ever known."*

David Marcum
April 6th, 2024
The 141st Anniversary of
the first day of
"The Speckled Band"

Foreword
by Daniel Stashower

"*This I am sure of,*" Arthur Conan Doyle once declared, "*that there are far fewer supremely good short stories than there are supremely good long books. It takes more exquisite skill to carve the cameo than the statue.*"

The comment reflected hard-won experience. Early in his career, while practicing medicine in Southsea, Conan Doyle seemed on occasion to begrudge the time he spent pursuing the short story form. "*I realized that I could go on doing short stories forever and never make headway,*" he would recall. "*What is necessary is that your name should be on the back of a volume. Only so do you assert your individuality, and get the full credit or discredit of your achievement.*"

He soon reversed course. In April of 1891, even as his novel *The White Company* was enjoying notable success, Conan Doyle's career as a medical practitioner reached a turning point. Having recently abandoned his practice in Southsea to study diseases of the eye, the thirty-one-year-old physician moved his family to London and declared himself ready to "*put up my plate as an oculist*", setting up a consulting room at 2 Upper Wimpole Street. His lease entitled him to a consulting room and a share of a waiting room, but, as Conan Doyle ruefully admitted, "*I was soon to find that they were both waiting rooms.*"

His thoughts naturally turned to literature, and he now approached the subject of short stories in a more congenial spirit. It struck him that there might be some benefit in writing a series of stories featuring a single, continuing character. This offered an advantage over the more conventional serialized novel, because the reader would not lose interest if one installment or another was missed. "*Looking round for my central character,*" he wrote, "*I felt that Sherlock Holmes, whom I had already handled in two little books, would easily lend himself to a succession of short stories.*"

This proved to be a life-changing decision. Not only had Conan Doyle made a canny marketing decision, but he had also found the natural showcase for the talents of Sherlock Holmes. In the two previously published Holmes novellas – *A Study in Scarlet* and *The Sign of the Four* – the detective had been obliged to trundle offstage for long patches of exposition. The short story format offered a compact execution and brisk pace, and highlighted Conan Doyle's singular talent for puzzle plots.

9

Within weeks, Conan Doyle began sending the first of his Sherlock Holmes short stories to a new magazine called *The Strand*, and the rest – in a cliché he would have abhorred – is history.

"*I've written a good deal more about him than I ever intended to do,*" Conan Doyle would observe in 1927, forty years after Holmes first saw print, "*but my hand has been rather forced by kind friends who continually wanted to know more. And so it is that this monstrous growth has come out, out of what was really a comparatively small seed.*"

The phrase "*monstrous growth*" admits a number of interpretations, with a heavy suggestion of Conan Doyle's ambivalence towards his famous creation. One naturally wonders what he would have made of the present volumes, the latest in a series of forty-five – *Forty-five!* – collections of short stories, all contributed by kind friends continually wanting to know more. Even so, I feel confident that Conan Doyle would look upon the MX book series with a kindly eye. "*If every man who receives a cheque for a story which owes its springs to Poe were to pay a tithe to a monument for the master,*" he once declared, "*he would have a pyramid as big as that of Cheops.*" Each of the stories in this series owes its springs to Conan Doyle – unabashedly so. As yet there is no Egyptian pyramid dedicated in Conan Doyle's name, but at last count these books had raised some $120,000 for the Undershaw school, which provides a specialist setting for children with learning difficulties and additional needs, under the banner of "*eliminating the impossible*". It is difficult to imagine a more fitting monument to the master; one that preserves the legacy of his Hindhead home even as it helps to insure – as someone once remarked – that education never ends.

Daniel Stashower, BSI
January 2024

A Letter From Scotland Yard
Discovered by Roger Johnson

My dear Dr. Watson,

Further to our correspondence of the 15th *ult* . . . .

No, scrub that. This is strictly unofficial and off the record, and if you so much as think of publishing any part of it, *I will have you, sunshine,* good and proper.

Right. Where was I? Oh, yes . . . .

I see that Mr. Sherlock Holmes has decided to pack in the detective business and retire to the south coast. Very nice, too! I also am about to become a gentleman of leisure, having been detecting, I may say, for quite a few years more than Mr. H, but I don't expect to be moving from my little house in Camberwell – not till they carry me out feet first, anyway.

Well, well! I can't say I begrudge Mr. Holmes his retirement. Goodness knows he's earned it, and I'm not too proud to admit that he was a great help to me on many occasions, and to some of my colleagues as well. Toby Gregson – He hates being called that! – *Tobias* Gregson is probably indebted to Mr. H. for his promotion. Did you know that? At all events, he became an Inspector shortly after the successful conclusion of the Arnsworth Castle affair.

Come to think of it, I may even owe *my* rise in the force to Mr. Holmes, though I like to think that my own good qualities had something to do with it. If I remember correctly, Mr. H. once said I was the best of the professionals, and I've always taken that as a high compliment, even if he did also call me "that imbecile Lestrade"!

Dear me, but we've seen some times, haven't we, Doctor – You, me and Mr. Sherlock Holmes! "We have heard the chimes at midnight, Master Shallow."

Hah! That surprised you, I'll bet: *Me* quoting the Bard! The fact is that I once saw Beerbohm Tree play Falstaff, and I've never forgotten his performance. I couldn't tell you which play it was – "The Merry Wives of Whatsit" or "Henry Ivy" – but it was the best evening I ever had in the theatre, outside of the Drury Lane pantomimes, of course. (I say, can you imagine Herbert Campbell as the fat knight and Dan Leno as Justice Shallow? That *would* be something, now, wouldn't it?)

We have seen some times, though, haven't we? That Norwood affair, the business out in Herefordshire, the Black Pearl of the Borgias . . . Great days, Doctor, great days! And, you know, I was right about that last case: The Mafia *was* involved, after all, even if its involvement did turn out to be a bit of a red herring.

Do you recall our first proper meeting? Well, of course you do. It was at an empty house in Lauriston Gardens, Brixton − empty, that is, apart from Toby Gregson and a *very* ugly corpse. Gregson was at his most pompous, I remember, and Mr. Holmes was at his most superior. I don't need to tell you that he was always keen to prove himself a better detective than any of us, and in those early days, I sometimes suspected that that outweighed his wish to see justice done. Later, of course, I discovered that I was mistaken, but it was a close-run thing on occasion.

That, as I say, was our first *proper* meeting, though we had seen each other a few times before then, without either of us knowing just who the other one was. I quickly realised that you were sharing digs with Mr. H., and in time he told you that I was − Let me see − "*a well-known detective, who got himself into a fog recently over a forgery case*". Yes, well . . . it's true enough, as far as it goes, though the case was a good deal more complicated than Mr. H. would admit.

You weren't exactly complimentary about me yourself, were you? A "*little sallow, rat-faced, dark-eyed fellow*" you called me then, and not so long after, you said I was "*lean and ferret-like*". Well, I suppose a ferret is a more useful creature than a rat! I rather like ferrets, as it happens. My old dad used to breed them − lithe, handsome things they were, very cat-like in their ways, wonderful for getting in and out of tight corners, absolutely fearless, and unbeatable for rabbiting. You know, I really don't mind being called ferret-like! A ferret's as good a model for a detective as any sort of *dog*.

Come to think of it, you've compared me to a dog on occasion as well. Not a hound − I think you kept that particular simile for Mr. Sherlock Holmes − but a "*small wiry bulldog*". That made my wife sit up, I can tell you! She's always the first to admit that yours truly is no oil painting, but even she couldn't work out how the same person can resemble both a *ferret* and a *bulldog*!

Let's see. That was the Dartmoor business, wasn't it? Why I ever let Mr. Holmes talk me into these things I shall never know. You wouldn't *believe* the trouble I had with my own Superintendent and the Deputy C. C. of the Devonshire Constabulary! I'm sure it put my career back two years. Ah, well, it's all water under the bridge, and I wouldn't have missed it for the world, though I don't know whether Sir Henry would agree. Still, he seems to be getting on all right these days, thank goodness.

12

What was that stuff about an *unsigned warrant*, though? "*Coming down with* unsigned warrant." I can only imagine that you had lost the telegram I sent and wrote the first thing that came into your head. After all this time I can't remember just what I did say, but I'm certain I never mentioned an *unsigned warrant*! What's the use of a warrant if it isn't *signed*?

And while I think of it, I've often wondered why you described me as *little* and *small*. I'm *thin* – always have been, eat like a horse and never put a pound on – and I'll grant you that I'm shorter than Mr. H. Well, most people are, aren't they? He's a fraction over six foot, I think, and, as you said yourself, he's so *very* lean that he seems to be considerably taller. (It's odd, but *my* leanness seems to have the opposite effect!) I'm shorter than *you*, if it comes to that, but only by half-an-inch. In fact I stand – or did, in my prime – exactly five-foot-ten, the absolute minimum height for an officer in the good old Metropolitan Police.

I hope you don't mind me letting off a bit of steam. It's not really anything personal, you know. Only things are rather slow here at the moment. If I weren't writing to you, I'd just be tidying up my desk and clearing out my cupboard, getting ready to leave the Yard.

I'll miss the old place, of course I will. Old, did I say? This is *New* Scotland Yard, mate, and they don't let you forget it, especially if you've been around as long as I have, and remember working at *Great* Scotland Yard, the other end of Whitehall! Well, you'll remember what that was like. We occupied half-a-dozen buildings around Whitehall Place and Great Scotland Yard. It was dark, poky, and uncomfortable. This place is like the Langham Hotel by comparison, but that's not why I'll miss it.

It's the *people*, the fact that every day is different, the knowledge that you're helping to keep London safe . . . but there's more to it than that. We work hard here, you know (and it is mostly brainwork, whatever Mr. Holmes may say to the contrary). Sometimes it can be dull, but *most* of the time – Well, you've written about the "Adventures" of Sherlock Holmes. I can assure you that the adventures of G. Lestrade have been no less exciting!

Still, I can't deny that the best of them have been the ones I shared with you and Mr. Holmes. The Baskerville case really was a corker, and it would have been hard to top that business of the stolen submarine plans. Police work isn't always appreciated, despite what you may read in the papers, so it's nice to get a bit of public recognition – Ah! I know what you're thinking, but you're wrong. True, there was no public recognition in *that* case: You said yourself that it was part of "*that secret history of a nation which is often so much more intimate and interesting than its public chronicles*". But we all knew, didn't we, that we'd done the country good service, and that we had the approval of the people who matter.

If anyone should ask me, though, what was the most memorable adventure in my forty years with the force, I'd have to say the arrest of Sebastian Moran. Not just because it cleared up a particularly baffling murder case. Not even because it put an end to the Moriarty gang at last, but because it rather gloriously confirmed my suspicions that Mr. Sherlock Holmes *was* still alive and that he would eventually come back to London. You know, Doctor, I was never so glad in my life as when I got his message asking me to be in Baker Street that night!

And now, even though only one of us has reached what I'd call retirement age, we're both packing it in. Goodness knows what Mr. Holmes will find to do down there in Sussex, but I intend to spend my time in the garden. Mrs. L has made it very clear that she doesn't want me in the house all day, getting under her feet!

You've got yourself a good practice now, haven't you, just off Harley Street, and I can't somehow see you retiring for a good many years. Well, if anyone deserves success, Doctor, I reckon it's you. You've said a lot in your memoirs about the remarkable qualities of Mr. Sherlock Holmes, and you've even come to appreciate that we in the C.I.D. aren't lacking in skill and intelligence! But you've rather tended to hide your own light under a bushel. On occasion, you've made yourself out to be a bit of a booby, which is something you're definitely *not*!

Your military service may have been fairly short, but it was by no means ignominious. You're intelligent, skilful and courageous. Unlike Mr. H, you have a gift for making friends – and you're a better shot than he is, for all his fancy pistol-work indoors. (My word, wasn't Mrs. Hudson's face a picture when she saw what he'd done to the wall of your sitting-room!)

Above all, Doctor, you're honest and straightforward. It's been a pleasure and a privilege to know you. If I may adopt the language of the streets for a moment, and use a phrase that I'm sure Mr. Holmes would recognise, you, Dr. John H. Watson, are a *Diamond Geezer*!

Please give my best regards to Mrs. Watson, and believe me to be,

Yours very sincerely,
G. Lestrade . . .

. . . by way of Roger Johnson, BSI, ASH
Editor: *The Sherlock Holmes Journal*
February 2024

An Ongoing Legacy
for Sherlock Holmes
by Steve Emecz

Undershaw
Circa 1900

With over six-hundred Sherlock Holmes books in print, we continue to have lots of fun publishing Holmes stories. *The MX Book of New Sherlock Holmes Stories* is by some way our largest and most successful project.

Since 2023, every book bought on our website means we donate a meal to a family in need through ShareTheMeal from The World Food Programme (WFP). I am proud to have been a member of the external advisory council and a mentor with the WFP for several years, and part of the team in 2020 that was awarded the Nobel Peace Prize. You can find links to all our projects on our website:

https://mxpublishing.com/pages/about-us

Coming into 2024, it is audio that has been the fastest growing segment – though we do see some fans still wanting print, so we will continue to produce paperback and hardcover versions – especially of this series.

Steve Emecz
March 2024

The Doyle Room at Undershaw
Partially funded through royalties from
The MX Book of New Sherlock Holmes Stories

A Word from Undershaw
by Emma West

Undershaw
September 9, 2016
Grand Opening of the Stepping Stones School
(Now *Undershaw*)
(Photograph courtesy of Roger Johnson)

"Until you spread your wings, you'll have no idea how far you can fly."
– Napoleon Bonaparte

There are so many attributes to an Undershaw education, both within the classroom and in the world beyond. Who we are and the strong Undershaw character we show to the world are as real on the outside as they are on the inside. We are who we say we are. Our sense of community, our strong culture, and the values which shape our behaviour all become the very tangible qualities of an Undershaw student.

We have had such a wonderful start to 2024, and at this juncture of being halfway through our school year, it's such a pleasure to recount some of our achievements that go so far in illustrating the cultural fabric of our school.

Under the leadership of Will Milner-Smith, Undershaw's Physical Education Lead, we have seen an exponential increase in participation in sports, particularly football. We have four teams across the school, all of

17

which compete across the county in accessible leagues. Our girls' team has just returned from a tournament hosted by Fulham FC (London's oldest professional football club, established in 1879) where they were not only triumphant, but congratulated for their 'tournament values' by the staff and students from the opposing teams. Illustrating their football skills alongside their inter-personal skills has been the focus of our physical education curriculum, and it was wonderful to see these skills shining through.

To continue the theme of resilience, a group of students have just completed their Duke of Edinburgh Award Bronze Expedition, which involved two days of walking and an overnight camp. The technical skills on show (map reading, setting up camp, fire lighting, and campfire cooking) were balanced beautifully by their life skills and school values of respect, kindness, and resilience – and obviously a huge dose of teamwork.

We are also excited to bring you news of our first collaboration with an international school: Kampinda School in Zambia. PEAS (Promoting Equality in African Schools) is one of our partner charities supported by the Leo Lion Foundation. This is the first of many opportunities of this type for Undershaw, and we're excited for the future of this partnership where we can share best practice and get to know more about the world, our friends in other geographies and cultures, and shape a new way of working.

Undershaw continues to recruit and retain the very best talent, and to that end, all our Teaching Assistants have just been awarded the Open University qualification in 'Understanding Autism'. Not only does this illustrate their significant passion and commitment to our students at Undershaw, but also Undershaw's belief and investment in our staff. Careers at Undershaw are sought after, and working at a Centre of Excellence for SEND education is an enviable role.

We are so proud of our school, and of the staff and students who showcase our vision every day. I continue to be proud of our relationships outside the gates too, some with people who have never set foot in the school but know from our reputation of the abundance of good that we do here. I thank you for sharing your talent with us and for your keen commitment to us and to our remarkable students. Thank you for being by our side as we look forward to end of the academic year, awash with all its celebrations, fun to be had, and the promise of the new beginnings in the year beyond. I look forward to writing again in the Autumn with more news from Undershaw.

Emma West
Headteacher, Undershaw
March 2024

"Undershaw," Hindhead Conan Doyle's House.

Editor's *Caveats*

When these anthologies first began back in 2015, I noted that the authors were from all over the world – and thus, there would be British spelling and American spelling. As I explained then, I didn't want to take the responsibility of changing American spelling to British and vice-versa. I would undoubtedly miss something, leading to inconsistencies, or I'd change something incorrectly.

Some readers are bothered by this, made nervous and irate when encountering American spelling as written by Watson, and in stories set in England. However, here in America, the versions of The Canon that we read have long-ago has their spelling Americanized, so it isn't quite as shocking for us.

Additionally, I offer my apologies up front for any typographical errors that have slipped through. As a print-on-demand publisher, MX does not have squadrons of editors as some readers believe. The business consists of three part-time people who also have busy lives elsewhere – Steve Emecz, Sharon Emecz, and Timi Emecz – so the editing effort largely falls on the contributors. Some readers and consumers out there in the world are unhappy with this – apparently forgetting about all of those self-produced Holmes stories and volumes from decades ago (typed and Xeroxed) with awkward self-published formatting and loads of errors that are now prized as very expensive collector's items.

I'm personally mortified when errors slip through – ironically, there will probably be errors in these *caveats* – and I apologize now, but without a regiment of professional full-time editors looking over my shoulder, this is as good as it gets. Real life is more important than writing and editing – even in such a good cause as promoting the True and Traditional Canonical Holmes – and only so much time can be spent preparing these books before they're released into the wild. I hope that you can look past any errors, small or huge, and simply enjoy these stories, and appreciate the efforts of everyone involved, and the sincere desire to add to The Great Holmes Tapestry.

And in spite of any errors here, there are more Sherlock Holmes stories in the world than there were before, and that's a good thing.

David Marcum
Editor

Sherlock Holmes (1854-1957) was born in Yorkshire, England, on 6 January, 1854. In the mid-1870's, he moved to 24 Montague Street, London, where he established himself as the world's first Consulting Detective. After meeting Dr. John H. Watson in early 1881, he and Watson moved to rooms at 221b Baker Street, where his reputation as the world's greatest detective grew for several decades. He was presumed to have died battling noted criminal Professor James Moriarty on 4 May, 1891, but he returned to London on 5 April, 1894, resuming his consulting practice in Baker Street. Retiring to the Sussex coast near Beachy Head in October 1903, he continued to be associated in various private and government investigations while giving the impression of being a reclusive apiarist. He was very involved in the events encompassing World War I, and to a lesser degree those of World War II. He passed away peacefully upon the cliffs above his Sussex home on his 103rd birthday, 6 January, 1957.

Dr. John Hamish Watson (1852-1929) was born in Stranraer, Scotland on 7 August, 1852. In 1878, he took his Doctor of Medicine Degree from the University of London, and later joined the army as a surgeon. Wounded at the Battle of Maiwand in Afghanistan (27 July, 1880), he returned to London late that same year. On New Year's Day, 1881, he was introduced to Sherlock Holmes in the chemical laboratory at Barts. Agreeing to share rooms with Holmes in Baker Street, Watson became invaluable to Holmes's consulting detective practice. Watson was married and widowed three times, and from the late 1880's onward, in addition to his participation in Holmes's investigations and his medical practice, he chronicled Holmes's adventures, with the assistance of his literary agent, Sir Arthur Conan Doyle, in a series of popular narratives, most of which were first published in *The Strand* magazine. Watson's later years were spent preparing a vast number of his notes of Holmes's cases for future publication. Following a final important investigation with Holmes, Watson contracted pneumonia and passed away on 24 July, 1929.

Photos of Sherlock Holmes and Dr. John H. Watson courtesy of Roger Johnson

The
MX Book
of
New
Sherlock
Holmes
Stories

Part XLIV
2024 Annual
(1889-1897)

Moriarty
by Kevin Patrick McCann

"My horror at his crimes was lost in my admiration at his skill."

I sense his presence everywhere
Spreading like a tumour,
In quaysides slopped out by the Thames,
Whisperings and rumour.

From Limehouse up to Whitechapel,
Deceptive as a fog,
His puppets strike without pity,
Each one's a soulless cog.

He is my dark Doppelgänger,
My mind's demented twin,
I detest him for this craving,
He fills my need for sin.

The Disputed Debutante
by I.A. Watson

A disturbing circumstance summoned us from a Theatre Royal [1] performance of Puccini's new offering, *Edgar*. Such are the dangers of attending a venue in the shadow of Bow Street Police Station. Holmes was not too concerned at vacating the performance at the first interval, expressing his disappointment with the debuting opera's "contradictory notation of phrasing, dynamics, and articulation," which seemed to have offended his musical sensibilities. [2]

"An honest mystery would be better than this confounded garble of noise," Holmes considered. "I had best eschew the remaining three acts of this cacophonic travesty and find useful employment."

The urgent plea came from Scotland Yard Detective Inspector P. Athelney Jones, [3] who had evidently been called to the Mayfair home of Lord Fouldenheath, [4] the Earl of Fenwick. An exclusive *soiree* at which half of our capital's society was attending had been rudely interrupted by the deaths of two of the guests. It appeared that a pair of ardent suitors of the same debutante had shot each other in a duel, but there were aspects of the incident which were troubling the policeman. Would Holmes be able to come immediately before any chance of a proper investigation was lost?

"You do not mind me missing *Edgar?*" Holmes checked with me, smelling better entertainment.

"You must go, of course. I am sorry I cannot accompany you."

My concern was that our evening out included my fiancée, Miss Morstan, who would become my wife within four weeks. I was loathe to let Holmes respond to Jones's appeal alone, but also to part with Mary's company, especially on an occasion designed to encourage my friend Holmes to socialise with my future bride. [5]

Holmes evidently discerned my dismay at our interrupted evening. "You must escort Miss Morstan home, of course," he told me. "I quite understand that you are unable to accompany me to Lord Fouldenheath's place." To Mary he said, "I trust you will excuse my sudden dispatch?"

"Oh, I would not part Mr. Holmes from his companion in detection," Mary teased us. "If there is need for Sherlock Holmes at Lord Fouldenheath's residence, there is need for Dr. Watson. If there has indeed been a death, then it behoves each of us to do what we can. I know that I should feel guilty to simply go home and do nothing. Besides, since we are dressed for the opera, we are fit to be presented at a society ball."

35

"*We* are fit?" I repeated, with a growing dismay.

"I was promised an evening out, James. [6] Since the opera has proved a disappointment, perhaps a Mayfair *soiree* might salvage the evening? Don't you think?"

She shot me a significant look, which I belatedly took as a reminder of a conversation we had shared regarding our concern about Holmes's growing reliance upon the use of cocaine to divert himself. Mary and I would be moving into old Farquahar's medical connection in Paddington once we were wed, but my fiancée and I had agreed it best that I remain close to my dear friend as he adjusted to my imminent departure from our shared Baker Street lodgings – hence Mary's unusual proposal to accompany us on our investigation.

"There have been *murders!*" I still objected. "Or if not murders, at least deaths! I can hardly drag my fiancée – "

"That's not the issue, James," Mary warned me. "It is whether you intend to forbid me to accompany you."

"But my dear – " I replied, glancing at Holmes.

"I have volunteered," Mary cut me short. "Come, James, you know that I have endured hardship and horror beyond anything one might encounter in a Mayfair drawing room. And if a young debutante is distressed by two suitors' deaths, who would be better to calm her – a gruff army doctor, or an experienced governess?"

I am unsure how much of our byplay and thinking Holmes noted. "The presence of a sensible female companion might be fortuitous," he admitted.

Mary was a soldier's daughter and an old India hand. Recognising the set of her fair eyes and the determination in her dainty jaw, I knew better than to put up more opposition. If she wished to see the rich chambers and fancy dresses of the noble set, then why should I prevent her curiosity? Besides, Miss Mary Morstan might match any woman in England, or in the world, for grace, charm, looks, and character.

So it was three of us who took his Lordship's carriage and responded to Athelney Jones's summons.

The scene at Fouldenheath's party was one of confusion. The unhappy events had occurred less than an hour before. Police had been summoned to the site and had arrived in a great swarm, although Inspector Jones had managed to herd them to some semblance of order. Guests were expecting to depart, their carriages already cluttering up the square outside, but had so far been prevented from leaving until statements could be taken from all present. A good number of Important Personages were outraged to be so discommoded, and were not reticent to say so.

Holmes, Mary, and I were greeted by the harassed inspector and by Lord Fouldenheath himself. His Lordship glanced dubiously at Mary. "I'll just go and find young Lady Constance, shall I?" my fiancée asked us brightly, and hastened off to offer the support she had intended.

The Stock Exchange peer was rather ruffled and red-faced, evidencing little affection for the police detective in charge at the scene. I could see why Jones might have wished for additional support outside his chain of command. In addition to Fouldenheath, there were at least two High Court judges present, along with almost a dozen members of the House of Lords. Any of threescore outraged guests might stir themselves to blight the inspector's career.

As soon as we were ushered into a private antechamber, settled in comfortable chesterfields, Jones and Lord Fouldenheath laid the facts as they knew them before us.

Jones reported with the aid of his notebook in fine judicial form. "Constables were summoned to Lord Fouldenheath's Mayfair townhouse at or about 8:42 p.m. tonight, after discovery of an incident in the library. Two fatalities were reported.

"Amongst Lord Fouldenheath's guests at his ball was Lady Constance Westcott, one of the debutantes of this year's season. Also present were several of her suitors, including Lord Winterly, Viscount St. Stephen, and Viscount Edward Fouldenheath, the Earl's eldest son.

"At or about 8:50 p.m., Mrs. Sanderson, Lady Constance's companion chaperone, was taken ill – to be blunt she had to retreat to a privy rather quickly – which allowed the debutante's admirers to press their suits. Winterly and St. Stephen accompanied the lady into the first floor library, which is a chamber at the far end of the long gallery where the dancing was taking place. His Lordship insists that the library was locked – "

"It *was* locked!" Lord Fouldenheath interrupted. "I secured it myself this afternoon before the caterers and guests arrived. I did not want idlers handling rare and delicate volumes or otherwise disrupting my collection. The door was locked."

Holmes gestured for Jones to continue his account.

"It seems as though Winterly and St. Stephen had determined to win some decision from Lady Constance regarding her matrimonial future," the Scotland Yard man reported. "Their mutually exclusive campaigns evidently led to a good deal of anger about the object of their desire. Lady Constance sought to intervene before they came to blows, but they ushered her into the connecting reading room, a small annex which has but one door and can be accessed only via the library. There is no lock on the reading room, but a chair was laid at an angle such that its back caught under the doorknob, effectively barricading the lady in while her swains roared at each other.

"The music was loud and the dancing vigorous. Nobody heard, or could have heard, upraised voices and harsh words. Lady Constance cried out for assistance and to try and soothe the conflict, then was startled to frightened silence by the sharp nearby sound of two shots.

"Shortly after this time, perhaps 8:20 p.m., Mrs. Sanderson returned to seek her charge. It took her a few minutes to learn that Lady Constance had retired to the library with her admirers, and then she discovered that the library door was locked. She appealed – indeed complained – to Lord Fouldenheath, who produced a key and gained entry to the room.

"This was when the tragedy was discovered. The two men were at opposite ends of the library, St. Stephen by the fireplace and Lord Winterly at the end nearer to the annex door. Both men were dead of gunshot. Each had a duelling pistol in or close to his grip. Lady Constance was still sealed inside the annex, frightened and distressed by the rapport of two bullets."

"It was obvious what had happened," Lord Fouldenheath broke in again. "The two hotheads had quarrelled, had produced pistols to settle matters, and had managed to shoot each other. A doctor present at the party declared them both dead of their wounds, one shot to the head, the other to the centre chest. Naturally the police had to be called, and so they were. But then Inspector Jones produced his fantastic theory and – "

"I shall determine my own theories," Holmes interrupted the interruption. "For now, I should like to have the facts as the inspector has noted them."

His Lordship bit down whatever comment he was about to retort and allowed Athelney Jones his piece.

The detective glanced at Holmes gratefully and went on. "There were a few problems with the scene," he told us. "First off, the library door. It was locked, yet I have not been able to find a key inside the library, either on the dead men or hidden in the room. Secondly, on the side-table there were three brandies poured, all partly drunk. Lady Constance does not drink brandy, preferring a light white wine. Thirdly, from your lessons, Mr. Holmes, I was able to read that Lord Winterly was left-handed – at least I think he was – but the revolver lay close by his right hand.

"I do not say that these observations mean that the death-scene was staged, but it raised doubts in my mind. For that reason, I was unwilling to draw the simplest conclusion and sought permission to send word to see if you might review the case."

Lord Fouldenheath sniffed. "I wouldn't have agreed except that Robert Walsingham argued that you might be the man to help us avoid scandal and disgrace. He said you were capable of a degree of discretion."

Holmes and I had encountered Lord Robert Walsingham de Vere St. Simon, second son of the Duke of Balmoral, a couple of years earlier, assisting him in discovering the circumstances of his absconded bride-to-be. [7] He had little reason to love us (since said bride was proved to be already married to another man) but had good cause to know our discretion. I was unsurprised to learn of his presence at the *soiree*, or that he too was one of Lady Constance's many suitors.

"I shall do what I may to discover the truth," Holmes replied. "Perhaps you might offer me an account of the evening from your Lordship's perspective?"

The Earl's lips tightened. He gathered his thoughts and said, "It has been my custom for over a decade now to host a gathering during the season, since the days when my own daughters came out. I do not believe I flatter myself in claiming that few people in good society would willingly miss one of my balls.

"Lady Constance has made quite an entrance into society. Her name is on many lips. I am aware of my eldest son's interest, but I doubt much will come of it. Constance Westcott is a pretty girl with good breeding, but her inheritance cannot be much more than seven-thousand a year. She will doubtless make a good match, but not with Edward."

Seven-thousand a year seemed a very great deal to me, an impecunious army surgeon seeking a larger practice that might sustain a wife, but I well understood how differences in wealth could be barriers to alliance. Indeed, had Mary's rich inheritance not been lost in the waters of the Thames, I should never have felt able to court her and marry her. [8] Viscount Edward, son and heir to the Earl of Fenwick, eventual inheritor of his family's entailed estates, would command an annual income of far more than seven-thousand, and would doubtless take a wife who could magnify his fortunes.

I wondered, though, if young Edward saw the matter in the cold business terms that his noble father, hard-headed Vice-Chairman of the London Stock Exchange, evidently did.

Fouldenheath continued, oblivious to my ruminations. "The girl received a good deal of attention tonight. I daresay her dance card was as full as any of the young ladies turned out in their dazzling array. Winterley, St. Stephen, Walsingham, Chapman, Morris, FitzHenry, as well as my Edward, all lined up to partner her across the floor. She is a heartbreaker, that one.

"She is evidently staying with the Dalrymples for the London season – the Kent Dalrymples, you know – it was they who brought her to visit previously, at Edward's invitation. Mrs. Dalrymple is not well today and therefore Lady Constance was attended by her *duenna*. It was that lady,

Mrs. Sanderson, who sought me out to object to her ward's sequestration in my library. I *do not* understand how the library was unlocked to be available for guests to occupy.

"Did Viscount Edward have a key?" I enquired.

"No. There are three keys, held by myself, my head butler Matthias, and the third in my private study on the second floor, which is also locked, in a locked desk. That last is the most secure of all, since it is that room where I retain those confidential files and correspondence regarding my work with the Stock Exchange. Matthias insists that he did not open the library or allow his key to be removed from him. I can attest the same."

"The key is a serious question," Jones affirmed, perhaps hoping for Holmes's support on the point.

"Alerted by Mrs. Sanderson to some oddity in the library, I left off my conversation with Sir Gabriel and Lady Kipps, collected Matthias, and proceeded through the long gallery ballroom to the library door. It was locked as it should have been, but I unfastened it and looked inside.

"That was when I discovered the tragedy. Mrs. Sanderson screamed, alerting the rest of my guests that something was amiss. She cried out for Lady Constance, with no reply. I told Matthias to take her in hand and to keep everyone back. The music had stopped, and many curious revellers would have otherwise swarmed in to look at the scene."

"The library has not been disturbed?" Holmes demanded jealously.

"Except by Scotland Yard and half the policemen of London," Lord Fouldenheath answered angrily. "Anyway, the points of interest were as Jones told you: The two men dead at extreme ends of the room, bloodied from gunfire that also stained my Turkey rugs. The three whiskies – which I own is odd. The desk chair propped to hold the annex door shut, and Lady Constance, distraught and fearful, cowering behind it. She was not short of people who wished to comfort her when her companion retrieved her."

I was rather glad then that I had brought sensible Mary to sit with the young woman, especially if Lady Constance's chaperone still suffered from a malady and might at any time have to make a hasty withdrawal.

The rest of his Lordship's account did not hold Holmes's attention. Having been apprised of the bones of the situation, he was eager to see the site of the incident. We moved upstairs, fending off the protests of guests who felt that their being retained by the police was an imposture better reserved for servants and commoners, and were shown to the library.

The Earl's library was larger than our entire flat at Baker Street, occupying the full length of one side of the house, if its annex reading room was included. Three banks of stately Georgian sash windows would offer excellent illumination in the daytime, For now, the room was illuminated by a dozen or more floor-standing branched candelabras, as well as the roof and wall-fitted gas lights. The full-length curtains remained undrawn. A grand fireplace with marble surround occupied one shorter wall, but the hearth was cold since no guests had been expected in this part of the townhouse.

The side-table, smaller than the polished circular reading table that had been pushed aside during the recent confrontation, was positioned quite near the connecting door to the gallery. A silver tray contained port, brandy, and whisky. The three glasses with their poured contents had come from a shelf below where five more identical cut-crystal glasses were still stored. There were two cigarettes stubbed out in the ashtray, whose brands Holmes immediately identified and later matched with the dead men's tobacco-cases.

We could see by the ruined floor-rugs where the corpses had laid. Holmes was put out that the bodies had been moved, but Jones pointed out that it was all he had been able to do to keep them from being removed from the premises. They had been shifted to the scullery under the supervision of Sir Gabriel Kipps, who before his retirement had been senior surgeon at St. Bart's Hospital, and my own supervisor during my time as a dresser [9] there.

Still present were the revolvers, a pair of single-shot duelling pistols from J. Beattie and Son of Portland Place. [10] Holmes sniffed them, confirming that they had been recently fired, and checked them for any other useful signs. He quickly traced the bullets' passages, retrieving one crumpled ball from the floor where it had ricocheted off the marble hearth leaving a chip, and another from a handsome collected edition of *Athenae Cantabrigienses* [11] behind where Lord Winterly would have stood. Both bullets showed grisly signs of their passage through their intended targets.

"You were correct to summon me, Jones," Holmes told the watching Scotland Yard inspector. "You may see from the line of the shots that something is amiss."

I tried the trigonometry myself. "If Winterly stood at the opposite end of the library to St. Steven and exchanged shots with him so that the ball penetrated the shelved book there, then he could not have fallen in the spot where the stained rug places him."

"Might not Winterly have survived long enough to stagger a step or two before falling?" Lord Fouldenheath objected.

"He might," Holmes accepted, "had he not brought his rug along with him. Look carefully. There is no second stain here, for the effusion had not then permeated the weave, but every trace of blood indicates that the victim dropped where he was shot, marring your Turkey carpet, and was then dragged three feet to the side on the rug itself."

"How so?" I objected. "Both men were shot. St. Steven received his bullet right to the head. His demise would have been instant. And yet the room was locked and empty, save for these two!"

Holmes waved aside that problem for another time. He examined the desk chair that had been commandeered to confine the unfortunate Lady Constance in the reading room, discovering scratches on the furniture's varnish complicit with being jammed under the doorknob. There was a corresponding abrasion on the mother-of-pearl door handle.

We tested the chair *in situ*, and I discovered that the arrangement was sufficient to bar me from the library. A young woman such as Lady Constance would have had no means of breaking out.

Holmes insisted that both rooms remain sealed, with a constable at the door, until he had opportunity for a thorough search. Lord Fouldenheath had so far demurred from allowing "grubby policeman" to handle the books on his shelves.

I was anxious to find Mary and assure myself that she was coping with our unexpected adventure. I need not have been concerned. She had taken charge of the disputed debutante in one of the sitting rooms off the other end of the gallery. In the absence of Mrs. Sanderson, who had again been taken with the flux and had been compelled to retreat to a water closet, Mary had proved a formidable defence for Lady Constance against well-meaning matrons, curious thrill-seekers, and hopeful swains.

"Constance is ready to talk to you," she told Holmes and me. "She will be sensible and discover what she saw and heard."

"Perhaps you might collate the statements of the other guests that your constables have taken?" Holmes suggested to Inspector Jones. "If you are satisfied that any useful witnesses have been identified and that we know where to find the rest if required, there is no reason you cannot now send the revellers on their ways."

That also neatly disposed of Lord Fouldenheath, who followed after the Scotland Yard man to ensure that none of his noble guests might be further offended by their interrupted evening.

"How are you faring?" I asked my fiancée as Holmes closed the door on policeman and peer.

"The plot seems better than that of *Edgar*," Mary told me with a twinkle. "I shall retain judgement until I have seen the last act."

Despite tear-reddened eyes, Lady Constance Amelia Westcott was a very attractive young thing, maintaining her composure in spite of the dead men whose lives had ended right before her. As always, my heart went out towards a damsel in distress.

"It is my coming-out season," she explained as we questioned her. She gestured to her ballgown of white silk, signifier of her availability for matrimonial alliance of the highest sort. [12] "I had half-expected proposals of marriage tonight, from Lord Winterly or Viscount St. Stephen or both. I had not expected them to kill each other over me."

"It is preferable to begin at the start of the thread," Holmes told Lady Constance. "Tell us of yourself. What circumstance brought you into the orbit of these two noble sprigs?"

The debutante set aside her mother-of-pearl fan and dabbed her eyes with a delicate handkerchief. She took a grip of herself, glanced at Mary for support, drew in a deep breath, then spoke as calmly and clearly as she could muster.

"In December before last, my father passed away of a long-term lung illness. He had been an invalid for some years and had kept to our country manor at Flaxhollow in Derbyshire. That was where I grew up, though as his illness progressed he deemed it better for me to be away from a gloomy house of sickness and arranged for me to be boarded at a private school for girls. He died shortly before my final term ended, but I was able to return home for his funeral. I am his sole heiress.

"It had always been understood that I should come out once I had finished my education overseas. My father made provision for it in his will, arrangements that when I turned sixteen, I should be sent for a year to a finishing school in St. Gallen, Switzerland, and then introduced to society. His executor, Mr. Hurstings, of Hurstings and Crewe, our family solicitors, has followed his instructions exactly.

"I am hosted in London by friends of my late mother, the Dalrymples of Mayfair. At Easter, I was presented to Her Majesty, along with the five-hundred-or-so other girls who are now entering society – all those carriages queuing along the Mall, awaiting their occupants' turn to show off their practiced curtseys to our monarch!"

Lady Constance dared a glance directly at the detective who interviewed her. "You must understand, Mr. Holmes, how important the Season is to a debutante's hopes of a proper future. For six months, between March and the opening of the red grouse season on the Glorious Twelfth, she is paraded through a calendar of social engagements, shown off to such men of quality as are seeking a wife. A successful debutante will be affianced before August when everyone leaves London for the shires. There will be a courtship, a period of not less than six months to prove the match is well-suited and to conclude arrangements regarding dowry and settlements, and thereafter an alliance of marriage.

Unsuccessful young women must rely upon the next Season or the one after that, or risk becoming old maids.

"I confess, I was prepared for my coming out no less rigorously than a thoroughbred racehorse from an exclusive stable is trained for the Derby. That is the purpose of a finishing school, of course. An accomplished debutante has perfect poise and manners, is fluent in several languages, plays the piano and sings, is skilled at needlepoint and painting, knows the classics, and is an expert hostess. A *wise* debutante is versed about every member of the monarchy, peerage, and gentry, their families and histories, along with regimental uniforms and insignia. We must be elegant, graceful, and lovely, demure but confident, innocent yet competent – the sort of woman who could run a grand estate and mother capable children, who can stand beside a great man and support him in his great endeavours.

"I say this not to boast but to illustrate how I was shaped to enter society. It is relevant to the enquiry you made of me, Mr. Holmes. It is perhaps the reason that two men now lie dead."

Lady Constance pushed back an artfully framed "stray" curl that hung fetchingly over her left eye, heedless now of her artifices. Her powdered cheeks were pale. "I met Viscount St. Stephen in the Strand as I was promenading on my little palfrey. You must understand, riding each day to be seen is an important part of the Season. A well-kept seat on a sprightly prancer may yet captivate gentleman who have no skill at or love for dancing. So long as the lady is escorted by a groom or male relative, there is no reason not to exchange words of greeting with a young officer or gentleman rider who is likewise exercising his horse. In such a manner, I encountered Arthur St. Stephen, eldest son of the Marquess of Castlepeak.

"Lord Winterly first noticed me in church as I sang a portion of *Ellens dritter Gesang* – 'Ave Maria'. I am especially fond of Schubert, and he suits my mezzo-soprano voice very well. [13] Thereafter he called upon Mr. and Mrs. Dalrymple and left his card, and shortly after invited them to call upon him at his St. James's Park address. Of course, his invitation included any houseguest the Dalrymples might choose to bring with them to return his compliments. So I was introduced to my second suitor, who has – had – a fine ear for a well-performed piece of music.

"This was all in the first days of my Season, There were other gentleman that courted me, several newly presented to Her Majesty themselves at one of her levees: Dear Edward Fouldenheath, of course, who particularly arranged for my invitation to the event tonight. Lord Robert Walsingham de Vere St. Simon, of the Balmoral line. Captain Morris of the Guards. Chapman, the diplomat. And Sir Maurice FitzHenry."

"Are any of those others here tonight?" I wondered.

"They are all here," Mary answered me. She had been required to fend several off them off from "attending" to the upset Lady Constance. "None of them seemed too distressed to have their two primary rivals gone from the field."

The debutante shuddered. "It should not be like that. I know that there is a distasteful aspect to the season's parade of girls for marriage, but it is also a great honour to be admitted to court, to receive Queen Victoria's regard, to be introduced to men of consequence and serious intention and to gain their attention. Now I am afraid that I was trained too well, prepared too rigorously. Two men are dead for it!"

"You have provided the context of your situation," Holmes told her. "Now describe the events of this evening as you experienced them."

"Say it as you told me, Constance," Mary advised.

The society beauty nodded. She sat up straight as if giving a recital or reading aloud at some salon event, and spoke in a steady, clear voice. "I arrived with Mrs. Sanderson at twenty-to-eight. That was a calculation. One must appear in time to be seen arriving – not too early, nor yet tardy. Mrs. Sanderson accompanied me because Mrs. Dalrymple was indisposed. We could not know that Mrs. Sanderson might suffer similar symptoms once she was here. It may have been the fish at last night's dinner, which I did not have since I do not care for turbot.

"I was greeted at the door by Edward – that is the Earl's son, Viscount Edward Fouldenheath. He was very eager to be the first to meet me, to escort me into the ball, and to be first on my dance card. He outmaneuvered both Winterly and St. Stephen on that count. I ensured that my other suitors also had their turns about the room.

"You can read my dance card for an exact timetable of my engagements at the ball. As I have been tutored, I was careful to allow intervals where I would sit out a measure so that gentlemen might approach me in pleasant conversation. In that manner, I had opportunity to exchange regards with all the suitors I have mentioned. I might perhaps preclude old General Grandier, who at sixty-one is unlikely to be my proper match and whose proposal should be discounted.

"After my fourth dance, which would perhaps have been at eight o'clock and was with Lord Winterly, he requested a moment's confidential speech with me in one of the side chambers. I looked about for Mrs. Sanderson but could not see her. I now know that she was indisposed. Seeing that I was unsure about being unescorted, Lord Winterley suggested that we might sit in the library, apart from the party crowd, with the doors open so that we could watch the dancers."

"The library was unlocked?" I checked.

"Certainly. Why would it not be?"

"And Lord Winterly knew it was available?" Holmes confirmed.

"Yes. He escorted me there with certitude." Lady Constance did not seem to understand why we would ask such a question.

"Tell them the rest," Mary urged her.

"Lord Winterly seated me at the large reading table. He remained standing. He was beginning to speak when Viscount St. Stephen stalked in, asking him what he thought he was doing. Winterley replied that he was having a private conversation with me, and that St. Stephen could go to – Well, that he could go to the Devil. St. Stephen retorted that he would be damned indeed if he left me alone in Winterly's clutches. There were no clutches.

"Were either of the fellows drunk?" I checked.

"No. I don't believe so. The party had hardly started."

"They did not pour drinks for themselves in the library?" Holmes ventured. "Did they perhaps offer you a drink? A brandy?"

"I had already drunk a white wine between the third and fourth turns. I do not care for brandy or any strong spirits."

Holmes gestured that she should continue her account.

"The gentlemen became agitated," Lady Constance recounted. "They were shouting, but that was partly because the music of the orchestra was quite loud. St. Stephen closed the doors to muffle it somewhat."

"St Stephen closed them?" Holmes verified. "Did he also lock them at that time?"

"I do not know. I admit to being somewhat alarmed that my suitors were becoming so enraged. I feared they might come to blows and harm each other. I did not even think . . . ." The lady paused a moment, gripping Mary's hand tightly.

"'We must settle this, then,' St. Steven said at last. 'We cannot expect Lady Constance to resolve our grievances. There is only one way.'

"'Not in front of Constance,' Winterley answered him. 'She should not see this.' I asked them what they meant, but Lord Winterly drew me up by my elbow and escorted me to the adjacent reading annex, that small room off the main library. Before I knew what was happening, he had closed the annex door on me – and I could not get it open again!

"I knocked and then hammered upon the door. I became angry, and then frightened. I could hear the men speaking in the next room, sounding cross, but I could not hear what they were saying."

"How many voices did you hear?" Holmes enquired.

"How many?" Lady Constance hesitated for a moment, licked her lips nervously, and replied, "Why, there must have been two."

"There was no third voice?"

46

"How could there have been? The . . . the orchestra was still playing a Viennese waltz – Strauss, but I cannot recall which one. I could not distinguish voices. Anyhow, I realised that I was being silly, hitting a door. I composed myself in a chair and awaited my release, intending to speak sharp words to the gentlemen who had confined me so. And then I heard the shots."

"How close together were they?" Holmes wanted to know.

"Close . . . but not simultaneous. One, two! Like that. I know now that they were shots. At the time I was unsure. I have never been close to gunfire of that type before, although I am properly versed in shooting game. But I began to fear that something terrible had occurred. It was when Mrs. Sanderson released me that my doubts were confirmed."

"Neither of your suitors had actually proposed to you yet," Mary clarified.

"I feel that Lord Winterly may have intended to before the quarrel. I would not have immediately accepted his offer, of course, without consulting the Dalrymples and my guardian. Indeed, I would not be able to contract marriage without my guardian's consent."

"Who is you guardian?" I wondered.

"Mr. Hurstings, my father's man-of-business and his executor, of Hastings and Crowe in Chesterfield. He administers my trust fund and ensures the terms of my father's will. Mr. Hurstings arranged for my placement with Mr. and Mrs. Dalrymple for the season. Mr. Hurstings must approve any contract of marriage that I enter into before my thirty-fifth year, and I am presently in my seventeenth."

"And he would settle issues of dowry, allowance, and so forth?" Holmes supposed.

"Yes. It seems silly now that men are dead, but I would have brought my husband – *will* bring my husband – around twelve-thousand pounds in cash and twenty in land and properties. [14] Subject to Mr. Hastings' approval."

Mary's brows rose. That was a lot of wealth for an orphaned debutante to command, although perhaps still not enough to justify the serious interest of nobles like Winterly, St. Stephen, Walsingham, or the cadet Fouldenheath, had she not also been so beautiful and accomplished.

Holmes asked questions of detail and seemed satisfied by the answers. He requested that Mary and I continue to support Lady Constance and hastened off to interview the attendants who had come with the deceased suitors.

"Am I responsible for these men's demises, Mary?" the disputed debutante asked my fiancée. "In Switzerland, we were taught how to

47

command the attention of admirers, to flirt and enchant. Did I lead these two to their deaths?"

"You did not ask them to shoot each other," my future wife assured the girl. Perhaps out of curiosity, Mary wondered, "If they had both proposed, for which suit would you have sought your guardian's blessing?"

The enquiry seemed to startle Lady Constance. "Well . . . if I had my choice of them all . . . That is, before this tragedy . . . and was being very candid, and trusting your discretion and confidentiality on this matter . . . I should have hoped for a proposal from Edward Fouldenheath."

"Ah," responded Mary sympathetically. When I glanced at her, wondering why she might so react, she clarified for me. "Since the tragedy, several of Constance's suitors have attended on her, seeking to offer her comfort and perhaps secure some advantage in her affections. Captain Morris was likely the most persistent, requiring me to be quite candid with him about offering a bereaved lady her privacy. Viscount Edward was not amongst those solicitous enquirers."

Lady Constance looked away, perhaps to hide another set of tears.

When Holmes returned, he beckoned me over to a conference with Athelney Jones, but without Lord Fouldenheath. "I have inspected the Earl's private office door," he told us. "There are no signs of tampering with the lock to gain access to the library key in the desk drawer there. And indeed, why would a murderer who can pick locks bother to break into a sealed room to steal the key to the library? Moreover, the security precautions and quality of lock on his Lordship's office are significantly superior."

"I have a mass of statement from the party guests," Jones reported. "There are plenty of contradictory accounts, much gossip, several 'expert' opinions and deductions, but nothing that seems of much value. A few people may have seen Lady Constance retreating to the library with Lord Winterly. Another thinks he saw Viscount St. Stephen enter and close the door behind him. On the whole, the rush of so many people dancing and the orchestra playing seems to have created enough confusion to obscure everything."

I confessed that I had dared face my old medical tutor, Sir Gabriel Kipps, who had been the doctor on the spot. He was convinced from the liquidity of blood and the temperature of the corpses that the deaths had only just occurred before their discovery. He would mark the death certificates as *"Termination by gunshot to the skull and torso, respectively"*.

"But we are no further on for all of this," Jones began to despair.

"We might try and discover the provenance of the pistols," I suggested. "Surely Beattie's will be able to identify the weapons, and discover from their records to whom they were sold?"

"It might be worth a try," Jones admitted. "This pair are quite elderly, perhaps twenty years old, so they may have changed hands, but we shall make enquiries."

"I have intelligence from the servants," Holmes briefed us. "It will perhaps assist us in penetrating the murk of this tangled little case."

"Mattias the butler could not account for the library's unlocking and relocking," Jones has already ascertained.

"But Holmes also spoke with Winterly's and St. Stephen's valets," I knew.

"And with some of the domestic staff on duty at the ball. Here, in brief, are the facts that I deem relevant: Lord Winterly was indeed taken with Lady Constance and was considering making an offer for her. He had gone so far as to consult his solicitor regarding questions of finance and entailment. He had also commissioned his man to discreetly identify a reputable doctor who might verify his bride's virtue. He had not yet made any proposal to Lady Constance.

"Viscount St. Stephen also had some hopes of matrimony. His manservant is aware of a conversation between his master and St. Stephen's father, the Marquess of Castlepeak, although he does not believe that the young viscount had yet won his father's blessing. The lady brings a fair fortune with her, but not an overwhelming one, and the elder Castlepeak would prefer a substantial influx of new money to retain their line's ancient privilege. If St. Stephen had sought Lady Constance as his bride without his father's consent, then he might have discovered himself cut off from his family's support.

"Viscount Edward Fouldenheath would also need to secure the agreement of his father, our host the Earl of Fenwick. The elder Fouldenheath has made his reputation as an astute financier. He is a major player on Threadneedle Street. [15] His Lordship's privileged position in our nation's financial institutions, as much as his high place amongst Britain's peers, makes his son one of the most eligible of bachelors."

"We have not yet encountered Viscount Edward," I noted.

"Viscount Edward is insensible drunk," Jones reported. "He was incoherent when my officers located him in his bedchamber, and has slept most of the time since. He is being served strong Turkish coffee to revive him so that he can be interviewed."

"He was sober enough to welcome and dance with Lady Constance," I pointed out. "That was less than half-an-hour before the confrontation in the library."

"A man my imbibe a lot of alcohol in a short time if he wishes to provide himself with an alibi. And the son of the house has every opportunity to avail himself of a copy key for his father's library."

This, then, was where Jones's suspicions had led him. "You think that Viscount Edward was the third man, with the third glass," I noted.

"I think . . ." Jones answered slowly, pondering, ". . . that it would have been easy for a jealous third suitor to follow the others into that library, either before or after Lady Constance was bundled out of the way. The library door could then be locked and pistols produced. The weapons might even have been waiting ready in a drawer in the writing desk. An armed man might order his rivals to assume the locations where they were shot. It would be simple to adjust where they fell to confirm the impression of a duel between two opponents, when actually they were both killed by another fellow present."

Athelney Jones fell short of making that last connection that condemned Viscount Edward, but he might as well have begun to plait a noose.

"This matter must be placed before Lady Constance," I declared.

"Another interview with the debutante might prove illuminating," conceded Sherlock Holmes.

"I will not answer!" Lady Constance cried out, distressed.

Jones took a stern approach. "Your Ladyship, this is a matter of murder. A police matter. Obstructing an investigation is a criminal offence."

The debutante's companion had now rejoined her. "Lady Constance is not required to speak to police officers, or to anyone else! If you wish to caution her for an official interview, then do so, and arrange a time with her guardian to question her when he can be present to represent her. But I had thought better of gentlemen such as Mr. Holmes and Doctor Watson than to badger a tender young girl with such brutal questioning."

"I only asked if Edward Fouldenheath was in the library," Jones declared unhappily. "It is a simple question. It should have a simple answer."

Lord Fouldenheath had also returned to follow the investigation, perhaps sensing that matters were now tending into areas he would prefer that they did not. "It is ridiculous to believe that Edward would be present," he scoffed. "I did not consent to investigators in my house so that they could cause trouble with idle speculation! Must I speak to the Commissioner? To the Home Secretary?"

"That would be unhelpful, your Lordship," Holmes told the Earl. "It might create an unfortunate and undeserved stigma that you tried to divert the course of a murder investigation. You are convinced of your son's innocence? Then allow me to pursue my enquiries to uncover the truth. What have you to fear?"

"The lady will have to answer the question sooner or later," Jones continued inexorably. "Either here and now, or in the witness box under oath, in peril of perjury."

"Can't you help us?" Mary appealed to Lady Constance.

"*No!*" the debutante insisted. "I shall say nothing that might harm Edward – I mean Viscount Edward. They cannot force me to it."

Lord Fouldenheath took a deep breath, appraising her. "They cannot, my dear. And if my son's suit prospers, well then . . . a wife cannot be compelled to testify against her husband . . . ." [16]

Lady Constance's brows rose in surprise. She flushed and looked away quickly.

"No arrangement of any kind has been agreed," Mrs. Sanderson insisted.

"Look here," Jones pressed on. "Someone unlocked the library. Someone locked it again with Winterly and St. Stephen inside. Someone brought duelling pistols, or had them to hand already. According to Mr. Holmes, someone shifted Winterly's body after his death."

Lord Fouldenheath replied sceptically. "Even if that is true – and I consider it unproven – any number of people might have slipped into the room at the last moment: Maurice, FitzHenry, Walsingham, Chapman, or any of their servants."

"But where did they get their key?" Mary puzzled.

"Some people can pick tumblers," the Earl insisted. "Or a wax imprint might have been taken of one of the actual keys any time before tonight."

Another thought occurred to me. "Mrs. Sanderson, I am sorry that you have been ill. I gather you suspect last night's turbot as the cause of your indisposition. But as a medical man I ask you: Had you eaten or drunk anything since arriving here at Lord Fouldenheath's *soiree*?"

"Only a glass of wine from – " the chaperone began and then clamped her jaws shut.

"Who gave you the wine?" Jones sprang, eagerly.

"I'm sure I don't remember."

"It was Viscount Edward who greeted Lady Constance at the door. Was he waiting with glasses of wine for the two of you?"

"I cannot now recall."

"You were feeling well before you drank?" I asked.

Mrs. Sanderson owned that she was.

"But Mrs. Dalrymple was similarly indisposed," I recalled.

51

Mrs. Sanderson supposed that she was, although she could not swear to the details of Mrs. Dalrymple's malady. Such details were not discussed in proper society.

"You drank a flute of wine, and soon after had to go apart for private ablution," Jones summarised, "leaving your charge unprotected and alone to be hauled away unchaperoned."

The *duenna* protested that this was not the case. She was a responsible and experienced companion for ladies of quality, well-versed in the etiquette and propriety of caring for the safety and well-being of her charges, as well as in guiding them in navigating the high society into which they were being launched. She had excellent references, as Mr. Hurstings would attest. He had interviewed her very thoroughly. She had never before suffered from such an unfortunate and embarrassing malaise, and to accuse her of inattention or unprofessionally was . . . .

Holmes had been silent all through the recent conversation, but he had watched and listened and now he spoke. "Mrs. Sanderson, what was your maiden name?"

"What?" the chaperone responded, caught off guard. "Why should you wish to know a thing like that? It was Miss Potter before I married in '75. My husband died in '78 at the sinking of the *Eurydice* off the isle of Wight. [17]

"You did not grow up in England," Holmes deduced. "Your English is very good, but it is a second language. I should say from your inflection that German was your mother-tongue, possibly with an Austrian or Swiss dialect."

"I was raised abroad," Mrs. Sanderson confessed. "I am often employed for my language skills – although Lady Constance speaks good French and German from her tuition and travels."

Whatever Holmes was asking for, we were diverted by the hasty arrival of Mr. Frederick Dalrymple, who had finally been made aware of the extraordinary events at the Mayfair party to which he had dispatched his charge. He bulled his way past Fouldenheath footmen and constables alike to discover Lady Constance.

"Connie?" he asked her, "Are you all right?"

"Yes, Uncle," she replied, "but Lord Winterly and Viscount St. Stephen are not." And she burst into tears.

Holmes and I finally got to speak with Viscount Edward, albeit with the looming presence of his protective and increasingly irate father.

"I have a horrid headache," the young man objected. "Don't look at me like that, *Pater*. I only had one drink, or perhaps two. For courage, I mean, before I danced with Constance. Not enough to land me with this beastly drumbeat in my skull. No, I was slipped something, you mark my words, by that rat St. Stephen or by Captain Morris. They probably bribed a footman! When I catch up with St. Stephen . . . Why are you all looking at me like that?"

Edward Fouldenheath's testimony was that he did not realise that two of his rivals were dead. He remembered little after his early dance with Lady Constance. He did not enter the library. He knew that it was locked. He did not possess a key. Why would he want one? He could have asked Matthias to open the door if he wanted to go in there. He did not like Lord Winterly, who was too old and stuffy for a bright bride, nor St. Stephen, who was too trivial and frivolous, but he would not murder them. He had no great opinion of Captain Morris, who lacked good manners. Chapman spent too much time talking with the French and was becoming entirely Continental. FitzHenry was a bore. Any girl would gnaw her leg off like a rat in a trap to escape an hour's conversation with him. As for Walsingham, one bride had already fled the country to avoid matrimony to him, and he didn't blame her. His (Viscount Edward's) head throbbed abominably, and when could he go and check that Constance was all right?

"There are irregularities about the duel and the deaths," the Earl told his heir. "More irregular than two fellows shooting off pistols in my library, I mean. This policeman here and his detective seem determined to drag us further into scandal, and would have it that you were also present. Give them your word that you were not and we can be done with it."

Edward Fouldenheath hesitated. "Umm, well . . ." he stammered.

"Well, what?" Jones demanded.

"Fact is, I don't really remember. I recall having a suspicion that Winterly and St. Stephen were up to something. Winterly can't avoid a smirk when he's playing a good hand, it's a useful tell. I remember deciding that I'd better keep a watch on those two after their dances with Connie. But then . . . that's all." The young lover blinked confusedly as if that might stir his thoughts. "If you ask me to swear to what I did next, I can't. Not a bit. I can't dredge up anything after that."

"Convenient," muttered Jones.

Lord Fouldenheath chivvied his son to "dredge" harder, but the desired assurance was not forthcoming.

Holmes and Jones interviewed Chapman the diplomat, a carefully spoken, circumspect witness, who had not yet had the opportunity to dance with Lady Constance before she retired into the library. They spoke with Captain Morris, a belligerent witness, who felt no need to co-operate with a "damned comic-opera rigmarole after a ridiculous pair of buffoons managed to shoot each other". They made enquiries of Sir Maurice

FitzHenry, an evasive witness, who invited them to make application with their questions to his family attorney. They had audience with Lord Robert Walsingham de Vere St. Simon, a supercilious witness, who was reluctant to again be associated with scandal and who preferred to withdraw from the whole affair.

By the time the necessary statements had been made or denied, the memorable society evening had drawn to a close. Even the most sensation-seeking of the guests had made their departure, gone to gossip word of the library scandal that would be in all the papers the next day. Staff were negotiating with policeman as to what they could clean away to set the townhouse in order after the revels and the search. Such hired help as the orchestra took their leave as soon as they were paid.

Having handed Lady Constance back to her London guardian Mr. Dalrymple and to the recovering Mrs. Sanderson, Mary rejoined Holmes and me as the detective inspected the library and annex one more time.

"Constance is recovering from her scare," Mary told me. "Indeed, she has done herself no harm tonight by her composure and compassion. Certainly the Earl of Fenwick seems more inclined to her after her defence of Viscount Edward."

"One must admire a lady who can handle herself well in adversity," I told Mary with a smile, for of course none had more demonstrated such qualities as my own dear fiancée.

"I am envious of her education," Mary owned. "That finishing school has given her a poise and polish that any debutante might covet. Mr. Dalrymple has known Constance since she was a child – he is a family connection of her late mother's – and remembers her as quite a shy, awkward little girl, especially after her mother's passing. Her father was scarcely a communicative man, evidently, after he became a widower and an invalid, and hardly encouraged her conversation. But Constance has blossomed into a vivacious and talented young woman."

Holmes had not appeared to be listening, engrossed in an inspection of the windowsills and the view out into the garden at the side of the house, but he added, "She was careful to conceal the identity of any additional person who might have been present in the library. She foresaw the advantages of discretion before any other did."

"You mean that she may have recognised the voice, Holmes?" I asked. "She knows who was there and is concealing it?"

"It may be affection, not ambition, that stills her tongue," Mary allowed.

Holmes made no comment on that, but left to search other parts of the house and grounds.

* * * * *

Miss Mary Morstan's call at 221b Baker Street the following day was perhaps slightly earlier than our luncheon appointment required. I think that, having seen the opening of Holmes's investigation, she was interested to witness whatever came next. In our married life thereafter, she never objected to my absence when Holmes required my help in an investigation, though many a wife might have. I believe it was the insights she had from the debutante duel case into Holmes's process and my part in it that softened her heart towards our detective endeavours.

She arrived in time to hear our conversation with Inspector Jones, who had endured a harassing morning pursuing enquiries and addressing a number of complaints from Important Personages who knew the Commissioner.

"I have undertaken further investigations of my own," Holmes mollified him. "If you must offer facts to your superiors to divert their ire, you may tell them the following: That the pistols utilised in the duel, the Damascus steel-barrelled Beattie set, were sold at auction in Hammersmith in July this year to a bidder who paid cash. That Lady Constance's gown was created especially for her by Gaiholm of Paris at the fantastic cost of four-thousand pounds. [18] That the Marquis of Castlepeak's debts are such that he is in danger of defaulting, and that it was therefore quite important for his son to make provident marriage with a bride of great wealth. That Mrs. Dalrymple fell ill the night before the ball and was in bed all yesterday, and that Lord Fouldenheath's hollyhocks were disturbed in the night. There are additional details that I will mention as they prove relevant. I am awaiting answers to other telegrams."

Jones absorbed this wealth of information slowly, taking his time to ponder it. "Castlepeak in trouble? But Lady Constance's fortune would be insufficient to help there. A four-thousand-pound dress? That's ten years' pay for a Police Superintendent! What's this about hollyhocks?"

"There is a bed of them beneath the library window," Holmes answered absently. He was riffling through one of his copious folders, though I could not read the label on the spine. "The flowers are somewhat broken down this morning. The markings were such as to indicate a weight of around twelve pounds was irregularly distributed over an area of three-square feet. There is one trace of a hob-nailed toecap close by that does not match the gardeners' boots."

"Someone was beneath the library window last night?" Mary considered. "Perhaps it was one of Inspector Jones's searching constables?"

"There was insufficient mess for it to have been a policeman," answered Holmes sourly. "Whoever was there had better sense about where to plant his feet, although he could not entirely avoided leaving a trace."

"Was something dropped from the window?" I wondered, confident that Holmes would know. "Another weapon, perhaps, or some valuable book?"

That did not mean that he immediately informed me, of course. Holmes is often reticent in rendering analysis until he in certain, and especially in the company of police officers with a tendency to rush to conclusions and perform dramatic arrests.

"It's answers I need, not more questions," Jones confirmed. "I've been getting roasted for making a case of this, and roasted again by the Marquis of Castlepeak about his son's death, and again by Lord Winterly's brother. And Lady Constance's legal guardian, Mr. Hurstings, is coming up to London to check on his charge and to meet with the Fouldenheaths. I don't doubt but what he will demand explanations also."

"Explanations may be forthcoming," Holmes assured us, "but patience is required. Extraordinary conclusions require secure proof."

"But am I to arrest Viscount Edwards or not?" Jones wanted to know.

"If he was there, it would be difficult to prosecute him without additional evidence or Lady Constance's testimony," I observed.

"And Constance seems reluctant to testify against him," Mary pointed out.

"Patience," Holmes reiterated. "'*Softly, softly, catch monkey.*'" [19]

Afterwards, as Mary and I lunched at Simpson's in the Strand [20], we discussed the clues that Holmes has reeled off. "There is something there," she puzzled. "The pieces must fit together. But how? Is Constance silent because she does not know or she will not say – or dare not say? Is Viscount Edward truly unable to recall his actions, or does he remember full well what he perpetrated? How did the duellists come to be in a supposedly locked library with a pair of pistols that must have been brought into the house for the purpose of their duel? Was Mrs. Sanderson made ill deliberately? Was Mrs. Dalrymple?"

"Jones said that he would interview the servants again," I mentioned. "If either Mrs. Sanderson or Viscount Edward were given drugs to cause malady or intoxication, then it would most easily have been introduced to their wine glasses. The staff are also the most likely way for someone to have acquired a duplicate library key, or to have unlocked the room."

"The key was not found inside the library, even when Holmes searched it. But it might have been dropped from the window."

"Whatever fell on the flower-bed was heavier than that. And someone was waiting for whatever it was, to take it away."

Mary addressed her salmon for a moment, and then ventured, "Constance seems to have no close confidantes, no female friends of her own age. Mrs. Sanderson is more coach than companion, and Mrs. Dalrymple is quite elderly and perhaps somewhat fussy. Do you think I might get Constance to confide in me?"

"You might call on her in a day or so," I supposed. "It would be a natural consequence of your care of her last night."

"I might convince her to speak of anything else she heard while she was confined in the annex. She may not realise that her reticence is increasing the suspicion upon Lord Edward rather than alleviating it – always assuming that she is not loyally protecting a guilty man whom she cherishes as a future husband-to-be. Or there may be other pressures on her to remain silent. The girl has been moulded to comply to instruction so as to be the model society bride. What other instruction has she received?"

"Holmes has counselled patience," I reminded my own bride-to-be. "It is generally best to allow him his methods."

"And you are part of his method, James," Mary smiled. "I trust that in time I shall become a part of yours?"

With that brave hope dashing from Mary's lips to my heart, it was only natural that I should escort her to call upon Lady Constance Westcott at the Dalrymple residence the following day, but our visit was in vain, for the disputed debutante was not at home. She was visiting the Earl of Fenwick and his family.

It was two more days before Holmes was ready to catch his monkey. In that time, he pursued a variety of other odd enquiries, about which I struggled to see any association with the case that Jones had brought him. Why he might need information from the Association de Taxi Parisien, from the verger of St. Hilda's, Borroknowle, or from Sedgemont's Naval and Admiralty Supplies baffled me. Additionally, Holmes dispatched his irregular street-myrmidons to eavesdrop on gambling dens, dock wharves, and dog tracks, while venturing out in a variety of grotesque disguises as an old tar, an itinerant knife-sharpener, a country pastor, and a Bohemian *bon vivant*.

I might have asked about these things, except that in our one long conversation at that time, Holmes led the discussion into an exacting description of the minutiae of my forthcoming wedding. While gratified that my best man was taking a creditable interest in the affair, I was surprised to have to detail the legal arrangements for marrying a bride with a settlement upon her, the church authority's requirements for documentation since Mary had been born and brought up overseas, and the ramifications of Mary having no close living relative to give her away.

On the fourth day after the Earl of Fenwick's disastrous society ball, Holmes warned me that Athelney Jones would be picking him up at one, "to resolve the minor mystery regarding Lady Constance's suitors", and that I should feel free to join him and to bring my intended wife with me if she cared to be there at the resolution. "She may prefer to avoid the unpleasantness," he warned me, "but I am certain that The Woman would wish to be there regardless, were she involved, and so may your Miss Morstan."

Consequently, it was four of us who took a hansom to Mayfair and knocked at the door of Lord Fouldenheath's townhouse. We were expected. Jones had evidently wired ahead. The family and their guests had just concluded their light luncheon.

The guests included Lady Constance Westcott, her *duenna* Mrs. Sanderson, her London hosts the Dalrymples, and now also her guardian and trustee, the dour family solicitor Mr. Hurstings, who had evidently been sufficiently alarmed by his ward's recent adventure to depart from his provincial practice to verify her safety, and had remained to negotiate the details of the Honourable Edward Fouldenheath's sudden and fervent offer of marriage.

At Holmes's insistence, the Fouldenheaths and their guests were all shepherded into that same library where Winterly and St. Stephen had perished. I noticed that the rugs had been replaced.

"This habit of interrupting my domestic affairs must cease," Lord Fouldenheath scolded Jones and Holmes. "Has not the Commissioner of Police made clear to you that you are barking up the wrong tree? Has he not called you to heel?"

"I am expected to hunt, your Lordship," answered Jones with what dignity he could muster. "I understand from Mr. Holmes that this may be the last visit that is required."

"I have solved the case," Holmes said plainly. "I have come to deliver my conclusions."

"There was no third man in this room when my suitors died," Lady Constance continued to insist. "At least, none that I heard."

"I believe you. I have only a few more clarifying questions for those of you here present and then I shall set out the solution to this puzzle."

Mary reached out and grabbed my hand, watching everything with worried wonderful eyes.

"What do you want to know?" the younger Fouldenheath demanded.

"First, Mr. Hurstings, what are the terms of Lady Constance's trust? When is her money released from its present attainder? Is it at the time of her marriage?"

The solicitor eyed Holmes suspiciously. "That's correct. There was a sum to complete her education, a sum to launch her into society, and there is an annuity. The remainder is released to her husband's control upon the occasion of her wedding. It is a common provision."

"When was this arrangement set in place? How long before her father's death was it?"

"The Last Will and Testament and its accompanying coda were put down during the last year of Lady Constance's boarding school days, a few months before Lord Westcott's passing. Despite his declining health, he was very clear in his wishes."

"How specific was he in the matter of Lady Constance's education? Did he specify the finishing establishment at St. Gallen, or was that your choice?"

Hurstings stirred unhappily. "I found the place. I fail to see the relevance of your questioning."

"I doubt it," Holmes told him. "Now, Lady Constance, would you be so good as to tell me what tune the clock on the Flaxhollow parish hall plays on the hour?"

The debutante's eyes opened in surprise at the question. "Why would you wish to know that?"

"Humour my curiosity."

"I cannot remember."

"Come," the detective chided. "The chimes sound quite clearly across your father's estate. They must have been a familiar companion of your childhood. Did they perhaps play *The Lass of Richmond Hill*?"

"Yes. I remember now."

"Not *Loch Lomond*?"

"I . . . I do not well recall my childhood. It was a traumatic time, with my mother's loss. I try not to think of Flaxhallow."

"Your mother's loss, yes. She was interred at Flaxhallow? Some family plot?"

"Of course."

"I'm afraid you misremember again. She is buried in her parents' mausoleum at St. Hilda's in Barroknowle. You recall the inscription upon her stone?"

"I cannot say. I am unaccustomed to such rude questioning!"

Holmes raised a finger to stay Viscount Edward's outraged defence of the girl. "My final question is for Mrs. Sanderson, and then I can reveal all. Frau Huber: *What became of the real Constance Amelia Westcott?*"

The lady's companion's teacup shattered on the floor, splashing out its contents, ruining another rug. She rose as if to flee. Only then did the people assembled in the library discover two unformed constables had slipped in to stand sentry at the exit.

"What do you mean, the *real* Constance?" Lord Fouldenheath demanded in a thunderous voice.

"This *is* Constance!" his son insisted loudly.

"It must be!" cried Mrs. Dalrymple. "How could . . . ?" She paused, confused and worried.

Mr. Hurstings made no response at all.

Lady Constance, if it was she, raised her noble chin and locked gazes with Sherlock Holmes. "You seem to have some wild and absurd theory, sir."

"I have facts," the detective replied. "Lady Constance was a shy, mousy girl at boarding school. She was a middling student, too quiet to be popular with her classmates, unregarded in all things, kept distant by a bereaved and ailing father, and finally fully orphaned. Yet when she arrived at her Swiss finishing school, she was a very different person: Amiable, talented, smart, and pretty – the perfect material to be groomed into a society wife."

"What?" I ejaculated, appalled by the implication.

"I have traced the quiet heiress to Paris," Holmes went on. "There she was met by Frau Huber, a tutor at the St. Gallen Academy. You would know her as Mrs. Sanderson, but that name was only adopted with her new passport on her return to England with her young charge. I'm afraid I can find no trace of the Miss Potter she claimed to once have been."

"I'll hear no more of this!" shrieked the alleged Mrs. Sanderson.

"We shall get to the heart of it!" the Earl of Fenwick insisted. "Carry on, Holmes!"

"Are you claiming, sir, that Lady Constance was exchanged for some other girl in Switzerland?" Mr. Hurstings asked Holmes caustically, with all the scepticism that the legal profession could muster.

"Indeed I am," Holmes agreed. "Once verification is sought, it will be easy to pierce the exchange of heiresses. Old classmates and teachers, inhabitants of Flaxhallow – all can attest to the identity of the true Constance."

Mary looked in horror at the debutante she had comforted. "Mr. Holmes, are you saying that the real Lady Constance was replaced with an impostor? But why?"

"The '*why*' is the key to all of this. The whole chain of events has been manipulated with significant expertise. The murders obscured the true purpose of the plot. I shall now demonstrate."

He rose and paced the room so that he could illustrate his points. The men and women assembled watched Holmes as if he was a venomous snake and they transfixed by his glare.

"Once we recognise that Lady Constance was *not* Lady Constance, and that her chaperone could not be trusted either, the whole affair becomes relatively simple. Here is the sequence of events:

"On the day of the ball, Mrs. Dalrymple is ill. It is a simple matter in a shared household for one trusted member of it to introduce *ipecacuanha* or some similar purgative into the drink or food of another member. Lady Constance, if we may continue to call her thus for now, must therefore be accompanied only by her *duenna*, Mrs. Sanderson.

"A number of things need to happen at the ball for Lady Constance to achieve her ambition of being asked to wed Viscount Edward. His father's indifference to the uneven match must be overcome. Viscount St. Steven's insufficient and impecunious suit must be dismissed. Lord Winterly's marriage negotiations had included a request that the bride's chastity be verified, which might perhaps have proved problematic. In any case, both of these suitors must be removed from the contest for Edward Fouldenheath to prevail in his quest.

"Just as it is easy for a household member to drug another, so it is to add an inebriant and sedative to a glass of wine while its owner dances with the object of his desire. Did Mrs. Sanderson hold your drink for you as you claimed the first waltz, Viscount Edward? In any case, soon after that you became insensible and were led off to your room by helpful servants. It meant that you had no alibi to prove you were not in the library at the occasion of the deaths.

"The library was unlocked around this time. Lady Constance and Mrs. Dalrymple had both visited the townhouse before, and might easily have found the chance to pickpocket or otherwise sequester the library key to gain a wax mould of it before returning it to place. It also gave them the chance to scout the layout of the premises and to set their plans.

"Given Winterly's and St. Stephen's pursuit of the lady, it was simple for her to persuade them to retire with her into the library for some private conversation. She already had a copy key to resecure the room. Once confined, the noise of the ball would drown out any gunshot. Lady Constance's expensive and elaborate gown was quite voluminous enough to conceal a pair of pistols."

"You are saying that she brought the weapons and made the men duel?" I asked.

"Nothing so baroque," Holmes dismissed. "She only held her suitors at gunpoint, put them in position, and shot them both dead. She merely needed to shift Winterly's corpse slightly to complete the illusion of two swains duelling to the death."

"No!" protested the Honourable Edward Fouldenheath.

"Her?" Jones gasped, staring at the winsome girl with new distrust.

"But the chair was jamming the door!" Mary protested. "Lady Constance was trapped on the other side."

Holmes went on dispassionately. "You will recall that Mrs. Sanderson was 'indisposed', the pretext by which Winterly and St. Stephen was able to enjoy a library liaison with the debutante without her chaperone. In fact, Mrs. Sanderson had a length of naval cord under her own skirts – I have traced the sale to Sedgemont's of Albany Street and have a good sworn description of the lady who purchased it – and she mounted to the roof parapet above the library. Constance opened the annex window. She secured the annex door with the chair, naturally remaining on the library side. Mrs. Sanderson paid down a looped, secured cord to the level of the library windows, into which Constance set her foot, and by that method was able to shift along the outside of the building and enter through the opened annex window."

"When the annex window was closed, there was Lady Constance sealed into the reading room with no escape, and her alibi established!" Jones recognised.

I saw the rest of it. "And the rope was dropped to the ground, crushing the flowers, and was removed by a waiting accomplice. The dead men seemed to be alone, each having killed the other."

"That was the intended first impression. However, the placing of the pistols, with the supposed error of left-handed Winterley's weapon being at his right hand, the discarded cigarettes, and the three whiskies were all intended to put doubt upon the obvious first conclusion of death by duel. Those were clues left for a shrewder investigator to become suspicious."

"Left to fool Scotland Yard, you mean!" spat Jones.

"Constance was quick to defend Viscount Edward," Mary recognised. "It was her fervent defence that focussed suspicion upon him. But it secured the good opinion of his doubting father the Earl for her, and she was quick to seize the legal point that a wife need not testify against her husband."

"And now an alliance of marriage has been contracted," Jones recognised. "All to gain the Fouldenheath title and fortune!"

Viscount Edward looked stricken, perhaps heartbroken.

"Indeed, it was not," Holmes contradicted Jones. "This gambit has been aimed not at the son but at the *father*. It was intended to place an agent in the bosom of the family of the very man who holds the secrets of the Stock Exchange."

Now the Earl rose to his feet. "A spy? In my own household? My son's wife?"

"There are fortunes far greater than those even of the Fouldenheaths, and secrets and contracts upon which the wealth of our nation depend. And once compromised, what blackmail might be brought against so senior a figure in our economic institutions? This substitution was long-planned and carefully prepared for. I read in it a certain touch of genius, the hand of a master, but cannot yet prove that. Suffice for now to say that suspicion must be cast upon the St. Gallen Academy. What others of its alumni are more and less than they seem?"

My eyes turned to the family lawyer who had chosen the Swiss academy, and who must have known of his ward's substitution. He avoided my glare.

"What did you do to the real Lady Constance?" I demanded of him. "Speak!"

Mr. Hurstings shook his head and made no reply. His previous feigned outrage mortified into sullen non-cooperation.

The disputed debutante answered for him. "Hurstings will say nothing. He has long been suborned. He is paid for and knows better than to betray his paymaster, even though he hangs for it. But since I am exposed, I shall make my due confession, to satisfy your minds on the detail."

"Then you did kill them?" Mary confirmed, aghast.

"I told you that I had been trained in all the proper skills of a hopeful lady. That includes shooting. I am a very good shot – although careful to disguise it so as not to surpass the gentlemen."

"Where is the real Lady Constance?" I repeated.

"Dead. Huber killed her, I believe, although she will not tell you. Huber too has her orders, and knows the consequences of saying too much. I never even met the poor child, but I was a better Constance Westcott than she ever was!"

"You . . . it was . . . ." Viscount Edward spluttered, pale and aghast.

"I fooled you all, you simple snobs! I convinced Mr. and Mrs. Dalrymple that I was the child they had known, 'so much improved' by her Swiss education. I entranced Winterly and St. Stephen, until it was confirmed that dear Edward should be my target. The murders were not part of the original conception, but became necessary for the reasons Mr. Holmes has deduced. Neither man was that great a loss to society."

The counterfeit Constance sighed dramatically. "Now it seems as though my Season has ended. For your kindnesses, Miss Morstan, I thank you, and wish you a happy marriage with your dashing doctor. For your deception, Edward, I apologise. I was pleased to be told to accept your suit over the rest. Had my plans unfolded properly, I should have made you a very happy husband. We might have had such joys. Mr. Holmes, you may regret meddling in this affair. There are greater schemes in which you should not trespass."

"Who are you really?" Inspector Jones demanded of the deceitful deb.

"Who I was doesn't matter. I was shaped and trained to be who I am now. The girl I was is as dead as the girl I impersonate. There is only me. And soon there will be no one. I shall not long survive this interview."

I have never seen so winsome a murderess make so guiltless a confession.

"Who set you on to this?" Lord Fouldenheath interrogated. "Who? Who?"

"Surely some foreign power?" she replied. "Some state with great resources to command, with capacity to plot the downfall of the great and the control of empires." She flicked a glance at Holmes. "Who else might it be?"

And then she too would say no more.

Along with the constables, Jones had brought a pair of severe matrons from Brixton Women's Prison to take charge of Mrs. Sanderson – Frau Huber – and her *ingénue*, but before the wagon arrived to remove them from Lord Fouldenheath's townhouse, the fake lady Constance was dead. The girl had not only predicted her death, she had caused it. This time her gown had contained an ampoule of cyanide.

"It's all so horrible, James," Mary commented as we walked together that evening. She had endured the library meeting and its interminable police epilogue with the character and resolution which made her so singular, but I knew she was disquieted and upset. "A shy orphaned girl betrayed by her guardian, done to death in a foreign city, never to be found. Another girl shaped like a weapon against noble men until she is used for murder and then destroys herself. Two suitors dead, another man and woman to hang, many lives blighted. Such wickedness there is in this poor world!"

"I wish I had not involved you," I admitted. "I meant to keep you from such things after Sholto. I shall be more careful henceforth."

She squeezed my arm. "I am glad to know that you and Mr. Holmes are there to bring such injustices to book. I should not love you so much if you were not the man who did that."

"Holmes does that. I am the fellow who follows behind, asking questions and taking notes."

She laid her head on my shoulder and smiled at last. "I am very content with that fellow, you know. I am going to marry him."

We set aside debutantes and duels and continued our stroll in peace.

NOTES

1. This historic theatre, built upon its site at Covent Garden in 1857-1858 after earlier venues from 1728 and 1808 burned down, has been known since 1892 as the Royal Opera House. The distinguished frontage and some rooms of Edward Middleton Barry's Victorian design remain, but renovations and reconstruction between the 1960's to the 1990's have largely replaced the remainder. It is the home of home of the Royal Opera, the Royal Ballet, and the Orchestra of the Royal Opera House.

2. Holmes was not the only person to give the work middling reviews. After many revisions, in 1905 Puccini himself declared the work irredeemable, describing it as "*warmed-up soup*". A copy of the score that Puccini sent to his friend Sybil Seligman included his scathing marginal remarks and he amended the title to read, "*E Dio ti Guardi da quest'opera!*" ("*And may God protect you from this opera!*").

3. The Scotland Yard detective Athelney Jones appears in *The Sign of Four* (1890), the novel in which Holmes and Watson encounter Miss Morstan. "The Red-Headed League" (Published 1891, collected in *The Adventures of Sherlock Holmes,* 1892) is investigated by Inspector Peter Jones, who refers back to "*that business of the Sholto murder and the Agra treasure.*" Various theories try to reconcile the similarly named policemen into one person.

4. Pronounced "*FOAL-den-eeth*" to rhyme with "*teeth*".

5. Watson may be mistaken in his recollection of which opera performance Holmes was watching. Giacomo Puccini's second opera, *Edgar*, only debuted at the Teatro alla Scala in Milan on 21st April, 1889. W.S. Baring-Gould's biography of Sherlock Holmes records that Watson's marriage to Miss Morstan, "*my wife within four weeks*" in our present narrative, took place on 1st May, 1889.

6. On the only occasion in the Canon when Mary addresses her husband by his Christian name, she calls him *James*, not *John*. This led none other than writer and scholar Dorothy L. Sayers to publish an article arguing that Watson's middle initial *H.* stood for *Hamish*, the Scottish version of *James*, and that Mary Watson, disliking the nomenclature *John*, chose to use the Anglicised form of her husband's middle name in addressing him. This theory has now accreted into Holmesian lore and is given due respect and credit here.

7. In "The Adventure of the Noble Bachelor" (*The Adventures of Sherlock Holmes*,1892).

8. The loss of "the Agra Treasure" occurs at the climax of *The Sign of Four*.

9. A dresser is a surgical houseman, what is nowadays called a Pre-registration House Officer, a newly qualified doctor working a six-month supervised probationary period prior to being fully registered with the General Medical Council. Watson's own dresser at St. Bartholomew's Hospital, London was Stamford, who introduced Holmes and Watson in *A Study in Scarlet* (1887).

10. Small arms manufacturer James Beattie's work is now very collectable. The gunsmith exhibited rifles, double guns, and duelling pistols at the 1851 Great

Exhibition. His fashionable London business was based at 52 Upper Marylebone Street, Portland Place from 1849 to 1879, becoming J. Beattie and Son from 1865.

11. *Athenae Cantabrigienses* was the work of Charles Henry Cooper, historian, lawyer, and town clerk of Cambridge in the mid-nineteenth century. Originally published in three volumes, the last posthumously, it was inspired by Anthony Wood's *Athenae Oxonienses* (1692) and contained around seven-thousand biographies of clergymen, military commanders, judges, artists, scholars, and benefactors of Cambridge University.

12. It was a custom of the age that debutantes wore white gowns to be presented to the Queen (and to Kings before that) and as signifiers of their status at other society events. Since the fabulous gowns in which they attended upon the Crown were likely the most expensive and elaborate garments they would ever own, these outfits were commonly reused as wedding dresses at the culmination of the debutante season's purpose.

   Queen Victoria herself probably set the trend for such gowns with an 1840 wedding outfit of white silk and lace that made white the fashionable colour for society marriages.

13. Franz Schubert's *Ellens dritter Gesang D*. 839, Op. 52, No. 6, 1825 ("Ellen's Third Song") was part of his Op. 52, a setting of seven songs from Walter Scott's 1810 popular narrative poem *The Lady of the Lake*. The most well-known part of the song is performed under the title "*Ave Maria*".

14. In today's currency, this would be around £2-million and £3.3-million respectively, or US $2.5-million and $4.14-million.

15. Since 1347, Threadneedle Street in the City of London has been home of the Worshipful Company of Merchant Taylors at the Merchant Taylors' Hall (where it is supposed that John Bull first conducted a performance of the British National Anthem). In Holmes's present context, however, "Threadneedle Street" refers to the site of the Bank of England (nicknamed "The Old Lady of Threadneedle Street"), the home of the London Stock Exchange until 2004.

16. Spousal privilege against being compelled to give testimony against a matrimonial partner is a very old point of law, stemming from the assumption that husband and wife are one legal entity with the right to avoid self-incrimination. By assumed rather than written law, communications between a husband and wife were also privileged by "*inviolability of domestic confidence*".

   The Evidence Amendment Act 1858 established that spousal evidence could be compelled in civil law cases but not criminal ones. The Evidence Further Amendment Act 1869 stripped additional protections in cases of adultery. At the time of our present story, 1889, a wife could not testify in the prosecution of her husband except in matters of domestic violence.

   Since the Criminal Evidence Act 1898, a series of legislations have eroded U.K. spousal privilege further, though it still exists in British law to the present day. U.S. laws on spousal communication and spousal privilege remain much firmer than their contemporary British and European counterparts.

17. *HMS Eurydice* was a 26-gun Royal Navy corvette commissioned in 1843. After several adventures around the globe, the then-elderly ship was converted to a training vessel. She capsized and sank in Sandown Bay off the Isle of Wight during a heavy snowstorm in March 1878, one of Britain's worst peacetime naval disasters. The tragedy was ascribed to "stress of weather", with all but two of her 319 crew and trainees lost.

The spectre of the *Eurydice* has often been sighted near the place she sank, with even a Royal Navy submarine once taking evasive action before the phantom ship vanished. Prince Edward, youngest sibling of King Charles III, claims to have sighted the vessel on 17th October, 1998. A film crew with him claimed to have captured the image.

18. That is around two-thirds-of-a-million pounds in today's money.

19. This phrase probably first found print in *Law and Lawyers; or, Sketches and Illustrations of Legal History and Biography* (Archer Polson, James Grant, 1840), which recounts, "'*Prudens qui patiens' was the motto of our great Coke: a motto which the negro pithily paraphrases — 'Softly, softly, catch monkey'*." By the time of "The Native Levy in the Ashanti Expedition, 1895-96" in *Journal of the Royal United Service Institution*, Volume 40, Page 305 (1896), Robert Baden-Powell records the "*West Coast [Africa] proverb*" as "*Softly, softly, catchee monkey.*"

The motto was adopted by the Lancashire Constabulary Training School and lent its name to the 1966-1969 BBC police procedural drama *Softly, Softly* and its sequel series *Softly, Softly: Task Force* from 1969-1976.

20. Officially named "*Simpson's-in-the-Strand, Grand Divan Tavern*" since 1904, the famous restaurant began in 1828 as Samuel Reiss's Grand Cigar Divan and developed into England's premiere chess-playing venue. For many years, white-coated silent waiters would quietly wheel meat trolleys between the tables so as not to disturb chess players, while boy runners waited to deliver game moves to opponents in other chess houses elsewhere.

Before 1984, women were not allowed to dine in the street-level dining-room at lunchtimes but were entertained in the first floor (second storey, U.S.) Ladies Dining Room, which was specially decorated in pastel colours (so as not to alarm females, presumably) and where louder general conversation was permitted. Women were also welcome in the first-floor 100-guest Victorian-era Banqueting Room.

P. G. Wodehouse called wood-panelled, serene Simpson's "*a restful temple of food*".

The Deaths on the Edge of Standish Woods

by Stephen Herczeg

"That was a horrible day," our host, Dr. Colton Lee, said. "So hot and dry." We sat at a small table in an outside area behind Lee's house, consisting of a wide circular area covered in fine gravel, and bordered by a wide expanse of closely cut lawn. It was a beautiful June day, with just a slight gust of breeze to dispel any of the heat.

Sipping my coffee, I replied. "I only remember the early part. The trudge from our overnight camp across the dusty plains towards Maiwand Pass dried my throat, and made my every fibre beg to return to the camp and safety."

"Yes. I'll admit that if my memory serves me well, I could only feel trepidation ahead of the day's events."

"I'm not much of a tactician, but I think the officers underestimated the Afghanis. In the thick of it, the 66th was forced into a retreat, and if it hadn't been for the poor blighter than copped it in the chest, I would have kept going."

"Yes. I was helping another injured fellow when I saw you stop and drop to help that private. When you were hit, I passed my patient off and hurried to you. Such a mess. Blood everywhere. I did what I could to staunch the bleeding until your devoted orderly, Murray, arrived with a pack horse he'd found amid the turmoil. The last I saw was you being carted off like a saddlebag."

"To that I owe you my thanks and my life." Nodding, I lifted my cup in a toast to my friend. We had come into each other's company as members of the 66th Regiment, which was pulled into a skirmish that became known as the Battle of Maiwand in the Second Anglo-Afghan War. A silly endeavour by our military chiefs, and the one that saw me sustain the nastiest of shoulder injuries and a tear to the subclavian artery. Afterwards, I came down with a bout of enteric fever and was sent back to England, never to return to active duty.

"Did you return to England along with Watson?" asked Sherlock Holmes. Looking across, I could see a tilt at boredom creeping across his face. My remembrances with my good friend were close and personal due to the period between visits.

"Oh, no, I survived that day unscathed. They needed me to stay and keep the boys fit and healthy for another few months anyway. I was even there at the end in Kandahar. Helped get the last of the boys out of Afghanistan." He shook his head in dismay. "I promised myself that I would quit the service on arrival in England, and true to my word, I did. I moved into a surgical position at Great Ormond Street, where I stayed for a few years before finally tossing it all in and coming out here."

"You've done well for yourself," I said, looking around the rear gardens of Lee's house.

Holmes and I had only just finished a little business in Ross-on-Wye, to help clear a young man named James McCarthy of the murder of his father. As we trundled slowly back towards Gloucester in a borrowed coach, I remembered that Lee had moved out to Stroud, and convinced Holmes to drop in and visit with my friend. He hadn't been impressed at the time, murmuring that there were cases that needed his attention, but I was able to persuade him to rest a day or two further before returning to London.

"Thank you, John. To be perfectly honest, I can definitely recommend a similar move for yourself. Small-town life is certainly quieter and much more peaceful than the hustle-and-bustle of London. I don't miss the regular distractions and need for my attention. Here I can set my own diary and know that nothing untoward will pop up at any moment."

"It does sound attractive," I answered, noticing an almost mocking look on Holmes's face, before adding, "But I do enjoy the adventures and higher paced life of the capital."

"Oh, yes, the adventures." Lee turned to Holmes, "How do you find yourself in so many perilous situations, Mr. Holmes?"

"I think they find me, to be honest. I have a history of solving mysteries that no other can solve, and the victims or casualties of such crimes tend to seek out the justice that I can bring them when all others can't."

Draining his coffee and reaching for the pot, Lee added, "I am intrigued, though. How does one do what you do?"

"It is an innate skill. I view a situation and my mind picks up on the minuscule clues hidden, while piecing them together into a story that fits the narrative of the puzzle. From those observations, I simply use deductive reasoning to determine the solution. I liken it a lot to what you and Watson do. A patient supplies you with evidence, spoken or measured, and it comes down to your knowledge of others who have presented similarly to conclude what ails them. Your wisdom then leads to a prescription of methods or medicines to alleviate those symptoms."

Lee thought for a moment. "Hmm. I suppose it is, isn't it? I face the same situation on an almost daily basis, I just haven't thought of it in that way before."

Our conversation was interrupted by a frantic ringing at the doorbell. Within a few moments, Carson, Lee's manservant, led a young, comely woman dressed in a slightly dishevelled nurse's uniform out onto the gravelled area.

Bowing, Carson started to introduce the woman, but before he could begin, she butted in and talked over him. "Dr. Lee, I'm so sorry to intrude, sir, especially on your Sunday afternoon, but there's been a horrible tragedy at the hospital."

Taking our coach, we ferried Lee and the young nurse back to the hospital. Vivian's ride, for that, was her name I discovered, had already made his own return journey. My old friend remained silent for the entire journey, except for asking the scant details about the patients from the nurse.

There were two couples. The Laugherys, James and Suzan, and their neighbours, Freddie and Verlene Euler. They had been found unconscious by the Laughery's farmhand upon his arrival just after dawn to perform the morning milking. Panicking, he had simply lifted each one into the Laughery's milk cart and trundled his way to the hospital, which luckily was only two miles from Lee's house.

We arrived quickly, and as I found somewhere to leave the coach, Lee leapt out and hurried into the majestic old building with Nurse Vivian in tow. Holmes followed him, keeping an eye on me and Lee until I was able to catch up and we both chased after him.

Finding my friend in a ward containing four beds, I was overpowered by the odours coming from the patients. None were in a good way.

Four people, two men and two women, obviously those Nurse Vivian had mentioned, lay in the beds. Each was covered in what was once a crisp white sheet, but was now stained with all manner of effluent from the poor unfortunate patients, most likely the remains of their last meals.

As I gawked at the afflicted quartet, another nurse beckoned for Lee to come to attend one of the women. He put the earpieces of his stethoscope in place and listened closely to the stricken woman's chest. I watched as he went still, even stopping his breathing and listening intently, before dropping his head and shaking it slowly from side to side before uttering one word. "Gone." The nurse gasped and raised a hand to her mouth. Lee pulled the sheet up over the poor woman's head in a moment of finality before moving to the next patient.

"Can I assist?" I almost shouted, hoping that more help would provide a quicker diagnosis and remedy.

The face that peered up at me wore an expression of absolute dejection before recognition dawned and he nodded. "That would be very helpful, John." He motioned towards Nurse Vivian. "Please fetch an apron and some instruments for Dr. Watson, here."

Taking the garment from the nurse's hand, and donning it to protect my day clothes, I moved to the nearest patient and began my assessment. The gentleman was well into his fifties and on the large side. His temperature was high. I could gather that simply from feeling his forehead, which was covered in almost a lake of sweat. His eyes were leaking tears profusely, possibly from the uncontrollable nausea and vomiting. Listening to his heart, it seemed to race far beyond the tolerances for a man of this size. His body was wracked either from disease or some consumed ailment.

The woman near him was no different. She had dark hair, streaked with strands of grey. I placed her at a similar age as the man. Her breathing was more controlled, the evidence of vomit, less. Her temperature was fierce, but not as high, and her heartbeat was fast, but well-controlled. She was certainly the healthier of the two, and as I found later, the healthiest of all four.

"Any clue, John?" asked my friend.

"These two are running high temperatures, the man especially. Obvious nausea and vomiting. Their hearts are beating faster than normal, the man's simply racing. The pallid complexion and sweat-soaked skin indicate they are fighting off an ailment of some kind. If it was a single person, I would think they had succumbed to a disease, but since there are four, I would put it down to a reaction to something they consumed or to which they were exposed."

"Good. My assessment as well."

"Where is the farmhand that found and brought them in?" Holmes asked from the doorway, his question aimed at Nurse Vivian.

"We asked him to stay in the waiting room. He did seem a little on edge and wishing to leave."

"Natural. This situation would stretch any person's resolve. If he has any fear of the police, then he would be downright terrified by now."

"Do the police need to be called?"

"I would think so. Four people are in a state of extreme physical distress, and found by a fifth, all alone. The police will only see a crime and nothing else."

"Oh, dear," said Vivian, "But William is such a nice, simple boy."

"That may be, but probably best to question him before he succumbs to any fear and becomes mute."

"It was horrible," said Willy, as he was called. "They were just lying there. In pools of . . . ." He grimaced instead of saying the word.

"Yes, we've all seen what comes next," said Holmes.

After assuring myself that Lee needed no further assistance, I accompanied Holmes and Nurse Vivian to the small but functional waiting area. It was a modest room, with two entrances and walls lined with simple chairs.

We found the young lad alone on one of the seats. He simply sat, waiting, a look of desperation on his face, with eyes that furtively glanced at both entrances and at the other two people in the room.

When his eyes fell on the three of us, he almost exploded from his seat. The nurse, who obviously knew him, calmed him down and told Willy our names and that we were there to help Doctor Lee diagnose the group's ailment.

He told his story quickly. He'd been working for the Laugherys for a few months and had taken over the milking of the cows. He generally came early on Sundays to give him time to milk and then get to church before the first service. After finishing with the cows, he placed the milk in the cool room before checking in with Mr. Laughery – something he always did in case there were any other chores to attend to in the afternoon.

Then he found them.

All were lying on the kitchen floor. He tried rousing each one in turn by slapping their cheeks and calling their names, but couldn't. Willy admitted that he thought about leaving and coming straight to the hospital, but decided that it would save time if he brought them with him. He was a strong lad, but I was still surprised to find that he had been able to carry each of the patients we'd seen. They weren't small people, but in times of stress, the body is capable of amazing feats.

The rest of the story was simple enough. He'd driven the Laughery's milk cart as fast as possible to the hospital and, with the help of the staff, brought each person inside.

His face was a mask of horror when told that one of the patients had died. Nurse Vivian announced her as Mrs. Euler, a fact I hadn't known until then. For me, they were simply unknown people that needed to be treated. To these locals they were friends.

"Oh, no!" Willy said, "She's been so nice to me for so long. I helps with their garden from time to time. It gives me a few coppers extra. Poor Mr. Euler. He'll be devastated."

If he lives.

I shook my head in silence to dismiss such thoughts.

"Watson!" Holmes's voice broke my morbid thinking and diverted my attention to him.

"We should visit the Laughery's farm. If Doctor Lee can see to the patients, I think we may be able to investigate and provide evidence or clues as to what afflicts these poor people."

"Yes. Yes, we should."

With a quick detour to inform Lee what we planned, we left the hospital and strode to our carriage. Nurse Vivian stayed behind to assist Dr. Lee, while Willy hopped into the Laughery's milk cart and led the way, with Holmes and me close behind.

The journey was over roads that had evolved to be taken slowly. Following Willy, who seemed to be urging his horse far beyond its normal pace, our backs and rears were much worse for wear by the time we arrived at the farm. The place was deathly still, with only the lowing of the cows in the near meadow, all milling around the gate in readiness for their evening milking. In the distance, a small wood ran off towards the horizon. My basic knowledge of the local area told me that was Standish Woods, one of the last wild places in Gloucestershire.

As soon as Willy drew up in front of the main house, we leapt down and proceeded through the unlocked front door. The young lad stayed behind, shaking his head and mentioning that he didn't want to enter the death house again. He would milk the cows instead.

The sight that greeted us was disturbing, to say the least. The locations that the two couples had laid on the ground near the kitchen table were obvious due to the pool of effluent. Each had succumbed to their nausea, and the debilitative effects of whatever ailed them, and had slid from their seats and slumped to the floor, as if they had been immediately struck down where they sat.

On the table were four plates, with the last remnants of their evening meal. The uneaten portion on the serving platter in the middle of the table appeared to be a pudding, from the scant remnants possibly bread and butter. My stomach growled at the sight, reminding me that we hadn't had our luncheon either. We were due to have it on the train, but my requested deviation had postponed that. However, when a whiff of the foul contents of the puddles beneath the table wafted across my nose, all thoughts of food were stripped from my mind.

A pitcher of water sat in the middle of the table, along with a stoneware flagon. It presumably held red wine, as each dinner setting had three glasses. The two larger ones were for water and wine. A bottle of port sat next to the flagon. Each person's port glass had remnants of the darker, sweeter liquor. The guests had been enjoying themselves, that was certain.

"What do you think?" I asked.

A squeal of hinges snatched my attention, I looked around and found Holmes standing near the stove and examining the interior of the oven. "Sorry," he said, "Just wanted to inspect this to see if it was gas." Shaking his head, he added, "It's a simple wood-fired oven. Gas poisoning is out of the question."

"Poison?" I nodded in agreement. "Four people unconscious at the same time, in the same place. Poisoning might be the answer. It looks like they had Beef Wellington," I said, pointing to the plates in the sink, plus the remains in the serving dish on the drainer.

"Beef?" said Holmes. "And mushrooms?" Moving to one side, Holmes scanned the meal preparation area. "Mrs. Laughery was far too particular about tidiness. Everything has been cleansed and put away. Only the eating dishes remain."

"The pantry must be through there." I pointed to an alcove with a simple curtain strung across it.

I joined Holmes as he crossed the entranceway. Pulling the curtain to one side revealed a well-stocked larder filled with fresh vegetables and some hanging game, probably obtained from the nearby Standish Woods. The baskets of vegetables contained several kinds of tubers, and indeed a small basket of mushrooms with brown-skinned caps and white stalks.

"Hmm. Tawny Grisette, if I'm not mistaken. A fairly common and quite edible species of wild mushroom."

"What were you expecting?"

"Well, in looking at the scene out there, we see four people succumbing to the same ailments all around the same time. They appear to have shared a common meal, Beef Wellington, a central ingredient being mushrooms. We are situated on the edge of Standish Woods, known for its divergent species of wild mushrooms. The symptoms of nausea and incapacitation, correlated to the meal eaten, give me reason to believe they have consumed the same poisonous wild mushroom, possibly Death Cap, Destroying Angel, or Funeral Bell – all of which are known to occur in the Standish Woods."

"But these are edible mushrooms."

"Yes, so it would appear that our cook hasn't mistaken one of the poisonous varieties for a common one. Annoying, as that was the most logical answer, and gives us a solution to those poor people's calamity."

A look of disappointment dwelled on Holmes's face as he scanned the larder for clues. Shaking his head, he moved out and stood in the kitchen for a moment, his head resting on one hand with a finger extended up his cheek – a familiar pose of contemplation. When he looked up and moved off into another part of the house, I resumed investigating the pantry.

I was also convinced that the solution lay in whatever the two couples had ingested. Nausea is a common reaction to anything that the body wishes to automatically reject. The fainting or abject collapsing was something more sinister, and suggested a substance with a virulent effect on the human physiognomy – that is, a poison.

My eyes fell on several small crates stacked on each other in one corner of the small room. The top one held some potatoes, which had begun to grow a little older than I would have wanted to use. The skin was slightly wrinkled with small green shoots sprouting from the eyes. Lifting the crate, I found another full of carrots in a similar state of age. Fine hairy roots had emerged along their orange bodies, and they held a slightly sweet smell to them, the odor of corruption. Moving the two top crates aside, I found something more interesting and possibly connected to the issue at hand.

The bottom crate held what appeared to be dried herbs of some sort – a lot of them. The oddity was that they weren't the finely cut shreds of leaves normally associated with common herbs. These were small, but almost cubic in appearance, as if someone had diced a larger, fleshier substance. However, it was the smell that hit me. Mixed into what reminded me of the odour of an aged forest, full of earthy, sweet decay, there was a strong hint of ammonia – the sort of smell that would ward off any potential eating of the offending item by any sort of animal.

I jiggled the crate and dislodged a pile of dried fragments in one corner, revealing two fully formed mushrooms. The caps were more conical in shape as compared to the tawny grisette, and the colour was lighter as well, though possibly discoloured by rot.

The question was, why were these mushrooms hidden away from the others used in the Beef Wellington? Picking up the crate, I moved out into the kitchen area and called out to Holmes.

A moment later, he appeared in the doorway on the opposite side of the room, holding what looked like, a sheaf of papers in his hand.

"I think I've found it," we both said at once.

A smile broke out on Holmes's face, and he indicated the nearby empty kitchen bench.

Placing my crate down, I asked, "What have you discovered?"

Holmes peeled off one of the sheets of paper and placed it down before us. It was a letter, written in a thin, delicate scrawl. I'm no expert in writing, but even I could tell that it came from a woman's hand.

It read:

Dearest Jim,

I fear my love for you will be the end of me. I cannot sleep on the nights we are not together, and every moment in your absence is like a stab to the heart. Please take me away from this drudgery, away where we can share our love and tell it to the world. These days of the concealment of our bond is a Hell that I can no longer endure. F. will be away next Saturday and Sunday. My bed longs for you to fill it.

Yours in enduring love,
Very

The other letters were much of the same sentiment. The names Jim and Very appeared on every single one.

"What were the names of the couples?" Holmes asked.

"Umm, the Laugherys were Suzan and James." My eyes lit up with realisation. "Oh – James. *Jim.* Could they be his?"

"I believe so. What about the others?"

"Euler. Verlene was the poor woman who died. Fred was her husband. The F. That must signify Fred."

"Yes, and *Very* must be a sobriquet for *Verlene*."

"Oh, my, so James and Verlene were . . . ."

"It would seem so. These were in a small drawer of one of the bedside tables. I can only imagine that only the most foolish person would leave something like this in such an obvious place."

"Do you think they were found by the wife?"

"That may be so." His eyes moved from the letters to the crate of herbs that I'd found. "Now, what did you find?" Holmes's hand went into his coat and pulled out the small glass he used for close examinations. His other hand opened a nearby drawer and pulled out a serving spoon. Gently, Holmes reached into the crate and picked up one of the mushrooms on the spoon, studying it intently, before sniffing the noxious odour it emitted. A broad smile crossed his face. "Well done, Watson, well done. Do you know what this is?"

"Mushroom. I must say, my knowledge is severely lacking. I've never had much call for knowing what kinds of mushrooms can kill you. London isn't exactly overflowing with that kind of tragedy."

"True. To let you know then, for later use, this is *Amanita Phalloides*, or the common Death Cap mushroom – the most poisonous fungus in all of Britain." He dropped the specimen back into the crate and then pushed around the flakes and fragments with the spoon. "This is excellent. You've solved two of the problems I was faced with."

"What were those?"

"Death cap mushrooms only grow in the colder months, November to April. If they were the source of poison, then they couldn't have been used fresh. The answer, they were dried. Which gives us intent."

"The other?"

"The rapidity of the poisoning. Death cap symptoms don't begin to show until after about six hours. But, if you dry them, you increase the toxicity by a factor of two."

"But that would also make the symptoms worse. Hence, why the poor woman died. Of what I know of death cap poisoning, any healthy person won't succumb for some time, and the symptoms still take several hours to show."

"Which begs the question: Were the mushrooms ingested as part of the meal, or . . . ?"

He rummaged around the kitchen and finally spied what he was looking for outside the window. Unlatching the back door, Holmes moved out into a small, paved area, similar to Dr. Lee's setup. A small table, surrounded by four chairs, sat in the middle of the area. A tea set, with a teapot, four cups, and small side plates, sat on top.

"Mr. Laughery was indeed fastidious about the preparation of the Beef Wellington, but not so much about afternoon tea." Holmes picked up one of the cups and turned it over on the saucer. Tapping it several times, he placed it on the table and proceeded to examine the contents left behind with his glass. "Hmm," he murmured, reaching for a teaspoon and pushing the dregs of the tea around to separate the leaves.

Standing up, he offered the glass to me and asked, "What do you make of this?"

Bending down, I held the glass so that the mess on the saucer came into focus. It now appeared several times larger than with my naked eye, and I could see what he was on about. Interspersed amongst the fine, black tea leaves were larger fragments of brown. It then occurred to me. "The mushrooms. The pieces of shredded death cap. They've been mixed in with the tea leaves." I stood and thought for a moment. "If they were brewed into the tea, the concoction would have been quite powerful."

"Yes, and when do the British folk generally have tea?"

"Around four o'clock."

"And dinner."

"Depends, but six, possibly seven in the evening."

"So, by about eight o'clock, the guests may have begun to feel the effects of a stronger version of the death cap poison. Add some more of the dried mushroom to the main meal, and you have a neatly set-up situation for the murder of your husband and his lover."

"This is horrible. Surely there would be other ways to resolve such a situation?"

"Perhaps. There were no dates on that letter, but I can only presume that this has been going on for some time. The Laugherys may have even tried to resolve the situation, or Mrs. Laughery kept her knowledge hidden. I cannot surmise. We would need to speak with her." His face became a little disconsolate. "And I fear, given the death of Mrs. Euler, which may not be possible."

"Should we return to the hospital?"

"Yes. The sooner the better, though I don't think there is much that Dr. Lee can do for these unfortunate people. If our knowledge can help, then by all means let us return."

Before we left, Holmes found a small empty canister and filled it with the dried mushroom flakes, mentioning that it was better to give the good doctor a sample of the poisonous matter than to simply explain it to him.

Stepping back into the ward from earlier in the day, we found it almost deserted. Three of the beds were empty and had been neatly remade with fresh linen. The fourth bed held the reposing form of Mrs. Laughery.

An immediate twinge of fear gripped my chest.

"Ah, John, bad news I'm afraid." I turned to see Lee standing in the doorway. His countenance showed extreme fatigue, mixed with sadness.

"The two men? Succumbed?"

Nodding, Lee added, "Yes, about half-an-hour after you left. I did everything I could." He looked down at his open hands as if accusing them of causing the poor men's demise. "I just didn't know what to do."

"I can only apologise that we weren't able to return quickly. We do have this." Holmes handed the little canister to Lee. "It seems to hold dried death cap mushroom pieces."

"They were poisoned by death cap mushrooms?"

"The evidence would suggest that."

Lee turned and yelled down the corridor. "Nurse, bring some activated charcoal, now. And more water." Turning back to us, he added, "I've already treated Mrs. Laughery with potassium iodide, I could only assume that this was some form of mineral poisoning. Mushroom poisoning would account for the horrible symptoms. Those poor men died in agonising pain."

"But Mrs. Laughery has been relatively fine?"

"Well, I don't know about fine. She's had severe vomiting and other ailments for the last few hours. Poor thing woke up when her husband died, then passed out before I could speak to her."

"Hmm," murmured Holmes, "I assume you'll need to wake her so she can take the charcoal."

"Well, yes."

"Good."

I noticed Lee give Holmes a slightly disgusted look, but before he could respond, Nurse Vivian arrived with the charcoal.

"Here, Doctor."

Lee moved around the bed and leaned over the poor woman. Gently, he slapped her cheeks with his right hand and called her name. "Mrs. Laughery, we need you to wake up!" When she was unresponsive, he repeated the actions and said a little louder, "Suzan – wake up!"

After several minutes, her eyelids began to flutter and open. As anyone who has been recalled from a deep sleep, she was confused and dazed. "Where? What? Doctor Lee? Why?"

"Relax, Suzan. You are in the hospital. You've fallen ill. I'm here to help you."

"Where is James?" Her expression was that of someone dazed, but her eyes darted around furtively as if seeking out her husband.

"He is resting, Suzan. I'm afraid he is ill as well. We've had to take him to a private room for closer care." He picked up some of the small black pellets from the tray Nurse Vivian held. "Here, please take these. They should help you." She took the pellets and placed them in her mouth, before taking the glass of water offered to her and washing the charcoal down.

A grimace came across her face. "Ooh, they don't taste very nice at all."

"Nurse, perhaps you could arrange some tea for Mrs. Laughery."

As Vivian moved away, the woman shook her head. "Oh, no. I don't drink tea. Water, or maybe a coffee if you can make that here."

"You don't drink tea?" asked Holmes.

Mrs. Laughery looked up at Holmes as if noticing him for the first time. "No. Never touch the stuff. Who are you?"

"Mr. Holmes," said Lee, "and the other gentleman is Doctor Watson, an old friend of mine. What do you remember, Suzan?"

She leaned back into her pillows and sighed. "We were having a lovely dinner. Beef Wellington. It's one of Verlene's specials. She loves to cook a nice Wellington. Gets the mushrooms from the woods, you know. Nice and fresh. She cooked it in our kitchen. She brought over all the veggies, and we provided the beef. She even cleaned everything up.

She's such a treasure. I must have had far too much wine or port or something. We'd finished the main and had a nice bread-and-butter pudding. That was mine. After about two hours, I think that I started to feel a little sick in the stomach. My head became very fuzzy. I remember leaning forward and heaving, I was disgusted with myself, but couldn't control it. Then I blacked out and woke up here." She glanced at Lee, an anxious look on her face. "Is James all right?"

"Not as well as you, I'm sorry to say," said Lee, still avoiding the unpleasant reality.

"You had tea earlier in the afternoon, did you not?" Holmes asked.

"No, I had coffee. Oh, my," her hands went to her face, "I left the tea things outside. That was my best set." She started to move, but Lee placed a gentle hand on her shoulder.

"Don't worry yourself, Suzan. That's all been taken care of. Your China is fine."

"Oh, thank you."

"If you don't drink tea, who prepared the pot?"

"Oh, that was Verlene again. She knows James loves his tea and makes it just as he likes it. Always has. James has a special blend that he prefers." She grimaced again, "I can't stand the stuff. It's too orangey for me. Much prefer a strong coffee."

Just then Nurse Vivian returned with a tray upon which sat a small pot with steam rising from it and a cup, with a milk jug and sugar. "Coffee, Mrs. Laughery? As ordered."

While the patient served herself, Holmes drew me and Lee away.

"What do you think?" Holmes asked.

His question was aimed at me, but Lee answered. "The poor woman will be devastated when she finds out about her husband."

"That was my assessment too," I added, "Which makes me believe she had no idea of the poisoning."

"What do you mean?" asked Lee. "Do you think this was intentional?" His face was a mass of confusion for a moment before his eyes grew wide. "Death cap mushrooms. It's June. They die out around May. And you mentioned dried mushrooms. That must mean that – "

"Yes," said Holmes. "Someone purposely collected and dried the mushrooms. Possibly for this moment."

"Good Lord!" said Lee, glancing back at Mrs. Laughery, who sipped her coffee and smiled to herself. "Do you think Suzan had anything to do with it?"

"I did, but now, I'm not so sure. Watson, I think we need to return to the Laughery farm, and possibly journey to the Euler house as well."

"That should be simple," said Lee, "They live right next door. The property just to the west, along the edge of the woods."

We found the Euler place, as Lee said, next to the Laughery property. It was a much smaller cottage, set almost on the edge of the woods, with only a small run of sheep to one side. The front door was unlocked, something unique to country folk.

The interior was similar to the Laughery house in layout, but a little more austere. It seemed that the Eulers led a much more modest lifestyle than their neighbours.

On the ride to the house, Holmes and I had discussed several possibilities.

"I have to admit, Watson, that I am always perplexed when it comes to affairs of the heart."

"How so?"

"At first, this case seemed to present as a simple act of revenge, but if I am to take Mrs. Laughery's word, it has turned into something confusing, if not more sinister."

"It does appear that way, if I'm reading it the same way you are. We have a love triangle involving an affair between Mrs. Euler and Mr. Laughery."

"Yes."

"At first, you were correct, it appeared to be an act of revenge by Mrs. Laughery, having found out about the affair. But her concern for her husband in a state of near-delirium gives me cause to believe she didn't know. As well as the fact that she stated that she didn't cook the Beef Wellington, and it would appear that she didn't provide the noxious herbs."

"Because of her preference, she didn't drink the tainted tea either. I also agree with your summation, but it will need verification."

"The next possibility would be an attempt at murder by Mrs. Euler on her rival. Which resulted in dire consequences for her."

"Indeed. The last scenario may be even grimmer and be understood by investigating the Euler's house." I was about to add to the conversation, but noticed we had arrived at the smaller cottage.

Holmes headed into the bowels of the house, toward the bedroom, and I went to the kitchen. The larder was significantly barer than the Laughery's. Some similar crates as I found there were stacked in the corner, but were empty of any other vegetables or herbs. On the thrawl, in the cooler part of the room, sat a small slab of butter and a jug of milk, which my nose told me was on the turn. On the shelves above sat a small selection of dry goods.

In the kitchen outside the larder, the preparation area was relatively clean, with a slightly dirty cutting board and knife the only evidence that it had been used at all. I bent forward and studied the items. The remains of something dry and flaky could be seen. With my naked eye, I could vaguely identify them as similar to the mushroom fragments I'd found in the crate next door.

I was startled by Holmes's voice behind me.

"Looks like more of the mushroom pieces. Perhaps diced even finer to be used with the tea leaves?"

"That was my supposition too." Turning, I noticed Holmes held a small book in his hand, and some more sheaves of paper. "More love letters?"

"Yes, and Mrs. Euler's journal."

"Hmm. Something that should stay private?"

"Normally I would agree, but I think circumstances require a different perspective."

"What does it say?"

Opening the book to the last page, he said, "It's all here on the last page, I'm afraid." He took a deep breath and read aloud:

> *Today is the day. We are to dine at his house. For so long I had hoped we would be together forever, but his love for her has dashed any hopes. I shall prepare a* special *meal.*
>
> *Goodbye.*

"Notice how the word special is written, with heavy emphasis. The writer wished to make it significant, even to her own mind."

"Yes. And the handwriting has changed from the elegant script we saw in those letters."

Holmes flipped back through the journal. The script became neater and less frantically written as the entries went back in time. Finally, he stopped at one page and showed it to me.

"Here is where it started."

> *I'm devastated. He has professed his love for her and no longer wishes to see me. I need to hide my sorrow from Freddie, though that shouldn't be hard. Bless him, he has never been the sharpest, and will probably never know of our dalliances.*
>
> *I so wished for us to simply go away, to be together forever, but now, I don't know what to do.*

83

"I dare say if we read through the rest of these pages, we will gain a deeper understanding of the poor woman's mental state," I said.

"Yes. It will certainly paint a picture of her motivation."

"Where to now?"

"The hospital. I think we've uncovered enough to inform the local constabulary of the circumstances of the poisoning. We can only hope that poor Mrs. Laughery is recovering."

"An affair? Oh, my word. And this was all deliberate?"

"I'm afraid so, Mrs. Laughery. It seems that Mrs. Euler wasn't quite of sound mind. When your husband turned away from her affections, she simply undertook a long act of revenge, which ended the lives of the other three, and almost yours. If you had taken the tea, then it would probably have been the end of you, too."

The poor woman's face was a mask of destitution. Tears welled in her eyes and ran down her cheeks in a torrent as the full realisation struck her.

"That silly man. We've been together for forty years. He's known Verlene for twenty of those." Her head shook slowly. "Wasn't I enough for him?" As the tears took hold, she laid back in her bed and stared at the ceiling. A single hand waved us away.

We had arrived at the hospital to find her looking slightly better after her ordeal and were informed that Lee had broken the sad news about her husband. Rather than keep her in suspense any further, Holmes and I, with Lee's permission, decided to explain our findings.

Outside the ward, we were accosted by the local constable, a young fellow by the name of Edward Rapp. He had the brusqueness of a young know-it-all who complained about us interfering in his case – even though anyone with enough knowledge of the ways of the constabulary would understand that an inspector would need to be brought in to investigate, and the young constable would be forced aside and ignored.

Once apprised of the circumstances, his eyes grew wider, but a wide grin grew on his face. "Two murders and a suicide?" His voice became so excited that several nearby nurses *shushed* him at the same time.

"Yes," said Holmes, handing the journal and sheaf of letters over to the young policeman. "A crime of the heart, it seems. The two houses are unlocked, but we haven't disturbed the scenes in any untoward way. When the inspector arrives, you will be able to show him all that I have mentioned."

"Right you are, Mr. Holmes, right you are." With the prospects of an exciting investigation in his sights, Rapp left the hospital.

Holmes simply stood and shook his head at the departing figure. "Good thing we were here. By the time he's finished, the inspector will be hard-pressed to even find the remains of the Beef Wellington."

I chuckled to myself, but was interrupted by the arrival of Colton Lee at my left shoulder.

"I'm sorry your visit wasn't as peaceful as you'd hoped, John."

"Never mind. Just something that follows Holmes and me around, it seems. Even the most innocent of trips somehow leads to an adventure. All I hope is that we have provided you with enough information to ensure that the unfortunate woman will be all right."

"I believe so. She ingested a smaller dose of the mushroom poison, so there is hope that the charcoal will clear it out. I'll keep her here for a few more days, just to observe if there are any longer-lasting ailments involved." He sighed to himself, "Though I think that the damage to her soul will be deeper than to her body."

"Yes. Matters of the heart can be worse than other forms of revenge." I shook my old comrade's hand and, with that, we left and walked out to our carriage.

It was a long trek back to Gloucester, and we would need to find accommodation there for the night. But all through the journey, I could think of nothing better than arriving home the next day. I had someone waiting there that meant the world to me. As much, though in a different way I thought, as the different players of the sad tragedy just past had meant to each other.

The Disappeared Doctor
by Paula Hammond

My dear friend, Watson, has a flare for the dramatic. In relating our adventures, his approach so often eschews that which I, myself, find the most interesting – the process, the science, the "nuts-and-bolts", as it might be termed, of the deductive practice. Indeed, I've often berated him for his lack of rigor, and insistence on injecting his accounts with elements of romance. However, when I come to lay out the facts of this case, I find myself in sore need of my Boswell. Analytical reasoning, cold logic, cause and effect – all seem a dull thing when the events I am to relate touch so closely to home.

I am no Dr. Watson, but I will do what I can to be true to his practices and processes, and I hope that the reader will be more forgiving of my literary endeavors than I have been of Watson's.

It is a fact that should you devote time to any study, you will quickly begin to develop what might be called a "nose" for the truth. Many doctors can spot a malingerer on sight. The humble beat copper has an unerring instinct for those generally classed as "a bad lot". And, in my rarefied profession, murder may be unusual, but its many and varied forms have become so perfectly familiar to me that, when faced with the grim work of the assassin, it's as though the one committing the crime had signed his name to it.

Of late, I had begun to recognize certain similarities in the style and execution of a number of deaths which were seemingly unrelated in every important aspect, bar one: They were all bizarre in the extreme.

These murders, of three men and one woman, had not attracted the attention of Scotland Yard. That the newspapers had mentioned them at all was thanks to their somewhat ghoulish nature. A priest had his skull crushed when a stone cross in his graveyard toppled on him. A solicitor's clerk was impaled through the eye by the nib of his pen after slipping on spilt ink. A banker was suffocated in his own locked vault.

The only woman had been poisoned while making eye-drops. The drops contained *Atropa belladonna*, whose usage dates back to the time of Cleopatra and has recently become fashionable again. Of all of the deaths, this was the one that most clearly screamed foul play. Yet the police didn't think it strange that a qualified chemist could poison herself – her sex seemingly the reason for her clumsiness.

The papers reported that all four had died alone. There were no signs of struggle, nothing was missing, and the victims themselves were so ordinary that it was only the strangeness of their deaths that made them notable.

The police investigations had been cursory. Friends and family were satisfied that the deaths were accidental. As for myself, I could neither prove nor disprove my growing conviction that these people had been deliberately disposed of.

A murder committed in the heat of the moment is a horrible thing. But there is nothing more abominable than when a life is taken – not in passion – but coldly, calculatedly, as a tick on a check list which forms part of a greater plot. Even for one as wedded to logic as I am, the fact that a life may be snuffed out merely because its owner is an inconvenience will never cease to shock.

I had, in my mind's eye, the very picture of the assassin I felt to be behind these peculiar deaths. He was arrogant. More than that, he was egotistical to the point of mania. Why else would he kill in such a conspicuous manner? It was as though he wanted his acts of daring to be noticed. There was a macabre humor to his choice of murder weapons, too, that was suggestive of some form of moral vacuum – a *manie sans délire*. This portrait indicated someone low in empathy, indifferent to morality, prone to act on impulse, with a Machiavellian streak of self-interest.

Could nature make such a man? Modern psychiatry would have us believe so. So, too, it seems, can Fate. Recall the case of the railroad man, impaled through the head by a metal bar, who was so radically changed that friends declared the equilibrium between his intellectual faculties and animal propensities had been quite destroyed. He became, in effect, a child, impatient of restraint, with the animal passions of a grown man. Such a man might, perhaps, kill four random people on a whim. What use, then, for logic and deduction?

I was at an impasse. There was no case to speak of. No official body had requested my help. All I had was a small collection of clippings in a manila folder. I had used my contacts to make enquiries. I'd spoken to the vicar's curate, to the banker's colleagues, as well as the clerk's and the druggist's, who did little but confirm events as laid out by the press. Even Gregson, who is the smartest of the Scotland Yarders, had too many pressing demands to indulge me. I was sure I could eventually win him 'round but, with the victims buried and the scenes cleared, I lacked that essential thing that all detectives must have: Proof.

Watson had been married but six months and, while I am solitary by nature, I found myself wanting a companion by the fireside with whom to share a pipe and puzzles.

I did not begrudge my friend his happiness. Matrimony suited him – but I sorely felt the lack of a comrade who had always been on hand to temper the more obsessive parts of my nature.

My attempts to follow the threads of this particular web had begun to task me. I was so deeply in the grip of the problem that morning had run into evening without my noticing. Breakfast, lunch, and a cold collation lay untouched on the dining table. My worthy landlady had presumably come and gone without my keen senses noting the fact. I would, perhaps, have stayed this way for days, had not a hand on my shoulder roused me from my reveries.

I looked up to see the kindly face of Mrs. Hudson. She retreated from the room without saying a word, but not before her expressive features had told me everything I needed to know.

I leapt to my feet, panicked. The blinds still covered the window so that the room's only illumination came from a pair of flickering oil lamps.

There, in the gloomy doorway, I saw the sweet lady who, such a short time ago, had captured the heart of my dearest companion.

Mary Watson's sensitive, blue eyes, regarded me intently. I could see she had been crying. Her face was pale and pinched, and those singular eyes of hers were red-rimmed and filmy. The gown she wore told me that she had clearly dressed for dinner, but had been so distressed she hadn't had the presence to change again before coming to my rooms. In her hands she clasped a basket, presumably taken from the kitchen, to carry some object of size that couldn't be accommodated in her usual reticule.

According to the clock on the mantel, it was eight o'clock. There could be only one reason for a visit so early in the morning. "Why, what is it?" I asked quietly, feeling a terrible hollow at the centre of my being. In reply, she shook her head, as though whatever needed to be said was too terrible to voice.

I took her hands in mine and led her, gently, to the basket chair beside the fire.

"My dear lady," I said, "please sit."

She looked at me, trembling. Then, her reserves exhausted, she collapsed instead into Watson's old chair in a paroxysm of tears.

At that moment, Mrs. Hudson reappeared with a tea tray, which she thrust in my direction.

"Now, now, my dear," she said to Mrs. Watson, "whatever it is, you've come to just the right place." Then to me, "Well, don't just stand there, Mr. Holmes. Pour the tea."

I did as instructed while Mrs. Hudson threw Mary a succession of concerned glances. She moved about the room, tidying away the previous day's food. Several times she opened her mouth as though to speak. Then, thinking better of it, closed it again. Finally, with one last glance, she bustled out of the room.

By then, Mary had composed herself and was regarding me with a wide, hopeful gaze.

"Tell me everything" I said.

"It's John," she began. "Oh, Mr. Holmes, what ever shall I do?" For a moment, she looked likely to succumb to her emotions again, but with a supreme effort of will, she paused, straightened her back, smoothed her skirts, and began to speak, quietly at first, then, with growing confidence.

"Knowing a little from John of your methods of working, I've been trying to piece together the events of the last twelve hours, in as much detail as I can. I cannot be as confident as I would wish on certain points. I can only tell you what I believe to be true – and I pray, for John's sake, that it's enough.

"In the last months, John's practice has grown quickly. So much so, that he's been in the habit, of late, of reserving one evening a week for just the two of us. Some time away from the early mornings and the late nights, when we can take our ease and enjoy each other's company. This Wednesday, we had planned on visiting Wilton's Oyster Bar. John hasn't been there since it moved to Duke Street, and was keen on doing so.

"We had planned to dine at eight, but by half-past the hour, there was still no sign of him. By nine, I had settled down to wait, certain he'd been detained by some emergency.

"However, as the minutes ticked away, I became increasingly worried. I checked his diary and, as I expected, there were no appointments past six o'clock. His last patient was an address in Old Quebec Street, just off Portman Square, which is less than thirty-minutes' walk away.

"Portman Square!" I cried.

"Why, yes. Does it mean anything?"

"It may mean everything. Pray, continue."

"I considered sending a telegram, but was loathe to disturb a patient who might, at that very moment, be undergoing some vital treatment. No, I determined that the oysters could wait – and so could I.

"By ten, my resolve had quite evaporated. I sent a telegram to Portman Square and received a reply within the hour. John had been delayed, but had left at half-past-six!"

"My first thoughts were to you, Mr. Holmes, but I was still hopeful that some forgotten errand had delayed my dear John. I determined to wait, but not to idle the time away.

"At eleven, I walked to Paddington Station and picked up a cab. For the next hour or so, we quartered the area, between the station and Gray Street. The streets are well lit, even at that time of night. Apart from a hawker and a couple of barrow-men, I saw no one.

"I was back home a little after one and set myself to telephone every hospital in London. There had been no admissions matching John's description. It was still possible that he was lying unclaimed on some mortuary slab, so my next call was to the local police station.

"I'm afraid that I was treated as rather a joke. Apparently, a missing husband is of little concern to the constabulary. I was told he was likely having a bit of harmless fun and would be home 'when the money runs out, or she kicks him out of bed!'"

At this my hackles rose, and it was all I could to restrain the urge head straight round to H Division and give them a piece of my mind.

"My dear Mary! Have you slept at all?"

"No. I couldn't. I spent the rest of the evening watching the embers burn, jumping at every creak and groan of the floorboards, imagining it was John. I would have hammered your door down at dawn, had I been able to get a cab! You know John – his habits, the sort of man he is. He wouldn't leave me worrying if it was in his power to a message to me."

"You have his appointment book in the basket?"

The lady started a little at that. "Oh, Mr. Holmes, I'd quite forgotten I'd brought it. I've been so worried, I can barely recall my own name. And his diary, yes, here."

She pulled out two heavy morocco-bound notebooks. What Mary had called Watson's diary contained a neat a list of appointments, listed by hour and day. The appointment book contained a more detailed list of patients, treatments, and observations.

"This Colonel Whetherby is the one in Portman Square? He's a new patient?"

"Yes. How can you tell?"

"He's only mentioned once in each book. What do you know of him?"

"He telephoned on Wednesday morning, wishing to be put on the books. His doctor had just retired and John came recommended. John took his details and promised to see him that very day, once he'd finished his regular rounds"

"What did you learn of him?"

"Not much. He was recently widowed. No children. Retired, but in business of some sort."

"How recently widowed?"

"A couple of months, I believe."

"Do you know who recommended Watson?"

"John wasn't given a name, but he assumed it was some old crony from Barts."

"He walked there?"

"Yes. He always does his rounds on foot, unless it rains."

I know what a capital mistake it is to theorize before gathering all the evidence, yet as Mary spoke, my mind had begun to conjure several unpleasant possibilities.

Lying in a pile beside my chair was a stack of papers, through which I had been trawling. I pulled a handful from the bottom and began scanning the pages. It wasn't long before I found it – a short piece in *The Illustrated Police News* from two months earlier, which finally gave me the missing link between the murders that had so tasked me.

"By Jove! If I'm right, Watson will be home by the evening. In the meantime, the best thing you can do now is go home."

"But you know something?" Mary protested. "Please, tell me. Even if it is the smallest thing. The smallest hope."

"Something I've been working on that also links to Portman Square. It may be nothing at all. I need more data to be certain. But there's always hope, my dear Mary." I took her small hand in mine and said, with more confidence than I felt, "Now, you need to rest. I should certainly catch it from Watson if I let you make yourself ill, worrying unnecessarily."

"You know where he is?" she asked, her grave face a picture of concern.

I didn't dare say more. Instead, I gave what reassurances I could, my mind already busy on the problem. "Please, there is much to be done, and time is of the essence."

I watched Mary Watson leave, and then began making arrangements. My nerves were worked up to the highest pitch and it appeared to me that time flew by an incredible speed. I had not lied. We were against the clock. The dear lady would have made a fine detective, but I sorely wished she had knocked my door down at dawn.

I'd barely had time to change when I heard the sharp clang of the bell, followed by Mrs. Hudson's tread on the stairs. She entered carrying a telegram. What I read turned my blood to ice: "*Watson is safe. If you wish him to remain so, desist. You have until this evening to make your decision known to me via the Personal section of* The Evening News."

I could see from her expression that Mrs. Hudson had already read its contents. "I'm sorry, Mr. Holmes" she said, shamefaced. "I did read it. I couldn't help myself. It is about the Doctor, isn't it?" she asked.

"I will not lie, it is. But – as you know me, know this: I will not rest until Watson is home, safe with his Mary. I promise you that."

Desist is such a small word, but I felt the weight of it fall on me. I had often feared for the safety of my companion. There were men held at Her Majesty's pleasure, thanks to the efforts of Holmes and Watson. There were men who had gone to the gallows, too, whose friends and families wouldn't quickly forget our names. Now, I knew for certain that the enquiries I'd been making had brought this upon Watson. I'm a lazy devil, but at that moment I felt a surge of energy – a cry for action. My friend needed me – and I would not fail him.

Portman Square is one of London's most desirable garden squares, boasting rows of town-houses, built in grand, Classical style. The Square's private, ornamental garden lies at the southern end of Baker Street – a peaceful oasis shaded by London plane trees – around which the town-houses nestle.

Walk past the garden, along Upper Berkley Street, and one reaches Old Quebec Street. A small chapel of ease lies on the corner, beyond which are neat rows of four-story Georgian houses.

The Colonel's home was No. 33 – an unremarkable looking mid-terrace made notable by its olive green door, and a brass knocker in the shape of a wolf's head. I thought it a curious choice of ornament, but was quickly to learn how apt it was.

I knocked, waited, and then knocked again. This time, a noise within revealed itself to be the sound of hurried footsteps and a heavy bolt being pulled.

The door was opened by a girl whose pretty face was marred by malnutrition and creased with worry. By her side was a dog, who she dismissed with a tap on the head.

"Is the Colonel at home?" I asked.

The girl nodded, curtsied as though greeting royalty, and then ushered me inside.

I was deposited in the day room, which was still in darkness. The girl motioned me to sit, while she busied around, opening the shutters. Having finally brought some light to the cheerless room, she thrust out her hand and stood, waiting expectantly.

Given her apparent mutism, and how uncoordinated her movements were, it seemed that the poor child was yet another victim of the *meningococcus* bacterium, which, if caught in infancy, can leave one deaf.

I reached into my jacket and pulled out a calling card, which the girl took.

The fire had not yet been lit, and my wait was a cold and thankless one.

The room was small and cluttered. An occasional table was positioned to one side of the fire, the armchair to the other. A battered, balloon-back chair was paired with a writing desk, while more small tables, carrying lamps, a humidor, and a brandy decanter filled the rest of the space.

This wasn't the room of a married man, or even a widower. It was the room of a bachelor – and a misanthrope – without even a spare chair for guests. And, while someone offering employment to a deaf-mute would otherwise seem laudable, Whetherby's choice of a domestic who could neither hear nor report what she witnessed seemed ominous.

The clock on the mantel ticked away five, ten, then fifteen minutes, before the door opened and the man I took to be Colonel Whetherby entered.

He was a spare specimen, tall and wiry, with cheekbones like chalk dusters, a long, wide nose, and a shock of black hair cropped close to this skull. A wicked scar ran from just above his right eye to behind his ear. Whatever had caused it, he was surely lucky to have survived the blow.

His eyes were the most striking part of his appearance. They were large, pale, copper-colored orbs, set so deep into his face that they looked like miniature moons. Here was the wolf indeed!

"Colonel Whetherby?" I asked.

"Mr. Holmes. I assume you've come about Dr. Watson? Based on last night's telegram, it seems he's gone astray?"

His tone was so flippant that it immediately set my hackles rising. "We're concerned for his safety" I said. "You had an appointment with him, I believe?"

"Why else would he call? I presume what you mean to ask is when did he leave, and did he give any indication where he might be going? As I told Mrs. Watson, he left around half-past-six and, no, I didn't feel the need to ask where he was bound."

"May I ask what time he arrived?"

"The appointment was for five. I don't recall exactly when he arrived, just that he was late. I told him that wouldn't do, thanked him for his time, and sent him on his way."

"Do you know what delayed him?"

"Good God, man, do you think I care about the small doings of everyone I do business with? If someone has disappeared your doctor, I suggest you go to the police, and stop harassing me."

The features are given to man as the means to express his emotions, and I have made it my business to be able to read those features. I knew the Colonel only feigned disinterest. There was about him a palpable tension – the stress of the unspoken.

"This morning I received a telegram from Regent's Street Post Office" I began. "Regent's Street is, I think, the closest post office to Portman Square. Portman Square also happens to be the location of Alice Potter's pharmacy – the same Alice Potter who died in such strange circumstances a week ago."

The Colonel smiled at me coldly. His face was a picture of calm, but his breathing was elevated and his cheeks began to flush. By God, he was enjoying this!

"You seem to have something to say," he replied in a breathless whisper. "Best get it off your chest."

I jumped to my feet. "I wonder," I continued hotly, "if you ever knew the lady's name? I imagine not. But you would certainly remember the name of Reverend John Hawker of All Saints Church in Margaret Street. Of Percival Williams, solicitor, and Ewart Temple, banker. A wedding, a will, or insurance policy drawn up, an apparent suicide, by poison, of a young newlywed, as reported in *The Illustrated Police News*, and monies then withdrawn by the husband, I'd vouch. What is of interest to me is that, at the scene of every one of your murders, no papers were missing. You do not care that there are documents in your name. You do care that people may identify you by sight. No mystery there: Names are easy to change, but yours is a face that's hard to disguise. Who you are you really, Colonel Whetherby?"

"That, Mr. Holmes, is for me to know and you to find out. But since you have taken the time to visit me in person, I will ask you, again, will you desist, or does Dr. Watson have to die for your stubbornness? Perhaps," the Colonel added with a small, low, laugh, "he's already dead."

"I don't believe that. You may have murdered five people and got away with it, but to kill Watson would bring the whole of Scotland Yard down upon yourself. Indeed, I don't believe you've ever met the Doctor. You wouldn't go to the trouble of killing four witnesses, just to land yourself with another. No, Watson was taken off the street and is being kept somewhere local. A long journey would be too much of a risk – too many opportunities to escape, and you'd have to rely on out-of-town help."

"You can talk all day, Mr. Holmes, and while you do, Watson lies dying."

At that moment, I felt the color drain from my face. I was filled with horror for Watson, and such loathing for the man before me, that it threatened to unhinge my reason. But I had no choice. I wouldn't ordinarily have tipped my hand so completely, but I needed to know.

I swallowed roughly, forcing myself to continue. "Colonel Whetherby may not be your name, but you are a military man. It's written all over your body, in the camp sicknesses that have ravaged you, in the sabre cut you carry, in the way you stand, and the way your muscles have been shaped by use and practice: You're a cavalry man. And it isn't difficult to imagine where someone with that background, living in this part of the city, might hide one he wished to do away with."

The mask of indifference dropped. Whetherby snarled, and before I could reach my Webley, he was on me.

He sprang forwards, landing a right hook squarely on my chin. My head snapped back and, for a moment, I reeled, staggering backwards, into the chair behind me.

He didn't wait on ceremony. Before I could stand back up, he was on the attack, arms flailing like windmill sails. He landed blow after blow – and I felt every one.

The Colonel was athletic, but was no foot soldier. He wasn't used to this type of hack and slash. He was already out of breath. I saw my moment – and took it.

I lowered my head and, using my arms to push myself back out of the chair, I roared at him. My head hit him soundly in the chest and he went down, winded, sending the small, occasional table clattering to the floor.

I stumbled on, unbalanced. Whetherby was at my feet, his hands tugging at the hem of my jacket as he attempted to haul himself upright.

I pulled myself free and, as I did so, I heard the cloth tear. My revolver flew from my pocket and landed, with a clang, in the fire place.

I saw Whetherby's body whip around. His hand snaked out towards the fallen gun and closed on the stock. For a second, he lay there, covered in soot, then, he rolled over, took aim, and fired.

I was already running. My hypothesis had needed data. Now that I had it, I had other places to be.

Half-falling, half-sliding, I ran, pell-mell, down the tiled hallway, hitting the front door with a jolt. I was heaving on the heavy bolt when I heard the unmistakable click of the sear on the revolver's trigger being thrown. I ducked – just in time. Wood and splinters exploded where, just a few seconds ago, my head had been.

I felt a searing pain, followed by a loud buzzing, as my ears protested the noise. I didn't know what had hit me – lead or wood – but could feel blood, hot and tacky, running down my face. I reached up for the bolt again. My fingers felt too big, too clumsy, but I finally managed to wrench open it.

So intent on the task had I been that didn't hear the next shot, but luck was with me. The door unaccountably swung open and, having been positioned directly behind it, the momentum propelled me backwards. I landed, winded, on the floor. My head hit the tiles with an audible crack, but thankfully the bullet that had been intended for it, merely clipped the doorframe.

I was still lying, prone on my back, when a flaxen-haired man, with a face the color of milk, exploded through the door. He had his own Home Office-issue Webley in his hand and, this time, I heard the shot.

Detective Inspector Tobias Gregson had every right to look satisfied with himself. A few hours ago, he hadn't even known a crime had been committed. Now, he had in custody a man who had certainly murdered five people, and had attempted to do away with two more.

He offered me his hand and helped me back on my feet. "Well, Mr. Holmes," he said, with a look of beatitude spreading across his face, "it looks like Scotland Yard has saved the day."

The barracks for the Second Troop of Horse Guards, just off Hyde Park, had been built during the Napoleonic Wars. The barracks had lain deserted since the Horse Guards were incorporated into the Life Guards. I had telegrammed Gregson on my way to Portman Square, reasoning that, if one wanted to spirit someone away, a familiar place, close to home, such as the old barracks, might suit. I hadn't known for certain that my reasoning was sound until Whetherby's actions confirmed it.

"Watson?" I asked, peering past Gregson's tall frame. "For God's sake, man, is he safe?"

"Here, Mr. Holmes!" Gregson made way, and there was my dear friend behind him, a little bruised around the temples – but alive and well!

"Good Lord, Holmes!" Watson cried clasping my hand in his with a look of intense concern. "Are you shot?"

"A graze, merely. And you?"

"Oh," he laughed, "I'll have a headache for a day or two. They set upon me as I headed down the Mews. Didn't know a thing until I woke in some old stables, trussed up like a Christmas goose. Gregson's men have the gang now. But what on earth – ?"

"Let's just say, I owe you my deepest apologies. Had I known my curiosity would lead you into danger, I would have left Whetherby to his machinations."

"Rot, and you know it. Besides, no harm is done, and you've made Gregson's year!"

"And your wife? Have you sent word to Mary?"

"Gregson messaged ahead, and I'm heading there now. But Holmes, I expect to hear the full story tonight – at Wilton's."

"I think you still owe your wife a meal, but I'll gladly take you up on that offer another evening."

"I will hold you to it," he said, regarding me with that calm, steady look I knew so well. I felt, then, that special bond between men who have been, not just friends, but comrades-at-arms. I have never been to war, but Watson and I had certainly fought our fair share of battles together. I knew then, as I know now, that he was, and always would be, my friend.

NOTE

Holmes's *"picture of the assassin"* includes many of the markers that modern-day criminal profilers ascribe to psychopathic personalities. While it isn't known how much Holmes was aware of the psychology of the day, the study of "psychopathy" had been an active field of research since at least the 1850's. Holmes would, however, have certainly been aware of the Mironovich Murder Case (1883-1885), which was one of the most scandalous cases of the period. During the trial, the eminent Russian psychiatrist, Professor Ivan M. Balinsky, described one of the defendants as "a psychopath".

Victorian medicine had a poor understanding of mental illness, which was often seen as a physical manifestation of some "moral failing". *Manie sans délire*, ("insanity without delusion"), was a catch-all term of the period, referring to a type of mental disorder, typified by what was seen as abnormal emotions and behaviors, without any accompanying delusions or intellectual impairments.

The case of the man *"impaled through the head by a metal bar"* refers to Phineas P. Gage (1823–1860), an American construction foreman, remembered for his surviving an accident in which a large iron rod was driven through his head. The impact destroyed much of his frontal lobe, dramatically changing his personality. His case formed the basis for early studies of the brain and its functions. It's interesting to note that Whetherby seems to have had a similar injury to the frontal lobe.

The Adventure of the
Heirloom Necklace
by Tracy J. Revels

Inspector Lestrade was many things to Sherlock Holmes. At times, Lestrade served as a foil. At others, he was a useful sounding board for Holmes's ideas. He was always eager to take the credit for my friend's work, allowing the press to praise him as the "professional detective" while Holmes was dismissed as merely a "talented amateur", but despite his ego, Lestrade could, upon occasion, admit that Holmes's intellect was the far superior one, and even invited Holmes to come to Scotland Yard and receive the accolades of the law enforcement fraternity. Most important, Lestrade was a loyal, if occasionally misguided, friend. I shared Holmes's fondness for the lithe, ferret-faced inspector, and therefore we were equally shocked and alarmed when he arrived at Baker Street in the wake of the outraged figure of the Countess of Ionne. Their entrance to our chamber was striking, for the lady, a grand dame of Amazonian proportions, charged through our sitting room door with Lestrade, hat in hand, trailing two miserable steps behind her. I was instantly reminded of a small schoolboy being towed by the ear towards the headmaster's office by an irate teacher.

"Inspector, Lady Ionne, welcome," Holmes said, schooling his face not to show his astonishment at this strange development. We had both been lazing about, and had just finished smoking our pipes, but my friend offered to ring for a fresh supply of coffee and biscuits. The countess shook her head forcefully, an action with nearly dislodged her sizeable hat with its long ostrich plume. She dropped onto the divan and shot a withering look at Lestrade.

"We do not have time for such pleasantries. Mr. Holmes, I have come to employ you in a most urgent matter. The inspector has handled the affair in a grossly incompetent style, and therefore I must place my trust in you. Otherwise, an item of great financial, sentimental, and historical value will be lost forever."

Holmes coughed softly. "Madam, I'm certain that Scotland Yard – "

"Is nothing but a circus, filled with clowns!" the lady snapped. "Or overflowing with monkeys, if you prefer that analogy. It was a simple-enough business, I think, to apprehend a felon and return my necklace. This cretin – " Here she waved a finely-gloved hand at Lestrade. " –

thought to make a grand presentation to me, to demonstrate his deductive skills. And what did he have? My valuables? My family's greatest heirloom? No – He brought me *this*!"

The countess pulled a string of pearls from her sizable handbag and flung them onto the rug. Warily, I picked them up and held them out for Holmes to examine. The pearls formed a long necklace bearing a golden pendant in the form of the letter *B*, with three more teardrop-shaped pearls dangling from the bottom of the initial. Holmes lifted his magnifying glass from the table and carefully inspected the object.

"It is a replica," he said. "Cunningly made, but artificial."

"It looks familiar," I said. Holmes smiled at me.

"That is because you know your history, Doctor. You are recalling the famous portrait of Anne Boleyn, the second wife of the notorious Henry VIII. She is shown wearing this exact necklace."

The countess puffed with pride. "Indeed, the 'Boleyn Letter', as we call it, has been in my paternal family for centuries. I am descended from the Howards, who were cousins to the Boleyns. The necklace was thought lost, until discovered by my great-great grandfather. It was gifted to me by my father just before my wedding. As you may know, my husband died two years ago, and I have only recently been freed from my mourning obligations. Saturday is the great Tudor Ball, the fancy dress party where all of society gathers. It is my second debut of sorts, and I had hoped to wear my ancestorial pendant for the occasion. But now this idiot has lost it. You must find my heirloom, Mr. Holmes. I will spare no expense and reward you handsomely."

Holmes looked across the room. Lestrade had borne the diatribe with his head hung down, and now, slowly, he looked up like a whipped dog.

"We were certain we had it. After all, the thief was dead, and this item was found in his pocket."

"Dead!" I exclaimed.

"As this fool of an inspector should be!" the countess snapped.

"Madam," Holmes interrupted, with more patience than any other man might have shown. Those who believe Holmes was a hopeless misogynist would have marveled at how well he held his temper in check. "Perhaps I can serve you best if you tell me the particulars of how your necklace was stolen. Afterward, Doctor Watson and I will discuss the matter with Inspector Lestrade, in a professional and *private* consultation."

"You are trying to spare his feelings," the countess sneered. "Very well, I shall do as you wish. But understand that if my heirloom is not recovered, before the Ball, the Queen shall hear of it!"

"If you will begin with the days before the theft?" Holmes coaxed.

"A week ago, I returned to London," the lady said. "I took a suite at the Savoy. My maid, Elaine Gilly, accompanied me. As you might imagine, I had much to do while in the city, especially as I had just come out of mourning and needed to refresh my wardrobe."

I said nothing, but in my notes, I jotted down my suspicion that the lady had made many dressmakers and milliners quite happy.

"At seven-thirty this morning, I had an appointment in Piccadilly to have my costume fitted, and I set out alone, for poor Elaine was quite exhausted and complaining of a terrible headache. Well, I had not quite reached Charing Cross when I realized that I had gone off without my spectacles, which I would require to inspect the quality of the stitching. As I returned to my room, I noted a poorly dressed fellow coming down the hall with his hat pulled low. I was alarmed, for he was clearly not of the class to be staying at the hotel, or properly uniformed to be working there. I put my hand to the door and found that it opened without the key. I stepped inside, calling for Elaine.

"She did not come. I frowned and went further into my suite. Imagine, Mr. Holmes, the horror I felt when I saw her lying upon the divan in a stupor, with sheets all bunched around her. I roused her by splashing cold water into her face. She told me that she had gone out to buy a newspaper, only to be seized by a ruffian who pressed a knife to her side and threatened to cut her if she screamed. He forced her to return to our suite and there she fainted, not reviving until I roused her. But all this I confess I learned afterward, for when I saw her senseless, and the door to my bedroom flung open, I knew a robbery had occurred. The box that held the Boleyn Letter was open upon the floor.

"Without a moment's hesitation, and leaving her in her faint, I ran downstairs and shouted at the clerk and – Mr. Holmes, if you can believe it – I saw the very man I had seen before, with his sly face and his tattered coat. I screamed '*Stop thief!*' and he bolted from the lobby. I heard a policeman blow his whistle, and when I stepped through the door, I saw two officers in pursuit. Of course, there was nothing I could do but to go back upstairs and wake my maid. Two hours later, Mr. Lestrade came up and took my statement. Then, as if he was so smart, he presented my necklace to me. I knew immediately there had been a substitution. I told him we would waste not a moment in seeking your help."

"Nothing else was stolen?" I asked. "Were your jewels riffled?"

"Not a one, though in truth I wasn't travelling with any other truly valuable pieces. Only the Boleyn Letter was essential to my costume. I looked about at the Inspector's request, but nothing else was missing."

Holmes nodded solemnly. "Is your maid hurt?"

The countess shook her head. "There isn't a scratch on her. She begged permission to leave for a rest at her mother's house in Spitalfields, for her nerves were badly shaken, and I told her to go. She was useless anyway, breaking into tears when she heard the man who assaulted her was dead."

"And how did he die?" Holmes asked.

The lady rose from her seat. "I will allow the inspector to explain it to you. I will expect results before the Tudor Ball, which is in two days' time, or I will lay my case before Her Majesty."

The countess stomped from the room, slamming the door behind her. Lestrade sighed and wilted onto the sofa.

"It is early for a whisky," he admitted, "but a cigarette would not be amiss."

Holmes opened his silver case. "You have my sympathies, Inspector. She is not a personage I would choose for a client."

"It's a bad business," he muttered. "And I'm sorry for Constable Rutledge, who's distraught over things, even though he's been assured he is not at fault." Lestrade drew smoke into his lungs, soothing his nerves. Holmes held up a hand.

"I presume you are having the maid followed?"

Lestrade scowled. "Whatever for?"

"Because she is clearly an accomplice," I said, enjoying Holmes's firm nod of approval. "She was feigning unconsciousness when her mistress returned unexpectedly."

"Watson is ahead of us," Holmes said, lighting a pipe as he spoke. "The girl's story is a shaky one. Why does a domestic so stricken with a headache suddenly develop an urge to read a newspaper? What evildoer would seize a young woman in broad daylight, and be cool enough to march her into a hotel? Surely someone would have noticed the respectable maid being forced upstairs by such a ruffian, or she would have cried out for help. Plus, there is the small matter of the thief knowing the valuable necklace from the worthless pieces of paste. No Lestrade, it reeks of being staged. Especially the part about the sheets."

"How so?"

"Why would the villain need to pull sheets from the bed if the lady had already fainted? I would suggest that the bedsheets were being set aside to use as bindings, so that when Madam returned from her fitting, she would find her maid helplessly trussed and a more convincing victim. The pair simply had no time to complete the tableau."

"But how would they know the lady was returning?"

Holmes gestured toward the street. "There is a wonderful invention known as a *window*. Does the countess's room face the thoroughfare she would return along?"

Lestrade looked pained but nodded.

"One of them alerted the other. They had but moments to scheme and prepare a story to replace the one they had concocted."

"I'll send a constable for the maid's address in Spitalfields."

"And if you find a concerned mother at the end of it, I will treat you to dinner at Simpsons," Holmes said dryly. "That bird is flown by now, though perhaps through much labor we may bring her to ground. Tell us what happened after the hue-and-cry was raised."

"By good fortune, two of our constables were standing at the corner, having a chat. Rutledge is new and has just completed his training. Tate, however, has been an officer for almost five years. His patrol is along the Strand, and within Covent Garden, and he's a reliable sort.

"Well, the bandit was fleet-footed, and for a time he got away from them, but then Rutledge – who stands nearly seven feet tall, a Goliath of a man – saw him turn a corner and run up into the warrens of stalls. Tate thought the rascal had gone into one of the theatres. Then there was a cry from a woman who'd been knocked aside, and the boys saw that he'd forced his way into Porter's Museum of Historical Curiosities. They have displays like those of Madame Tussaud, except all the statues are of English kings and queens. Not a very bright place, but they say it is popular with the lower sorts. It's closed on Thursdays, so no one was about except the proprietor's daughter, who was in her family's rooms, working on some accounts. She was shocked to hear the museum door open, followed by the tramping of boots on the stairs. The girl climbed to the exhibit room the room on the third floor and found the thief there, looking through the window, as if trying to make up his mind whether he might risk jumping through it. She gave a cry of alarm, and he was on her like a wolf, with a knife to her throat.

"Rutledge and Tate had followed him in. They heard the girl's squeal. Rutledge ducked into an open doorway off the second-floor landing, and at just that moment the criminal appeared at the head of the stairs, his arm around the terrified girl. He started down with her as his prisoner, shouting threats. Tate tried to talk some sense into the fellow, but he kept moving, lower and lower, and there was blood on the girl's neck. Tate felt he had no choice but to step aside, in hopes the dastard would release his hostage, but Rutledge saw his chance, and once the fellow was below him on the stairs, Rutledge sprang from his hiding place and delivered a mighty blow with his club. The girl darted loose, and the man toppled over. Tate stepped forward and realized that Rutledge – so much stronger than the average officer – had literally bashed the thief's brains in."

"My word," I whispered.

"I was summoned from the Yard and came as quickly as possible. It was a clear-enough scenario. Poor Rutledge was distraught. He swore he only meant to stun the man, but seeing the innocent girl in danger made him angry and careless. We'll need to investigate the matter further, and we've sent Rutledge home for a few days, but he will be exonerated. The girl practically worshipped him, as well she might. But here's where it all becomes strange: We found the necklace in the brigand's pocket, just where you would expect it to be. I was relieved, and so I tried a bit of your showmanship, Mr. Holmes, producing it from my coat at the end of my questioning of the countess. Once she took it from me, she . . . Well," Lestrade lifted a hand and rubbed his head, "I hope never to be hit by a reticule with such force again."

Holmes's lips quirked, but he did not smile. "Was the maid in the room when this assault upon your person happened?"

"She was, but at the next moment she was a puddle of tears, bemoaning that anyone had died for a 'foolish bauble'. If the countess had not been so upset with me, I feel certain she would have turned her rage upon her maid."

"As well she should," Holmes muttered.

"So, tell me – How does a thief run out of one building with a valuable piece of jewelry in his hand and be captured ten minutes later with a splendid replica of the same?"

"I have an idea," Holmes said.

"Then share it!"

My friend shook his head. "Several possibilities are associated with this idea. Allow me time to tug upon the thread that seems most likely to lead to the necklace."

"There isn't time. You heard what the lady is threatening to do."

"How fortunate for us that the Queen is currently at Balmoral. Do not despair, Lestrade. I'm confident I can bring this case to a successful conclusion before the opening promenade of the Tudor Ball."

Lestrade hurled the butt of his cigarette into the fire. "Very well. But I don't want to find myself wearing a uniform and walking a beat in Whitechapel."

I waited until Lestrade made his exit. Holmes stood at the window, wreathed in smoke. He spoke with a low chuckle.

"A simple-enough matter. Barely worth wearing out one's shoe leather."

"Simple! I concede it is obvious that the man had an accomplice, but how will you ever track her down?"

"Watson, I feel certain that the individual who most aided our felon cannot move at all. Still – there might be amusement in it, and maybe even a reward. My last chemical experiment went a bit awry – " Here he gave a quick glance toward a burnt patch in the ceiling. " – and Mrs. Hudson has been speaking of raising our rent. Into your coat and let us get to work."

"And where shall we go first?"

"To the police morgue."

It was a dull and gloomy room that we entered, a portal to the underworld lit by flickering gas lamps and reeking of the foul odor of decay. Several unfortunates were laid on boards beneath rough sheets, with only their bare feet protruding. A grim-faced attendant directed us to the table in the furthest corner, where a young doctor in a gore-soaked apron was just finishing his examination of a corpse. A slender, dark-haired, and pale-faced policeman stood just a few steps beyond, watching the work in silence.

"You are Mr. Sherlock Holmes, are you not?" the physician asked. "I am Doctor Strauss. Inspector Lestrade sent a note, instructing me to provide any help that I can."

"Ah, I see my professional colleague has anticipated my path," Holmes said, with some pleasure. "I take it this body belongs to the thief who was killed earlier this morning. What can you tell us about him?"

"Not very much, I fear. His cause of death is unquestionable." The doctor gestured towards the crushed area of the man's skull. "Had he not turned a fraction to look back, he might not have caught the officer's weapon as he did. And Rutledge is a bear of a man. I'd hate to be on the receiving end of his fist, much less his stick. As for other aspects – well, there was no identification on him, and all his clothing is second-hand. He had but a single shilling and a sliver of soap in his pocket. Judging by his skin color, and the general reek of dissolution, I'd say he was a confirmed drunkard. Sir? Mr. Holmes?"

I had been appraising the body and agreeing with the doctor. I was startled to look up and find my friend staring not at the figure beneath the drape, but at the policeman who was watching the procedure.

"Your name, officer?" Holmes asked, but it was the physician who answered.

"This is Constable Tate. He came in with the body."

"And has stayed," Holmes whispered, half to himself. "You were a witness to his demise?" Holmes asked, even though we were certainly aware of the answer. The man stepped forward with a brisk nod.

"I was. And while I'll not take a brother officer to task, Rutledge used unnecessary force. Had he just given me another moment, I believe I could have persuaded this man to halt and release the girl he was holding."

"You are sorry for a criminal's death?"

The policeman rubbed his face, resting his hand about his mouth. "I was raised a Quaker, sir, and though I am no longer affiliated with the Society of Friends, I do not wish to see any man's life ended prematurely. Even a thief or bad sort has family who love him and wish him alive."

"An admirable sentiment," Holmes said. "What a shame we shall never know this individual's identity."

"His name – " the officer began, and then doubled over with a spasm of coughing. "Pardon me, sir, this environment is oppressive. I was only going to say that while his name will never be known, I have offered to pay for him to have a decent burial. I feel I failed the man. The least I can do is put him away properly."

"Our assistant can see to those details," the doctor said. "Rest assured, that if no one claims him in three days, you will be notified."

"Thank you," Tate said. "Gentlemen, good day." And then he drifted out through the passage.

"An intriguing study," Holmes observed. "What a mystery is man."

I confess I was relieved when, a short time later, we emerged into the afternoon sunlight. Holmes consulted his pocket watch.

"We have just enough time to visit Rutledge, I think."

We journeyed to the officer's abode, which was not far removed from Audley Court where we had encountered Constable Rance, all those years ago. The neighborhood was sadder than before, but Rutledge's small flat was tidy and, as best any bachelor could make such a place, warm and welcoming. The man himself was so large and burly that a teacup looked like a child's plaything in his monstrous hands.

"I feel terrible," Rutledge rumbled. "They train us in the proper ways, of course, but something about how that dirty villain was handling that poor little miss – it brought out the savage in me. I wonder if I will be arrested and go to prison."

"You saw blood at her throat – the suspect had wounded her," Holmes said, and the constable nodded. "No stout-hearted Englishman would ever convict you," my friend prophesied. "But I am curious as to the chase itself. Can you describe it?"

"I was talking with Tate," he said. "I was surprised to see him, for I thought his patrol was further along the street. We were chatting of one thing or another, and he told me he thought I should follow a cab that had just passed, as he was certain the driver was a felon we'd been looking for all week. Then, I heard a lady screaming '*Stop thief!*' The rascal shot out of the doorway of the Savoy and ran into the Strand, not fifty feet from where we stood. Tate caught my jacket in alarm, we both blew our whistles, and we were off. We lost him for a moment in the crowd. Tate tugged on my arm, and said he thought he'd seen the man slip into the Lyceum, but I spotted him darting into an alley. We trailed him to Covent Garden, lost him again amid the stalls, and Tate had just suggested we should backtrack and summon more assistance when we heard another scream. I charged up and found a flower-seller knocked to the ground. She was unhurt, but very angry, and she pointed right to the door of the museum. The rest . . . ."

"Yes, Inspector Lestrade provided those details," Holmes said. "Constable, I find that I will require your services in an unofficial capacity."

"For what, sir?"

"To apprehend a dangerous criminal. My address is 221b Baker Street. If you will come there tomorrow, at five, we shall go hunting together."

"We have one more stop," Holmes said, as he hailed a cab. "Let us hope that our interview will go as I anticipate – or I shall have engaged our sizable assistant for nothing."

As always, I was astonished by my friend's ability to plan his movements several steps ahead of any opponent. A short time later, we arrived at Covent Garden, stepping out of our vehicle at the door of the wax museum. Lestrade had, rather thoughtfully, left a man stationed there. The officer admitted us and assured Miss Rose Porter that we were known to Scotland Yard and were there to help her.

"You are alone?" Holmes asked softly, for the girl was clearly still shaken by all that had occurred that day. She was no more than twenty, and her face was deathly pale, a shocking contrast to her beautiful dark hair. There was a bandage upon her throat, and she showed us the bruises on her wrists from where she had been cruelly handled.

"I fear so, sir. My mother is dead, and Father has gone to France to purchase – " She abruptly shook her head, placing delicate fingers on her brow. "No – I shall not lie. I have read the stories about you, Mr. Holmes, and I know that you always see the truth. My father is a drunkard, and he is in Edinburgh with his brother, who is equally dissolute. He does this so frequently I think little of it. I spend my days attempting to keep our little museum open. But now that there has been a crime committed here, I feel that we must surely close, and that Father will blame me for the misfortune."

I heard many fears in her trembling voice. Holmes gestured toward the stairs.

"May we see the room where you found the culprit?"

Miss Porter bit upon her lip but obediently led the way. I noticed a damp spot upon the second-floor landing, where she had been forced to clean away the blood and gore from the attack. She turned her head and pointed into adjoining galleries.

"On the first floor, we have the statues of the Stuart and Georgian kings and queens. The Plantagenets are here on the second. But the third floor is our pride, for it is filled with the glorious Tudors, including Henry VIII and all his wives."

We stepped into a single long and narrow chamber. The wax figures stood on a low stage, illuminated by gaslights. Their false gems twinkled, the velvet and satin of their clothing warmly glowed. Holmes stepped forward, musing over the figures.

"These are expertly done."

"Thank you, sir. In his youth, Father was a master craftsman who trained at Tussaud's studio. And Mother was the finest seamstress in London, as well as an artist. She would spend hours studying famous paintings, so that she could exactly reproduce the costumes and jewelry."

"And you share these gifts?" Holmes inquired, studying the tableaux of the notorious Henry VIII and his many spouses.

The girl meekly bowed her head. "I fear not, Mr. Holmes. My only talent, as Father is quick to remind me, is for sweeping the floor."

Holmes turned, his expression one that – to a stranger – might have seemed cold and unreadable. But I, who knew him so well, instantly discerned his sympathy for the young woman, and his determination to help her.

"Miss Porter, I believe that we may yet recover the Boleyn Letter, which has been the cause of so much suffering. To do so, however, will require your assistance, and all your courage."

The girl gasped in astonishment but straightened her spine. "What can I do?"

Holmes began to scribble upon his notebook. "You will allow me to place this story in the morning papers. A constable will remain here tonight, and first thing tomorrow, my friend will come and serve as a guard in this room. Watson, do you think you know enough about the Tudors to entertain any final visitors to the museum?"

"Final?" Miss Porter asked.

"Entertain?" I said.

Holmes smiled and showed the lady his note. She looked up in wonder.

"Destroy the figures! But sir – if Father should return . . . ?"

Holmes placed coins in her hand. "If he does, make sure that he goes to the nearest pub and bemoans his misfortune. But tomorrow, the word will go out that Porter's Museum of Historical Curiosities is having its final day of operation. Close the doors promptly at five. I will come shortly afterward, with Constable Rutledge, and we shall keep a special vigil. I am certain that our villain will return to the scene."

The young woman nodded her ascent but favored my friend with a skeptical look. "Sir, that man is dead."

"Is he?" Holmes inquired.

Back at our lodgings that evening, Holmes explained my role, but not its ultimate purpose.

"I have inserted a dramatic announcement in the newspapers," Holmes said. "The press can very valuable, when properly manipulated. In the early editions, readers will learn that due to a tragedy at the Porter Museum, the proprietor has decided to retire. The attraction will therefore be open for one last day, and afterward all the waxworks will be summarily destroyed, to prevent them from being exhibited under any other name."

"It would be a foolish plan, if it were real!" I objected.

"Foolish plans can inspire desperate actions," Holmes agreed. "I am counting on it."

I shook my head. "It is a pity you weren't able to retrieve the Boleyn Letter."

"My dear Watson, you wound me! I know exactly where the Letter lies. I could be holding it in my hand at this very moment."

"What! Then why did you not act?"

"For two reasons – the first is that the Countess of Ionne needs a comeuppance. I will not allow her to abuse my friend Lestrade with impunity, so she shall pass one more day without her precious bauble. But, more importantly, I wish to bring an evildoer to justice by catching him in the act of committing another crime."

"But – "

"Let us leave it at that, Watson. Off with you, as you shall have a long day tomorrow!"

The next morning, at an unseemly early hour, I was shaving, and it occurred to me that perhaps Rutledge was somehow involved. The big man had seemed innocent and broken-hearted, yet he had slain the thief without hesitation. Young Miss Porter was clearly in his thrall, for when Holmes had mentioned that Rutledge would be returning with him, her cheeks turned rosy, and her smile was almost giddy. Could the two of them, in league with the dubious maid, have engineered a theft and a murder? I had little time to mull it over, for Holmes picked me up, giving me my instructions as we rode to the museum with London awakening around us.

"You are to take a chair in the Tudor gallery. Serve as a docent, but whatever you do, never leave the figures unguarded, not even for a second. I'll send Wiggins and some of the Irregulars to relieve you for lunch and at tea, but otherwise you must not abandon your post. Is that clear?"

I responded with a mocking salute. Miss Porter admitted me and made me comfortable on a veritable throne, elevated on the stage, amid all the figures.

"Does Mr. Holmes think our waxworks will run away?" Miss Porter asked, as I settled in for my duty.

"He's probably concerned that the thief's accomplice will return. I should recognize her if she did." I disliked telling a falsehood to a lady, but the more I considered it, the more I felt certain Miss Porter was duplicitous and somehow involved in this bad business. The girl nodded and hurried back downstairs. In ten minutes, the chamber was filled with patrons.

"You there," one man, a stout fellow in a checkered coat, called out. "You look lively enough. Are you the guide? Tell me all about these dummy folks. I'll be hanged if I ever paid attention in history class."

And so, my new career began. I quickly exhausted my store of tales from school days and fell back on the many romances I had read, as well as plots from Shakespeare. My audience grew, fell away, then swelled again. After a time, and confident that my listeners were of the most ignorant classes, I began to embellish the tales, adding even more victims, until Henry VIII had slain all his wives, and Bloody Mary had burned half of England at the stake. I was midway through a depiction of Richard III strangling the Princes in the Tower with his own hands when a bewhiskered elder in a shabby coat called me out as an ignoramus.

"Richard and the princes were of the House of York, not Tudor, and there is no proof that Richard ever did such a vile deed," the old man whined, his voice shrill and reedy. "Lies spread by Sir Thomas More! I'll not hear my favorite monarch so belittled."

The man waved his cane above his head. The other patrons quickly scattered, except for a handful of naughty boys who urged the "professor" to thrash me. As soon as the last onlooker hurried through the door, the lads bent double in laughter.

"I am not amused," I grumbled at Holmes. "Really, I knew it was you the moment you hobbled inside."

"But I never tire of the game! Wiggins," my friend said to the tallest of the lads, "deploy your troops. You have the watch for an hour, while I treat Watson to lunch and, hopefully, correct his rather bad history."

We made a quick meal at The Punch and Judy pub while Holmes updated me on his activities.

"I spoke with our friend, Constable Tate, this morning. He was saddened to hear the tragic event would cost the young lady her livelihood."

"I'm not convinced she is a victim here."

"Indeed?"

"I am merely wondering . . . If she and Rutledge are in it together, then are we taking a terrible risk?"

"Perhaps. But think how boring our lives would be without an occasional indulgence in recklessness."

I could not be so blasé, especially when I considered how large and frightful Rutledge appeared. I whispered for Holmes to be sure he slipped a pistol into his pocket before leaving Baker Street again.

I returned to my post, noting that the Irregulars were "telling porkies" with gusto. Their relish for beheadings and elaborate tortures was disturbing. The remainder of the afternoon passed without incident, except for one child who seemed intent on stealing Good Queen Elizabeth's crown. Fortunately, Miss Porter had just entered the room and deftly retrieved the naughty girl before she could scale the queen's bejeweled skirts. Shortly afterward, the museum closed, and the last patron wandered away. I was assisting Miss Porter in shuttering the ticket window when we heard a light rapping in the rear of the building. I hurried to open the back door, which gave access to a narrow, filthy alley. I admitted Holmes, Rutledge, and – much to my surprise – Lestrade.

"I felt the Inspector might enjoy our little party," Holmes said, gesturing to the large basket he carried on his arm. "A cold supper and two very excellent bottles of wine. Ah, Miss Porter – I believe you and the constable have met?"

The lady had hurried up to us in the corridor, but now she nodded shyly. I noticed that the big man immediately snatched off his cap, and was offering an awkward, boyish smile. Lestrade snorted angrily.

"Will you tell me the point of this, Mr. Holmes, or are you determined to be mysterious?"

"Patience, Lestrade. Let us go up to the family's rooms, in the front of the museum. Miss Porter, be good enough to light a lamp and pass before the window a few times. Gentlemen, we must stay back and not be seen."

I knew that Holmes was attempting to lure an accomplice to the museum. I watched Miss Porter and Constable Rutledge carefully and saw only two young people whose attraction was both immediate and charming. Holmes was at his wittiest, telling anecdotes of his many adventures, while Lestrade grumbled about the possibility of receiving a demotion from the rank of Inspector. Holmes pulled out his watch just at ten.

"Late enough, I think. Miss Porter, we will now retire to our stations inside the museum. Go about your normal routines, extinguish your light, and lock yourself inside your chamber. For your safety, do not emerge until one of us comes to your door and summons you. Is this clear?"

"Yes, sir. And do please . . . be careful."

I buried a smile, as she had directed this instruction to the gargantuan Rutledge.

"Where shall we lurk?" Lestrade asked.

"Constable Rutledge should remain on the first floor, behind the curtain of the exhibits, to guard the lady. Lestrade, you will slip into the darkened alcove on the second floor. Be certain that you both remain silent until – " Holmes suddenly smiled, as if struck by a delightful idea. "Lestrade, can you imitate a cat?"

"What?"

"A single meow will suffice. Do not utter it until you witness someone pass you on the stairs. It will provide an alert to Watson and myself. We shall raise the alarm the moment the prize is obtained."

Lestrade fumed but agreed to the plan. Holmes and I continued to the long gallery at the top of the stairs.

"Holmes – who are you expecting?"

My friend had brought the picnic basket with him. Now he pulled a long, hooded robe from its depths.

"Is it not obvious? The thief had an accomplice, one who knows that, on the morrow, all the figures will be destroyed. Therefore, if this villain wishes to obtain the prize, the job must be done tonight – "

Holmes threw the robe over his shoulders, lifting its hood to shield his face. He then extinguished all the gaslights, plunging the room into nearly total darkness. We waited, allowing our eyes to adjust.

"I will stand just here, behind King Henry," Holmes said. "You shall move to the window and place yourself behind the curtains.

"Of course. But why should we – "

Holmes held up a hand, signaling for silence. I heard something below us. It was a tinkling, as if glass had been broken. We stood frozen, waiting for more. Perhaps two minutes later, a cat gave an irritated cry. Holmes shoved me toward my place, then tiptoed to the stage. As always, I was astonished by how noiselessly my friend moved. Just as I concealed myself behind the drapes, I saw Holmes lower his head and fold his hands, becoming a silent, prayerful priest standing behind the great king.

The gallery door opened. I peeked through a slit in the curtains, but the figure who entered the room was still indistinct. The intruder plodded forward awkwardly, and I frowned. Was it the countess's maid, in boots and trousers? The mysterious form paused for a moment, then struck a match and lit a candle. A gloved hand reached out toward Queen Anne Boleyn's slender neck, and dark fingers closed on her necklace.

"Unhand her!"

A terrible scream cut the air. The thief skittered backward, nearly falling. Holmes was on the phantom like a panther, seizing a wrist. With a blistering curse, the man twisted and hurled the candle toward the waxen tableaux. Holmes shouted for aid as he fell to the floorboards, wrestling with the intruder. I heard Lestrade and Rutledge on the stairs. My first though was to aid my friend, but then I saw the candle had ignited Queen Katherine Howard's skirts. I seized King Henry's massive cape from his shoulders and beat back the flames as the policemen hauled the dark figure up, fastening handcuffs upon him.

"And who do we have?" Lestrade growled, as his officer opened a dark lantern.

"Why – My God! It's *Tate*!" Rutledge exclaimed.

"Yes. Our constable is the thief's brother and partner in crime," Holmes said calmly. "My only question now is whether the maid is their sister, or a lover to one or both."

"You keep little Ellie's name off your filthy lips!" the constable sneered. Holmes nodded.

"Sister, then. Lestrade, you may yet capture the entire gang."

"This affair truly ranks among the annals of unusual crimes," said Sherlock Holmes the next morning, as we sat in the four-wheeler with Lestrade and Rutledge, on our way to an appointment at the Savoy, where we would restore the Boleyn Letter to the Countess of Ionne. "I cannot recall one like it, with perhaps the exception of the Latimer case in Charleston."

Lestrade made no comment, but the young officer, who sizeable physique took up half the vehicle, leaned forward eagerly.

"I still do not understand how you knew it all, Mr. Holmes."

"It was elementary," my friend said, with gentle authority and no hint of mockery in his tone. "It was obvious from the start that there was collusion between the countess's maid and the thief. Their elaborate, though interrupted, staging of the crime made me wonder whether another accomplice might be involved. The inspector gave me some details on the chase and the killing of the thief, and then you provided the rest. Think back to Tate's actions. You mentioned it was strange that he was near the Savoy, when his assigned patrol was around Covent Garden. He tried to send you away on a wild goose chase after a cab driver, and when that failed, he grabbed your sleeve and attempted to hold you back, all in the guise of being startled. He sought to send you to an area he knew the thief would not be hiding, and then urged you to leave and summon reinforcements. I hope, Rutledge, that Scotland Yard will recognize you for your doggedness in staying after your man."

The big constable blushed. Lestrade spoke up.

"How did you know Tate and the thief were brothers?"

"I spotted the resemblance between them in the morgue. That, and Tate's clumsy lie about his Quaker roots compelling him to take responsibility for the body made me certain that he was the late man's sibling."

"But the crime was a poorly planned thing!" Lestrade snorted. "Even if the brother knew he could hide the necklace on the statue, in plain sight, why bother? Why not just trust that his sibling would allow him to escape?"

Holmes opened the case that now held the antique necklace. "This is not an item that could be readily sold. It is both antique in style and instantly recognizable. The goal was never possession of the necklace."

"Then what was it?" I asked.

"Monetary reward," Holmes said. "And, for Constable Tate, professional acclaim, and promotion. Here is what the trio planned: The maid would be left in the rooms, staged as a victim. Once the thief departed, Tate would blow his whistle and give chase, but not too speedily. The thief would slip into the museum. Constable Tate made sure to pick the lock earlier so that it would be accessible. Thief Tate would exchange the necklaces, then run out and be 'captured' by his sibling. The replica necklace would be found in his pocket, and the case against him would collapse, especially as the maid would claim he was not the man who assaulted her. The thief would then disappear into the underworld, even as the maid also conveniently removed herself from the countess's employ. In a few days' time, Tate would make a brilliant deduction as to where the actual necklace had been hidden. He would recover it and receive the accolades of his colleagues, as well as a sizeable reward from the countess, which he would divide with his conspirator siblings."

"I ruined the plan," Rutledge whispered.

"Indeed – by your determination, you threw everything into disorder. The arrival of Miss Porter only made things worse. Thief Tate panicked, taking her prisoner, wounding her in the process. I have no doubt that Constable Tate was trying to calm his brother, using some code, perhaps even trying to alert him to your presence."

"The man was turning," Rutledge said, "looking back. But I had begun to swing my stick . . . ."

Holmes shook his head. "You performed your duty. Do not allow it to haunt you, for if you had not intervened, Miss Porter might have come to greater harm. Ah, I see we have arrived. I wish you well, gentlemen. Perhaps the countess will not be armed with her reticule this time."

"You are not coming?" Lestrade asked. "But any reward – "

"Belongs to you, and to Constable Rutledge. My work is its own reward. Good day!"

Holmes thumped his cane upon the roof, and we drove on.

"What about the damage to Mrs. Hudson's ceiling?" I asked with a smirk.

Holmes shook his head. "I am certain some further remunerative business will come my way soon. I received a note from Mycroft just this morning, and government work is always profitable. I wished Rutledge to have his share of the countess's gratitude, for unless I have completely lost my ability to see and observe, the strong attraction between Rutledge and Miss Porter leads me to the deduction that Rutledge will soon have a wedding and a new home to finance."

Anne Boleyn and the Boleyn Letter

The Case of the
Ignoble Cuckold
by Tom Turley

Readers of my early chronicles will recall "The Adventure of the Noble Bachelor", in which Lord Robert St. Simon lost his bride. The affair was something of a nine days' wonder, but it was not, alas, the last of that distinguished family's marital woes. Whereas the original case's implications affected only the unfortunate aristocrat, the scandal I shall now relate might have shaken the British monarchy to its very core, had not Mr. Sherlock Holmes succeeded in putting matters right. Over twenty years have passed since these events transpired, and many of the principals involved are now deceased. Even so, I have directed that the following account shall not be published in my lifetime.

His desertion by Miss Hattie Doran – or, rather, by Mrs. Francis Hay Moulton – was the beginning of a momentous period for poor Lord Robert. [1] Later that year, his elder brother, the Marquess of Backwater, died without issue in a hunting accident. Their aged father succumbed soon afterwards. So it was that the Ninth Duke of Balmoral came into his title, though hardly in the manner that he might have wished. [2] It was not long, moreover, before Lord Eustace St. Simon married the daughter of a Scottish shipbuilder, securing thereby both a handsome dowry and the promise of a fortune such as his ducal brother had unsuccessfully aspired to gain. For Holmes and me, who retained a certain sympathy for our former client, his succession of misfortunes made dismal reading in the society pages of *The Times*.

It was in May of 1890 [3] that I called at 221b Baker Street one afternoon when I had no patients scheduled and my wife was absent on a shopping spree. After the obligatory enquiries regarding married life, and an appreciative silence as we consumed the viands Mrs. Hudson had provided, Holmes mentioned casually that he was expecting a client to arrive upon the hour.

"Indeed? Well, I must leave you to it." I feinted at rising, amused and gratified when my friend lifted a protesting hand.

"Don't go, Doctor. If Mrs. Watson can spare you for another hour, I should much prefer you to remain."

"Knowing how Mary dithers over choosing a new hat," I laughed, "I'm unlikely to see her before nightfall. Who's your client, then?"

"Only a prospective one at present. You're familiar with Sir John MacPherson, the shipbuilder? I understand his yard on the Clyde produced our latest class of battleships."

"I first heard of 'Jock' MacPherson as a first-class cricketer," I irrelevantly noted, "although naturally he played long before my time. By now, he may be the richest man in Scotland. He's held a seat in Parliament since the last Glasgow by-election, just after his daughter married into the St. Simon family."

Sherlock Holmes smiled with satisfaction. "Excellent, Watson! I can always depend upon your sporting knowledge and your fascination with 'The Great'. Indeed, Miss Fiona MacPherson wed Lord Eustace St. Simon some three years ago, and last week the happy couple welcomed their first child – a girl, alas. I do *occasionally* read the society column of *The Times*, you know."

"Ah, there's the bell," he added eagerly. After the usual delay and noise upon the stairs, Billy showed the Scottish baronet into our sitting room.

Sir John was then in his fifty-second year, a stocky man of middle height, only a stone heavier, perhaps, than when he last stepped from the cricket pitch. He wore a rust-coloured tweed suit and the flowing side-whiskers fashionable thirty years ago, turning now to grey from russet. From his countenance, I should have judged him of a bluff and hearty disposition, but an unnatural pallor overlay the ruddy face, and the prominent green eyes looked dull and lifeless. My medical instincts told me that "Jock" MacPherson had suffered a great shock, some disaster that had all but overwhelmed him. No doubt we would soon learn what it was.

"Mr. Sherlock Holmes?" He gazed uncertainly between us, finally settling on my companion.

"Quite so, Sir John. This is my friend and colleague, Dr. Watson. Pray take a seat and explain how we may be of service."

"I am here, Mr. Holmes, on behalf of my daughter." With a groan, the distracted father collapsed on the settee. "They have sent my bonny lass to an asylum." He shook his head in wonderment, accepting the tumbler of whisky I offered him.

My friend's reply conveyed less sympathy than ill-suppressed excitement. "Your 'bonny lass' is, I believe, the wife of Lord Eustace St. Simon?"

"She is. Had I kenned of him what I ken now, I'd have drowned Fiona in the sea before the blackguard married her!"

"*Well*, Doctor," remarked Holmes, "so there's a black sheep in the St. Simon flock! I take it, then, that the union has not been a success?"

"Can you ask that, sir, when things have come to such a pass?" MacPherson glared indignantly at the detective, who had the grace to look a little discomfited.

"My apologies." Holmes took shag tobacco from the Persian slipper and began to fill his pipe. "Assuredly, asylums do not figure in a happy marriage. Let us start, Sir John, at the beginning. *How* did things come to such a pass?"

"It's a sorry tale," MacPherson sighed, "and my puir girl has made a mess of things. But she's not mad, Mr. Holmes, no matter what they say of her." He emptied his glass and held it out to me. "I'll need another dram of that, if you please, Doctor." Once I had provided it, our client began to tell the "sorry tale".

"Fiona, gentleman, is my only child. My dear wife died in birthing her, and I never wished to find another. For all her life before her marriage, Fiona had only me for family, and I spent my days at the shipyard or the docks, leaving my daughter in that grey, grim house in Govan, with only the servants there for company – and those Murrays as dour a pair of Presbyterians as ever sucked the joy out of a young girl's heart. Yet, Fiona seemed to grow up happy: A little shy and innocent, perhaps, but loving and sweet-natured for all that. And even then, I could see that one day she would be as lovely as her mother."

My friend was already growing restless. "As touching as these childhood memories are," he said, "an account of recent events would be more useful to the case at hand."

"Very well," the Scotsman growled, "I'll move along. Back in '86, when my firm was assigned to build *Trafalgar* and her sisters, my financial future was assured. Better still, the government contract brought with it court connexions and a baronetcy. I decided to buy a house in London, so that my Fiona could make her debut in society. She was sixteen then, and a rare beauty, and I thought it time that she saw something of the world. Puir lassie." He broke off with a kind of sob. "God knows she's seen it now!"

Holmes stolidly ignored his client's lapse into emotion. "Your residence," he asked, as I took out my notebook, "is located where?"

"Tryon House, not far from Hounslow Heath, which is as close as a man can get in London to a Highland moor. But it was from that heath that all our troubles came." In response to our enquiring looks, he added furiously: "*The bluidie 10th Hussars!*"

"Indeed? That is an élite regiment, if I am not mistaken, Watson?"

"The Prince of Wales served in it," I confirmed, "as does his son and heir, Prince Albert Victor."

"Aye, that dunderhead 'Prince Eddy'!'" sneered MacPherson. "He has darkened our door at Tryon House on more than one occasion."

"I think you had better explain yourself, Sir John," suggested Holmes, "lest Watson and I charge you with *lèse majesté*."

"I've nought against the Prince himself," the baronet relented, "but those damnable Hussars have trailed Fiona like a pack of dogs ever since she came to Hounslow. His Royal Highness is by no means the chief offender."

"*The Daughter of the Regiment*, eh, Doctor?" My friend's reference to Donizetti's opera was lost on our disgruntled client, who grumbled that this was no laughing matter. Again Holmes pressed him for an explanation, and this time Sir John complied.

Shortly after their arrival in Hounslow, MacPherson and Fiona had been taking an innocent stroll upon the heath. Suddenly, two troops of cavalry came thundering down on them from opposite directions, for (unbeknownst to them) the 10th Hussars had scheduled that morning for a training exercise. The troopers barely reined up before they overran the interlopers, whom their officers began berating soundly – until they noticed Sir John's lovely daughter. For her part, Fiona was thrilled by the handsome, gorgeously uniformed horsemen who surrounded her. As her father drily put it, "I doubt she'd seen so many young men, together or separately, in all her sixteen years!

"After that day upon the heath, nothing would do for Fiona but that we must plan a party for the 10th Hussars and invite their officers to Tryon House. And so we did. From that night onward, Mr. Holmes, I dinna think they ever left it!"

Although Sir John acknowledged this remark to be exaggerated, the élite regiment continued to play a major role in the MacPhersons' lives. Their acquaintance with Prince Eddy opened the exalted doors of Marlborough House, and Fiona, despite her youth and inexperience, was soon moving in the highest social circles. After her debut at seventeen, the Scottish beauty was besieged by suitors. Initially, her interest focused upon Captain "Reggie" Elliott of the 10th Hussars: A well-born, personable, but virtually penniless officer a decade older than herself. Sir John had considered him the best of a bad lot. However, his daughter's head was belatedly turned by the attentions of Lord Eustace St. Simon, whose outward charm and proximity to a dukedom were eventually decisive. They were married in the autumn of 1887, just before Fiona's eighteenth birthday.

Following their honeymoon, the couple took up residence at Birchmoor, previously Lord Robert's small estate in Hounslow, which he (now duke) had gifted to his brother as a wedding present. It was soon evident that Lady Eustace St. Simon intended to maintain an active social life, and in particular her friendships among the 10th Hussars. Conversely, her husband's taste ran more to cards, horses, and the pleasures of the hunt. Though Lord Eustace could hardly balk at receiving His Royal Highness and other officers while he was at Birchmoor, the fact that such visits continued in his absence soon became a source of strife. Not surprisingly, he objected most strongly to the dashing Captain Elliott, whom Fiona admitted even on afternoons when she was otherwise alone.

Her father regarded this conduct with deep foreboding. The Murrays, now serving as Birchmoor's housekeeper and butler, kept him apprised of his daughter's indiscretions with pious regularity. Despite appearances, MacPherson at first believed Fiona guilty of no more than carelessness. "She swore to me that her friendships were entirely innocent. She seemed shocked that I should think her guilty of adultery. But she wouldna give them up, even though I warned her that the *appearance* of sin can be as deadly as the sin itself. Fiona heard that admonition more than once from Morag Murray."

"I have to say, Sir John," remarked Sherlock Holmes, "that I fully understand Lord Eustace's concern. *Tête à tête* meetings with a former suitor? However innocent she may have been, your daughter was playing a very foolish game."

"Do you think I dinna ken that?" MacPherson plaintively replied. "But you must remember that Fiona was eighteen! Before she came to London, she'd hardly spoken to a man. Now they crowded 'round her like bears around a honeypot. These flirtations *were* a game to her. She couldna see the danger. If it's anybody's fault, it's mine. I never should have let her marry young."

"Surely, there was more to the affair than this," I interjected. "It was nearly three years ago your daughter married. Mere flirtations would not have justified Lord Eustace in placing her – the mother of his newborn child – in an asylum. What precipitated that decision?" Holmes gave an affirming nod, impatient to reach the matter's crux.

One precipitating factor had occurred ten months before. Lord Eustace had come home a day early from a fortnight's hunting trip in Austria. On arriving at Birchmoor, he found Fiona exercising a magnificent bay stallion on the lawn, while Captain Elliott and another officer looked on admiringly. Informed by his delighted wife that the stallion was "a gift from the 10th Hussars", the furious aristocrat ordered the two officers to depart his property and not return. Once they reluctantly obeyed, he immediately – and in Fiona's presence – shot the horse. Sir John's face, as told this shocking story, reflected something of the horror his young daughter must have felt.

"After that," MacPherson went on grimly, "things went from bad to worse. Though Fiona thought him no better than a murderer, St. Simon began demanding that she have a child. 'It is vital to my interests,' he kept telling her, 'that you bear my son.' I dinna ken what all the hurry was. He'd made no fash about a bairn before. Yet, he kept himself apart from her and treated her like a common strumpet on the rare occasions he was home. Is it a wonder Fiona decided to commit the sin he'd judged her guilty of before it happened?"

Holmes's face evinced his discomfort, as was usually the case when sexual matters were discussed. "So, I take it there was some question as to the child's paternity?"

"Aye."

"And the other possibility was presumably this Captain Elliott?"

Now it was MacPherson's turn to look uncomfortable. "I would to God it were that simple, Mr. Holmes."

When Sir John had visited his daughter on the previous Sunday, she had seemed tired but calm and happy with her infant daughter. It was the last time he had seen Fiona. What happened afterwards was reported to him by Lord Eustace, who had stormed into Tryon House on Thursday, the day before our client came to Baker Street.

"There was something amiss with the wee lassie's eyes," MacPherson informed us, "a runny discharge the doctors said was caused by an infection. They feared she might go blind. Everyone tried to keep this worry from Fiona, but she kept asking if the puir bairn was 'diseased'."

In response to my friend's enquiring glance, I said reluctantly, "Ophthalmia in newborns can sometimes be the sign of a venereal infection, passed on from the mother."

"Aye, Doctor. When she finally heard the truth from Morag Murray, Fiona became hysterical. She insisted on speaking to her husband and sent everybody else away."

"And what was the nature of this conversation?" Holmes demanded quietly.

Recounting its nature brought tears to Sir John's eyes. His daughter had admitted to adultery with Captain Elliott and others – "often, and in open day". While she would not disclose the identities of her other paramours, she was certain that one of them must be "diseased", resulting in her baby's eye infection. Having confessed, Fiona lapsed into a sullen silence, ignoring her irate husband's accusations and insults as though he were not there. She stopped eating and, over the next two days, alternated between fits of weeping and an almost catatonic lethargy. She also showed no interest in the child. On Thursday, Lord Eustace had overruled his family physician and consulted a psychiatric specialist, Dr. Samuel Drake, who urged that Lady Eustace be placed in his private asylum. Only then did St. Simon inform his wife's father (who had just returned from the launch of a battleship in Govan) of the week's events.

"To give the man his due," MacPherson grumbled, "I dinna believe he did it purely for revenge. Drake's an acknowledged expert in the field, and Fiona couldna go on as she was. But Eustace told me that he intends to divorce her in a public trial, naming Captain Elliott as correspondent. If my daughter's not well enough to testify, he'll keep her in the madhouse 'til she is. If there's na divorce, he'll keep her there until she dies!"

Holmes sighed and rose to knock his pipe against the grate. He turned back to our client with a quizzical smile. "But why have you come to *me*, Sir John? As I view the situation, you are less in need of a detective than a barrister."

"It may yet come to that," the baronet acknowledged. "I'mna opposed to a divorce, if it's done quietly – God knows I'd like to be rid of that St. Simon – but I canna let my only child spend the rest of her life in an asylum. I need you to find out more about what happened: For one, who her other lovers are. Likely they willna wish to be exposed."

"Can you not ask your daughter?"

"Her doctor presently allows na visitors, and Fiona mayna agree to see me. Like as not, she's too ashamed." A quaver returned to the grieving father's voice.

My friend relapsed into his chair. "There's something in what you say about the other lovers," he said thoughtfully, "and there's also the new Duke of Balmoral. I doubt that he'll look kindly on adultery, but – as you may recall – His Grace's abortive marital venture became public several years ago. Another scandal of the kind could ruin the St. Simon family socially. He might be used to moderate his brother's conduct."

"Aye."

"Very well, Sir John," Holmes concluded briskly. "Give me a few days to look into this matter, and I should be better able to advise you. To be frank, it's not the sort of case most suited to my talents, but I shall do what I can to save your foolish young Fiona. However disreputable her conduct may have been, she hardly deserves a husband cruel enough to shoot a horse in front of her! I am glad to have Lord Eustace St. Simon called to my attention before he chances to do something worse."

Our client seemed not best-pleased with portions of this speech, but he took leave of us with a gracious word of thanks. Once the door had shut behind him, my friend turned back to me.

"Well, Watson, you will note that I did not commit you to involvement. Even so, I should be very glad to have your counsel, particularly regarding the medical aspects of the case. Does your practice permit you to accompany me?"

"I daresay Anstruther could take my patients for a day or two. We are neither of us very busy at the moment."

"And what of Mrs. Watson?"

"She is tolerant of our adventures. Should she ever grow cross, I need only remind her of what I gained by one of them!"

"Excellent! Then return in the morning at your earliest convenience. We shall begin our investigation in Hounslow. Pray give your wife my kindest greetings."

With these cordial words, we parted. I returned to 7 Praed Street, [4] where I found dear Mary eager to show me the most charming hat in London.

Early the next day, Holmes and I boarded a train at Paddington on the Underground Railway, exiting at the station on the Birchmoor Road. He had previously despatched a letter to Lord Eustace St. Simon, "ensuring that we shall be expected, though perhaps unwelcome, guests."

A ten-minute walk brought us to Birchmoor, a small but handsome Jacobean manor surrounded by a wooded park. There, my friend's prescience regarding our reception was confirmed. When the butler Murray responded to our knock, he informed us with sour satisfaction that His Lordship did not find himself at home.

"At least to us," Holmes muttered. Proffering his card before the door shut in his face, he promised to return at the same hour tomorrow. As we turned away, he nudged me sharply and gestured at a tall figure walking up the drive.

"That is surely the family doctor," he apprised me, though I can generally recognise a member of my own profession. "See what information you can glean from him."

The young man approaching apparently intended to pass us without speaking, but I called out "Good morning, Doctor . . . ?" in response to his brief nod.

"Dr. Walter Ormond, Lord Eustace's physician. And you, sir?"

"Dr. John H. Watson. My associate and I – " A careless nod towards Holmes. " – have called on behalf of Sir John MacPherson, Lady Eustace's father."

"Indeed? I trust you found the child improved?"

'In fact, we had not had the opportunity of observing her before."

"The discharge from her eyes has cleared remarkably in the last two days. I see no reason to suspect incipient blindness or venereal disease.

Lady Eustace's fears upon that score were no more than *post-partum* hysteria, which I feel certain will soon pass."

"That is excellent news. We shall inform Sir John immediately." I bowed, and my earnest young colleague continued towards the house.

"You might also inform him," he suddenly called after us, "that my observation of Lady Eustace convinces me that she is no more insane than you or I. She is heartbroken, guilt-ridden, and extremely fearful of her husband. From a medical standpoint, there was no necessity at all for her to be confined."

We bowed again, acknowledging Dr. Ormond's blatant violation of his Hippocratic Oath. "That fellow," I remarked, "is very confident of his opinions."

"He has fallen under Lady Eustace's spell." I turned to find Holmes regarding me – for once – with admiration. "I must admit, Watson, that you are developing a degree of guile. Without telling an untruth, you managed to create an altogether false impression. Dr. Ormond could not have conveyed more useful evidence even on the witness stand. Well done!"

"Thank you, Holmes." Praise from Caesar was a relatively rare occurrence in our friendship, but it was always welcome when it came.

After an early luncheon at a local inn, we again took the District Railway to the new station outside Hounslow Barracks. It had been years since I had visited this installation, built during the French Revolution as a bulwark against foreign invasion and a possible rising by the London populace. Nowadays, it was used primarily as a training facility for cavalry, and for this purpose had incorporated large portions of the ancient boundaries of Hounslow Heath. From the moment we stepped through the Barracks' wrought-iron gates and crossed the parade ground, I found myself squaring my shoulders and adopting a military stride, insofar as my game leg permitted. My friend's chaffing was sufficient to deter me, but for us old campaigners such habits are ingrained.

During my service, I had always been attracted to the cavalry. As a medical officer, my equestrian experience was too limited to achieve true skill, but I had enjoyed the days I spent on horseback. There is something thrilling in the coordinated action of a mass of mounted men, performing their evolutions at the trot or gallop. At the time we visited, the day's formal drill had been concluded, but small groups of lancers or Hussars still moved back and forth in échelon from column into line, their manoeuvers finally culminating in a simulated charge. I had to restrain myself from cheering, but Holmes, as ever, seemed entirely unimpressed.

Our object was to interview Lady Eustace's acknowledged lover. Holmes had sent Elliott a telegram the night before, explaining his commission from Sir John MacPherson. To my surprise, the Captain had agreed to meet with us. He, unlike most of his wealthier or married fellows, resided in the officers' barracks instead of a private house in London. We made our way into a large, pedimented building across the parade ground from the gate, opposed on either side by barracks that housed the enlisted men above the stables. Inside, few soldiers seemed to be about, but we were able to obtain directions to the Captain's quarters.

We found him preparing to depart for an evening's entertainment. Immaculately attired in his dress regimentals: Blue jacket elaborately frogged with gold. Busby, pelisse, and sword-belt near at hand, this darkly handsome hussar looked well-equipped to steal the heart – and virtue – of a naïve young wife who, by then, must have regretted allowing a mere title to dissuade her from her heart's first choice.

Captain Elliott greeted us genially as he stood before a mirror fastening his collar. "Come in, gentlemen, come in. I can give you twenty minutes. Then I'm off to meet some fellows at the Empire. Old Capel's booked a pair of French songbirds who – so I've been told – are well worth the price of admission on their own." He motioned us to a settee and offered whisky, which Holmes declined for both of us. It was apparent that my friend was in no mood for cheerful banter.

"We shall not detain you, Captain, longer than required, but you should understand that this is a serious enquiry. I am acting on behalf of Sir John MacPherson."

"Yes, so your telegram informed me." Elliott now assumed a thoughtful demeanour and took the chair across from us. "I'm sorry this trouble has come upon old Jock, for he was always kind to me. What I *don't* understand, Mr. Sherlock Holmes, is why he felt the need to employ a detective."

Before Holmes could reply, the Captain turned to me. "What regiment, Doctor?"

"Fifth Northumberland Fusiliers," I answered in surprise, "although I was with the Berkshires when we fought at Maiwand."

"The Gallant 66th," the Captain smiled. [5] "But you must stop carrying your kerchief in your sleeve, if you object to being marked as an old soldier." He rose and offered me his hand, which I accepted. "It is an honour, sir."

"Unless you two plan to start comparing war wounds," the detective snapped with some asperity, "I propose we return to the matter at hand."

"Of course." Elliott resumed his chair and put on a face of patient enquiry.

126

"I think we can take it as established fact," Holmes began sententiously, "that Lady Eustace St. Simon is, or has been, your mistress. She has told her husband that you are the most likely father of her child."

The Captain flushed but managed to respond with equanimity. "If the lady has said we are lovers, it would be ungallant of me to say she lies – although," he added quickly, "in any other circumstance I should deny it to my dying breath!"

"Your gallantry is noted," my friend remarked ironically, for there was something slightly frivolous in our host's manner. "Unfortunately, there is also evidence that Lady Eustace – and, through her, her infant daughter – have contracted a venereal disease. Are you suffering from such a disease, Captain?"

This time Elliott did not suppress his anger. "I am *not*, Mr. Holmes. The suggestion is outrageous."

"Then evidently the infection was contracted from another source."

"Have you enquired of the lady's husband?"

"No, for – as much as I dislike discussing it – Lady Eustace has admitted that there were *others*. Other lovers, that is, besides yourself. Can you offer any suggestions as to their identities?"

"As you are surely aware, sir, it would be highly dishonourable of me to speculate, or to reveal such information if I knew."

"Well, I am relieved to learn there is honour even among adulterers. Yet, I have also been informed that another officer accompanied you on the afternoon you presented Lady Eustace with a stallion as a gift from the 10th Hussars – before, of course, you were both evicted by her outraged husband. Presumably, you are aware of this officer's identity?"

At last Holmes had pierced the Captain's armour. With a curse, he sprang to his feet and glared at us, eventually relapsing in his seat with an exasperated sigh.

"D--n Lord Eustace! I would have challenged him over killing that beautiful beast, had we all been living in another century. As things stand, Mr. Holmes, I have decided to 'do the decent' and allow myself to be named as correspondent if the bounder proceeds with a divorce. But I will *not* reveal my brother officer's identity, even should it come to perjuring myself upon the stand. There are higher loyalties, you know, than even to one's honour. Doctor, I appeal to you!"

I could not but answer him honestly. "Speaking personally, I would find it difficult to place any other obligation above honour."

"You might not, if you knew – "

"But what of the lady whose honour you have taken? What is to become of her?"

This shot hit home as well. Elliott rose once more and turned away from us, looking out upon the empty parade ground that lay beyond his window.

"I would have married that lady, Dr. Watson, had she not chosen another, but what help can I provide her now? I *will* do what I can to see that she obtains a quiet divorce. But even when she is no longer bound, I cannot tie myself to a known adulteress whose mind and body may both be diseased."

"Especially," Sherlock Holmes put in sharply, "when there is no longer the prospect of acquiring her fortune."

Once more the Captain sighed. "I am a poor man, Mr. Holmes. My father's business ventures ruined our family, so I must marry well to set things right. Alas, poor Fiona can no longer aid me in that goal."

As we stood to take our leave, we were distracted by a low growling in the hallway. Elliott opened the door to find – of all things – a small badger eyeing him expectantly.

"Hallo, Teddy. Is this my night to take you for your constitutional? Well, I suppose that's one obligation I must honour before leaving for the music hall." He took a dog leash from a nail beside the door. "Gentlemen, this is our regimental mascot. [6] Would you like for us to walk you to your station?"

"Frankly," my friend answered, "I would prefer you to choose another destination." Nodding curtly, he evaded Teddy and strode off down the hall. After offering the Captain my own parting comment: "Your hypocrisy astounds me, sir," I followed Holmes. We left Hounslow Barracks and took our train to Baker Street.

Before I returned home, the detective outlined our agenda for the following day. He would regress to Birchmoor and insist upon being admitted, invoking the authority of His Lordship's father-in-law. When I asked what Holmes expected to accomplish, he replied, "If nothing else, to test my hypothesis concerning this mysterious officer Captain Elliott was so determined to protect. I believe St. Simon will be more forthcoming."

My own task would be to visit Chisholm Asylum. If permitted, I would examine the unfortunate young lady who was central to the case. If not, I would again glean whatever information her doctor was willing to impart.

"Do you know this Dr. Samuel Drake?" my friend enquired.

"Only from hearsay. His methods are said to be humane, based on not restraining or confining patients. Those who are not 'acute' live as normally as possible, and are even allowed to leave the grounds. The facilities and care are reputedly excellent. Naturally, all of this comes at a cost – several hundred pounds a year – so Drake's clients come mostly from the wealthy classes. Some, I've been told, even bring their servants!"

"Ha! Perhaps I shall retire there, Watson, on the day I lose my wits. No doubt Mrs. Hudson would happily verify the need for such a change of residence."

That night, I apprised Mary of my intentions for the morrow. I had already told her something of the case, and, with typical kindliness, she had expressed great sympathy for Lady Eustace. Now, my wife made a proposal for which I was unprepared.

"May I come with you tomorrow, John?"

"To a madhouse? Certainly not!"

"Pooh! It isn't a madhouse. It's 'an orderly and well-run sanitorium for patients who require only minimal supervision'. You said those words yourself to reassure me."

"But why should you wish to go to such a place?"

"To help with your examination. It may be that a woman's touch is needed."

"Why should you think that, my dear?" My smile, I must admit, was condescending.

"Why, from everything you've told me, I feel quite sure that Lady Eustace has had enough of *men*. Neglected by her father, then rushed into society and married at eighteen? Bullied by a beastly husband and forced into motherhood when she was hardly older than a child herself? Seduced by lechers who took full advantage of her inexperience – to say nothing of giving her disease! Is it any wonder the poor girl broke down?"

"Lady Eustace is receiving the best of care," I replied feebly.

"Is she? Even in the asylum, she's in the hands of Dr. Drake – another man! Let me try to reach her, John, if she won't respond to you. I'm only thankful that Mr. Holmes decided not to go. Heaven knows what she would have made of *him!*"

So it was that Dr. and Mrs. Watson arrived at Chisholm Asylum the next morning. Originally an Italianate villa built in the last century, it had been woefully disfigured by the addition of two wings that housed the patients' rooms and hospital. The grounds were spacious and attractive, and we noticed several inmates strolling at ease under the benign observation of their keepers. Having explained our visit's purpose, we were escorted to the eastern wing and left to wait in Dr. Drake's consulting room. He joined us after an interval no longer than required to demonstrate the many calls upon his time.

The asylum's director appeared to be approaching seventy, his cavernous, dark eyes observing us beneath a balding dome. A straggling beard obscured the remainder of his countenance. Having shaken my hand, he took a seat behind his desk, regarding Mary with what appeared to be professional concern. To remove any misconception, I thought it best to state our business promptly.

"We are here, sir, at the request of Sir John MacPherson, Lady Eustace St. Simon's father. Lady Eustace was admitted in his absence, and he has received no information regarding her condition. Would it be possible for us to see her?"

Dr. Drake elected to evade my question. "Why has Sir John not come himself?"

"He was apprised, several days ago, that Lady Eustace was not permitted visitors. However, as more time has now passed, and as I am a doctor. . . ."

The psychiatrist offered me a sceptical smile. "Do you usually bring your wife on consultations, Doctor?"

Mary, I am proud to say, answered him with spirit. "As you insinuate, sir, I have no medical qualifications whatsoever. I have come only in hope that my feminine presence will provide some comfort to that poor young lady, and perhaps induce her to speak more freely to my husband."

The smile my wife received was slightly tinged with admiration. "Well, the proposal is highly irregular, but I suppose there is no harm in it. I warn you both that Lady Eustace is likely to be unresponsive. Neither I nor her attendants – including feminine attendants, Madam – have been able to get much out of her so far.

"When you have finished your examination, Doctor," Drake added as we rose to go, "I shall be happy to provide such information as I think appropriate for you to relay to Sir John MacPherson. I regret, Mrs. Watson, that you cannot be included in our discussion of the case." A respectful bow, before he rang the bell for an attendant, served to confirm the sincerity of his regret.

We followed the attendant up two flights of stairs and down a long hallway, halting at the third door on the right. There, a uniformed nurse admitted us. After announcing our credentials, I looked past her to see a young woman seated in a rocking chair and gazing out a window. She did not turn to greet us, so I took a moment to observe the details of the room. It might almost have passed for a lady's bedroom in a London house. Besides the chair, the furnishings included a brass bedstead, a chest of drawers, a basin and ewer, and a screen that hid the water closet. There were lace curtains at the windows and a bright, patterned carpet on the floor. Having introduced us, the nurse retired discreetly to a corner, leaving us with Sir John MacPherson's daughter.

She was truly as beautiful as rumoured. Fiona had inherited her father's colouring, his russet hair here softened into reddish-blonde, her green eyes far surpassing his in their intensity. Her delicate features still held a child-like quality. Indeed, she looked closer to sixteen than twenty. I was reminded of my first wife, Constance, who had retained this mien of youthful innocence until her death at twenty-four. Unlike my wife's, however, Lady Eustace's face remained unmarked by suffering. Her steady gaze, still focused out her window, was as untroubled and serene as that of the Egyptian Sphinx.

The interview itself was disappointing. Instead of questioning the patient regarding her condition, I tried to direct her mind towards the people in her former life. She did not respond when I passed on her father's greetings, and my mention of her husband elicited only a fleeting grimace of disquiet. In search of inspiration, I noted Dr. Ormond's opinion that her baby was not, in reality, "diseased". Lady Eustace answered softly, "But I am." Thereafter, she showed no interest in anything I had to say. I finally turned to Mary in despair.

"Let me try, John." Kneeling alongside the impassive girl, my wife placed an arm around her shoulder. "It's a beautiful morning, Lady Eustace," she said gently. "Would you care to go for a walk in the garden?"

"She likes 'er outings," the nurse put in from the corner.

"Why don't you finish your discussion with Dr. Drake, my dear?" Mary suggested. "I'll meet you in the foyer when Lady Eustace and I have returned." Accepting my dismissal, I turned towards the door. As I left the room, I heard the two ladies conversing quietly as they prepared to take their leave.

My second consultation with the director was equally discouraging. He explained his diagnosis of "puerperal mania" (a rare but severe form of *post-partum* hysteria) and opined that Lady Eustace's condition was much worse than his initial examination had led him to believe. "Although it seems clear that she had intercourse with Captain Elliott, I cannot say with certainty that the other adulterous 'affairs' are not delusions. In any case, Dr. Watson," Drake concluded dolefully, "I now fear that she will not recover, or ever again be a normal wife and mother." Based on my own brief observation, I was compelled – however reluctantly – to agree.

As she promised, my wife awaited me in the asylum's foyer, but with a much more favourable prognosis. Lady Eustace, she reported, had brightened immediately in the out-of-doors, taking Mary's arm in a confidential manner and remarking on the beauty of the trees and flowers as they strolled along the garden path. As they passed a cricket pitch, where a contest between staff and patients was in progress, she called out gaily, "That's the game that Father used to play!"

"I began to wonder, John, whether it is not you and Dr. Drake who are being led along the garden path. For when I turned the conversation back to her own troubles, Lady Eustace at once grew vague and affected not to understand. We walked on in silence for a time, until suddenly she blurted out, 'I dinna see why they keep me here when I've done nothing wrong!'

"'Nothing?' I repeated in astonishment.

"'No,' she insisted, 'for all my friends at Marlborough House assured me that affairs outside of marriage are usual for people of our class. Still, I shouldna have done it, hadna Eustace shot my horse. That was very wicked of him!'

"I hardly knew what I should reply to *that*. In one way, she was conversing sensibly, but her reasoning was like a child's. So I simply asked her, "What is it you *want*, Lady Eustace?' She looked at me calmly and replied, 'I want to go home.'

"'You mean to Birchmoor? Home to your husband and your daughter?'

"'No, *home*. Home to Scotland. I canna be happy here.' Surely," my wife added, "'home' would be the best place for her, John. Given agreeable surroundings and time, I believe the girl Fiona could recover. I doubt that Lady Eustace St. Simon ever will."

In Baker Street that afternoon, I related this account to Sherlock Holmes. Rather to my surprise, he congratulated me upon my wife's participation in the case.

"If you recall, Doctor, I recognised Miss Morstan's qualities before you married her. She is a woman of considerable intelligence, as well as a remarkably sympathetic nature. Indeed, she has outshone both you and Dr. Drake in revealing Lady Eustace St. Simon as less likely to be a lunatic than a wanton, devious child."

Whoever had a sympathetic nature, it was not my friend! "Your verdict," I objected, "is unduly harsh. May she not be, instead, a wronged young woman who found a singular means to extricate herself from problems not entirely of her making?"

"Perhaps it is a matter of perspective," replied Holmes, "but fleeing to Scotland may not enable her to escape her husband's wrath. Unhappily, the welfare of MacPherson's daughter can no longer be our first concern. The case has taken the turn that I anticipated, and greater issues are at stake. Let me tell you how I spent *my* morning."

The detective had returned to Birchmoor and this time was admitted. Lord Eustace received him in what Holmes described ("for your inevitable literary effort, Watson") as a drawing room of unusual magnificence, the ornate plasterwork of its white mantelpiece and ceiling set off by elaborate candelabra and French blue-papered walls.

"St. Simon is a good deal younger than his brother – a few years short of forty – and no doubt considered handsome. When in good humour, he has (so I am told) an unctuous charm that might appeal to an inexperienced young girl. His Lordship's charm was *not* displayed to his father-in-law's emissary. He showed no sympathy for Sir John's anxiety and spoke of the Scotsman's daughter and his own in terms no gentleman should employ. Indeed, the man's conduct throughout his marriage convinces me that regardless of his lineage, he is no gentleman.

"Remembering what MacPherson had told us, I began by asking why, in view of his wife's age and immaturity, he had importuned her so relentlessly to bear a child. His Lordship answered, quite coldly and correctly, that the issues of his marriage were none of my concern. However, when I mentioned the 10th Hussars – and a certain quadruped – it was immediately evident that I had struck a nerve. Lord Eustace slammed his fist upon the mantelpiece. (We were both standing, Watson, for I had not been invited to sit down.)

"'Ah, the highwaymen of Hounslow Heath!' [7] he cried sarcastically. 'That d----d Elliott wasn't the only one sniffing 'round my little wifey on that afternoon. Do you think *he* could have paid for that stallion? Fellow hasn't got a farthing to his name. Oh, no, Mr. Meddling Holmes. Another highwayman was there as well. One who, so dear Fiona told me, had likewise been a frequent visitor. Someone higher up the social ladder, who could have given her a *thousand* chargers if he'd wanted to. I believe she called him "Eddy".'"

"Good Lord, Holmes! The Prince?"

"His Royal Highness, Prince Albert Victor of Wales. St. Simon now threatens to name him, as well as Elliott, as correspondent in his public suit for a divorce, in which case the Prince undoubtedly will be called upon to testify."

"This is terrible! His Royal Highness could not admit to adultery on the stand, so he would be publicly known as an almost-certain perjurer."

"Quite so. Yet, I have heard it said that when a gentleman has taken a lady's honour, he must defend it thereafter, even at the cost of his own. As you remember, even Captain Elliott paid homage to that code."

"But the gentleman in question is the future King of England! What can we do?"

"I have notified the palace and await instruction. I shall also consult our client to see whether he is willing to meet St. Simon's terms."

"Which are?"

"A financial settlement equivalent to the inheritance Sir John would otherwise have left his daughter. In return, Lord Eustace will agree to a private divorce. As he elegantly expressed it, 'Jock won't get out of paying up just because his daughter is – ' Well, let us say, a woman of low virtue."

"The blackguard! I think I would have struck him."

"I'm sure you would have, Watson. I contented myself with remarking, as I left his drawing room, that the last highwayman in Hounslow was not upon the heath."

I was called out on a medical emergency after leaving Baker Street, returning home too late at night to see the evening papers. Thus, it was only at breakfast the next morning that I noticed this item in *The Star:*

> *It is reported that a young and highly placed member of the Royal Family may be called to testify in the pending divorce trial of an aristocratic couple. The wife's indiscretions, we are informed, have caused her to be placed in an asylum. Her husband is the sole surviving brother of a duke whose nuptials, several years ago, were nullified when it was discovered that his bride already had a living spouse. Assuredly, the last scions of an eminent and ancient family have been most unfortunate their choice of wives.*

"Great Caesar!" I could not forbear exclaiming.

"What is it, John?" my wife cried in alarm, for I had all but choked upon my kipper. Wordlessly, I handed her the offending page and tried to catch my breath. After scanning the relevant column, she sighed, "The poor Duke of Balmoral, to have all *that* brought up again." Naturally, I had told her of "The Noble Bachelor" case.

"Bother the Duke!" I coughed. "What about the *'young and highly placed member of the Royal Family'*? Lord Eustace must have spoken with *The Star's* reporter, in order to threaten the palace with exposure unless MacPherson meets his terms."

"Of course! Lady Eustace's 'Prince Eddy'." She began leafing through the morning journals. "There don't seem to be any similar articles in *The Times* or *Standard.*"

"The respectable press would hardly stoop so low. But Holmes, I recall, was furious with *The Star's* sordid coverage of the Ripper Murders. Speaking of Holmes, Mary, I must return to Baker Street."

Just at that moment, the maid brought in the early mail, which included a note from Holmes summoning me to call on him at nine o'clock. It was past that hour before I left Praed Street, and fifteen minutes later when I opened the door to my old quarters, after no more than a preliminary knock.

There I found Mrs. Hudson removing the remains of a light breakfast, which she had served to her lodger and two gentlemen whom I knew by sight but had not met. One was Sir Francis Knollys, private secretary to the Prince of Wales, the other Dr. James Reid, our medical liaison in London when we had visited the dying German Emperor two years before. [8] Invited to the table, I waited more patiently than Holmes until his landlady departed. After my introduction to the courtiers, Sir Francis opened the discussion.

"I am here, Dr. Watson, instead of General Ponsonby, [9] because His Royal Highness wishes to keep his son and heir's involvement in this matter from Her Majesty. After the Cleveland Street Scandal, [10] another of the kind could have an unfortunate effect upon her health. As you may know, rumours surrounding the Prince have led to his removal from the public eye. He has been touring India for the past seven months.

"*Seven* months?" Holmes queried. "The Prince was still in England, then, at the time Lady Eustace St. Simon conceived her child, presumably last July or early August?"

"Yes, but there is little reason to suppose he was its father. His Royal Highness was occupied throughout the summer with official duties. In mid-July, he was at Windsor for the Shah of Persia's visit, and at Osborne for the Kaiser's during the first week of August. Afterwards, he went to Scotland for the shooting season."

"So, it would have been difficult to slip away to Hounslow for an assignation?"

"Indubitably."

"But not impossible?"

"Well, no, particularly if it was before the Shah arrived."

"Then pardon my indelicacy, gentlemen, but has the Prince shown signs of having a venereal disease?"

Knollys and Reid exchanged a troubled glance. "At the time, he was treated for . . . a *fever,*" the latter said reluctantly, "while visiting the cavalry barracks at York in late July. Naturally, His Royal Highness had recovered his health fully before he left for India."

"Are we to understand, Mr. Holmes," enquired Sir Francis, "that Lady Eustace has named Prince Albert Victor as the father of her child?"

"No, that honour has fallen to a Captain Elliott. Nor has her husband made a public claim, at least so far. But the child *has* exhibited symptoms of a venereal infection."

The detective looked to me for confirmation, but I felt compelled to add, "The St. Simons' family doctor doubts that diagnosis. It should be possible to settle the question when the baby can be thoroughly examined."

"The question of disease is neither here nor there," snapped Knollys. His normally mild countenance had turned florid, his bushy mustache quivering in indignation. "So long as St. Simon threatens to involve His Royal Highness in a public trial, the monarchy's future is at risk. The timing of this scandal is especially unfortunate, for when the Prince returns from India, it is intended to begin the preparations for his marriage."

"Indeed!" said Holmes. "Are you at liberty to name the lucky lady?"

Knollys' glare informed my friend that levity was not appreciated. Dr. Reid quickly intervened. "Does Lord Eustace understand the social cost of the course he is pursuing? Whatever he may gain financially, he will become a pariah until the day he dies."

"The Prince of Wales is always loyal to his friends," Sir Francis growled, "but some have learned that he can also be an unrelenting enemy. His enmity shall redound upon the whole St. Simon family."

"I have some experience of Prince Albert Edward's *misplaced* loyalty to friends," Holmes noted, recalling a case from early in our detective partnership, [11] "so I also have no doubt of his vindictiveness. Unfortunately, nothing I have seen or heard of Lord Eustace St. Simon persuades me that he values social standing more than wealth. Nor do I believe him amenable to reason."

"Then – as much as I regret to say it, Mr. Holmes – Sir John MacPherson must resign himself to meeting his blackmailer's terms. It is an unconscionable sacrifice to require of him, I know. Yet, he could not perform a greater service to Her Majesty if he built a hundred battleships!"

"And what of his daughter?" Holmes demanded quietly.

Knollys turned expectantly to Reid. "So I have heard from Dr. Samuel Drake," the court physician answered, "Lady Eustace's condition is unlikely to improve. If that is so, then surely it is best for everyone if she remains in the asylum."

"Oh, no, *no, no*, gentlemen!" cried the detective, his anger growing in proportion to each repetition. Rising, he strode to the bow window and stood looking down on Baker Street, his back to the two visitors. I have seldom seen my friend so moved. It was some moments before he regained his composure sufficiently to turn and face the courtiers with an ironic smile.

"It would be poor service to my client," Holmes proclaimed, "were I to advise that he and his daughter take upon *their* backs the sins of others, and allow the *truly* guilty parties to profit from their wickedness or walk away scot-free. Oh, no. There is one party still to be heard from in this business, and it is long past time that I consulted him. I shall communicate

136

with you gentlemen again when I have done so. Until that time, I have the honour to wish you both good-morning."

He turned again to the bow window, and it was I who escorted Reid and Knollys to the door.

For the next three days, I was preoccupied with my neglected practice, and I heard nothing in the interim from Sherlock Holmes. On the fourth day, I received a letter in the morning mail that bore the ducal arms. It invited me to a conference in Balmoral House, [12] to be held at six o'clock that evening. Needless to say, I revised my schedule to attend. It surprised me that my friend had not suggested that we leave together, but I surmised that he intended to consult independently with the Duke and others associated with the case. Accordingly, I took my own cab into Piccadilly, arriving just at the appointed hour in a shower of rain.

Balmoral was a large but stark and rather ugly house, built in the Palladian style. I had heard one critic sneer that it looked more like a warehouse than a mansion. A high wall hid its lower storey from the street, and scaffolding had been erected to repair the roof. Once inside the gates, the yard was bare, unadorned by shrubs or statuary. The same Spartan appearance characterised the interior, for it was evident that much of the house's former grandeur had departed. Although several paintings still adorned the walls, there were obvious gaps where others had been taken down. I recalled the reports of Lord Robert's ill-starred wedding mentioning that his father had been "compelled to sell his pictures." It looked as though the present duke had been unable to reclaim them.

I was led by a servant wearing faded livery into the library, an impressive room that also showed the ill effects of recent poverty, for many of its shelves had been denuded of their books. Once more I appeared to be a late arrival. The meeting's other attendees were seated at an ornate table in the centre of the room. Holmes caught my eye and motioned to the empty chair beside him. At the table's head sat our friend Lord Robert, now Ninth Duke of Balmoral. On either side of him were Sir John MacPherson and Mr. Sherlock Holmes. Seated across from me was Sir Francis Knollys, and at the table's foot was a younger, handsomer version of His Grace, who could be none other than Lord Eustace. Obviously, he had been seated as far from his brother as possible, a fact that seemed to be reflected in his scowl.

In the years since our last meeting, the impression of age Lord Robert had conveyed had markedly increased. At forty-five, the Duke's pale face had thinned to gauntness. His hair was also thinner and more grizzled than before. Lines of care upon his brow and cheeks had deepened into permanence, giving him the aura of a morose and disappointed man. His attire likewise had deteriorated: The black frock coat was no longer in the latest fashion, as well as slightly frayed in the lapels. Even so, His Grace retained impenetrable dignity, and he cleared his throat meaningfully as I took my chair.

"Good evening, gentlemen," he began, his voice as cultured as I had remembered it. "Thank you for attending. Most of you, I know, are busy men, so I intend to conclude this distasteful matter as expeditiously as possible. As anyone who knows me can attest, I am highly averse to discussing my personal affairs in any public manner. However, as my brother has seen fit to expose our family's manifold misfortunes in the press, it seems that I have little choice."

Lord Eustace smirked and started to reply, but his brother cut him off immediately. "Be silent, Eustace. You are here, solely as a courtesy, to be informed of the settlement that has been made. Nothing you can say will alter that decision in the slightest."

When his cadet reluctantly subsided, the Duke sighed as though steeling himself to undergo a great ordeal. "I have now, gentlemen, to tell you a most humiliating story. Four years ago (as *The Star* has recently reminded us), I wed an heiress, only to lose both wife and fortune to an American whose prior claim superseded mine. This event was naturally a disappointment to our father, who had counted on my marriage to restore the solvency of his estate. Then came the death of our brother Thomas, Father's heir. That blow, alas, proved a fatal one to him as well." By now, tears glinted in His Grace's eyes, and even Lord Eustace seemed affected.

"It was soon after my accession," resumed the Duke, "that Eustace succeeded where I failed. Once more, a favourable marriage seemed destined to restore the family fortunes. However – and *as* ever," he added in a harsher tone – "my brother's expectation was that any contribution he might make would come at a high price. The bargain I was offered came to this: He would advance the money needed to restore Balmoral House and our country home in Devonshire, using part of the generous dowry Sir John MacPherson had provided him." (Here His Grace nodded respectfully to the Scottish baronet.) "In return, I would refrain from further efforts to contract a marriage, so that Eustace's descendants should eventually acquire the ducal title and the residue of my estate."

An audible murmur, not quite a gasp, went round the table, and Sir Francis Knollys shot Lord Eustace a contemptuous glance. That aristocrat looked as if he wished to speak, but under the general opprobrium chose silence. Only Holmes remained impassive.

"You may wonder why I should accept such terms. My motive has always been to preserve our properties within the family, of which Eustace is, of course, a part. I should have been content had he held to his side of the arrangement. But in the three years since his marriage, my brother has yet to offer any funding for the maintenance of the estate."

This time, Lord Eustace did venture to reply. "Our bargain is a moot point, Robert, until I have an heir. Why not blame the little tart I married?"

Jock MacPherson turned scarlet and, with an oath, half-rose in his chair before the Duke's consoling arm restrained him. After muttering an apology to the irate Scotsman, His Grace turned to his brother with a visage of cold fury.

"One more word from you, Eustace, and I shall have you evicted from the house. I have nothing to say regarding your marriage, although from what I have been told, your own conduct has been unworthy of a British gentleman, much less a would-be Duke of Balmoral. It only remains to explain the agreement Sir John and I have come to, thanks to the good offices of Mr. Sherlock Holmes." He turned to the detective to provide this explanation, as it was evident that MacPherson did not trust himself to speak.

"It is simply this," my friend began quietly, for as always the emotions of the others had not affected him. "Sir John will transfer two-thirds of the inheritance he had intended for his daughter, in the amount of – " He named a sum that took my breath away. " – to His Grace the Duke of Balmoral. In return, the Duke – Well, perhaps I should ask Your Grace make this part of the announcement. . . ."

"In return," the Duke intoned, looking sternly at his brother, "I shall make adequate provision for your future, Eustace – *provided* that you agree to your wife's immediate release from Chisholm Asylum and to divorce her *privately*, without any public notoriety that would dishonour her, the St. Simon or MacPherson families, or the Crown."

Lord Eustace snorted in derision, but he answered only, "Just what would you call 'adequate provision', Robert?"

"Well, I presume you have something left of your wife's dowry. You are also free to retain any profits from the sale of Birchmoor."

"Sale? What sale?"

"Those funds should more than suffice to finance your removal to Johannesburg. There – thanks to contacts provided by Sir Francis Knollys – you will have opportunities for investment in the gold and diamond mines. I shall assist in purchasing the shares."

"I assure you," the courtier informed Lord Eustace coolly, "that your opportunities in South Africa are far superior to any you have left in Britain."

"There's one thing more," MacPherson growled. "You'll allow my granddaughter to accompany her mother and myself when we return to

Scotland. You'll have nought to do with the wee lass from this day forward."

"Do you think I want the little ----- ?" the younger St. Simon cried out wildly. "You're mad, Robert, if you think that I'll submit to this. I'll see you all in Hell first!" He leapt from his chair and, without a backward glance, stormed out of the room and down the hallway, calling for his carriage.

The Duke of Balmoral looked 'round the table with a weary smile. "I beg you to take no notice, gentlemen. Eustace has been subject to such tantrums from his childhood, but he's not a fool. I have no doubt that on reflection, he'll accept the opportunity that we have offered him. Quite soon," he sighed, "I shall be the last St. Simon left in England.

"And now," His Grace added, rising, "I trust that all of you will join me for drinks while we await our dinner. Whatever else Balmoral House has lost in recent years, it still employs a most excellent cook."

As the Duke had prophesied, Lord Eustace overcame his fury and, after his divorce, departed for Johannesburg. There he prospered, and in later years the brothers reconciled. Sir John MacPherson gave up his seat in Parliament and retired to Glasgow permanently, where he lived with his daughter and granddaughter until his death last year. Fiona never remarried and remains a virtual recluse. Her daughter – despite not having inherited her mother's beauty – wed the heir to an earldom earlier this summer, possibly owing to the unfounded rumour that she has royal blood. It had been confirmed before they left for Scotland that neither MacPherson lady had contracted a venereal disease.

The Ninth Duke of Balmoral lost his status as "the Noble Bachelor". As an heiress was no longer required, he married the eldest daughter of an impoverished aristocratic neighbour. She provided him with a St. Simon heir, presently Tenth Duke of Balmoral.

Prince Albert Victor (created Duke of Clarence and Avondale just before he left for India) returned from his tour without further damage to his reputation. By that time, the Cleveland Street rumours had died down, and, thanks to his Royal father's influence, The Star's offending article was the only mention of any impending scandal by the press. The next year, Prince Eddy became engaged to his cousin (now Queen Mary), but His Royal Highness succumbed to influenza in January 1892, before the marriage could take place. This tragedy I hardly noticed, for I was still mourning not only Sherlock Holmes but my beloved Mary, who had died suddenly the month before. Fortunately, the loss of Holmes was not a lasting one.

140

Our second case involving the St. Simons represented something of a triumph for my friend. The Duke of Balmoral sent us both handsome gifts soon afterwards, and the palace offered Holmes a decoration, which he naturally declined. Even so, his prejudice against the Prince of Wales declined somewhat, and in their encounter some years later (which I have chronicled as "The Adventure of the Illustrious Client"), his references to that Royal personage were most respectful. Of course, the case occurred after Edward VII had become his king. Today, Holmes honours His Late Majesty as sincerely as he does the last Queen Regnant, a lady whose memory will always be hallowed among all those who served her.

NOTES

1. Although, in "The Noble Bachelor", Conan Doyle has Holmes address his client as "Lord St. Simon", this form of address would only be correct if His Lordship held an actual, rather than a courtesy, title. Younger offspring of a duke were properly addressed as "Lord" or "Lady" with their given name, or as "my Lord" or "my Lady". A parallel case would be Sir Winston Churchill's parents, who were always known as Lord and Lady Randolph Churchill. Randolph was the third son of the Duke of Marlborough.

2. Sadly, Lord Backwater's heir had died in childhood. Readers of the canonical story "Silver Blaze" (which W.S. Baring-Gould dated as September 1890) may recall that Lord Backwater is mentioned as the owner of Mapleton Stables and Silver Blaze's rival, Desborough. Based on the present account, it appears that the widowed Lady Backwater was the actual owner at that time. Moreover, the Duke of Balmoral whose horse Iris ran a poor third in the Wessex Cup, would seem to have been none other than the Noble Bachelor.

3. In "The Noble Bachelor" (published by *The Strand* in 1892), the Doctor wrote that the case had taken place four years before. However, the chronologies of both Baring-Gould and Craig Janacek place NOBL in October 1886. It seems, therefore, that when Watson referred to its occurring *"a few weeks before my own marriage"*, he meant his first marriage to Constance Adams (November 1, 1886), not his second one to Mary Morstan (May 1, 1889). Possibly concluding this reunion with the St. Simons in May 1890 led the Doctor to write "The Noble Bachelor" two years before its appearance in *The Strand*.
   https:// craigjanacek.wordpress.com/2015/09/13/a-chronological-order-of-sherlock-holmes-stories/

4. Although John and Mary Watson's address in Paddington was not specified in The Canon, the Doctor did mention it in David Marcum's story "The Adventure of the Treacherous Tea" (p. 40). When Watson left No. 7 Praed Street after Mary's death, he sold the lease to a Mrs. Johnson, who turned the building into flats. Siger Holmes, the great detective's nephew and successor, later rented flat 7B and became known as *"The Sherlock Holmes of Praed Street"* under his alias (first revealed by August Derleth), *Solar Pons*. Siger's transition into Solar is recounted in Marcum's "The Adventure of the Other Brother", pp. 292-294. Page citations for the two stories refer to Marcum's collection *The Papers of Sherlock Holmes*, Volume One & Volume Two (London: MX Publishing, 2014).

5. Officially, the Berkshires were Her Majesty's 66th Regiment of Foot. Their role at the Battle of Maiwand (July 27, 1880) was immortalized by *"the last stand of the Eleven"* when a portion of the regiment was cut off in a ravine by the Afghans and fought to the last man. Watson's medical duties occupied him elsewhere before he, too, was wounded.
   https://www.britishbattles.com/second-afghan-war/battle-of-maiwand/

6. In his book *My Early Life, 1874-1908: A Roving Commission* (Glasgow: Fontana Books, 1980 [1930]), Sir Winston Churchill provides an account of his exploits in the late-Victorian British cavalry. He served in the 4th Hussars under Colonel Brabazon and at the Battle of Omdurman (1898) with the 21st Lancers. On p. 98 of his memoir, Churchill recounts the kidnapping, years before, of the 10th Hussars' badger by a young officer of the 12th Lancers. Evidently, Teddy succeeded it or later badgers as the 10th's regimental mascot.

7. Although it had been used as a military camp and training ground since Roman times, during the late seventeenth and eighteenth centuries Hounslow Heath became notorious as a lurking-place for highwaymen, who robbed and murdered there with relative impunity. A brief but well-illustrated article on the subject may be found at:
https://londonist.com/london/history/when-hounslow-was-the-most-dangerous-place-in-london

8. As told in "The Case of the Dying Emperor" from my collection *Sherlock Holmes and the Crowned Heads of Europe* (London: MX Publishing, 2021), pp. 1-96.

9. Sir Henry Ponsonby, Queen Victoria's private secretary, with whom Holmes and Watson had dealt during the "Dying Emperor" case.

10. The Cleveland Street Scandal had arisen in mid-1889, when Scotland Yard Inspector Frederick Abberline (better known for his investigation of the Ripper Murders) arrested several teenaged "telegraph boys" who were also employed in a male brothel at 19 Cleveland Street. Among the aristocratic clients the boys named was Lord Arthur Somerset, an equerry of the Prince of Wales. Facing prosecution, Somerset hinted to the police that a member of the royal family, "*P.A.V.*", had also visited the brothel. While there was no other evidence to support his claim, the rumors persisted even after Lord Arthur was allowed to flee to Germany and the Prince was sent to India. His name was further blackened in the 1970's (and later in two excellent films, *From Hell* and *Murder by Decree*) by a theory that Albert Victor and/or his physician, Sir William Gull, were candidates for Jack the Ripper. Andrew Cook's biography *Prince Eddy: The King Britain Never Had* (Stroud, Gloucestershire: Tempus Publishing, Limited, 2006), absolves His Royal Highness of the two worst slanders his reputation has endured.

11. See "A Yuletide Tragedy" from my latest book, *Watson's Wives and Other Tales of Sherlock Holmes* (London: MX Publishing, 2023), pp. 1-18.

12. Balmoral House was not, of course, Balmoral Castle, the Queen's Scottish residence, which Prince Albert had purchased from members of Clan Farquharson in 1852. What is less clear is how the St. Simon family (which, as we learn in "Silver Blaze", was based in Devonshire near Dartmoor) acquired a ducal title that apparently had Scottish origins. Possibly the St. Simons had some marital connection to the clan, or (perhaps more likely) Watson was indulging for discretion's sake in obfuscation. The true name and title of the "St. Simons" may have been something else entirely.

The Midsummer Murders
by Paul A. Freeman

During the sultry summer of 1890, I was returning one morning from a professional visit to old Colonel Sanderson, whose bullet wound from the Crimean War had been causing him discomfort, when I found myself in the vicinity of Baker Street. Feeling somewhat nostalgic, I diverted from my homeward route and joined the crowds thronging one of the larger arteries of our great metropolis until I stood opposite the apartments I once shared with my friend, Sherlock Holmes.

The renowned sleuth was at one of the upstairs sash windows of 221b, his clay pipe clenched between his teeth, a sure sign he was engaged in a case. In one hand he held his magnifying glass and in the other was a rather nondescript-looking green book. Due to the oppressive weather the sash was open, and when Holmes eventually spied me, his rapt expression lit up. With a beckoning wave, he invited me to join him. And so, sidestepping the hansoms and other horse-drawn traffic, I crossed the dung-strewn road and was welcomed by Mrs. Hudson, my former landlady, to my old abode.

"How is Colonel Sanderson?" Holmes asked, without preamble, as he admitted me to his apartments and seated me beside the unlit hearthplace. "Still suffering from his encounter with Russian infantry at the Charge of the Light Brigade, I imagine." To the perplexed spluttering of my reply, he explained: "Colonel Sanderson is one of your only patients living within walking distance of Baker Street, and the only one whose treatment – of seasonal, muscular impairment, I believe – does not involve you requiring your bag, which I observe is conspicuously absent."

Indeed, the Colonel's left leg was more prone to swelling and to painfulness in the summer months, the nature of his complaint allowing me to leave my doctoring paraphernalia at home.

"The man needs a masseuse, not a physician," Holmes declared.

Unaccountably miffed at my friend's unwavering insight, I said, "I could merely have been making an impromptu visit to you."

Holmes chuckled. "Then why were you mooching about with such a wistful countenance on the other side of the road?" And before I could mumble another stammered reply, he introduced me to his own pressing business. "What do you make of this?" he asked, handing me the book he had been examining at the window.

I found myself holding a cheaply-produced novel titled *A Midsummer's Fortune*, whose bottle-green, cloth-and-cardboard cover bore lettering impressed in gold. The author was given as "*Les Cotis*", and the sheets were imperfectly cut, making it difficult to leaf through the volume's three-hundred-and-thirty pages smoothly. All this intelligence I conveyed to Holmes, who, as I expected, was less than impressed.

"You *see*, Watson," he berated, "but you don't *deduce!*"

"Then pray educate me," I said, excising what sarcasm I could from my voice and placing the book, face up, on the sitting room table.

Rubbing his hands together, Holmes began: "Let's start with the name of the author, '*Les Cotis*'. '*Cotis*' may be from the Italian, '*De Cotis*'. Such shortenings are often practised by Americans to conceal their ethnic origins. The forename, however, '*Les*', seems at first glance to follow that appalling trend nowadays of abbreviating one's moniker. We therefore have the possibility that the author is a '*Lester*' or a '*Leslie*', or alternatively that *Les Cotis* is a *nom de plume*."

At this point, Holmes became silent and contemplative. Knowing better than to disturb his meditations, I looked on as he pondered some burgeoning point of interest. Finally, he picked up the book, sniffed and examined the binding, and opened it seemingly at random at around two-thirds of the way through the volume's text. He regarded the selected page for a minute or two before closing it with a thud.

"The novel, for a novel it is, is bound with a glue whose deep amber colour, hardness, and adhesive composition indicates it came from a horse glue factory in the Midlands. Meanwhile, the quality of printing on the pages, as on the cover, is imperfect, that of a cut-rate compositor, printer, and publisher, whose name doesn't appear on the title page, nor anywhere else in the book. Such anonymity is suggestive of hefty remuneration, considering publishers both crave and sustain themselves by publicity. It appears this is a pre-publication edition of *A Midsummer's Fortune* – an advance copy I imagine, aimed at critics and reviewers, or else to impress those closest to the author."

After another spell of quiet introspection, Holmes spoke again. "The cover is, as you noted, rather poorly imprinted, with the title of the work and the writer's name both appearing in deplorably and unevenly applied gold leaf. Look! You can see the flakiness of its application."

Grudgingly, I nodded at the obvious feature that I had overlooked during my own perusal.

"The cloth-and-cardboard cover is equally instructive," Holmes continued, testing its pliability, "as is the ink utilised to attain the cover's peculiar bottle-green sheen. I recently wrote a monograph on industrial printing ink, and without doubt, this colour and hue originates from the Lake District – Keswick to be exact."

"And to what purpose is all this supposition?" I asked, "unless this book is a clue in some ghastly case upon which you're engaged."

In reply, Holmes leapt to his feet and handed me a letter that had been lying folded on the hearth mantelshelf. "This arrived yesterday, hand-delivered to Mrs. Hudson, along with this unassuming literary offering."

All the missive said, scrawled in an untidy hand, was: "*SH. Will call on you tomorrow at 10:30 a.m., J.J.*" Yet before I could interrogate Holmes any further, there came a knock upon the front door, and on checking my pocket watch I discovered it was precisely half-past-ten.

"That will be the enigmatic Mr. '*J.J.*'," said Holmes, striding across the room.

We heard a brisk step upon the staircase, followed moments later by an equally brisk rap on the sitting room door, which Holmes made answer to immediately.

With the slightest of bows, Holmes admitted a gentleman of early middle age. He had an expression of forced joviality on his face that somehow belied an impression of deep unease. He was attired in a light summer jacket, waistcoat, and trousers, his only concession to the mugginess in the air being a loosened necktie. He had his visiting card at the ready, gave it to Holmes, and noted with an appreciative grin that Holmes was cradling the book he had left in Mrs. Hudson's care the previous day.

"Mr. Jefferson James, of J.J. Publishing, Bermondsey," Holmes read out for my benefit.

On becoming conscious of my presence, Mr. James vacillated. As I made to depart, Holmes cajolingly suggested I should stay, insisting that I was both a discreet third person and a valuable additional string to his bow of detection. Swayed by Holmes's rhetoric, Mr. James took the seat Holmes proffered and, after introductions, the three of us sat about the long-extinguished fireplace, enjoying what little breeze came through the open windows.

"I observe," said Jefferson James, rocking nervously back and forth and clenching and unclenching his hands, "that you have examined the volume of crime fiction I received last week through the post."

"I have indeed perused *A Midsummer's Fortune*," stated Holmes, "though regretfully I have only read a single page in any great detail. The writing, on first glance, seems most proficient."

"It is! It is!" Mr. James enthusiastically replied, and, looking more at ease, began his story. "Though I barely read until halfway before sending the book to you, four years ago I received an earlier, handwritten

146

manuscript of *A Midsummer's Fortune*, composed in a neat, flowing hand. It arrived as a much rougher, less-literary iteration of this present version. Since J.J. Publishing isn't one of the leading national publishing houses, we charge for the numerous services we offer – reading, editing, book compositing, distribution, and publicity fees. Additionally, we appropriate fifty percent of any profits that may accrue from a book we back. I therefore sent an invoice cataloguing such costs to the return address."

"Then you're a publisher who is paid by your clients to produce books, instead of the other way around," Holmes clarified.

"Please, Mr. Holmes. Ours is a co-operative publishing house. We make literary dissemination a joint venture between author and publisher. We take a coarse gemstone, cut it to perfection, and buff it up until it outshines its competition. We give hope of literary success to the layman."

"A most colourful description of your profession," Holmes said incredulously. "Pray continue."

"This book I sent you, *A Midsummer's Fortune*, has been 'polished to perfection', apparently through a tremendous effort, by Les Cotis, the formerly anonymous author. As it now stands, given the right marketing, this novel would likely be a lucrative investment to a publisher."

"So, the author has sent you a copy of his polished book as a sort of vengeance," I ventured. "To rub in, as it were, the opportunity you turned down."

"Not at all. At that time four years ago, this Mr. Cotis paid a deposit to J.J. Publishing's services to privately publish his book. I believe he must have already been cognisant of the book's potential, for he said he had pitted three co-operative publishing houses against each other in a bidding war, to get a better, more traditional publishing deal."

"And you dropped out of the bidding," Holmes surmised.

Jefferson nodded. "I had my overheads. I couldn't take a chance on an author who was an unknown quantity, even for a hefty, non-returnable deposit."

"Why didn't the author just submit his novel to a regular publisher?" I enquired.

The visitor shrugged. "A lurid past? A criminal conviction? Or maybe 'Les Cotis' is a *nom de plume*, used because the author's real name is recognisable."

At this juncture, a smile played on Holmes's lips and a gleam shone in his eye. "Do you know the proprietors of the other two publishing houses that Les Cotis approached?" asked Holmes.

Jefferson shook his head.

"Then perhaps could you elucidate further on how you communicated with this anonymous client of yours with the neat, flowing handwriting."

Jefferson James looked sheepishly into the empty fireplace. "The Lewisham Dormitory for Eastern European Migrants was the return address," he replied. "For the attention of '*Midsummer*', which was also obviously a pseudonym."

"You've been exploiting the neediest denizens of our metropolis," I said, stunned by how low these "co-operative" publishers went, "preying on their hopes of literary fame and fortune, knowing how unlikely such hope may be. Your monetary demands from such people is tantamount to theft."

Holmes held up his hand, indicating that I should desist from my recriminations and that the floor should remain his.

"I noticed upon your presenting me with your card, Mr. James," said Holmes, "that your hand is ink-stained and displays the marks of both fresh and old injuries indicative of an unskilled compositor. Additionally, since your attire, notably your necktie, is of a style two years out of date, I can infer that co-operative publishing isn't as lucrative as it formerly may have been, and that your own participation in the business stretches from managerial tasks to mundane shopfloor work, which might well explain why you wished to consult me."

Jefferson seemed reluctant to continue, but finally took the plunge. "As Doctor Watson has suggested, there may be an element of revenge in my being sent this book since I accepted a non-returnable deposit from one who could least afford to be parted with even a few shillings. On the other hand – "

"On the other hand," Holmes interrupted, "acquiring publication rights to this book could earn you a tidy sum and make J.J. Publishing a major name amongst London publishing houses. You now have a possible golden goose of a book to publish, but are uncertain of the author's motives. Ergo, you wish me to investigate them.

"Mr. James," Holmes said, returning to Jefferson the book, "you're a greedy, unprincipled charlatan who isn't averse to defrauding the most disadvantaged members of society by having them aspire to be great writers, even if they have none of the abilities required. So no, I will not be accepting your case. Here is your pre-publication edition of *A Midsummer's Fortune* back."

Once the despondent Jefferson James had vacated the premises, brandishing *A Midsummer's Fortune* like a cudgel and mumbling darkly about exposing to public scrutiny Holmes's inflated and undeserved reputation, Holmes clapped his hands and chuckled. "We have Mr. James just where we want him, Watson – totally unaware he has fully engaged my services."

"I don't understand," I began, but Holmes was in no mood to explain.

"Where do you think we should start?" he asked.

"The migrants' dormitory in Lewisham?" I hazarded.

"A good place, indeed! However, as you may recall, the Dormitory for Eastern European Migrants in Lewisham burned down over three years ago due to an ill-starred fellow smoking a cheap pipe in bed. His actions caused much death and disfigurement."

"And you're sure it was an accidental fire?"

Holmes scrutinised me from beneath his hooded eyelids as if I were a doltish schoolboy. "My services were retained by the fire brigade to assist in their investigations. I'm sure. No, our start point should be the mysterious murder of a publisher of Mr. Jefferson's ilk who was killed last summer, and another of that disreputable profession who died by another's hand the summer before that. Two publishers killed in two years, and a third feeling distinctly threatened, cannot be coincidental. We therefore need to ascertain whether the deceased publishers were the other two participants in an apparently unresolved bidding war over *A Midsummer's Fortune*."

While Holmes searched his indexed files for the newspaper reports of the two murdered men, I asked him, out of interest, which page of *A Midsummer's Fortune* was the one he had read in detail, and what, if any significance, that page held.

"Ah, yes," Holmes said. "Page two-hundred-and-sixteen. Even you should be able to comprehend that number's importance?"

"Two-one-six," I repeated over and over to myself until I did indeed divine its significance. "The twenty-first day of June, June being the sixth month, is midsummer, as in the book's title. How on earth did you fathom which page to single out?"

He rolled his eyes. "You're coming at this from the wrong way. The clue is on the book's cover, in the author's name – '*Les Cotis*'."

"An anagram!" I cried, after a short cudgelling of my grey matter. '*Les Cotis*' is an anagram of the word '*solstice*'."

"And the summer solstice is – "

"The twenty-first of June!" I cried. "Hence, page two, one, six."

"Spot on, my dear Watson. We'll make a detective of you yet," Holmes said, just as he secured the second of the newspaper reports. Handing the first to me, dated 22nd June, 1888, I read:

> *The puzzling death, yesterday, of Sheridan Cawley, a Kentish publisher shot dead in the library of Witton House, Pilston, is under investigation. Anyone with pertinent information is urged to call on Pilston Police Station, where a twenty-pound reward is being offered by the victim's widow.*

In reply to my narration of *The London Clarion* article on Sheridan Crawley's untimely demise, Holmes read a report from *The Capital Gazette*, dated 22nd June, 1889:

> *Police at the two-man constabulary outpost at Marborough, Sussex, are mystified at the apparent murder by bludgeoning, yesterday, of Mr. Reginald Boltraine, proprietor of Boltraine Publishing Company, a producer of questionable self-published novels and memoirs. Discovered in a rose garden not far from his residence, any witnesses to this heinous crime are urged to come forward.*

"As may be expected with rural constabularies, they are more concerned with sheep-stealing than homicide. Hence, neither slaying has been resolved," said Holmes. "I therefore propose, it being the 20th of June, the day *before* the solstice, that you pay a visit on Mr. Cawley's beneficent widow in Pilston, Kent, while I drop in on the police post at Marborough, Surrey, and learn more about the scene where Mr. Boltraine was bludgeoned to death."

I was about to protest Holmes's attempt to coerce me into joining him as his co-investigator, but realised I was already a hooked fish, and at the mercy of a skilful angler. As such, I found myself two hours later on a train from London Bridge to Pilston village, my overnight portmanteau at my side, while Holmes took a locomotive from Victoria Station through the rustic countryside of Sussex to the hamlet of Marborough.

By midafternoon, I found myself seated uncomfortably on a dogcart transporting me from Pilston Station to Witton House, the country seat of the two-years' deceased Sheriden Cawley. The fields were golden brown with wheat crops bathed in sunshine, under a canopy of fresh air. It was an idyllic English summer's day – as compared to the oppressive stickiness of the London heat – as I wended my way to the sprawling limestone-block monstrosity that is Witton House, residence of Mrs. Bernadette Cawley, the widow of the late Sheriden. Here I left instructions with the dogcart driver to take my portmanteau to the local inn and continued on foot.

I saw immediately that Mrs. Cawley had been experiencing difficult times since her husband's death. The driveway to Witton House was unkempt and the gravel unraked, with weeds poking their unsightly heads through the surface. As for the house itself, the masonry was discoloured by soot, no matter we were in the countryside, and several roof tiles were missing and unreplaced.

After longer than convention dictates, a slovenly-dressed parlour maid answered my ring and admitted me to the sitting room where a dusty armchair awaited me. On the chaise longue opposite, Mrs. Bernadette Cawley was lounging, hand dramatically held against her forehead as if affected by a malaise.

"He left me nothing!" cried Mrs. Cawley once I had explained the purpose of my visit. "Nothing but debts and unfulfilled promises."

It transpired, over afternoon tea, that apart from a few assets, including the much-diminished nonreturnable deposit to publish *A Midsummer's Fortune*, that Sheriden Publishing, now under the inconsistent management of Sheriden's brother, was in a financial quagmire. Meanwhile, upon the subject of Sheriden's death, Mrs. Cawley had little to say, though what she did say was noteworthy.

"My husband was an incurable philanderer, Dr. Watson," she explained. "He died while I was visiting my sister in Leatherhead, shot through the heart in the library, in broad daylight, and I just know a woman was involved. One of his tavern wenches who he'd tossed aside, I suspect."

I delicately steered Mrs. Cawley away from the subject of her husband's illicit liaisons and on to the known facts about his murder.

"The local constabulary contacted Scotland Yard," she informed me, "from where one Inspector Lestrade came down from London and examined the murder scene."

"And did the inspector discover anything?" I inquired, knowing from past experience the policeman's limitations.

"He did. There was no sign of forced entry, nor of a violent struggle. Meanwhile, on the library table lay a book which had arrived in the post a week prior to Sheriden's death, alongside a bar of gold that alas turned out to be made from lead covered in a film of gold paint."

This was more than I expected, and I asked if I could be shown the book that had arrived in the post.

At first glance, Sheriden Cawley's copy of *A Midsummer's Fortune* by Les Cotis seemed identical to that of Jefferson James's, what with its bottle-green cover, poor-quality gold-leaf lettering, and cheap glue binding. However, Holmes's last instruction to me before I left Baker Street was specifically to examine page two-hundred and sixteen if I happened to find a copy of the book, as I had in Witton House library, and to telegraph him at Marborough with my discovery and my thoughts on the page.

On reading the specific page, I was amazed to find a description of a library, of a publisher named Sheriden Cawley accepting a bribe there in the form of a bar of gold, and of a wronged author, one Randolph Ventner, on a mission of vengeance. The literary scenario was essentially a forewarning of what occurred a week after the book's arrival at Witton House, bar the shooting to death of the house owner.

Having gained permission from Mrs. Bernadette Cawley to take the book away with me, at the consideration of a twenty-pound compensatory payment, I headed on foot to the King's Head Inn, Pilston. There, over a pint of ale and a late ploughman's lunch, I composed a telegram containing all my salient intelligence, which, for a one-shilling gratuity, the innkeeper's son took to the nearest telegraph office to forward to Holmes, in Marborough.

In the interim, after making myself as comfortable as possible in my cramped but homely room at the inn, I got down to the business of reading *A Midsummer's Fortune* in its entirety while awaiting news from Holmes. The wait wasn't long however, for the landlord's son returned with a telegram from Holmes just as I was looking forward to taking a nap and anticipating the tavern's evening fare. Apparently, the detective had been anticipating my message and had read and immediately responded to my telegram.

His telegram to me read thus:

Marborough, Sussex. 20 June, 1890 – 5:47 p.m.

Watson. Local constabulary showed me where Reginald Boltraine died, struck on head with gardening spade in Perrington Sedgewick Memorial Rose Garden. Boltraine body found with fake diamonds in frockcoat pocket and copy of A Midsummer's Fortune *(which Marborough Police have gifted me from their evidence locker) next to body. Page 216 set in rose garden, with book's anti-hero, Randolph Ventner, offering corrupt publisher a bribe of diamonds. No time to lose. Believe J.J. in gravest danger. Cannot trust resolution of case to Scotland Yard. Am taking next train back to London and on to Baker Street. Do likewise.*

Holmes

With a resigned sigh, I re-packed my portmanteau, paid the landlord for a night's lodging I would not be enjoying and for a dinner of which I would not be partaking, and, finding myself so preoccupied with reading Sheriden Cawley's volume of *A Midsummer's Fortune*, got precious little sleep on the 6:28 slow train from Pilston to London Bridge railway station.

Arriving in Baker Street, I found Holmes in ebullient mood as he strode back and forth in his dressing gown, puffing on his cherry-wood pipe, and mentally juggling the puzzle pieces of the case.

"Ah, there you are," said Holmes upon my entry. "Your presence is most welcome, what with you being somewhere between an artist's muse and a much-needed sounding board." With this dubious compliment concerning my usefulness ringing in my ears, he continued: "Just as when you figured out the significance of page 216 *prior to* working out that '*Les Cotis*' was an anagram of '*solstice*', I fear I've been coming at this case from the wrong side." He ushered me into my own armchair before resuming his pacing up and down. "When your telegram arrived at Marborough, I was there, in the telegraph office, in intimate contact with one Mr. Haversham, of Haversham Compositing and Printing Company, a cut-rate publisher in Birmingham."

From the table on which Holmes often conducted his chemical experiments, he picked up and flourished what I presumed to be the copy of *A Midsummer's Fortune* found beside the body of Reginald Boltraine a year earlier, almost to the day.

"Before venturing to Marborough, having ascertained that the relatively common glue binding of the two copies of *A Midsummer's Fortune* I had so far examined originated in the Midlands, I contracted a London publisher of my acquaintance to compile a list of low-cost printers operating in and around that corner of our fair British Isles. The list was awaiting me at the hamlet's humble telegraph office when I returned from Perrington Sedgewick Memorial Rose Garden. It was then only a matter of time, enquiring directly from each compositor-printer listed, whether they had ever used the distinctive bottle-green ink from the Lake District that is on the covers of the three copies of *A Midsummer's Fortune* we've encountered. There was only one who did."

"Haversham Compositing and Printing Company," I guessed.

"Exactly. However, first to a little theory I evolved in Marborough. The anagram of the author's name, '*Les Cotis*', and page 216 of Boltraine's copy of *A Midsummer's Fortune* directed the man to a nearby memorial rose garden, which, though somewhat secluded, boasts sweeping views in every direction, thereby negating any possibility of his being ambushed or otherwise taken by surprise. Furthermore, the mysteriousness of the situation must have put him on his guard, yet he was apparently easily overcome. What do you deduce from that?"

"You believe he didn't consider his killer to be a threat," I posited.

"I do," Holmes affirmed. "Just as Sheriden Cawley didn't consider *his* visitor, a visitor to his very home, to his Englishman's castle, to his inner sanctum – his library – to be a threat, either. The assailant was able to take both victims unawares. In each case, there was no indication of a struggle, nor of any defensive injuries consistent with a man who's in jeopardy or is fighting for his life."

An incandescent light bulb of comprehension suddenly illuminated my mind. "You imagine that the *murderer* is actually a *murderess*. You think the killer is a woman."

"Yes. I imagine a slight, demur, couldn't-harm-a-fly type of a woman. Les Cotis is a '*Lesley*' with an '*e-y*' rather than with an '*i-e*'."

I wanted to scoff at the ludicrousness of this notion, and yet Holmes's pronouncement made perfect sense. The neatness of the handwritten manuscript that Jefferson James and, I presume, Sheriden Cawley and Reginald Boltraine had received four years ago, bolstered Holmes's theory, and the fact that many female writers weren't taken as seriously as they perhaps should have been. The author of *A Midsummer's Fortune* had to approach seedy publishers rather than the more reputable purveyors of literature based in the City.

"And what of Haversham Compositing and Printing Company?" I asked. "Did they confirm this theory of yours?"

"They did, indeed," Holmes said, pulling a telegram from the pocket of his dressing gown. "In almost all respects."

He handed Mr. Haversham's reply to his enquiry to me. It read thus:

Dear Mr. Sherlock Holmes,

> *What an honour it is to address such a famed and respected personage as yourself, and to be of service in some small way in one of your cases. I did indeed take delivery of a shipment of Keswick, bottle-green ink which was used in the preparation of cloth-bound covers for a three-copy book order. The author, a young lady, writes under the pen name* Les Cotis. *Her real name, however, which is printed on the sixty-pound cheque she wrote for the extensive professional services I provided, is Rozina Varga.*

> *For this sum, we typeset and published three copies of* A Midsummer's Fortune, *though in the furtherance of some personal intrigue, Miss Varga insisted that page number 216 contain an altered text in each of the three versions, though not so as to affect the storyline.*

> *As to a description of the young lady, Mr. Holmes, apart from noting Miss Varga was a petite woman, I can tell you little since on the one occasion I met with her when she collected her order, she was wearing a veil – not the type of veil for mourning, but out of modesty.*

154

"Modesty, my foot!" said Holmes, but expanded no further on this point. Turning to me, he said: "At last we have a name for the perpetrator behind two killings, and a third planned killing. Not '*Les Cotis*', and not '*Midsummer*', but a woman named Rozina Varga."

"This would be Jefferson James's mystery correspondent at the now defunct Lewisham Dormitory for Eastern European Migrants," I speculated.

"Undeniably. Why, Miss Varga and her book's fictitious anti-hero, Randolph Ventner, even share the same initials."

I enquired whether or not we should alert Scotland Yard as to our concerns for the safety of Jefferson James, what with the solstice being the following day, and, by Holmes's admission, the publisher being in the gravest of danger. Once again, however, Holmes would have none of it.

"Those clodhoppers might well frighten away our *femme fatale*?" he said. "No, we need to catch Miss Varga actively perpetrating an attempt to commit murder. So far, we have only circumstantial proof, supposition, and hearsay. We have no hard facts demonstrating the lady's guilt. And as for Mr. James, a lesson in the consequences of preying off of peoples dreams and aspirations would do him good."

"In other words, you're using him as bait to lure out the killer," I said in disbelief.

"Semantics, Watson. Mere semantics. However, as a precaution, let me contact Lestrade, one of the few Scotland Yard detectives who demonstrates any amount of initiative, to accompany us on our adventures tomorrow. We should be in place at our Miss Varga's self-prescribed venue for murder – which, according to James's version of *A Midsummer's Fortune*, will be the old stone bridge on the outskirts of Tulverton, Norfolk, not far from Jefferson James's country abode, well before the prescribed hour she plans to do away with him. So as long as Mr. James has completed reading the book and has realised the significance of page 216, which I have no reason to believe he hasn't, all is safely in hand. In the meantime, Mrs. Hudson is preparing a meal of hand-basted roast goose with roasted potatoes and assorted green vegetables. After dinner, I suggest you go home, make preparations for tomorrow's jaunt, get a good night's sleep, and meet Lestrade and me at Liverpool Street Station in time for the 6:20 train to Norwich. Oh, and – "

" – bring my service revolver."

"You read my mind."

That night, instead of enjoying a restful slumber, I felt obliged to complete my reading of *A Midsummer's Fortune*. The novel concerned an aspiring author, one Randolph Ventner, who resorts to bribery, blackmail, and eventually murder to get his debut novel published and to secure a three-book publishing deal. I had retained the copy of the book I'd purchased from Mrs. Bernadette Cawley, and Holmes had stated he currently had no more use for copy that was on permanent loan to him from the constables at Marlborough Police Station. I was therefore able to scrutinise page 216 of both versions of the novel and note down the similarities and differences.

It transpired that both Sheriden Cawley and Reginald Boltraine appeared in cameo in the novels sent to them, as the heads of fictitious publishing houses. On page 216 in Cawley's copy of the book, he was in his library, where Randolph Ventner bribed him with a bar of gold to publish his book. On the other hand, in Boltraine's copy, he was approached at Perrington Sedgewick Memorial Rose Garden, his bribe being a handful of cut diamonds. Neither man died during these fictional scenarios. Yet it was these fabricated texts that enticed the real Sheriden Cawley and Reginald Boltraine, through greed, ego, and the promise of acquiring a best-selling novel on their publishing lists, to their deaths.

So, at 6:10 the next morning, I found myself on Platform Three of Liverpool Street Station, face-to-face with the usually sceptical Inspector Lestrade. He was sporting a somewhat luxurious moustache of the type then currently in fashion. Holmes had just finished updating the inspector on the case of the veiled lady, Rozina Varga, as well as notifying him of the true facts surrounding the death of Sheriden Cawley, whose murder Lestrade had unsuccessfully investigated two years previously. The Scotland Yard policeman accepted news of his shortcomings with equanimity, and ten minutes later we were in a private train carriage on our way to the interminable flatlands of East Anglia.

Apart from the two copies of *A Midsummer's Fortune* that were in my possession, and which I had brought along with me on the trip to Tulverton, we also had the relevant page of Jefferson James's version, the page Holmes had read on the day of James's visit to Baker Street, imprinted on his memory like an image on a photographic plate. And as we chuffed through the awakening East Anglian countryside, Holmes appraised us of the page's more salient particulars, as well as his own estimations of the case.

"The venue Miss Varga has chosen to dispatch her third victim is Tulverton's old stone bridge, a crossing located, according to James's version of the novel, on the edge of Tulverton village," Holmes said. "As in the other two versions of the book, Mr. James is being offered a literal midsummer's fortune, though not in gold, nor in diamonds. On this occasion, rather vulgarly, James's patronage is to be paid for with what no doubt will be a fictitious wad of money. Just note how cleverly our temptress is luring her prey. She appeals to each publisher's avariciousness with the promise of wealth, as per the book's title, what with the enigmatic anagram of the novelist's pseudonym leading them to the page featuring a cameo of Miss Varga's next victim – not being murdered, but being enriched at their summer solstice meeting. Miss Varga is a Venus flytrap *par excellence*."

As the heat of the day set in and the mercury in the thermometer rose, and with a new and grudging respect for the ingenuity of our prey, Rozina Varga, we carried on across the monochromatic fecundity of the Norfolk Fens towards the straggling village of Tulverton, a settlement built within a bend in the River Tul, a tributary of the great River Yar.

We disembarked at Tulverton at nine-fifty-five, emerging into the sweltering humidity of the fenlands. We were the only passengers who stepped down from the train. There was no veiled lady, nor unveiled lady for that matter, so it appeared Miss Varga had either arrived the previous evening and lodged in the village, or at a nearby farmstead, or had camped overnight in a barn or a copse.

From the station platform we could see an old, two-span stone-block bridge straddling the River Tul. We therefore waved aside the stationmaster's well-intentioned though prying overtures and, using what few trees and hedgerows there were for cover, made our way surreptitiously to the bridge.

As we took up our positions in a brush-concealed bird hide close to the near end of the bridge, I noticed the slightest of frowns furrowing Holmes's brow, a sure indication that all was not right.

"The bridge!" said Holmes, his frown deepening. "In James's version of *A Midsummer's Fortune*, it's a single-span construction that is mentioned. This bridge has two arches."

Lestrade shrugged off Holmes's concerns. "I expect Miss Varga read of the old stone bridge at Tulverton in the *Encyclopaedia Britannica*, or in a travel book, or perhaps in a newspaper or magazine, and hasn't actually seen it."

"I don't deal in 'perhaps'," Holmes snapped back, and with some reluctance settled down for the wait. Even so, the detective seemed increasingly unhappy at the seed of doubt that had been sown. And as the hour wore on and the heat increased, he became ever more agitated.

"Come on!" he eventually said, leaping to his feet, our watches showing 10:20. "Jefferson James is unguarded and we're in need of local intelligence." With that, he broke cover and ran for the train station, Lestrade at his heels, while I struggled to keep up, my leg wound from the Afghan campaign telling.

157

When he was within hailing distance of the station, without breaking step and pointing back to where we were coming from, Holmes called to the stationmaster, "Is that the only old stone bridge in the vicinity?"

"Nay, sir," the railwayman shouted back. "Tulverton has *two* stone bridges. One at either end of the village on account of the bend in the river."

With a brusque thank you, and without reducing his pace, Holmes carried on along the dirt lane bisecting the ribbon-like rural settlement towards the other end of the village, cursing himself as he went for his complacency and ineptitude.

Huffing and puffing, limping a tad and in some discomfort, I hastened after the two so dissimilar detectives until I got to that part of the village most distant from the train station. At my first sight of it, the bridge took up my consideration – a single-arched packhorse bridge over a narrowed section of the River Tul. Then my attention shifted to a man in his middle thirties, informally dressed for an outdoor excursion, standing precisely in the middle of the bridge. It was Jefferson James. With a jaunty, self-satisfied demeanour, he was rubbing his hands covetously together as he looked down on a stack of banknotes tied together with string, resting on the bridge parapet. So absorbed was he with his acquisition and with his greed that he hadn't registered Holmes and Lestrade's shouts of warning and alarm. Nor was he paying attention to the reason for those alarums – the veiled woman who had apparently gifted him with what I presumed was a fraudulent fortune, and who was now standing, unregarded by him, at his side.

As Jefferson James picked up the wad of banknotes and undid the string, his eyes blazed with avarice. He proceeded to flick through them like a card sharp riffling through a deck, and his delighted expression changed to one of mortified rage. Too late, he turned to the veiled lady as she stepped forward and seemingly punched him in the side.

The publisher staggered away from her, swayed back and forth, and collapsed to his knees. However, before Rozina Varga could make another thrust with the long-bladed knife grasped in her hand, Holmes had hold of her by the blade-wielding arm and Lestrade wasn't far behind, flourishing his police pistol.

"Watson!" yelled Holmes, wresting the bloody knife from the assailant as I stumblingly ascended the arch of the bridge. "Your professional ministrations are required."

Jefferson James was in better condition than he could have hoped for. Though the stab wound he suffered to his right flank was deep and bleeding quite heavily, the knife had punctured no internal organs. Nor had it severed an artery. Yet when Holmes and I went to his aid, James

158

initially waved us off, angrily accusing us of staking him out like a sacrificial goat to be eviscerated by a madwoman.

Holmes magnanimously accepted responsibility for using the publisher as bait, and thereby facilitated permission for me to tear open James's blood-stained shirt and staunch the flow of blood. This I did with a compress I fashioned from the oblong-cut pieces of paper that were now scattered about the footway of the bridge and which had formerly been masquerading as five-pound notes.

"The top one!" the ever-avaricious Jefferson James cried out, his left hand searching through the mass of rectangular pieces of blank paper that surrounded us, and in spite of his serious injury. "The top banknote. It was real!"

At the sight of Mr. James feverishly looking for a single genuine banknote amidst a sea of white paper, Rozina Varga began laughing. At first it was a snigger, then a throaty guffaw, and finally with abandon, like the madwoman Jefferson James had labelled her to be.

Under Lestrade's custody, guarded both by the Scotland Yard detective's close scrutiny and his pistol, Rozina Varga suddenly went unnervingly quiet and, with great deliberation, lifted her veil, revealing a hideously fire-disfigured countenance. Her upper lip had melted away and was uplifted at either end like a horrible smile, while two vertical holes, separated by the remnants of her nasal septum, stood where her nose and nostrils once were. Her eyes protruded from sockets surrounded by shiny flesh of an unhealthy pink colour, and her ears were stumps of skin-covered cartilage enclosing the red-raw wells of her earholes.

As Jefferson James shrank back in horror, and as Lestrade took an unconscious step away from his charge, I couldn't but feel pity for this young woman whose visage had been defaced so terribly during the blooming years of her life.

"You were a victim of the fire at the Lewisham Dormitory for Eastern European Immigrants," Holmes said, more as a statement than a question.

"I was," the unfortunate woman replied. "By day, I toiled in London's dockside factories along with my fellow immigrants to sustain my poverty-stricken existence. At night, I was caretaker of the ladies' section of the Lewisham dormitory. During those long nighttime hours, I worked on the handwritten manuscripts of my debut novel, *A Midsummer's Fortune*. However, because I was a woman, I was unable to place my manuscript with a traditional publishing house and was forced to negotiate terms with three untrustworthy knaves, heads of publishing companies who were more concerned with swindling their customers than nurturing art."

159

"Look here – " Jefferson James began, irked by Miss Varga's description and summation of him.

"Those knaves," noted Holmes, "would be Sheriden Cawley, Reginald Boltraine, and this gentleman who you just stabbed, Mr. Jefferson James."

"That's correct," said Rozina Varga. "If it weren't for this trio of conmen, the book they later all believed in their stone-cold hearts could become a publishing sensation, and for which they each took a non-returnable deposit from me four years ago, would have been published long before the Lewisham fire marred me. I would still be a whole person, and a well-known novelist, to boot. This is why, once I had recuperated enough to resume labouring in a factory again, I hatched my plan of revenge. I bought a typewriter, learned to type, composed a second, a third, and a final draft of *A Midsummer's Fortune*. I saved up enough money to have three custom copies printed by Haversham Printing. Only then did I decide to utilise the annual fortnight off work permitted me by my employer to exact vengeance, one by one, year after year, on each of those putrid specimens of humankind who ruined my life."

"Was your vengeance worth it?" Holmes asked, stepping forward and readjusting her veil with an unexpected show of tenderness and compassion, while Lestrade secured handcuffs to his prisoner's wrists. "Now you are set to swing at the end of a hangman's noose."

Rozina Vargas chuckled. "I think not. When you account for the pity of a jury, I expect to be sentenced perhaps to a life's term of imprisonment instead of the gallows, maybe not even that. And as it stands, just look at me. My current existence is little better than imprisonment, hiding away from my fellow human beings lest my appearance frighten them or elicit ridicule. In the meantime, I've done away with two men who thought of publishing as a game in which authors were to be fleeced, and I've given a third such man the scare of his life. Added to which, there's presently no law preventing me from profiting from my crimes. With all that time on my hands, who knows – I could still obtain a three-book deal: A trilogy, one volume for each of my two victims, and one for the third, intended victim."

At this point, the disreputable Mr. Jefferson James sheepishly raised his hand and took a deep breath, no doubt preparatory to offering Miss Varga literary representation. This prompted me to haul him painfully to his feet and guide him to the nearest inhabited Tulverton cottage, to further treat his wound until he could be transported by cart to the county infirmary.

As it turned out, Rozina Varga was indeed spared the rope, and did write her trilogy. It was published to much fanfare, her case giving folk pause for thought when contemplating the lot of women in modern-day society.

As for Mr. Jefferson James, proprietor of J.J. Publishing: He attempted to sue Holmes for wilful endangerment. However, since Holmes had saved his life, this was difficult to prove and James's case was dismissed. To avoid the threat of counter-litigation for slander, Holmes demanded that the publisher give him, as compensation and as a memento for his private museum, the custom-printed copy of *A Midsummer's Fortune* that Miss Varga had sent to him.

A piece I wrote on the Rozina Varga case appeared in the illustrious *Times* newspaper in December of 1890. And so, in observance of my achievement, we found ourselves – Holmes and Inspector Lestrade and myself – seated around a roaring fireplace at 221b one chilly winter's evening. We each had retained one of Rozina Varga's customised books to remember our adventure by and reminisced well into the night – a glass of brandy continually at hand – about two solved murders and a murder prevented, with Holmes closing the evening with a toast.

"Gentlemen!" he said. "To the case of the veiled lady!"

The Adventure of the
Absentee Officer
by Daniel Lenois

It was in October of the year 1890. I had been much caught up in my medical practice at the time. Changes in weather, particularly the shift away from the warmer seasons, always seemed to bring with it an ever-predictable onset of various illnesses among my patients. Luckily, most of these cases were of a mild nature, so my efforts were rarely put to a more serious test.

This particular day plodded along sedately. Save for one singular patient at my door from the moment I strode in that morning, I had since been left entirely to my own devices. I henceforth dedicated myself to pursuing nothing more urgent than making my way through a particularly dense volume on the Napoleonic Wars. While no doubt enormously faithful to known historical records, the author's command of the mind's eye through the boundless linguistic dexterity of the English language was admittedly rather limited, making what otherwise might have been a compelling narrative instead come across as a rather tired lecture.

It was then that I heard a knock at the door. Rising and crossing the room, I opened the door to find myself face to face with my dear friend, Mr. Sherlock Holmes.

He smiled genially as we shook hands warmly.

"I hope I didn't greatly disturb your studies into the imperial prerogative of our brothers across the channel," Holmes remarked sardonically.

"Not at all," said I.

"I was wondering whether I might persuade you to set aside your practice for some little time," Holmes continued, "as there is a rather promising matter that has come to my attention, and I should be lost indeed without my faithful biographer."

"I should be glad indeed!" I declared enthusiastically.

I hurriedly scribbled a note to my neighbour. It had often been common practice between us to see to the other's patients in just such situations as this, were it necessary for one of us to be out for any extended period of time, although I privately doubted that this afternoon would prove of any greater activity than the morning had.

It was only when Holmes had escorted me into the carriage waiting outside that he clarified his purpose in calling upon me.

"Not an hour ago, I received this wire from Mycroft." He handed the telegram to me. Upon its face was typed the following:

> *A most sensitive situation has arisen, one that may, as of yet, prove of some passing intellectual merit to you. Kindly report to me at the Diogenes Club at your earliest possible convenience.*
>
> *M*

"Whatever do you think he means by this?" I asked, turning over to the other side, so as to be sure I had read the intended message in its entirety.

"There is little evidence upon which to build any lasting foundation for speculation," Holmes responded. "However, Mycroft is not one to bandy words. The distinction between emphasizing this matter as being 'most sensitive', as opposed to its more benign alternative of mere 'sensitive', is highly indicative. We must then go above and beyond the conventional standards of confidentiality here, Watson. Whatever case Mycroft intends to lay before us, it's more like than not to involve persons and events with good reason not yet intended to fall within that narrow awareness of that habitual creature, the British subject."

As good as I was to my word, it was only following the passage of some three-and-twenty years before Holmes finally relented and begrudgingly allowed me to begin setting this narrative to written record, and then only a marginally modified account of those true events which ultimately came to pass.

So furiously aroused was my curiosity in that carriage that our gradual traversal through the thriving streets of London felt to my restless spirit akin to a perpetual Purgatory, which was aided in some part by the fog that hovered low, obscuring the finer details of the streets and buildings surrounding us. However, it wasn't more than ten minutes until we arrived before the front door of the Diogenes Club, that ever-present centre founded upon the strictest of misanthropic principles.

Upon catching sight of Holmes, an attendant stepped forward perfunctorily and, without a word, led us to the Stranger's Room. Having already before accustomed myself to the rather extreme formalised eccentricities of the club, including its absolute prohibition against speaking for any reason outside of the guest room, I took no offence at being so curtly ignored by its attending staff.

Mycroft awaited us serenely in a comfortable armchair as we strode in. His light grey, almost-transparent eyes studied us with acute interest as the attendant behind us slowly closed the door, so as to cause almost no perceivable noise.

Mycroft shifted in his seat, causing his protruding waistline to wobble perceptively.

"Ah, Sherlock. So good of you to have come. And Dr. Watson – I trust your reading of this world's histories was not so compelling as to leave your mind behind at your offices when my brother appeared at your door?"

I started noticeably. While I was well familiar with Holmes's own extraordinary perceptions and deductive prowess, I was, as of yet, nevertheless considerably more unfamiliar with those of his elder brother.

Mycroft chuckled. "It is no great thing, Doctor. The crease upon your left wrist indicated a book of some weight had laid upon it for some time, so as to impress itself upon your person. The lack of activity evident upon your person, along with the lack of any physical or psychological strain upon your features, which would be expected were one reading with any great intensity, indicates said reading wasn't for the benefit of your, shall we say, very generalised approach to the doctrine of British medicine. What variety of commonplace book, then, is most widely associated with such girth? And of those, which were you most like to read upon this admittedly most dreary day? Surely not an exploration of common law, nor an exploration of scientific hypotheses. A medical man of your military standing would, more than most, have developed a more thorough appreciation for the complexities and intricacies of man's past than the average bricklayer, shopkeeper, or other citizen of Her Majesty's government – a solution upon which I have no doubt my brother here would have eventually availed of you." Mycroft's eyes twinkled with amusement. However, this soon faded away to instead be replaced with an expression of utmost seriousness. I glanced to the armchair across from him, which I hadn't originally noticed.

Holmes had already begun examining the second man with a flicker of surprise crossing his face, as if the figure were familiar to him. Mycroft caught the look.

"Indeed, Sherlock, indeed. Gentlemen, may I present the esteemed Lord John Beaumont, a man of high station within the British Army's Intelligence branch. It is on his account that I sent for you."

As he spoke, the other man rose with the stiff solemnity of the trained officer, nodded to Holmes and me grimly, shaking Holmes's hand, then my own. He was a tall man of a broad, muscular build. His hair was coal-black and neatly parted. Flecks of verdant colouring were visible in his otherwise-azure eyes. Mycroft waved a hand at us, indicating that we be seated, and we returned to the business at hand.

"I am much indebted to you for having come, Mr. Holmes," Beaumont began, relaxing his posture somewhat. I was taken aback by the quiet, almost harmonic melody of his voice, given his imposing physical presence. "There is a matter of some concern within the intelligence community at present that, I fear, we may all come to rue if its cause isn't made clear with the most urgent of expediency."

"If you would be so good as to lay the facts before me," Holmes responded graciously, "I would be glad to be of some small assistance."

"The matter, at least on its face, is rather simple," Beaumont continued. "However, the implications are all the more complex for that fact." He took a brief drink from the glass on the small table next to him.

"Three months ago, I dispatched one of my agents to Paris, under orders to pick up the scent of a certain gang of robbers." He shook his head. "Had it just been ordinary robberies of some few thousand pounds, as is the case so often elsewhere, the incidents would have proved of little interest to our department. However, in robbing the safe-boxes of their contents, the thieves also made off with certain documents whose nature would prove more than slightly discomforting to our nation's allies and trading partners.

"The documents themselves had been stored there temporarily, waiting for transition to a new facility of the highest governmental security. The bank's proximity and rather local nature made it, to our consideration, a frankly limited safety risk." He grimaced. "Obviously, we miscalculated, to our cost." He took a breath. "I sent one of my agents, Arthur Barrett, to intercept the thieves and recover the documents before their true nature was made clear, and then their contents sold to the highest bidder. Given his hereditary standing as both a true-born British citizen, and his familial links as a Parisian, he was ideally situated to make the inquiries needed in order to attempt such a feat."

Beaumont swirled his glass idly. "Approximately six weeks later, we received word through channels that Barrett had obtained all but three of the documents, sending notable surviving fragments as confirmation that the latter had been destroyed through some external act. It was expected that Barrett would promptly return back in order to deliver a full accounting of events. However, he never showed. Nearly a month went by with no communication from him or any of his contacts acting on his behalf. Then, out of nowhere, he reemerged here, in the heart of London. When my men looked into the records, we found that he had returned some weeks prior under an alias and, by all accounts, was publicly behaving no different than normal, so far as we could tell. However, he had made no effort to come forward.

"When I sent two of my other agents to collect him, they found his home empty and dust-strewn. Despite sending several of my other men to follow him closely, we have yet to learn where he disappears to, or why. One of the downsides of having an agent well-versed in his trade, I suppose, is that should he not desire to be found, there is very little one can do to run him to ground.

"What I don't understand, Mr. Holmes, is why a man such as Barrett would take the trouble to return to London, give rampant evidence of his presence here, and yet make every possible effort to avoid us, once we aim to lay our hands upon him. There is something in the air here of which I most strongly dislike. I ask you then, as by formal station, as you are a civilian and not a person the likes of which would be immediately familiar by sight to Barrett, can you pull loose the curtain obscuring this mystery?"

Holmes was silent for a moment, his fingers interlocked as he considered Beaumont's report with the utmost attentiveness with that studied introspection for which he was at times so known. Then, his features cleared, and he stood up.

"I believe I might be capable of shining some light on your particular problem, my Lord. Set your mind at rest. I shall send word to you as to our progress. Come, Watson, I believe there is work yet to perform."

Holmes was silent for much of the ride back. Only when we had halted before my front door did he finally rouse himself. "Here we must part for some time. I must work this ground alone. I expect I shall soon lay my hands upon certain clarifying information which, by its very nature, may bring us forward."

"Can I not be of some other assistance?" I asked, a trifle irked at the dismissal, although inwardly I understood the impersonal nature of his decision. I hardly needed reminding of my own blunt-spoken manner and comparative inexperience in such fieldwork. Caution, improvisation, and general adaptability were all crucial functions in the area of professional practical observance.

Holmes shook his head. "I shall be the better for going unaccompanied on this particular venture. However, if it's at all agreeable to you, let us aim to meet once more this evening. I shall send you the specifics at some later time."

I stepped down from the carriage and strode to the door, not looking back as the sound of the horses' feet renewed clopping down the street informed me of Holmes's departure.

My afternoon was livened some by a house call to treat a moderate case of influenza. After diagnosing the condition and providing the patient with what medications I deemed appropriate, I left her with strictest instructions to remain in bed until the worst of the symptoms had passed, packed my things, and returned home to my wife.

Having informed her of Holmes's intentions, Mary and I enjoyed a quiet hour in our sitting room, she sewing a partially formed blanket of some design, and me catching up on my letters. It was then that there was a ring of the bell.

I stood up, setting my remaining letters to one side, and strode to the door. A messenger awaited me at the stoop, handing me an envelope before promptly departing. I closed the door and then opened the letter. I immediately recognized Holmes's writing, directing me to where I might find my friend, as well as instructions to bring with me my old service revolver. While I readily conceded that the years had never made me remotely near the equal of Holmes in all matters concerning the art of investigation, I couldn't fail to observe the apparent inferences from such a request. It was with an unconcealed thrill of excitement coursing through my limbs that I carefully loaded and stowed away the revolver in my coat pocket.

A half-hour later, I found myself striding into a small nondescript restaurant which almost directly bordered the River Thames. I found Holmes already seated and cutting into a finely grilled herring.

"Ah, Watson," said he as I sat down opposite him. "Very good. I went ahead and ordered for you, as we have but a little time to ourselves before we must once more set off. It will be a long night, I fear. However, if we're lucky, we may soon see all set right once more."

"You have found our man?" I asked intently.

"I have found traces of him," Holmes responded carefully. "With any luck, we should expect to behold the gentleman himself within this very hour."

"Surely you aren't serious!" I exclaimed.

"Quite." He lifted another piece of herring from his plate and swallowed it before continuing. "Following our brief separation, I took to the field, to find out what more I could. Mycroft gave me the initial lead, and only Mycroft, not to mention our newfound client, Lord Beaumont, could verify those necessary details and inferences that led us to the precipice upon which we now gaze down upon our elusive quarry." He raised the glass he now held and sipped at the contents. "There are certain specifics of which I should be more than willing to share with you, were it not for the sensitivity of their nature. At some future date, I should be more than pleased to satisfy your every branch of inquiry that you should decide to put to me. However, for the moment, we must allow actions to speak for us, and let what else come what may."

"It shall be as you say," I declared, my curiosity momentarily tempered by his words.

A few minutes later, my own plate arrived, and we dedicated ourselves to nothing more important than finishing them off while conversing of other matters of little significance. We remained at our table for some little while after paying for the meal. I could see Holmes keeping careful watch out through the window as we spoke, as if waiting for a certain sequence of events to be set into action.

With a gesture of his head, he indicated toward the window.

"See there, Watson? But mind you to look with studied indifference, as if you were merely disengaged with all around you. That man there – he who so carefully follows his assigned pattern."

"Assigned?" asked I.

I gazed at the man. His frame was neither taller nor shorter than what was commonly expected of the typical Londoner. His auburn, almost strawberry-coloured hair gleamed in the fading sunlight. He strode without the accompaniment of a walking stick or other accessory to compliment his figure. His suit was of a respectable fabric, but lacking in those finer details that bespoke the master tailor.

"Just so. Observe the precise, scripted nature of his movements. He walks neither with purpose nor with a lack thereof, so as to indicate idleness. He portrays himself so distinctly as unremarkable, taking it to such dramatic effect that, by its very nature, it draws eyes upon him as nothing short of remarkable. It is not a *person* we gaze upon, Watson, but an *actor*, and the streets of London are as his stage."

Finally, as the man began to pass from our sight, he stood up.

"The horn of battle has sounded. Now we must needs confront the enemy directly. Did you do as I asked?"

I nodded and gestured toward my pocket.

"Very good. Follow me, and upon your life, make no move out of the ordinary until I give such word as to the contrary."

I nodded again, and we set off.

The street was bustling with the everyday carriages and foot traffic that so well reflected the inherent normative state of the City of London. With a singular glance, Holmes indicated toward a medium-built man ahead of us, whose back was to us. His head was bare and marked with a vivid colouring of auburn hair, although it had begun to fall away in his present middling years. I glanced to the side where Holmes had been, but he had already disappeared into the crowd behind us.

I followed as the man strode further down the street. However, something in my gait must have betrayed me, as with only the most fleeting glance, the figure ahead of us burst into a dead run, hurling himself

168

down a narrow side alley in between two neighbouring residential buildings. I tore after him, although I was certain that the more-than-marginal difference in our respective speeds would ensure this to be but a fleeting pursuit. Putting everything I could summon into forcing my legs into yet more violent efforts, I gradually gained on the man and, just as he slid, trying to take a corner, I pounced upon him with what I perhaps extravagantly deemed the roaring ferocity of the hunting African lion.

We struggled back and forth for several moments, I grabbing him by the front of his collar, and he rolling first from one side then to the other in a desperate attempt to shake me loose, all the while raining down upon me a flurry of blows and kicks. It was then that my army training came back to me. While my role had been that of a field doctor, one doesn't survive long on or around a battlefield long without having developed the means by which to defend one's self. With effort, I managed to subdue my struggling adversary, with only nominal injury to either of us. It was only then that I noticed several curious faded scars at various points along his face, so faint as to be entirely unremarkable at a casual glance.

"I trust you didn't over-exert yourself, Watson," a familiar voice reached me from behind. I turned. Sherlock Holmes stood standing above me, smiling with some bemusement.

"Mary has remarked that I am perhaps over-in-need of some physical exertion," I responded lightly. I stood, panting, waving one hand at my fallen opponent. "My dance partner here was courteous enough to oblige."

Holmes laughed.

"I trust that you didn't take serious offence to my absence in your struggle. I myself had laid seeds of some promise some hours ago, and it was directly thanks to your actions that I now have begun to reap the fruits of those labours."

I then saw, pulling up some distance away and on the side of the main street from which I had so hastily dove off of some minutes prior, a carriage, from which emerged a quartet made up of Scotland Yard officials, led by Inspector Lestrade, and one prisoner.

"We have him, Mr. Holmes," Lestrade declared, his chest puffing with self-evident pride. Two of the officers behind him led between them a man of medium height, who in every respect bore an almost identical likeness to the man I had just apprehended in the alley. Bruises and dried blood obscured his hands and face, and he struggled to walk even with the aid of the officials.

Lestrade's mouth fell open as he stared at the bloodied but otherwise clearly distinguished face of the man behind me, as did mine at the sight of the man led behind him. We both turned to Holmes.

169

"What is the meaning of this, Mr. Holmes?" the inspector demanded with unabashed astonishment.

"I should very much like to know myself," I insisted, struggling to form the words through my shock.

"Everything shall be explained," Holmes promised. "For the moment, however, I believe two destinations take precedence: A hospital bed for our much-beleaguered Mr. Barrett, and a holding cell for his counterpart. Then I expect, with Barrett's assistance, all may soon become clear."

It was a few hours later, after the hospital staff had finished attending to Barrett's most serious injuries and had assured us that, given a few weeks in bed, he would readily recover, we were then permitted to speak with him. The doctor assigned to Barrett's care had shown a more-than-passing disinclination in regards to the prospect of our interview with his newest patient. However, such was the unquestionable authority of Scotland Yard that we were permitted a brief window of time to speak with the patient without further delay.

Barrett's fingers, encased in tight gauzed wrappings to accelerate the mending of several broken bones on his right hand, were immobilised, forcing him to rely upon his more lightly bound left in order to light a cigarette clutched firmly between his teeth. His left hand shook from some case of nerves, either physical or psychological. Lestrade kindly took the matchbox from Barrett and, taking out a match, struck it twice, igniting the flame. He lit the end of Barrett's cigarette and then set the box down upon the bedside table.

Barrett nodded in appreciation and smoked in silence for a few moments before removing the cigarette and putting it out in the ashtray next to him. "I hear it's to you I owe my life, sirs," he said to Holmes and Lestrade, "and to you also," he noted to me, "for so thoroughly running down my *doppelgänger* back there." He grinned tightly. "What I wouldn't have given for the opportunity to have joined in myself – although, I must confess, I might have applied a more lingering penance, for all the inconvenience brought down upon me." There was a roguish, almost youthful energy about him, far different in manner than that of the man I had pursued.

"Would you be so good as to elucidate the events which brought you hence?" Holmes asked him patiently. "While I have surmised most of the essentials, there are a few finer details that haven't quite become entirely clear."

Barrett nodded. "It was of my own doing," he admitted. "I had been tasked with recovering certain documents by my superiors. These documents had no military application. However, they involved trade negotiations between Britain and certain Eastern European nations –

Prussia, Romania, the like. I can say all this with full transparency, for the broadest details were widely known. However, there were more than a few specific clauses that escaped wider diplomatic circulation, which I would not mention openly thus, and which were known only at the highest levels of operational governance." He leaned back in his bed as he spoke, wincing.

"I managed to make contact with a certain individual who the criminals – I never quite discovered their exact identities – had determined to be their middleman. His intent, and theirs, was to go through surreptitious means and auction off the items to any one out of a number of various representatives of rival governments and independent agents."

"How did you establish yourself among them?" Lestrade asked sharply.

"I posed as a French national," Barrett explained, "and through the funding of my superiors, managed to obtain the documents for a sum of just over twelve-thousand pounds. This was no easy feat, as I had been only given fifteen-thousand, and I tell you true, every raise in price produced new beads of sweat upon my brow. Upon exchanging the money for the documents, it came to my attention that several of the documents were missing from the rest.

He flexed the fingers of his left hand as he spoke. "I deposited the documents I had so dearly purchased into the hands of a trusted contact. I knew he would see to it that they were immediately transported back to London for safekeeping. I waited until late into that night, and then silently broke into the office of the man who served as the unofficial auctioneer, searching for any sign. It was then that I had found that he had burned the remaining documents. This was curious, as before I had departed upon my assignment, I had been briefed in some explicit detail as to the precise contents on those pages."

He frowned reflectively. "Those particular pages had much to do with an impending private negotiation between England and another power – I dare not say its name. Nothing else in the pages I held made any mention of said tentative agreements. It was then that, upon checking the still embers in the fireplace, that I caught a few fragments of paper. I recognized them. The papers I sought had been burned."

Barrett stared grimly off into the distance for a moment, as if seeing something beyond our vision. "Scouring the office still farther, I discovered evidence that the contents had been copied out in excruciating detail. Whether there was but one copy or a multitude, I couldn't tell, although my instincts told me that, were the duplicates commonplace, their price would be negatively impacted in the extreme. Searching through the man's desk, I found a certain letter, dated nearly a week prior, from a

London buyer who was interested in procuring those specific pages. The letter included explicit instructors for how the documents were to be delivered, and when. I checked the date and time, and I knew I had no time to waste. I hurriedly replaced all I had found and made for the door. However, it was then that I heard footsteps. Devoid of other recourse, I dove to the open window and scaled my way down."

He laughed, then caught himself as a sudden spasm of pain surged through him. "My unexpected departure, unseen by the guards inside, along with some remnant sign of my presence in that room, must have sent word ahead of me that I was upon their track. When I reached the predetermined spot, I was violently apprehended by a group of men. There were four of them, and only one of me. I held my own as best I could, killing one of them by forcing his clutched knife back into his own heart, and injuring another with my fists. One of the others grabbed me and clubbed me unconscious."

His eyes went dead. "What happened next wasn't pleasant. They interrogated me harshly for some time, as much for the pleasure of my writhing as for whatever limited information they could glean from me. There was little I could tell them even had I wanted to. It is standard policy in my profession to ask nothing more than what is necessary to know."

He indicated his wounds. "The less one knows, the less one may reveal under such conditions. It was in their mind to kill me, I believe. However, a message eventually reached them informing them that, for whatever reason, it was advantageous to them that I be kept alive. Not released, mind you, but it was certain that I would not, as yet, die. Possibly whoever was in charge intended to hold me for ransom. They brought in an artist of their acquaintance who painstakingly captured my every bodily detail, for use in locating my double. Then a hood was placed over my eyes, and I was left alone. I couldn't swear, not at the Gates of either Heaven or Hell themselves, how much time passed. It was as a blur. I became conscious of little besides the steady beat of my own heart, and the pain emitting from my frame and limbs." He looked to Holmes and Lestrade. "It was only when you and the others appeared that I became aware of aught else."

Holmes nodded. "I believe we can extrapolate the rest, in conjunction with your narrative. The man that was captured was hired effectively as an actor, a pretender, to play the role of Mr. Barrett here. He lacked many of the hardened features of a true spy. However, as is so often the case with career criminals great or minor, he knew enough to escape the loose inattentive net of the everyday authorities that followed him, who so in assuming that he was who he seemed to be, were entirely taken aback and didn't display due diligence in adapting to the situation when the pretender initially escaped their grasp. Someone with connections in both high and low places very specifically wanted our Mr. Barrett kept alive, in order so the fake Barrett might better replicate the outward attitude and mannerisms of the authentic article while the others determine what the next step in their operation will be."

Holmes looked at me with some amusement. "I must confess, Watson, that should you have insisted upon accompanying me, following our interview with both Mycroft and our client, you would have found the subsequent work tedious and trying in the extreme." He clarified. "I took the time to tail our criminal pretender. While I make no allusions to my capabilities as a member of the official intelligence community, one benefit of having no direct links to such agencies is that my name and description would be most unlikely to appear in any official records of those individuals known to have been, or actively are still, affiliated with such.

"So while my name has brought with it a certain local celebrity, the odds were still reasonably good that my presence, at a more than discreet distance, would go not necessary unnoticed, but certainly disregarded. That fine line between *seeing* and *observing* may occasionally work as much to one's advantage in certain practical instances as it can far more often to the opposite in theoretical explorations. Without by any means intending to, it took merely a few hours before our prey led me right back to his preferred den, at which point I removed myself from the area, that we might spring the trap I had thus far laid.

Holmes paused for a moment, and turned back to Barrett. "One particular detail stands out quite strongly in your explanation of said events. Given that you had begun to search the office, as you say, late into the night, did it not strike you as curious that, within minutes of your arrival into the room, one or more others attempted to burst in, when there was no particular need for said rush, given that they had no reason to believe the room was occupied at the time? Unless, of course, you might have unintentionally made some noise so as to give away your presence therein?"

"No, I had not." Barrett insisted firmly.

"Then either those upon the other side of the door had the most extraordinary case of fortune smiling upon them, or alternatively, your presence there had been made known to them."

"But then, that would mean – " Barrett's face went pale.

" – They knew who you were, where you were, and your purpose in being there."

Fearing that Barrett might very well be on the verge of outright fainting at the revelation, I intervened.

"It could have been that they were conducting an ordinary patrol, of no relevance to him personally. We have no evidence to be sure, in any case." I stared meaningfully at Holmes.

Whether he caught my meaning and overrode my objections, or whether it missed him by altogether, I couldn't be altogether sure. Nevertheless, he persevered.

"This is too elaborate a scheme to be the work of a mere few street thieves, aided and abetted by a singular acting auctioneer of questionable scruples. Consider the artist who clearly so altered the appearance of that man you so excellently subdued. There is a structure here. A web upon which we have only strummed an individual string. Wherein lies the spider at its centre, this is the question we must answer."

"I think we have enough at present to satisfy my superiors, at any rate," Lestrade observed. "Whatever other strange and unwholesome secrets lie at the bottom of this well, we have our man, and with your help, Mr. Barrett, I can all but promise you we shall lay our hands upon the rest, and put the fear of God himself, and that of the noose, upon their soul."

It was but a week later that I read in a newspaper clipping sent to me by Holmes himself, that Scotland Yard had, upon information from a strictly confidential source within the high ranks of British Intelligence, obtained a warrant for the arrest of Mr. Silas Walker and Mr. Oscar Chambers, and had entered their homes, only to find the former empty, and the latter containing the bodies of both respective men. It was publicly believed that both men had fatally shot one another in a heated dispute. Holmes, however, had his own private doubts as to the validity of this conclusion. He himself went to the scene and, over the mild objections of Scotland Yard, thoroughly examined both bodies for some sign that all wasn't as it appeared. However, the few indications he raised were not substantial enough to sway the firmly held position of the officials, and he soon abandoned the effort.

While the police were content with the finality of their own written report of the events I have here disclosed from my own perspective to the reader, and the geopolitical maneuvering that entailed soon ceased to be of significant importance to national stability, Holmes was ever after reluctant to allow me to publish this account. Only in his retiring days, following the full dismantlement of the criminal enterprise directed by the malignant Professor James Moriarty, has my pen now been granted authority to set to paper these finer details of this particular expedition. Whether the now-thankfully deceased Professor himself was the spider Holmes had so acutely envisioned, involving himself in this affair as he did so many others, was never made definitively clear to either Holmes or myself. The answer to that question, as does uncounted others, lies at the bottom of the Reichenbach Falls.

A Bucket's Worth of Help
by David Marcum

Chapter I

At that time of night, Fleet Street, with its various legitimate commercial interests paused until daylight, was mostly deserted. But not entirely, for that thoroughfare, like every street in London, was never truly still, even at three o'clock in the morning, and there were those afoot whose tasks were best completed in darkness.

As Sherlock Holmes and I walked westward through the autumn fog that had settled in from the nearby river like a slow but inexorable overland flood, an ephemeral tide that rose almost before one was aware of it, our footsteps echoed from the pavement and walls of the surrounding buildings in a lonely way that would have never been perceived during the tumultuous daylight hours.

Thankfully the claggy mist was not the choking and acidic sort, or one of the thick and impenetrable white banks of dense oily vapor piled higher than a man's head that left the throat raw while burning the lungs, forcing one to progress forward only inches at a time, one hand held outward so as not to walk into a building or lamppost. Heaven help someone who had to move at speed through such a *ceò* as that. I'd once come upon a man who had been running through such a fog, in terror for his life, and hit a common lamppost straight on. His end was mercifully quick, but the instant of his death must have been terrible. Thankfully on this night, we trod through a mere swirling vapor lying just two or three feet above the ground, giving the setting a dreamlike feeling – but also a sense of heightened awareness, as if one were being hunted.

If Sherlock Holmes's plan had worked, we were.

Ahead of us, under distant gaslights, we saw occasional movement as solitary figures appeared, walking in front of us in the same direction for a moment, or crossing a street from one side to the other, or perhaps tarrying under a lamp to light a cigarette or consider which direction to take. They were but passing shadows, dark shapes that one could only assume held some spark of eternity within them, identifiable as human beings only by their upright carriage. Seen in a different place on such a night – a distant village cemetery during the witching hour, perhaps – they might have been liches or wraiths.

But our prey this night was not any supernatural creature, and whoever was stalking us from ahead and behind was under the mistaken impression that we would soon be victims. As usual, Sherlock Holmes was three steps ahead, and when Richard Magellan made his play, the trap snapped upon him before he quite knew what had occurred.

We paused under the dim gaslight at Chancery Lane, on the northern side of the street. Holmes, as was typical of him, made no sudden move when we heard steady and intentional footsteps approaching us, louder as the distance decreased. There was no need for reaction, as he was already prepared. He had been since our walk had begun just five minutes earlier, when we'd stepped out of Silas Haynor's hovel in Tudor Street, having made our visit quite obvious, and then started walking north to Fleet Street. From there we'd turned west, knowing that we would be accosted long before reaching the Strand. Our pace along the north side of the street had been slow but unremarkable, as befit the conditions. We passed the Mitre Court passage on our left, leading down into King's Bench Walk, and my thoughts imagined the opening as it must have been just a month earlier, jammed with red-headed men, spilling back into Fleet Street. I considered, when writing the matter up, whether I ought to change to name of the location to spare the residents any bother. [1] This thought led me to recall our old friend, Kirbishaw, the attorney who lived at 5A King's Bench Walk. [2] He would be fast asleep now, and I wondered if he'd be surprised at knowing the drama transpiring just a few hundred feet north of his front door.

But those thoughts were chased away when we heard the purposeful and distinctive strides of someone getting closer. Richard Magellan's limp was unmistakable from the echoing footsteps, but such a large and vigorous man as he wasn't slowed by it.

He was tall and broad, by then just forty years of age (although he'd never see forty-one, as he would be predictably murdered in his cell on the night before his trial), with thick black hair and a matching beard, long and lying tangled down his chest. He maintained a fierce scowl under twisted wiry black brows, and one expected that every word from his mouth would be expressed as a towering roar of rage – but in fact, his tone never rose above a low purr, a sly and insinuating voice that demonstrated both his intelligence and his bitter malevolence.

He was from a fine family, with ancestors and brothers who had all served the Realm with distinction for generations. But as Holmes often had occasion to note, sometimes an otherwise healthy tree will form a branch that, for no apparent reason, twists and deforms. Such was the life of Richard Magellan, matriculating at both Oxford and Cambridge (while graduating from neither) and then, by way of dark connections and owed

177

favors and a fair amount of blackmail, establishing himself a successful attorney before a series of scandals inevitably left his career in ruins. And yet, having lost his wife and children – she returned with the boy and girl to her family, who were powerful enough to protect them – and his apparent source of legitimate income, he demonstrated no diminishment of financial resources, continuing to reside in a comfortable home in Bruton Street, on the Conduit Street end, not far from a certain Colonel's house that was located there.

None of Magellan's background seemed immediately relevant, however, when the man himself appeared out of the darkness, his black suit the same color as the night behind him, his legs invisible in the swirling mist. He seemed to glide toward us, and I pondered how such a big man with a limp could move so oddly, his upper body showing no motion as if he were rolling forward on wheels like some levitating *nosferatu*. His angry face appeared to float a fathom above the ground, equivalent to the same distance in the opposite direction that a man at death is supposed to be buried in the earth. The expression on Magellan's bitter face just then put one in mind of death. He had ours fixed in his mind, but Holmes's plans were otherwise.

"Did you think you could just stroll down here and then walk away?" Magellan asked in his low cunning voice as he stopped before us. He waved a massive hand. "As soon as he received your wire, Haynor told me you were coming to see him. Surely you didn't think that he would simply answer your inquiries."

He said it as a statement rather than a question. Holmes nodded, his eyes deeply shadowed from the lamplight by the bill of his fore-and-aft. "Of course not. But apparently you did believe that we were that foolish – else, you wouldn't have broken cover just now to accost us."

Magellan laughed, but there was no joy in it. He suddenly seemed a bit more tense, as if dimly starting to become cognizant that he'd made a mistake by approaching Holmes in such a way. Still, thinking he had the advantage, he pressed on, waving a hand once more, this time, indicating that those unseen should join him.

And they did – six or seven shadowed brutes who appeared from various nearby alleys and narrow passages. They converged slowly, in a tightening circle on all sides. Some carried cudgels or life-preservers, while a few just clenched their fists. It was with effort that I didn't draw my service revolver then, knowing that there were other factors at play here.

"We were waiting," said Magellan, becoming confident once again as his troops assembled. Above the greasy smell of the fog I grasped a new sour smell – the promise of violence wafting off the barely restrained pack surrounding us. And yet, Holmes showed nothing but polite amusement. Still, knowing him as I did, I could see that he was as tense as a tightly stretched wire, the stored and restrained potential energy there ready to snap loose at the slightest instant.

"We followed you right along from Haynor's," Magellan continued. "It wouldn't do to take you there – the old man has been too loyal for your killing to happen upon his own doorstep, within hearing of the neighbors. But the river is close enough from here. You can both toss a prayer toward Temple Church as we pass by." His voice lowered even more as the intensity increased. "Take them, boys!"

And his trained beasts began to move.

But their motion was short-lived as Holmes raised a hand and said, his voice sharper and commanding, "The Professor won't be very happy with you this night, Magellan."

We were outmatched and outnumbered and hadn't made any defense, nor pulled any weapon, and yet mention of James Moriarty stopped the looming thugs in their tracks. To a man, they looked toward Magellan, seeing how he would react.

He didn't change his stance, and yet he was suddenly taut, in that way a hunted animal will freeze with all senses alert for the direction of the fast-approaching threat, ready to jump and flee, but uncertain of his direction. Then he swallowed and asked, his voice softer now, and undoubtedly uncertain, "What do you mean?"

Mention of the Professor in this way, aloud and unexpected, had served to shake our foes on previous occasions. Fear of Moriarty, a name that that those in the shadows dreaded to hear or mention, was a powerful tool.

"You made a mistake this night," replied Holmes. "The mistake of allowing yourself to be removed from the board. The Professor will miss his Bishop – able until now to cut diagonally through any number of difficulties."

"You have nothing," was Magellan's low reply.

"I have everything," countered Holmes. "All three of the railway employees have provided sworn statements. But that isn't all. I also have the evidence in hand of your complicity in the Lyles forgery, the Umbershot explosion, the Connaught Street blackmail affair, and the murder of Jenny Elnathan twenty-one years ago behind the Bodleian Library. Ah, I see that that one stings. You didn't think anyone would ever connect you with poor Jenny, but there's really no escape."

Magellan's face had raced through a plethora expressions before settling on rage, and he was starting to step toward Holmes, his great hand folded in a fist and any fear of the Professor forgotten, when Holmes raised his voice and cried, "*Now, Patterson!*"

And from the same alleyways and passages and nearby streets that Magellan's men had just vacated boiled two-dozen policemen of all ranks, surrounding us in a matter of heartbeats.

With a roar, Magellan reached into his coat, certainly attempting to retrieve a gun. I moved at the same moment, finally pulling forth my own revolver, but neither of our efforts mattered, for Holmes was quicker. With a one-footed pivot and lift, he whipped his own lead-loaded stick savagely across Magellan's raging face, laying out the devil with a flat smack upon the stones, his now-unconscious form licked and tasted by the delicately curious tendrils of fog while the blood from his laid-open face pooled beneath his shaggy head.

We had been uncertain as to how many men Magellan might bring with him. It seemed that he'd felt he could finish us with seven, besides himself, and now it looked as if there were far more policemen than necessary to load them all into the Black Marias which soon joined us, harshly disturbing the silence. But there was a method to bringing so many officers. In those exponentially escalating days of Holmes's struggle against Professor Moriarty, it was sadly uncertain exactly who could be trusted, so extra officers were on hand to keep any that might be on Moriarty's payroll from doing something against our interests – such as stealthily unlocking Magellan's cuffs when no one was looking and letting him scurry away into a nearby alley. With so many officers present, no mischief was possible. And in any case, Magellan was going nowhere fast on his own.

Magellan was roughly placed into a separate Black Maria by himself, slid unconscious along the floor at the feet of four policemen. The seven hoodlums were to be questioned at the Yard, but their leader was set for a more demanding performance. He would be taken to the Woolwich Arsenal, where, upon receiving medical treatment, the Government was most interested in questioning him regarding the recent theft of the prototype for the Caiden-Keller naval gun, a bold and audacious act which would have certainly compromised the national safety and interest in countless spots around the globe had the theft been successful.

Holmes had been recruited by his brother Mycroft when the gun went missing, instructed to work separately from the official Government investigation, as it was uncertain whose loyalties could be trusted. The gun, so far the only one built, had vanished while being shipped from the Arsenal to Portsmouth. The special train upon which it was loaded had passed through the Three Bridges Station without incident or question, but when the train arrived in Crawley [3] just a few moments later, the car with the gun was missing, with the two cars that had been on either side of it now joined to one another. The method used to steal it had been fast and clever, as the train had arrived in Crawley within a minute of being on time.

It had taken very little for Holmes to determine that the gun and its car had been shunted onto a hastily constructed temporary siding when the train was stopped, broken apart, and reassembled. He saw no need for false modesty, pointing out that the signs he observed would have been initially missed by most involved, though seen eventually, and the gun would have been completely removed from its hiding place before the scheme of misdirection was fully comprehended and investigated.

Of greater interest and effort was how a squad of a dozen soldiers and the train's crew could, to a man, have been suborned into being complicit with the theft – for they must have been in order for the train to have been so efficiently stopped and the car with the gun moved along the abandoned siding where it was found. Holmes, recognizing in the plan Professor Moriarty's arrogant and ambitious signature, had quickly nudged the investigation into verifying that every one of the men set to guard the gun, as well has the crew of the train, had been mercilessly pressured into cooperation by vicious threats to their families, as well as the selective taking of hostages. As the truth was uncovered, with one man and then another breaking down and confessing his unwilling involvement, it became apparent that no direct connection could be made with Moriarty. With the great naval gun recovered and the hostages already freed following the theft, Holmes recommended leniency toward all those involved.

Holmes recognized from questioning the train's engineer that the man he described, waiting in a carriage and watching while the engineer's part in the plot was explained and proof provided that his daughter had been taken, was unmistakably Robert Magellan. Holmes had long known that the great bearded villain was one of the Professor's trusted lieutenants, and it was then that he decided to make use of a long-withheld resource of his own: Silas Haynor, a man who had spent his life dabbling poorly in many criminal activities, and who had some connections to Magellan. But older than those were Holmes's own connections with Haynor, whom he had met and aided years before, when living in Montague Street.

In those days, Holmes had been attempting to commence his career as a consulting detective, but with cases quite thin on the ground, he'd spent a great deal of time in study, pursuing topics that he felt might be of use as his profession became more successful. Much effort was spent pursuing mastery of various subjects in the British Museum, located adjacent to his Montague Street rooms, but he also managed to make connections and associations with individuals of varying degrees of wickedness within London's criminal community, convincing them to teach him a surfeit of useful skills. Silas Haynor was one of these, and during the course of their association, Holmes had found opportunity to rescue Haynor's wayward daughter from a particularly verminous master in the East End – earning Haynor's eternal, if secret, gratitude.

Knowing that Haynor was associated with Magellan, it was easy for Holmes to make himself seen when asking Haynor for information. It could only help Haynor to shore up his own reputation within the criminal community when he, as a good soldier, immediately reported this to Magellan, who lost no time in arranging his aborted trap for Sherlock Holmes – and me as well, the satellite of little interest to Magellan who happened to be carried along to the meeting.

Inspector Patterson, the Scotland Yard inspector who was so deeply involved in building the case against Professor James Moriarty, was speaking with Holmes, arranging that he and I would be at Magellan's questioning in Woolwich in the morning – now just a few short hours away – when Holmes glanced over at the men being loaded into the Black Marias. He held up a hand to pause Patterson's comment and then stepped that way, apparently recognizing one of the seemingly anonymous fellows.

"McMurdo?" Holmes asked, surprised. "What in Heaven's name are you doing mixed in with this lot?"

He stepped over and pulled the shackled man to one side. I joined them. Patterson looked as if he would as well, but then he turned a different direction and began giving instructions to a sergeant.

The deep-chested man, who I recognized as one who had brought no weapon, choosing instead to rely on his fists, was somewhat shorter than his compatriots. He had been facing in the direction of the carriage in which he was to climb. He seemed at first as if he didn't hear Holmes's question. Then it became apparent that he did, but instead wanted to ignore it. He paused, and his great shoulders heaved with a deep sigh. He turned to face my friend, his protruding and heavy-set features carrying an expression of shame.

"Hello, Mr. Holmes," he rumbled, his broad shoulders slumped in defeat. "I'm sorry."

"Sorry?"

"For being part o' this – for being here tonight to attack you. I should ha' known you'd be out in front of us. I . . . I hoped you wouldn't recognize me when we . . . when we walked you down to the river . . . ." His voice faded.

"Why are you here, McMurdo?" Holmes asked, his voice dropping significantly. "You don't have any association with these people – or you shouldn't. What happened?"

The big man closed his eyes, and then squeezed them tight. A teardrop formed at the corner of one eye, just visible in the nearly useless lamp light. "What does it matter, Mr. Holmes? I'm fair caught."

Rarely had I seen someone appear to be so defeated. McMurdo was much changed from when I first met him a couple of years before, when he'd answered the door of Pondicherry Lodge in Upper Norwood. [4] On that night, the big man had looked at us with distrustful yet twinkling eyes, reflecting in the light of the lantern he held to investigate the unexpected visitors. That day had been a dreary one, with a dense and drizzly yellow fog lying low upon the great city, and mud-coloured clouds drooping sadly over the damp-slicked streets, and by sunset a great slimy vapor hung over the capital and the surrounding counties. McMurdo's suspicion of strangers had been in accord with the day's weather.

"I don't know none o' your friends," he'd explained to our guide, Thaddeus Sholto.

"Oh, yes you do, McMurdo," Holmes had replied. "I don't think you can have forgotten me. Don't you remember that amateur who fought three rounds with you at Alison's rooms on the night of your benefit four years back?"

"Not Mr. Sherlock Holmes!" exclaimed the big man, now clearly identified as a former prize-fighter, and apparently one of the bodyguards employed at Pondicherry Lodge. "God's truth! How could I have mistook you? If instead o' standin' there so quiet you had just stepped up and given me that cross-hit of yours under the jaw, I'd ha' known you without a question."

After he and Holmes exchanged a few further comments about the old days, we were admitted to the great house. My observations of McMurdo during that short period of time had led me to the conclusion that he was a good man, salt of the earth and a stalwart citizen, despite being on the sometimes-shady side of the law in terms of prize-fighting. And yet, now we found him under the orders of Professor Moriarty, by way of Robert Magellan.

"What happened?" repeated Sherlock Holmes.

McMurdo shook his head. "I can't say. It's . . . I have to stick to what I agreed."

Holmes was silent for a long moment, while McMurdo's eyes kept glancing at him, and then away, like a cowed dog who cannot directly meet one's gaze. Finally Holmes replied, his voice now almost too soft to hear.

"As I recall, you have a daughter. Is that not so?"

McMurdo's eyes widened then, almost in terror as if some secret had been exposed. He wasn't afraid to look at Holmes now, and he started to shake his head.

"Not to fear," whispered Holmes, his tone low but reassuring. "I understand. We'll speak to you soon, at Scotland Yard. No one will know. In the meantime, stay strong."

Then he backed away and raised his voice. "I should have known you'd come to such a sorry end, McMurdo. You always did scoff at the law." He turned toward Patterson. "Get this one to the Yard along with the rest of them."

He stepped away. McMurdo gave no sign of acknowledgement, instead allowing himself to be turned by a constable and shuffled into one of the prisoners' wagons.

Holmes stepped over to Patterson and whispered a word, and then walked five feet or so down the pavement, stopping to rub the bridge of his nose. I joined him and he said softly, "I'll apologize to Mrs. Watson tomorrow for extending your day even further. I'm afraid, if you're willing, that there's more work to be done – Now. Tonight. We need to get about disentangling McMurdo and his daughter from Moriarty's nets."

Chapter II

"A daughter," I said as Holmes and I walked down the Strand, the night still pressing around us, but now without the apparent threat of Magellan's troops slowly encircling us. "You believe that McMurdo has been forced into Moriarty's service by threats against his daughter – in the same way that the soldiers and train crew were manipulated into helping steal the naval gun."

"It seemed a logical leap," Holmes replied, "and if I'm not mistaken, McMurdo's reaction confirmed it. I've known him for a long time. He isn't the type to willingly involve himself in this type of work."

"Just how deep does Moriarty's influence extend?" I asked with angry exasperation, although after observing the Professor's pervasive influence for a number of years, the question was rather rhetorical.

"Deeper every day," was the weary answer. "Initially, he was a shadowy figure at the top of a large criminal pyramid, known only to the few lieutenants who have access to him – Moran, Magellan, Bassick, and a few others. You'll recall when I first became aware of him and would try to explain this arrangement to various inspectors – Lanner and MacDonald for instance – they would be skeptical. Thank Heavens Lestrade and Gregson and Bradstreet had more sense from the beginning, and were willing to work with us. MacDonald was convinced soon enough

– he has a sharp mind – but I still have some questions about Lanner. Keep that in your thoughts, Watson, as we move forward."

"But my question stands," I answered. "How deep have Moriarty's tentacles twisted through society's fabric? We couldn't even be entirely certain of the loyalty of the constables on scene tonight."

Holmes nodded. "Tentacles is an apt image at this point. My initial description of Moriarty as a thin-legged spider sitting at the center of a web, feeling every vibration upon every strand, seems rather simplistic now. In those days, he was aware of everything, but rarely needed to involve himself – only when some complicated question arose. He mostly sat back, taking his financial cut that drifted upward to him from the many London's crimes, as inevitable as capillary action draws a liquid up a thread-like tube, defying gravity. But as his ambitions have grown, he's allowed his existence to become more widely known, using it as a force for intimidation, and increasing his influence.

"I believe that he changed – that he *wanted* people to be aware of him – after he fell from the Tower while trying to steal the Crown Jewels. [5] Before that, he'd treated his organization as an intellectual game – with me as the player on the other side of the chess board. After that affair, and his injuries, he could no longer pretend to be the innocent and persecuted mathematics professor, just trying to live a quiet life as an Army coach. He was known, and he realized the value of his reputation in coercing people to his will that hadn't already voluntarily joined him. And when he'd swelled his ranks all he could by that method, he became more aggressive still – using threats against family members."

He shook his head, and I asked, "Can he not be stopped?"

"You've asked me that before," Holmes replied, a tightness to his voice. "And what has been my answer? *You must give me time.* We have progressed quite far from five years ago, when this menace first became much more apparent. From his initial mistakes, I've been able – with the help of a number of good men such as yourselves and trustworthy policemen and Government officials, and a number of anonymous citizens whose aid will never be acknowledged – to slowly force Moriarty into a corner. But he will fight – like a rat, he'll fight harder now than ever. The next few months . . . things are going to become much more complicated. And dangerous – for all of us. There are so many pieces to watch. In many ways, the moves and counter-moves with Moriarty are even more complex than when we fought the Rippers." [6]

"But there were many of them," I said, "an abundance of killers, each with their own motives, working loosely in harness when it suited them to fulfill their various conspiracies. In the end, Moriarty is but one man. You've already removed Magellan, one of his lieutenants, and two others as well. His supporting base is being crumbled, one pillar at a time. Unlike the Rippers who hid in a dozen different rat-holes, you know where to find Moriarty – his house in Russell Square, or the Limehouse tunnels. And every day, just as he intimidates someone into his unwilling service, you free two more of them – and they will see that. They'll see that he isn't invincible. That he can be beaten."

"Ah, but they'll also wonder and worry if it will be their own daughters whose throats are cut before I'm able to bring him down." He sighed. "Regardless, Watson, it's all coming to a head, and will be over in a few months. Moriarty is incommoded and inconvenienced and hampered, and with any luck, he'll be finished sooner rather than later."

Our conversation, not the first upon that topic, but rather a repetition of an oft-discussed subject meant to give us some comfort during the battle, had continued as we progressed down the Strand, turning left onto Wellington Street. Although offered a ride in a police vehicle, Holmes had wanted to walk, giving as his reason that he didn't want to arrive at Scotland Yard too quickly, forcing us to loiter while the prisoners were brought in and separated. I realized, however, that he also wanted time to think.

From Wellington we had emerged onto the Embankment, keeping up a steady pace until we reached the new Yard buildings, just across the road from Westminster Pier. Like everyone, I can never see various spots without associating them to memories of what occurred there, and I suppose that I'll never view that pier with recalling the night of 10 September, 1888, when Holmes and I boarded a police launch to follow Jonathan Small as he began his dash for freedom on the *Aurora*. Now, with the river fog rising to the level of the roadway, there was nothing to see but an undulating white blanket, shining with a faint luminescence in the darkness. If not for the gentle creakings of the moorings, the dock and the boats tied there might not have existed.

Scotland Yard is never truly quiet, even in the hours before dawn. Officers of all rank are always going here and there, quickly or with more leisured steps, all intent on their tasks. That night, a number of them were known to us, and they nodded in our direction – some more friendly than others – but none spoke as we moved deeper into the building, recognized and unhindered, toward the area where the inspector's offices are located.

Holmes has occasionally told me of his early days as a consulting detective, when interactions with the police were often frustrating at best. In his early twenties then, and fresh up to London from his abandoned university pursuits, I could imagine the impression he made, frequently, when bursting into the Yard, demanding to speak to someone with authority, either sharing information that wasn't requested or trusted, or demanding assistance or some fact toward completing his own investigation. (In truth, I had met him just a few years after this, first encountering him mere days before he turned twenty-seven years old, and he'd still displayed many of those traits.) There were some inspectors, back in those long-past days of the 1870's, who did listen to him and learned to trust him, and then to make use of his unique skills, realizing that his assistance would be invaluable toward clearing their own cases and obtaining justice – Inspectors Plummer and Nettings, for instance, and Lestrade and Gregson.

Patterson's office was empty – but that wasn't unusual, as he did not follow the typical inspector's way of doing things. Often out in the city, in disguise and amongst the lower elements to a great degree, he had made himself an expert on the subject of the underworld – a spider, in his own way, comparable to Moriarty at the center of a web. Initially Patterson hadn't fit in at the Yard at all, but it had made no difference to him as he set about his tasks, and as his successes steadily accumulated and his usefulness became apparent, he was left alone to carry on as he saw fit. He and Holmes had formed a good working relationship from Patterson's early days, especially after the matter of the Dicky Ferrin embezzlement scandal, and I always believed that Holmes had done much to help inculcate Patterson in the methods of the London criminal element, giving advice and instruction in many ways, including that of successful disguise.

Based on Holmes's whispered instructions in Fleet Street, Patterson had placed McMurdo into a separate interrogation room along a less-used hallway in the building's basement. It was there that we found him, after being admitted by Constable Wilkins, one of the officers that we most trusted. If Wilkins had been compromised by Moriarty, we were indeed in deep difficulties.

Wilkins shut the door behind us, leaving us alone with the prisoner.

McMurdo was no longer the defeated slump-shouldered man we'd encountered in Fleet Street. Instead, he was alert, tense, barely able to stay seated. His eyes were wide now, with the whites showing 'round the pupils as if he was on some sort of stimulant. I wondered what had come over him, and if we would soon be in a physical confrontation should he choose to make some move against us, but it was quickly apparent that his motivation was basic fear.

"My daughter," he said, his voice scraped hoarse with tension. "You mustn't – You can't cross these people, Mr. Holmes! Just let me take my punishment! It's the only way they'll let her be."

"So they don't have her yet," Holmes replied. "It's just the threat of harm that's been keeping you on the lead.

McMurdo nodded. "She's watched – all o' the time. I couldn't ha' taken her away if I'd tried. They're too many of them – everywhere. It was easier to do what they bid and then just hope . . . I'm always hoping. Watching – for a way, you see. But I can trust no one, and have nowhere to go . . . ."

"You can trust me, McMurdo," replied Sherlock Holmes.

"Tell us about her," I interjected, hoping to calm him as he became more agitated at his intolerable situation.

McMurdo nodded and closed his eyes, perhaps sensing that relating his story was more productive. He licked his lips and locked the fingers of both hands together, large arthritic knuckles white underneath ancient scars.

"It was just over twenty years ago," he said. "I was but a lad in my twenties. Oh, I see your surprise, Doctor. I know I look to be sixty if I'm a day, but I've lived rough. Back then I wasn't so unpleasant to gaze upon, and I won the heart of a beautiful girl, my Lydia. We were both in service then, at a manor decorated with fine old copper beeches, not five miles on the far side of Winchester. It was a fine place back then. She worked as a maid, and I was in the stables. It's not great story one way or another – we were married and had a good life, and a year or so later we had a little girl, Jane. When our girl was but three, Lydia sickened and died. It was a tragedy, of course, but no different than what drops into other's lives. My heart wasn't in that place any longer, so I found another job closer to London, another manor south of the city doing the same work, and I settled in with my daughter.

"I married again, a good woman – a childless widow – who was already working there as the assistant cook. She helped raise Jane – as good a second mother as a girl could have. It was then that my size became of more interest – I became more broad as I aged and worked – and I became involved in the fancy – bare-knuckle boxing, and then prize-fighting. The owner of the manor had a fascination for it, and I was his fighter. It was just enjoyable, and nothing wrong, and I earned some extra money. You'll recall that's how you and I met, Mr. Holmes. My second wife died in '84, and you fought me at Alison's, at the benefit they arranged for me.

"I wasn't as broken up by Edith's death as I had been Lydia's. Edith was a good woman, but I'd never loved her like Lydia. Jane and I did fine and the next years passed. I continued to fight for a while, but I was getting too old and knew it. I was already worn out from the other work, too, truth be told, and when young Bartholomew Sholto put about that he was hiring bodyguards for the Lodge, not far from where Jane and I lived, it suited me down to the ground. He was an odd fellow, was Mister Bartholomew

– though not as odd as his brother, Mister Thaddeus, I'll swear – but the work was easy beyond telling. I just had to be present, you see, in case some danger might show itself. None ever did – not until that terrible night. Meanwhile, the two brothers tore up the grounds of the lodge like terriers digging for rats – never saying why, but we all knew they thought that their old dad had buried an Indian treasure.

"Then, after that night in '88 when you visited, everything changed. After Mr. Bartholomew was found dead, and that there had truly been a real treasure, there was no longer a place for me – for any of us. Mr. Thaddeus sold the lodge and went back to India. He'd always had a fascination with that place. The land developers knocked down the house and started cutting up the grounds into little streets and lanes, and building tiny cottages everywhere. I always half-suspected that Major Sholto really might have hidden some part of his treasure there on the grounds – he was ever a canny and suspicious sort – and that some house-builder maybe found it while scraping and digging and kept his mouth shut and is now living fine from the proceeds.

"In any case, Jane was of age then, and I found her a position with a seamstress off the Holborn, and moved us up to London. I've been working for a pub in Clerkenwell. The work is harder than I'd been used to for many a year with the Mr. Bartholomew, but I had to do something, and I was making do. Then, during the middle of this past year, a man who said he worked for Magellan came by, letting me know that my muscle would be working for them from now on."

His voice had grown dry, and I rose and opened the door, asking Wilkins to find some water. He nodded and departed, and I returned to my seat.

Holmes gave McMurdo a chance to pause, stating, "I've heard variations of this before. You were to keep your regular job, but be available when called upon for whatever little task was required. You might have initially resisted – " McMurdo nodded. " – but it was quickly explained to you that they knew where your daughter was. Who she was working for, her place of residence, her schedule, her routes to and from work and other errands – everything that they would need to know, should they choose that some harm would befall her. And the only way this might be prevented was if you capitulated to their requests."

McMurdo blinked while he followed Holmes's explanation, but seeming to decide that it was correct, he nodded again.

"Is she safe right now?" I asked.

McMurdo nodded, but a bit of the wildness came back to his eyes. He leaned forward. "I think so. She was as of last night. They don't call me very often, but when they do, I jump. I went to see her last night before

189

joining Magellan's men – he'd heard of your meeting with Silas Haynor, and planned to put an end to you." He looked at Holmes, a pained expression twisting his face. "I've been with them before when a man has been beaten, or his shop ransacked. I was ashamed. But I've never . . . I was never in on a killing job. A few were like me – they had no choice. But some of the others were looking forward to it."

As Wilkins returned with the water and I poured him a glass, McMurdo looked back at me. As the constable departed, the old fighter continued. "My daughter was safe at home last night, in a small lodging house not far from where she works. But I fear, now, that since tonight has gone wrong, they'll punish us – all of us – by taking it out on those who are precious. You know how . . . you've heard how the Professor is." He whispered Moriarty's title, as if saying even that word aloud would attract the man's fiery gaze from whatever eyrie he was perched upon. "It wasn't our fault. We were just there to do as told. But he might think that one of us turned traitor, or got word to you ahead of time. Or he might just decide to teach a lesson to everyone – to show what a hard man he is."

He knotted his fingers tighter. "I'm being ground between two stones, Mr. Holmes. I did what they asked to save my daughter, to keep her safe, and still she may be punished. And what can I do? I'm in here, and there's no one who can protect her. No one!"

Holmes leaned forward, catching McMurdo's panicked eyes, and holding them until the big man had calmed himself.

"I will protect her, McMurdo. You can count on that. Now, I have many questions, and there is work to be done."

Chapter III

Although it was well after six a.m. when we walked out of the Yard, the November sky was still dark. Holmes frowned, muttered that, "It cannot be helped," and walked to the carriage that had just been arranged for our use. He'd already used the telephone inside to call and let his brother Mycroft know that we were on our way, though without providing a great deal of detail.

I've remarked elsewhere about the fixed rails upon which Mycroft Holmes carried out his day: From his lodgings at No. 48 Pall Mall to his unassuming office in Whitehall, and then back to Pall Mall, this time to No. 78, the Diogenes Club, just across the street from his rooms. [7] He had set times when he might be found at each and, like every normal man who wasn't out all night hunting criminals, he would be at home at this particular early hour.

Mycroft Holmes had cultivated a routine for himself that thoroughly suited his tastes, and especially the time spent at the Diogenes Club reflected the luxury-seeking aspect of his personality – but one ought never make the mistake from observing this aspect of his life that he was indolent or lazy. His heavy-set frame might prefer time spent seated in his specially made red-leather chair in the Diogenes Stranger's Room over movement, and he certainly appreciated the finer aspects of food and drink, but in no way was this to be taken for lethargic or shiftless loafing. His mind was always working, making connections and seeing patterns, wherever he was and at whatever time of day. Even as the clock over Parliament was chiming the seventh morning hour, we found Mycroft Holmes awake and alert, awaiting our report and the reason for our visit.

Once we were seated in Mycroft's study and had accepted strong black coffee and warm buttered scones, Mycroft gestured for his brother to speak. Holmes succinctly explained what had occurred during the previous night, leading to our interview with McMurdo.

"After we gained the basic points of how he was being pressured into assisting Magellan," Holmes stated, "it became apparent that three of the other men arrested tonight are in similar straits. Watson and I then spoke to each of them as well, although gaining their trust – all of them strangers to us who only know us by reputation – was initially difficult. We soon confirmed that in each case, however, that ongoing threats against their family members are what is keeping them in the Professor's servitude."

"What sort of threats? Death?"

"Or worse. McMurdo has a daughter. He was told that she would be taken and sold to an African brothel. The same for another man, Kildeane. The third, Belmont, has a sick wife that he adores and is terrified of losing – it was the simple threat of her particularly grim murder that keeps him in line. The fourth, Theobald, has a wife and small children. Their deaths, trapped in a house fire, were guaranteed if he doesn't cooperate."

Mycroft's eyes narrowed. I recalled discussions two years earlier, held during the months when we'd been attempting to catch the various Rippers, and how Mycroft and I had agreed that there was more suffering in the world – and the nation's capital – than could be helped. We'd each felt the same frustration, and Mycroft had commented, "It's as if one were trying to stop the incoming tide with a bucket." But in this instance, there were specific people that needed help – Holmes and I had met them and seen the anguish in their faces – and help could be provided, though it only be one small bucket's worth.

"What would you have me do?" Mycroft asked.

Holmes answered without hesitation. "I want you to take these men and their families away – in the same way you offered an alternative to the train crew and the soldiers and their families."

Holmes hadn't hinted to me his intentions, and I looked at him with some of the same surprise that Mycroft evinced.

"Take them?" I asked. "Where? Who is being taken?"

Holmes glanced at me, and then re-fixed his gaze upon his brother, who replied, "In the end, the only way that we could convince the soldiers and the crew to explain why they had helped Magellan carry out Moriarty's plan was to promise them safety – absolute safety – and the only safety that they believed possible was to completely leave England in secret to escape Moriarty's sphere of influence – at least for the foreseeable future – and take on new identities far away."

Holmes glanced at me. "They all felt – rightly so – that there is no safety on the Continent, and they instead insisted on relocation to America. They didn't realize that the Professor has reciprocal agreements with American criminals. We saw that in '88, when Moriarty provided assistance to the killer who came looking for Birdy Edwards."

I recalled the matter – and how Holmes had still ended up beating Moriarty in the end. [8]

Meanwhile, Mycroft and started to purse his lips, compressing them in and out while nearly closing his eyes as he considered Sherlock Holmes's new request. After a moment he took a massive deep breath and released it, almost with a sigh, before pulling himself straighter. His right finger was slowly inscribing a circle upon the arm of his chair, the only sign that he was somewhat perturbed.

"The plans to remove the fifteen men – soldiers and crew – and their entire families is already in place. In fact, tonight they'll be quietly taken by train to Liverpool, where they'll be discreetly placed on a ship bound for South Africa."

"Were there any problems extracting everyone?"

"Not at all. None of their families were actually being held hostage, only watched, and we were careful to spirit each person away at some moment yesterday when they were alone. The soldiers' families were easier than those of the railway men, obviously. There were a few unmarried soldiers whose parents were being threatened, but they have been approached and are willing to cooperate, with the understanding that when Moriarty and his organization have both been eliminated, they can return to England and resume their normal lives." He let a short silence fall into the conversation, as if reminding his brother that this immense task still needed completion, and the sooner the better.

A look of understanding passed between them, and then Mycroft asked, "How many more people are we talking about?"

"Not that many. The four men, two wives, two grown daughters, and two small children."

"Removing them may be a bit more difficult than the others," replied Mycroft, "as they are certainly being watched more closely, even as we speak. Yet it can be done, and adding ten more individuals to our plans isn't a burdensome problem. But the ship leaves *tonight*, Sherlock. It cannot be delayed. We used only our most trusted men to extract the families and transport them to Liverpool. You must do the same. They must be at the dock on time, and undetected. If any whiff of this is understood by Moriarty's agents – "

"I understand," said Holmes.

"And have you considered," added Mycroft, "that Moriarty may use this to his advantage? Once these people disappear, seemingly vanished without a trace, he can falsely spread the word that *he* was the one who removed them, making him seem even more omniscient and dangerous? And how can such a claim be countered without revealing the truth and possibly placing the families in new danger?"

"I believe that I've worked that out as well. We'll get out in front of Moriarty, leaking that each of the men has provided sworn statements of his involvement – not for the public press, but to be spread as gossip across London. After all, it's true that we'll have their statements in return for our help, and we can imply that they've been relocated to the Continent. Moriarty's attention will be misdirected, and it will undermine the notion that he's invincible. Once a few start to lose their fear of him, more will follow."

Mycroft nodded, but I could see he wasn't entirely convinced. "It won't fool Moriarty. I suspect hinting that everyone has headed east to the Continent will only serve to alert him that they are anywhere else *but* the Continent. Still, we can only try." He leaned forward, to emphasize, "But you must have them in Liverpool by *tonight*. The ship won't wait."

We returned to Scotland Yard by way of the waiting police vehicle. Holmes remained in quiet thought, his only comment being, "Patterson will not be pleased."

And he was correct. The inspector, living as he did with absolutely fanatical dedication toward stopping Moriarty to the point that he spent more time undercover than as himself, had an absolute black-and-white vision of justice and punishment. In his mind, the seven men arrested with Magellan were equally guilty, whether they had willingly joined Moriarty's cause or been coerced. He understood the pressure the men were under, forced to accompany Magellan on his various villainous outings, but that made no difference to him.

"They had a *choice!*" he whined irritably. I was reminded of some hint of gossip I'd once heard from Lestrade or Gregson that Patterson's father had been some low-level criminal. "And last night wasn't the first time they've assisted Magellan. We have confessions from all of them – the coerced and otherwise – as to numerous earlier beatings and other destructive mayhem. It isn't right to let some go free and for others to pay their debt!"

"Maybe not," agreed Lestrade, who along with Gregson and Bradstreet, were using their seniority to overrule Patterson. "But this is the way it's going to be."

"Think of it," added Gregson, "as tactically withdrawing from a skirmish to win the war."

"And rescuing these men and their families," Bradstreet contributed, "can be used as a tactical move against the Professor."

The six of us were crowded into Lestrade's small office, a secret meeting to explain what needed to be done. Patterson had erupted against the plan from the beginning, but when he realized that he had no choice in the matter, he shifted positions to add his practical knowledge toward safely extracting the various family members.

As the plans were developed for rescuing the families of each of the four men, Holmes indicated that his Irregulars, that band of street urchins who were pledged to being his eyes and ears, seeing everything, would be of great assistance. This time Lestrade disagreed.

"I'll admit their usefulness over the years," he stated. "But Mr. Holmes – do you think it's wise to keep using them right now? A few of those lads, such as Wiggins and the Peake brothers, are your known associates. I'm not just speaking of involving them in these current events. If Moriarty decides to push back, he's going to use whatever leverage he can find – and him trapping and hurting those boys, no matter how canny they are, is a very real possibility that you must consider."

It isn't often that Sherlock Holmes has failed to take all the factors of a problem into consideration, but I believe that this was the first time this particular concern had surfaced for him. I knew that he'd taken precautions – both those I knew about and others that I didn't – to protect my wife and Mrs. Hudson, and likely me as well, but to him, the anonymity of the Irregulars was such a given that anything to the contrary had escaped notice. He'd always been proud that he'd recruited these lads (and lasses) who could so effortlessly vanish into the shadows – but Moriarty commanded creatures whose normal demesne was those same dark and lonesome places.

Holmes nodded. "You're right, Lestrade. I believe that for the next few months – until this matter is resolved – the Irregulars should maintain a very low profile. And there are a few who should specifically rusticate in the countryside for their own safety."

With information provided by the four prisoners who would be leaving, we soon had a clear idea of who to retrieve and where to find them. Without the use of his Irregulars to create distractions, Holmes pivoted to some of his older associates, including Porky Johnson and Burton Scott, two semi-criminals who both owed Holmes more than they could repay. They were not reformed, and they were not above recidivism in their day-to-day lives, but in their own ways, they were trustworthy, and neither had any love for Moriarty, nor were they under any obligation to him. Holmes had verified this on several occasions, and he was satisfied with their loyalty.

In each case, Holmes's agents were the first to quietly infiltrate the streets and alleys and passages around where the family members were to be extricated. When Moriarty's observers were located, word was passed back to waiting policemen, who just happened to walk by a moment later. Then, Lestrade or Gregson would initiate a conversation with the individual in question, phrasing questions offensively so that the matter quickly escalated to the point where the watcher was led away under arrest, allowing the family member to be approached.

McMurdo's daughter was the first. When informed that the coast was clear, the prize-fighter met her as she left home to walk to her place of employment. Without wasting any words, he told her to return inside immediately and gather what she needed to go away – clothing and valuable personal items – and to be back in five minutes.

"And be sure to bring your mother's photograph," he added.

"What? But Papa – I don't understand! Who are these men? Can you come inside too?"

McMurdo looked at Holmes, who was standing there with Bradstreet and me. Holmes shook his head.

"No," replied McMurdo. "No time. Things are in a hurry. I'll be waiting right here – and don't tell a soul inside what you're doing!"

She was back in ten minutes – understandable, given her confusion, and, as Bradstreet commented while we hurried away, impressive that she was able to quickly determine what was needed and what could be left behind.

"It wasn't so difficult," Jane McMurdo replied, nearly out of breath. She nodded to the carpetbag that Bradstreet was carrying for her. "We don't have very much, so packing what was needed was easy and obvious."

The procedure was completed successfully three other times, gathering in Thomas Kildeane's daughter from her job at an Aldgate pub, Michael Belmont's sick wife from their lodgings in Varden Street, not far south of the London Hospital in Whitechapel, and Andrew Theobald's wife and two young children from Rotherhithe.

It was only at the latter where any complications arose. Gregson had started conversing with Moriarty's watcher, heating the encounter to the point where the suddenly angry young man would be temporarily taken into custody by the accompanying constables. But unlike the previous three instances, this young man, a lanky and greasy specimen in his early twenties who resembled a long-faced feral dog, instead chose to run. Fortunately for me, as I was feeling rather underused, he chose to escape by way of the street in which I was waiting with Holmes and Bradstreet.

Holmes, I'm certain, would have moved quickly and effectively in order to stop the fellow, but I stepped forward first, shoving my stick between the legs of the Professor's man, causing him to take a hard sprawl onto the pavement. After he was in custody, my quick examination showed no serious injuries. The sudden loss of his front teeth upon the roadway was only an improvement to his appearance. As we left, several children ran from the nearby shadows to collect them.

By noon, all four families were reunited and had been safely smuggled undetected into the cellar of the Royal Albert Hall. A special train car had been arranged for the 1:43 from Euston Station, and everyone was transported and safely placed aboard with time to spare. Having gone this far, Holmes and I agreed that we wished to see the matter through to the end – at least, the portion that was the end of how we could help. After the ship departed, the safety of all concerned would be in Mycroft's hands.

I sent a wire to Mary and rejoined Holmes on the platform, just minutes before we were to depart. We were both scanning surrounding crowd intently, as were the three police inspectors who had accompanied us. We observed nothing to concern us, and we were aboard and seated as the train left the station. Three hours later, our party had joined those already sent ahead by Mycroft, and not long after, the ship set sail.

"I don't know how to thank you, Mr. Holmes," said McMurdo before we took our leave of him. I could see that he was rather dazed at how quickly events had moved, but that was no different than the rest of the group. Anyone would have reacted the same way – going about one's business as normal in the morning, and then suddenly plucked out of routine and re-routed to the other side of the world. Around us, some of the families were just learning why such a move was necessary, having had no previous idea that Moriarty had gained a hold upon the men by so effectively threatening their family members.

I knew that for Holmes, no thanks were necessary, and that he was already considering the next move in this deadly game of chess where there would be only one winner.

Not long after, as we partook of a small meal in the station buffet, waiting for our return train to London, Gregson looked at Holmes, a frown darkening his light features.

"We can't rescue all of them, Mr. Holmes. This strategy worked this time, but what about the next? And the time after that? And this solution was only successful because these men were being forced into Moriarty's service. How do we stop those who join him willingly? What do we do about them?"

Holmes, who had only picked at his food in a distracted fashion, didn't answer for the longest time. But finally his gaze rose, and he looked at each of us in turn.

"We are restricted by laws, and decency, and doing the right thing. Moriarty is not. We're constrained by the fact that we are unwilling to cause damage and hurt. He is not. We're limited in our responses, lest we cross the line and use Moriarty's methods. He has no such limits.

"But what we can do," he added, "is to be *better* than Moriarty."

"How?" responded Lestrade. "How do we do that? We don't even know who we can trust. He has probably infiltrated the police. He probably has agents within high levels of government, and even some of the nobility may be under his sway. What advantage can we find?"

"We have the numbers," answered Holmes. "Do not forget that there are more good men than bad. When we find Moriarty's agents, we can convert them or prosecute and incarcerate them – or if necessary, legally execute them if warranted. That may not seem like much when they have no qualms at executing those who oppose them, but in the end, right will be victorious. But as we've seen, victories come with cost, and while victory will eventually be ours, there will a price to pay."

And victory was ours, but it required a terrible payment. Less than half-a-year later, Moriarty's organization was destroyed, and the Professor along with it, atop a remote Swiss waterfall. As Holmes wrote, just before he joined Moriarty in mortal and final combat, "*I am pleased to think that I shall be able to free society from any further effects of his presence, though I fear that it is at a cost which will give pain to my friends, and especially, my dear Watson, to you.*"

The cost wasn't just the personal one suffered by Holmes and the friends who miss him. England, though free of Moriarty's pervasive evil, was left without one if its greatest champions. Still, as McMurdo and I were discussing the other day, following his recent return from Africa to his home now freed of threat, how the good accomplished by Holmes during his lifetime is a powerful and enduring testament not only to himself, but to all of those who suffer and sacrifice to protect what's good and decent in the world.

JHW
12 April, 1893

NOTES

1. In fact, Watson did change the name from "Mitre Court" to the fictionalized "Pope's Court". (See "The Red-Headed League", October 25, 1890.)
2. For more about Kirbishaw, the resident of No. 5A King's Bench Walk in the 1890's, see "The Curious Cardboard Boxes" in *The Collected Papers of Sherlock Holmes – Volume V: Chronicles*, and *The Strand Magazine*, Issue LIX, 2019. To learn how the later more-famous resident of No. 5A, Dr. John Thorndyke, came to inhabit those rooms, see "The Inner Temple Intruder", found in *The Collected Papers of Sherlock Holmes – Volume III: Accounts*, and also in *Sherlock Holmes and the Great Detectives.*
3. This map shows the area in West Sussex between the Three Bridges Station (top right) and the Crawley Station (bottom left). Though not specified in Watson's manuscript, it's possible that the temporary siding used to hide the train car was constructed in a wooded area about halfway between the stations, on the south side of the tracks. This area is still there to the present day.

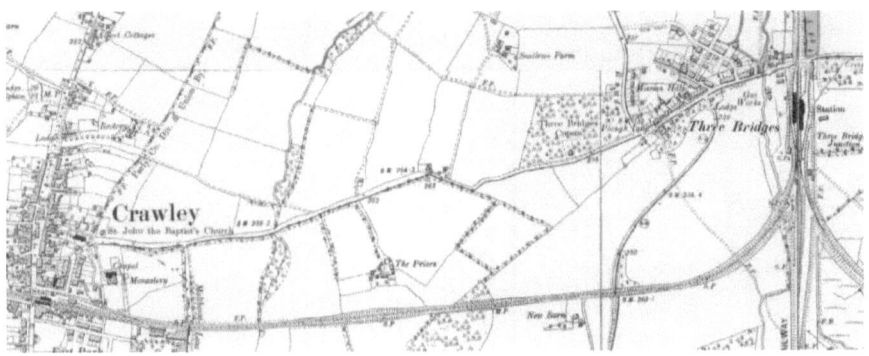

4. As related in *The Sign of the Four*, September 7-10, 1888.
5. These events, taking place from September 7-10, 1887 (one year exactly before *The Sign of the Four*) were later dramatized in the 1939 film, *The Adventures of Sherlock Holmes*.
6. A further examination of Holmes's overall investigation into the massive Rippers Conspiracy during the terrible Bloody Autumn of 1888 can be found in "November, 1888", published in *The Collected Papers of Sherlock Holmes – Volume III: Accounts*. It was originally published in *The Watsonian* (Fall 2015, Vol. 3, No.2) and in my online blog, *A Seventeen Step Program* at:
    https://17stepprogram.blogspot.com/2017/02/sherlock-holmes-versus-jack-ripper.html
7. An examination determining the exact location of Mycroft's rooms and the Diogenes Club can be found in my essay, "Pall Mall: Location the Diogenes Club", originally published in *The Baker Street Journal*, (Vol. 67, No. 2, Summer 2017).

8. For more about this affair, see "Some Notes Upon the Matter of John Douglas", available in *The Collected Papers of Sherlock Holmes – Volume III: Accounts*, and also *Beyond Holmes.*

Magic Squares
by Marcia Wilson

*"My dear Watson, Professor Moriarty is not a man
who lets the grass grow under his feet."*

Chapter I – 24 April, 1891

Tea steamed in the pot by the window – Mrs. Hudson's welcome back from his trip abroad. In return, he had passed to her a sachet of lavender and was trying to hold the peace at Baker Street by not soothing his nerves in ways that would damage the landlady's. That meant bullets were out. It was a deep pity. He wondered if Moriarty's people would hesitate to attack him if they could hear another *V.R.* being added to the walls.

> *If change in plan, come to Oxford rendezvous.*
> *If no change, I will see you at our agreed location.*

Sherlock Holmes dropped the day's Agony Column [1] – and with it Patterson's ciphered advertisement – to the breakfast table with a pensive expression. It added more years to his face than the absent Watson would have wished. Holmes personally had little concern for trying to look younger than one's years. This was just as well. He was aging at a sorry rate this fateful spring.

Patterson's caution was justifiable, but standing in the comfort of his own rooms with soft spring airs breezing open the lace curtain (but not standing too close). Holmes wondered if it was advisable to make the rendezvous.

They were all being watched. Holmes sensed eyes in all directions as soon as his foot left the French ferry and set upon English soil. At this point, no one had yet accosted him, but Patterson was in a precarious position – perhaps even more precarious than himself. Holmes did not pretend to omniscience, but Moriarty was still struggling to divine the identity of Holmes's "Man in the Yard".

Patterson's importance was still minuscule in the scheme of things. To all appearances, the man was beneath his reptilian contempt: A prematurely aged, brittle man bearing scars in his mind and soul from too much work under deep cover. That he had been regulated to tasks of the most superficial importance spoke of that damage. He had no appearance of being a man in charge or responsible of a case of longstanding powers. Common gossip as well as reports said the man was little respected by his own peers. Even the hard-shaped older policemen avoided his company. Years of work had gone into this deception, and Holmes had helped it every step of the way.

It was another reason for which he was grateful for the tapering-off relations between himself and Watson. Watson was a good man. His wife admirable. The two deserved peace and quiet. They certainly did not deserve to be under the chill gaze of a criminal spider within his web.

There was a bedrock weakness to Moriarty's brain: The man believed Holmes worked largely alone and had little use for the Watsons of this world. What love did Moriarty keep of sentimentality, or affection and deep friendship? Nothing, for he had no comprehension of such things. That Holmes had all but stopped his connections to Watson meant, to Moriarty's brilliant if flawed mind, that Watson was no longer important to Holmes – if he had ever been.

A biographer. A tamed teller of tales. Perhaps a blind harper in the halls. He left Watson alone because he had mistaken this war as purely intellectual.

Holmes hoped Moriarty didn't see the mistake in this assumption, and yet to him it was as clear a logic as seeing through clean water. Against a war of pure wit, Holmes would be doomed to fail under Moriarty's hand because Moriarty had an army at his command. Therefore, if he were to even those odds, he must needs keep a different sort of army: An army that was invisible to Moriarty's fathom.

That would be the bonds of the irrational, the honest, the friendliness, and the intangible.

Moriarty has enjoyed this game as much as I, but for different reasons. I have long craved a challenge of my worth . . . but for him? He sees me no more as an intriguing little distraction from his usual work. What a mind, to be so cold! It is all a game of Magic Squares to him – the beauty of finished numbers inside cages and boxes, creating a pattern . . . while I must spoil his lovely arithmetic by taking his numbers from him. War is the only outcome of this insult to his intellect. And if he truly understood what I was planning, he would act with far more speed than he is now. I wouldn't have been given the courtesy of a greeting and a chance to back away.

A glass bottle tumbled out of a passing cab. It burst and he flinched. His reflexes were strung high, not unlike piano wire. He was still wearied from his trip abroad. The notes he had sent Watson probably misled him into thinking he was still there. Yet not a moment after sending the second wire in Nimes, a strong feeling of apprehension had caused him to change his plan.

London's April was colder than that of France, and Holmes felt the thin chill sinking into his bones. The Professor's visit that morning had unsettled him to his very core. He needed to rest, but he also needed to have some peace and quiet.

If only this were but a confrontation between himself and Moriarty! But Moriarty had achieved his status as criminal mastermind by manipulating many people to work as one unit under his control. Each of his men stood as a separate tendril upon a monstrous web. Holmes's employment upon others was nothing upon this level of organisation. He used the small, the forgotten, and those who were weak if clever and able to remain invisible. And Holmes had no interest in risking another's life.

At last, Holmes weighed no better or worse in his mind, and reached for his hat. It was turning the midday of a clear and warm April day, and there would be some bit of refuge within the mass of four-million citizens.

I went out about midday to transact some business in Oxford Street.

His luck held for many long minutes. He knew the city well, but the living macrocosm was disturbed. His nerves prickled under the strain of mere walking as each step created and destroyed infinite possibilities of his personal future. The chaunters' cries rang against his ears, pressing more and more feverishly for sales against their rivals. Holmes tightened his lips, knowing the evening papers' release would be a repeat of this chaos. He hurried as best as he was able through the uneven stream of humanity.

He stopped several times, merely waiting in discreet places where a single man might observe without being himself being observed. It was an old habit of his, and the familiarity comforted his unease. Not for the first time, he thought of Watson's steady presence at his side. Give the man a task and he would do his best, single-mindedly and hard-headedly.

How he missed him.

Even now, his old friend was an absence in his rooms like a missing pipe or broken lamp by his chemistry table. So accustomed to his habits, Holmes would reach out his hand for either object without thought. He found himself doing the same for Watson.

But these were not the old days. Watson was now better fit with his slow-mending wounds dissolving over time – but he was older. They both were.

Missing Watson may have helped to save his life. His nostalgic loneliness kept him moving – wandering, almost, without appearance of aim. And his nervous sensation had not dispersed as he passed the busy corner of Bentinck Street to Welbeck Street.

As I passed the corner which leads from Bentinck Street on to the Welbeck Street crossing, a two-horse van furiously driven whizzed round and was on me like a flash. I sprang for the footpath and saved myself by the fraction of a second.

When the van rounded the same corner on all but two wheels, Holmes was already moving quickly. He moved faster, sprinting for the other side, even as he clutched his walking stick for futile protection. Eight metal-shod hooves pounded the brick all the way to the lost Westbourne River beneath. He reached safety without a moment to spare. About him people cried out in variations of indignation and fear. A woman screamed. A man swore. The hot breath of foam-flecked horses passed by a hair, steaming the back of his sweating neck.

It was over as quickly as it started. Holmes blended in with the dazed crowd, listening to the confused demands for the van's number or had anyone seen them before. What of the horses?

Holmes said nothing, absorbing the dwindling chaos.

He didn't recognise the horses, but he had gotten their symbolism all the same.

They had been a perfectly matched pair of blacks: *The preferred horses for funerals.*

His hands were too tightly wrapped about his stick. He made himself stop and release one hand as he reached for his handkerchief. He wiped both hot and cold sweat off his face.

There would be no going to the Oxford Street rendezvous now. He was not sorry. In this storm-charged atmosphere, it would be unsafe for himself and for Patterson, who would merely go along as they had originally planned.

He would keep to the pavement and take a slightly different route. Already he thought twice of heading back to Baker Street.

No, not Baker Street. Not safe for himself or for Mrs. Hudson and whoever would be helping her. Best to keep the personal warfare private. He would go to Mycroft. Eventually.

Holmes swallowed and adjusted his hat and collar, shot his cuffs briskly, and started walking. No cab. A cab would be foolish if he couldn't trust the driver. He would have to make other arrangements . . . .

Constable Church was too long a policeman not to know Sherlock Holmes by sight. Every form of plain-clothed detective needed constables with them for their work, and every detective needed to put upon the advice of the man sooner or later. Church had seen Holmes twice in the line of duty and countless times as he was patrolling. He was hard to miss – he was a striking gentleman – and Church thought of hawks whenever he caught that pale, thin face among the crowd. Hawks were hot-blooded birds, but they had cool eyes.

Vere Street meant much to Constable Church. It was amusing but true that his name was tied to his reason for loving his beat. Marylebone Church (in all its variations of spelling and pronunciation) had history that drew people right and left. Plenty of curious folk came from all over the world to see the chapel. The Duchess of Portland had married *herself* there back about a hundred years ago, leaving her name behind for Bentinck Street. People were drawn to that too.

Men and women liked a good story, and she had been the richest woman in the country. Possibly a bit of a daft collector, but she had been the keeper of the Arundel Marbles, and Church could expect to hear the gawpers talking about the pieces. The closer one got to the chapel, the more the gawping. With spring, men thought of love and women of marriage. In between was the sermon, and the draw of the memory of Vere Street's children, such as the holy Frederick Dennison Maurice.

Church was a self-taught historian – he knew which side buttered his bread – and someday he would have to find out if it were true that his Vere Street was named after Aubrey de Vere, who likened one of Maurice's famous sermons to eating pea soup with a fork. If so, it would be a tit-bit of cheerful gossip good for a tip or three. For now, he strolled his beat, being sure to look neat and trim within his long moustaches and buttoned-up coat.

Today had been a profitable day for pleasing the sight-seers. The warmish weather had brought in a few groups – young people mostly – and using the excuse of April and a little history lesson as cause to display the new season's colours. Church was fond of these, for if one was properly respectful, they were generous with their rewards. Young men liked to impress their ladies, themselves, and each other in no particular order. The extra coins rattled in the little bag he kept sewn inside his coat. The three shillings meant the week's butter and flour were taken care of and the Missus would be pleased. They might have it in their potatoes tomorrow.

Church was thinking of potatoes because his shift was ending soon and his feet hurt. It therefore surprised him just a bit to hear a whistle go off across the street and down towards the commemorative sign of Rysbrack's. [2]

He was surprised a lot to see the ruckus was coming from Sherlock Holmes.

I kept to the pavement after that, Watson, but as I walked down Vere Street a brick came down from the roof of one of the houses and was shattered to fragments at my feet. I called the police and had the place examined. There were slates and bricks piled up on the roof preparatory to some repairs, and they would have me believe that the wind had toppled over one of these.

The gentleman was standing stiff as iron with his back up against the wall of one of the fancy brick houses, hands spread apart at his sides as if he could press himself into the wall. Church trotted forward his eyes narrowing to a bushy frown, for it seemed odd that there be such a large pool of people around him. Vere Street was busier than this at any given time, yet here he was standing by himself like he had the plague.

"What's this now, Mr. Holmes?" he called out before he finished puffing up the street.

Mr. Holmes shot a pale face up, and there was something tight and ferocious about his eyes. Calm as ever, cool as you please, but he wasn't happy.

"Constable Church," he declared. The man always sounded like one of Church's old Sunday school teachers. "I believe there may be a problem." As Church joined his side, he moved the toe of his left shoe to the side. Fragments of brick rattled against the concrete and set stone of the pavement.

Church looked without fully understanding. "Looks as though you got lucky, Mr. Holmes."

Holmes almost – but not quite – blinked. "Yes," he drawled slowly. "One might think so. And yet, I would like to have the cause for this . . . fortuitous accident . . . examined."

Church had almost forgotten how Holmes talked. He re-listened to the words in his head until he was certain he understood it. "Are you suspecting foul play, Mr. Holmes?" Even as he asked this, he lifted his own hand and whistled for the next man over – ought to be Jamison today.

"I am saying that at this point my brush with death does not have a clear cause. For my own satisfaction, you would understand that I would like to rule out foul play."

Church thought this over, even as Jamison panted up to his side. The two policemen discussed the particulars quickly, and Jamison volunteered to enter the building and examine the roof. Through it all, Holmes stood stock-still, his hands upon his walking stick as though he intended to use it. Twice he glanced back up to the roof, and Church was almost certain be saw the man shrink backwards each time.

"I'm sure there's nothing, sir." Church said the moment Jamison tapped on the front door and was given entrance. "Repairs are always going on in London. Sometimes they don't hire the right sort of worker for the job, I fear. Mistakes, they happen."

"Mistakes most certainly do happen." Holmes answered back. He looked as though he were speaking of something else. Those cool grey eyes were far away into the crowd. "Nevertheless, I feel I should satisfy my curiosity."

Church chuckled lightly. Laugh it off, he'd been advised time and time again. Laugh it off. Even if it is something, and it probably isn't most of the time, you don't want people scared. "As you say, sir, but accidents happen to people as much as the blackguards do."

"Hallo!"

Both Church and Holmes craned straight up. Jamison was leaning forward, the winds battering the folds of his coat as he stretched his long neck down.

"There's no one up here, gennulmen!" Jamison screamed down over the rising wind. "Just some bricks and slates piled up for repairs! Wind must've knocked a bit over!"

"That," Holmes grumbled, "would be a considerable wind indeed."

"These things happen." Church assured him. "Especially if they was placed wrong."

Holmes turned his head slowly, and measured Church with his cool, grey hawk's eyes.

"So you say," he answered quietly. "Nevertheless, I expect you to make a full report to your division, Constable."

"A report? For this?" Church started to laugh, but stopped. "You're serious."

"As you say. It appears to be an accident, but blackguards kill as much as accidents." Holmes sounded as if he were biting off each word with great effort. "It would bring me comfort, Constable, if a report would cause greater caution upon this street." He lifted one swift, white hand as Church opened his mouth. "I am an unattached man, Constable. And I have swift reflexes. I hesitate to think of what would have happened if it had been a woman or child walking past this same spot."

207

Church went white to his chin strap. He swallowed hard. "Yes, yes. You're quite right about that sir." He pulled out his notebook and pencil with due haste. "At what time would you estimate this accident?"

Of course, I knew better, but I could prove nothing.

Chapter II – Such Is The Feud

I took a cab after that and reached my brother's rooms in Pall Mall, where I spent the day.

Only a man such as Mycroft Holmes took comfort and safety from being utterly predictable.

But then, there was only one Mycroft Holmes.

The large man stepped from his Whitehall office without a sound, graceful despite his weight and not-inconsiderable height. He walked patiently through the building, across rooms carpeted with designs from across the globe, a different world within each chamber. These were the rooms in which the truly powerful meetings took place – the filtration between politicians who sorted out the needed and not-needed affairs before they were sent to Parliament or Palace.

In four breaths, he traversed Africa's deserts on a Bedouin rug and ignored the maneless lion stuffed in the comer. On the wall rested a clay tablet, beautifully inscribed:

If you hear hoofprints, do not look for zebras.

So many politicians needed that advice. The room was popular and that was but one of its reasons.

With a single step out of Africa, he was crossing the woolen gold-and-green jungle of Sumatra, avoiding the long slim table and chairs made of mahogany bamboo, and paying the respect of a fellow traveler to a gleaming black-and-silver cockerel captured in oils. The Meiji Emperor's experts had come here late in the year of 1889, following their young ruler's command to learn the ways of Naval power. Mycroft remembered how they had chosen this room above the others for their tea-time discussions and admired the rooster's show of strength. A letter addressed from Sultan Alauddin Shah of Aceh, King of Aceh and Samudra, to Elizabeth rested under glass – the only obtrusive example of three-dimensional art in the room besides the furniture.

Mycroft stopped long enough to ponder the letter beneath the glass. Others commented on the realistic facsimile of a letter written in 1602.

Only he and select others knew the letter was genuine. Where better to hide something in plain sight? Pretty though it was, no one would steal an imitation.

This was but one of Mycroft's little touches upon Whitehall. The Diplomatic Assemblies had their own circles and their meeting halls, but it made common sense to create places where the world's dignitaries would draw comfort (or perhaps intimidation) in the same place where England made her day-to-day decisions on paper.

In each room was a statement – always subtle, always layered. In Sumatra was a framed silk calligraphy of *Samudra* in gold paint. It was the Sanskrit for the island, but that was not as important as what Samudra meant: *"Gathering together of waters, sea, or ocean."*

Whitehall was where many waters met. How better that they do it underneath a neutral ground, within small representations of their own lands, with meaningful symbols of their lands around them. The created atmosphere was conducive to productive thought, and a mind cast to the future ensured the reminders of his peoples' past hung on the four walls and floor and even the ceiling: China's room held a red silk kite of a bat in the corner, its silk teeth bared against rude intruders.

Sumatra melted behind him. Sweden possessed a carpet as blue as the deepest of seas, trimmed with golden chains of tiny isles and fine fringes of land. Books demonstrated this room. A leather-bound and monstrously-sized copy of *Tacitus* sat on its own table, vellum pages open upon that ancient man's accounting of the Suiones tribe. Black fox skins, their main export to Rome, hung at one wall in glory. Mycroft appreciated the symmetry of the skins placed close to an ivory carving of a longship. Britain was the supreme sea power, and had been since Elizabeth. But once upon a time, Sweden had held that title . . . and had held it for millenia, not centuries.

Britain would be a very long time in catching up . . . if ever. But at least they could comfort themselves with the example of the very best.

A Vendel-era helmet, battered by time's teeth more than the enemy's sword, stared sightlessly and unnervingly across the microcosm that was his world. Below its mount rested an engraving from ancient *Beowulf*:

> *Þæt ys sio fæhðo and se feond-scipe*

> *Such is the feud, the foeman's rage . . . .*

Mycroft breathed the cool London evening as stepped outside and he crossed the front steps. A commissionaire tapped his uniform cap in respect and offered to call for a cab. Mycroft said no.

From Whitehall he normally went straight to the Diogenes, and this dusky evening was no exception. He never bothered to hide where he was. The very uniqueness of his post ensured that he be as predictable as possible. Luckily for the rest of the world, Mycroft thrived in being predictable, and, save for a few minor indiscretions – He felt it was important to have a few every year. – he was as straight in his paths as a train upon the tracks.

The wind swirled about his legs and he slowed, waiting for a lull into the crowd to cross the street.

"I beg your pardon!"

"I am sorry, sir. It was most unintentional."

Mycroft hadn't seen Lestrade until that moment, but he was hardly surprised. The crowd was full of above-average-sized men, and the faint surprise in the detective's voice proclaimed he had seen Mycroft no better.

The man Lestrade had accidentally jostled returned to his perusal of the evening paper, willing himself to block out the recent unpleasantness. Lestrade was just as willing to learn invisibility. He stood huddled within his long coat – a coat that should have been replaced months ago. Mycroft idly wondered about the level of debt the man was in, recalling Sherlock's comment about ill children.

"*Good evening, Mr. Lestrade,*" Mycroft would have said, had the man not desired to be unseen. "*Departmental meetings are so tedious, are they not? Dullness combined with the usual fears of being bitten by one's superiors . . . A decent ale is a reasonable reward for surviving them.*"

Lestrade looked up into the darkling sky of the city as giants swirled about him. He smelled of the less-pleasant gas lamps in the basement of the very building Mycroft had just left. There had been a meeting involving the Home Office today – a meeting not deemed important enough to bother Mycroft about. Mycroft glanced about with his peripheral, seeing no one else that he recognized from the records of the Yard. That meant whatever the outcome of the meeting, Lestrade had left alone. Not a fortuitous indication of one's professional career.

The lamp-lighters stepped one by one down the street, throwing haphazard pools of flame against the streets. Lestrade was all small and spare and slim and dark where Mycroft was the opposite. They even dressed apart, within the best of what their divergent incomes could afford. Lestrade had changed his cuffs and collar while at work. The clean white of starched cloth glowed in the dwindling light Mycroft knew from observation that Lestrade kept an eternal supply of clean replacements in his office.

There was a hard, weary set of the man's mouth that matched his unseeing eyes. Lestrade's meeting had gone ill and he was smarting. Lestrade was preparing for a sacrificial altar.

He was a sensible choice for culling. He was the best because of his determination, not his intelligence. The Yard operated under the Home Office, and thus wanted men who were smart enough to bow to the word from the higher offices. Lestrade did not have that sort of intelligence. He must have stepped over someone's lines today. That stifled expression was too similar to that of a first-level clerk upon finding they had revealed an indiscretion about a departmental mentor.

A horse bus emerged, slowed in a thickening fog, and for a wonder it was half-empty. Several people boarded the brightly coloured contraption without a word, the men stoically taking the seats up top and under the elements while the few women and children sheltered below. Lestrade remained standing, too oblivious within his own internal world to notice Mycroft, but at last, the small man shook himself like a bird beneath rainfall and pulled out a cab whistle. Somewhat curious despite himself – he shared his brother's need for amusement – Mycroft watched as the policeman lifted a beaten whistle to his lips and winded.

Mycroft admitted to fascination. A police inspector could hardly afford the luxury of a hansom. [3]

Sherlock preferred the hansom and its ability to show the city around him. He was a loving observer of London, fascinated by its smallest eddies, and he liked the fact that the hansom could navigate faster than any other method. For a man who preferred the telegram over the note, the hansom was his logical conveyance.

Likewise, Lestrade wanted to go home without being around another living person, and he did so with haste. He simply took the nearest available vehicle to Paddington Street, despite the high cost to his purse. He was too deep within the discomfort of his own thoughts to pay mind to his budget. As Mycroft watched, the hansom clipped away with its blank-eyed passenger.

A man who would spend on a swift ride home but not on a warm coat was a troubled man. Mycroft made a note to look into the affairs at the Yard in the morning. Lestrade's reputation was of confidence, even when he was wrong about something. Here he was behaving like a Hindoo pariah.

Mycroft took himself to the Diogenes and ate an unadorned meal of roast with potatoes. In concession to spring, he enjoyed a green onion salad with tiny feathers of red oakleaf lettuce and curls of tender watercress.

The cress reminded him of the French markets of his youth, when the greengrocers rolled the dark green leaves within their bundles of lighter-tasting lettuces for the morning purchases. He missed the personal exposure to the outside world, but then he knew what the price would be when he accepted his post.

He travelled within his lines, straight as a tram, but within his mind he travelled in every way conceivable. For him numbers sang. For his eyes statistics and markets opened their treasures, and under the retention of his memory, England's equity remained stable.

Politicians came and went. Rulers passed to forgetfulness or they were assassinated. England was still a jewel of worth, and so many greedy eyes coveted anything of hers that it was a wonder anyone of importance could work in safety. Wars were brewing, and brewing with enthusiasm. England would be involved yet.

But no one, not even the ruler of the most Anglo-hating country in the world, would harm Mycroft Holmes.

No one wanted to seize control of a shattered country.

It was Mycroft's habit to leave his club before eight. He did so, and this time walked home – not an unusual event as the evening lacked rain. Thick fog crept upon the streets, smelling of both the Thames and the factory smokes that added the slimy yellow texture to the fog. Pall Mall gleamed with bright, clean lamps and religiously polished metal. A surgeon's red lamp hung ahead, a sullen red eye in the distance. Mycroft thrust his key into his lock in the front and stepped in with only a faint pause.

Upstairs, he saw that Mr. Melas' room was firmly shut. Soft musical syllables rose and fell on the other side of the door. Melas did adore reading aloud. Tonight, he must be in a restless mood. Antipater of Sidon was positively Old Testament in his loquacious attitudes.

Mycroft loosened his coat and prepared to thrust his key into his lock, but hesitated. He waited the span of a breath and merely pressed the door open.

Sherlock was sitting in the guest chair, long legs drawn up as was his thinking habit since childhood. Neither man was surprised that Mycroft intuited his presence before walking in.

"You appear to be in straits, Brother." Mycroft rumbled.

"As always, you are correct." Sherlock answered just as quietly. "And for that matter, you would be wise to hesitate before leaving your silhouette before the windows, no matter how well drawn they are. I have been a popular man of late, and an assassin's fevered imagination might mistake you."

Mycroft grunted, hung up his coat, turned, and locked the door. "Tell me what has happened."

Sherlock did.

The fire burnt low, Sherlock hopped to his feet and rebuilt the embers to hot red coals. It never took him long to recover his energy after a trial – and today had been a trial. Mycroft remained sitting with his hands drawn across his waistcoat, Sherlock's narrative was typical Sherlock: Finely detailed, but to the point.

"How unlike the Professor to tip his hand." Mycroft said at last. "From what you have said to me of him in the past, this is a most uncharacteristic choice of actions."

"If you mean by which he took the trouble to warn me off, I agree." Sherlock's grey eyes were clouded with apprehension. "And there was some risk to himself for coming to my rooms this morning."

"You were armed." Mycroft reminded him. "Clearly this was more than a meeting of the minds, Sherlock."

Sherlock agreed by nodding once, sharply. He was troubled as his thoughts multiplied within each other, over and over.

"Moriarty is a brilliant man, but he is still just one man. And he has powerful clients." Mycroft rose long enough to pour himself a drink. Sherlock had already helped himself with a well-watered brandy. "You have made yourself too powerful, Sherlock. You now have but one competitor in the field, and that is a man who is your inevitable enemy."

"'*Competitor*'," Sherlock mused. "An unexpected comparison, Mycroft."

"You were ever the idealist of us." Mycroft said it kindly. "You had the luxury of being exposed to Plebian thought and different minds. I was trained for other things. The first lesson I ever learned was that Monarchs do not look for kindness."

Sherlock sighed. "I know."

The brothers fell silent before the crackling fire. It was some long minutes and two brandy snifters later that Mycroft spoke again.

"You are the future, Sherlock. Moriarty is the past. In his day, anyone of importance consulted experts who were expected to be criminals. From bankers to barons and all levels of royalty, everyone needed the likes of Moriarty to work their wonders. You represent a newer time, and a newer thinking. If this newer way is to survive, then you – yourself or at least your methods – need to survive too."

"Moriarty seeks to keep the world within tight lines." Sherlock practically spat. Anger glittered in his eyes against the spots of high colour upon his cheeks. "He seeks a rigid method without flexibility. There is no room to breathe in his ways."

Mycroft almost smiled, for Sherlock could forgive much, but not the rigidity of thought.

"He is fighting for his crown, Sherlock. He knows that if you are to destroy him, it will be *you* the heads of state consult for their solutions. And that is intolerable. His sort *causes* wars. You seek to *prevent*. The two of you will meet no more than the two poles."

"Brother," Sherlock smiled with thin-lipped fondness. His emotions were always restrained, for that was how they could bear it. "You give incontestable advice."

"If only that were my position in life. Then I daresay I would have a more interesting time of it. Yet I would be worried for my life as well as yours."

Sherlock chuckled lightly. "No one would dare assassinate you for the fearsome consequence. A rival country would no more order your death than they would the murder of the one man at the bank who can make sense of the books."

Mycroft grunted his agreement and settled back, hands folded and fingers dovetailed within each other on his large belly. "I may be safe, but that is because my oath declares me loyal to the government no matter what the government decides. There is always the question of what I know and how I would serve the ruling party. I did not choose this post for myself, but it was my duty. Better that one of us lives completely within his lights."

Sherlock sighed once, and it was a thin, barely audible sound against the low snap of the anthracite in the grate. He was looking more than tired. He looked tired to death.

"You are too indispensable to kill, and indeed – no one would kill the only man who can make sense of British governmental trade lines, politics, and the thousands of threads of ridiculous matters that tie all together. But that does not mean you have forgotten how to play tricks."

Mycroft chuckled at last, and his thoughtful grey eyes stirred – the way mercury glimmers when it has been forcibly moved from one vessel into another.

"I forget little, Sherlock. How may I be of service?"

"I seem to recall you once had a remarkable starting post in coordinating the licensed cabs throughout the city."

Mycroft chuckled again. "You recall correctly – " He stopped for a moment "But you need to really talk to the Good Doctor before you draft him into this plan.

"That is the next thing on my list." Sherlock smiled.

And they conversed until the fires were all but dead. Sherlock had fallen asleep, worn out from the attack upon his nerves. Mycroft watched him and judged his brother warm enough this close to the grate. The silence between the two was comfortable and steady.

Since childhood, they had been able to exist for hours without the need to talk.

Several hours later, Sherlock stirred. He stretched a bit and examined his collar and cuffs for stains. Mycroft ordered a light meal sent up, and they ate quietly. Just as quietly, they left the building together. In the middle of the street they parted ways.

Mycroft watched his brother go, a thin, erect frame of singular power in a large city.

Unbidden yet inevitably, his mind cast back to when he had stood before the Swedish helmet in Whitehall. The inscription in English translated all-too-well to the situation:

Such is the feud, the foeman's rage,

And because he thought of the first line, he could not help but recall the rest of the poem:

> *death hate of men: so I deem it sure*
> *that the Swedish folk will seek us home*
> *for this fall of their friends, the fighting – Scylfings,*
> *when once they learn that our warrior leader*
> *lifeless lies, who land and hoard*
> *ever defended from all his foes,*
> *furthered his folk's weal, finished his course*
> *a hardy hero.*

The lines were drawn. Mycroft could see it as clearly as he could read the world within a stock market. His brother stood upon one side of the chessboard, Moriarty another. In his mind, Mycroft could see the different countries lined up, each country choosing their loyalty to one man or the other . . . The rest of the world waited, watching to see which would be the winner before they declared their loyalty.

Sherlock was right in his actions, but the proving it would be hard, and the odds were high his proof would be fatal. Mycroft knew this, and accepted it. There were many things worse than death. Many things. For his brother, failure was the first of them.

Sherlock could afford to die, but he could not afford to fail.

Nor, Mycroft knew, could England. If Sherlock did fail, then it would be upon Mycroft's shoulders to create the future.

Mycroft was not optimistic about his abilities in that project.

Commercial Street

Constable Church was dead tired. He fell into step with the rest of London and made his way for home, too poor for a cab but rich with the comfort of a netted sack swinging from his gloved fingers. A quarter-pound of butter and a week's worth of flour [4] would brighten tomorrow's supper. It was possible they could even spare a pat of that butter on the morning porridge.

He was off duty, if such a thing ever happened to a policeman. Church doubted it. His father had never taken time off. Nor had any of the men in his family that wore any uniform. The uniform stayed on, if only in the mind. At least they could remove their uniforms when off duty in this enlightened day and age. He approached the humble flats nested over each other like so many dishes above the hundreds of tiny shops of Commercial Street. The closer he was to his own, the louder the local children yelped. He belonged to the people here, just as they belonged to him.

From a full street away, one of his brethren lifted a white-gloved hand in a distant greeting. Church returned the wave. It looked like Goldsworthy. Church frowned in ready compassion. Goldsworthy was usually paired with the other Cornishmen on this side – there were enough of them as disgruntled former miners that the Yard wanted coppers who knew the language – but Jory had been laid up from a clumsy garrotter almost a fortnight and Gay was still under reprimand for taking his wife to hospital when he was due to work. That left Roach and Tyack for the nightshift, but here was Goldsworthy all on his own self

Better that Goldie be the one alone. There was only one of the man, but he was large enough to be three average constables put together. He was possibly the only copper on the beat that could walk by himself without fear of molesting bludgers.

A vegetable cart wheeled away the evening's losses for a pig farm. Church knew the driver from childhood and grinned when a bundle flew through the air in his direction: A half-good leek and two twigs of celery with a leftover sprig of parsley was his reward. Mrs. Church would be pleased as the flour and butter. Church's belly grumbled at the thought of celery soup for the night. He'd no idea what she was planning, but she could always work out a miracle with an iron pot by the grate. For that matter, so could he.

Commercial Street's urchins slithered past as he circled a disgrace of a pothole. He recognised them all, and mentally noted which the orphans were and which had different troubles. Rich or poor, the poorest of all were the motherless and fatherless – regardless of who else had the raising of the children. They were all united in singing some silly-minded little ditty at the top of their lungs:

"There is no lady in the land
Is half so sweet as Sally.
She is the darling of my heart,
And she lives in our alley . . . ."

Church coughed and waved his large hand in the air, sending children shrieking with laughter even as they scattered, still singing.

"The only Sally you're old enough for is Sally the stray cat!" he growled. The older boys flipped him saucy grins and they were off, melting into the dwindling evening crowd. *Children,* Church snorted. *Always trying to prove they're grown.*

He fished his key out of a small loop sewn inside his pocket and unlocked the front door. A quick check showed the absence of rats in the hall – hopefully the rat catcher had done the job this time. They were all getting tired of the fuss – the horrible little terriers the man carried, and the reek of too-strong peppermint oil to repel the vermin.

Boards creaked under his clamshells, and he was quick to pause at their narrow door, balancing the vegetables, sack, and keys amongst only two hands.

"There you are!" The door opened, and who was on the other side but his brother, Matthew Church, fresh-faced from a day off the grueling demands of Westminster proper. "Tess and I were hoping you'd be in soon! How was the beat?"

Church sniffed good-naturedly and passed the heaviest of his burdens to his brother. "Long enough. The gentlemen are showing their appreciation now that it's warmed."

"That's good news, Sam!" Matthew Church was a constable himself, only his shift was rougher and deeper into the East End. For that reason, he and his wife shared rooms against theirs. "I got a tip today for helping a woman cross the street."

"You didn't take it, did you?"

"Oh, she insisted." Matthew shrugged in one of those "What do you do about that?" sort of movements. "Our loving wives are off to get some tea for the eggs. I think they're bored with the children gone."

Church sniffed. This time of year the children were better off in the country with the grandparents.

"Well, it could be they just wanted to get out and stop looking at me."

"How long have you been home?" Church demanded.

"Not e'en an hour."

"Well, that would be long enough to see your face."

Church had finished wrestling his shoelaces off. He ignored the friendly slap on his shoulder. In a few moments the brothers were bending over his street-battered uniform, examining each inch for any repair-work or bits that needed cleaning.

"Anything interesting?" Matthew wondered.

"Doubt it'd be as interesting as your twenty mile." Church retorted.

"I doubt it too, but I'm trying not to think about what supper might be."

"We could start on a celery soup. Did Green steal your tin again?"

"Lord, no. He was kept over at the St. James today."

"St. James? What's he doing all the way over at Haymarket?" Church stopped brushing dried mud from his hem to frown.

"Forgot why, but it's just as well. He was on his way back to his reports when he got into an altercation outside of Pall Mall."

Church listened to his brother – half-report, half-complaint – with half an ear. Matthew picked up the vegetables and with a tiny pen-knife was cleaning the rotten bits off into a pail. "Been an odd enough day. Men shuffled over half of London – at least my half. How was yours?"

"Can't say I noticed . . . . "

"Well, you're too far away from the Thames. That's where all the interesting things happen." Matthew splashed the celery in water and started on the parsley. Against the homemade wallpaper, his silhouette shaped the attributes of a deranged scarecrow. Their rooms were so small that even the shadows appeared to take up room, but they all took pride in sticking together as a family.

"The Irish Twins were off their usual spot by the Threadneedle's corner, and Brook Street just had replacement coppers!"

"I saw Goldie further down the street." Church admitted. "Didn't see nobody else with him."

"He doesn't need anyone else with him." Matthew laughed. "That's why Lanner speaks for him. Those Cousin Jacks [5] stick together."

Church's earlier fatigue renewed its gravity upon his shoulders. He slumped into his corner chair and finished removing his uncomfortable shoes while his brother fashioned the handful of vegetables and two of the largest potatoes in their rooms into a pot full of celery soup. Like all children brought up in the country, they knew how to cook – and if necessary, how to go find the ingredients for themselves.

"Just a queer day all around," he heard Matthew mutter. It was unusual to see a cloud pass over his brother's unquenchable chipper humour. "Just a queer day."

"Pardon?"

"Nothing, Brother. Nothing." Matthew's face remained a touch clouded and he threw chopped vegetables together to cook into smooth chowder. "Just a queer day . . . all those men out or shuffled about London like your girl's paper dolls. Probably doesn't mean anything . . . probably aren't testing us again."

Church rubbed at the throbbing spot on his forehead. "Maybe they are. You know it's about the right time for it. Don't worry about it, Matthew. If we weren't tapped in all that, it should mean something, right? The Yard tests us all the time to see if we've got our mettle. Shouldn't think anything of it."

"I suppose so." Matthew mumbled some more. Church didn't hear it at all over the sudden pop and hiss of the cheap sea-coal against the grate. The sound made him thirsty. He got up and went to the grate to pour up a cup of red tea.

"I had an odd day too. Gentleman nearly got hit from above by a flying brick. Got me to make a police report about it and everything!"

Matthew chuckled. "What's he going to do, press charges against the building?"

Church chuckled too, but slowly. "Man was all shook up. Had to go check out the top of the building, but there was no one there but the wind. I s'pose he has his enemies." He hadn't truly thought about that fact before . . . not until the words popped out. His hands stilled about his cup as the new consideration came to him. Self-conscious, he went back to his brush and resumed working on a bit of dry mud.

"Going around, then." Matthew leaned back comfortably in his slippered feet, chewing loudly on a scrap of raw potato. "At least Green wasn't around to nick my tin because he had to take a report. Some bludgeoner was daft enough to take a swing at that Sherlock Holmes fellow."

Church's heavy wool brush skidded across the back of his uniform on the narrow table, and down the hem. A cloud of fine dust burst into the air. He sneezed, which did a fine job of covering his alarm.

"You bring dust in here, and both the wives will smoke us in the chimney!" Matthew exclaimed.

"Sorry, hand slipped." Church lied. "What was that you just said?"

Matthew told him.

"That's very peculiar." Church muttered. "Because it was Sherlock Holmes who had me write that report up about the brick."

The brothers looked at each other in growing silence. "You did write the report up." Matthew stated.

219

"Yes . . . yes of course." Church stammered. "But I didn't think anything of it . . . I thought he was just barking. You know how odd he can be at times."

"Well." Matthew said at last. "He is a queer sort – but so is his profession. I'm certain I don't know a fragment of what the man does."

Church pulled out his little notebook and read aloud the details. In light of his brother's gossip, the small story sounded far more sinister.

Matthew nodded when he finished. "All I really know is, a man went up against Mr. Holmes, and got a flatter face for his troubles."

"Serves the fool right. I saw that left hook a' his once underneath Old Nelson!" Church shook his head.

"Holmes could kill a man with those fists if he wanted to."

"Ah, but he won't." Matthew dismissed that. "He wouldn't kill anyone. That gun he carries East of Aldgate's more for show."

"You're not helping." Church spoke sharply out of guilt "This is too much a coincidence, Brother."

"We could send a note over." Matthew offered. "Let someone know up front. You know they won't notice anything if it ain't pointed out."

Church sighed. "I'd rather sound like a man caught in fancies than have blood on my hands. Holmes has a rough tongue, but he deals fair and he don't ask for rewards."

"We'll go together." Matthew shrugged. "It'd look better."

But when they got to the station, all was chaos. A weary-looking clerk half-slumped over his tall desk and greeted them with a pale-faced nod.

"Belt?" Church asked timidly. "Is that you under all that?"

Beltmaker nodded with a ghost of his usual humor and pushed aside a paper tower of work. "Been quite a day," he said wearily. "Half our best were pulled off the streets and put on a confidential run to sweep up some bloody gang."

The brothers whistled softly, understanding everything. It was rare that the C.I.D. needed a lot of people, but when they did, things were exciting. "How did it go?" Matthew asked eagerly.

Beltmaker managed to smile. "Everything seemed all nice and normal most of the day. Then, suddenly, coppers start coming in with their Derbies bulging. It's like suckin' em off the streets with a straw!" The elderly clerk was amazed. "They're still coming in, if you can imagine." He caught the envy of his audience. "I take it you two were part of the coppers patrolling and makin' it all look normal."

"We were looking for the Inspector." Matthew began. "Ran into a queer mess today, and we thought he should know about it."

"Well, I don't know where any of those are right now." Beltmaker admitted. "They're in and out of the door like leaves in a rain. But I'll see who I can find."

"Thank you," Church said quietly. Matthew read his expression and nodded. They didn't feel like they were being foolish now, but the troubling sensation had increased. The police couldn't pull in a ring of criminals this successful without outside help. Sherlock Holmes was one of the few willing, and one of the fewer capable.

"Wonder where Mr. Holmes is now?" Matthew muttered under his breath.

Dr. Watson's practice had closed for the day. No one had darkened his doorstep for nearly an hour. Behind his desk he could hear the lowering murmur of traffic. It was a perfect spring evening, he thought to himself.

The doctor was in a pleasant mood despite the absence of his wife, but Mary had the excellent excuse of visiting her friends in the country while passing on to them the little gewgaws she didn't want to take when they soon relocated to Kensington. She was looking forward to the move as much as he. Kensington was a rise in his career, and the area a better place for Mary's health.

Soon, he reminded himself. Soon they would no longer deal with the hustle and blare of the trains and odd-hour visitors.

His office was trimmed down and freshly cleaned. When they left, the entire building would be in far better shape than it had been when he'd made his first payment!

Watson was still smiling to himself as he went to his desk and settled back to his papers. He was just reaching to the brass dial-calendar by the lamp, thinking to move it to tomorrow's date, April 25th, when a familiar and completely unexpected visitor walked through his doorway.

Ch IV – 14 March, 1891

Six Weeks Earlier

The four-and-twenty hours after the storm attacked us – as ferocious as that of a hamadryad – will live in the dwindling memory of my remaining years. I am aware that in London you had all the "pleasant" concomitants of a snowstorm (as if it is automatically an honour and convenience to be within city limits). I both sympathise and envy your position, for you were no doubt miserable where you were. There were no conveyances such as cabs or omnibuses at work, and I wished nostalgically for the skid-sledded cabs of my youth. Perhaps you remember them from your own youth, John, when winters truly were cooler and not a figment of the old man's memories?

The streets smothered first in deep, muddy snow the colour of pale oysters, and then a pool of dirty slush, which no man seemed even to wish to remove . . . only the most miserably and objected, unpoetically short-cut and inadequate means were employed to clear the streets – an easy task, for the snow did not freeze – and to make them passable for the unhappy horses . . . I tell you in perfect truthfulness, John, that I saw wooden ploughs!

John Watson lowered Colonel Hardesty's letter to his desk and exhaled with the gratitude of a man who can finally do this in the privacy of his own home without a cloud of frost drifting across his blotting paper. For days, the storm the world titled "The Great Blizzard" had raged – starting with sound and fury upon the ninth of the month, the day before the unfortunate full moon – Watson inevitably glanced at his brass calendar, surprised. Was it only four days ago? He shook his head at the days-old paper and rubbed his hands together in the memory of the chill that had preyed against London. He felt far older than the four days.

They had been fortunate. Devon and Cornwall had been utterly severed from the rest of Britain. At the last count, Watson recalled more than two-hundred people were dead and more than six-thousand animals.

Their countryside friends, such as Mary's old employer, had written to them with horrors of below-zero temperatures and trees leveled by terrific gales:

In some places, the snow is still piled over five yards in height! Roads were impassable and the church hosted the stranded travellers of two full-length passenger trains! We heard from the vicar that the ships of Falmouth harbour ran through the very face of the blizzard for shelter . . . . But not all of them made it.

Mrs. Forrester, widow and survivor of four children and three sisters, wrote with simple compassion that held no patience for self-pity.

It was terrible. Afterwards, the countryside grew black with the scurrying movements of small hares and rabbits that had escaped the storm in their burrows. They played amongst

222

the sad corpses of the cattle and horses, dead under their cold mantles. It was indescribable, really, to see such a thing and feel only gratitude that something had survived. The gardener found birds frozen to their branches, yet at the base of the same tree, a flock of sea-drakes and hens were perfectly unharmed! In the end, I believe we were all in awe of both Nature's terrors, and the wonders of her survivors.

The doctor sat with the weariness that follows a soldier who, only at this point, has the luxury of knowing his battle has ended. He could feel the firmness of the padded chair against his back and the pressure of a mended shirt against his old shoulder wound.

Weariness still creased caverns into his brow when he rose at last and reached for his hat and coat. It was only a moment's work to speak to Mary and he was free to examine the city.

John, my boy, you will scarce believe this, but when the winds over the Channel blew over the snow, bits of it thawed so quickly my poor old butler found on one of his jaunts a bit of tile peeping from the soft earth – tile that the vicar and my own amateur research – calls identical to that of the Rosehill site. [6]

And John smiled in recollection, both to be called "*my boy*" by the avuncular if overly bearing Hardesty, and also because Hardesty's butler was worth quite a few stories in his own right That poor man . . . and yet Hardesty could hardly have an ordinary man working for him. Not a perfect butler to be sure, but a remarkable human being.

London was a grey city beneath a grey sky and faced by grey seas receiving the greyest waters of all: The Thames, flowing from purer fits and starts from the West. This time of year, the land itself was grey. The blue clay that formed the typical London brick baked grey. Grey was his mood, because he was glad to be alive but beaten down from being unaware of the city's next test. For the first time in months, he was forced to use his walking stick for simple balance. On the same token, he was grateful to just be able to move.

Watson prided himself on being clever with numbers, but he could not hope to calculate the tons of snow that had been carted off by weary workers. Even now he had to walk around mismatched and oddly-sized lumps of snow, from cobbles-small to shoulder height. Children found the snow lumps to be fine mounds upon which to wage war. He passed more than one late-evening battlefield where the King of the Mountain had to

223

fight for his throne. While the adult within his breast wanted them to stop and consider the folly of what they did, he also knew the ridiculousness of such actions. These were street urchins, poor and barely lettered, defiant and legion.

He smiled suddenly, for it came to him that there had once been another mound of snow piled in a very similar way upon their kerb at Baker Street.

Coming home one night, he had come across the charming sight of Irregulars romping over the mound like kittens, and above their heads he saw the pale face of his friend smiling down upon the happy melee.

"There is a fascination to watching the apparent chaos and finding laws and logic beneath," Holmes had said later that evening once they were sitting and digesting a late hot supper. "Can anything look less organised than a pack of children, running helter-skelter? And yet, they are making perfect sense according to their lights. Like moths they swarm, or perhaps bees. Take a little time to know the language of each, and you may be rewarded by the simple accomplishment."

"I find charting out the paths of children or insects hardly simple." Watson had chuckled. "But leave it to your considerable powers of patience.

"Patience? Not at all. Am I an example of patience to you? Have I ever been? It is curiosity, my good fellow, which is confused for patience. It is a quality with which I am both blessed and cursed."

Watson paused now, years after this event. He stood amidst rough mountains of dirty snow in light growing swiftly blue in the evening's fall. He remembered that he had laughed at this, shook his head, and pulled out his pipe to add to the smoke.

Watson often passed by Baker Street in the night as he came or went to house or tasks, and each time he looked up in hopes of glimpsing Holmes through the window. It was an inevitable reflex – a reassurance that his old friend was still about and, at the same time, a homage to their days as financially struggling lodgers.

Tonight, there was nothing to see. The windows were cold and still, devoid of life, and he knew Holmes was off on one of his cases. That he would return at its conclusion, but for nothing less.

Watson wondered how the storm had affected Holmes's part of France. If it was worthy of note, he was certain to receive it in the post or by a telegram. Experience led the doctor to suspect the weather had been no more than an inconvenience to his friend – if he had noticed it at all.

Watson felt his tired face crease into a smile, and a chill, dank wind brushed against his temples. The past would always seem brighter in places, more cheerful or more sunny – more *everything*, as his old friend Stamford would have said. And there was some truth to it. When he had first stood on his own two feet after Maiwand, it had been in the centre of the Lauriston Gardens mystery. It was in the company of Holmes and (indirectly) Scotland Yard that he looked down and saw to his astonishment that he was standing on his own power, and he felt alive . . . more alive than he had been for perhaps the first time in his life.

The realisation came sharp. He should not have felt that way. He should have measured the supreme moments of his existence within the spheres of family – in the baked desert of Australia, or under the shadow of his father . . . or at the least, the penumbrance [7] of his brother.

Perhaps the proverb rang true, and a man was not truly a man until he had his own hearth and home. Try as Watson may, he could not recollect a higher contentment before the small fire at Baker Street . . . and later the comforts of his small practice with Mary . . . .

. . . Holmes, of course, was the indirect source of this final peace. A path to his bone-deep happiness.

Watson's two lives bled together like two water-colours painted on the same paper. He could not separate the one without the other, and least of all when he stood here, underneath the fey crossroads under the lamp at Baker Street.

Holmes's features had been sharp and lean in their younger years. That sharpness had grown more pronounced. When Watson could look up from the kerb on Baker Street, he would see his friend pacing back and forth, back and forth on these nights. That aquiline nose was unmistakable. That receding brow and hard shoulders part of being Holmes.

Watson could see the modern Holmes, but not without a superimposed image of Holmes as a younger man, ten years ago.

He wished he could see either Holmes now.

Mary was waiting for him when he made his way home. Before his soles finished scrubbing off the packed crust of blackened ice and soot, she was there with his old slippers and a small hand wrapped about a cup of steaming red tea. For a moment, the weary doctor sighed and bathed his face inside that sweet-smelling steam, thinking that the miseries of his late walk had been worth it, if only for coming back to this small domestic bliss.

"Do be careful," Mary chided as she smiled. "You don't want ice crystals floating in my tea!"

"Not at all, dearest." He pulled the cup away and bent slightly to kiss her smooth cheek. Her skin felt like the smoothest of damask, or a delicate palimpsest he had been allowed to touch as a boy visiting a monastery outside – but Watson stopped the memory before it could finish and put it back in the brain-attic where it belonged.

"What news, my dear?" he asked.

"Precious little," Mary said, and smiled even as she said it. "But you will be most pleased to note that the International Copyright Act has been passed as of the third of this month."

"Really?" He was pleased and surprised. "I suppose the storm kept us from knowing about it sooner."

"Good news for a man who hopes to send his 'humble writings' to other countries, such as India, Afghanistan, Prussia – or perhaps even Saskatchewan."

"You tease me, Mary." Watson chuckled and drew her into the parlour with his slippers. As he tugged them on, he continued to smile. "And what would an Indian Flower know of Saskatchewan?"

Mary sighed. "You make those syllables flow forth so effortlessly," she complained.

"You can speak Tamil, so I can hardly share your self-recriminations."

"Flatterer."

They sat together inside the horsehair embrace of the sofa, listening to the fire crackle. Behind them the thin glass pressed and groaned as the barometer dropped.

"Oh, my." Mary's voice, always soft and deep, hushed. "John . . . look at the weather case."

Watson turned his eye from the glamour of the fire lapping about the coal and followed her rapt gaze. Mounted upon the wall in a gleaming glass tube, the viscous liquid inside . . . was forming slow and silent feathers of crystal. Winter was still here.

"I do hope Mr. Holmes fares better than London."

Watson reached for his wife's small hand. Holmes surprised him every day, but he and Mary shared the same directions of thought.

"I am certain he is well, Mary. He would have said something otherwise."

NOTES

1   Ciphered notes, telegrams, and Agony Column advertisements were quite common in an era of telegrams and hand-delivered notes – both open to the scrutiny of strangers, and it was a way of passing confidential information in plain view.

2   John Michael Rysbrack, a famous Flemish artist who died at his Vere Street address in 1770.

3   "Very Hansom of You, Mr. Holmes: A Look at the Old Two-wheeler and its Place in the Recorded Cases of Mr. Sherlock Holmes" by Brad Keefauver (1982): *"Cabs could be hired by distance or time, sometimes at the passenger's choice. The fares for distance at the turn of the century were a shilling for the first two miles, then a sixpence for each mile or part of a mile after that. To travel further than the four-mile radius from Charing Cross, the cost rose to a shilling a mile. Items such as luggage and waiting time cost extra, at a fixed scale of charges."*

4   This is far more flour than most people use today. Bread was of the highest importance in diet. Higher even than meat at the majority of meals. Even the poorest of the poor might not have meat, but they would at least have bread. Because potatoes (peels and all) were a common additive to the dough, the bread did have some staying power to diners.

5   West-country slang for Cornishmen. It is worth a note that in "The Resident Patient", Dr. Trevelyn completely avoids being mistaken as a criminal in the case. Perhaps Inspector Larmer, another Cornishman, was sympathetic to Trevelyn, a fellow Cornishman?

6   The Rosehill site was a venerated old archaeological site in Surrey.

7   From *penumbra*: *"almost shadow"*

The Adventure of the
Moving Pictures
by Shane Simmons

There was a light on at 221b Baker Street once more.

The return of Sherlock Holmes from the dead was a miracle, though we all should have realised the great detective would figure some way to clever himself out of the clutches of the Grim Reaper. Not so much could be said for Mrs. Watson, I'm afraid. I suppose it was inevitable that Dr. Watson would move back into Baker Street with his friend once Mr. Holmes had risen from his grave and Mary Watson had been put in hers. Their partnership renewed, even under such sad circumstances, meant great things were expected from 221b once again.

"Dr. Watson will have a host of new adventures to write in his notebooks, I expect," commented Mrs. Hudson when I came to the door, answering an urgent summons.

"I've been trying my hand at writing up some of Mr. Holmes's mysteries I've been privy to myself," I said of my first efforts, primitive though they were at the time.

"Have you now?" said Mrs. Hudson. "Well, then, I've a mind to tell you about a mystery of my own if you need material."

"What's that then?" I asked, wondering at the insight she might have living in the same house as the famous sleuth.

"It's called 'The Mystery of the Missing Rent Money', and it baffles me every month."

"Are you having a laugh?" I said, when she elaborated no more.

"I find nothing the least bit funny about it."

Mrs. Hudson wasn't one for making jokes. Or laughing. Or smiling.

"Mr. Holmes and Dr. Watson are good for their debts, surely," I said in their defence.

"The state of their funds isn't the issue. It's the matter of their forgetfulness. Dr. Watson has his patients, Mr. Holmes has his clients, and they're off solving puzzles more often than they're in. And what gets forgotten in all that hubbub and bother? My rent! I haven't been paid for my rooms on time since the days Mr. Holmes was dead and the rent was made regular to keep them empty. Now that he's alive and living under my roof again, and the doctor has returned following his terrible loss, I'm back to chasing after them once more. Not that I wish Mr. Holmes dead, you understand. It's only that life was easier when he was deceased."

"Can I go up?" I asked. "He's called on me."

"Wipe your feet," were Mrs. Hudson's only words of welcome.

Bounding up the stairs, I arrived at the first-floor landing and knocked.

"Come!" came the commanding invitation.

I opened the door and entered, only to find myself plunged into darkness. The curtains were drawn and Sherlock Holmes's rooms were vastly dimmer than the London gloom I had just left behind.

"Shut the door behind you, Wiggins," I was instructed.

The rooms grew blacker still when I did so.

"Now," said the familiar voice in the dark, "observe the wall."

I could see by the faint light that Mr. Holmes had a covered lantern poised on a table. He opened the shutter and adjusted the flaps so that the beam was focused on a single narrow point. Then, producing what looked like a long ribbon, he held the bottom tip in front of the light, pulling it taught until there was no slack left. The ribbon was transparent, and as the light shone through it, an image appeared on the wall. It was a photograph of several men in a barber shop. One was leaning back in the chair, having his whiskers shaved.

The detective advanced the ribbon so the light could shine through the next section, and I saw what looked like an identical image – the perfect twin of the previous picture. Or was it? One by one, Mr. Holmes kept advance the strip, pausing on each new image, and I began to perceive differences. There were subtle changes in the positions of the men. One was stepping to the side. The barber was moving his arm. And the razor in his hand was slicing through the shaving cream on the customer's chin.

"Those pictures," I observed. "They change from one to the next."

"Precisely so," confirmed Mr. Holmes. "Each one proceeding a fraction of a second in time. Pulled through a mechanism at a rapid enough pace, the eye is tricked. A shutter lighting each still image in sequence creatures a perception of movement for the spectator."

He set the strip of photographs down and raised the light on the gas lamp on the wall so we could see each other better.

"Has the veil been lifted at last?" I heard Dr. Watson mutter from his chair.

"The demonstration is over," confirmed Mr. Holmes.

"If you're sure you're done playing at shadow puppets, perhaps I can finish this article," said the doctor, straightening out the morning paper and resuming from where he left off.

"Does such a machine exist?" I wondered, far more enthused by the prospect than the doctor was.

"It does indeed," said Mr. Holmes. "This filmstrip is only a sample that was provided to me. The device itself is too large to be easily portable, but the so-called *Kinetoscope* has been a sensation in New York, Paris, and Buenos Aires. It seems London is the next target."

As Mr. Holmes pulled the curtains open, I held the filmstrip up to the outside light and saw a tiny version of the barber-shop scene I had just seen cast upon the wall.

"I have yet to see the Kinetoscope in action," the detective continued, "but I understand the illusion is most astonishing."

"Given your distaste for illusion," said Dr. Watson, "I'm surprised you are so enthralled with this device, Holmes."

"It depends entirely on the sort of illusion."

"I once took him to an illusionist show at the Albert Hall," Dr. Watson told me. "I thought it would make for a distracting evening."

"A puerile waste of time," declared Mr. Holmes.

"Holmes sat there all evening deducing how each trick was done."

"I work in the realm of reality," said the detective. "As there is no room for magic or miracles in my mind, I cannot offer the necessary suspension of disbelief to appreciate such theatrics."

"It was infuriating," Dr. Watson recalled. "Not only for myself, but for everyone else within earshot. The show was sold out and we were sitting shoulder to shoulder, so the night was spoiled for dozens in all directions."

"I might have saved everyone the cost of admission if I had exchanged my seat for a pair of opera glasses and a less expensive placement in the balcony. They could have relaxed in the upstairs lounge while I relayed how each sleight of hand was accomplished."

"You seem to know well enough how this Kinetoscope performs its trick."

"My dear Watson, that is what makes its potential so fascinating. Such technology does not *deceive*. It *documents*."

"For what purpose? I have seen the inside of a barber shop."

"That is but one example of its application. You must think ahead to foresee all the uses such a device could be turned to."

"It seems a passing fancy to me," said Dr. Watson.

"Then I take it you don't wish to accompany us to the Kinetoscope parlour."

"I said nothing of the sort!" protested Dr. Watson. "I assume if it holds your interest, there must be some crime associated with this new technology."

"Indeed," agreed Mr. Holmes. "It may have already photographed one."

The year 1894 was full of miracles. Not just resurrections from the dead, but mystifying advances in scientific wonders as well. I didn't know why Mr. Holmes wanted me along on his trip to the Kinetoscope parlour, but I wasn't about to turn him down. If he needed me, that was enough. And if I got to have a preview of the next great wonder of the modern age, all the better.

The parlour was down a side street and didn't stand out from any of the other shops. The signs were still being painted, and it wasn't open to the public yet. The windows were papered over with old editions of *The Times*, keeping inquisitive eyes out and suspense up. The grand opening was a week away, and the inside was still being prepared for the expected influx of customers.

A man waited outside. Impatiently. Dressed like an off-duty barrister, he didn't look like the showman or carnival barker I expected to be fronting a novel entertainment. That's because he wasn't.

"Which one of you is Holmes?" he demanded.

"You aren't the proprietor of this establishment, I gather," said Mr. Holmes, mirroring the deduction I'd already made myself.

"Most certainly not!" he huffed.

Of course, Mr. Holmes had already deduced more than that at first glance.

"It isn't the exposition business that occupies you," he said. "Your calling is political. I see you are the alderman of this borough, recently elected by the council, but already at odds with them. You disapprove of this new business and would sooner see it shut down before it ever opens, despite the money it promises to attract to the district. You have already expressed your concerns to the proprietor, the debate has become heated, and your disagreement has reached an impasse."

"You know much of my affairs, Mr. Holmes," said the man. "What else have you been told about me?"

"Nothing at all. In fact, you have me at a disadvantage, sir. I don't even know your name."

"I am, as you say, Alderman Emrys Privett, at your service. That, I hope, will suffice filling in the blanks, since you already seem informed about everything else."

"I have merely made a few simple observations, I assure you. Dress and demeanour tell me much, logic and reason cover the rest."

"Including the state of my mind?"

"Your disapproval was clear enough the moment you spoke. I trust it was the proprietor, James Arliss, who informed you of my involvement during your last exchange."

"Indeed it was! Though why a famed consulting detective should be consulted at all in this matter is beyond me."

"I expect Mister Arliss will be happy to explain his concerns to us both once he invites us inside."

With no more words, Alderman Privett rapped on the door with his cane, not so much knocking to let the owner know we had arrived, but beating at it like he meant to break it down if it wasn't promptly opened.

"Ah, Mr. Holmes. I see you've brought company," said the man who greeted us a moment later.

"My associates, Watson and Wiggins," said Mr. Holmes, presenting us at his side. "You are already acquainted with the representative of your local council."

"Regretfully," said Arliss. "He means to put me out of business."

"Only if you persist in the matter," said Privett.

"I take it you refer to a specific matter, and don't object to the Kinetoscope as a whole," said Mr. Holmes as we all stepped inside the parlour.

"I see little good that can come of this picture machine, but most of these film strips I have seen thus far have been innocuous in nature," said Privett.

"The sample from a broken strip you sent to my rooms this morning has already caused a sensation," Mr. Holmes said to the owner. "I look forward to seeing the full effect of a complete film run through one of your machines."

"It is a marvel!" said Arliss. "Even Mr. Privett was impressed."

"Initially," agreed Privett. "The likeness of a woman feeding grain to birds makes it easy to imagine being surrounded by the flock on all sides. If the public wishes to pay for such trivial amusements, I find no grounds for objection."

"Gentlemen, if you care to see for yourself, select a vantage point and peer down through the lens," said Arliss, directing us to a row of wooden cabinets lining the wall.

Each one was little more than a wooden box, standing about four feet high, with a protruding peephole viewer sticking out of the top. They were all labelled differently, with simple titles such as *Shoeing a Horse* and *Newark Athlete*. I was drawn to one called *Savage Braves* simply because I didn't know what to expect. I'd seen my share of horse shoeing and athletics, but brave savages sounded out of the ordinary.

I wasn't disappointed. Once Mr. Holmes, Dr. Watson, and myself had assumed our positions over three of the spyglasses, Arliss turned on the machines and images began to flicker before us as we looked down into the guts of our individual cabinets. Before my eyes, I saw the great feathered headdresses of a tribe of American Injuns, dancing about like they were trying to make it rain. Or maybe they were getting ready to go on the warpath. I couldn't say which, but it was mesmerising, and over too quickly. This glimpse into another world lasted less than half-a-minute, and I was left wanting more.

"How does it work?" I asked the moment it was over. Mr. Holmes had covered the basics back at Baker Street, but this was something else entirely.

Arliss opened the side of my cabinet so we could all have a look at the inner workings.

"An electric motor moves the loops of film past this narrow slot beneath the viewing lens while the lamp shines light through the individual photographs. It all happens so quickly, our mind perceives the images as genuine motion."

"Thus far, I see no cause for controversy," said Mr. Holmes.

"That one," said Alderman Privett, pointing his cane at the last machine in the row. "That is the source of my objection."

Serpentine Dance was the name of the film strip contained within.

"I take it the film in question doesn't involve a trip to the reptile house at the zoo," said Mr. Holmes.

"It is, perhaps, best if you see for yourself. But I must warn you, Mr. Holmes, prepare yourself for a shock. I am certain you have seen many a horror in your line of work, but this . . . This is simply beyond the scope of God's good graces."

The alderman lowered his cane and turned his head away, like he was absolving himself of further entanglement with the terrible thing.

Even the fearless Sherlock Holmes seemed to have a moment of trepidation, suspicious of what he might witness, but unable to deduce exactly what. He stepped up to the machine and gave a curt nod to Arliss. The proprietor switched on the display and Mr. Holmes put his eyes to the viewer.

We all waited for the film to play out. Like the others, it ran for less than half-a-minute, but it felt like an hour as we tried to read any hint of change in the detective's expression. When at last he stood back from what he had just seen, he had a ponderous look on his face I couldn't interpret.

"It is, as you say, a shock," he said. "Yes, quite shocking. I shall have to ask for a second opinion from my associate."

He gestured for Dr. Watson to step forward and take his turn.

"The fewer who see this abomination the better," interjected Privett.

"Rest assured, he is a doctor. The most professional of medical practitioners."

"If you think it best, Mr. Holmes."

"Go on. See for yourself, Watson."

Dr. Watson approached the machine and seemed hesitant to put his eyes to the task, concerned by what he was about to experience, but determined to subject himself to the evidence in his good friend's latest case. He had, after all, seen war. How bad could this be?

"Oh, my!" he said, after only a few moments staring down the viewing lens and seeing the film spool out before him.

"What is it?" I asked, unable to hold my curiosity in check.

"It is filth!" the alderman bellowed. "Scandal and disgrace! Why, not only are her ankles on full public display, her entire leg is exposed with each kick she makes throughout that wanton vulgarity of a dance!"

"My turn next," I called out, perhaps too eagerly.

"Certainly not!" I was told, in no uncertain terms, by the council representative. "You see what wretched sin this contraption has been set to! I pray we never see a time when our women will become so immodest as to permit photographers to document them in even more intimate and revealing of circumstances."

"This dispute between alderman and exhibitor is a matter of morality, not legality," said Mr. Holmes. "At least, it isn't a crime that falls within my area of expertise. Why then have you summoned me so desperately today, Mr. Arliss?"

"But a crime *has* been committed, Mr. Holmes," protested Arliss. "I have been robbed!"

"The crime," Privett insisted, "was the very act of pointing a camera at that harlot and capturing her lasciviousness. I seek to prevent the further crime of showing it to the unwitting citizens of London."

Mr. Holmes ignored the alderman in his search for more details about the sort of crime that held his interest.

"You say there has been a burglary?"

"A dozen Kinetoscope cabinets were supplied as part of our contract with the Edison Laboratory in New Jersey," Arliss explained. "With them came a baker's dozen of film strips to display. I would be pleased to swap out the *Serpentine Dance* if Alderman Privett finds it so objectionable, but the one and only spare has been stolen. All our signs and advertisements promise the paying public a full dozen entertainments for their admission fee. They will be most upset if they don't get the complete bill."

"I take it you will have no objection if the more lurid film is replaced before the grand opening," said Mr. Holmes to the alderman.

"Provided the replacement if suitably inoffensive," said Privett. "I would have to judge it on its own merits."

"Everyone's a critic," commented Arliss.

"Do you know the nature of the missing strip?" Mr. Holmes asked.

"It was stolen before I could load any of them into their machines, so I never had the chance to see it myself."

"Then we shall have to hope it is harmless in nature once we recover it. Thank you for your diligence in this matter, Alderman," said Mr. Holmes, directing Privett to the door, like he had already been on his way out. "The moral fortitude of England, I perceive, remains in firm hands."

The head councilman was shown out with no further objections raised, moral or otherwise. Once he was gone, Arliss was more vocal with his desperation.

"Can you recover it, Mr. Holmes?" he asked.

"I have been known to lay my hands upon a thief or two in my time," said Mr. Holmes.

"Money or jewellery I understand," said Arliss, "but who would steal such a thing as this? It isn't as though the thief can display it on his own Kinetoscope. There are but twelve of them in all of Britain, and every one stands before you."

"Where were the films stored when the theft occurred?"

"The afternoon of their delivery, I left them all in their shipping cans and stacked them in the back room while I worked on assembling the cabinets. They sat unmolested for three days. When I arrived yesterday morning, I found the rear door had been kicked in overnight, and one of the canisters was gone. Another had been opened, and the film inside vandalised."

"The one featuring the barber shop," said Mr. Holmes, removing the few feet of coiled film from his pocket.

"That's the one. I thought you might want to have a look at the damaged section," said Arliss.

"It was a clean cut," said Mr. Holmes of the severed end. "I expect you will be able to mend it and display the film in its entirety."

"That shouldn't be a problem," said Arliss, accepting the severed strip back from the detective. "The trimmed piece only amounts to a couple of seconds of the full display."

"The films, though short in length, are quite long in form," observed Mr. Holmes, looking at the one in the open cabinet that was looped up and down multiple times on various spindles in order to fit it all inside.

"A single roll of film is a good fifty feet, and runs through forty frames each second," Arliss informed him.

"So, a mere twenty seconds is composed of no less than eight hundred individual pictures," calculated Mr. Holmes.

"That's about spot on," agreed Arliss.

"Most telling."

"Telling of what?"

235

Whatever it told Mr. Holmes, he didn't bother to tell the rest of us.

"If I might see the room where the theft took place," he said.

"Of course," said Arliss, and directed us to the storage room in the back of the parlour.

Confirming the detective needed nothing else from him, the proprietor left Mr. Holmes to his investigation. Once we were alone, we were free to discuss the case more candidly amongst ourselves.

"I can't say I much cared for that Privett fellow," said Dr. Watson, "representative or not."

"What do you make of the local alderman?" asked Mr. Holmes. "Have you any observations to add to my own."

"Only that he's never been to Paris. One needn't go as far as the Moulin Rouge to see more flesh than what has outraged him here. If he is so offended by a picture, I pray he is never shown a French postcard."

"Ah, but these pictures *move*," said Mr. Holmes, "and will have far more reach than a single saucy postcard, or a can-can in a darkened cabaret. He seems affronted more by what he imagines is yet to come, and indeed his concern for the potential of moral degeneracy may be warranted. This technological advancement may easily be employed to venture leaps and bounds beyond the questionable modesty of a Pigalle showgirl. Not all moving pictures will seek to document the mundane or the inspirational. There will be more than a few that will cast their lens upon the salacious and the lewd."

"Well, I wouldn't put it past him to be the one who had this whole enterprise sabotaged by a break-in and theft."

"To what end, though?" said Mr. Holmes. "The main source of his contention remains on the premises. Surely that film would have been the target for destruction or removal instead."

"The thief might have simply made off with the wrong one."

"My thoughts exactly, Watson."

"Could it be this one?" I asked, holding up a freshly painted sign that was a match for the others affixed to the cabinets in the main room.

Cat Fight was the name of the film it boasted.

"Wiggins, you have happened upon the key to this entire intrigue."

"Have I?" I asked, looking down at the sign in my hands and seeing no great revelation.

"I confess, I wasn't as surprised by the subject of *Serpentine Dance* as I might have been," said Mr. Holmes. "I have closely followed news of the Kinetoscope since it was first announced to be coming to our shores. The ability to photographically document movement promises many applications to the field of criminology in the future. Attuned as I was to any mention of the machine, I couldn't help but happen upon the controversies surrounding its subjects. One film, in particular, was said to be criminal in nature. Alderman Privett isn't the first public official to take exception, either here or abroad. Rumours about this photographic affront have been bandied about town for weeks."

"I have seen no mention of it in the papers," said Dr. Watson.

"Word of mouth spreads faster than the work of any typesetter," said Mr. Holmes. "Calling the film *criminal*, as you could see for yourself Watson, was an exaggeration. But the rumour has served its purpose as free advertising. The parlour will fill up as soon as the doors open."

"Short one film, if Privett's objection stands and the substitute isn't located in time."

"If the thief was after the dancing-girl strip," I said, "how'd he make such a blunder?"

"The title *Cat Fight* would suggest any number of unwholesome acts to a mind inclined towards the perverse," said Mr. Holmes. "*Serpentine Dance*, however, more readily suggests the image of a snake charmer, and might be overlooked entirely by someone seeking titillation."

"If they mean to destroy the film based on moral objection, the lost film is likely already burned to ash or tossed in the Thames," Dr. Watson speculated.

"Destruction wasn't the objective of the theft," said Mr. Holmes. "We know this thanks to the only film that was damaged."

"But why tear off a piece of the one about a barber shop?" I asked.

"It wasn't a tear," said Mr. Holmes. "Rather it was a test cut, to see how easily the film stock could be separated. It was only then that the thief seized what he thought was his prize. That one amusement was whisked away intact, to be dissected thoroughly and precisely at a later date, in better controlled circumstances."

"He means to cut it up?" asked Dr. Watson. "Whatever for?"

"You yourself invoked the idea of the French postcard, Watson. What is the going value of one of them?"

"Rather more than your typical picture postcard with Parliament or Big Ben on it, I'd say."

"Imagine happening upon the equivalent of eight hundred of them in a single pile, all neatly coiled together, just waiting for you to trim them off, one at a time, with a single snip of a pair of scissors."

"You could sell eight-hundred dancing-girl pictures, all ankles and legs, to any number of keen-eyed boys and men," said Dr. Watson, calculating the windfall. "It might take a while, but it would be regular pay for quite a stretch, once word spread."

"Many a thief has stolen and fenced things of lesser viability, to be sure," said Mr. Holmes.

237

"So how do we catch him and get him to give us back the goods he stole?" I asked.

"That falls to you, Wiggins," said Mr. Holmes. "I initially expected I would need you to run about town, to any pubs or gambling houses or establishments of ill repute, to see how many of the severed individual frames you could locate for reassembly. It promised to be an arduous and costly affair, with many a satisfied customer unwilling to part with his newly purchased pocket postcard. We have had a stroke of luck however. The thief will, doubtless by now, have held up his acquisition to the light of day and discovered he has the wrong film roll."

"He's coming back," realised Dr. Watson.

"Almost certainly so," said Mr. Holmes.

"So criminals really do return to the scene," I said, recalling a bit of common wisdom.

"Not as often as would be convenient for the police," said Mr. Holmes. "But when a criminal endeavour hasn't panned out, and the profits remain unclaimed at the original location, a thief may be sorely tempted to return to try his hand at it again."

"What do you want me to do?" I asked, ready to obey any orders to the letter.

"I want you to remain perfectly still, Wiggins, and let the pictures do all the moving."

Mr. Holmes was busier than ever since his return, and the doctor had a full load of patients complaining about gout and sniffles. With both men needed elsewhere, and the specifics of the case all but solved, it fell to me to be on the lookout overnight. I was to hide in wait for the thief's return. Once he broke in a second time and took the other film, I would follow him back to his lair and get word to Mr. Holmes. The police could handle the rest.

It was a simple enough plan. But the thing about plans is they never pan out quite as you expect. Sometimes they have to get tossed away entirely when circumstances change.

Past midnight, I heard scratches at the back door of the Kinetoscope parlour. The lock was still broken from the first robbery, so it took small effort to work the latch from the other side and breech the storeroom again. The visitor soon saw that all the films had been cleared out since last he'd come around, so he had to venture into the main room and snoop about there.

The whole time I was crouched behind the remains of the shipping crates. What hadn't been broken up and turned into kindling yet was enough to make good cover. As the thief paced the parlour, trying to locate the valuables he was after, he took what seemed like forever to figure out how best to determine which was the right one. At last he decided on the most obvious course of action and turned on the power so he could run the machines and see for himself.

The electric lights came on overhead as the row of Kinetoscopes clattered to life. That's when I got a good look at who our mastermind criminal was. I recognised him at once. As suspects went, he was no Moriarty, but he was infamous just the same if you knew your way around the underbelly of the East End. Neither a master nor much of a mind, "Freddie Fiver" was the name he went by back in the day when he was getting his start as a petty pickpocket. These days, he was mockingly referred to as "Freddie Fourver" after he tried to jimmy his way into somebody's flat and had the door slammed on one of his fingers no sooner than he popped the lock. His misadventures were the stuff of legend, and fodder for many a joke at his expense. Thieves don't have a harder run of bad luck without ever getting pinched. A long stretch in gaol might have improved Freddie's fortune if only he had the sense to get caught. Maybe his fellow prisoners could have taught him a trick or two of the trade.

The thing was, I didn't want to be the one to finally bring him in. Some criminals are so bad at breaking the law, their greatest crime is being too stupid to give it up and get a proper job. I felt sorry for the poor fellow. Sure, I'd laughed at all the cruel jokes, but he wasn't a rotten sort as underworld miscreants go. Just misguided. And unlucky. And thick.

Watching Freddie fumble about the parlour, previewing film after film while the place was lit up like a beacon to any passing bobby, made me want to slap some sense into him. I didn't much fancy waiting around for him to make his way through the whole gallery, until he arrived at the last in the row, so I crept over to the *Serpentine Dance* cabinet and gave that a good slap instead. Freddie nearly jumped out of his skin when he heard the loud band, and almost fell off his feet turning around to see who had discovered him.

"This is the one you want," I told him.

"Wh – what?" Freddie fumbled.

"You're here to steal the girlie film, right?"

"Am I?" he said, playing innocent.

"So you can cut it up into pieces and sell it around town, one picture at a time."

"How do you know that?"

"Deductive reasoning," I said.

"Duck seasoning?" he wondered.

"Never mind," I answered, not wanting to confuse him any more than he already was. "Come and see."

239

Freddie crept forward, suspecting some trap or betrayal that would thwart his latest heist, like so many before it. He carefully put his eyes to the viewer. Once the film began, he knew he had the goods at last.

"Oh yes!" he said. "Very nice. This'll do. This'll do well."

The moment it was over, he pulled open the panel in the side of the cabinet and seized the strip inside, spooling it out as he pulled it free of the mechanism. I grabbed his hand, stopping him, and felt the finger stump that had turned Freddie Fiver into a Fourver.

"Not so fast," I said. "You already got your mitts on one film. Where is it?"

"Back at the flophouse where I'm staying," said Freddie. "But it's useless. Just a bit of nonsense with not a single girl in it, dancing or otherwise."

"Sounds perfect. The alderman should be pleased."

"The who now?"

"I want it back," I demanded. "Tonight. In one hour is fine. Less would be better."

"Sure, sure," agreed Freddie. "Just as soon as I pull this one out, you can have it."

He tried to resume reeling in his catch but I held him fast.

"Bring the other to me first. All in one piece. Be quick about it and I'll make sure you get your money maker. Or would you rather get charged with two counts of burglary over the one you've already been caught at?"

"You keep the peelers out of this," he vowed, "and I'll get you your picture strip."

"Off you go then."

There's no honour among thieves, but Freddie Fourver knew how to hold up his end of a fair deal. Before the hour was out, he returned, lugging a heavy film canister that was labelled *Cat Fight* on a plaster stuck to the side. Once I'd opened it up and confirmed Freddie hadn't been at it with a pair of clippers, I let him have at his *Serpentine Dance*. It only took him a few minutes to have all fifty feet of it unwound all over the floor in a giant tangled mess. Bundling it up in his arms, he nodded his thanks for a successful transaction and dashed out the front door with the whole jumble of pictures. I watched him awkwardly stagger away down the street, trailing the final six or seven feet of film behind him, until his tail vanished around the corner a few moments after he did.

"What did you do, Wiggins?" I was asked the next morning, once all the involved parties had been summoned for the resolution of the case.

"I made a fair trade," I explained, as simply as I could.

James Arliss had spent his time loading *Cat Fight* into his one free cabinet while I reported the evening's events to Mr. Holmes. Minus the exact identity of the perpetrator, of course. Freddie Fourver already had enough misfortune in his ill-chosen vocation without me siccing the likes of Sherlock Holmes on him.

The detective was dissatisfied with my compromise, but the parlour proprietor was outright infuriated.

"That film wasn't yours to give away to some bandit in the night, young man! It was and remains property of the Edison Company, and I shall have to pay them for its loss."

"It isn't like that fellow from the council was ever going to let you ever show the dancing-girl to anyone. I offered Mr. Sticky Fingers a good deal, and it saved me following him all over town or trying to lug around a pile of stolen goods."

Mr. Holmes saw my reasoning for the swap, even if he didn't care for how I went about it.

"I have no doubt, Mr. Arliss, that your Kinetoscope parlour will be a highly gainful success now that you have a full complement of entertainments again," he said. "Your returns should vastly outstrip your expenses in this matter. Although I cannot approve of Wiggins's methods, the results have satisfied the needs of all parties."

"Not all parties, sir," came a voice from the doorway. "At least, not yet." Privett had returned, and looked as displeased as usual.

"Good morning, Alderman," Mr. Holmes said. "You have arrived just in time for the premiere of the latest motion picture to have landed on English soil. May I present to you, *Cat Fight*."

Arliss had only just finished loading it into the cabinet. Shutting the door, he stepped aside to permit the chief councilman access.

"Am I to assume this one is suitable for public viewing?"

"Assume nothing and judge for yourself," invited Mr. Holmes.

Freshly cued up, none of us had had a chance to test it out yet. It fell to Privett to be the first man in the nation to lay eyes on that final film in all its splendour, if there was splendour to be had at all. What little I'd seen of it without the benefit of proper lighting and magnification through a Kinetoscope had been confused and indistinct. I could only hope I'd made a trade for something that would satisfy the stuffy old tosser better than a pair of shapely legs.

The film unfolded for him, and several long seconds passed as he took in what was happening before his eyes. And then something extraordinary happened. He laughed. Loud and long and repeatedly until the whole strip had expired. Even after it was done, he was left chuckling and breathless for a good long while. Longer than it had taken to watch the thing in full.

241

"Most edifying!" he said at last. "Mr. Arliss, I wish you great triumph with your parlour."

"Then you approve of the entire bill?" asked the owner.

"Consider this my official seal," said the alderman. "In fact, I may have to return as a paying customer for another viewing the next time I need to brighten my day."

With no further critical evaluation, Privett excused himself and departing the building, leaving us all baffled.

"Run it through again, if you please, Mr. Arliss," said Mr. Holmes. "I must see for myself what has so captured your alderman's affection."

Arliss did as he was requested, restarting the film for another cycle. It only took Mr. Holmes a few seconds to understand what had amused Privett, though it provoked not so much as a grin out of the detective. He waved me over.

"Come, Wiggins, and see what your transaction with the criminal element has wrought."

I stepped forward and peered down into the viewing port Mr. Holmes had just vacated. What I saw looked like something out of a strange dream. Not a nightmare, but the sort of nocturnal phantom that would make you wonder what you ate before bed that was disagreeing with you. The film featured a pair of cats, in a miniature boxing ring, wearing teeny-tiny boxing gloves as they swatted and hissed at each other. A man, serving as referee I suppose, held them both by the scruff of the neck to better facilitate this clash of pugilist titans. As main events went, it weren't no Smith versus Pritchard, but the felines held the Marquess of Queensberry rules in equally low regard.

"Holmes!" I heard Dr. Watson say just as the film came to an end. "I was held up with a most unfortunate abscess that needed draining. What did I miss?"

"Nothing of great significance," said the detective. "The matter has been resolved and the replacement film discovered."

"Should I have a look?"

"For my part, I cannot give it my recommendation," said Mr. Holmes, tipping his hat to Arliss and ushering us towards the door. "You will have doubtless found your patient's abscess more entertaining. What did you think of it, Wiggins?"

I gave the film I'd just watched a thumbs down and a raspberry that summed up my thoughts.

"I would say the alderman, despite his puritanical streak, is possessed of a rather base sense of humour."

"Here now!" said Dr. Watson, crossing the road to get to the narrow connecting street on the other side. "Isn't this another piece of one of the moving pictures?"

A length of film lay in the walkway, looking like a discarded ribbon, if not for the sprocket holes lining the sides.

"It seems Wiggins's trading partner didn't abscond in the night with the entirety of the *Serpentine Dance*," said Mr. Holmes, collecting the fragment of a dozen frames.

A final foot had been severed from the print – not carefully sliced, but roughly torn away. It must have got snagged on a crack in the bricks as Freddie Fourver rounded the corner.

"Can I have a look?" I asked of the bit of evidence. "I never got to see so much as a second."

Mr. Holmes was considering my request when Dr. Watson objected.

"Don't you suppose the lad is a touch young?"

"Young!" I burst out, more than a little offended. "After all the dead bodies and nasties I've seen on the job for years?"

"A fair point," conceded Mr. Holmes. "I'm afraid Wiggins has had the youthful innocence squeezed out of him by his duties as an Irregular. Exposure to one more scandal will hardly condemn him to moral turpitude at his late date. Go on then, satisfy your curiosity."

He handed me the strip and I held it up to the sky to let as much light as the cloudy day would allow to shine through. What I saw amounted to a few hints of bare skin and a gauzy dress to cover the rest.

"Who is she, I wonder?" I said as I squinted up into the tantalising image.

"An object of desire," said Mr. Holmes. "A fleeting fantasy, immortalised in the moment. A moment that may outlive us all."

"Do you really suppose such trivial distractions will hold any interest so far down the road?" asked Dr. Watson.

"One must hope the potential will be recognised in future," said Mr. Holmes, "and that the people of the next century and beyond will push the artistic boundaries of moving pictures past the base depiction of exposed female flesh and the humorous antics of felines."

"You can hope for it, sure enough" I said. "But don't be expecting it."

Death of a Mudlark
by David MacGregor

It will not come as an earth-shattering revelation to my readers for me to declare that living in close proximity to another human being means that over the course of time, we are increasingly able to accurately gauge their mood and general frame of mind without a single word being uttered. This was most assuredly the case with my good friend Sherlock Holmes who, for all of his considerable gifts, did not include concealing his feelings among them. Or to be more accurate, his inclination to conceal his state of mind within the cosy confines of our rooms at 221b Baker Street was minimal. As one might judge the weather by a drop in the barometric pressure, one could measure the days he had been without a case by the degree of chaos to be observed in our living quarters. This was usually accompanied by spontaneous grunts or growls of general dissatisfaction, and long periods spent looking out our window with his hands thrust deeply into the pockets of his dressing gown.

In the late spring of 1894, a full week had passed since any client or official representative of the police had called upon us, and only small patches of our floor were visible amongst the sea of scattered newspapers that Holmes had flung this way or that after a perfunctory reading. It was a delicate business landing upon a conversational salvo that wouldn't be met with either silence or pointed sarcasm, but at length Holmes's dark mood became a boil needing to be lanced, and as both his friend and a member of the medical profession, I knew it was my duty to execute the unpleasant task. Bracing myself as he stood at the window looking out at the gathering dusk, I addressed Holmes's back in what I hoped was a pleasant and carefree manner.

"Looks to be a pleasant day tomorrow," I began. "What do you say to a stroll through Hyde Park? Get a bit of fresh air."

With no response immediately forthcoming, I gathered my reserves and pressed on. "Or perhaps the British Museum? Don't they have a new exhibit on display? Something or other about whales?"

At this, Holmes turned and came a step or two toward me, kicking at a crumpled up edition of *The Times*. "You and I both know that it's ridiculous. Perfectly ridiculous. And no stroll through Hyde Park or museum display featuring our cetacean friends will make it any less ridiculous. We live in a city with some six-million inhabitants, and you

244

mean to tell me that in the past week there has been no crime or mystery worthy of my attention? Not one? Absurd."

"You haven't seen anything to pique your interest in the newspapers?" I enquired.

"Hints here and there," answered Holmes. "Whiffs of various forms of malfeasance. A fire at a haberdashery that was most certainly arson, the pilfering of three furs from a shop in the Strand, no fewer than six unexplained deaths, three outside pubs in Whitechapel – two in the vicinity of Trafalgar Square, and one not fifty yards from the Thames – yet neither the police nor anyone else has been inclined to seek my advice or assistance. And here another day has come and gone, and nothing. Nothing . . . ."

Holmes trailed off, and just as I was pondering the possibility of embarking upon a crime spree myself to give him a case to work on, I heard the downstairs door open with force, a cry of surprise from Mrs. Hudson, and then footsteps pounding up the steps to our rooms. When our door was flung open it was a young, pale-faced boy who stood there, panic and exhaustion in his features, with his clothes and hands covered in greyish mud. Right behind him was Mrs. Hudson, uttering all manner of cries of distress at the appearance of this filthy intruder, but Holmes merely waved her away, closed the door, and then directed his full attention to our visitor.

"Why, it's Bisset, isn't it?" declared Holmes.

With a nod, the young man confirmed his identity, and then with a rush of movement he ran to our window to scan the street below before turning back to us. It was no great feat to read the fear and agitation in his expression. I had little doubt that he had just been running for his life, and now, instead of making any kind of remark, he opened up a clenched fist to reveal what appeared to be a sizable emerald in the palm of his hand. Its green colour stood out all the more radiantly given the grey mud caking his skin, and Holmes plucked the jewel from him and held it up to the light. Turning it this way and that, Holmes flashed a glance in my direction, then addressed the boy.

"I want you clean yourself up, compose yourself, and I will have Mrs. Hudson prepare you some food. At that point, I would be most interested in hearing how this object happened to come into your possession. Would that be agreeable to you?"

At a nod from the young man, Holmes ushered him in the direction of some soap and water, then handed me the jewel before venturing downstairs to give instructions to Mrs. Hudson. When he returned, I was still gazing at the sizable emerald with some disbelief. Opening a drawer in his desk and removing a magnifying lens, Holmes took the gem from me and proceeded to examine it closely under a strong light.

"It can't be real," I offered. "It must be glass. A genuine emerald of that size . . . ."

"I do note some imperfections in it," began Holmes. "A tiny crack here, for example."

"Well, there you are, then," I said. "It's a fake."

"To the contrary," Holmes continued to turn the gem in his fingers. "Real emeralds typically contain flaws of some kind, or what are known as *inclusions*. It is when a stone appears to be perfect that it is usually a fake. The colour of this stone is ideal, what an enthusiast might call a 'velvety' green. The weight feels correct as well – that is, it's heavier than an object of this size made of glass. I would put it at about twelve carats, and with its classic emerald cut, a truly first-rate example of the gem."

Taking to his armchair, Holmes tented his fingers and looked at me.

"Well, what do you make of it?"

"If what you say is true," I began, "if this a genuine emerald, it must be worth a small fortune."

"I concur," answered Holmes.

"And you know this boy?" I asked.

"I do. He has been of use to me on no fewer than three occasions as part of the Baker Street Irregulars. Quite excellent when it comes to following people that I wish to have followed. But this . . ." Holmes gazed into the heart of the jewel. ". . . this takes young Mr. Bisset into very deep waters indeed. We may assume that he hasn't stolen it, because he would scarcely come here if that were the case. However, it has somehow come into his possession, and that possession has put him in fear of his life. It is that fear which has brought him here, as presumably he has nowhere else to turn."

In short order, Mrs. Hudson brought up some tea and sandwiches, and a few moments later, a somewhat cleaner and calmer Bisset entered our sitting room. Holmes waved him toward the food, and the young man did not require a second invitation, immediately tucking into a ham sandwich and availing himself liberally of the biscuits which Mrs. Hudson had been thoughtful enough to include.

"You have had an evening of some excitement, Bisset," observed Holmes.

"I should say so, sir," answered the young man, taking a healthy gulp of tea. "And not the kind of excitement I am anxious to repeat."

"How did this gem happen to come into your possession?"

"Luck, sir," answered the boy. "Pure, blind luck. At first I assumed it to be good luck, but my opinion on that score changed quickly."

Getting up from his chair, Holmes packed some tobacco into his cherry-wood pipe, lit it, then sat back down as the boy continued to gorge himself.

"Please do your best to describe the sequence of events as clearly as you can. Omit nothing."

"I'll do my best, sir." Bisset turned his chair toward Holmes, who had now closed his eyes. "Are you familiar at all with mudlarking?"

Holmes nodded. "Scavenging on the banks of the Thames."

"Right you are, sir," answered Bisset. "If you venture down there after the tide has gone out, there's no telling what manner of things you are likely to come across. Clothing, old clay pipes, coins, dead animals, even the odd dead person. People throw themselves off bridges or lose their way after a night in the pubs or opium dens, and if you happen to get stuck in the mud as the tide is coming back in – Well, that's the end of you. I do my best scavenging at either dawn or dusk, because the angle of the sun hits anything metal and you can see the shine."

"Interesting strategy," I remarked as I scrawled down some notes. "It's quite remarkable that the pickings from the river replenish themselves on a daily basis."

"Well." Holmes opened his eyes. "The tidal pull on the Thames is a very powerful one, practically scouring the riverbed every day, with the result that all manner of objects, both ancient and modern, may find themselves deposited on the banks in full of view of anyone with enough enterprise to come along and pick them up. Given that, mudlarking can provide a meagre income for the adolescent boys whose youthful nimbleness and light frames allow them to skip to and fro across the slick surface. How long have you been at this, Bisset?"

"Almost a year now, sir. Some of the bigger lads can be a bit territorial, but as they get older and slower, they move on to some other enterprise. I do all right. I like the excitement of it, never knowing what might turn up. Just last month I picked up a Roman coin, neat as you please, sitting there like Julius Caesar himself had dropped it. Took it to a dealer and got two quid for it."

"And what happened this evening?"

"I was out at my usual time, down by Wapping Pier, but a bit nervous to be honest, because of what happened to Dickie Bentham just a few days ago."

Holmes looked up sharply. "Dickie Bentham, you say? He was most useful to me in the Keown case. Do you happen to recall that sordid affair, Watson?"

"All too vividly," I replied, with an involuntary shudder.

Holmes returned his attention to Bisset. "What happened to Dickie?"

"He's dead, Mr. Holmes."

A flash of emotion crossed Holmes's features. "I'm sorry to hear that. Very sorry, indeed. There was a rather perfunctory article in the paper that said a drowning victim had been found, but no name was given."

"Drowning victim," repeated Bisset. "You'd drown too if some great lummox was holding your head in the river."

"Start from the beginning," instructed Holmes.

"It was Dickie's first time mudlarking," said Bisset. "He was a bit young and not keen on the water, but then he saw some of the things me and the other lads were finding. He asked if he could come with me, so we went down there together . . . ." Bisset paused, the memory of events overwhelming him. "It was my fault what happened."

"How so?" asked Holmes.

"I never warned him, see?" continued the boy. "When you find something, you don't make a fuss. You keep your mouth shut and slip into your pocket or a bag. So, Dickie's down a bit from me, maybe a hundred yards or so. I'm minding my own business, about to pack it in because the sun has just gone down, and then I hear this yelping coming from Dickie. I look his way and he's waving his hand in the air like he's found a sovereign in the mud. As he heads back to dry land, I see these two big blokes heading his way, with an even bigger bloke standing well back . . . Big Jamie."

"You know this man?" asked Holmes.

"Know enough to avoid him," answered Bisset. "Complete nutter from Glasgow. He's got razors sewn inside the lapels of his coat in case anyone tries to grab him and half an ear from a knife fight. He's shouting directions to his men, and when they get to Dickie they start throwing him back and forth like a doll, tearing the clothes off him, searching for whatever he's found. When they find it, they head back to Big Jamie and hand him something. He looks at it, waves those two away, then goes down to where Dickie is and pushes him face down into the mud, then holds him there until he stops moving. It was horrible."

By this point I had had the good sense to bring out my notebook to record this story, and I paused in my writing, "And what did the police say when you reported it?"

As Holmes opened his eyes and young Bisset looked at me in mystification, I immediately realised my error. Young gentlemen of Bisset's class made it a practise to avoid any and all contact with the constabulary, regardless of what crime has been committed. I returned my attention to my notebook as Holmes addressed Bisset.

"And yet despite the crime that you witnessed, you made the decision to return to the spot where Dickie had been murdered."

"Yes, sir," answered Bisset. "Whatever he found, it was something valuable. And you know how it is: If there's one thing there, well then, maybe there's something else worthwhile nearby. Sure enough, after an hour or so of poking around, I saw this flash of green and picked it up. Just as I was splashing some water on it to get a better look, I see these two blokes heading in my direction, and I see Big Jamie standing further up the bank. I didn't want to end up like poor Dickie, so I scarpered right quick and managed to get away from them. I couldn't go to the police and there's no one else I can trust, so I came straight here, Mr. Holmes. You've always been more than decent to me, and you always seem to know what to do in, well, peculiar situations."

Holmes offered a thin smile. "You're too kind, my boy. But yes, I do specialise in, as you call them, 'peculiar situations', of which this is most definitely one." Holmes paused, his grey eyes shifting pensively before returning his full attention to the boy. "Would you trust me for a day or two with your quite remarkable find?"

"Of course, sir. To be honest, I wouldn't be able to sleep a wink if I had that on me."

"Then I'll be in touch," said Holmes, slipping the lad a few coins. "In the meantime, I would recommend avoiding the foreshore near Wapping Pier."

"Right you are, sir. And will you . . . ?" The boy hesitated.

"Yes," answered Holmes, reading his mind. "I will most definitely see what I can do about the scoundrel who murdered poor Dickie."

"Thank you, sir!"

And with that, the boy grabbed another sandwich and exited as quickly as he had arrived. I looked up from the few notes I had managed to scribble down.

"Well?" I asked. "What do you make of it all?"

"We have enough information with which to proceed, but precisely *how* we proceed is the question. There is nothing to be done tonight, so we will attack the problem with all of the vigour at our disposal tomorrow."

When I awoke the next morning, I found Holmes already up and dressed, sitting at his desk and staring at the emerald before him. How long he had been there I had no idea, but I imagined he was running one scenario after another through his mind, calculating where the jewel might have come from, and what sort of action he might embark upon that day. There were the various issues of preserving the identity and safety of young Bisset, finding the murderer of Dickie Bentham, and solving the mystery of how and why a jewel of this splendour wound up on the banks of the Thames.

"Well, there is nothing else for it," Holmes suddenly broke his silence. "I shall have to call on Mycroft. Would you care to accompany me to Whitehall?"

Upon indicating that nothing would be give me greater pleasure than to call upon Holmes's older brother, Holmes and I set sail across the city on a clear and brisk morning. Mindful of the fact that Holmes was not a man who enjoyed repeating himself, I held my tongue during our journey, quite certain that all of my questions would be answered during the conference with Mycroft.

Upon entering at Whitehall, we were swiftly and silently escorted to Mycroft Holmes's office. Aside from some well-stuffed bookshelves and a scattering of papers on the desk, there was little to indicate that it was there that the most serious business of the country was decided. From private conversations with Holmes, I had learned there was scarcely any matter of national or international importance upon which Mycroft was not consulted, and we had only waited a matter of moments before his considerable bulk navigated itself into our presence. There were no greetings or niceties exchanged between the brothers. Instead, Holmes reached into his vest pocket, removed the emerald, and held it toward Mycroft in his outstretched hand.

Taking the jewel from Holmes, Mycroft strolled to a window and held it up to the light, turning it this way and that.

"Quite a pretty little bauble," began Mycroft, "and genuine, of course. You would scarcely be here otherwise."

"Quite right," answered Holmes as Mycroft returned the stone with a shake of his head.

"There is simply no accounting for the various whims and desires of humanity," observed Mycroft. "We like to think of ourselves as being the masters of the planet, but when it comes down to it, our interests aren't any more complex or profound than those of a crow. Thinks of the wars that have been waged and the countless lives ruined thanks to nothing more than the lust for a shiny rock or piece of metal. We are, I'm afraid, quite a ludicrous species."

"There have been no police reports of missing jewels," remarked Holmes, "and I take it that no one in your august circles have reported such a magnificent emerald missing?"

"No," answered Mycroft, "and I would most assuredly have heard about it if Lord So-and-So or Duchess Whomever had been robbed. Personally, the whereabouts of a stone formed from hydrothermal fluids containing beryllium is of little interest to me, but as you are well aware, there is a class of people in our society to whom nothing is more important or valuable. How did the stone happen to come into your possession?"

At this, Holmes recounted the tale of Bisset almost verbatim. When he was finished, the Holmes brothers settled themselves across from one another, and what followed was a consultation that apparently required no speaking whatsoever. After some thirty seconds of this, Mycroft leaned back in his chair and drummed his fingers on the armrest.

"Not an injudicious assumption."

"So you agree?"

"No other series of circumstances fits the facts at our disposal."

"Although that possibility does exist."

"Certainly."

"Then I shall move forward with that as a working hypothesis."

"Agreed. Do keep me posted."

At this, Holmes got to his feet and Mycroft did the same. Holmes looked at the emerald in his hand. "A jewel such as this will no doubt excite a general feeling of acquisitiveness in any number of individuals, both through legal machinations and otherwise. However, it is my considered opinion that young Bisset, having risked his life to acquire it, should be the sole beneficiary of whatever monetary value it possesses. May I trust you to see to that with the expertise and discretion for which you are so justly fabled?"

A whisper of a smile crossed Mycroft's face at this gentle jibe from his younger sibling. "You may."

"Excellent. Then I shall retain the jewel for the time being, but return it to your care at the earliest opportunity."

Exiting the building, Holmes waved down a hansom cab, and a moment later we were travelling at a brisk pace back to Baker Street. I pulled out my notebook and readied my pencil.

"'Not an injudicious assumption,'" I quoted Mycroft. "Would it be indelicate of me to ask what, precisely, that injudicious assumption might be?"

"You were there," returned Holmes. "You witnessed the climax to the entire affair. Not only that, you thought sufficiently of it to write it up as one of your tales in the somewhat lurid fashion that your readers seem to enjoy."

Now I was even more at sea than I had been previously.

"I enjoy riddles, allusions, and hints as much as the next man," I answered, my pencil hovering over my notebook, "But if you would be so kind . . . ."

Holmes turned his gaze toward me. "The Agra Treasure. The chest of priceless jewels smuggled into this country from India, and the story which was so ably recounted by you in *The Sign of the Four*. As we pursued

251

Jonathan Small and the Andaman Islander Tonga down the Thames, once Small despaired of making his escape – "

"He threw the Agra Treasure overboard into the Thames!" I fairly shouted. "Yes, of course! And now it's those individual gems that are somehow being dredged up by the tide and deposited on the banks of the river."

"Not an injudicious assumption," answered Holmes with a smile.

"Well then, what do we do next?" I enquired. "Should we bring Scotland Yard into it?"

"I think not," answered Holmes. "While there would no doubt be some excitement at the prospect of recovering lost treasure, they would have little interest in pursuing justice on behalf little Dickie Bentham. Even if they did, that would put young Bisset in harm's way as the only witness to the crime. No, Watson, I think we shall need to expand the horizon of possibilities in this particular case, perhaps even venturing into extralegal waters."

"Then what do you propose?"

"I propose a stroll along the banks of the Thames near Wapping Pier later today, perhaps just as the sun is setting to more readily reveal whatever the tides have dredged up for a watchful observer."

"Excellent!" I agreed. "I'll bring my revolver should any of the brigands show their faces."

"Which is precisely why you will not be accompanying me on this particular expedition, Watson." Reading my confused expression, Holmes continued. "I am sincerely hoping that the brigands do show their faces."

"But Holmes," I objected, "you'll be putting yourself in harm's way!"

"To a certain extent, I suppose," agreed Holmes, "but in my profession there is bound to be a little bit of danger now and then. Hazard of the trade. All one can do is be prepared for whatever obstacles present themselves."

I was not at all pleased with Holmes's plan for the evening, but I held my tongue, well aware that a wide streak of obstinacy was a particularly salient part of his personality. As the hour of his departure neared, Holmes took the time to tidy up some of the mess he had created in our rooms, then puttered around with some sort of chemical experiment as I pondered the odds of my following Holmes without being detected. It was with some consternation, therefore, that I heard him pronounce, "The clever thing to do, of course, would be to leave before me rather than attempt to follow my footsteps. My destination is no secret, and perhaps there is some kind of structure behind which you could obscure yourself with me none the wiser."

"I am merely concerned for your safety," I returned, not bothering to try and refute Holmes's deduction.

"And your concern is duly noted and appreciated." Holmes abandoned his chemical experimentation to put on his coat and slip a revolver into his pocket. "I must confess, Watson, I'm rather excited about this expedition. I do enjoy looking for things and fancy that I have a certain facility for finding them. In this case, the possibility of turning up both a priceless gem and a murderer has my appetite rather keenly whetted. Back in a bit."

And with that, Holmes exited our rooms. I moved to our window and a moment later watched his lean form crossing Baker Street with long strides. This is what he lived for – the hunt – and I could only hope that this was not an occasion in which he would become the hunted. It was everything I could do not to follow my first instinct which, as Holmes had correctly deduced, was to shadow his footsteps, but if Holmes wished to evade me, there was little question that he could do so with ease. There was nothing for it but to wait at Baker Street and hope that he returned safely and with an interesting tale to tell.

Not surprisingly, I was more conscious of the movement of the sun than usual, and as the day waned, I pictured in my mind's eye Holmes scrambling down to the shore of the Thames, and then picking his way amongst the debris. Even as his eagle eye scanned this way and that for anything interesting or untoward in the muck at his feet, I knew that he would also be mindful of anyone watching his movements. This ability of his, a kind of spatial awareness that allowed him to focus on the *minutiae* of a location and yet retain a bird's-eye-view, as it were, was something that I had never encountered in any of my other acquaintances. Still, my nerves were on edge as darkness fell and the minutes of the clock ticked past.

Just as I was of a mind to put on my coat and head toward Wapping Pier, I heard our downstairs door open, and a moment later a somewhat disheveled and mud-spattered Sherlock Holmes entered our rooms. His faced was flushed with excitement, and the blood from a gash above his left eye was still glistening.

"Holmes!" I cried. "You've been wounded!"

"I'm perfectly fine," he answered. "The greatest wound is to my vanity. Let me just clean up and I shall tell you all. Fetch us a brandy, will you?"

By the time Holmes emerged from his bedroom, I had stoked the fire and his brandy was waiting for him. I had already indulged in one glass and had another at my elbow as Holmes approached me, then held out his open palm.

"Not a bad evening's work, eh?"

Looking at the contents of Holmes's hand, I expected to see diamonds, a ruby or two, or perhaps a smattering of pearls. Instead, there was a Coldstream Guards button, some kind of copper badge, and a George II halfpenny which had been bent in two.

"Note the Georgian halfpenny, Watson. Young men of the period used to bend these coins to demonstrate their strength to young ladies they wished to impress. Who knows the full history behind this coin? Were I not a consulting detective, I feel quite certain that I could quite happily spend my life as an archaeologist or museum curator."

Holmes sat down and picked up his snifter of brandy.

"And your wound?" I asked. "How did you come by that?"

"Well," he answered, "I picked up my little prizes, then gave a loud shout of delight to suggest that I had found something quite valuable and remarkable. This immediately brought two antagonists into my vicinity, demanding that I come toward them and show them my treasure. I delayed, hoping to see the form of Big Jamie further up the bank, but there was no one. My new acquaintances became increasingly agitated at my hesitation, and so a brief but difficult conference ensued. One of them took to his heels almost immediately, but the other fellow remained and caught me a neat blow with a small cudgel he was carrying. I was concerned that the fellow who ran away might be summoning reinforcements, so I made arrangements to speak with my remaining assailant tomorrow."

I paused in my note-taking to look up. "Come now, Holmes. You don't mean to suggest this fellow introduced himself and handed you his card."

"Nothing quite so civilised, I'm afraid," answered Holmes as he finished his brandy and got to his feet. "But you would do me a great favour tomorrow morning if you could possibly contact some of your medical acquaintances to find a gentleman recently admitted to a hospital with a broken left fibula, a fractured orbital socket, and dislocated right thumb. Now then, if you don't mind, it has been an evening of some exertion, and I would like to rest up for tomorrow, which promises to be of an extremely stimulating nature."

I was still registering the meaning of Holmes's parting words and trying to picture the scene as I heard his bedroom door close behind him. There he had been, on the edge of the Thames, dusk gathering, as an armed assailant stood before him and one of his assailant's confederates was in the process of gathering reinforcements. Far from panicking or lashing out indiscriminately, Holmes had quite coolly calculated the very specific injuries he was about to inflict upon the man, in full knowledge that those injuries would allow him to track the man down to a hospital the next day.

It was, I daresay, cold-blooded in the extreme, but only one way in which Holmes made for a far more formidable opponent than most people dreamed. He was an extremely civilised and well-mannered gentleman – up until the moment he wasn't – and not for the first time it occurred to me how happy I was to be on his side.

The next morning, as London Hospital was only a little over a mile north of Wapping Pier, I made my first enquiries there and wasn't particularly surprised to learn that a gentleman with the precise injuries described by Holmes had been admitted the previous evening. His name, or at least, the name that he gave the hospital, was William Brown. Subsequently communicating this to Holmes, we made our way to the hospital in the early afternoon, with Holmes silent and thoughtful, at one point pulling the emerald from his pocket to gaze upon it, as if all the answers to this particular case lay concealed within its deep green interior.

As we strolled the hallway of the hospital toward the infirmary, I was curious as to what information Holmes wanted to get from the man, and precisely how he would go about getting it. The beds were filled with all manner of patients with all manner of injuries or other ailments, and as he spotted us approaching, Brown's eyes went wide and he made an effort to sit up in his bed. This effort was made with some difficulty, as various bandages and plasters covered three parts of his body, and he looked every inch like a man who had been hit by a train.

"Mr. Brown, is it? I believe we made one another's acquaintance yesterday evening," said Holmes politely, only to be met by a frightened and uncomprehending stare. "No matter if you don't remember my face, but I wonder if I might have a word with you regarding your activities between Blackwall and the Plumstead Marshes, and your acquaintance with a gentleman known as Big Jamie? I am most anxious to locate him."

At this, a guttural sound of contempt emerged from the man. "I don't know nothing. Nothing. Never heard of Big Jamie."

"Ah, I fancied that might be your response," Holmes nodded, then turned to me. "Watson, I wonder if I might have a private word with Mr. Brown."

"Of course," I agreed, and with the rapid motion known to every doctor and nurse, pulled a set of curtains around the bed, leaving Holmes and the man alone. I stayed nearby, keeping an eye out for any medical personnel who might interrupt this conference and simultaneously endeavouring to hear whatever might transpire, but could make nothing out until Holmes emerged from behind the curtains less than two minutes later.

"Most illuminating," was all he said, and then I found myself trailing after his rapid stride as he made his way out of the hospital and we emerged into Whitechapel Road. As Holmes blinked into the bright afternoon sunshine, my curiosity got the better of me.

"What did he tell you?"

"Apparently, Big Jamie does consider that particular portion of the shore to be his personal stomping grounds, as it were, but last night he had overindulged in a local pub to the extent that he was unable to patrol his territory as usual. This was likely a result of him pawning whatever jewel or valuable he stole from Dickie Bentham before murdering the poor lad."

"And Mr. Brown simply volunteered this information?" I asked.

"Watson, you are a perceptive man and you have known me for some time now. In your estimation, would you say that I am a good man to cross?"

"No," I said, then added, "I should say you were the last man in London I would wish to cross."

"A conclusion that Mr. Brown apparently reached as well, with commendable alacrity, I might add." Holmes began walking and I kept by his side as he glanced at me. "Any plans for the evening?"

"No, none," I answered.

"Would you care to accompany me to the vicinity of Wapping Pier? I fancy trying my luck at a bit more mudlarking on the Thames."

"Nothing would please me more," I returned, glad that I was finally to be included more actively in this most interesting case.

By the time the sun had begun to dip toward the horizon, Holmes and I were on our way. I was pleased to see that he had armed himself, and I had my trusty Webley in my pocket as well. It is always preferable to anticipate rather than react, and if Big Jamie had somehow managed to avoid drinking himself into a stupor, I felt fairly certain that he would make an appearance before the evening was through. For some reason not quite clear to me, Holmes had brought along a bullseye lantern for the expedition, and as we neared Wapping Pier, he paused to take in our surroundings.

"I'm just going to go down over there," Holmes began, pointing to a spot some fifty yards away. "Be a good fellow and slump down against this wall like a drunken sailor, will you?"

"What?" I objected. "Let me go down with you. You have no idea what will happen. What if that murderous ruffian shows up with a gang of his men?"

"I highly doubt that. He'll have one or two assistants at the most, because he won't want to share whatever treasures are found. In fact, I'm willing to wager that Big Jamie will be entirely on his own this evening. Given that, I would prefer to have you as my reserve force, if necessary, and fancy that a single figure poking around in the mud will make a much more attractive target than two of us. Just keep an eye out and act as you see best."

And so, with some misgivings, I watched Holmes make his way to the shore while I sat myself down in the shadow of an old warehouse and kept one hand on my Webley. It was a grim spot to be sure, and it was only far up the river that I spotted any other human activity at all. The slow-flowing Thames glowed deep orange beneath the rays of the setting sun as Holmes made his way carefully across the mud, stooping every now and then to retrieve a new prize of some kind. Or was he actually retrieving anything, I wondered? Perhaps this was all a show for whatever hidden eyes might be watching him.

An enormous barge floated silently downstream as the sun finally disappeared and darkness began to gather with disconcerting rapidity. I could still see Holmes as a silhouette in the distance, and then saw the light in his bullseye lantern sending out a strong beam of illumination. This made his movements much easier to follow – not only for me, but for anyone else who might be watching him. My unease continued to increase as the minutes passed, until at length an excited cry from Holmes carried its way across the gloom. Peering into the distance, I saw him hold up the bullseye lantern, then place the emerald directly in front of the single point of light streaming from it. The gem glowed in the darkness like a green beacon and I found myself getting to my feet involuntarily.

At the same time, I became aware of a large figure disengaging itself from a tangled mass of flotsam and moving Holmes's direction. I somehow managed to stifle the cry of warning in my throat, knowing full well that Holmes had intentionally lured his adversary into the open, but the sheer size of the man was a shock to my senses. Well over six feet tall and clearly weighing nearly thirty stone, he lumbered with surprising speed toward Holmes, yelling something indecipherable to my ears. Holmes immediately began moving away from the man, getting closer to the now black waters of the Thames as the tide began to creep back in.

This failed to deter his approaching antagonist, whose greed for the green stone he had seen in Holmes's hand had overwhelmed all his senses. Reaching into the folds of his gargantuan coat, his hand emerged holding a knife as he closed in on Holmes. No longer willing to stay in my hiding place, I rushed forward with every intention of helping Holmes fight off the giant, when the sharp retort of a pistol shot reached my ears and I saw Big Jamie stumble and then fall into the mud clutching at his leg. Holmes stood only a few feet from the man, and I could see Holmes bending down to speak to him. Whatever Holmes said, his words were met with a roar of anger followed by a torrent of abuse. A moment later the light of the bullseye lantern was bobbing in my direction, and soon Holmes had scrambled up some stairs to stand by my side, somewhat out of breath.

Like some kind of beached sea monster, the writhing figure of Big Jamie was struggling to stand up, but the thick mud of the Thames had begun to hold him fast. The tide was rushing in more rapidly now, and it was a cry of fear and terror that emerged from the giant's throat.

"Holmes," I began, "should we help him?"

"I did offer my assistance," answered Holmes, "on the condition that he confess to the murder of Dickie Bentham. You witnessed his reply."

Turning to search the pier for any associates of Big Jamie's rushing to his rescue, Holmes nodded in satisfaction as he observed that we were quite alone. Out in the darkness, Big Jamie continued to thrash helplessly in the dark muck, like a musk ox who has stumbled into a mud pit, his cries growing more feeble and hoarse as the tide continued its inexorable course toward shore and gradually engulfed him.

"He's beyond our help, Watson, and I greatly doubt that the world will mourn the passing of such a murderous ruffian," remarked Holmes as he extinguished the light in his lantern. "Let's go home. I should like to clean up."

It was several days later, as I was consolidating some notes from Holmes's previous cases, that he entered our rooms, hung up his coat, and poured himself a cup of tea.

"Would you like to hear the resolution to our little adventure near Wapping Pier?" he asked.

"I most assuredly would," I replied, turning my notebook to a blank page.

"I have just returned from a meeting with Mycroft, and you will be gratified to learn that all loose ends have been tied up."

"Mycroft's specialty," I observed.

"Indeed," answered Holmes, sipping his tea. "The body of a large but unidentifiable man was pulled from the Thames two days ago. The emerald found by young Bisset has been exchanged for a quite respectable bank account in his name at the Bank of London. At Bisset's insistence, a small portion of that money was used to purchase a headstone for Dickie Bentham. He's a good lad, Bisset. Would that more of our so-called 'respectable' fellow citizens had his sense of honour and decency. I predict a bright future for him."

"And – ?" I asked. There was one aspect of our adventure that Holmes had neglected to mention, and it was an aspect that my mind had returned to with unsettling frequency since we left Big Jamie to his fate.

"Calm yourself, Watson," answered Holmes, as he strolled to our window to look down at the hustle and bustle in Baker Street. "I don't recommend any further expeditions to Wapping Pier in search of the scattered remains of the Agra Treasure. Certainly, portions of it may wash ashore here and there over time, but I suspect that most it has already been washed to sea. Besides, as you are well aware, ravenous greed for the Agra Treasure has led more than one man to his unpleasant demise. I shouldn't like either one of us to come to a premature end in pursuit of some shiny stones."

"True," I muttered, my dreams of running my fingers through a treasure chest full of jewels dissipating rapidly.

"But don't despair," continued Holmes, leaning more closely to the window as he continued to stare out of it. "In the first place, money, as you are well aware, isn't everything. And secondly, I suspect that the recently widowed leech collector heading in our direction will present a most interesting case."

The Adventure of the Serpent's Head
by Arthur Hall

It was, as I recall, several months after Holmes's return from his long absence that we settled into our armchairs after breakfast in order that he could fulfil his promise to me. This was that he would relate some of his experiences in foreign parts, for he knew well that I was eager to hear of his adventures.

We had lit cigars, and he leaned back in his chair and blew smoke rings into the air. I could see from his expression that he was formulating a narrative in his mind, possibly with a view to excluding certain incidents which, for reasons of his own, he did not wish to disclose.

"You did promise," I prompted, "even if you mentioned that some of your revelations would not be permitted for publication."

"Quite so. My hesitation is merely to use a few minutes to assemble the facts in the manner which you will find most interesting."

I put aside my cigar and prepared to listen to my friend's exploits. He took a final puff and ground the remnants of his tobacco into an ashtray. Through the cloud of smoke surrounding him, I saw that he had settled on the form that his presentation was to take and was about to begin. With my notebook poised, I leaned forward with great anticipation –

At that moment, the doorbell rang.

We immediately allowed silence to fall between us, straining our ears to hear the conversation between Mrs. Hudson, our landlady, and our visitor.

"It may be the butcher's boy," I suggested, hoping that the caller wasn't about to interrupt our conversation.

Holmes shook his head. "No, Watson, it's a young lady, and Mrs. Hudson is already leading her up the stairs to us. I'm afraid that my experiences that you are so keen to hear about will have to wait – for now."

Inwardly, I scowled, but I was obliged to present a pleasant face as our landlady knocked upon our door before leading in a young woman who I judged to be no more than twenty-five years old.

I'm certain that my friend would already have deduced much more about her, but my own observations revealed that she was of medium height with hair of a rich dark brown shade, and that she was far from unattractive.

"Miss Agnes Lorimer, to see Mr. Holmes," announced Mrs. Hudson before leaving.

We had both risen as she entered, and now Holmes approached her.

"Miss Lorimer, welcome. I see that you are a little chilled, so pray come nearer the fire. I think you'll find the basket chair to be comfortable."

"Thank you, sir," she replied. "I hope I have done right to consult you. It would grieve me to have wasted your time."

"I'm sure that will not be the case," my friend smiled. "Shall I call for tea?"

"Thank you, sir, but no. I have to return to my work at the earliest moment."

"I'm aware that a seamstress is expected to produce a daily quota if she expects to retain her employment."

"How on Earth – ?"

"It is simplicity itself. The indentations on your fingers from the constant pushing of needles into resistant fabrics are quite unmistakable."

She gave him an astonished look. "You amaze me, sir!"

"To notice such things is a necessity of my profession. Now, I take it that the box you carry is in some way connected to your reason for visiting us today?" He paused, suddenly remembering my presence. "Forgive me. I should have introduced my friend and colleague, Doctor John Watson, whose help has proven invaluable in many of my enquiries. I assure you that he is the soul of discretion."

I moved towards her and we shook hands.

When we were seated, she elaborated. "This box arrived with the morning post at my home in Hampstead. As you see, it is sealed. I have made no attempt to open it because of this accompanying note." She passed an envelope to Holmes, who immediately held it up to catch the light.

"Rather cheap quality paper," he observed as he withdrew the enclosed sheet, "with no watermark. But let us see what this tells us."

He gave the paper a momentary glance before holding it up so that I could read it:

Miss Lorimer,

Do not open the box.
See Sherlock Holmes.

"So," she said then, "you see why I have brought it to you."

She held the box out to Holmes, who took it and shook it slightly while holding it near his ear.

"It weighs much less than I would have expected. In fact, it is very light." He paused before asking her, "Is there no one known to you who could have sent this?"

"No one, sir. I spend most of my time with my mother who lives with me, or at my place of employment. I have few friends or acquaintances."

"Then it's unlikely that this could be a practical joke?"

"I cannot imagine who would play such a trick."

"Is there – Forgive me for asking this – a suitor, perhaps?"

"I have had but one, sir, but we quarreled and he went to sea. I haven't heard from him since, nor do I wish to."

Holmes regarded her thoughtfully. "Tell us, pray, how long ago was this?"

"Almost three years, now."

He nodded, rose, and went to his desk, where he picked up the straight-bladed knife that he often used to open letters. He ran the sharp edge around the box, beneath the lid.

"As I thought. It was secured by nothing more than common wood glue."

Nevertheless, he raised the lid slightly with caution, peering into the box through the narrow space that was created. After a moment of inspection, he folded it back to its fullest extent, visibly becoming more relaxed and with the ghost of a smile playing on his lips.

"Why," I said with some bewilderment, "it appears to be empty."

"Not quite," Holmes corrected, taking from it a piece of white card.

Miss Lorimer and I leaned forward, to see that the card bore nothing but a symbol. It was a serpent's head, but unlike any serpent that I have ever seen. It had horns, and fangs much longer than what is normal, and its eyes glittered unmistakably with vengeful hate.

My friend stared at the card, then turned it over in his hand. His face was expressionless as he held it up so that our visitor and I could obtain a better view.

"Does this device have any significance for you Miss Lorimer?"

She shivered visibly. "None. It's a horrible thing."

"It is a mythological or imaginary creature, I am sure, but you're quite certain that this is the first that you have seen of it?"

"I am. Why would anyone send such a thing to me?"

"In order to bring you here, as I will demonstrate in a moment. The real question is, I think, why was this meeting desired and arranged?"

Holmes placed the card on a side-table and took up a volume of his index.

"This is where I retain details and objects connected with enquiries from prospective clients which fail to develop. When I saw the card, I knew at once that the device was familiar."

He withdrew a similar card and replaced the file. I saw that the embossed hideous head was now underlined with an address. Both Miss Lorimer and I craned our necks to read it:

J. Farrar
Solicitor
42 Clapham High Street

"When did this arrive?" I asked him.

"A few weeks ago. When I received no explanation I put it aside, in case clarification was to follow. None did – until now."

"So, are we to visit Mister Farrar this morning?"

"That would seem to be an obvious first step of our enquiry." He turned to our visitor. "Miss Lorimer, we will see what can be learned from this, today. I see that you are anxious to return to your work. If you will be so good as to leave your address with Doctor Watson, I think I can promise that you'll hear from us very soon. No," he anticipated her next question, "you need not be concerned about fees. On this occasion, there will be none."

He brushed aside her effusive thanks and gestured for me to accompany her outside, where I was able to quickly procure a hansom. She appeared much relieved as she left me.

Mr. Jonathan Farrar was huge. As Holmes and I seated ourselves in front of his desk, I saw that he literally overflowed from his chair. The buttons of his waistcoat strained against his bulk, and the excess flesh of his cheeks quivered as he spoke.

"No, sirs," he rumbled in answer to Holmes's enquiry, "this rather frightening illustration isn't my doing. I was instructed to add my details to the card and send it to your good self by a client. It was some little time ago, as I remember."

"You were given no explanation?"

"None. When I attempted to extract one, the client said that you would understand – eventually."

"Do you recall the name of this man?" I asked, anticipating Holmes's next question.

Mister Farrar nodded. "Oh, I do, sir, I do. It was Mr. Alwyn Doubleday. I fear you will learn nothing from him though for, as you have doubtless read in the newspapers, he died recently in Newgate."

"Consumption, I believe."

"Breathing was a great effort for him, as I recall," Farrar confirmed.

"Is there anything more you can tell us, to assist our enquiry?" Holmes asked.

Mr. Farrar shook his head, his jowls s quivering as he fingered his mustache. Then his expression brightened. "Of course. It almost slipped my memory, sirs. The very reason that Mr. Doubleday consulted me was to instruct me to retain an envelope until you came here, as you have today."

With that he rose from his chair, the effort reddening his face. He waddled across the room to a picture of Her Majesty upon the panelled wall and slid it aside to reveal a small safe. The envelope that he withdrew was handed to Holmes, who gave it a momentary glance before placing it in his pocket.

Mr. Farrar closed the safe and smiled at us expectantly, and I formed the impression that he had become curious about the contents of the envelope after having retained it for some time. Holmes had no intention of opening it in his presence however, for he rose immediately, and I did likewise.

"My thanks to you, Mr. Farrar. Doubtless this will be of considerable aid to our investigation. Good morning to you, sir."

We departed from the solicitor's premises then, leaving him with an expression of sad disappointment. My friend said nothing more until we had walked a short distance along Clapham High Street. I made to raise my stick as an empty hansom passed, but he placed a restraining hand on my arm.

"One moment, Watson. The contents of this envelope may determine our next destination."

He tore at the flap with a thumbnail, after remarking on the lack of weight of the envelope.

"Perhaps it's empty." I suggested. "But then, what purpose could there be in all this?"

We stood aside to allow a woman accompanied by five children to pass, and then he withdrew a single playing card.

"So," he said, "what have we here?"

He held it up so that I could examine it. It was a ten of hearts, but the figure had been added to by a scratchy pen, so that it bore the legend: *+1*.

"What can it mean?" I asked.

He smiled. "It seems we have eleven hearts to consider then. Does that suggest anything to you?"

I shook my head, but in a few seconds it came to me. "Of course! There is an inn of that name in Chelsea that I noticed when we were there recently. It was once called 'The Plough and Sickle', but has been renamed after restoration from fire damage."

"Excellent! Now we can proceed, if you will be good enough to summon that cab which has just turned the corner."

He was silent during most of the journey, which is often his custom. I also made no comment, except to exclaim as an elderly beggar crossed the road without raising his head, the horses' hooves narrowly missing his thin body.

We alighted and the cab left us. I saw that the inn nestled between a saddlery and the premises of a maker of walking canes. Holmes looked up at the sign above us that swung slightly in the breeze.

"Not quite as we envisaged."

I saw his meaning. The sign bore the image of eleven *harts*, animals quite distinct from the typical depiction of the human heart that we had imagined. Nevertheless, he appeared to be satisfied that this was the place we sought.

We entered through a door that was propped open. The air was heavy with smoke and several tables were occupied by men talking quietly. Behind the bar a man who could have been an ex-boxer stood polishing glasses with a dirty towel. Holmes wished him good day and he nodded silently.

"What can I get you, gentlemen?" he asked then.

A man in a crumpled suit who had been leaning against the bar nearby pushed himself upright and staggered past us, sodden with drink. My friend waited until the fumes had dispersed before answering.

"First tell me, Landlord: Have you been here for some time, or have you taken up your post since the recent fire."

The man raised his eyebrows in surprise. "Well sir, I have owned this place since long before that. Why do you ask?"

"I wondered if this is familiar to you." He produced the card that our client had brought.

"I have seen it before," he said with a puzzled expression. Then his brow cleared. "Of course! Just wait a minute, sir. I remember now."

With that he vanished through the beaded curtain that presumably concealed his living quarters. He reappeared after a few minutes, bearing a flat cardboard case with a wax seal. I saw that the serpent's head symbol was embossed on both sides.

Holmes made to reach for it but the barman held it back.

"No, sir. My instructions were to open it in your presence, should you call, and read to you the contents." He broke the seal and folded back the flap.

"Why," he said after extracting a small sheet of cheap paper, "it's just an address. It says '*19, Paradise Street, Hammersmith*'."

"Can you recall the person who left this with you?"

The barman adopted a thoughtful look, excused himself, and left us for a moment to serve a customer. He quickly returned looking pleased with himself.

"I can't rightly remember when it was, sir, but the man who paid me to keep this for you was about as tall as your friend here. I thought at the time that he had been in a fight. I used to be in that game myself, so I know what a man who's had a good battering looks like. His lip was swollen or scarred. I can't think of anything else, except that his voice was queer."

"Do you mean that it was deep," I asked, "or hoarse?"

He shook his head. "Not deep, sir. The very opposite. It was more like a squeak, and I can't say that I'd ever heard another like it."

"Can you recall anything more?" Holmes enquired.

The innkeeper reflected. "I can't say that I can, sir. He wore a long coat, I think, and his hat was pulled down over his face so that I could hardly see his eyes, but that's about all."

"My thanks to you, Landlord."

"Can I pull you gentlemen a drink, sir?" He placed a hand on the handle in anticipation.

Holmes glanced at the dirty towel. "Not now, thank you. We're involved in matters that require us to keep a clear head." He produced a half-sovereign from his pocket. "But pray take this for your most valuable help."

The landlord accepted this with thanks and we left.

We emerged as a hansom delivered its passenger to a house across the street. Before it could take off, we were there in a few quick strides. Holmes gave our destination as Baker Street, and the horse broke into a fast trot.

"I have observed the signs of impending hunger in your expression, Watson," he explained, "so I thought it best that we should consume the late lunch which Mrs. Hudson is undoubtedly keeping for us before visiting Hammersmith."

The roast duck was indeed welcome, although Holmes ate little of it. No sooner had I finished my gooseberry pie and coffee than he rose quickly from his chair to put on his coat before handing me mine. In moments, we were strolling along Baker Street, awaiting the appearance of a cab. Our wait was a short one.

"Well," Holmes said as we set off, "we will now see where the next clue in this rather ridiculous paper chase leads us."

Paradise Street cannot have been named by anyone who was familiar with the place. It was no more than a short block of adjoined dwellings, both sides of the street being similar, situated at the very extremity of Hammersmith where the countryside resumed. The pavement was uneven

266

and muddy, so that we had to tread carefully.

"The house second from the end is Number 19," I remarked as we progressed.

He nodded. "And the occupier is already aware of our impending visit. The curtains moved as he observed our approach."

We stepped over the puddles along the short path, and Holmes rapped upon the door with his stick. The owner, a young fellow barely into his twenties, I judged, must indeed have been expecting us, for he emerged immediately.

"What are you gentlemen wanting here?"

My friend ignored his coarse manner. "Good afternoon. We are conducting a legal investigation." He held up Mr. Farrar's card for the man to see. "Kindly tell us, does this symbol have any significance for you? There seems to be some connection with this district."

The man peered at the card with a blank expression and shook his head. I knew instantly, as Holmes certainly did, that we were confronting the individual described by the landlord of The Eleven Harts, whose hare lip (not the result of blows, as the landlord had surmised) was very noticeable.

"I know nothing of this," he replied in a high-pitched voice that was further proof of his identity. His eyes took on a shifty look as he added, "You must have the wrong place."

"So it would appear," my friend retorted. "Yet our informant was quite certain. You are quite sure, Mr. – ?"

"Edward Knell. I told you that I know nothing." He scowled at us and sarcastically wished us, "Good day," before closing the door firmly.

"Surly fellow," I remarked as we retraced our streps. "He is undoubtedly the one the innkeeper spoke of."

"His appearance confirms it, as does his response when he set eyes upon the serpent's head. I feel sure that we'll see more of him before long, but for now we will walk into Hammersmith in search of a hansom."

Holmes poured two glasses of port from the crystal decanter. We had returned to Baker Street without incident, and dinner was still an hour away.

"As far as I can tell," he said when we had settled into our armchairs and taken our first sips, "presenting this symbol has acted as a kind of signal for a sequence of events to begin. Miss Lorimer was directed to involve us. Then we in turn were sent to Mr. Farrar, who supplied us indirectly with the name of the inn. From there we visited Mr. Edward Knell. I confess that I cannot yet see the reason behind this."

"Perhaps," I answered after taking a further drink, "someone with a strange sense of humour wishes to waste our time."

"Possible, but unlikely, I think. Ah, of course, I should have remembered earlier." Holmes reached for his index and turned its pages rapidly. After a moment he stopped to read, nodding his head silently. When he replaced the volume he had the look of someone enlightened.

"What have you learned?" I enquired.

"You will recall that Mr. Farrar mentioned a client who died in Newgate."

"I believe he named him as Alwyn Doubleday."

"Precisely, although that was but one of the identities adopted by this adept professional jewel thief. I knew I had heard of him before, but the details escaped me. His method, it seems, was always the same: The victims were invariably widows or elderly women, always with a sizeable collection of valuable jewellery. He was known to have been disturbed on several occasions during nighttime burglaries, and to have viciously attacked the helpless owners of the gems he was in the process of stealing. It was his last escapade that landed him in prison, for the lady screamed loud enough to attract the attention of a passing constable. Doubleday was arrested, and the lady almost died."

"Hardly a gentleman," I commented. "It sounds as if Newgate was no more than he deserved."

"Quite," Holmes agreed. "He was of course given a long sentence and was reported to have become insane as a result of his incarceration. Perhaps that was when he devised this little puzzle."

I was about to reply, but was interrupted by the doorbell. Mrs. Hudson's answering voice preceded a heavy tread upon the stairs.

"It's Lestrade," my friend said with certainty.

We rose expectantly, as the inspector entered after knocking.

"Come in, Lestrade," Holmes said in his most welcoming tone. "Place your hat on that side-table, then be seated and help yourself to a cigar."

The inspector complied, except for the cigar, which he declined.

"No thank you, Mr. Holmes. I haven't much time. I'm here because we received information from an anonymous informant that a young woman, a Miss Agnes Lorimer, is in possession of the stolen tiara belonging to the Countess Woolby. We called at Miss Lorimer's address and, after calming her hysterical mother, searched her room. It didn't take us long to discover that the information was correct. I arrested her, of course, but she claims innocence and to be your client."

"And so she is," Holmes shifted his slim form in his chair. "But more importantly, did Miss Lorimer's mother mention any visitors of the last few hours?"

The official detective looked confused. "Yes. As a matter of fact, she referred to a gas fitter who called earlier to attend to a suspected leak in her daughter's room. When we arrived, she at first thought it was him returning."

"Did the lady draw your attention to anything unusual about him?"

"I think . . . ." Lestrade consulted his notebook. "Yes, here it is. She said he had a squeaky voice, like a character from a Punch-and-Judy show."

Surprisingly, Holmes laughed. "Inspector, I suggest that you ask Miss Lorimer if she knows of this man. If she denies it you may release her, for the visitor was an associate of a deceased criminal who is the subject of my current investigation. The object was to implicate her, for reasons I expect to discover shortly, in his past crimes. I'm sure that the Countess will be grateful for the return of her property."

Lestrade nodded after some little consideration and left soon after. Holmes smiled as he lit his clay pipe.

"Miss Lorimer will soon be back at her home," he said, as he sat wreathed in fragrant smoke. "I think Mr. Edward Knell must have acted immediately after we left him. This affair appears increasingly as a predetermined sequence of events, begun by the appearance of that serpent's head symbol. Alwyn Doubleday, in his madness, must have planned them carefully."

"If that's the case, I wonder how the sequence will develop."

"Doubtless this will be revealed to us soon, possibly tomorrow."

Holmes said little during dinner. I saw that he was preoccupied, and had no doubt that it was on some feature of the case that Miss Lorimer had brought to us.

"What perplexes me," he murmured, more to himself than as an opening to a conversation, "is the link between our client and myself. Why was the box sent to her, and why was she instructed to bring it to me?"

This didn't occupy his thoughts for long, however. When our meal was concluded, we adjourned to our armchairs as was our custom, to spend the remaining hours before retiring in the promised discussion of his foreign adventures. Holmes was in that rare mood where he would elaborate on his past exploits, so I took notes as we smoked cigars and partook of some excellent brandy.

The evening passed surprisingly quickly. Before we were aware of it, midnight approached and we parted.

Holmes had already finished his breakfast before I joined him the following morning.

"I see that you have enjoyed a very large kipper," I remarked after greetings had been exchanged.

He nodded. "You deduced that from the size of the bones that remain on my plate. Excellent. Allow me to summon Mrs. Hudson so that you may consume a similar meal."

This he did, and we spoke sparingly as I ate, until our landlady appeared to ask if we required more coffee and to bring the early editions of several newspapers. We declined the additional beverage, and she cleared the table with her usual efficiency. I was about to adjourn to my armchair and to enquire of Holmes his intentions for the day when his expression suddenly became grim.

"This affair becomes more curious still." He handed me the folded newspaper. "Look at this."

He retrieved his old briar and began to fill it as I gazed at the headline he had indicated:

Clapham Solicitor Found Strangled

I didn't need to read the accompanying article to know that it was Mr. Farrar who had met a sudden and violent end. More curious still, as my friend had said.

"What can this mean?" I asked him.

He put his pipe aside. "Clearly, Mr. Farrar was part of this pattern that is proving so elusive to define. Very well. We have one certain connection to this affair, and this morning we will make use of it."

"Are you referring to Mr. Edward Knell?"

"I am. We know that, despite his denial, he is involved in this affair, since he visited Miss Lorimer's house soon after we questioned him. Let us see what he'll tell us when confronted with his actions." He rose and approached the hat-stand. "Here, Watson, put on your hat and coat, and we'll attempt to procure the hansom that I've just seen from the window before it's taken."

We were back at the outskirts of Hammersmith before mid-morning. Our driver had controlled his horse with difficulty, as the animal was skittish and, I would have said, without much experience of hauling cabs through the streets of the capital.

This time we saw no indication that Knell had observed our approach. Again, Holmes rapped urgently on the door with his stick, but it was more than a few moments before it was flung open to reveal the occupant half-dressed and with traces of shaving-soap behind his ears.

His face changed from expectation to fury as he recognised us.

"I told you yesterday that you are wasting your time!" he said in his shrill voice. "If you don't leave instantly, I'll have the law on you."

"That, I think, would be more to your inconvenience than ours," my friend answered.

"What do you mean by that?" Knell's face reddened as he scrutinized Holmes. "And who are you anyway?"

"My name is Sherlock Holmes."

His manner changed instantly. Fear showed in his eyes.

"You said before you were from the legal people."

"I said that Doctor Watson and I are conducting a legal investigation, which is true. I see from your expression that you have heard of me, so you are possibly aware that you will fare better by being straight with us now than you would at Scotland Yard."

"Why should I? I ain't done nothing wrong!"

Holmes gave him a look of mock disappointment. "You believe then, that entering the house of my client, Miss Agnes Lorimer, in order to leave false evidence against her before informing the official force was a lawful act? Come now, Mr. Knell. Many of your recent activities are known to us, but a full account is necessary if I'm to conclude this case successfully. For my part, I will guarantee in return to give no aid to Scotland Yard in their investigation into the affairs of the late Alwyn Doubleday."

At this last it must have come home to the young Knell that we were in possession of much that could be used against him. At Holmes's words his expression changed, then collapsed into a countenance of despair as he put his hands to his face and sat down heavily on his doorstep.

"Alwyn Doubleday was my uncle," he told us in his squeaky tones. He took a moment to collect himself and I saw that he fought to restrain tears. "More of a father to me than my own, he was. He was a thief, I know that, and that he had a temper that was easily roused, but murder he wouldn't have done, and neither would I." He looked up at us like a hunted beast, with the scar on his lip swollen and vivid.

"Who then, since you are aware of the crime and deny your guilt, is the murderer of the solicitor, Mr. Jonathan Farrar?"

"The same as who threatened and blackmailed my uncle, and is the blight of my life."

"You must tell us his name," I specified.

He spoke slowly, not meeting our eyes. "It's Roger Burcott, and a worse scoundrel you will never meet."

"Rarely, at least." Holmes agreed. "I had thought him dead, or retired from his wicked pursuits."

"You know of this man?" I asked my friend.

"By reputation only, for our paths have never crossed. He was suspected, some years ago, of the kidnapping of a six year-old child who was subsequently found dead despite a ransom being paid, but the charge was never proved. He has a history of extortion and the heinous crime of 'adopting' children from the orphanages of our city, only to sell them to foreign clients to work as slaves in the fields of distant lands."

"The man is a blackguard!" I exclaimed. "An absolute disgrace."

"Quite so, but let us hear what Mr. Knell has experienced."

"Years ago," the young man began, "my uncle was discovered in the early hours burgling a house on a small estate in Kent. He was about to leave with his booty when he was attacked by an elderly butler. My uncle didn't hurt the man, I swear, but shook off his restraining hold in order to make his escape. The butler fell and struck his head, which killed him just as his master entered the room and held my uncle at gunpoint. My uncle was certain that this would mean the law and a long sentence or the rope, but was amazed when Roger Burcott – for it was he – that told him that he was free to go. Burcott explained that the body would be disposed of in such a way that my uncle would be seen to be responsible, and in addition several witnesses could be paid to testify to his guilt. All this could be avoided as long as he remembered that he now worked for Burcott, who was to be his master until the day he died."

I found this appalling, but Holmes seemed to experience no surprise.

"This is despicable, but no less than I would expect if the man's reputation does him justice. Tell us, then, the significance of Roger Burcott's involvement in this affair."

Knell appeared to struggle with his recollections before continuing. "When he learned of my closeness to my uncle, he drew me into his web, as I began to see it. His further threat was that I would meet with a sudden 'accident' if either of us failed to obey his every word. My uncle's skills as a burglar continued to be controlled by Burcott, as did my life. Under his direction, I have committed crimes of which I will always be ashamed."

Holmes nodded. "But how does our client, Miss Agnes Lorimer, feature in these events?"

"Do you gentlemen recall Kathleen Dinwell, the murderess?"

"It would be extraordinary if we did not. The dailies were full of her crimes and subsequent execution, less than a year ago."

"She was engaged to be married to Burcott, but that didn't prevent him from sending her to do his dirty work when he felt she could be useful. There was a debt to be collected from a party in Whitechapel, a man whose luck had deserted him at a card game. In some way, I don't know how, the money became due to Burcott, and he sent Miss Dinwell to collect. She also was a hard and dishonest woman, but the debtor believed he could be rid of her by force. He knocked her to the ground and told her to inform her master that he wouldn't pay and that was the end of it, and she replied by burying a kitchen knife in his chest. By the time the constables arrived she had fled, and was arrested in Hampstead later that day. Before she was captured, she attempted to find a hiding-place by forcing her way into the house of a young woman who had looked out in response to the commotion and sounds of police whistles."

"Miss Agnes Lorimer," I ventured.

"It was. That lady slammed the door and the fugitive was captured. Burcott swore revenge on her, for he attributed her refusal of assistance to the loss of his mate. All this my uncle knew, because Burcott planned to use him to ensure that the girl met a painful death, but he had no stomach for it. Secretly he devised a plan in which I was to be instrumental. You would be drawn in to protect her. Then, the situation would be revealed to you in stages through the solicitor and others.

"It was intended to end with you receiving enough evidence to send Roger Burcott to the gallows, but before that could be arranged, my uncle was apprehended by the official force and himself imprisoned. Before long he was afflicted by consumption and then insanity, and his plan was left incomplete. During his last days, I visited him in his cell so that I might further his intentions, but he hardly knew me. By this time Burcott had discovered my uncle's treachery, as he saw it, and concocted an alternative scheme. When he demanded that I implicate Miss Lorimer in the theft of the tiara, it was because he had already arranged that she should be murdered in prison, and Mr. Farrar was disposed of because of his part in my uncle's plan."

"By whom?" I interrupted.

"In truth I know not, but Burcott was so enraged that it's likely he could well have acted personally."

"And the serpent's head symbol?" Holmes enquired.

"That was a simple device to ensure that the events were understood to be a succession. Such a hideous depiction isn't easily forgotten by most. My uncle was determined that every stage of his plan should be connected in the correct manner, as it would have been if things had turned out as he intended."

"Why did you not confess this to us yesterday?" Holmes fixed him with a stern glare. "Mr. Farrar's life might have been saved."

Knell shook his head. "You do not understand, sir. If Roger Burcott orders that you shall die, then before long, you will. That is why I wouldn't talk to you yesterday – because of my fear of him. He has already threatened my life, and will doubtless end it when our conversation becomes known to him, as it surely will. One of his boasts is that he has ears everywhere, but I have relented and spoken out for my uncle's sake."

His narrative ended, the young man sat with his head bowed.

Holmes was silent for what seemed a long time, and I didn't intrude upon his thoughts.

"So, Mr. Knell," he said at last. "I can see nothing to indicate that you haven't been truthful. Your criminal acts cannot be condoned, but I will keep my word to you, and Scotland Yard shall hear nothing of this from me. You can be assured that Roger Burcott's days are numbered, for he cannot be allowed to continue, even if the law has no grounds to prevent him. As for you, I accept that you are in mortal danger since Burcott's accomplices may strike before I'm able to deal with him." He reached into his coat and produced several banknotes. "My advice to you is to lock up your property and leave without delay. If you spend several weeks abroad, it may well be sufficient for me to remove the threat that hangs over you, but we will see. Here is enough to sustain you for that amount of time plus a little more. I suggest you repair to the docks immediately. Come, Watson."

With that we turned away abruptly to leave the dejected follow stammering his surprised thanks. We had made our way to the nearby road in search of a cab before I spoke.

"You never cease to surprise me."

He shrugged. "His crimes were mostly forced upon him. I don't think that he will continue them when he returns. But now we have a new adversary to deal with, and I must give some thought to what must be done. This Burcott must be a man of some ability, both because he is the head of an organised criminal gang with some influence, and because he keeps himself concealed to the extent that I haven't heard of his activities lately. After we have fortified ourselves with Mrs. Hudson's chicken pie, I think a visit to our friend Inspector Lestrade is indicated."

Mid-afternoon had arrived by the time we found ourselves seated in the inspector's office. We had already refused his offer of tea, which we knew from past experience to be an appalling concoction.

"Well, gentlemen," he said from across his battered desk, "I hadn't expected to see you again so soon. What brings you here today?"

"First," Holmes answered, "I would like to know the outcome of your dealings with Miss Lorimer."

"She was released. Acting on your recommendation, I accepted her denials. Unfortunately, we haven't yet apprehended whoever placed the stolen tiara in her room. The Countess Woolby, by the way, was delighted at its return."

"Doubtless you will discover some connection between that theft and the subject of my current enquiry."

"Ah, yes," Lestrade remembered, "you mentioned that you were

274

investigating the misdeeds of someone deceased. Really, Mr. Holmes, here at the Yard we have enough to do looking into the crimes of the living."

"That is all over. The man I would like to discuss is Roger Burcott."

The conversation paused as there occurred a burst of activity in the corridor outside. Heavy footfalls and shouted protests faded into echoes before the official detective continued.

"Now there is a man I would dearly like to see behind bars," replied Lestrade. "Without consulting his file, I can tell you that he is guilty of kidnapping, the robbery last year of two solid silver statuettes from storage as they awaited exhibition in the British Museum, and, quite possibly, murder. The worst of it is that we can prove nothing against him. Every charge has been dropped because he has produced witnesses who claim he was in their company when the crime occurred."

"Drawn from members of his gang, no doubt." I speculated.

"Naturally, Doctor. Are you investigating any incident in particular?"

"We believe him to be implicated in the murder of a solicitor, Mr. Jonathan Farrar," Holmes said.

The inspector's surprise was evident. "But that was only yesterday! You are quick off the mark with this one, gentlemen. Gregson took several constables to Clapham but learned little, so I understand."

He failed to keep the satisfaction out of his voice, and I reflected that the old rivalry persisted.

"So, nothing has been discovered to indicate who is responsible?"

"Not yet, but we'll get him, Mr. Holmes, you can be assured."

"But in the interval, are you able to disclose to us Burcott's whereabouts?"

"As always, we have no reason to suspect a connection, but seeing as it's you, I can tell you that he lives at No. 21 Galatia Gardens, Knightsbridge."

"Our thanks to you, Inspector." Holmes got to his feet as did I.

Lestrade called after us as we retreated. "You will inform me of any significant developments?"

"As ever. Good afternoon."

We emerged from that drab building looking for a hansom.

"Are we bound for Clapham, or Galatia Gardens," I asked my friend.

"Mr. Farrar's Clapham office is unlikely to tell us much, since Gregson and several heavy-booted constables have trodden all over any evidence that might have remained. Galatia Gardens we will leave until tomorrow, I think. For now, I believe that a brandy in anticipation of a hearty meal will be in order."

Our dinner was indeed excellent. Surprisingly, Holmes ate unusually well, though he appeared weary. After only an hour or two of smoking and conversation, during which we discussed once more the disturbing rise of German influence in Europe, he announced his intention to retire. As the door of his room closed behind him, I began the final chapters of a rousing sea saga that I had been attempting to read for some weeks, but fell asleep before I reached its conclusion.

My friend maintained a thoughtful silence during breakfast. I made only the occasional remark, since it became apparent that he was making plans towards our progress in this affair. Finally, with our landlady having removed the remains of our meal, he took up his violin. For almost an hour, I endured the mournful tones of what must surely have been one of his own compositions, all the while attempting to reduce my accumulated pile of medical journals.

When the appalling noise suddenly ceased, I knew that his mood had lifted.

"Ho, friend Watson!" he said cheerfully. "Time to leave, I think. There is heavy rain to contend with, so let us not forget our umbrellas."

Unusually, our driver seemed uncertain as to our destination. It was received with a puzzled look, and we eventually arrived after fruitless visits to addresses adjoining Hyde Park and Sloane Street, before Beauchamp Place proved to lead to the place we sought. As we alighted, it was immediately apparent why our youthful driver had experienced such confusion. Galatia Gardens was all but hidden from the road, the only access being through a narrow corridor between two stately mansions. Anyone visiting here would have stated the main thoroughfare as their destination, then walked beneath the sprawling oak and along the passage to reach the crumbling structures beyond.

Gripping our umbrellas against the incessant weather, we emerged into a three-sided square. The remaining side featured a path leading to communal gardens which were now bereft of vegetation, but must once have been more extensive, since classical statues bearing evident signs of neglect stood atop a slope in the near distance. Number 21 appeared to be the sole inhabited dwelling, the other four appearing equal in age but now obviously derelict.

"A dull place," I commented.

"Possibly not without purpose," Holmes observed. "Someone with as much to conceal as Burcott undoubtedly has would do well to purchase adjacent buildings to his chosen lair, especially in such an out-of-the-way location. His activities wouldn't fare well with public exhibition."

The house at first appeared deserted, but after we had ventured a few yards along the path, the door flew open. A rough-looking fellow in worn tweeds called to us angrily, "What are you doing here? This property is private!"

He strode up to us aggressively, but Holmes replied in a calm voice.

"Our apologies, sir. We are strangers here who have been given directions to Hyde Park, apparently incorrectly."

"Well, the way isn't here, is it? Be off with you before I make you sorry!"

"Very well. Tell me, is this the only exit?"

The man scowled. "You can't see that, can't you? Get out of here!"

We retraced our steps, saying nothing until we reached Beauchamp Place.

"Offensive brute," I remarked then. "A lesson in manners would not go amiss."

Holmes smiled. "I do so agree, but he has inadvertently provided us with a possible way to conclude this case. I had considered six separate more elaborate paths for us to follow, but hopefully these will now be unnecessary."

"I cannot see that we have learned anything."

"On our return to our lodgings, I may be able to enlighten you after consulting my index."

I shook my head as we regained the main road. "I confess to being all at sea regarding this."

Holmes adjusted the angle at which he held his umbrella. "My first thought, on entering that square, was to obtain an overall view of the house with the intention of paying Mr. Burcott an overnight visit in search of evidence – hence our venturing a short distance along that path." He signalled and a passing hansom came to a halt a short way ahead. "The appearance of that ruffian curtailed that, however, but replaced my plan with a better one."

"Holmes, you mystify me. Nothing else occurred."

"Ah, but it did! Had you looked beyond our offensive friend, you would presumably have seen several more of Burcott's henchmen lurking in the open doorway at the ready. One of these I recognised as 'Fingers' Wood, a safecracker of some renown. He is our solution, and the way by which Burcott will finally be punished."

Holmes was still in the midst of his records as Mrs. Hudson appeared bearing our luncheon. He waved away her warning that his food would quickly get cold if he didn't partake of it soon, but joined me a few minutes later after finding the information he sought.

"I have information on Nathanial Wood's past. Not enough to secure a conviction, but perhaps he can be made to believe otherwise."

I pushed away my empty plate. "We are to visit him, then?"

"He's likely to stay in Galatia Gardens for some hours, since his most likely reason for being there is that Burcott has included him in some new crime he is planning which will require a small amount of his time. He's called 'Fingers' because of his skill in opening safes and vaults, so most likely they intend an assault on a bank. I think we'll allow him sufficient time to receive his instructions before we interview him. He lives in Highgate, so how do you feel about an evening jaunt after dinner?"

"I am at your disposal."

"Good old Watson!" he said before proceeding to eat. "We have the afternoon free. I see from *The Standard* that there is a recital at St. James Hall – one of those little-known Lassus compositions, I believe."

"I would be delighted to accompany you."

The rain had long since ceased as we set out for Highgate. Clouds scudded across the sky, obscuring the moon at irregular intervals.

Holmes paid off the cab a short distance from our destination which, he explained, was a rather run-down street of terraced houses near the gasworks. We walked through several foul-smelling alleyways and two silent thoroughfares before being confronted by a range of unlit dwellings with peeling paint and the occasional broken window repaired with newspaper.

"Mr. Wood doesn't appear to have been a very successful criminal," I concluded. "At least, he has spent little of his ill-gotten gains on accommodation."

"I know of at least six bank robberies, here and in the north of England, in which he was a definite participant," Holmes replied. "He has only served two jail sentences, however, for minor crimes. Almost certainly he has a considerable sum hidden away, perhaps intended for his retirement."

We crossed the empty street to a house my friend indicated. A cat emerged from the shadows and preceded us before disappearing up a passage, which presumably led to the rear entrance. The place appeared to have once been a shop, for its window was large and square. Holmes peered through it from several angles before pronouncing the dwelling occupied.

"There is a glimmer of light in the room beyond the parlour. Let us see whether Mr. Wood has returned."

He rapped upon the door with his stick several times. After what seemed an age, I heard movement within.

Hinges, long starved of oil, creaked, and I caught a glimpse of the shadowy figure that was revealed. Holmes placed his foot where it would serve as an obstruction, as an attempt was made to slam the door hard.

"Good evening, Mr. Wood," he said lightly. "After failing to meet you earlier, I thought we might make your acquaintance tonight."

Cautiously the occupier stepped out into the street, and I saw that he was a hulking brute of a man, heavy-set and hairless with small eyes that reflected the meagre glow from a nearby lamp post.

"I don't know you," he said in a voice that was almost a growl. "What do you want?"

"I'm surprised that you fail to recollect our visit to Galatia Gardens earlier, since your current employer, Mr. Roger Burcott, will undoubtedly have identified us. If he hasn't, you will certainly have heard of me. My name is Sherlock Holmes."

He shook his head. "That name means nothing to me." But his eyes belied his words.

"We are here to discuss your future."

At once, he became outraged. "What have my affairs to do with you?"

"Since I am aware of many of your past activities – the Newcastle Industrial Bank, for example, and the London and Provincial Mutual Society robberies – it might be to your advantage to listen to what I have to say."

"I wasn't there, when they were done."

"Ah, but you *were*! It hasn't been proven until now, but I can do so conclusively. Consider what that would mean in court, in addition to whatever you are involved in now." He glanced at me. "What would be your estimation?"

"Oh, best part of thirty years, I should think." I shrugged nonchalantly. "Unless anyone is or has been killed, of course. Then it's the rope."

In the poor light, I saw Mr. Wood's expression change.

"If you want a cut of the loot," he said in subdued tones, "I might be able to arrange it."

"My dear fellow," Holmes laughed. "That isn't the case at all. You misunderstand our intention completely."

The safe-cracker appeared confused. "What do you want from me then, for you to keep quiet?"

Holmes let a few seconds pass. "It would be as well for you if you were to exclude yourself from Mr. Burcott's current project, for our purpose is to ensure that he pays the penalty for his many crimes. Before you do this, it would be to your advantage – and ours – if you were to secretly procure evidence, perhaps some incriminating documents of his more serious misdeeds, and deliver them to us. An opportunity may well occur during your next visit to his house, or on a subsequent occasion."

279

Mr. Wood was visibly shocked. "I can't rat! Do you know what you're suggesting? I've heard about those who've tried this on him before, and none of them are alive now! I have never known of a more bitter and unforgiving man, and I've no wish to offend him."

"Yet if you continue on your present path, you will certainly spend much of the rest of your life in prison, and I cannot imagine that you would relish that. Mr. Burcott's intentions are known to Scotland Yard, as is your involvement, but if you follow my instructions, nothing will be proved against you."

"Maybe the Yard couldn't touch me, but if I betray him, then Burcott certainly would. If I don't do my part, he'll know something's up."

"Listen to Mr. Holmes," I advised him. "He has said that we are here for the sake of your future. Follow his directions and you will stay a free man."

The safecracker turned his gaze on me momentarily, then looked at Holmes with narrowed eyes.

"You say the Yard knows about Burcott's job?"

Holmes nodded. "I have this from Inspector Lestrade himself."

"And if I get you something to put him away and don't take part in the job, I'll be left out of it?"

"I personally guarantee it."

"If I do this, how will I protect myself from him if he discovers what I've done before the job is finished?"

"One moment," I interrupted. "How could it take place without you anyway? Is there another with your skill?"

"Burcott leaves little to chance. He's got Archie Berry as a reserve."

"Another of your trade," Holmes confirmed, "but with a criminal history far worse than yours, I fancy. As to your question, my suggestion is that you take the *Glasgow Express* immediately after handing over the evidence to us. It departs from the capital every day, and you will be conveyed to the station under my protection. When you arrive north of the border, you can decide upon your destination – Ireland, or if you wish to travel south after the misdirection, France may serve to conceal you until Burcott and his henchmen are convicted."

Mr. Wood now appeared bewildered as he wrestled with his dilemma. I feared that we had presented him with too much to consider.

"All right, Mr. Holmes," he said at length. "I can see that I'll be better off doing as you say – provided that Burcott can't get his hands on me before he's captured. Where shall I bring the goods if I can get them?"

"To Baker Street, or any other place you prefer."

"Baker Street will do."

"Are you certain that you will recognise the sort of information that is required?" Holmes asked.

For the first time, a faint smile crossed the safecracker's face. "I will know."

"Then we will expect to hear from you."

"As soon as I get something, you will have it."

"Then we'll leave you. Good evening."

As we passed an unlit lamp post I looked back once, but the street was again deserted.

"Do you believe we can trust the man?" I asked when we were settled back in our lodgings.

"Usually, I would have the gravest doubts," Holmes replied as he filled his clay pipe, "but the fear I saw in Woods' face when I explained what awaited him after the certain failure of Burcott's plan reassures me. He may change his mind, of course, when he's considered further, but that's the risk we run."

As it was, a week passed and no word came. Holmes concerned himself briefly with the affair that I have described elsewhere as "The Incident of the Broken Promise", but otherwise he spent much time adding to his index. The atmosphere in our rooms had, I felt, become one of anticipation. Daily, I saw his restlessness increase.

Then, late one stormy evening, a frantic rapping on our front door disturbed our peace. It ceased suddenly, to be instantly replaced by the repeated rings of the doorbell. I lowered the medical journal I had been reading to see that Holmes was already on the landing and about to descend the stairs. The urgency was apparent but, not wishing to disturb Mrs. Hudson at this hour, he elected to answer the call himself. At once I put my reading aside and rose with the intention of following. As I left the sitting room, I heard the front door close, and by leaning over the bannister rail was able to see a bedraggled figure in oilskins preceding Holmes in its ascent.

"Come in," my friend invited our visitor as they approached. "Watson, kindly be so good as to pour Mr. Woods a brandy."

Our visitor removed his hat and I saw that he was indeed Mr. Nathanial Woods. I handed him a full glass as Holmes directed him to the basket chair.

"Thank you, sir," he said with an air quite unlike that he had displayed previously. "This really is most welcome."

He reduced the contents of the glass by about half in a single gulp.

When we were all three seated, Holmes leaned forward eagerly. "I see that you are quite upset, Mr. Woods. Take some time to calm yourself while your drink has its restorative effect, and then tell us from the beginning what has transpired since our last meeting. I perceive that you had some difficulty in performing your task."

"You are right there, sir. There was me thinking I'd got away with it, when one of Burcott's closest accomplices walked in on me. I was shocked because of the care I'd taken, but something unexpected must have gone wrong. I gave him a good uppercut and left the place before the alarm was raised, but by now they'll be after me like a pack of hounds."

Holmes nodded. "As I have assured you, we will help you to leave the capital temporarily. Kindly be so good as to reveal what you were able to discover."

At this, Woods plunged a hand into an inside pocket of his long oilskin coat, and he retrieved a thick wad of papers. Some, I observed, were crumpled, while others seemed quite unused.

"I hope these are sufficient, Mr. Holmes."

My friend accepted them and at once began to examine one page after another. Three or four minutes passed as Woods and I waited in silence.

Finally, Holmes raised his head, and I saw triumph in his grey eyes.

"You have done well, Mr. Woods. These are plans and outlines of crimes that haven't yet taken place, as well as details of some which Scotland Yard are still investigating. Presumably Burcott retains these records for future reference, and that will prove to be his undoing. These documents will hang him, for they are in handwriting which is undoubtedly his own."

"Then I have done as you wanted?"

"Certainly. Now, unless there is anything else, it's time for us to arrange your departure."

Woods drank again and put down his empty glass on a side table. He got to his feet and ran a hand over his hairless head in a nervous gesture.

"Gentlemen, despite everything I'm grateful for your help, but I am now a marked man, for certain."

Holmes said nothing but strode to the window and looked out from an oblique angle. After a few moments, he turned away and picked up his *Bradshaw*.

"Baker Street appears to be clear. I cannot see that we are under observation." He turned some pages quickly. "I had intended that you should leave London on *The Glasgow Express*, if you recall. I now see that it departed hours ago, but we are fortunate in that a slower train leaves Euston in a little over an hour." He replaced the book and turned to me. "Watson, our hats and coats, if you please. We'll set off at once."

We left our lodgings quietly, to avoid disturbing our landlady. For some reason not disclosed to me, Holmes carried a small dispatch-case. The rainfall was much reduced, but the strong wind remained. I had expected some difficulty in procuring a hansom at such a late hour, but to my surprise there were many in evidence. Holmes refused the first that presented itself, then the second, and we finally boarded a cab that discharged its passenger before us as we neared the end of Baker Street.

Little was said during the journey, but Woods was visibly afraid. Every time a dark-clad figure appeared at the side of the road I could have sworn that he trembled, and every shadow in the ill-lit streets held terror for him. Holmes was vigilant in his many glances into the night, and I knew that any indication that all wasn't well would have produced a change in our destination, so I was relieved at our arrival.

The cab came to rest and we alighted, Holmes immediately inspecting this new scene as I paid our fare. We entered the station and purchased the ticket from a sleepy clerk, before ensuring that Woods safely boarded the train that arrived after a short wait. The attending official raised a green flag and gave a blast on his whistle, before turning away as the last of the coaches disappeared into the darkness. Moments later all sounds of the conveyance ceased, and I saw that Holmes was studying the few travellers remaining on the platform. He turned his attention across the line, towards the waiting room and benches at the opposite side of the track, and then left abruptly with me in his wake.

"Did you detect any observation?" I asked him as we left the station.

"No, there was no one. However, there is the possibility that Woods was followed and observed entering our lodgings. The watcher could then have immediately left to report before I looked out on Baker Street. This may or may not be the case, but if so, then Burcott is now aware of our interest in his affairs."

"My hand is on my service revolver at this moment."

"I also will be armed constantly until this affair is over," he said as he selected a hansom from several nearby, awaiting the next exodus from the station.

I had anticipated that this affair, or the echoes of it, would be with us for some time. As it was, it came to a violent conclusion that very night. As our cab entered Baker Street, I saw Holmes become alert at once. His body stiffened as a hunting dog's does at the first sight of its prey.

"What is it?" I asked.

He shouted for the driver to halt. "Woods seems to have been rather careless when he visited us. There are at least three roughs waiting for our return near our lodgings. I can only suppose that whoever followed Woods reported to Burcott immediately, as I surmised earlier."

I peered into the darkness ahead. One of the lamp posts held no illumination, whether because of malfunction or deliberate damage for the purpose of concealment by our adversaries, I couldn't tell. I saw movement against the unlit buildings. The shadows would serve them well.

"I see them," I said, "and I'm ready."

"You would serve me better by leaving, I think."

In the dim interior, I stared at him in surprise. "Whatever can you mean? As always, I'm here to fight side-by-side with you."

"I don't doubt that for an instant, but you must believe me when I tell you that to seek a constable or continue in this hansom to Scotland Yard would be by far the best course." He reached into his coat and extracted what I recognised to be the collection of papers provided by Woods. "These must reach the Yard tonight. I beg you to take them before we are accosted."

His intention was plain to see – that the evidence was delivered to Lestrade was clearly for the greater good. Yet I was reluctant in the extreme to leave my old friend to face an unknown number of opponents.

The decision, however, was quickly taken from me. Holmes leapt from the cab and shouted to the driver, "Scotland Yard, with all speed!"

The hansom lurched forward as the driver cracked his whip and the horse went into an immediate gallop. From the shadows a burly shape appeared and attempted to attach itself to the side of the conveyance, but I struck at the unshaven face through the open window and heard a scream as a wheel passed over the body. The driver shouted something that was lost on the wind as several shots pierced the silence. I looked back as best as I could, but we were now too far away. Fear gripped me as I wondered whether my friend still lived, and the hansom leaned heavily to one side as we jolted around a sharp corner.

Then, and I thanked God for it, a young constable appeared out of the darkness. I shouted to the driver who brought the cab to a screeching halt, attracting the attention of the officer immediately. I leaped to the pavement, hurriedly explaining that the documents I placed in his hands were vital. He appeared confused. Possibly he was new to the official force, but at the mention of Holmes's name and that of Lestrade, he voiced his understanding and promised to send assistance, as well as to effect delivery. I ushered him into the hansom before instructing the driver to resume his journey. I found myself alone in an instant. I began to retrace my steps, running in the ill-lit street from shadow to shadow and dreading what might lie ahead.

I slowed my pace to a cautious walk as I neared the scene. At once relief flooded over me because Holmes stood defiantly facing a tall man wearing a top hat, surrounded by four prone bodies and five vicious-looking roughs who appeared anxious to resume the assault.

I was by now breathless and still too far away to assist my friend, but as my heart slowed its beat I could hear what passed between them.

"You really must give it up, Mr. Holmes. As soon as my agent brought me the news, I realised the difficulties I would face in retrieving my property. No bullets remain in your weapon, you have only your swordstick with which to defend yourself. Be in no doubt that we will compel you to reveal to us where Nathaniel Woods is hidden, and that it will be extremely painful, unless you choose to be sensible."

Moving silently, I drew nearer. In the meagre light, I would swear that I saw Holmes's expression change to one of relief. His keen eyes had noticed my return. My service revolver was in my hand as I advanced further.

"Your criminal career is at end, Burcott. If I cannot end it, Scotland Yard will ensure it."

"You believe so?" He shifted his position, and the poor illumination revealed a thin, cruel face. His narrow moustache enclosed a mouth that snarled its evil intent. "Consider your situation, it doesn't support such an outcome." His voice took on a harsher edge, and he advanced towards my friend slowly. "Now return those papers if you wish to die quickly."

In answer, Holmes flung the dispatch case at his antagonist's feet obediently. As Burcott bent to retrieve it he screamed, and I saw that Holmes's swordstick protruded from his thigh. The others, armed with cudgels and knives, rushed forward, and the blade was withdrawn and buried in the chest of the first of them. The next man slashed at my friend and succeeded in drawing blood because Holmes's evasion came an instant too late, but no second attack was forthcoming. The assailant fell with my bullet in his heart, and another with blood gushing from his throat. The two remaining turned and saw me, and I was able to fell the nearest of them before he could get closer. The last man standing confronted me, and I levelled my weapon at him but never fired, since he dropped his cudgel and fled into the night. I went to Holmes, who wiped blood from his face while holding his swordstick at the ready.

"Holmes!" I cried. "No!"

He glanced at me, unperturbed. "Oh, do not concern yourself. I have no intention of taking Burcott's life, only of ensuring that he doesn't attack further. You surely cannot imagine that I would cheat the hangman of so worthy a subject."

Before I could reply, a police coach hurtled towards us out of the gloom, and then another. I counted eight armed constables emerging the instant their conveyances came to halt, accompanied by Inspector Lestrade.

He strode up to us, but stopped short to look at what surrounded him.

"I see that you and Doctor Watson have been busy, Mr. Holmes. I

285

was at the local station when Constable Bramwell reported the urgency of the situation, and I assembled these men before setting out at once." He turned his attention to Burcott, who was attempting to stem the flow of blood from his thigh. "But who have we here? I tell you, gentlemen, that if you have secured evidence against this man, you have done a good night's work indeed. The Yard has long hungered to see him behind bars, but our attempts until now have failed."

"You saw the papers that your constable delivered?" Holmes enquired.

Lestrade shook his head. "Not yet. He told me of their importance, so I placed them in our safe. It seemed to me that to furnish assistance was the most immediate issue."

"Quite so, Lestrade," he nodded. "And we thank you for it. The papers contain details of crimes past and present, written in Burcott's own hand. You should now have no difficulty in obtaining a conviction."

"We owe you a debt, sir," The official detective advanced upon us and saw my friend clearly for the first time. "But, Mr. Holmes, you are wounded! Accompany us back to the station, where a police doctor will attend to you."

"My thanks," said Holmes, "but it's little more than a scratch. I think Burcott is in need more than I."

"I shall see to it. We want him to be in the best of health when he mounts the scaffold." A burly sergeant had approached, and Lestrade turned to him. "Askins, leave two constables on guard here, while the rest of us return to the station. I will send out a conveyance to remove the bodies later."

The officer saluted and rejoined his men. Several windows nearby had been illuminated briefly, the residents disturbed by the reports from the firearms, but now all was dark once more.

"If there is nothing else, Inspector," said my friend, "Watson and I will be away to our beds."

"Of course. I would appreciate a visit at the Yard tomorrow, to furnish a full report."

Holmes glanced at Burcott, whose stare exuded hate.

"It will our pleasure to do so."

We wished each other goodnight, and the little detective set about organising their departure. Holmes and I walked wearily to our lodgings, and I saw that his bleeding has ceased.

"I confess to being glad to see the end of this day," I remarked.

Holmes placed his key in the lock. "I as well. But, tired as we are, I'm certain that you will have no objection to a brandy before we surrender ourselves to a well-earned good night's sleep."

The Adventure of the
Aged Actor
by Tracy J. Revels

It is with a heavy heart that I write this tale. My friend Mr. Sherlock Holmes has bidden me to record it and then seal it away. It makes him sad, to think on its conclusion, but he feels it should be documented, even if it is never published due to the pain it might cause a certain innocent young lady. Once completed, I shall lock it in my box and, perhaps when all of us are only memory, it shall then be read.

Theatrical patrons once adored Mr. Peyton Fox, the actor crowned "The King of the Melodramas" by the London Press. Though melodramas have fallen out of fashion in this modern, cynical age, the overwrought productions which featured tales of murder and supernatural revenge were previously favored by the city's laboring classes, who felt free to express their pleasure with loud cheers and their disgust with rotten tomatoes. Fox began his career playing dashing heroes: Handsome princes, stouthearted soldiers, and debonair cavaliers, with the occasional romantic bandit thrown in for good measure. By the final act, Fox would have slain his wicked rival and swept the fainting maiden into his arms. In his later years, Fox transitioned into secondary yet memorable roles: Outraged fathers, compassionate priests, and noble monarchs. During the curtain call of his final public appearance, he boasted he had played over five-hundred roles, but never once been cast as a villain.

It was therefore rather ironic when Sherlock Holmes received a visit from Fox's lawyer, who blandly stated that his client had been accused of arson and murder in the tiny village of Biddenbrook, two days previously. And so, early on a fine summer morning, we found ourselves in Fox's cell, given permission to interview him as associates of his legal representation. He was a wreck of a handsome man. His pale face, with its dark-circled, haunted eyes framed by long white hair, was a startling contrast to the striking visage which had once graced a thousand theatrical broadsides. He was dressed only in his shirt and trousers, as his wild behavior upon confinement made his keepers fear he might attempt suicide. Upon hearing my friend's name, he rose and offered a dignified hand.

"God bless you for coming, sir, and so soon. Mr. Jones has advised me to hold nothing back from you. The man has given me up, you see –

287

even he, who should be my staunchest defender, thinks I killed my wife. He finds my story too fantastical to believe."

"Fantastical storytellers are rarely liars, unless they are published authors," Holmes observed, with a wink in my direction. "A successful liar must stick to the mundane if he is to succeed." My friend leaned against a wall and opened his cigarette case, holding it out to his new client, but the prisoner demurred. Holmes snapped a vesta with authority. "Give us your tale, Mr. Fox – but be aware that we are only permitted an hour for this interview."

The man sighed as he folded himself back onto the narrow bunk. "I cannot be as concise as you might wish, for to understand my current trouble, it is necessary to know my past ones. For the first twenty years of my career, I was a bachelor, with no thought of ever entering the blessed state of wedlock. Then I met my beloved Rosita – she played the Indian princess to my valiant conquistador in *The Treasure of Ponce de Leon* – and we married after the play's final performance. For many seasons we knew only happiness. But then, some twenty-five years ago, Rosita was brought to bed, and perished while giving birth to our daughter, Juliet.

"What was I to do in such a predicament? The infant was small and weak, there were no suitable nurses among the theater troupe to which I belonged, and backstage was certainly no place to raise a baby. Desperate, I reached out to my sister, Suzanna. We had been estranged, as she was very religious and disproved of the life I led. Despite being a spinster, she adored children, and I couldn't imagine that she would turn her back on my precious little girl. However, I was shocked by the condition she laid upon me. She agreed to raise Juliet with loving care, but only if she could claim Juliet as her own, the offspring of a mythical, recently deceased husband. I would be demoted to the status of an affectionate uncle, forbidden to interfere with any of Suzanna's decisions concerning Juliet's discipline or education.

"You no doubt think me a wicked man for allowing my daughter to be taken away under such demands, but I felt Juliet would have a better life with my sister. Shortly after she took Juliet into her care, Suzanna moved to Canterbury, where no one would question her story as to Juliet's origins. From time to time, I visited them. In all those years, I performed from the script Suzanna had written for me, even though it broke my heart to do so.

"After Suzanne's departure with my girl, I experienced a terrible dark time in my life. I took to drinking, I was often debauched, and while in this state I had a brief liaison with a young *danseuse*. We soon quarreled and she left the company, but seven months later she appeared at my dressing room door, carrying a swaddled baby. One glance at his hair – as red as mine was at the time – revealed the truth of her claim. Then, much to my astonishment, she told me she had fallen in love with another man who adored both her and the child and would give the boy his name. She was honest and asked only for my blessing, so that her conscience would be clear. I gave it willingly, for I knew she and my boy would be better for having found a home far from the stage."

Holmes waggled his cigarette. "Mr. Fox, your personal dramas – "

"Are essential, I tell you! Bear with me, I beg of you." Fox combed one nervous hand through his hair. "I came to my senses, and for the next two decades I devoted myself to my craft. Perhaps you have some sense of the fame I achieved. When I left the stage, I wanted nothing more than to live quietly, puttering in a garden and writing my memoirs in some picturesque village. I took a bride, a Miss Helen Hitchford, a young dresser in our company. She assured me her dreams aligned with mine, but less than a year had passed before our love soured and she grew bored with me and with our life here in Biddenbrook. Without children to raise, I suppose it was inevitable that we would drift apart, and I didn't attempt to stand in her way when she travelled to London alone. Oh, I saw through her claims of visiting friends, or comforting an invalid relative. I knew what she was about, with younger men. It was unimportant to me. If she remained my wife and brought no open scandal on my name, I would look the other way.

"You grow impatient, Mr. Holmes, so I shall come to the crux of the matter. Three months ago, I received a message from my sister, telling me that a suitor had proposed marriage to Juliet. Suzanna said the boy was a newly licensed physician, and from a good Canterbury family, but I was incensed that I hadn't been alerted to the courtship. In the letter, Suzanna mentioned that Juliet's beau and his mother would be visiting with them the next Saturday, and so I made a point to travel to Canterbury on that morning, determined to judge the young man's suitability. I arrived at my sister's home just at luncheon and heard the voices of a merry party having a picnic in her little garden. I stormed in and was nearly struck dead with horror.

"For you see, Mr. Holmes, my eyes fell first on the youth, and noted that he possessed the same great wreath of red hair that had been my trademark on stage. My gaze shot to his mother, and despite her increased girth and wrinkled face, I recognized the *danseuse* I had known years in the past. There was no question – this was the son I had seen but once, as an infant in her arms. And my daughter was engaged to him!"

Holmes arched an eyebrow. "The plot does indeed thicken."

The man leapt from the bunk, waving his hands about, as if forgetting he was in a jail cell rather a music hall theater.

"There were cries and screams and two separate incidents of fainting. But I had to tell them the truth. As innocent as their love was, it dared not be consummated. Juliet wouldn't be comforted, and both my sister and my former lover turned on me like harpies. The young man fled, his face crimson with shame. I hurried home, but when I told my wife this terrible twist of fate, she merely laughed at me. I hated her from that moment forward . . . but I swear to you I didn't kill her."

"You have an alibi for the night of her death?"

"I do – I was in Canterbury."

Holmes sighed. "Then surely there is someone who can verify your presence in that city."

"It isn't so simple . . . Allow me to continue my tale."

Holmes waved for him to go on.

"Five days ago, I received a note from my son, indicating that he and Juliet wished to speak to me, but only in the greatest confidence. He said they would meet me in Canterbury at the Hotel Caliban at nine the following evening, but that I should come incognito. I didn't question the note. I imagined my shame had become theirs, and they wouldn't wish any friend to know who they were meeting. I burned the letter and told my plans to no one, just as my son had requested. The next day, I shaved my rather stately beard and placed a dark wig upon my head. My wife had gone to do her charity work at the Refuge for Young Mothers, so she didn't witness my transformation, and I left her a note stating that I would be spending the night in London, meeting with old actor friends. I boarded the afternoon train and arrived in Canterbury several hours before my appointment. During that time, I loitered about the cathedral like any other tourist. I doubt anyone who saw me would remember me, for I did my best to remain inconspicuous.

"At last, with only an hour to spare before the all-important rendezvous, I hailed a cab and asked the driver to take me to the address from the note. He gave me a rather hard look but cracked his whip. It seemed we travelled endlessly until we reached a dreary, lonesome place outside of town. The vehicle halted and I stepped out, handing up the exorbitant fare.

"'But – wait – Where is the hotel?' I asked, for the cab had stopped before the massive wrought iron gates of an ill-kept cemetery. 'Where is the Hotel Caliban?'

"'There is no such place in Canterbury,' the brutish driver shouted. 'But this is the address you gave me.'

"He snapped the reins, and I was left alone with the realization that I had been the victim of some nasty prank. I dropped to my knees and wept for an hour. By the time I recovered, the blackest night had fallen. There were no streetlights, and I feared that I was in a dangerous location. The dead seemed safer companions, so I climbed the fence and passed the lonely hours atop a marble slab, with a lichen-covered angel for a companion. The next morning, I woke up cold and weary, aching in every joint. I must have walked for more than two hours before I found a friendly tradesman who directed me back toward the town and the station. Though I was famished, I was also so disheveled that I wasn't presentable in any café, therefore I sat alone at the station until my train arrived and whisked me back to Biddenbrook at just past noon – only to walk into the arms of the police, who arrested me for the terrible crimes of murder and arson."

"And how did the police recognize you?"

"I felt no need to remain incognito. I had thrown my wig into a bin in the Canterbury Station."

"Has your advocate reached out to your children?"

"He has. My daughter denies any hand in luring me away from home. My son's mother said he is travelling abroad, so he could have nothing to do with the matter."

"Very well, Mr. Fox. I shall make inquiries. You case is a most unusual one."

"Do you give me any hope, sir? Or should I prepare to climb the gallows?"

"There is always hope, Mr. Fox, if you have told us the complete truth."

"I assure you that I have."

We left the old fellow brooding in his cell and invited the local inspector across the street for a coffee. Inspector Jack Walker was a young man, with blond hair, exceptionally bright eyes, and a firm jaw.

"Your reputation precedes you, Mr. Holmes," he said. "But I feel certain there is no need for you to concern yourself with this ugly business. The matter is quite open and shut."

"Then it will do no harm for you to share it with us, Inspector," Holmes said, his lips twitching into a momentary smile, "so that we may admire your methods."

If the young man heard the edge of sarcasm in my friend's tone, he didn't acknowledge it. Instead, he plunged into his tale with great enthusiasm.

"Everyone in the village knew that the Fox marriage was an unhappy one, and that she regularly placed the cuckhold's horns upon his foolish old head. Mrs. Fox is – I mean *was* – an exceptionally beautiful woman of some thirty years, tall and raven-haired, with a witch's black eyes. Many a morning I have seen Mrs. Fox walking to the station, dressed in her finest, and seen her return late in the evening, with her hair loose, her

291

blouse half unbuttoned, and such a look of dissipation on her face that even an innocent child would have known what sins she had been committing! And their quarrels! I have heard them shouting abuse at each other, in their front garden, with only the high hedge to obscure their domestic woes."

"Was this unhappiness also a source of violence?" Holmes asked.

"Well, it appears that Mr. Fox has a rather savage temper. I know this because my wife – who served with Mrs. Fox in the Friends of the Refuge for Young Mothers – told me that for almost a week before her death, the lady was nursing a black eye which she said her spouse had given her.

"But you wish to know what happened three days ago. Fox claims he left our town the day before, but no one noticed him going to the station. His missus came to donate some items to the Refuge the morning her husband supposedly departed. She confided to my wife how she feared her husband's increasing wrath. She was never seen again. At six the next morning, Mr. Fox purchased a ticket for London at the station, departing on the six-ten train. Some twenty minutes later, the nearest neighbors noticed smoke roiling from the windows of the Fox cottage. Before the firemen could assemble, the house was almost entirely consumed. I believe that the fire was set amid the covers and hangings of the couple's bed."

"What leads you to this conclusion?" Holmes asked.

"The fact that Mrs. Fox's body was found amid the ashes. It was reduced to a charred skeleton, but clearly the lady had been most horribly murdered. We found handcuffs around her wrists and heavy chains upon her ankles."

I confess I gasped at this statement. Some part of me had hoped it might all be proven to be a mistake – a tragic accident unjustly labeled a homicide. But how could one argue for such when evidence of restraint was obvious? I shuddered to imagine any man so vicious he could leave his wife to die in such a manner.

"Did the couple employ any servants?" Holmes asked softly.

"Just one, a young girl named Abby. She is staying in the cottage by the station."

"It may be worth paying her a visit," Holmes said. "I take it you have already cleared her in the matter?"

"Yes. Her mother had been ill, and Mrs. Fox had given Abby three day's leave to tend to her."

Holmes nodded and finished off his coffee. "You are quite convinced of Mr. Fox's guilt in the matter?" he said to the inspector.

"Surely you don't believe that fanciful tale of his! Siring two children, abandoning them both, and then claiming they were planning to wed? It reads like a melodrama, Mr. Holmes."

"A genre with which he is clearly familiar."

Inspector Walker nodded eagerly. "Here is what happened, I am certain: The man tired of his wife's promiscuous behavior, which had made him the laughingstock of the village. When words and fists failed him, he completely lost his temper and decided to do away with her in a suitably horrific manner, one perhaps suggested to him by all his years upon the stage. He left the fire to burn and fled the scene before the alarm was raised. He was bold enough to return, just hours later, with his face and clothing altered, in hopes that we would believe his fanciful alibi."

My friend's gaze was locked to the ceiling beams. "One more question, Inspector: Have there been any other crimes in the village, in the days surrounding the lady's untimely death?"

"You'd think arson and murder would be enough!" the young man stated, then chuckled ruefully. "Well, let me think . . . Abernathy's sheep got out of their pen the night before Mrs. Fox was murdered, and we had a devil of a time chasing them out of Mrs. Wrenlay's flower garden, as she threatened to shoot the lot of them with her late husband's elephant gun. And the vicar told me, just before the alarm of fire went up, that he feared some youngsters had been impudent in the churchyard, for the lovely flowers which the matron of the Refuge left upon a poor girl's newly dug grave had been rudely cast aside. Ah, and there was the theft of a barrel of whisky from The Horse and Hound pub, the day after the fire – I almost forgot about that. I have my eye on our local gravedigger, though discovering when he was sober enough to roll away an entire barrel would be a test for your skills!"

"Perhaps I shall apply myself," Holmes said. "Come, Watson, it is a lovely day. Let us have a stroll."

We set out, and Holmes steered us immediately to the station. The clerk in the ticket office swore to selling Mr. Fox a ticket for London early on the day of the murder, and to noting his departure aboard the train.

"Did he speak to you in that morning?" Holmes asked.

"No," the ticket agent said. "It was blustery, and he had his hat down and his collar up, and dark spectacles shielding his eyes, but of course I knew his white hair and his long beard and that cape with the red-satin lining. He always wears it, even when it's hot and uncomfortable. He asked for a ticket and slid the fare across without another word. He seemed a bit preoccupied, and I didn't wish to intrude upon his thoughts."

"And when he returned?"

The ticket agent shrugged. "He was agitated, and his face was pale as a ghost's. I noticed he had changed his attire and shaved his beard, and I wondered if he had lost his fancy cloak. I almost called out to him, then decided it was no business of mine."

"I had hoped for a more curious fellow," Holmes muttered, as we walked away. "Perhaps the young maid might shed light upon the matter."

We found the girl in her mother's neat little cottage. She was small and slight, no more than sixteen years of age, but calm and dignified as Holmes told her his mission.

"I am grateful to learn it, sir," she said, asking us to sit in the tiny parlor. "Mr. Fox has always been a good and kind master to me, and I don't believe, for one instant, that he would do his wife harm."

"They were a devoted pair?" Holmes asked. The girl's face turned red. My friend leaned forward, speaking softly. "You will help Mr. Fox only if you tell the truth."

The girl swallowed. "I don't wish to speak ill of the dead, but Mrs. Fox didn't love her husband. She showed him no affection, and I have heard it said that she kept company with other gentlemen. However, sir, they never quarreled. They might have been cool toward each other, but that was all."

Holmes arched an eyebrow. "The inspector swears he heard them having a loud row in their garden."

The girl's hand flew to her mouth. "Oh, sir, no! They were only acting."

"Acting?" I asked. The girl nodded vigorously.

"It was a scene from a play. They used to go into the garden – it was her suggestion, that he stay in practice for the stage, and perform outside where the air was better. They would hide behind the tallest hedge, where no one might see them, but I stood at the cottage window and giggled because it sounded like a real 'lover's spat', if you will. But I never knew anyone else was listening."

"And your master wasn't violent with his spouse?" I asked.

"Never, sir. She had a bad black eye, not long ago, but I was with her when she slipped on the stairs and banged her head against the doorframe."

Holmes thanked the maid for her time. We were on the pathway, drawing on our gloves, when the young girl rushed back to us.

"Wait, sir! I didn't wish to say it, but seeing how my poor lady is dead, I suppose she has no more secrets. For the past two month, Mrs. Fox was very ill with complaints of a *womanly* nature," the girl stammered, her face turning red. "She hid her pain from Mr. Fox, but she visited the Refuge to consult with Dr. Furore, who she told me was a specialist in such matters. I hope I'm not betraying a confidence, but perhaps this doctor might know more, and could help you bring whoever killed Mrs. Fox to justice."

Holmes thanked the girl, and we set off down the main thoroughfare of the village.

"I must remember, from this day forward, to take more time to allow nervous young ladies to speak," Holmes chuckled. "I wonder if Mr. Fox was completely ignorant of his wife's visits to a specialist."

"If he suspected an affair, it gives him more motive to be the killer."

"And if there was an affair, another individual had a motive to free the lady from an unloved spouse."

"By killing her?" I protested.

Holmes favored me with an enigmatic smile. "I believe there has been a murder done in this village, but we undoubtedly have the wrong victim." He gestured down a side street with his cane. "I perceive that august building at the end of the lane is the Refuge for Young Mothers. Let us see what we can learn within its walls."

The institution was lodged in a much-patched and repaired structure that had once been a monastery. In a notable change from its former usage, a large sign at the door announced that no males were allowed inside without special permission. Fortunately, a young girl was just returning from the market, and she agreed to carry Holmes's card and request for an interview within. A short, stout, apple-cheeked matron in a dark dress and spotless apron quickly appeared and ushered us into an office, a chamber made homely by several religious paintings and tapestries, as well as a rather untidy pile of children's toys on the floor.

"Oh, I see I shall have to scold the girls again," she sighed. "It will hardly impress our patrons if we don't keep things neat!"

Holmes took a chair, and the sharp-eyed detective was suddenly replaced by a pious potential donor. I struggled to look as self-satisfied as Holmes did, with nothing more than a relaxation of his facial muscles, and the careless way he folded his hands.

"I am very interested in supporting your institution. There should be more homes for those the world has cruelly discarded."

"Oh yes!" the lady, who quickly introduced herself as Mrs. MacAllister, beamed. "We began our work five years ago, strictly as a sanctuary for young women who found themselves in despair and disgrace, and who might otherwise have become mothers on the street or in the workhouse. We currently house ten to twenty girls at a time, and we care for them when their babies are born. Meanwhile, we teach them useful domestic trades."

"You seem to have enlisted a number of community ladies to your cause."

Mrs. MacAllister's face turned rosy. "Biddenbrook's ladies are good to us."

"How sad, then, that you have recently lost Mrs. Fox. I hear she was dedicated to your work."

All the matron's pride suddenly vanished. "Sir, her terrible death is a disgrace to this town. But I will always remember her with gratitude, for it was she who told Dr. Furore of our needs and brought him to our village, about two months ago. He has been a blessing to all the girls in their confinements."

"I presume the presence of a resident physician has greatly reduced your institution's mortality."

Mrs. MacAllister nodded. "Indeed, though sadly we recently lost Miss Lacey Dwight. Such a beautiful, striking girl, so tall and with lovely black hair. She gave birth a week ago, to a darling boy. We thought she was well past any danger – then she abruptly took a turn. There was nothing poor Dr. Furore could do for her, as it was childbed fever. She was buried the next day."

Holmes frowned like a man trying to dreg up a memory.

"I believe I have met your esteemed physician. He is an older man, bald, with a limp?"

"Oh no, sir! Our doctor is a young man, with very dark hair, fresh from the University of London."

"They train excellent physicians there," Holmes said, "or so I have been told."

"He did his best, but is completely broken-hearted over Lacey's passing. He told me just this morning that he intends to return to a metropolitan hospital, to further his training, but will send a colleague to help us."

"A wise decision. Perhaps my friend Doctor Watson might offer advice on the best institution for him?"

"He would welcome it, though not today, I'm afraid. Another girl was brought to bed just an hour ago, and I know he wouldn't want to miss the delivery."

"Of course not." Holmes rose, ignoring the lady's look of disappointment at the lack of a donation. "I seem to have forgotten my cheque book," he said, with a distressed patting of his jacket. "But I shall send a suitable tribute to your good work as soon as I return to London."

"And where shall we go now?" I asked, as we once again found ourselves on the village thoroughfare. Holmes paused, rubbing his chin.

"I wonder if the gravedigger is thirsty. Be a good chap, Watson, and return to the tea shop and order some refreshments – I will be along momentarily."

I buried my frustration at my friend's refusal to give a simple and clear answer, but dutifully did his bidding. Some ten minutes later, he returned to the shop, directing me to change my seat so that we could watch the street through the large front window. For almost an hour we talked of meaningless and disjointed subjects, from the upcoming favorites in the Queen's Cup to the newest fashion in gentleman's hats to the historical reputation of Henry II. Holmes abruptly went rigid and gestured to the glass.

"My new friend has done his work!"

A dirty, disheveled man approached the shop. He halted, seeing us inside, and shook his head. It was clear, from his expression of dismay that whatever he was reporting upon, he found the matter disturbing.

"What do you mean?"

"Finish your tea, my friend. We have an appointment."

Holmes hustled me from the little restaurant, dropped some coins into the man's filthy hand, and led the way to the gaol, where we found Inspector Walker sitting behind a desk.

"The coffin was empty."

"What?"

In his masterful way, Holmes brushed aside all the informality of his approach. The inspector sat spellbound as my friend spoke.

"The village gravedigger inspected the internment of a girl who died at the Refuge, a week ago. Her eternal rest was disturbed because her corpse was the 'understudy' for Mrs. Fox's final performance."

"My God!" Inspector Walker cried. "How could you have known? And what does it mean?"

"It means, Inspector, that you and I are about to bring this dramatic case to a satisfying conclusion. You must deliver an urgent message to the Refuge."

The inspector stared. "And what message is that?"

"You have arrested a young woman for a petty crime, but she is suffering from violent hysterics. You require Dr. Furore's assistance immediately, as you fear the lady will die without immediate aid. Impress upon him the severity of the case to make him return with you."

"But there is no woman . . . ."

"Surely you possess an imagination, Inspector."

The man's cheeks reddened, but he hurried out upon his mission. Holmes plucked down some overcoats which were hanging upon pegs.

"A pity there isn't time to go shopping. These will have to do and – A-ha! I see that some lady has lost her bonnet! A bit of luck."

I felt as confused as the inspector, but I followed Holmes to the cells at the rear of the building, where the aged actor was sitting upon his bed. Holmes held out the garments.

"Mr. Fox, I know you have retired, but surely you long to tread the boards again. Have you ever performed a female role?"

He shrugged. "Once or twice, in comedic pantomimes."

"Excellent." Holmes passed the items to the prisoner through the bars. "Bundle yourself in these and turn your face to the wall. When you hear the door opening, give us your finest damsel in distress. No, don't ask why. Simply perform."

The old man nodded, quickly curling onto the bunk, and wrapping the cloaks around his body, with the bonnet pulled low, shielding his face. Holmes and I returned to the office, where Holmes settled into the inspector's chair.

"You see it all, of course," he said. "What a bizarre chain of events."

"I see nothing."

"Consider . . . a wife no longer loves her husband. She wishes to be free of him. She learns a scandalous secret. She reaches out to the offended party and together they devise a cruel plot to achieve their mutual goals."

"I am still in the dark."

"Not for long. Here comes the inspector with the doctor."

A moment later, the door opened. Doctor Furore was a tall, spare young man, with unnaturally dark hair and a look of panic on his pale features.

"Bleeding profusely," the inspector said. "Bashing her head on the bars. Never seen anything like it."

"Very well, but I must hurry. The confinement at the Refuge seems a complicated one and – who are these gentlemen?"

Holmes shook his head. "Friends of the young lady. Please help her!"

The doctor nodded and the inspector opened the passage that led to the cells. The moment the key rattled, we heard the most ear-splitting wail, followed by shrieks and cries for aid, all delivered in the high-pitched voice of a woman.

"Please! Please help, oh, I am dying! Dying! Help me, Doctor! Doctor!"

It would have taken a hard heart indeed to resist such entreaties. The inspector threw the cell door open. Doctor Furore knelt beside the bed, dropping his medical bag to the floor.

"Now, Madame, please – calm yourself. I will ready a sedative and – Good Lord! *Father!*"

Mr. Fox had rolled over at the touch, the bonnet sliding from his head. Furore fell backwards, his arm over his face.

"Son! My boy!" The old man's expression contorted from one of shock to dismay. "What have you done to your splendid hair?"

"More importantly," Holmes said, "where is Mrs. Fox?"

The young man skittered away, slamming into the wall of the cell. He stared up at us with the wild eyes of a cornered animal.

"I do not know."

"Come now," Holmes chided, with a sharp clap of his hands. "Tell us where she is. Or are you willing to be hanged alone for the murder of Miss Lacey Dwight, who you poisoned to procure a corpse of a suitable size to replace your conspirator upon the pyre? I have always held that when a doctor goes wrong, he is the first of criminals, and here is proof."

"The girl died naturally! I swear it! And it was all Helen's idea, to steal her body and send Father off to Canterbury and . . . ."

Furore suddenly realized what he had said, and dropped his head into his hands, weeping copiously. Slowly, Fox rose from his bunk, the coats and bonnet falling away from him. He voice was an agonized whisper.

"My wife is still alive?"

"Explain it to me," Inspector Walker said, as we settled into our seats aboard the train. "How, by all that is wonderful, did you put it together?"

"I began," Holmes said, "by accepting my client's story." Here he nodded to Mr. Fox, who was accompanying us on our journey, while his errant son took his place in a cell. "It was simply too bizarre to have been concocted. A man who wished to be rid of his wife, even in such a cruel fashion, would have devised a more believable alibi. There was always the possibility that Mr. Fox was insane, but our conversation convinced me otherwise."

"I am grateful," Fox whispered, "to hear you say so."

"We live our lives within our conventions," Holmes said. "You have spent a lifetime playing melodramatic roles. It is only natural that your delivery might be a bit . . . *overwrought*."

"But from there – ?" Walker prodded.

"The next question in my mind was who would wish Mrs. Fox ill? There were no likely candidates beyond her husband, and if I accepted his innocence as a working premise, then who would wish him incarcerated, and perhaps even hanged? Who would benefit from his suffering? Immediately, I recognized the possibility that either of his children might hold a potentially lethal grudge, for in their minds, his revelation had destroyed their lives. When you told me that flowers upon a recent grave had been disturbed, and I later learned from Mrs. MacAllister that the occupant of said grave had been a woman of relative dimensions to the incinerated corpse of Mrs. Fox, I was certain I knew how the trick was done. The maid's admission that her mistress often sought the help of the young doctor at the Refuge – a doctor she supposedly procured for the institution – confirmed a possible conspiracy, and Mr. Fox had earlier told me his son was a physician. Inspector, you revealed that on the night before Mrs. Fox's murder, there was a disturbance which kept you and your officers occupied: Trying to rescue a flock of sheep. I would further suggest the animals were unpenned by Mrs. Fox or Dr. Furore, as a cover for their grave-robbing – an event that conveniently took place on the evening Mr. Fox was lured away, incognito, for a false appointment in Canterbury."

"But – Who was the man who bought the ticket for the train on the morning of the fire?" Walker asked. "The fellow at the station recognized him as Fox!"

"It was Helen," our client murmured. "It had to be."

"Indeed," Holmes said. "The lady has theatrical experience and has made a keen study of her husband. She is tall, slender, and with a good pair of boots could easily mimic his height and gait. Long white hair, a false beard – she didn't know he'd already shaved it – plus a hat, unturned collar, dark spectacles, and probably gloved hands, made for an easy disguise, especially as Fox's cape was immediately recognizable. This garb allowed her to flee to London, while her paramour arranged the corpse in shackles and set the fire, staging the scene."

"Paramour?" Fox asked. "Oh, surely not!"

My friend's stern face softened. "I am sorry, Mr. Fox, but it is the logical explanation. She had no funds to offer him, and from his weakness of character, and his sudden breakdown in the cell, I don't believe he would have acted simply to gain revenge for a disappointed engagement. There had to be a more potent incentive. Mrs. Fox – from all evidence – is a woman of great cunning, drive, and purpose, as well as immoral character. Upon learning of the youth's existence, she laid the groundwork to convince the village of trouble at home – the loud staged arguments, the false wounding to her face – even as she seduced her prey into blindly doing her bidding." Holmes gently patted the old man's shoulder. "I am sorry that you should hear this, but it will all come out at the trial."

"I cannot bear it!" Fox moaned. "I will die in disgrace."

"It will be the trial of the century," Walker said. "Every newspaper in London will cover it. Think of it this way, Fox: You will be famous once again, at the center of the stage."

I glared at the callous inspector for, despite the aged actor's strange experience, I felt myself drawn to him, much as his former audiences had been. His distress was heart-breaking to witness. Nothing about it appeared feigned or insincere. Even Holmes, who was the most stoic of men, seemed moved by the elder's painful display of emotion.

"Let us talk of happier things," Holmes said. "Mr. Fox, I have long been a student of the theatrical arts. What is the most challenging role for an actor?"

"Hamlet, of course," the old man sniffed. "His frightful indecision . . . His struggle between right and wrong . . . How he wrestles with his conscience . . . Whether he should avenge his father's murder or . . . ."

We passed the remainder of the journey discussing Shakespearean roles, of which my friend was an expert critic. It seemed to ease Fox's mind. At last we arrived, and Holmes offered Fox the comforts of Baker Street, but he refused, saying he wished to be present for the arrest of his traitorous spouse. We stopped at Scotland Yard, where we found Inspector Gregson, who was willing to accompany us in an official capacity.

"What a tale!" he said as we made our journey. "It will certainly make the cover of *The Police Gazette*!"

Mrs. Fox was staying at rather seedy rooming house on the south bank of the Thames. The decrepit structure's windows overlooked the dull, fetid waters, and I could only imagine the oppressive smells that leached from the river in the height of summer, when that great watery thoroughfare collected the city's careless garbage. We were directed to a room on the fourth floor, and Holmes's firm knock was met with a shrill reply of "Well, is it all done?"

We had asked Fox to wait behind us in the corridor. I looked back and saw him nod, confirming that it was his wife's voice. Holmes replied in a nervous tenor.

"It is. Let me in."

The woman threw open the door. She had clearly been expecting her lover's return, for she was clad in a satin nightgown with a plush-trimmed robe, her inky hair spilling about her shoulders. She gave a startled gasp and tried to slam the door shut, but Gregson instantly stepped up and wedged it open.

"Helen Hitchford Fox – You are under arrest."

She fled to the rear of the room, where the open window gave some relief from the sweltering heat. Like a cat, she hissed and bared her teeth.

"Who are you, to be forcing yourself on me? I shall scream!"

Walker stepped inside. "Mrs. Fox, you know who I am. I have come to take you back to Biddenbrook."

She clutched her robe to her chest. "Why?"

"For the abuse of a corpse, arson, causing false imprisonment – Let us add attempted murder to the list."

"What nonsense is this? I am merely visiting a friend. I have done nothing wrong and – "

"You witch! You fiend! You seduced my son!"

Fox shot into the room, moving with a speed that belied his age and weakened health. He shook a gnarled fist at his wife, spitting out accusations of unfaithfulness and cruelty. As he advanced, she climbed into the high, open window, shaking her head.

"You are mad, old man! Insane! Come no closer or . . . or . . . I will jump!" She wobbled on the treacherous ledge. "You hateful fool! Go to the Devil!"

"You first!" he snapped and, before any of us could restrain him, he rushed at the window. He threw his arms out and wrapped his wife to his chest, one instant before he plunged them both through the opening and into the air. We raced after them but saw only the splash their bodies made. Gregson and Walker turned and ran out of the room, to attempt a rescue, while Holmes and I remained at the window. We waited for some time, but nothing rose above the murky, tainted water except a sodden scrap of the lady's gown.

The Stratford Street Lodgers
by Naching T. Kassa

Following that remarkable April of 1894, when Sherlock Holmes made his triumphant return, I found myself once again in Baker Street. The void left by my dear Mary had made living in my empty home unbearable, and it was with some relief that I sold my Kensington practice to young Verner and returned to my old lodgings and my friend.

The cases which came to Holmes's attention during this period were many and presented a wealth of material from which I could pick and choose. My notes regarding the Bishop of Bath and Wells would be of great interest to the public, as would the story concerning the vessel, *Mercury Queen*. However, I believe the tale I am about to relate will be far more fascinating, for all of its strange and macabre elements.

Our involvement in the matter began on a cold morning in October, as a chill rain fell outside our windows. Holmes and I had just taken our breakfast when Mrs. Hudson entered bearing a card on her salver. Holmes took it and, having read the name upon it, handed it to me.

"'*Mr. Mordecai Pettigrew*'," I said aloud.

"He says his business is most urgent, Mr. Holmes," Mrs. Hudson said. "I told him you were having breakfast, but he insists on seeing you."

"Show him in, Mrs. Hudson," Holmes said.

Moments later, a short man of forty, dressed in a smart suit, entered our rooms. He removed his hat, revealing a head of well-kept ginger hair, and stood trembling before us, his gaze shifting from myself to Holmes and back again.

"Won't you be seated, Mr. Pettigrew?" Holmes said, motioning to a chair. "I am Sherlock Holmes. This is my friend and colleague, Dr. Watson. You may speak freely before him."

Mr. Pettigrew took the chair opposite Holmes. "Thank you, Mr. Holmes. I'm so grateful you've agreed to see me. If you hadn't, well, I don't know what I should have done. I am – "

"A solicitor," Holmes replied. "And a practical and self-sufficient man, one who lives his life in an orderly fashion. And yet, something has changed all of that. What has frightened you, Mr. Pettigrew?"

The little man's eyes widened. "How on earth did you know that? Has my sister been to see you? It was her suggestion that I should come here."

Holmes smiled. "I am not acquainted with your sister. When you removed your hat, you told me all I need know of your profession. There are strands of white amongst the ginger, but they are not from your head. Rather, they are of the horsehair wig you often wear in court. The weight of said wig has given your hair that peculiar, pressed look. Your shoes and suit aren't particularly expensive, but presentable. Only a practical man would choose such functional clothing in your profession. There is a smudge of shoe polish on the index finger of your left hand, demonstrating your self-sufficiency – you polish your own shoes. This same smudge is incongruous with the state of your dress, as your suit is impeccable, save for the button which you have torn away in your haste to come here."

"It appears I have found the right man," our visitor said. "As to your question regarding my fearful state . . . Well, my tale is a dreadful one. I can scarce believe it myself. My friends, Mr. Oscar Harris and Mr. Edgar Bromley, have been murdered."

"If that is the case," Holmes replied, "then you must relate your story immediately."

The little man nodded. "Let me begin by saying that I own a thriving law practice with several clients. My landlady, Mrs. Bennett of 71 Stratford Street in Kensington, was one of these. She passed away two months ago. This information may not seem important now, but I assure you, it will become so during the course of my narrative."

"Details of are the utmost importance to me," Holmes said. "Please, proceed."

"Mrs. Bennett possessed a small fortune, one afforded her by her late husband. He had been killed in a carriage accident, and she had used the money from his insurance to purchase a boarding house. I lived there for nearly five years.

"I was not alone, of course. My friends, the aforementioned gentlemen, resided there as well, and we three were the only tenants. Mr. Harris and I lived on the second floor, Mr. Bromley on the first, and Mrs. Bennett lived on the ground. Mrs. Bennett referred to us as her 'little family', and a truer word has never been spoken. Though Mr. Bromley was several years my senior and Mr. Harris many years my junior, I considered them the brothers I'd never had. Mrs. Bennett was very much like a mother to us all.

"It was, therefore, no surprise to me when one morning about two months ago, Mrs. Bennett came to me and asked if I might draw up her will. I had performed other duties for her in the past and, as she trusted me, it only made sense that I should help her in these matters as well."

"'I have done wrong in my life, Mr. Pettigrew,' said she, 'and it is time I made it right. Though we share no blood, I have come to regard you,

Mr. Harris, and Mr. Bromley as family. It is my wish that the three of you inherit my fortune and this house, and that you split it equally between you.'

"You can imagine how astounded I was by this. And, though I did argue with her, I found she wouldn't be swayed. I made the will exactly as she specified and thought no more of it. Mrs. Bennett had always been in excellent health, and I believed she would be with us for many more years to come. Little did I know how short her time would be.

"Not long before she died, I returned home to find a gentleman in Mrs. Bennett's parlor. He was a fellow of medium build and stone-white hair, with a sour expression on his face. When I entered the house, I heard them arguing, though I couldn't make out what was said. They ceased the moment they heard me shut the front door, and their voices grew hushed. Mrs. Bennett didn't call out to me as I passed the parlor door, and so I continued up to my second-floor room. When I came down for supper, the gentleman had gone, and Mrs. Bennett didn't see fit to mention his presence to me. It was only later that I would come to understand why he had visited.

"As for poor Mrs. Bennett, she became quite ill soon after that. So ill, she took to her bed and never rose from it again. One morning, while Mr. Harris and I were out, Mr. Bromley found her. They always took breakfast together, even when she was ill. Poor man. It must've been a great shock to find that she had passed during the night. I am rather glad Mr. Harris and I weren't at home when they took her away."

"Who took the body?"

"The undertaker. Mrs. Bennett left strict instructions. Her casket was to be closed during the funeral. I found it rather peculiar, but we honored her wishes when we made the arrangements. She was laid to rest in a nearby cemetery. However, before the will could be read and our inheritance portioned between us, that same, strange old man arrived at the house. He introduced himself as Homer Balantine, a solicitor from Wimpole Street. He had a most astonishing revelation for us: He claimed to have Mrs. Bennett's *new will*."

"A new will?" Holmes said, leaning forward in his chair. "Who was the beneficiary?"

"The sole beneficiary was my friend, Mr. Harris."

"Was the new will written in Mrs. Bennett's hand?"

"It seemed so. If it was not, it was an excellent forgery."

"And when was it dated?"

"Two days following the will I had made for her."

Holmes leaned back and stretched his legs out before him. "What was Mr. Harris' reaction to this new will?"

"Complete bewilderment. When he asked Mr. Balantine why he had been chosen, the man said Mrs. Bennett had wished it so. He gave no other reason."

"An odd state of affairs," I said.

"And it became odder still," Pettigrew agreed. "Soon after inheriting the house and Mrs. Bennett's fortune, a change came over Mr. Harris. He began to spend more and more time with Mr. Balantine and less time with Mr. Bromley and myself. And the more time he spent, the more his disposition suffered. Mr. Harris had been a generous and even-tempered fellow for as long as I had known him. But in the company of the older man, he became stingy, suspicious, and quarrelsome. Why, only weeks after he had gained his inheritance, he increased the rent by ten pounds. This posed no difficulty for me, but for Mr. Bromley – Well, it was more than he could afford. He and Mr. Harris had a terrible row about it, and in the end, Mr. Bromley left the premises. I believe he took more affordable rooms in Shelton Street."

"And Balantine took up residence in Mr. Bromley's rooms?" Holmes asked.

Mr. Pettigrew nodded. "Barely a week after Mr. Bromley had gone. Things grew steadily worse after that. And though it was Mr. Harris saying the words, I knew they had come from Mr. Balantine. He would always appear after my exchanges with Harris, his face bearing a smug expression. Last week, I found I could take no more, and so I gave Mr. Harris my notice. I departed immediately for the home of my sister, Mrs. John Mansfield, and have lived there ever since.

"Yesterday, to my great surprise, I received a letter from Harris. He asked to meet me in the lobby of the Bailey Hotel at seven and, because his request seemed urgent, I agreed.

"He was more himself when I met him. He apologized even before I had taken the chair beside him.

"'I do hope you'll forgive me, old man,' said he. 'I fear that Mr. Balantine's advice regarding you and Edgar hasn't been particularly charitable. I realize now that I should never have accepted his counsel.'

"'I am glad to hear it,' said I.

"'I don't suppose you would consider returning to the house? The amount of rent shall be the same as before – less if you like.'

"'I cannot return while Mr. Balantine lives there.'

"'I asked him to leave this afternoon.'

"'You did? This very afternoon?'

"'He is packing as we speak.' He gave me a sheepish grin and ran hand through his sand-colored hair. 'He suggested I make a new will – and make *him* the beneficiary. It all became clear to me then. All the things he

306

told me, the dreadful things about you and Edgar – all lies.' He sighed. 'I am very sorry for how I've behaved.'

"'That is good news indeed. Very well. I shall be there tomorrow.'

"'I am glad. It is probably too late to mend fences with Edgar, but I will make the attempt.' He rose and shook my hand. 'You still have your key?'

"'I do.'

"'Then come as early as you please.' He took his leave, and it was the last I saw of him alive.

"Unexpected business, in the form of a client, kept me from the house the next day, and I didn't arrive until late that afternoon. A chilling silence greeted me as I entered, and though I called out Mr. Harris' name, he did not answer. I made my way to the stairs, intending to climb to the first floor, when I noticed the parlor door was open. I peered inside and – Mr. Holmes, what I found in that room shall haunt me until the end of my days!"

Mr. Pettigrew had gone quite pale by this point of his narrative, and so I poured him a small brandy. He drank it gratefully and then continued his tale.

"Mr. Harris, poor Mr. Harris, lay face up on the floor, his chest covered in blood, a revolver near his right hand. Mr. Bromley lay face down nearby, also dead. He had been shot in the face and was quite unrecognizable. Were it not for his clothes, I wouldn't have known it was he." He lowered his eyes to the hat in his hand. "And here is the strange thing, Mr. Holmes. Though the evidence is very much against him, I don't believe Mr. Bromley could have killed Mr. Harris."

"What leads you to such a conclusion?" Holmes asked.

"Mr. Bromley was armed with a carving knife, the very weapon which killed Mr. Harris, but he clutched it in his right hand. To kill a man in such a manner would have been an impossibility, as Mr. Bromley suffered a terrible injury as a young man. It left him with a scar upon his cheek and a damaged right hand. He couldn't make a fist, let alone clutch a knife in that way."

Holmes leaned forward, a bright and eager light in his eyes. "You are very observant, Mr. Pettigrew. What else can you tell me?"

"Well, Mr. Bromley was a most fastidious man. He dressed more immaculately even than I. So you might imagine my surprise when I noticed what he wore on his feet. Instead of shoes, he wore a rather drab pair of slippers. It was hardly the kind of footwear one might wear when going out, let alone on a journey from Shelton Street.

"I brought these same particulars to the attention of the police, but they weren't interested. They seem to think the case solved." The little man fidgeted with his hat and then looked up into Holmes's gaze. "There is one other thing. Before she passed, Mrs. Bennett disclosed a secret to me. There was a hidden panel in the parlor, just above the fireplace. She kept her jewelry there, and she assured me that I was the only person she had ever revealed it to. When I entered the parlor, the panel was open and the jewelry had been removed."

"Did you inform the police of this fact?"

Mr. Pettigrew shifted in the chair. "I know it was foolish, Mr. Holmes, but I did not. Mrs. Bennett intimated that the jewels had been acquired dishonestly, and I had no intention of besmirching her good name. I had intended to give the jewels to the police at a later date."

Holmes nodded.

"Mr. Holmes, will you investigate these circumstances? I don't have much, but I will give all I have to find the truth."

"I shall investigate the matter," Holmes said, rising to his feet. "Will you indulge me by answering one or two more questions before you go?"

"Of course."

"What was Mr. Bromley's reaction when Mrs. Bennett died?"

"He was, like the rest of us, quite overcome by grief. As I said, they often breakfasted together. I think, of the three of us, she favored him most. But then, he was closer to her age and had known her longer. He had lived there a year before me and two years before Mr. Harris."

"You have been of great help, Mr. Pettigrew. Now, I must ask you for one more thing: The key to the house – Do you still have it?"

"I do." He reached into his waistcoat pocket and removed a large, brass key. He handed it to Holmes.

"I shall send word when there is news," Holmes said.

Holmes took his leave soon after our client and didn't return until later that evening. When he entered our rooms, he bore an expression of triumph. "I have spent a most profitable afternoon in Bishopsgate and at Scotland Yard. Lestrade was a great help to me, though I fear I have greatly annoyed him. Mr. Pettigrew's case grows more interesting by the minute."

"What have you learned?"

"A great deal, though there are one or two items which still require my attention. Ah, I see Mrs. Hudson has prepared roast chicken this evening. If you are agreeable, Watson, we shall visit Stratford Street after we've dined."

The house at 71 Stratford Street seemed welcoming on the outside. A more modern affair, it stood tall, its large windows looking out on the street. No constable waited outside, and the place seemed quite deserted.

The sun, which had finally made an appearance, began its decline as we stepped up on the porch, and I could see a growing haze which promised fog. It afforded Holmes enough light to examine the keyhole before he unlocked the door. As we slipped inside, I realized how accurate Mr. Pettigrew's description of the chilling silence had been. Holmes lit a dark lantern which he'd wisely brought and, together, we made our way to the parlor. The room, which might have been quite pleasant on any other day, seemed cold and lonely now. Two chairs stood near the fireplace, their dark upholstery matching the settee which sat on the left side of the room. Blood stained the well-worn rug which covered the floor.

Holmes lit the lamp on the table and, ensuring the drapes had been pulled, began his investigation of the room. He examined the floor first.

"I see the usual herd of bison have made their rounds in this room," he observed. "When will the London constabulary inspect the floor before they allow their inspectors upon it? Hello! What is this?"

He plucked something from the rug and held it up for my inspection. The object was a small boot nail, coated with mud.

"Very suggestive," Holmes mused. "You can find this sort of mud at only three locations in London. Shelton Street is one of them."

"I suppose that would be understandable, Mr. Bromley's rooms were in Shelton Street."

"If you remember, Watson, Mr. Bromley wore slippers, and this nail could only have come from a boot."

Holmes moved to the fireplace next, and the hidden panel Pettigrew had mentioned. He peered into the little chamber, examined it for several seconds, and then turned to the mantel.

"See here, Watson," he said. He ran his finger over a small chip in the stone. "And here."

Blood had spattered the hearth. I could barely make it out against the red stone.

"Whatever does it mean?" I asked. "This blood . . . How did it come to be here? It's too far away, and in the opposite direction of the gunshot."

Holmes didn't answer. Something in the nearby chair had caught his eye. It proved to be a small tear in the upholstery.

"It seems our friend climbed up on the chair shortly before he lost the nail in his boot."

"Our friend? A third man?"

Holmes paused. Somewhere in the house, a door had closed. The sound had come from the floor above.

Holmes rushed to the lamp and extinguished the light, plunging the room into darkness. I stood near the open parlor door as footsteps descended the stairs. Moments later, Holmes joined me, the shuttered dark lantern in hand.

Upon reaching the ground floor, the footsteps paused. I cursed myself for failing to bring my revolver, missing its comforting weight in my pocket.

The footsteps moved toward the front door. It opened and then closed.

"Come, Watson!" Holmes cried, dashing down the hall.

We rushed out of the house and into a now-thick wall of fog. It filled the street, obscuring our quarry, whose footsteps now faded into the distance.

"Can you make out the direction, Watson?" he asked.

"No."

"Go up the street and see what you may. I will go down."

I hurried, hoping that I might hear the tell-tale footsteps, or glimpse a shadow in the mist. I saw nothing.

When I returned to the house, I found Holmes waiting for me.

"Did you see anything?" I asked.

My friend shook his head. "This fog – it is a bosom friend of the criminal class, and a bane to those who seek justice. Though I found his footprints, I didn't find our quarry. He is the same man who visited the house before. The boot is missing a nail."

"He has already removed the jewelry. Why should he return here?"

"That is what we must discover," Holmes said, opening the shutter on the dark lantern. "Our friend had a key. I found no scratches upon the outside lock. It could be he had a duplicate made or – "

"He lived here in the house."

"Excellent, Watson."

"And Balantine took the first-floor rooms after Mr. Bromley had gone. Could it have been he we pursued just now?"

"Unlikely, for one simple reason."

"And what is that?"

"Balantine is dead."

"Dead!"

"Come now, Watson. Mr. Pettigrew has given us the clues. I am always suspicious of such a grisly death as a shot in the face. When a face is destroyed, it is far more likely to be a method of hiding identity than a means of killing. A shot in the heart can do that. And as you recall, Mr. Bromley couldn't have killed Mr. Harris because – "

"He couldn't clutch the knife!"

"Capital, Watson! Bromley also had a distinctive scar upon his cheek."

"Which explains why Balantine was shot in the face."

Holmes nodded.

"Then Bromley is the murderer of both men?" I shook my head. "It isn't possible. Bromley could not hold a knife, how could he pull the trigger of the revolver?"

Holmes shrugged. "Awkwardly with his other hand? In any case, I have theory, but no facts to support it. Not even an examination of the evidence at Scotland Yard could aid me – though it was rather pleasant to see Lestrade's face when I revealed the complications of his simple case. He was very displeased when I pointed out the tattoo on the supposed body of Bromley. It was a sailor's tattoo and could never have belonged to Bromley. Let us see what we may find upstairs."

The first floor consisted of a large sitting room and bedroom. Holmes examined the former carefully, and finding nothing, entered the bedroom.

A bed stood at the center of the room, flanked by a wardrobe and a squat cabinet. The wardrobe stood open and several suits lay upon the bed, along with a suitcase and a small trunk. Upon opening the trunk, we found two pairs of boots. Holmes studied them both before setting them back inside. Next, he turned to the cabinet. Several framed photographs filled the shelves within. Two featured a beautiful young woman who resembled the matronly one in the others. I soon realized it was the same woman.

"One is missing," Holmes said. He indicated an empty frame. "It isn't in the suitcase or the trunk. Nor is it on the bed."

"Why would Bromley come for this picture?" I asked.

"An interesting question. Come. We have learned all we can from this place."

We once again made our way to Baker Street. Holmes retired to the chair before the fire, his cherry-wood pipe between his lips. There he remained for the rest of the night.

When I awoke the next morning, I found Holmes seated at the table. He had scarcely touched his breakfast but urged me to eat mine. He held a telegram in one hand.

"It is from Lestrade. We now know the true identity of Mr. Balantine."

"'*It is Frederick Steele*'." I read. "'*Tattoo on upper left arm identified by informant.*' Frederick Steele? Where have I heard that name before?"

Holmes pushed one of his commonplace books across the table to me and I paged through it until I found the correct passage.

"Ah, yes. Frederick Steele, the confidence trickster. He swindled Lady Helen Merryweather out of her entire fortune."

"And was imprisoned for it. He was locked away for two years, and after they released him, he vanished – no doubt to sea. Later he resurfaced as the rather dubious solicitor, Homer Balantine."

Footsteps thundered up the stairs then, followed by a shout from Mrs. Hudson. The door opened and a tall boy burst inside.

"Ah, Wiggins! You have news?"

"We've found him, Mr. 'Olmes!" the leader of our Irregulars cried, quite out of breath. "'E's at the Westwood Arms, just down the street from 'is old digs. And you were right all along. He's still using the same name – Bromley."

"Clever," Holmes said. "He is hiding in plain sight. Very good, Wiggins." He handed the boy a handful of coins. "Share it amongst the others. Come, Watson. Have you your revolver? We may have need of it."

The Westwood Arms was a tumble-down hotel on the outskirts of St. Giles. The proprietor, a seedy fellow with a grimy gold tooth, seemed rather reticent when answering our questions, but soon changed his mind when plied with a five-pound note. We were directed to a room at the top of the stairs.

The upstairs hall seemed strangely quiet when we reached it, and I felt several pairs of unfriendly eyes upon me, though I couldn't see the observers. Their doors shut with a quiet *click* as we stepped up to Mr. Bromley's door.

Holmes knocked and receiving no answer, pushed upon the door. It was unlocked.

We entered a small room furnished only with a bed, table, and chair. A washbasin stood on the table alongside a lamp, and under the table, a pair of boots. The rest of the room was empty.

Holmes snatched up one boot and turned it over, revealing the sole and its lost nail. He tossed it to the floor in disgust.

"He has gone. And it will be impossible to track him now."

"It is very like chasing a ghost," I remarked. "Each time we are at Bromley's heels, he vanishes."

Holmes stared at me and suddenly, his expression transformed from one of vexation to that of a hound who has caught the scent.

"I have been a fool, Watson!" he cried. "The answer has been before me the whole time and I've been too blind to see it. Blind as a beetle! I only hope we aren't too late."

We took our leave of the Westwood Arms and made for the nearest telegraph office. Holmes sent a telegram to Mr. Pettigrew and we returned to Baker Street to await the reply.

Hours passed. And as the daylight dimmed, and the streetlamps outside came to life, his agitation grew. He paced the floor like a caged lion, and when the knock came upon the door, he vaulted over the settee and rushed down the steps two at a time.

Moments later, he returned with the telegram in hand, a triumphant expression upon his face.

"Let us venture into the fog once more, Watson," he said. "If we are fortunate, we may capture our ghost at last."

"I am ready," I replied. "Where are we bound?"

"Brompton Cemetery."

A maze of stone and marble awaited us. Holmes, however, had little trouble finding his way through it. He weaved through the tombstones, much in the way a bee might thread its way through a forest in search of a flower. Our flower proved to be the gravestone of Mrs. Cora Bennett.

Despite being a recent burial, the grave, unlike many in the cemetery, had been well-cared for. October leaves had been brushed away and a bouquet of daisies, perhaps a day old, lay beside the stone.

Holmes directed me toward the back of a small sepulchre, and here, we concealed ourselves. The fading light of day gave way to fog, and a strange and somber ambiance filled the graveyard. We waited.

"You think he will come here?" I asked.

"I am counting on it."

"But why? A lodger couldn't be so aggrieved by his landlady's death."

"Mr. Bromley is much more than a lodger. My inquiries at Bishopsgate revealed as much. It seems that, fifteen years ago, a coachman called Bennett was injured in a terrible accident. His right hand had been impaired and his face damaged. He later died from his injuries and his wife collected the insurance. A solicitor supervised the matter for the good lady."

"Frederick Steele?"

"The very same. This occurred shortly before his efforts to cheat Lady Merryweather. Would it interest you to know that an anonymous witness exposed Steele to the police? I thought it might. And it is no coincidence that soon after Steele's imprisonment, Mr. *Bromley* took up residence in Mrs. Bennett's boarding house. The reason he breakfasted with her, kept a cabinet of her photographs in his room, and knew where the jewelry was hidden, is that he is her *husband*."

The crunch of boots on gravel silenced us.

Holmes held his hunting crop at the ready as a figure materialized from the fog. Clad in a tall hat and ulster, a heavy scarf obscuring the

313

bottom half of his face, he walked up the path. Holmes and I peered from behind the stone sepulchre as he approached the grave and laid a fresh bouquet atop the stone.

Holmes leaped out and laid a hand upon his right shoulder. The man turned and, as he did so, the scarf fell aside. We looked into his frightened face and at the long scar which ran from beneath his eye and down his cheek.

"What's all this?" he cried.

"Do not try to run," Holmes said. "If you flee, it will go very hard on you indeed."

"Who are you?"

"I am Sherlock Holmes."

At the mention of my friend's name, the fellow slumped as though defeated. He nodded. "I suppose it is no use then. I have heard of you, Mr. Holmes. You are like a bulldog when you get your teeth in. I give you my word, I will not run."

Holmes allowed the man to rise to his feet. "I know you were present when Mr. Harris and Mr. Balantine were killed."

"And you think I murdered them."

"On the contrary, I know you did not."

The man stared at Holmes, his eyes wide.

"It will be dark soon, and I should like to end this quickly. Are you agreeable, Mr. Bromley? Or shall I call you *Bennett*?"

"How could you know this? Any of it?"

"It is my business to know. Answer my questions, and we shall see how this ends."

"Very well."

"Fifteen years ago, you feigned your death with the aid of your wife and Frederick Steele. Your wife collected the insurance money."

"Yes. It was Steele's idea. He convinced me no one would hire a one-handed cabbie. My poor girl told me not to listen. But I did, and I've been ashamed of it ever since."

"Is that why you exposed Steele to the police?"

"No one knows that. Not even Steele. Not even at the end. He finally found us and tried to blackmail my wife. She was a sensitive soul and more ashamed than I. He drove her to the grave – "

Holmes laughed at these words. "Come now, Mr. Bennett. We both know your wife is alive and well, living in the rooms at Shelton Street. The woman in this grave, judging by the dates, is your mother. It's no wonder your wife gave instructions for a closed casket." He frowned. "I warn you, Mr. Bennett. Do not lie to me again."

Humbled, Bennett nodded. "I will not. I swear it."

314

"Steele blackmailed you."

"Yes. We knew he would never let us be."

"So you 'arranged' Mrs. Bennett's death and her will. Which should have been ensured her fortune was shared equally between you, Mr. Harris, and Mr. Pettigrew."

"I knew Steele wouldn't be fooled for long. But I hardly expected him to forge a new will naming Harris as the beneficiary. And when he turned the boy against me, I knew I had no choice but to leave.

"Ivy had already rented rooms in Shelton Street, so that was no trouble. But we had both forgotten the jewelry. Had it not been for Harris' apology and invitation to return, we might never have recovered them. Of course, if I had ignored the invitation, as I was inclined to do, I never would have been involved in what happened.

"The note Harris had sent informed me that Balantine had been barred from the house, and when I arrived that morning, I thought only Harris might be at home. No one answered my knock, and so I used my key to gain entrance.

"The ground floor was empty. I found no one there, and so, instead of climbing the stairs to find Harris, I hurried into the parlor. I stood upon one of the chairs to reach the panel and quickly opened it. It was then that Balantine rushed into the room. He must have been upstairs, packing his things when he heard me. Perhaps he visited the kitchen first. It is the only explanation I have for his holding the knife.

"He threatened me with it, demanding that I give him the box and flee the house or he would expose me and Ivy. I'd hardly had time to refuse before Mr. Harris entered and a dreadful row ensued. So heated did their exchange become that Steele stabbed Mr. Harris in the chest. The poor boy fell to the floor and I fell upon Steele."

"You pushed him, and he fell against the mantel."

"Yes. He was dead before he struck the floor. I left him and rushed to Harris' side. I tried to staunch the blood but couldn't."

"'I am sorry, Bromley,' he said, as I gripped his hand. 'Balantine lied to me. So . . . so many lies. I don't know what I should . . . believe.'

"'It's all right,' I said.

"'You . . . can't stay here. You'll be blamed.'

"'I can't leave you.'

"'You should go. Disappear. Live . . . your life.'

"Mr. Holmes, I swear to you, on the grave of my mother, that it was Harris who planned the way I might escape the blame. He who told me to once again feign my death. I switched clothes with Steele but found there was a problem."

"The boots didn't fit," Holmes said.

"Yes. Damn the man. Even in death, he was nothing but trouble. I was forced to leave the slippers on his feet. Then, Harris shot him. It was the last thing he ever did."

"You left the knife in Steele's right hand. You are left-handed. Did you think that would go unnoticed?"

"I figured the police would be satisfied with what they saw, so I didn't think to move it. I never figured on you."

"You didn't figure on Mr. Mordecai Pettigrew. He was the one who noticed."

"Pettigrew, eh? He was always the cleverest of us three." He paused. "That's all there is to my story. After Harris died, I took the jewel box and fled."

"But you returned," Holmes said. "Just last night."

"You are a sorcerer, you are," Bennett said in a hushed voice. "Yes, I came back. There was a picture of my wife and me in the cabinet. It was the only other thing she wanted from the house. I couldn't leave it, just in case someone knew me. The frame was too bulky so I took the photograph out." He lowered his eyes. "Mr. Holmes, I know I haven't got the right to ask, but I beg you, let my Ivy be. Let her live what's left of her life. That money has been nothing but a bane to the both of us."

"I am not an agent of the police," Holmes said. "I am, however, an agent of Mr. Mordecai Pettigrew. It is he who engaged me, and he who wished me to prove Mr. Edgar Bromley innocent of Oscar Harris' murder. Have I satisfied the conditions set by my client, Watson?"

"You have," I replied. "It has already been established by the police that Mr. Frederick Steele, in the person of Mr. Homer Balantine, died in the act of murdering Oscar Harris."

"No one but Watson and I are aware of your presence at the murder. Nor do they know how you defended Mr. Harris at risk of your own person. I believe the young man has given you a gift. I suggest you do not take his sacrifice lightly."

"I . . . I can go?"

"Only if you give me your word you will return if an innocent is tried in your stead."

"I give you my word. I swear it!"

"Then go on your way, Mr. Bennett. It is my hope that I never see you or your good lady again."

"Thank you, Mr. Holmes!" the old fellow cried. "Thank you!" He turned and vanished into the fog.

The next day, we received a visitor in the person of Mordecai Pettigrew. Holmes had informed him by telegram that a solution had been obtained and he was quite pleased to hear of how the great detective had solved the case.

"I knew it couldn't be Mr. Bromley," he said, when my friend had finished his selective account of the affair. "But if he isn't dead, and was not present at the murder, how did Balantine – or Steele as he was called – come to be wearing his clothes?"

"Perhaps they were left in the wardrobe," I volunteered. "They were, after all, of the same build."

"Ah. That is quite possible." He turned to Holmes. "I am most grateful for your aid in all of this Mr. Holmes, but now I must ask another favor of you. Mr. Bromley has disappeared. Ever since I received your telegram, I have sought him out. Unfortunately, the address he gave me in Shelton Street has been vacated."

"How very odd," Holmes said.

"I must find him, Mr. Holmes. You see, I received this letter today. It is from the office Steele claimed to work for. It seems the will naming Mr. Harris beneficiary was forged. Poor Harris. If only he hadn't been so taken in by that confidence trickster."

"It is well he came to his senses in the end," Holmes said.

"Indeed. However, I am now left with a new problem. The will I drew up for Mrs. Bennett is now the only legitimate one – which means Mr. Bromley and I are the only beneficiaries. I must ensure he receives his share."

"I wish I could be of assistance," Holmes said, blandly, "but a new case has come to my attention, and I find I am not available. Here is the key to your house, Mr. Pettigrew. I suggest you return there. Perhaps, one day, you will meet Mr. Bromley again. However, I sincerely doubt it."

The Other Woman
by Susan Knight

It was the middle of November, a bright clear morning. Frost flowers overlaid the windows of our first-floor sitting room, so that the incessant bustle of Baker Street was, for once, hidden from us. I sat happily enough reading a journal, but my companion was sulking, buried in his armchair, and puffing clouds of smoke into the room from his noxious pipe. Holmes was ever thus when he had no case to solve, and experience had taught me it was better to avoid conversation when he was in this mood. Whatever I said would be met either with a disparaging contradiction or dismissive silence.

Suddenly Holmes rose from his seat and hastened to the window.

"I thought I heard something," he said.

Not feeling the need to respond, I merely turned the page of my journal.

"Watson!"

"I heard nothing," I replied reluctantly.

"You never do," he remarked with unnecessary asperity. Then: "Damnation upon this frost. One cannot see a thing."

To my astonishment, he took a coin from the pocket of his smoking jacket, blew upon it for some moments, rubbed it between his hands, and then pressed it against the window. After a minute, he removed it. A clear circle had been made on the glass. Holmes peered through it, then withdrew in disgust.

"Nothing!" he said, sinking back into his chair.

I tried not to appear too self-righteous.

However, almost immediately a sharp knock sounded on the front door.

"A-ha!" Holmes exclaimed. "I knew it."

He was suddenly energised. Leaning forward, he grasped the arms of his chair. His eyes sparkled, his nostrils trembled. The greyhound I knew so well, ready to burst from the slips.

In no time, heavy steps were heard pounding up the stairs and then, without ceremony, our door burst open. Behind the very large personage intruding on us in this uncustomary manner, Mrs. Hudson stood on her tiptoes, peering over his shoulder, and gesturing apologetically, as if to say, *I couldn't stop him.*

Attempting to emulate Holmes's deductive powers of observation, I studied the newcomer carefully. Despite his disregard for the conventions of polite society, he looked to be no uncouth denizen of the street, but, by his dress and bearing, a gentleman. Aged about fifty years, with a trimmed grey beard, he was clad in a suit of high quality that, despite being well-cut, only managed partially to conceal the fact that he was overweight to obesity. Just now, in addition, there was a somewhat dishevelled aspect to him, indicative of one who has been so eager to hasten to his destination that he has omitted to check his appearance. His hair, under the homburg he threw off, was unkempt, his coat ill-buttoned. Perspiration coated his face like a layer of grease, and an unhealthy flush coloured his complexion. I judged him to be choleric in all senses of the word.

"Mr. Holmes," he boomed, striding towards me, "I am at my wit's end. You are my last hope. You must help me."

"I am sorry – " I started to correct his misapprehension as to my identity.

"Do not refuse me, sir!" he interrupted, even seizing hold of my hands. "You must hear me out! If it is a question of money, don't doubt that I am prepared – "

Holmes coughed. The man looked round, taken aback. Apparently, he hadn't noticed my friend, ensconced as he was in his armchair. Holmes now stood up.

"My dear sir, please calm yourself," he said. "Take a chair, will you. I am Sherlock Holmes. This gentleman is my colleague, Dr. Watson."

"Oh, God help me! I am so bewildered, I must be going mad. Or else everyone else is." The man fell into an upright chair that rather groaned under his corpulence. "Believe me, I don't know what to do, who else to turn to. You must help me. The world is gone upside down."

He grasped his head in his hands as if to still his fevered brain.

"You have several advantages over us, sir." Holmes's tones were calm, although I sensed the excitement beneath at the prospect of a challenging new case. "In the first place, you now know our names, but we remain ignorant of yours. And secondly, we will not be able to help you unless you tell us exactly what is the matter that has brought you here so precipitously."

"Of course. Of course. I am Montgomery Beresford." He spoke with some pride, and indeed I had heard of him – head of a merchant bank in the City of London, and a man reputedly of astronomical wealth and a ruthless iron will. Something serious indeed must have happened to reduce him to his present state.

The banker paused, as if to let the eminence of his name sink in.

Holmes was unimpressed. After all, he had assisted more illustrious clients than this man in the past.

"I must again request that you explain why you are here, Mr. Beresford," he said. "What problem is exercising you to such an alarming extent?" Holmes regarded the man fixedly, no doubt hoping to hear of some intriguing mystery.

"It is my wife, Veronica. She has disappeared."

Holmes gave a great sigh. A banal-enough case, after all.

"Can I suppose," he said languidly, "that your wife is somewhat younger than you?"

"Yes, she is twenty-two."

"And no doubt pretty."

"Very. I should never have chosen to wed a frump."

Holmes sighed again. I could guess what he was thinking: An attractive young woman married to a much older and, to be frank, somewhat unprepossessing man. Wealth or no wealth, she had no doubt had enough of him.

"No, she hasn't just run off, Mr. Holmes," the banker insisted, reading our thoughts, "What happened is much stranger than that. Fantastic, even."

"Go on."

"Veronica is a child in many ways." Beresford shook his head. "Innocent and trusting. At least, so I thought. A girl of simple interests, easily diverted. To be honest, I picked her off the street. Well, not exactly. She was working in the florist shop where I buy my daily buttonhole."

He wore no buttonhole that day. Another sign that he had hurried to us without delay.

"A simple soul, do you see? A flower in her own right, ready to be plucked – By me."

It was a strange and not altogether pleasant way to be talking about his wife. I couldn't help myself from frowning, as did Holmes. The banker pressed on regardless.

"It was a pleasure and challenge for me to lift her out of the gutter, so to speak, and make a lady of her." He sighed. "I judged that I was making headway in that respect, albeit more slowly than I had hoped. However, I liked to relax the strict regime imposed on her from time to time and indulge her little whims."

He paused, shaking his head again.

"The point, please, Mr. Beresford."

The banker didn't care to be interrupted and continued in a sharper tone. "The point here, Mr. Holmes, is that when a circular arrived at the house announcing a forthcoming performance of some kind of a magic show, she pleaded for permission to go to see it, saying it was her favourite entertainment in all the world."

He cast brooding eyes upon us.

"Of course, such a spectacle wouldn't be to my taste at all, and I tried to argue her out of it, but you know the pretty wiles women use." He looked to us for concurrence. "Soft words and tears, promises and accusations . . . ." He mimicked a foolish girlish voice: "'Oh, I get so lonely here, Monty, without you.'" Adding somewhat dismissively, "'Monty' being her pet name for me, do you see? Of course, it is true gentlemen," he continued, "that I am a very busy man, and that she has to spend much time sequestered in the house."

We nodded to express understanding, although I couldn't but recall that my dear Mary had been well able to find plenty to occupy herself in my absence. Oh, how I missed her, dead far too young.

"And so," the banker was saying, "last eve I finally agreed to take her to the show. The Devil take it!" he exclaimed, clenching a fat fist and hitting it off the arm of his chair. "If only I had refused."

The theatre in question turned out to be a seedy-enough establishment in a less-than-salubrious part of town.

"I was in favour of turning back, but Veronica begged me. 'Now we are here, Monty, dear,' she said, 'we might as well go in.' So we did. An unforgiveable weakness I shall regret for the rest of my life." To our consternation, he began hitting himself repeatedly on the forehead with that same clenched fist.

"My dear sir – " Holmes began. Beresford took a deep breath to recover himself and continued his account.

"The show was as tawdry as I had expected, and attended by a very low class of patron. All sorts of vulgar acts of the music hall variety. The worst was the magician, a sleazy individual, by his name and execrable accent some sort of an Italian, whose tricks were crude and obvious." He shook his head. "An out-and-out scapegrace, gentleman, who would be abhorred in polite circles."

Veronica, however, according to her husband, was enchanted, applauding every silly sleight of hand and illusion.

Then, at a certain point, the magician invited a member of the audience to come up and assist him.

"The fellow was requesting '*una bella donna*', and had the cheek to look quite pointedly at Veronica. Well, Mr. Holmes, before I could stop her, she had jumped to her feet, rushed forward, and climbed on to the stage! I was both flabbergasted and shocked. The ruffians in the audience laughing and pointing at my wife in the most indecorous way. *My* wife!"

He spluttered angrily at the memory.

321

"What happened next?" Holmes asked.

"The fellow got her to go into some sort of upright box. A vanishing cabinet, as I understand it is called."

"And she vanished."

"Indeed she did." Beresford paused, looking at us significantly.

"Yet," Holmes rejoined, "as I recall from visits to such spectacles myself – and Watson will confirm this, for he has been present as well – after the *Ooh*'s and *Aah*'s of amazement have died down, the magician will close the door of the cabinet again, before reopening it, whereupon the disappeared person will return. Did this not happen in your case, Mr. Beresford?"

"Oh, the fellow closed the door all right, waved his wand, and babbled some incomprehensible nonsense before finally reopening the door with a flourish. And there she stood."

Holmes frowned. "I don't quite understand," he said.

"A woman stood there, dressed as my wife and very like her. But it wasn't Veronica."

For once Holmes, no less than I, was rendered speechless.

"Not her?" he said at last.

"I can assure you of that, Mr. Holmes. I know my own wife."

A broad smile lit up Holmes's face.

"How wonderful!" he said.

Beresford was less than impressed with this response.

I can assure you, Mr. Holmes," he replied coldly, "that it wasn't wonderful at all. It was frightful, particularly since no one else seemed to notice the difference. Not the audience, not the magician – even when I seized the fellow by the scruff of his neck and gave him a good shaking."

"Apologies, Mr. Beresford. I meant no belittlement of the seriousness of the matter," Holmes said ruefully. "I used the word in its original sense of inspiring wonder. You have presented us with a most intriguing conundrum."

The other nodded, somewhat appeased.

"Of course, I have to confirm," Holmes continued, "if you are absolutely sure that the person who emerged from the box wasn't Veronica."

"How many times must I say it? She bore a close resemblance to my wife, though without Veronica's bloom, if I might say so, or the refinement I have been so assiduous in cultivating. This person wore identical clothes and jewellery, dressed her hair in the same way, and yet without a scintilla of a doubt, it wasn't she."

Holmes rubbed his hands together. This was exactly the sort of mystery he had been hoping for. There was a long, thoughtful pause.

"We can rule out magic, I suppose?" I asked to break the silence. Not because I believed it myself, but because heretofore I had felt somewhat excluded from the interchange. The other two looked at me with disdain, and I smiled shamefacedly.

"Of course, it couldn't be," I mumbled.

Another explanation, which I hadn't been inclined to voice, was that Beresford was indeed mad, or at least mistaken for some deeper personal reason. Could it be that subconsciously he wanted rid of the wife to whom he professed such attachment? A wife who had turned out to be a disappointment to him? I had recently become aware, through my reading, of the most interesting notions of Herr Sigmund Freud regarding *displacement*. Perhaps Beresford had projected the image of a stranger onto his wife because he quite literally felt estranged from her. I wondered what Holmes would make of my theory.

He, meanwhile, was avidly questioning our visitor.

"How many minutes passed between Mrs. Beresford entering the box and the emergence of this other woman?"

"Long enough, I suppose."

"Long enough for someone to change clothes with your wife?"

The man looked exasperated.

"I cannot say exactly how long it was. I was beside myself, Mr. Holmes, thinking of how strongly I would chide her on her return for making a fool out of me."

He clenched his fist again, a gesture not wasted on Holmes.

"I have to ask, Mr. Beresford," Holmes asked, "is there any reason why your wife might wish to disappear?"

Again the man looked as if he might explode.

"None! After all I have done for her? She has been abducted. That's the only possible explanation."

"Yet you haven't received a ransom demand,"

"Not yet."

"Hmm," Holmes said. "Well, who do you think this woman is, if not your wife?"

The man sighed deeply.

"I have no idea, except that she has the audacity to claim to be Veronica. As I said, none of the audience believed me. Nor did the policeman who came on the scene while I was – I was questioning the magician."

Apparently, it was only after Beresford had revealed his identity to the constable that he avoided being arrested for affray.

"The Italian chappie was making an enormous fuss about nothing. I had hardly touched him. In fact, I am sure that, given a little while longer,

I could have got him to tell me exactly what had happened. Only the woman who was pretending to be my wife whispered something to the constable, presumably spinning some yarn about my state of mind, for they all started looking at me with pity as if I was stark staring mad – the very way you are looking at me now, Doctor."

He stared balefully at me. Holmes often tells me that my face is an open book.

He now murmured in soothing tones, "Not at all, my dear fellow. What you say might seem fantastic now, but I can think of at least three rational explanations for what has happened here. Abduction is certainly one possibility. But," he admonished before the man could interrupt him, "before I elaborate, I should like to visit the theatre to talk to the magician, and also to confront the woman in question. Where is she now?"

"In order to avoid a scandal, I took her home with me last night. But the situation is intolerable. It cannot be allowed to continue, Mr. Holmes."

"Clearly not."

"Thank you so much for believing me. It is a great relief."

Holmes gave an enigmatic smile. I knew that he wouldn't fully believe this extraordinary tale until he had examined all the evidence for himself.

"I imagine you have many servants, Mr. Beresford," he said. "How did they react when you arrived home?"

"The woman would only have been seen by the butler who opened the door for us. Baines is old and short-sighted, so would hardly have noticed anything was amiss. In any case, she hurried up to her room, her face half-concealed by a scarf, claiming a throbbing headache."

Holmes held up a forefinger. "She knew the way, then."

For the first time, Beresford was silenced.

"My God!" he said at last, clutching his head. "Am I mad after all?"

"Do not distress yourself, sir. I am sure you are as sane as Watson here." Holmes's lips curled in a not-completely pleasant smile. "Again, I can think of good reasons why the woman in question might be aware of the layout of the house."

"Was she not at least attended by her maid?" I asked.

Holmes looked at me for once with appreciation.

"A good point, Watson."

"No," Beresford replied. "She said that she was far too upset to see anyone."

"Interesting and telling. Clearly, she wished for no one to regard her too closely."

Or, on the other hand, I thought to myself, she was utterly distraught at the unreasonable behaviour of her husband.

"I am inclined," Holmes stated, making a steeple of his fingers, "to first visit the theatre and interview this magician – What is his name?"

Beresford pulled a paper from his pocket.

"This was the circular that was delivered to the house," he said.

"'*Maggiorino the Magnificent!*'" Holmes read aloud, chuckling. "Clearly the fellow doesn't suffer from false modesty."

"He hardly lives up to the title. A seedy little man in grubby velvet," the banker remarked scornfully, adding, "Do you wish for me to accompany you to the theatre? I have to say, I should rather not after last night."

"No," Holmes replied. "Watson and I will go. You will be better off staying at home, keeping a watchful eye on this supposed imposter."

Once more, Beresford reared up. He really had a very short fuse.

"There is nothing *supposed* about it, Holmes," he said.

"Well, well. Let us trust we can get to the bottom of things, and quickly."

The establishment in question, Jabot's Music Hall, was situated in Shoreditch, a squalid and overcrowded area of the city, though also home to many theatres and other places of entertainment, catering to the largely working-class inhabitants of the locality, as well as to members of the upper classes wishing to "slum it", as the saying goes. I fully comprehended Montgomery Beresford's distaste at having to visit such a place.

Jabot's presented a run-down exterior, its peeling plasterwork resembling some chronic skin condition, a lantern with a broken glass pane hanging over the entranceway. The dilapidation persisted to the inside, although I could imagine that, by night, the faded and tattered red velvet of the upholstery, the dust on the curtains, the filth on the floor, would be tempered by the soft effect of the gaslights.

We were soon accosted by a stout red-headed, red-faced individual, pulling a jacket over his less-than-scrupulously clean shirt even as he hurried towards us. This, as it turned out, was Jabot himself. He muttered cryptically something about "'Aving to see to the dogs". It turned out later that he had been referring to one of the regular acts, Miss Dimples and her performing poodles. He explained, before asking us our business, that since Miss Dimples had been laid low by an attack of the vapours, Jabot had to feed the dogs and look after their animal needs.

"Maggiorino, is it. 'E's gorn."

"Already?" Holmes asked.

"Up and left first thing. After that unpleasantness last night, see. 'E got on 'is 'igh 'orse and legged it."

"Do you know where he went?"

Jabot spat on the floor.

"Don't know and don't care. Bringin' a mutton shunter to the premises – gives it a bad name."

"The constable, you mean." Holmes was all sympathy. "Yes, I heard. What exactly happened here?"

"'Oo wants ter know?"

The man was suddenly suspicious.

"This is Dr. Watson," my companion replied amiably, "and I am Sherlock Holmes, acting on behalf of the gentleman present here last evening, who, as I understand it, had some sort of altercation with Signor Maggiorino."

Whether it was this explanation that had the desired effect, or perhaps it was the production of a golden guinea, Jabot suddenly became quite overly loquacious.

"Sherlock 'Olmes, is it. I 'eard o' you, Guv'nor. Often wondered if you'd be up to doin' a turn 'ere."

Holmes burst out laughing.

"Doing what, exactly?"

"Oh, I 'eard 'ow you can read people like a book from appearances alone. Go on, then. Tell me about me."

"I hardly think – "

"Go on. For a larf. Then I'll tell you what you want to know."

Holmes sighed, and studied the man from head to toe, turning him about in a theatrical way that I had never seen him employ in the past.

"Well," he said finally, "I hope you enjoyed your breakfast of ham and fried eggs, washed down with a goodly glass of – " He sniffed. " – small beer." Judged perhaps from certain fresh stains on the man's jacket. "You don't live here on the premises, for your boots and trousers display recent signs of the sticky yellow mud found on the banks of the Thames, so I imagine that your abode, though not far, is situated somewhere between Tower Bridge and Limehouse. From your distinctive gait, I deduce that you have spent time at sea, and from your complexion – the skin of persons of red-hair suffering unduly from exposure to the sun – that you have in the past travelled to southern climes. The tattoo on your arm, that I noticed before you put on your jacket, looked to be the work of a Pacific islander – perhaps someone from Tahiti?"

Jabot's mouth hung open, displaying an unfortunate absence of healthy teeth. "Astonishin'!" he exclaimed. "Correct in every pertikular, Mr. 'Olmes. If you ever wanted a turn in Jabot's, just say the word. I can see the poster now." He looked dreamily into the distance.

"Thank you," Holmes interrupted the revery. "I am most honoured by your offer, Mr. Jabot, although I am far too busy to consider it at present. But speaking of the poster, how is it that my client received a circular regarding your theatre at his house in Hampstead, so far distant from here?"

The man looked puzzled.

"Can't answer that one. We don't post out nothin' like that, Guv'nor. Only stick a few notices up in the locality. People 'ere abouts knows we give a good show."

"Hmm. Most enlightening." Holmes nodded thoughtfully. "Well, perhaps you will be so good as to describe what happened last eve, as you recollect it."

The man scrunched up his face in an attempt to remember.

"Maggi's act was goin' on as usual," he said finally. "Then 'e called for some person in the audience to join 'im on stage."

"'*Una bella donna*' as I understand it. A beautiful woman. This, I take it, was his usual practice?"

"Not at all, Mr. 'Olmes. But see, the assistant what usually done it, she took poorly of a sudden, so 'e 'ad to hextemporise."

"I see."

"'E asked for the *bella donna* coz the audience likes to see a pretty girl on stage. And this one what come up last eve – a right basket of oranges, she were."

He grinned appreciatively at the memory.

"And when she reemerged, did she look anyway different to you?"

Jabot scratched his head.

"See, that's what the gent claimed. To me, at first anyway, she looked hexactly the same."

"At first?"

"'Onestly, Guv'nor, I couldn't say she looked different in any way, but then I 'adn't 'ad a good dekko before. But ask yourself: 'Ow could she not be the same one what went in?"

"Magic?"

I looked sharply at Holmes for stealing my line.

Jabot wheezed a laugh. "Yeah, hexactly right, Guv'nor."

"But now you say you have doubts it was indeed the same woman?"

"Only coz the gent was so very sure of 'isself."

"Tell me, where exactly were you standing during the performance?"

Jabot pointed to the side of the stage. "Just there, behind the curtain, like what I always do."

"So if some exchange had taken place at the back of the stage, you wouldn't have seen it."

"It wouldn't 'ave 'appened like that anyway. The lady would 'ave gone down under the stage on a lift, and then be brought up again minutes later."

"I see. Can you show us?"

Jabot led the way up on to the stage and indicated the position of a trapdoor, about three feet square. He explained how the cabinet would have been neatly positioned over this and a lad below the stage would, at a given moment, set in motion the lift mechanism to lower the volunteer out of sight of the audience, raising her again when required.

"So if any exchange were effected, this lad would have known about it."

"You'd think so, wouldn't you, but, see, Tommy isn't the sharpest knife in the drawer. Just shook 'is 'ead when I asked. Said 'e didn't see nothin'."

"May I speak to him anyway?"

"'E ain't 'ere just now. See, 'e only comes in for the show."

Holmes frowned.

"Curiouser and curiouser," I ventured.

"Not curious at all, Watson," Holmes retorted, though not unkindly. "We aren't in Wonderland now. If indeed there has been a switch, then the whole thing must have been carefully planned. Let us go and speak to the person claiming to be Beresford's wife."

"We all thought the gent 'ad gone off 'is rocker," Jabot put in. "Then, when 'e started with the fisticuffs, it stopped being a joke. No wonder poor Dimples took bad. See, she was due on after."

"Was she, indeed? Might I have a word. Perhaps she saw something useful."

Jabot shook his head. "Can't see 'er agreein' to that, but I'll ask."

Miss Dimples, as it turned out, didn't only agree, but proved utterly thrilled to meet the great detective, Sherlock Holmes, and couldn't stop giggling girlishly and fluttering her eyelashes at him. Indeed, the very sight of him brought about a miraculous recovery from her purported attack of the vapours – a condition, incidentally, absent from any of my medical textbooks.

We had found her reclining backstage on a dingy ottoman, surrounded by her performing poodles – six absurdly clipped white canines – one tiny white-gloved hand pressed over her eyes.

No, she uttered in a faint voice, she couldn't possibly face visitors. However, after I identified myself as a doctor, the same little hand beckoned me over. A perilous enterprise, for the dogs, small as they were, stood guard over their mistress, and started yapping so aggressively that I quite feared for my ankles. However, in a more commanding voice than before, she told them to sit and stay, which they obediently did, all in a row, though continuing to eye me with suspicion and malice.

She made room for me on the edge of the ottoman. I rather reluctantly perched there and asked what was the matter.

From a distance I had taken Miss Dimples, in her frilly and beribboned white dress, ivory complexion, rosy cheeks, and golden curls, for a very young woman. But now I discovered her, on the contrary, to be well-advanced in years, heavily powdered and rouged, and the curls, quite obviously, a wig. Speaking in the false accents of one attempting to show herself better bred than she was, she explained the source of her malaise, a weakness caused by shock at the sight of a huge gorilla of a man attacking poor little Maggi.

"With may overly sensitive nature, Doctor, Ay 'aven't been able to exercise the image from may mind. Good 'Eavens, would the creature turn on me next? Ay was quate terrified."

I assured her in soothing tones that we had come to find out exactly what had happened, and were hoping that she, as an invaluable witness, might be able to help us.

"Ay fear not, Doctor," she replied. "Ay was quate blinded by terror."

"Now, now, Dimples," Jabot said. "'Ere's Mr. Sherlock 'Olmes, come all the way from Baker Street to talk to you."

"Sherlock 'Olmes," Miss Dimples sat up abruptly, the poodles cocking their heads expectantly, pompom tails hitting the floor in counterpoint. "Not *Mr. Sherlock 'Olmes*, the famous detective?"

"None other, Madam," Holmes replied, stepping forward and holding out his hand.

The dame seized it and covered it with kisses, much to my amusement and my friend's discomfiture.

"Oh, Mr. 'Olmes!" she said, smiling broadly – and one of her cheeks indeed dimpled. "What a 'onour!"

He somewhat warily took my vacated seat beside her.

"Now Miss – er, *Dimples*, I am sure, if you put your mind to it, a clever and observant lady like yourself will be able to recollect something useful."

She gazed up at him soulfully, one of her gloved claws still clutching his hand.

"Well," she said, "that's as may be."

"Good. Now," he urged, talking as if to a child, "why don't you lie back down, close your eyes, and imagine that you're standing behind the curtains."

Dutifully, she did as she was told.

"The magician has just invited someone from the audience to join him on the stage," Holmes continued.

"Yes, that were different. Usually 'e'd use 'is assistant. She weren't on that night for some reason."

"So I understand. In your opinion, did he single out one particular lady?"

Miss Dimples frowned in an effort at remembering. She shook her head.

"'E said something in 'is own lingo, but – "

"*Una bella donna*," Holmes prompted.

"That's it. Yes. But Ay don't think 'e looked nowhere special. In any case, with them footlights, you know, it's 'ard to see into the audience."

"Of course. So Mrs. Beresford – "

"'Oo?"

"The lady in question. She comes on to the stage."

"Gawd bless 'er. She was that excited. Laughing and smiling, she was."

"Good. Well done. So then she entered the box."

"Maggi told 'er not to be afraid when she disappeared."

"I see."

"Ay 'eard 'im add that 'e would make sure she was safe."

"Not that she would get back safely?"

"No, Mr. 'Olmes, but, being a foreign gent, poor little Maggi's command of the English language leaves much to be desired."

She clearly assumed her own command of it was flawless.

"Hmm," Holmes said. "What next?"

"Well, she disappeared, didn't she?" Miss Dimples opened her eyes and looked at Jabot. "Can Ay say 'ow, Alf?"

He nodded.

"I showed the gents already," he replied.

"Right you are. So she went down as always and, as far as Ay knew, she come up again. Like what always 'appens."

"Can I stop you there for a moment, Madam?" Holmes said. "How long was she under the stage?"

"Oh, quate some time. You see, Maggi likes to draw things out. So 'e opens the door and if she ain't there, 'e pretends surprise, closes it and waves 'is wand some more. 'E's a real showman, is Maggi. Anyway, after she come back for real, next thing, that 'orrid man comes rushing on the stage and starts knocking poor Maggi about while the lady tries to calm 'im. You stepped up then and pulled him orf, Alf, didn't you? So very brave."

Holmes smiled at her. "Very vividly described. Now, I can tell by looking at you that you are a lady of fashion." She giggled. "Think hard. Was there anything at all different about the lady's appearance when she returned?"

Miss Dimples closed her eyes again and kept them closed for so long that I started wondering if she had fallen asleep.

"'Er bonnet," she said at last.

"Yes?" Holmes leaned forward.

"It was tilted to one side when she went down. When she come up again, it was tilted to the other." She opened her eyes, making them big. "Is that what you want to 'ear, Mr. 'Olmes?"

"If that is what you saw," he replied dryly.

"Ay think so." She gave a little frown. "Oh, Ay don't know! Ay can't be sure. She looked just the same to me." Miss Dimples lowered her voice. "If you ask me, Ay think 'er 'ubby was jealous that Maggi 'ad laid 'is 'ands upon 'er."

Holmes raised his eyebrows.

"Laid hands how?"

"Oh, just took 'er 'and to 'elp her down from the box. Though 'e 'eld on, Ay thought, a little too long. But then, Maggi likes all the pretty ladies." She smirked and fluffed up her fake curls. "The naughty man. Eyetalian, don't you know. Didn't Ay 'ave to tell 'im over and over, Alf, Miss Dimples isn't that sort of a girl?"

She gave Holmes a nudge, and while he recoiled and hastily stood up, Jabot remained expressionless.

"Thank you," my friend said. "You have been most helpful."

"'Ave Ay?" The dimple twinkled in her faded cheek. "'Ave Ay, Mr. 'Olmes? Oh, come and see the show, do. And visit me in may dressing room after. May *un*-dressing room, I should say." She winked suggestively.

"What an absolute horror!" I exclaimed as we made our way out of the theatre. "I think she would have gobbled you up if she could."

"I rather feared the same thing myself," Holmes replied ruefully. "At least she told us something useful."

"Did she?"

"Seeing nothing amiss is good negative information."

"The bonnet business – "

"Made up, probably. She wanted to tell me something and it was all she could think of. However, maybe it was true. If so – " He knitted his brows in thought.

"There's the hand-holding," I continued, adding with a grin. "The magician's, I mean. Not Miss Dimples'."

Holmes glared at me. "Please don't remind me, Watson. This isn't an occasion for frivolity."

"I was just wondering: Could Mrs. Beresford have run off with Maggiorino?"

"It seems most unlikely from what we've heard of the man. And how would they have had a prior occasion to meet? It sounds as if Beresford keeps his wife well tucked away."

I then proceeded to describe my own theory as to what might have happened.

"Displacement – ?" Holmes asked.

"Herr Freud is most convincing on the subject."

"I know that, Watson. I have, of course, read his paper for myself. Well, it's a theory. Let us see what happens when we meet the lady, whoever she is."

A cab carried us all the way across town to the wealthy suburb of Hampstead, where Beresford's elegantly white-plastered house stood in a street of similar dwellings. An aged and bent individual, attired in the neat black attire of a butler, opened the door to us. This must be Baines. He was clearly expecting us, for he admitted us readily, showing us into an empty salon, and requesting us to wait there.

Holmes prowled the room which was decorated, to my eyes, in an impeccable, if somewhat impersonal, style, as if a professional decorator, rather than the residents, had been responsible for the furnishings. A piano stood in one corner, its lid open and a set of exercises by Herr Czerny on the music shelf. I imagined the bored wife sitting before it, reluctantly picking out notes for a husband who wished his flower-girl wife to become accomplished. On a wall nearby hung a large portrait of a very pretty young woman, presumably the self-same Mrs. Beresford. Holmes stood in front of this image for a good while, as if imprinting it on his mind.

We were left waiting at least fifteen minutes, as measured by the ormolu clock on the mantelpiece. I supposed the lady was unwilling to descend and submit to scrutiny, perhaps from fear of being revealed as an imposter, or perhaps bitterly offended that her husband should even suggest such a thing.

At last, the door opened and a slight young woman entered, the banker at her heels. It proved impossible to see her face, however, hidden as it was by a heavy veil. In a low and melodious voice, she explained, that she was suffering from a bad headache and couldn't tolerant bright lights.

"But Madam," Holmes replied, "your husband has boasted so much of your beauty that we should be sorely disappointed not to witness it for ourselves, even for a brief moment. Don't be cruel, I implore you! Lift the veil, so that we can gaze upon you."

I should add here that the lady was so far not aware of our true identities. Beresford had introduced us as colleagues, visiting on business, who had expressed a burning wish to meet his wife.

She reflected on Holmes's words for a few moments. Then she raised her veil. Because she was standing in front of the portrait of Beresford's wife, it was a simple matter to make the comparison. The resemblance was striking, even if the image in the painting showed a young woman happy and relaxed, her cheeks rosy, her eyes bright, while the person before us looked strained and pale, a difference explained easily enough by her headache, not to mention her husband's rejection of her. I hadn't the slightest doubt that this was Veronica, the true wife of Montgomery Beresford, with Herr Freud's theory becoming ever more likely as an explanation of what had transpired.

I looked across at Holmes, who also, frowning, was evidently comparing the woman in front of us with the portrait. Surely he would come to the same conclusions as myself.

He spoke at last.

"Tell me, Madam," he asked in a soft voice, "where is your sister?"

The woman gasped and let the veil fall over her face once more.

"What sister?" Beresford exclaimed. "My wife doesn't have a sister!"

"So you agree, then, that this woman is your wife."

"Not at all." An angry flush mounted to the man's cheeks. "I don't know what rubbish you are talking. You say Veronica has a sister. Why? To what end?"

Holmes smiled.

"You claim, sir, that this isn't your wife. However, you cannot deny that an extraordinary resemblance exists between her and the portrait of Mrs. Beresford. If she isn't your wife, then she must be a very close relative – a sister in fact."

The banker was beside himself with fury.

"How many times must I repeat that my wife has no sister? I would know of it, were it true!" He banged a fist on the top of the piano, forcing out a groan of protest from the instrument. "The Devil take you, Holmes! You are like all the others, after all, trying to make me out a liar or a madman."

"*Holmes*, Montgomery?" the young woman exclaimed, clearly shocked. "You have brought *Sherlock Holmes* here to question me?"

The man, ignoring her outburst, was pacing about the room liked a caged animal, all but foaming at the mouth. The high colour had risen to his cheeks again, rendering them more purple than red. I quite feared he might explode.

Suddenly he picked up a vase and threw it at the portrait. It smashed against the canvas and, falling to the ground, shattered into pieces. The young woman flinched as if she herself had been hit, while even Holmes was shocked into silence, I reflecting that if Beresford weren't a madman, then he was doing a very good job of imitating one.

The banker spun around, strode over to my friend and would, I reckon, have seized him by the lapels of his jacket, hadn't Holmes, an expert in the art of baritsu, raised his fists. Beresford then collected himself to some extent and continued in quieter tones, "I invited you here, Holmes," he said, "because I expected you to clear up the mystery. Instead, you have started prattling on about a non-existent sister. I don't claim to know who this woman is."

"Precisely," Holmes interrupted him. "So instead of 'prattling' your own denials, please let me do my work and interview this person, whoever she is, to get at last to the truth."

Beresford shrank back, as much as a man of his height and girth could manage.

"Go on then," he said begrudgingly.

Holmes turned back to the young woman.

"I repeat, Madam," he said softly, "*Where is your sister?*"

"I assure you, sir – " she started to reply in a trembling voice.

"No," Holmes interrupted. "No more lies, if you please."

The woman stood silent for a while.

"Very well," she said at last, her voice almost inaudible. "It will make no difference now, anyway. Veronica is long gone from this vile marriage, from this cruel man. By now, she is far from here in a place where he will never find her."

"A-ha! The truth at last." Beresford swung around. "I knew it! So Veronica's run off with one of her many lovers, has she? Fool that I was, I should have known better than to try and force a rose out of a ditchweed." The man's face having become deformed into a mask of hate, far from that of the respectable banker the world knew. With a sudden rush, he launched himself upon the young woman. "You will tell me, Miss, where she is right now, or it will be the worse for you!"

Holmes and I managed to pull him away with some difficulty, the man displaying almost superhuman strength.

"This will not do, Mr. Beresford," Holmes told him. "If you wife had a good reason to disappear, I need to hear it. Violence has no place here."

"Thank you, Mr. Holmes," the woman said with dignity. "Yes, indeed. I am, as you have guessed, the sister of poor Veronica – her twin in fact. My name is Madeleine Swann. She, having all too soon discovered the truly monstrous nature of her husband, kept my existence from him, for my own safety. Not that he showed any interest in her family."

"Why should I bother with low-lifes?" the man muttered. "Anyway, Veronica said she was an orphan."

"That is true, "Miss Swann continued sadly. "Both our parents are dead."

"You have accused this man of cruelty towards your sister. With justification, I trust," Holmes remarked. I wondered how he could doubt it, having just witnessed the man's intemperate behaviour.

"If you hadn't come here today, Mr. Holmes," she replied, "there is no doubt that he would have beaten me black-and-blue as he did my sister so very often."

"Is it true?" Holmes turned to the banker. "You beat your wife?"

The man shrugged his shoulders. "Fuss and bother over nothing. I laid no hand upon her unless she was asking for it. The girl is obstinate, you know. She doesn't seem to comprehend that a wife's duty is to obey her husband in all things, at all times. The result, I suppose, of ill-breeding and bad example."

Holmes looked at me gravely.

"You who have been married, Watson. What do you say to that? Do you agree with Mr. Beresford?"

My beloved Mary had been dead for over a year, but my heart was still utterly broken.

"Not at all. I respected my wife as an independent individual. We were best friends – partners in life."

The banker sneered.

"Words of someone who isn't a real man. A foolish weakling."

"If you like," I replied amiably. "But you know, I prefer to be considered that. I would never have raised a hand against Mary."

The banker shook his head, a mocking expression on his face.

"But why, Miss Swann," Holmes continued, "did you take your sister's place in such a dramatic fashion? Why did she not just escape when out of sight under the stage?"

"He would have gone after her immediately. She wouldn't even have had time to leave the theatre. You should know that her husband is absurdly jealous and guards her like a prisoner, with the connivance of all but one of his servants, who agreed to carry notes between us."

"Who? Which one?" Beresford struggled to free himself from our grip. "It's Nancy, isn't it, the little traitress! I shall dismiss her instantly without a reference."

Of course, he would.

"You will find that she is already gone," Miss Swann continued with dignity. "Nancy too is better off out of this place." She turned to Holmes, "My poor sister was never permitted to leave the house without an escort, so it was lucky for us if it was Nancy's turn, because then we could arrange a brief meeting. It was on one of these expeditions that we devised the plan for Veronica's escape."

"What if Beresford had refused to take her to the theatre?" I asked.

"It was only with the greatest difficulty that my sister managed to persuade him," she replied. "How she debased herself in the attempt to win him over!" She glanced at the simmering banker in distaste. "What he made her do, I'd be ashamed to relate." Verily the man was a monster. "We were hoping," she continued, "that he would fail to notice the switch at once, since we are almost identical. Alas . . . ."

"As if I cannot recognise my own wife," the banker growled. "As for my practice of keeping your errant sister under my thumb, Miss, it has been shown to be clearly justified by what has happened."

"But the theatre?" Holmes asked. "The magic show? Why that?"

"Oh, didn't I say? Apologies. I am Maggiorino's assistant. Usually I'm on stage with him, but to effect the switch, I had to tell Jabot I was taken poorly."

"Did no one, Jabot himself for instance, notice your extraordinary likeness to your sister?" I asked.

"Stage make-up and a wig change my appearance considerably. And I don't usually present myself as a lady."

"I suppose you persuaded Maggiorino to go along with the substitution," Holmes said.

"Yes, but he didn't know why. I told him that it was a practical joke."

"A practical joke!" The enraged banker once more tried to free himself from our grasp, but we held him firm. "I wish I had killed the snivelling little trickster while I had the chance! And when I get my hands on the ungrateful slut I took into my house for a wife, it will be all the worse for her." He reared up. "I hereby charge you, Sherlock Holmes, to bring my wife back to her lawful place."

Holmes shook his head, which exasperated the man even more.

"If it is a question of money, man, the sky is the limit!" Beresford bellowed.

"It may well be," Holmes replied, "but no amount of money would persuade me to force any woman to live in a state of fear and violence. I wish Veronica a long and happy life far from you, sir. Come Miss Swann. Your work here is finished. Ours also."

336

Leaving the wretched banker grinding his teeth, he offered the lady his arm, which she took gratefully, and together we left that splendid, heartless house.

Looking back at it, I remarked, "It is so true that money doesn't buy happiness."

"Thank you, Watson," Holmes replied drily. "Ever ready with an original thought." He addressed his companion, "So what will you do now, Miss Swann? Continue to work with Maggiorino the Magnificent?"

"Possibly," she replied smiling. "Or maybe I will join my sister and Nancy, our faithful friend, wherever they are . . . ."

We were walking down the high street and soon reached a little tea shop.

"Before we go our separate ways," Holmes remarked, as if the notion had suddenly taken him, "let us go in here and share a refreshing pot of Darjeeling. Perhaps I can press a cake upon you, Miss Swann."

I couldn't say which one of us was the more surprised, the lady or myself, but we followed Holmes into the shop. With all appearance of satisfaction, he helped her into a seat at a small round table before settling himself into another. I did likewise.

"Well," my friend said, "this is all very charming. Do you not agree?"

A white linen tablecloth and napkins, chintz curtains, and cream cakes were hardly objects I had deemed close to Holmes's heart. He was up to something.

It was while we were sipping the tea and Miss Swann and I were preparing to consume our Victoria buns – Holmes eating nothing – that he sat back.

"You are a very clever young woman indeed, Miss Swann."

She looked up at him innocently. "Am I?"

"You thought you could fool everyone – even Sherlock Holmes."

"What do you mean?"

"Spin a yarn, no matter how far-fetched, with sufficient confidence, and people will believe it?"

She neatly cut her bun in quarters.

"I still don't know to what you are referring."

"Who is this person, Watson?"

"Why, she is Madeleine Swann, twin sister to Veronica Beresford." I was bemused at the question. Had he himself not got her to admit her identity.

He smiled and shook his head.

"She isn't?" I asked.

"This chit of a girl has skilfully performed what I think might be termed a 'double bluff'. While insisting she was *Veronica*, by using various tricks and devices she managed to convince her husband, and then even you, that she was an imposter. That the real Veronica is long gone. But in fact, she sits before us now. Am I not right, Mrs. Beresford?"

She stared at him in silence.

"Oh, don't worry," Holmes continued. "I have no intention, as I already informed your husband, of forcing you to return to him. Once I realised what kind of a man he really is, I was content to connive at your deception of him."

"How did you know?" she asked. "And when?"

"Apart from the sheer preposterousness of the tale, do you mean? Apart from the unlikelihood that, had Veronica a sister, her husband wouldn't have known it, despite what you tried to suggest? I knew it when I viewed you before the portrait."

"But Holmes," I said, "they were supposedly identical twins."

"There is no such thing," he replied. "There will always be little differences. However, in this case there were none at all. It would be beyond belief that the little mole above Veronica's eyebrow, as depicted in the portrait, would be exactly replicated in her twin – and yet that is what she would have us believe."

Miss Swann's hand strayed to the spot.

"You must be applauded, as I have said, at managing to change your appearance and bearing so subtly between going into the box and emerging from it."

"I didn't know if it would work," she said finally, "but I was desperate to escape before he killed me. I was sure he would eventually, you know, in one of his rages. My accusations against him would never be believed. He is powerful, with influential connections, while I am friendless and alone – apart from dear Nancy, of course."

"No doubt he chose you for that very reason, hoping to mould you into the willing little slave he wanted."

She nodded.

"But how," I asked, "did you happen to visit the theatre on the very night when Maggiorino's assistant was unable to perform? Surely you could not have foreseen that?"

"Oh, that was the easy part, Doctor. You see, it is *Nancy's* sister, Madeleine, who is actually the magician's assistant. That's what gave us the idea in the first place, and Madeleine proved only too happy to accommodate us.'

She laughed.

"So now, gentlemen, I am free of that monster forever. With the money from the pawning of the jewellery I have managed to bring out with me, my faithful Nancy and I shall emigrate to America and start a new life there."

Upon which final note, she popped a small piece of bun into her mouth. "Delicious," she said.

The Adventure of the Surrey Revenant
by Alan Dimes

The year of 1894, which had seen the return of Mr. Sherlock Holmes to 221b Baker Street, and his resumption of his role of consulting detective and last court of appeal, was drawing to a close. The seven months since he had brought Professor Moriarty's deputy, the formidable Colonel Sebastian Moran, to justice, had been amongst the busiest of his professional career, and I had been privileged to accompany and assist him on many of his most important cases, even as I had in those days before his seeming death amid the swirling waters of the Reichenbach Falls.

I had left our lodgings on a brief shopping expedition in search of a new razor, my old one, which I had bought shortly before my attachment to the Fifth Northumberland Fusiliers, having given up the ghost after many years' service. As I climbed the steps to our rooms on my return I heard Holmes's clear, high voice coming through the door. I had passed Mrs. Hudson in the hallway, so he was presumably conversing with a client.

"I'm very sorry, Mr. Bridges, but I don't think I can take your case. While you have my complete sympathy, I think you should consult an exorcist, or at any rate a priest of some kind. Your situation really doesn't come within my purview. Ah, good morning, Watson."

I had entered our sitting room and saw what appeared to be a sane and competent middle-aged member of the rentier class, respectably dressed and well groomed, his straight brown hair neatly combed to the back of his head and his upper lip adorned with a meticulously trimmed moustache.

"Am I interrupting?" I asked.

"No, Doctor, I believe Mr. Bridges is about to leave."

Bridges rose to his feet, his regular features writhing in frustration.

"I came to you because I was told you help people – those who cannot go to the police. People who need things kept out of the papers. People who have nowhere else to go. Obviously I was misinformed. Good day, sir."

"I, at least, would like to hear your story, Mr. Bridges," I interrupted. "Surely there is no harm in that, Holmes."

The detective leaned forward in his chair.

"Please sit down, Mr. Bridges. Perhaps I was a little hasty. I have rather more human weaknesses than one might imagine from reading about me in my friend's accounts of our cases. But you would admit that most people, hearing your story, would find it incredible, and might well come to the conclusion that you were, at the very least, suffering from some kind of delusion. Surely the simplest and most logical solution to the situation is that it was a case of mistaken identity."

"I've known the man for twenty years, I tell you. It was him, not just somebody who looked like him. And as I said, I've seen him more than once."

"Excuse me, gentlemen," I interjected, "but I have yet to hear the story."

"My apologies, Watson. Please repeat what you have told me, Mr. Bridges, and I assure you I shall make no more observations until you have finished."

He reached for his pipe and Persian slipper, and Michael Bridges began his tale.

"Fifteen years ago, I started a business with my friend, Arthur Atwell. We specialised in the production of agricultural machinery. I don't suppose you've heard of us, but amongst farming folk, Atwell and Bridges have a pretty solid reputation. Do you know anything about Haiti, Dr. Watson?"

"Beyond the fact that it is part of the island of Hispaniola, I know virtually nothing of it. Why do you ask?"

"Well, most people don't even know that much. After a rough time of political and social chaos, Michel Domingue introduced a fairer and more democratic constitution in 1874, resulting in a stability which has lasted to this day. In such circumstances, one can usually expect to see an improvement in agriculture, with greater efficiency and higher yields. But Haiti has virtually no industry, and is consequently unable to produce the machinery which would facilitate this. Now, Arthur and I always kept an eye out for potential new markets, and we came up with a plan for Haiti which we believed would be beneficial to both parties. We would sell them our products at greatly reduced prices in exchange for a guaranteed percentage of the profits from their exported goods."

"That sounds like an eminently sensible scheme," I remarked.

"Well, we thought so too. Most of the small-holding farmers there are dirt poor, but we were sure that there were enough big landowners who were rich enough to be interested in what we had to offer, and would have some influence in government circles. The only way to meet those landowners and convince them was for one of us to go to Haiti in person. Arthur was always better at that sort of thing, so he went. It was a long

341

journey – Portsmouth to New York by sea, New York to Miami by train, and then Miami to Port-au-Prince by boat. I received a letter from him, posted a few days after he arrived, telling me that not only had we made a big mistake, but he was in personal danger and was returning home as soon as he could and catching the first available boat to Miami. The mistake we had made was that the landowners had hundreds of people working the land for them, using primitive methods and in conditions of virtual slavery, and the owners liked it that way. So Arthur had to get out, and he did get out, but not alive. It was his dead body that took that long journey back."

"Was there a death certificate?"

"Yes, Arthur's son and daughter made the journey to Port-au-Prince as soon as the news reached them from the British representative there, and it was given directly into their hands. The cause of death was diagnosed as a heart attack. I couldn't believe that at first. Arthur was fifty-five, a few years older than me, but he was pretty fit for a man of his age. But then I thought, he had that long journey, all that time in a hot country, the failure of our enterprise, the threat of death, and even eating food he wasn't used to – all that must have combined to put a strain on his heart. I must confess, I felt – and feel – rather guilty. I should have gone. I'm not married, you see, and I've no one to grieve over me.

"That's the background, but it's time I came to the point. The part you won't believe – that Mr. Holmes here already doesn't believe. It was dark, and I had just been to see Edgar and Amelia, Arthur's children, in Sutton in Surrey, about ten days ago. I suppose it was about eleven at night. I'd gone over there with some documents connected with the business that they needed to sign. The door of their house is at the end of a narrow cul-de-sac, so I had parked the carriage on the main road near the other end of it and now I was walking back down the street. I heard footsteps behind me. I turned, and someone came out of the darkness into the light of a streetlamp, and I thought my own heart was going to stop when I saw Arthur's face. His face, I swear it, but deathly pale and bearing an expression of unutterable horror. His eyes seemed to be staring into the very pits of Hell. I scuttled backwards away from him, then I turned back and ran off as far and as fast as I could."

He took a couple of deep breaths then continued. "I found a cab and got home. The next day, I told my coachman to go and fetch the carriage. I couldn't stand to go back there."

"Why didn't he drive you the night before?" I asked.

"It was his night off, that's all. Wednesday night. I didn't tell anyone what had happened. As you said, if I told most people, they'd think I was insane."

Holmes broke his silence.

"I didn't say that, exactly."

"Well, my own first thought was that I was going mad. I tried to tell myself I'd been tired, or overwrought because of Arthur's death, or that I'd drunk too much while dining with Edgar and Amelia, but none of that was true. If I wasn't insane, the only alternative was that it was really him. I'd had a supernatural experience. Do you know what a zombie is?"

"I've heard the word, that's all," I said, "but perhaps you can enlighten me."

"Certainly. I have done some research into the matter in the past few days. If Arthur had died in Haiti, then the root of the situation was to be found there. As you may know, the religion of Haiti is voodooism. There is no central authority, no Pope or Archbishop, which I imagine stems from the fact that the Negroes who were transported there as slaves came from many different tribal cultures. Their priests are called *houngans*, and some of them are good and virtuous, while others, known as *bokors*, follow what some call 'The Left Hand Path'."

"That of evil."

"Precisely. The *houngans* disinter dead bodies and reanimate them by the use of magical rituals. In this state of half-life, they can perform simple duties for long hours, needing no food or sleep. Being turned into a zombie is a form of punishment. Instead of being borne to the realm of the *loa*, the gods, the perpetrator of a crime – rape, say, or murder – is resurrected from the grave to a living death and condemned to carry out the most menial or irksome tasks until the *houngan* who has created the zombie, or his successor, deems that the zombie has expiated his or her crime."

His use of language suggested that he was quoting verbatim from a book, or books, on the subject.

"My opinion is that the large landowners on Haiti form a small group of *bokors*, or have some working on their behalf, who turn the innocent dead into zombies to use as workers in their fields. You can't get cheaper labour than that – they don't need food, they don't get sick or ask for improved pay and conditions. That would also explain why the landowners rejected our offer."

"You mentioned earlier that you had seen your friend more than once since his death," said Holmes,

"Yes. The second occasion was in the garden of my house in St. John's Wood, the night before last. I was awakened by the garden gate banging at about one in the morning and went down to close it. Arthur stepped out of the shadow of the trees into the moonlight. I wasn't quite as scared this time, because, as I said, now I had an explanation of sorts."

"Did you try to speak to him?"

"I called him by name, and his expression lightened a little, but zombies only fully respond to the one who has been given power over them."

"And you alone heard the garden gate making a noise?"

"My bedroom is on that side of the house. The servants" rooms are all on the other side."

"Did you try to restrain him?"

"Certainly not! Zombies are possessed of preternatural strength. He would have torn me to pieces. No, I let him go, by the garden gate."

"You didn't attempt to follow him?"

"Follow a zombie and their master becomes aware of you? You don't want that to happen."

"Even though they are on the other side of the Atlantic Ocean?" I asked. I confess that I was beginning to find Mr. Bridges' apparent gullibility somewhat irksome.

"It seemed quite possible to me that it might be the work of someone in this country, who had made a deeper study of voodoo. Or, of course, a native *bokor* could have come here by ship."

"Just a few more questions, Mr. Bridges," continued Holmes. "First, do you know where Mr. Atwell is – or rather *was* – buried?"

"In the churchyard of St. Botolph's, near the house in Surrey."

"Which now belongs to his son and daughter?"

"Yes."

"When?"

"The first available day after his body arrived. I was at the funeral. A Saturday, it must have been."

"The Saturday before the Wednesday you first saw him?"

"Yes."

"Did you see Atwell's body before it was interred?"

"No, the coffin was closed. Apparently the facial distortion caused by the pain of the sudden heart attack was beyond the ability of the undertakers to alter, because *rigor mortis* had set in during the transportation of the corpse."

"And his grave is now empty, if your suspicions are correct."

"An exhumation order would prove that one way or another," I said, "but I doubt the authorities would credit the reasons for requesting one. Why do you suppose he has appeared to you, and not his children?"

"We were great friends, don't forget."

"But what do you think he, or whoever may be controlling him, wants of you?" asked Holmes.

"I couldn't say."

"Did you and Mr. Atwood have any enemies?"

"Business rivals, certainly, but none of them knew about Arthur's trip to Haiti. Even if they had, I can't imagine any of them being behind this."

"No others?"

"None that I am aware of."

"Have you visited Mr. Atwood's children since that Wednesday?

"Yes. They invited me again the following Wednesday. All the papers transferring their father's interest in the business to them have been signed and dealt with, but since Arthur's death I think I may have become something of a substitute father for them."

"Did you drive the carriage again?"

"No, this time I asked my coachman to drive me there. He was a little put out, as Wednesday is also his lady friend's night off, but he agreed when I promised him the whole weekend free. He drove me to dinner, and I left at eleven again."

"Now, lastly," said Holmes, "what do you require of us? That we wait with you for a further visitation and witness that your tale is true? Or that we track down whoever is behind this?"

"Oh, no, Mr. Holmes. I want you to help me kill him – or rather, destroy him, since he's already dead. Put him out of his misery. As an old friend, it's the least I can do."

"I see. We shall give you whatever assistance you need, but first I shall give you some instructions you must follow to the letter. Do you have any other residence besides your house in St. John's Wood?"

"Yes, I have a cottage just outside Studley in Warwickshire."

"Excellent. I take it you can leave your business to run itself for a few days?"

"I have a very reliable man who is often left in charge."

"Then here is what you must do: Go home and pack a suitcase, then go to your office and inform them that you will be at your cottage from the eighth onwards – "

"But today is the fourth."

" – and then return here and give me the keys to the property in St. John's Wood, not forgetting to provide us with the address. Then take the first available train to Studley. Tell no one else of your departure. Stay there until we arrive on the seventh."

"But what is your plan, sir?"

"Mr. Bridges, if I am to bring this matter to a satisfactory conclusion, then you must trust me and allow me to keep my own counsel. Mrs. Hudson will show you out."

Reaching across to the bell-pull, he rang to summon that estimable lady.

"Thank you, Watson, If not for your timely arrival, I might have missed out on what looks to be a most interesting case. Mr. Bridges clearly found you a more sympathetic listener, as he told his story at greater length and in more detail than when I was his sole audience. By the way, I trust your quest for a new razor was successful."

"Yes, I went to Hayworth's in the Bayswater Road. But how – ?"

My hand flew up to my face.

"Relax, my friend. Your shave is but an hour or two overdue, and only the trained eye of one who knows of your habits would notice the very slight stubble on your cheeks and chin. Your reputation for scrupulous neatness remains intact. Now, what do you make of Bridges' story?"

"I find it very surprising that an apparently sane man could credit such nonsense for a single moment."

"Well, Watson, a rich vein of supernaturalism runs beneath the surface of our scientific, mechanized society, and as belief in the established religion wanes, folk become susceptible to more *outré* modes of thought. You and I are agreed that these visitations cannot be due to necromancy. How then, may we explain them?"

I thought for a few seconds.

"There is a certain amount of evidence that persons of a hypersensitive nature may be prone to hallucinations, particularly where the individual is suffering from a strong negative emotion, such as guilt."

"There were certainly a few indications that there is more to Mr. Bridges than his stolid exterior would suggest. Anything else?"

"Both these events took place at night. Perhaps whoever is behind this found someone who resembled Atwell enough to pass for him in a bad light. Or even," I continued, warming to the theme, "someone took a cast of his face after death and used it to construct a mask of rubber that would serve a similar purpose. Bridges did say that Atwell's face had an unnatural pallor."

Holmes looked down with a fixed, introspective look in his grey eyes.

"No," he said after a few seconds, "no. There is something else at work here, something deeper."

He looked up at me once more.

"Are you aware, Watson, that some have explained the Greek legend of the Centaurs by saying that they were simply men on horseback, as seen through the eyes of those who had never encountered such riders before?"

"I'm sorry, Holmes, I don't see your point."

"If zombies exist – "

"Oh, come now, Holmes!"

346

" – then there must be a rational, scientific explanation for their existence."

"If there is one, I have no doubt that you of all men can find it out. But what is our first move? I take it you were not serious when you agreed to help him destroy whoever or whatever it was he saw."

"I would if there were an absolute necessity for such action, but I think it highly unlikely that there will be. You realize, of course, that I sent him off to his cottage in Warwickshire principally to get him out of the way?"

"I imagined that was the reason."

"The presence of one who is convinced of the supernatural nature of these visits, to say nothing of his murderous intent, would hamper our investigation. Here is what we shall do: After Bridges has returned with the key and departed for the station, we will go to his house and take up temporary residence there until the seventh. If we see no zombies, we shall take the train to Studley and stay with our client until we see one there, though I have greater hopes of St. John's Wood."

"And during the days?"

"I will spend the first at the Reading Room at the British Museum, consulting Eckermann and whatever else I can find of relevance. And have no fear. When the hour of action does arrive, your presence will be crucial, or I should not have asked you to come."

Michael Bridges returned a couple of hours later with the key to 83 Perceval Gardens, St. John's Wood.

"I will give you a note to take to my servants," said Bridges when Holmes informed him of our plans regarding his house.

"Servants, indeed," I remarked as I gazed out of one of the windows at our client climbing into his carriage on the street below us.

"You heard him say so earlier. It is hardly remarkable that a rich man would have them."

"True. Has he any inkling of the reason we are sending him out of London, do you think?"

"As long as he obeys my instructions, it is immaterial to me whether he has or not. Now, Watson, have you packed enough for our short stay?"

"Of course."

"And I have already informed Mrs. Hudson of our impending absence, so we can be off without delay, and you can christen your new razor in the bathroom of 83 Perceval Gardens."

Bridge's house was a fully-detached villa-style building of the late eighteenth century with a large L-shaped garden that ran along its left side and back. Between the wall separating the garden from the next-door neighbour and the front of the house ran a set of iron railings with a wrought-iron gate at the centre. Rather than using the key Bridges had given him, Holmes rapped on the door with its brass knocker.

The door was opened by a tall, dark-haired young woman in a maid's outfit.

"Good afternoon," said Holmes.

"Good afternoon, sirs. I am afraid Mr. Bridges is not in."

"He gave us this," said Holmes, proffering the note.

It read:

> *This is to inform you that Mr. Sherlock Holmes and his colleague, Dr. Watson, will be staying at the house for the next few days in my absence. You will obey their orders as you would mine and serve them in the same manner.*
>
> *M.A. Bridges*
> *4th November, 1894*

"Sherlock Holmes!" said the young woman in a tone of awe.

"You have heard of me, then. Perhaps you would bring the rest of the staff here so that we can meet them all."

The household consisted of a butler, a cook, two more maids, and a boot-boy.

The butler, Wheatcroft, had a slight whiff of brown ale about him and his collar was slightly askew, as if it had been buttoned in haste. While the cats away, the mice will play, as the old adage has it. The cook, a dumpy, maternal woman with a Scots accent, was called Mrs. Guthrie. The maid who had opened the door to us was Mortimer, while the other two, both shorter and pale-skinned, answered to Mullins and Ratcliff. Jackson, the boot-boy, was a scrawny, somewhat-underdeveloped youth of sixteen, who looked two or three years younger. There was also the carriage driver, but Bridges has given him the week off.

"Before you go back to your duties," said Holmes, "I have a request to make of you: From tomorrow onward, if anyone calls at the house during the day, whether you know them or not, you are to tell them that your master is from home, but will be back in the evening. Is that clear? Good. You can go now."

"Dinner will be at half-past-seven, sir,"

"Thank you, Mrs. Guthrie."

I came down to dinner after a short rest, freshly shaven, to find Holmes waiting for me. As we ate the excellent three-course meal served us by Mullins and Ratcliff, Holmes informed me of the part I was to play. I had been given the role of Bridges because my moustache made it possible for me to be briefly mistaken for him, and also because my medical experience made me slightly more qualified for the task I must perform.

When we had finished, we repaired to the smoking room and chatted leisurely about other matters unconnected to the business in hand, smoking panatelas and drinking from a decanter of brandy brought to us by Wheatcroft.

Both of the guest bedrooms were on the same side of the house as Bridges' room, so if our visitor announced his presence by banging the gate, at least one of us would be sure to hear it. He did not call on that first night, nor on the second. Both of us were prepared for our separate tasks, but he didn't arrive until one in the morning on the seventh.

When Holmes returned from his researches at about three o'clock on the afternoon of our first full day, I scarcely gave him time to remove his topcoat before I began quizzing him on the subject. I had had a pleasant enough day leafing through the books in Bridges' library, to say nothing of consuming a splendid lunch, but I was most eager to know what he had learned.

Holmes gave me an indulgent smile.

"Background and colour for your coming account of the case, eh?"

"Well, I've given it a little thought, yes."

"Let us at least discuss it in comfort."

I followed him into the spacious living room, where we each sat down in one of the large, mahogany-brown padded-leather armchairs.

"Well, to begin with, voodoo is not just the religion of the common people, but permeates the professional classes there to such a degree that virtually every lawyer, doctor, and landowner is a *houngan*. One might even say that, despite those democratic reforms Bridges mentioned, they are the country's true rulers.

"As to zombies, they are never seen outside their work area, or at night. Unfortunately, discussion of the whole subject is prone to sensationalism, and it is entirely possible that Bridges consulted some unreliable texts. Even those writers I read who seem to believe that zombies are indeed resurrected corpses said nothing about their masters being able to divine where they are when out of sight, nor do they simply appear and disappear like ghosts."

For my part, the event which took place in the morning of the seventh of November, though brief, is indelibly imprinted on my memory. I had stood beside Holmes on more than one occasion when we appeared to be

349

in the presence of the supernatural, and although he had always proved that there was a rational explanation for the phenomenon, nevertheless, each time I had experienced a chilling moment of atavistic fear, during which, for all my scientific and medical training, it seemed to me that such things might somehow, after all, exist.

We heard the banging of the garden gate – in fact, it was opened and closed with a clatter more than once, doubtless to ensure that Bridges would be awakened by noise. In accordance with our plan, Holmes and I sprang into action. We both hurried down the stairs, and I went into the garden by the back door while Holmes went into the street by the main door. The air was filled with the chill of the late autumn as I took up my position.

A figure moved toward me, its pale, hollowed face ghastly in the circle of light cast by a nearby street lamp, its eyes full of a desperate and terrible sadness. I took a hypodermic syringe from my pocket, but as I raised it to plunge the needle in, the figure caught my arm and held it with an unanticipated burst of strength, such strength as a madman might possess. I flung the whole weight of my body against him, bringing us both to the damp earth. For a moment my hand was free, and I stuck the needle in his neck and depressed the plunger, flooding his system with 300-milligrams of chloral hydrate. For a second or two I feared it had had no effect, but then Atwell fell back in a stupour, his eyes closed and his face somewhat relaxed.

As I pulled myself to my feet, I heard cries and the sounds of a struggle coming from the street.

A minute or so later Holmes appeared, his revolver was in his hand. It was trained upon a tubby, bespectacled young man with his hands cuffed in front of him. He had a hard, spoiled face, and his eyes were filled with malice and frustration, and perhaps fear at what must now lie ahead of him.

"Watson, allow me to introduce Mr. Edgar Atwell, the perpetrator of this little plan."

He reached into the pockets of the man's coat and produced a vial of a colourless liquid.

"Ah, my surmise was correct. You carry an extra supply, in case the last dose proved insufficient. Watson, let us get this fellow inside and restrain him more fully. Then we can bear his unfortunate father inside and lay him on one of the beds."

His arm in Holmes's iron grip, the young man didn't struggle. Once inside, we tied him to a kitchen chair with a length of washing line, and he spoke for the first time, in an unpleasant rasping tone.

"I hope you realize that this is illegal restraint."

350

"Preventing a criminal's escape isn't illegal. Whereas your treatment of your father is a form of assault, and I don't doubt that a charge of attempted embezzlement can also be laid at your door, at the very least."

We brought the older Atwell inside and laid him on the bed of the room I had been occupying. We then woke Wheatcroft, telling him to summon an ambulance and the police.

While we waited, I said, "What was that liquid you took from young Atwell's pocket?"

"Oh, that? Nothing less than the key to this whole business, and a lot more besides. I'm not yet sure of its chemical composition, but you have seen for yourself what its effects are. Once Atwell Senior has been taken to hospital and his son to the police cells, we must return to Baker Street and analyse it." He took a small bottle from his own pocket and poured half the contents of the vial into it. Seeing my questioning glance, he said, "We must give the police a chance to come to their own conclusions."

We returned to Baker Street the following morning, and while our stay in St. John's Wood had undeniably had its pleasant aspects, I was happy to be back in our humble lodgings, and I was sure that Holmes, who was never completely content when away from his files and reference books, felt the same.

"You played your role to perfection, Watson, said Holmes as we took our accustomed armchairs in our sitting room," and it is only fair that I give you a complete explanation of the case as I understand it."

"May I take notes?"

"Of course."

I went to my desk and pulled a notebook and pencil from a drawer. When I was seated once more, Holmes began.

"Now, as you know, when one is in search of a motive for a crime, a good starting point is the question, "'*Cui bono?*', and it seemed to me that the only possible beneficiaries of this situation were Edgar and Amelia Atwell. By getting rid of both their father and Michael Bridges, full ownership of the firm would come into their hands. Their plan had the advantage that all the possible outcomes would serve their ends. If Bridges shared his belief, he might be considered insane – indeed, with sufficient persecution, he might actually *become* insane. In those circumstances, all that remained was to dispose of the father, who was already thought dead. If Bridges killed his partner in the belief that he was saving his soul, again, it wouldn't matter that the victim was already supposed to be dead, there would be a *corpus delicti*, and Edgar on hand as a witness. In fact, they might even claim that the entire hoax had been engineered by Bridges, rather than by them."

"Diabolical!"

"Indeed. My suspicions were supported by several facts. The first visitation took place near the house in Surrey, and Bridges was alone in the quiet street when he saw Atwell. In all probability, he had told the pair in passing that he had driven himself that night, but the following Wednesday, he was with his coachman, and he didn't see the older Atwell. Either he had told the son and daughter of the coachman's presence, or they had made a point of asking him about it. In St. John's Wood, much closer to the centre of the metropolis, Edgar waited until one in the morning for the street to be clear before bringing his father into the garden.

"Then there was the burial. As Atwell Senior hadn't died, of a heart attack or anything else, I think it likely that he was secreted somewhere in the house, and the coffin was full of stones, or perhaps even a genuine corpse they had somehow obtained. Let us not forget that even before this plan went into action, they received a considerable allowance from their father, enough to indulge in some selective bribery."

"And still that wasn't enough for them. They wanted it all."

"Quite. Now, as I told you before, the professional classes in Haiti are almost exclusively comprised of *houngans*. The Atwells might have obtained a falsified death certificate, and a supply of that liquid you saw me take from Edgar's pocket, from a corrupt medical man. I believe that they crossed the Atlantic before they claimed to have, once they learned their father was *en route*. That is, something that can be confirmed or disproved by the shipping lines" records of passengers to New York. Whether they formulated their plan in London, or during the crossing, or created it with the aid of a *houngan*, or perhaps more correctly a *bokor*, remains to be seen."

"You have yet to tell me exactly what that liquid was."

"Have you heard of the puffer fish?"

"It is poisonous, is it not?"

"Well, parts of it are edible. Those are known to the Japanese as *fugu*, and can only be prepared by specially trained chefs who know exactly which parts of the fish to cook. The rest contain a deadly neurotoxin called *tetrodotoxin*. If you eat the liver, for example, or the skin, you will die very quickly, and in great pain. Well, the *genus* the pufferfish belong to, the *tetraodontidae*, are found all over the world, including the Caribbean, and many of them have the same toxic properties as the pufferfish. What about *datura*? Do you know what that is?"

"No, I am afraid you have me there."

"It's also known as Devil's Trumpet – Jimson Weed, Hell's Bells, Thorn Apple, and a few other colourful names. Whatever name you give it, it's a plant which also contains deadly toxins. In smaller doses, it can cause hallucinations and temporary paralysis. The liquid in that vial contained both tetrodotoxin and tropane alkaloids, the active ingredient of *datura*, in significant amounts. It is my belief, though I will need to consult a neurologist to be completely sure, that in the right combination they would produce the classic zombie state, which Atwell manifested. Suspension of the higher brain functions with the autonomic system unaffected. To maintain this state, one would need to dose the subject on a regular basis, and if this dosage is stopped, he or she should eventually revert to normal."

"So Arthur Atwell will recover?"

"That is to be hoped for, but I don't envy him on the day he finds out what his own children did to him and Bridges. '*How sharper than a serpent's tooth it is, to have a thankless child!*' as Shakespeare says in *King Lear*. Now, before I forget, we must send a telegram to Studley and summon Mr. Bridges back to London.

Contrary to Holmes's hopes, Arthur Atwell never fully recovered. His mental faculties permanently impaired, he was placed in a private nursing home. Michael Bridges was ready to pay for his care, but the costs were instead met by an anonymous donor, with the condition that Bridges never visit his old friend.

Neither of the Atwell siblings was ever brought to trial. When the police arrived at the house in Surrey to question Amelia, she was nowhere to be found. Her brother's failure to return must have warned her that the game was up, and she fled to save her own skin. As to Edgar, we heard no more of him once we had handed him over into police custody.

These codas to our investigations would have struck both Holmes and I as odd, had it not been for an event which took place a few days after the case was concluded, and from which much might be inferred.

We had just finished our lunch when we heard a heavy footfall on the stair, and the door opened to reveal the bulky figure of the saturnine Mycroft Holmes on the threshold.

"Mycroft! How pleasant to see you! Please take a seat. Would you care for a whisky?"

The older Holmes brother remained where he was.

"This isn't a social call, Sherlock, and while the matter affects you, it is chiefly to Dr. Watson that I wish to speak."

"Me?"

"Yes, sir, you. I am aware that you and my brother have recently concluded what you would no doubt term an 'adventure' concerning a certain substance that has a particular effect upon the human nervous system. No doubt you plan to publish an account of the business."

"Well, I was – "

"No such account must ever be written. Or, if written, it must never be published. Should you ever do so, I promise you that there will be consequences of a most serious nature."

The younger Holmes got to his feet.

"I will endure much from you, Mycroft, but when it comes to threatening Watson, that is something I will not tolerate."

Mycroft's expression softened a little.

"Your loyalty to your friend does you credit, Sherlock. But I must ask you both to seriously consider the results of making the existence of this drug known. As long as these 'walking dead', as one might call them, are considered fables, and confined to a small and inconsequential island, they represent no danger. Imagine, however, what might happen if the story is credited in the palaces and chancellories of the great foreign powers. Surely you can see that they would do everything they can to manufacture or obtain supplies of the mixture. I trust you wouldn't wish to see it fall into the hands of the Kaiser, or of the Sultan of Turkey."

"Very well," I said. "I accept your reasoning, and I will not send the story to be published."

"You have made a wise decision, sir."

"Goodbye, Brother. It was, as ever, a pleasure to see you."

"Sarcasm ill becomes you, Sherlock. Good day, gentlemen."

A Generous Helping
of Deceit
by DJ Tyrer

Sherlock Holmes looked up from the letter he was reading as the door opened and Mrs. Hudson directed Inspector Lestrade into the room.

My friend indicated for the police detective to be seated.

"You've come about the Thewlis case," said Holmes, with an almost-pained air.

All London, or so it seemed, was preoccupied with the mystery of the robbery and death of the wealthy banker, Harrison Thewlis.

"Yes. You will know the generalities of the case, for the newspapers have made much work of them."

The respected banker, Harrison Thewlis, had gone into town with one-hundred pounds in his pocket to settle a debt,. For reasons unaccounted, he never arrived at his destination, but, according to the testimony of his wife, he instead apparently took a train out of London. Late that same afternoon, passengers aboard a train bound for Waterloo heard a crash and a man cry out in pain, and discovered the banker in the next compartment, dead from a blow to his head. The money and his gold pocket watch were missing.

Other than the details of those who had found him, Lestrade had little more to add.

"It's a complete mystery, Mr. Holmes. We have no idea who killed him. I was hoping you would help."

Naturally, the brutal murder of an influential man and the theft of such a sum had the city in an uproar, and there was pressure on Scotland Yard to produce the culprit for punishment.

Holmes shook his head. "My dear Lestrade," said he, as if explaining matters to a particularly dull-witted child, "there is nothing about the case to suggest any great mystery. It was, without doubt, the work of an opportunist thief. That you have failed to make any progress is due to that very lack of any deeper meaning."

"I don't follow," said Lestrade, rubbing his chin as he sought to unpick my friend's words.

"Simply put, there is no significant clue that you have overlooked, because there is nothing of significance about the death. It was robbery – most likely robbery gone wrong when Thewlis sought to defend his property. Had there been some plot, a plan of assassination, I am certain there would be hints of it – a more effective means of killing, for a start."

I couldn't help but exclaim that the means seemed most effective in this case.

Holmes conceded the point, but said, "A blow to the head is less reliable than a knife or bullet to the heart. An assassin would surely have wanted to make certain his attack was a killing one. The contusion that the inspector has described was, in my opinion, not intended to kill."

"But," interjected Lestrade "what was he doing aboard that train, eh? Answer me that."

Holmes gave him a narrow smile. "You know as well as I that there are many reasons why a man might take a train into the suburbs when his wife believes him to be about his business. Few of them are likely to be ones that the widow would care to be informed of."

Lestrade blinked at him, defeated, then sputtered, "Surely you aren't saying the case is unsolvable!"

It did seem quite unlike the Holmes we knew.

"Oh, quite the opposite, Inspector. I am saying it will doubtless be resolved without any effort from myself. The evidence suggests is that this was nothing more than an opportunistic theft. Probably the robber saw the man's watch and took a fancy to it. It's unlikely he was aware that he carried a small fortune upon his person, and it's unlikely that such a thief, surprised at his good luck, will be able to conceal his delight for long.

"Soon, he will tell another and word will spread, or his overly-generous spending will betray him. Then, Lestrade, you shall have him. Mark my words."

"I suppose you're right in that," he conceded – not entirely satisfied, if his tone was anything to go by.

The inspector left, as if defeated, and Holmes returned to his letter, his insouciance upon the matter leaving me somewhat baffled. Even if the crime were, as he declared, entirely run-of-the-mill in nature, it seemed to me that running down the blackguard ought still to have caught his attention. Clearly, whatever news the letter contained interested him more. I enquired as to its contents.

"The letter is from a Mr. Roger Strand and concerns his uncle, Marcus Strand, an optician domiciled in Surbiton."

"In what way?" I asked.

"It appears that his parents have made some outrageous claims against his uncle which have been aired in a local newspaper and are the subject of a planned lawsuit against him. He wishes that these claims be proved baseless and his uncle's reputation restored."

"It seems strange that a son would side against his parents," I observed.

"In this case, the son blames himself for his parents launching this attack against his uncle. Apparently, he had sought out his uncle's assistance in a dispute over his plan to marry in opposition to his parents' wishes. His uncle did indeed take his part, and he believes the lawsuit is their retaliation."

"Well, it's understandable why he would desire your assistance in this, but what is your interest? A petty family squabble hardly seems the sort of thing that would ensnare your attention."

"Did I not mention the accusations were outrageous? And the events that preceded them just as much. I am intrigued, Watson, intrigued."

I have described before how my friend would often ignore cases that offered wealth or fame in order to pursue those presented by humble clients which happened to more invigorate his sense of curiosity. It seemed that the mystery contained in this letter was one of these.

"Very well, but what happened?"

Holmes smiled. "Don your hat and coat, for we have a journey to make. I'll explain more on the train."

I followed my friend downstairs, bidding *adieu* to Mrs. Hudson as we passed, and so out into the street where he waved down a cab. A short time later, we were aboard the train travelling towards the town of Surbiton.

Holmes went on to explain that, according to the nephew and corroborated in the newspaper clipping that had accompanied the letter, the optician had a patient, his brother, and his brother's wife arrested for a burglary that had never happened.

"You mean to say that evidence of a burglary was fabricated against them?" I queried.

"No, Watson, I mean exactly what I say: There was no burglary."

"Well, I've heard of someone being arrested for a crime they didn't commit, but never for a crime that didn't happen."

"Oh, it does happen. Misinterpretation of a scene or misapprehension of the law. But in this situation, neither was the case."

"I don't understand."

"Neither, I must admit, do I. Not fully. Which is why I'm intrigued."

It was my turn to smile. I could understand what had caught his attention and had to admit my own curiosity was piqued.

"Still, we shall have all the details we require shortly, for I've arranged to meet young Roger Strand at Surbiton Police Station. Then, we shall learn the full background."

Roger Strand was a tall fellow, thin and possessed of a nervous energy that caused him to twitch awkwardly and constantly flex his fingers as he awaited us. His suit was neat, but had surely seen better days. The impression I took of him was of a lowly but respectable clerk.

"Mr. Holmes?" he asked in a somewhat-squeaky voice as we approached, wiping his hand on his jacket before thrusting it forth in greeting.

"Yes," said Holmes, taking and pumping the proffered hand. "And this is my colleague, Dr. Watson."

"I'm so glad you could come. My uncle is a most kind and generous man. He doesn't deserve such calumny to be heaped upon him."

"Quite so," said Holmes, diplomatically, before leading us inside and making our introduction to the desk sergeant, who hurried off to fetch the detective handling the case.

Detective Inspector Lanthorn was a bluff older man who was clearly pleased at the prospect of another relieving him of what was, in his words, "a most-perplexing case".

He introduced our *dramatis personae* with a brief description of each. Marcus Strand was a local notable, one of those opticians who insisted upon expanding the scope of their occupation beyond the provision of spectacles to the diagnosis and treatment of eye disorders, as if they were on a par with doctors. As far as Lanthorn was concerned, he was unimpeachable.

Mr. Edwin Davies, the patient, was a local butcher, and also considered quite respectable. Mr. and Mrs. Strand, the parents of Roger Strand, were from Chelmsford in Essex and unknown to the detective, who could only state that the optician's brother was a banker, apparently considered a steady man in his locality, and whose wife was, as Lanthorn put it with an apology to her son, "a disagreeable woman".

I noted that Roger Strand did not dispute the point.

Inspector Lanthorn then proceeded to explain what was known, saying, "I must admit it took quite some unravelling to understand, and I'm still uncertain what really happened, but, in short, what transpired was this . . . .

"Mr. and Mrs. Strand arrived to speak to the optician concerning a family matter – " Lanthorn glanced at our companion. " – and met with a man on the doorstep that they took to be him – having been long estranged from him – but who instead said he was a patient and told them that the optician was inside the house with the new maid he had just hired. He further claimed that the maid was shortly due to be married to the optician's nephew – that is, their son, Mr. Roger Strand.

"Enraged at this apparent interference in their parental authority, the couple rushed inside to confront Mr. Strand, and began to abuse the pair they found within. These, however, proved to be another patient, Mr. Davies, and the optician's long-term maid who had never met young Mr. Strand here."

"Such confusion," I acknowledged, and Lanthorn nodded.

"As this was occurring," he continued, "Mr. Strand – the optician – arrived home, having been absent, and met a man he described as 'unwell-looking' at his gate. It is presumed that this is the first man that his brother and his wife had met at the door, although they didn't describe him as looking unwell. Taking this man for his patient, Mr. Davies, who had been due to arrive about then, he spoke to him, concerned for his health.

"The man brushed aside his concern and claimed that the maid had just caught a trio breaking into the house and stealing the silver, and that he was on his way to fetch a policeman. An officer being visible a short distance away, Strand hurried over to gain his attention, and in that moment, the man he had just spoken to disappeared.

"With the accusation made, the officer went inside and, after a brief struggle in which Mrs. Strand put in the most effort at fighting him off, arrested the trio on suspicion of burglary. He escorted them here for questioning, with Strand and his maid in tow to give their accounts."

Lanthorn paused and produced a handkerchief with which he mopped his brow, as if telling the story were a physical exertion.

"Their contradictory accounts then emerged and, eventually, it was realised that the couple were the optician's family and the other man, Mr. Davies, his actual patient. It was confirmed that there had been no break-in and nothing had been stolen, and, so the three of them were released and apologies made.

"It can hardly be called unexpected," he added with a weary roll of his eyes, "that threats of lawsuits were then made."

Holmes considered what had been explained, and then asked, "And as for this other man, the one who made the accusation of a burglary, or indeed two men, if he and the other met by the couple should prove not to be the same person, no trace has been found?"

The detective shook his head. "No. Although it seems everyone met him, and it also seems nobody paid him much regard and their descriptions are vague to the point of uselessness: Just an older, bewhiskered man, quite ordinary. And, as he was repeatedly misidentified, we have no hint as to his name or identity. He's a dead end, I'm afraid, Mr. Holmes."

My friend chuckled. "One I shall endeavour to resurrect. Thank you, Inspector. You have been very helpful." He turned to Roger Strand. "Come, let us away to your uncle's house and speak to him and his maid."

Holmes strode through the quiet streets of Surbiton like a bloodhound on the scent, and those locals we passed turned their heads to look at him in consternation at his out-of-place vigour.

Reaching the house of the optician, he stepped up to the door ahead of us and pulled on the bell.

After a brief wait, the jangle was answered by a young woman in a maid's uniform.

"Miss Eliza Barnum?" asked Holmes, quoting the name that Lanthorn had provided.

She shook her head. "No, sir. Miss Barnum is no longer employed here. The master let her go and took me on in her place."

Holmes gave a snort of annoyance, then asked if he could see the optician.

"I'm sorry, sir, but no. Mr. Strand is seeing nobody. Right fed up with all the nosy callers he's had."

"I'm his nephew," said Roger, stepping forward and speaking imperiously. "Surely, he'll see me."

"He won't see family, no. Especially not family . . . ."

"Well," said Holmes in an ameliorating tone, "that is disappointing. Is it possible that Miss Barnum left a forwarding address?"

The maid responded to his smile simperingly, telling him to wait just one moment, and returning with her predecessor's address.

Holmes thanked her and we went on our way.

A short time later, we were seated in the rented room of Miss Eliza Barnum, enjoying a cup of tea.

The young woman hadn't been entirely disposed to speak with us, almost shutting the door in our faces, but a crown had convinced her to allow us across her threshold and to answer my friend's questions.

Although she clearly recognised Roger Strand by face, it was only once we were seated and Holmes had introduced us that she knew his name or his connection to her employer. Indeed, as the questioning proceeded, it became more and more clear that she knew very little about what had happened and understood less, an all the more distressing predicament given that her former employer had chosen to blame her for the entire embarrassing situation, leaving her without employ.

"It really is most unfair of him," she wailed into her kerchief.

Young Strand sniffed at this and opined that this seemed most unlike his uncle, whom he considered a fair and generous man.

Eliza Barnum laughed bitterly at his words. "Oh, it is very much his nature, sir, I assure you! The pompous old bully!"

This set the two to arguing, each continuing to aver that their impression of the optician was the correct one, until Holmes finally managed to shush them, as if they were a pair of squabbling children.

"I find their difference in interpretation of the man's nature most intriguing," Holmes said in an aside to me, before turning to the task of calming and placating the young woman so that he might continue his interrogation. In the end, it was his assurance that the resolution of the mystery would likely assist her by pouring oil upon the troubled waters between her and her former employer that, currently, prevented her from receiving a favourable reference that did the trick.

Nodding and drying her eyes, she agreed to answer his questions.

The morning had begun quite normally, she told us, with her employer having gone out early upon some personal business and the cook having taken her day off, leaving Miss Barnum to undertake some housework before the optician's first patient of the day, Mr. Edwin Davies, arrived for his midday appointment to have his eyes examined.

"Then," she continued, "the doorbell rang, and I answered it to find a gentleman there, asking for Mr. Strand. I assumed it to be Mr. Davies and told him that the master was out for the morning, but that he was welcome to come inside and wait in the lounge for his return. He did so, and I made him a pot of tea. Of course, as I learned later, he wasn't."

"Wasn't?" I asked.

"Wasn't Mr. Davies."

Holmes steepled his fingers and leant towards her. "And this man – did he actually say he was Davies?"

She considered for a moment, then shook her head. "I don't believe he did, no."

"So," Holmes said to Young Strand and me, "it was unlikely this was a deliberate impersonation, but rather a happy accident for the conman." He turned back to Miss Barnum. "Could you describe this man you mistook for Mr. Davies?"

"Only that he was an older gentleman, very respectable looking, with heavy whiskers and ruddy cheeks. Quite ordinary, really. Had he seemed a rogue, I would never have left him alone in the house."

"He was alone?"

She nodded. "Yes. Just before he rang the bell, I had discovered I was running low on laundry soap. Expecting Mr. Davies, I was unable to leave for the shop, but believing him to be present, I left him and went upon my errand."

"Quite understandable," Holmes reassured her and she continued.

"When I returned, I passed him – " She gestured toward Young Strand. " – leaving the house as I went in. I was perplexed as to who he was, but he hurried off before I could collect my wits and ask him. He appeared quite delighted."

Holmes glanced at Strand, who gave a nod of corroboration.

"My interview with my uncle had gone most favourably."

Holmes asked Miss Barnum to continue.

"Well, I went inside and saw the man I had taken to be Mr. Davies in the lounge. He asked me to make some more tea. When I returned, he was gone and a different man, whom I later learned was actually Mr. Davies, was sitting in the lounge in his place.

"I was quite perplexed, sir! I was attempting to find out who he was and where Mr. Davies, as I'd thought him, had gone, when a man and woman rushed into the room in great agitation and began to abuse us most vociferously."

"My parents," said Young Strand with a wince.

"Indeed," said Holmes. "They took Mr. Davies to be your master, I believe."

"Yes, it seemed so. It was difficult to be certain, as they were so upset I could hardly follow their words, and they wouldn't allow us to interrupt."

It was at that point that Mr. Strand and the policeman had entered and the couple and a bemused Mr. Davies had been arrested and taken to the police station. Miss Barnum had followed after them with her employer and was questioned there, but had no more to add. She began to sob again as she described how Mr. Strand had dismissed her.

I patted her gently on the shoulder and told her, "I'm sure we can straighten all this out, Miss."

Our next visit was to Mr. Davies. Unlike the optician or maid, he was happy to speak to us from the moment we introduced ourselves, expressing his hope that an opinion from the respected detective would surely benefit the lawsuit he was arranging against Mr. Strand. At his words, Young Strand's expression soured, but he held his tongue, and we entered the rear of the butcher's shop and settled down in a small parlour and began our questioning.

Davies' story was shorter and simpler than the maid's.

"I arrived a little early for my appointment with Mr. Strand and my ring was answered by the optician – or at least, the man who answered the door identified himself as such."

"You hadn't seen Mr. Strand before?" asked Holmes.

Davies shook his head. "No. At least, I think I was briefly introduced to him at a business luncheon, but only the briefest of nods and greetings. I had arranged my appointment with his maid."

Holmes asked for a description of the man. It was the same man who had been described to the inspector and by Miss Barnum to us.

"How did he seem to you?" Holmes asked.

The butcher looked at him, quizzically. "In what way?"

"Did he seem agitated or calm? Was he straight-backed or weary? Healthy in appearance, or did he seem sick to you?"

Davies considered. "Calm. Perfectly normal. Respectable. Maybe a little tired. I cannot recall."

I looked to Holmes. "There is that word again – respectable."

He nodded. "Yes. Our villain strikes the pose of a man of utmost probity, which is how he lulls his victims before playing his outrageous pranks upon them."

Looking back to Davies, Holmes asked him what occurred once he was inside.

"Well," said the butcher, "he led me through the lounge to his consulting room, where he seated me and set about examining my eyes."

"Did he appear to know what he was doing?" I asked.

Looking a trifle embarrassed, Davies said, "To one such as I, who has no idea about medical things, he seemed quite expert."

"Did he complete your examination?"

"No. The doorbell rang and he left to answer it. I remember him saying his maid was out on an errand. He was gone for some time, then returned and said something about his nephew. He then took me out into the lounge, apologising for the interruption and that we would resume shortly. A pot of tea was there, and I sat down to await his return.

"A minute later, the maid entered and asked who I was. She seemed confused when I said my name. Before we could speak further, a couple ran in and began ranting most outrageously at us. For some peculiar reason, they appeared to think that I was the optician."

"And then Mr. Strand arrived with the policeman?" said I.

"Indeed. I was arrested! It was most outrageous."

"I can quite imagine," said Holmes. "Still, I believe I shall have this entire affair explained soon. Now," he said, looking at Young Strand and me, "I think it's time for us to find a local hostelry and have something to eat."

Once we had fortified ourselves for the afternoon, Holmes said, "The story told by Mr. Davies is at odds with those told by the maid and her employer to Inspector Lanthorn, who claim that Strand was absent from prior to the arrival of the man she took to be the patient until the very end of the events. However, it does match with what you – " He nodded at Young Strand. " – have said about going to see your uncle that day."

363

"Most odd," I said. "It's as if two different days had occurred in tandem."

Holmes chuckled. "Certainly, from the point of view of those who experienced them, they did." He looked at Strand. "Perhaps you could give us your account of your visit in full?"

He nodded. "Very well. There isn't much to it. I had gone to see my uncle because I had fallen in love with a young lady who works in a factory, a job that my parents felt was demeaning and below me. They had threatened to disinherit me if I went ahead with the union. I had hoped that my uncle might be able to persuade my parents to accept my choice."

"From what we've been told," interrupted Holmes "your parents and uncle were estranged. They didn't recognise the imposter wasn't your uncle."

Strand nodded. "Yes, there had been a long estrangement between them, but he was the only family I have, and it was my hope that his support might yet sway them."

"Had you seen your uncle before?"

"No, but he was most welcoming and attentive when I arrived at his door. Such a kind and generous man. He invited me in and offered me tea – the maid was absent, but a pot was ready on the table with two cups." Strand chuckled. "I might almost have imagined I was expected. We sat and chatted for a while and I explained my predicament."

Strand smiled to himself. "He beamed with delight and declared that love was the most important thing in the world. Then, he proceeded to tell me the scandalous story behind why he and my father had fallen out as friends. To my shock, my mother was revealed to have been a chorus girl. He had fallen madly in love with her, only for his brother – my father – to woo her away from him." He shook his head. "Such hypocrisy!

"When he was done, he pronounced his blessing upon my nuptials and produced one-hundred pounds to allow me to marry, regardless of my parents' opposition." Strand chuckled. "He just plucked it from his pocket, like that! Can you imagine, a hundred pounds, as if it were small change? His business is clearly doing splendidly.

"As you can imagine, I was most delighted when I left. That was when I passed the maid, who was returning home."

He looked at Holmes. "As you can see, in spite of my circumstances, I have the money to pay for your assistance, sir."

"One-hundred pounds, to be exact," said my friend. Looking at me, he said, "Now, Watson, everything is become clear."

"Sorry, but you've lost me."

Holmes laughed. "All shall be explained. Come, we must return to London."

"London? Why?"

"I'll explain on our journey."

Having paused to cable Inspector Lestrade to meet us at Waterloo, we boarded the train and settled ourselves in a carriage with a man who was reading a newspaper.

"May I borrow this for a moment?" Holmes asked, glancing at the front page, startling the poor fellow from his reverie.

The man handed it over to him without murmur.

"Strand," said Holmes with a flourish, "I suspect you haven't kept abreast of the latest news, with thoughts of marriage and your uncle's reputation filling your mind."

"No, not really," said the bemused young man.

Holmes held the paper before him. "Take a look at the image of the man on the front page. Do you recognise him?"

"Why, yes. That is my uncle!" He groaned. "Don't say the scandal is front page news!"

Handing the newspaper back to its owner, Holmes said, "Quite the contrary. That photograph wasn't of your uncle."

"Sorry?"

I, too, looked at Holmes, bemused.

"Oh, Watson, I am disappointed. Surely, the hundred-pounds was the clue? No?"

He shook his head. "The photograph I just showed Young Strand, here, was that of the murdered banker that so befuddled Inspector Lestrade."

"Thewlis?"

"Indeed." He shook himself. "Oh, when he learns that I turned down his case, only to return full circle to it . . . Should you recount this investigation, Watson, I trust you shall portray it as my plan all along."

"I promise nothing," I said, with a chuckle. "But I don't really follow."

"Neither do I," said Strand. "Who is Thewlis, and what has he got to do with my uncle?"

"Harrison Thewlis was a banker who was believed to have been murdered on the same day as the peculiar events that overtook your uncle. He was also, we now know, the man whom you met under the impression he was your uncle. The man, indeed, who set in train the whole series of events that has left your uncle so embarrassed." He settled himself back in his chair. "I shall now proceed to recount what I believe was the true sequence of events on that day.

"Oh, and, Strand, I think you should banish any thoughts from your head of your mother having been a chorus girl. That was no more than an old man's idea of a joke.

"Harrison Thewlis," continued Holmes, "told his wife he was taking the hundred-pounds to settle a debt, but instead took a train from Waterloo to Surbiton, where he apparently strolled about for a while before arriving at the home and workplace of the optician, Marcus Strand.

"Now, at this point, all is conjecture. Did he truly intend to pay the debt and change his mind or, perhaps, intend to do so on his return journey, only to give the money away to his *faux* nephew here? Or was the talk of the debt merely a cover for his day trip? We shall never know. Nor, it seems, shall we be able to determine whether he arrived at Strand's home by chance or by deliberate choice. Should Inspectors Lanthorn and Lestrade wish to pursue it, I am certain we would learn that the late banker has played numerous tricks like this before."

"But why?" exclaimed Strand. "He was a wealthy and respected man."

Holmes gave a shrug. "Who can say for sure? As an escape from the pressures of his position? As an outlet for a sense of humour that was allowed little escape due to that very respect? Whatever his motivation, this was how he liked to entertain himself.

"For our purposes, the reasons why are unimportant. What I shall explain is the *what* – the course of events."

"Indeed, do go on," said Strand, shaking his head as if dazed.

"Thewlis rang the doorbell and, when the maid opened the door, he asked for the optician. Assuming him to be Mr. Davies, she let him in and asked him to await her master's return. Leaving him with a pot of tea, she left the house on an errand.

"A short time later, the real Mr. Davies arrived and Thewlis, pretending to be Strand, invited him inside and commenced to carry out an 'examination'.

"A further ring of the doorbell introduced you," said Holmes, nodding at Young Strand. "You mistook Thewlis for your uncle and he offered you the tea that the maid had left for him."

Strand was shaking his head, but couldn't deny my friend's words.

"You discussed your marriage plans and he spun you a fiction about your parents to encourage you before giving you the hundred pounds he carried. You left, delighted at your good fortune, passing the maid.

"Thewlis sent her for more tea and, while she was absent, brought Mr. Davies back to the lounge. The banker then left the house, leaving the butcher for the bemused maid to discover.

"On his way out, Thewlis encountered your parents," Holmes told Strand, "who mistook him for your uncle, just as you had, due to their long estrangement and, doubtless, a general similarity of appearance due to age, build, and whiskers. This time, however, he didn't maintain the impersonation, but indicated he was a patient, and that your uncle was in the lounge and about to take tea with the young lady, whom, Thewlis indicated, was engaged to you.

"Outraged at this perceived interference in their domestic affair, your parents rushed inside to confront them, abusing the confused patient and maid." Holmes clapped his hands together. "Uproar!"

"What of the optician's evidence?" I asked. "He said that the man he encountered, whom I presume you will tell us was Thewlis, appeared sickly, something nobody else has said."

"Indeed! And there we have the crux of Inspector Lestrade's case. Whom, I trust, will be awaiting our arrival." Holmes glanced out of the carriage window to confirm that we were nearing our destination.

"I believe that if you, Watson, were to speak to Thewlis's doctor, you would learn that he was far from in perfect health. A weak heart, perhaps. I would conjecture that the mental exertions of his prank, or perhaps a surfeit of mirth, caused him to suffer a bad turn as he was leaving the house. Indeed, it is possible that this was why he dropped his act as Strand, finding the mood of Young Strand's parents more than he felt able to make play of.

"Regardless, it was in this state that the optician found him. Playing one last prank, Thewlis invented the story of a burglary that brought the police into the situation and caused everyone such distress and embarrassment. Doubtless, he looked forward to reading some account of the results, not realising that it was he who would make the newspaper pages."

It was at that point that we drew into the station, where Inspector Lestrade was waiting for us. Holmes waved him aboard the carriage and gave a *précis* of the account he had explained to us.

"Which," Holmes said, upon reaching the conclusion of the banker's adventure, "brings us to the man's death. Thewlis, just as we did, boarded a train back to London. Alone in a carriage, I believe his health continued to worsen until, desperate for assistance, he did what anyone would do in the circumstance: Thewlis reached for the emergency cord. As he did so, he collapsed with a cry, striking his head and dying."

Turning to Lestrade, Holmes knelt and half-prostrated himself. "He was laying like this, wasn't he?"

The inspector nodded. "Yes."

"As I thought."

Holmes drew in a sharp breath across his teeth as he rose, as if annoyed at himself.

"The assumption of assault, based on the absence of the money, coloured the interpretation of the scene. A more thorough and unprejudiced examination would surely have shown that the spilt blood was from his head hitting the side of the carriage or seat, not a weapon's blow. But," he conceded, "the assumption was too easy to make and we ignored the other possibility."

"Although you may have answered the question of what happened to the missing money – " Lestrade glanced at Young Strand, adding, "I shall need a statement, but your account is the truth and you came by the money honestly, if abnormally. Tell me, Mr. Holmes, what happened to the man's pocket watch? You have given no account of that, and it remains missing. And, before you ask, it wasn't lost somewhere in the compartment, or in some nook, for my men searched it thoroughly."

Holmes conceded the point with a nod.

"However, Inspector, you didn't search the banker's would-be rescuers, did you? No? Of course not! Naturally, from the scenario, none of them could be murderer or thief because they had entered his compartment after the attack had occurred."

"Except," I added, "there was no attack."

"Precisely," said Holmes. "While all thoughts were upon a vanished thief, someone stole the watch for themselves – an impulsive act. Look at those who came to the banker's assistance and you shall find your petty thief – a good Samaritan gone bad."

Lestrade dispatched his men to question everyone who had been present in the compartment and, we later learned, a young man was found in possession of the watch and arrested for the theft.

I shook my head at the *denouement*, Holmes having been proved correct yet again.

"You make the complex and confusing web of events seem most simple," I told my friend.

He smiled. "When viewed in the correct order with all the pertinent facts in line, even the most extraordinary series of events are quite simple. It is only because we so often view them in disordered fragments that they appear as mysteries to us."

"Well, I am glad that everything appears to have been resolved to the good. Nobody is being sued now that it is known that their ills were the work of a dead man, and London can rest safely knowing a killer isn't on the loose. Lanthorn's case is closed and Lestrade is a hero, now that a thief has been apprehended and punished. Young Strand is marrying the woman he loves and starting his new life without trouble, and I believe he has offered to take on Miss Barnum as their maid."

"Yes," said Holmes. "A most satisfactory outcome, indeed."

Hollingbourne Grange
by Mike Chinn

"I feel as though I have been summoned by Her Majesty in person!"

These were the first words my friend Sherlock Holmes uttered as I joined him for breakfast on a prematurely autumnal, bleak summer's day. He held a crumpled telegram between two narrow fingers and thrust it carelessly at me as I sat. I took it, noting as I did so that the kippers on the plate before him were completely untouched and no doubt absolutely cold.

Holmes lit a cigarette and leaned back in his chair. "Well, Watson, what do you make of it?"

I read the telegram quickly. That it was brusque and to the point could not be argued. "'*Husband vanished under strangest circumstances,*'" I quoted. "'*Require your attendance immediately. Hollingbourne Grange, Kent. No answer required.*'" I placed the paper on the table, smoothing it flat before helping myself to kippers of my own. "There is certainly an imperious tone to the message. Someone who isn't used to being gainsaid, I imagine."

"The only Hollingbourne Grange I have been able to discover in Kent is owned by Sir Lenham Kingswood. You will be familiar with the name?"

I smiled at Holmes's outward insouciance. Clearly he had wasted no time consulting his library of notes and reference works to bolster any knowledge his remarkable brain already contained in order to greet me fully primed with information. I did know the name. There would likely be few in England who did not.

"Baron Hollingbourne, of course. A man with the ear of the British Government and many Crowned Heads of Europe." The importance of those words struck me. "He is the one who has vanished? Then the telegram can only be from – "

"Lady Louise, the Baroness Hollingbourne herself. It would explain the tone, at least."

"Indeed." I took a mouthful of kipper as I carefully arranged my thoughts and what I knew of the Baron and his wife. "I believe she is related to King Christian of Denmark – a distant cousin from the Hesse-Kassel branch of the family. And did His Majesty not recently spend some time with Sir Lenham during a royal visit to Britain? A meeting orchestrated in the main by the Baroness herself."

"Bravo, Watson! You excel yourself. A troubled crown on the head of a troubled country. Prime Minister Estrup was himself the victim of a failed assassination attempt a decade ago. It is hard to be sure who is presently the most unpopular: Monarch or minister." Holmes crushed out his cigarette on the congealed body of an unfortunate kipper. "So we may infer that her Ladyship is a resourceful woman: Determined, brooking no argument. This terse message would seem to confirm that conjecture." He leaned across the table and tapped the telegram. "But why such a direct appeal to me? Why not Scotland Yard? The disappearance of such a man – even under the most mundane of circumstances, which I imagine this cannot be – is of national importance."

"Should it then be redirected towards the police, or even your brother? You are extraordinarily busy at the moment."

"You know me better than that, Watson. I thrive on work and abhor stagnation." His lips twitched in a thin, momentary smile. "Besides, what man would dare ignore such an imperious summons? Finish your breakfast while I consult *Bradshaw*. We are bound on a trip to Kent."

Our train deposited us at a small, sleepy halt deep within the Kent countryside. It was the sort of station that I imagine existed only to service the Hollingbourne Estate, with sidings and attendant cranes for unloading goods and freight, the area of which was easily three times that of the platform upon which we stood. All were presently deserted, and there was no ticket office or waiting room. Passengers were clearly not a priority.

There was a small carriage standing by the station exit, however. An indifferent driver greeted us, saying the Baroness had despatched him to await our arrival. When I asked how he or his mistress could know upon which train we would be arriving – or indeed if we were coming at all – he shrugged and replied he was charged to wait nonetheless. I wondered if his surly manner was the result of being compelled to carry out what might be a long and pointless task, or because he had grown used to such a careless waste of his time.

The journey was thankfully brief. The driver said nothing, and I was left to watch the passing countryside as Holmes sat in equal silence, his lean form muffled against the unseasonal chill. His brows were drawn down in thought and I knew better than to disturb him at such a time.

The narrow lane down which we drove was bounded by overgrown banks, tall hedges, and lined by trees, the leaves of which glistened with condensation. A tenuous mist hung about the trees' topmost branches, and there was a dampness to the air which made its chill all the more penetrating. I felt a deep sense of relief and gratitude when the carriage turned into a driveway and passed between high, impressive wrought-iron gates. For a moment more trees blocked the view. Then the road turned to the left, the trees parted, and beyond was a small yet impressive mansion, surrounded by wide gardens. If this was Hollingbourne Grange, it transcended its lowly title by many degrees. I couldn't help but think its design had been suggested by Oxfordshire's magnificently baroque Blenheim Palace in its pomp, although on a less-grand scale.

The carriage wove around the gardens and pulled up outside a tall portico. A liveried footman came down the steps to greet us, opening the carriage door and standing to attention. Holmes raised his head as though starting from a deep sleep, looking up at the mansion's sandstone façade with a critical eye. After a moment he grunted, as though answering a private question, and sprang lithely from the carriage.

Once we were disembarked, the footman motioned that we should follow him indoors.

The interior was much smaller than I had expected. Although the reception hall was as grand as the outside, with a sweeping staircase and panelled walls, it was compact and dark, the only light supplied by the entrance. Over a dozen large portraits stared down from the walls with varying degrees of censure. Five were of proud, handsome men with splendid beards and dressed in military finery of a style I was confident wasn't British. Danish relatives of the Baroness, perhaps. I imagined the rest to be members of Sir Lenham's family, although I wasn't familiar enough with his features to tell if there was a resemblance. The only other adornment was a magnificent longcase clock, nestling in a corner beneath the rising stairs. Its deep, regular tick filled the hall with a peaceful, calming heartbeat.

A maid took our coats, hats, and sticks before the footman led us into another grandly decorated room with barely any furniture – although the few pieces were of the finest quality – and more paintings upon the walls. Some depicted landscapes – I recognised a view of the gardens in one – while others were undoubtedly of ancestors, dating back as far as the seventeenth century, if my knowledge of dress and armour was up to the task. The footman left, closing tall double doors behind him.

Not daring to sit or smoke, I gave the many paintings an inexpert eye, while Holmes stood gazing out through one of the high windows which punctuated the outer wall.

"The house is well maintained," he observed after a moment, "with a modest number of staff. The portico and frontages are clean and in excellent repair. The sparsity of furniture is of interest, however. Is it customary in Denmark to have the bare minimum, do you think?" He paused as the great doors once more swung open. "And here is our hostess, unless I am very much mistaken."

The woman who joined us was one of the most striking females I think I have ever set eyes upon. She was tall, dressed in a plain, deep-brown dress with little adornment. I wouldn't describe her as beautiful, but her heart-shaped face was dominated by large violet eyes that were quite breath-taking, demanding the observer's full attention. Her hair – almost the shade of her dress and shot through with silver – was drawn up by a plain clasp. She swept into the room, waiting until the doors were closed behind her before casting those remarkable eyes upon Holmes and myself. Her stance and expression were commanding.

"Mr. Holmes. Dr. Watson. I am pleased you responded to my request so promptly."

Holmes sketched the briefest bow. "Lady Louise. I sensed from its brevity there was some urgency, and since you have vouchsafed to contact only Watson and myself in this matter, I admit to being somewhat intrigued."

She met his gaze steadfastly. "How can you be sure I have contacted no one else?"

"Because if you had telegraphed Scotland Yard, it is more than likely that more than one of its senior representatives would have been knocking on my door before I had taken the first sip of my morning coffee. The same would be true if you had decided to approach, shall we say, more *elevated* departments."

"You think highly of yourself, Mr. Holmes."

"I know my worth, your Ladyship, and the best use to which the capital's police may put me. And I can be discreet, as you must know – else you wouldn't have contacted me in this matter."

"My husband's absence must not be general knowledge. If word should escape – "

"I understand perfectly, Lady Louise. Therefore, to details."

"Of course." She crossed to a chaise longue and sat, stiff-backed, failing to offer either Holmes or myself a seat on what furniture remained. "The Baron retired after dinner, as is his habit, to his private study. He has been working long and hard these past months on matters of great importance to both our government and to that of Denmark. You will be aware of my family connections, of course."

Holmes acknowledged her query with another curt bow.

"Shortly before eleven, Maybridge, the footman, took him a brandy. The Baron has taken to imbibing a glass before bedtime. It helps calm his mind, he claims. Maybridge found the room entirely deserted. Of the Baron there was no sign."

"Was the door locked?"

"Yes."

"Could the Baron have left his study and locked the door behind him?"

"You will be taken there shortly, Mr. Holmes. You will see that no one can exit through that door without being observed."

Holmes grunted softly. "The room was undisturbed?" He placed both hands flat together and tapped them against his lips, closing his eyes.

"The window was open – although it is likely my husband opened it himself. Nothing was disturbed. His bureau was shut. It was as though he had walked into the study, locked the door behind him, and promptly vanished."

"People rarely vanish, your Ladyship. Even such notorious cases as LePrince and Bathurst have mundane explanations once all the facts are assembled and unsubstantiated claims and hearsay dismissed. Is that all?"

She hesitated a moment, brows drawn down in thought. "There was, I thought, an odd, astringent odour about the place. I did not recognise it."

"Such as ether, or chloroform?" I suggested.

The Baroness nodded, still deep in thought. "Perhaps. Do you think my husband was rendered senseless?"

"At the moment, there are few facts upon which to build a hypothesis," Holmes interjected before I could speak. "I would like to see this study now."

"Of course." Lady Louise rose, pulling at a silken cord. Moments later, the footman Maybridge reappeared. "Show these gentlemen to the Baron's study. Answer any and all of their questions, and show them every courtesy."

He bowed to her deeply before indicating that we should follow him.

Once more we were in the reception hall, the slow, friendly tick of the tall clock filling the air.

"That is a magnificent timepiece," I said.

Maybridge half-turned to glance at the clock. "It is a Tompion," he said. It was the first time he had spoken, and his voice was slow and soft, yet precise as the pendulum swinging within the case. "A favourite of the master's, and the heart of this household. All things are measured by its regular progress."

He led us to another set of double doors at the back of the hall, no more than five feet from the corner in which stood the clock. If this was the only entrance to the Baron's study, then it was true he could hardly expect to leave by it without attracting some attention. For one thing, the hinges were in need of a little oil: In such a confined space, their creaking could just be heard over the ticking clock.

All three of us entered the study. It was a simple room, illuminated by two sash windows which faced the doorway. The walls were panelled with more dark wood – matured oak I imagined – and generally unadorned. Gas lamps were fitted to the walls on our left and right, two to a wall, and two more on the wall behind us, on either side of the doorway. As with the room we had recently left, there was little furniture, just a plain leather armchair with a small circular table adjacent to its right armrest, and a polished bureau – presently closed – and chair. A thick, Indian-pattern carpet covered much of the floor, not quite reaching the skirting, and exposing a foot or so of gleaming, stained floorboards all around. There were no bookshelves – which I confess surprised me a little – or any sign of reference material. In all it was quite a plain and simple room, one in which a man might retire to work or think, with no distractions. The one indulgence was the armchair and table, upon which my imagination placed the Baron, at day's end, sitting back and enjoying his late-night brandy.

Holmes stood in the room's centre and slowly turned, taking in every aspect. He pointed at the circular table. "The brandy would be placed there?"

The footman nodded silently.

"And where is the glass now?"

"Washed, sir – or so I imagine. The maid will have removed it."

Holmes made a brief, irritated sound. "The open window?"

"This one, sir." Maybridge crossed the floor, moving to the left of the armchair, and indicated one of the windows. The sash was down and secured.

"By how much was it open?" I didn't miss the level of annoyance in my friend's voice.

Maybridge unsecured the window and slid it up almost fully. Holmes went to it, gesturing the footman impatiently aside, and – taking a small lens from his waistcoat – inspected the sill and frame. After several moments of examination he leaned through the open window, his lithe frame fitting comfortably, and glanced down. He grunted and pulled himself back into the room, sliding the window shut once more.

"Is the bureau locked?"

Maybridge nodded.

"Then if you would be so kind . . . ."

The footman walked to the desk, removing a set of keys from his tunic, and unlocked it. He was about to pull down the front when a sharp rebuke from Holmes made him pause.

Before opening the bureau himself, my friend took his lens and examined every smooth, polished surface. Satisfied, he pulled down the front, turning the piece of furniture into a simple writing desk. The back of the bureau was a honeycomb of pigeonholes, all stuffed with a variety of paperwork. A half-full glass inkwell and five pens were placed to the left, just in front of the filed documents. The lowered writing surface was covered by a well-used blotter, and a dried ink stain as large as my fist had spread across an area close to the top right-hand corner. Holmes looked at each of the pens carefully, raising one in particular.

"The nib of this is coated with dried ink, the rest have all be carefully cleaned. Was the Baron in the habit of leaving his writing materials unwiped?"

"He was meticulous, sir."

"Then we must theorise he was engaged in writing something and was disturbed. Was this bureau open?"

"No sir – locked, as you first saw it."

"Capital. Watson, help me look through whatever documents are still in these drawers. I doubt we will find anything as helpful as an unfinished letter or memorandum, but we may always hope."

The footman took a step forward. "I am not – "

Holmes turned to him. "Your mistress bade you answer our questions and extend to us every courtesy, did she not?"

Maybridge stared back, his face unreadable. "She did, but I'm not sure – "

"Do you want me to uncover what has happened to Sir Lenham or not?" snapped Holmes. "Already potential evidence has been removed or interfered with. I must have full co-operation or none at all."

After a heartbeat, Maybridge nodded.

"So." My friend returned his attention to the bureau. "Examine everything, Watson. The smallest thing might prove vital. Although – " he added with a tight smile, " – if you uncover any draft treaties, please try to curb your natural curiosity and refrain from reading them."

The Baron's papers were organised with admirable orderliness. Hand-written notes were filed to one side of the pigeonholes, finished documents elsewhere. Clearly not meant as a secure location wherein such items might be kept on a long-term basis – other than the notes, perhaps – the papers were still filed in a regular manner, sometimes bound together by ribbon. Holmes sifted through his half of the desk, barely reading each paper's contents before adding it to a small pile he was building on the blotter. I was equally circumspect, only glancing at whatever I held to be sure it hadn't been abandoned half-composed before consigning to my own pile.

Holmes abruptly paused in his reading, and I felt sure he had uncovered that which we sought, but he placed the sheet he held on the blotter and pushed it wordlessly towards me. He held a forefinger to his lips to indicate I too should remain silent. It was a typewritten letter, and although I didn't peruse the contents, the one thing to which Holmes wished to draw my attention was abundantly clear.

At the bottom was my own signature.

I glanced up at my friend, and he gave an almost imperceptible shake of the head. When I looked down once more at the letter, it had gone – spirited cleanly away by some sleight-of-hand.

"I think the events are clear," spoke Holmes. "Sir Lenham was working at his desk, writing, when he was assaulted. This stain bears testimony to the suddenness of events: The inkwell was no doubt overturned or jolted sufficiently to splash a little of its contents. I think it quite likely that whatever he was composing would also be stained." He turned to face Maybridge. "You are certain there was no sign of any letter or note anywhere within this room? Not even a torn scrap?"

The footman shook his head.

Holmes pursed his lips. "That is too bad, although not a surprise. Whoever attacked the Baron and spirited him away through that window was thorough, leaving nothing tangible for us to get our teeth into. This was no of-the-moment action, but planned and executed in a most professional manner. Indeed, they have tidied the scene of the crime quite admirably."

"But can you help her Ladyship, Mr. Holmes?" asked the footman.

"I will try, Maybridge, to the best of my abilities. There are lines of enquiry I must first pursue." He slipped both hands into pockets and gave the study another careful perusal. "Is there an inn or such close by, where Watson and I might spend the night?"

"I am sure the Baroness would be only too happy to let you stay at the Grange – " Maybridge began.

Holmes began walking towards the doors. "That will not be necessary. I wouldn't care to impose . . . ."

"Then I will summon the coachman. There is an excellent inn not two miles from here – simple but comfortable."

"Thank you. That will be more than enough for us."

I looked at my friend, seeking clues, but his features were inscrutable.

As Maybridge went in search of the coachman, the maid returned with our coats and hats. As I slipped on my overcoat, I once more heard the deep, soothing tempo of the longcase clock. I slipped out my watch and found, to no great surprise, both timepieces were in agreement to within less than a minute.

"It's behaving itself today," spoke the maid, noticing. She handed me my hat and helped Holmes with his heavy overcoat.

"Is it not reliable?" I asked.

"Most of the time." She was dismissive. "But it's getting like the rest of this house, sir."

"In what manner?" asked Holmes.

"Well, sir, you know how old buildings settle at night. The faint groans and odd noises. I imagine this old clock's much the same: Past its prime and losing its voice."

"I thought it was the beating heart of the household," I said.

"It is, sir – or *was*. Over the past month or so, it's started to lose time. Just on the odd occasion. Its chimes aren't what they were, either. I thought a mouse might have got inside and died there, though I daren't look. Once it even stopped altogether. Every time it was spotted before it could throw us all out – never do for me to be late for my duties and such."

"Quite irksome," remarked Holmes with a faint smile.

"I expect Mr. Maybridge will get it seen to, eventually – " She glanced up, dropping her eyes and curtseying.

"That will be all, Forbes. I am sure these gentlemen do not wish to be detained by your chatter." Lady Louise was descending the stairs, her keen eyes watching us all over the banister.

"Very good, my Lady." The maid curtseyed again and hurried away.

The Baroness reached the bottom of the stairs. "I understand you will be staying overnight at a local tavern, Mr. Holmes." Her tone was neutral. I couldn't tell if she was pleased or put out by my friend's decision.

"Indeed. A single night of contemplation."

"Quite. Then you hope for some resolution."

"There is always hope, my Lady, and I flatter myself that this matter isn't so complex."

She favoured him with a keen look. "Indeed? Then we look forward to the morning, and your conclusion, Mr. Holmes." With that she swept by, tacitly dismissing us. A moment, later Maybridge informed us that the carriage was ready.

The drive from the Grange was conducted in thunderous silence, the taciturn driver saying nothing, while Holmes sat brooding, his shaggy brows drawn down over closed eyes. For myself I offered no comment – even though I was eager to discuss the letter and its forged signature – but recognising my friend's mood, I had to be content for it to lift.

The inn was an ancient, half-timbered building nestling among the tall hedgerows. A stout, hirsute innkeeper showed us to a small room crouched under the eaves. Its low, sloped ceiling was undershot by gnarled beams, most likely of oak, and to approach the only window it was necessary to duck, or risk striking one's head. There were two narrow beds, a wash stand, an empty hearth in one corner, and a tiny wardrobe which was barely wide enough to take our overcoats.

Once divested of his hat and outer garment, Holmes threw himself lengthways on a bed. He pinched the bridge of his nose between thin

378

fingers and let out a great groan. "Am I such a simpleton, Watson? Are such transparent lies meant to impress or befuddle me?"

I seated myself on the other bed. It felt quite hard and lumpy. "You refer to the letter?" I began.

"For one." He pulled the note from a waistcoat pocket and held it up in the thin light entering through the window. "Cheaply made paper, no watermark. Available from any stationers." He brought it closer. "The signature is a passable forgery, likely to temporarily convince anyone who isn't so familiar with your physician's scrawl as I, but by no means longer than a day or so."

"I am relieved to hear it." I lit a cigarette and tried to make myself comfortable.

"Observe: The downstroke on the '*A*' is too precise, the '*T*' crossed with a careful stroke rather than the negligent slash of your hand. This is the work of someone making a painstaking but slow copy from an example of your signature. They haven't set aside the time necessary for practice so that it becomes habitual. There is no spontaneity."

"But where did they obtain such a specimen?"

Holmes sat up, supporting himself by an elbow resting negligently on the bedhead. "I can easily imagine a consultation with a patient – one who hasn't seen you often, if at all – who requires some simple remedy for a minor ailment. Nothing remarkable. Nothing that would strike you as in any way memorable. There upon the prescription form will be an instant example of your signature, to be copied and distributed at will."

"You are describing any one of a dozen or more consultations."

"Therein lies the guile." He gave the letter one last inspection before thrusting it back into a pocket. "The only such example, however. All else is clumsy and transparent lies which wouldn't deceive a simpleton."

"The smell of chloroform, or ether, for example – "

"Ha! I knew you had spotted that. How could the scent of such volatile liquids linger in a well-ventilated room unless a soaked rag was still in evidence? There was no such rag."

"And it takes a considerable period of time to render someone unconscious with either anaesthetic. Twenty minutes or so."

"You are on form, Watson. Quite so. What's more, the ground below that open window is undisturbed. The weather has been quite damp for the last two days. Anyone simply standing at the window – least of all manhandling an unconscious form through it – would have left a trace. An unnecessarily washed brandy glass. A closed sash window which I doubt had ever been open, despite claims to the contrary. Last night was unseasonably cool. The squeaking study door hinges which no one heard – because the doors were never opened. Added to which was the melodramatic and unnecessary flourish of the spilled ink. It is all so insultingly obvious. Sir Lenham was never in his study last night – I doubt he remained conscious long after dinner. There was the real anaesthetic: In his food or drink." He shook his head. "And the letter to which we were so obviously led, adorned with your forged signature, is the screen behind which such transparent subterfuges are meant to hide."

"To what end?"

"A self-evident attempt at tying my hands, Watson. There can be no doubt that Sir Lenham has been abducted by some means. The manner of his disappearance is a curious one. Even had I not been involved so swiftly, it is almost certain that those whose purpose it is to investigate such a case would eventually consult with me." He produced a cigarette of his own, and I lit it for him as he searched his pockets for a match. "The abductors dared not risk my uninhibited involvement, so they resolved to place me in a position whereby I am constrained from interfering – no matter how temporarily."

"How?"

He stared at me directly. "By impugning the honour of my dearest friend. Don't imagine that this blatant forgery is the only copy? Or indeed the worst they can fabricate? In this, you merely implore the vanished Baron to intercede on the behalf of certain elements within the Danish government: Reformers who are presently trying to force the king to accede to their requests. Embarrassing for you and mildly irritating for our own government, but nothing my brother doesn't encounter on a regular basis and deal with most efficiently. Instead, they have chosen to show their hand, daring me to raise the stakes. They have announced hostilities, Watson. Admitted to us – albeit tacitly – their criminality, then challenged me to proceed with what I know, all the while suspending a Damoclean sword above your head."

I admit his words unnerved me somewhat. "But you said the forgery couldn't stand for a day or more – "

"Indeed it cannot – nor could any similar document. But time isn't our friend. They are demonstrating that they can – and will! – produce any evidence of your interference in another country's politics should we persist further. An investigation must follow, one that will inevitably clear your name – but it will take time. Time in which Sir Lenham will be taken far beyond our reach."

"Murdered, you mean?"

"I hope it will not come to that, but our adversaries have shown themselves to be ruthless, if not subtle. It is quite possible the Baron will be removed permanently, should his wife feel it necessary."

"That is dreadful, Holmes!"

"It is the way of modern politics. I have already said that King Christian is presently unpopular, while his Prime Minister is considered by many to be little more than a dictator. I suspect Sir Lenham's sympathies align more, in reality, with the reformers mentioned in this letter. While his wife – who is likely of a more forceful Danish heritage, along with Maybridge, if that is his true name, and whoever else is involved in this plot – side with the Prime Minister. When the Baron recently hosted King Christian at the Grange, it occurs to me that the direction of Denmark's future, and the role of the king and his ministers within it, was the central topic of conversation."

"Then what are we to do? If you continue to investigate, they will publish some libel against me which must, by necessity, delay you, giving them a chance to flee and deal with Sir Lenham as they will. If you bow to their threats, the outcome will be much the same."

"You have it in a nutshell. However, all is not lost. As I said to Maybridge, there are still avenues which I must pursue. And I'll wager that maid – Forbes – isn't a part of the scheme. She was most informative." He gave a tight smile. "We aren't beaten yet, friend Watson. I do not believe they will move tonight: They will first need to be convinced I am made powerless and no longer a threat. Tomorrow, we shall demonstrate just how wrong they are and move against them." He stubbed out his cigarette. "And now, I imagine you are in need of some dinner."

We occupied a small table in a corner of the taproom, just wide enough to accommodate us both. The room itself was rustic and in need of some revitalisation. Apart from Holmes and me, the only other soul was the innkeeper himself. When that worthy approached and asked what our pleasure was, I remarked on the quiet.

The man's bewhiskered face set into doleful lines. "Business is poor, sir, and that's a fact. Work is hard to find around here nowadays, and many folk have moved to places where it might be more easily sought. Truth be told, I reckon me and the missus will be closing up ourselves in a year or two." He shrugged and the ghost of a smile tugged at his lips. "In the meantime, what might I get you?"

I ordered two dinners, and a glass of the local ale for Holmes and myself. The drinks were brought first, and although I took an experimental sip – it was an excellent brew: Crisp and refreshing – I decided to await the serving of our meals before enjoying it further. When our dinner arrived – mutton chops with vegetables – Holmes spoke to the innkeeper with an air of detached interest.

"You know Hollingbourne Grange, of course?"

"The Old Grange sir? Indeed so. His Lordship is our landlord – and a fair-minded one, most of the time."

Holmes nodded thoughtfully. "And yet the house doesn't look so very old."

The innkeeper laughed briefly. "There has been a grange there since . . . well, the Elizabethan days, I believe. Perhaps earlier. It's been expanded and added to ever since. What you see now is probably no more than seventy or eighty years old. The outside of it, anyway."

"The kernel of the house remains?"

"Somewhere, sir. Over time, they just stuck on more rooms, and most recently a fancy exterior."

"Indeed." Holmes gave a tight smile. "Is it possible that I might have a telegram sent?"

"Certainly, sir. There's a boy who will be happy to run whatever message you require to the nearest post office."

"Capital. Have him sent to my room in an hour. Let him know there is half-a-crown to cover the cost, and what remains is a reward for his trouble."

"I will, sir. That's most generous." The innkeeper bobbed his head. "Well, enjoy your dinners, gentlemen. If there's anything else you require, the missus and I will be pleased to accommodate you." And with that, he left us to eat.

"That is generous," I observed.

"The boy's feet will move all the swifter for it, I'm sure." He lit a cigarette and half smiled.

I smiled myself and began to eat. I found the humble repast well cooked and quite delicious, and set to with a will. Holmes, however, ignored his own generously piled plate, instead smoking and sipping thoughtfully at his drink, his eyes distant.

Eventually, as I finished the last morsels of my dinner he placed the glass upon the table, the level reduced by barely an inch, and said, "It is quite the problem, but I am confident of my solution. An early night is called for, Watson, for I have a telegram to compose, and tomorrow Sir Lenham must be restored to us without hindrance."

Despite the lumpen bed and the fact that I was still partly dressed, I managed a good night's sleep. I awoke to the smell of charred paper and found Holmes, fully dressed, with the makings of a good fire in the corner hearth. He heard me and half-turned, raising a folded paper spill to his pipe.

"Morning, Watson. I trust you are well-rested."

"Better that I expected. And you?"

"Suitably refreshed, my friend. Make haste, now. I have already taken the liberty of ordering us some breakfast."

I arose and poured water into the bowl on the washstand. "You could have asked the innkeeper to lay the fire for you," I commented before I splashed cold water onto my face. "I'm sure he would have been happy to oblige."

My friend shrugged, threw the remains of the charred paper spill into the flames, and puffed on his noxious pipe. I needed no greater incentive to finish dressing and quit the small room. Minutes later we were downstairs, at the corner table, enjoying a breakfast of lightly boiled eggs, fresh bread, and a rich butter which tasted so much finer than that normally to be found in London.

Unlike the previous evening, Holmes took a hearty breakfast, devouring four eggs and washing them down with tea. It was a heartening sign.

After we had eaten, we once again put on overcoats and hats, I settled the bill and we left the inn, Holmes assuring our host that he had memorised the route to the Grange, and it was a fine morning for a walk. Indeed, the weather had improved greatly, and a bright summer sun hung low in a clear sky at our backs. Thus we set off to walk the two miles at a brisk pace.

I enquired of Holmes whether the boy had returned with an answer to his telegram. My friend did not reply – remarking instead that a vehicle identical to that belonging to Lady Louise was approaching down the road. It was indeed the same carriage, with the same surly driver. He spoke only to inform us he had been dispatched to collect and drive us to the Grange.

As Holmes pulled himself up he paused and turned to me, a roguish twinkle in his eyes. "Her Ladyship is certainly eager to reacquaint herself, Watson."

"After being so dismissive yesterday," I replied.

"Just so." He settled himself in the seat and I joined him. "How long will that humour last, I wonder."

We were back at Hollingbourne Grange in no time. We dismounted and went indoors, Holmes striding ahead of me.

In the reception hall, all was quiet except for the mellow ticking of the old clock. It was on its best behaviour that morning, the hands on its ornate face exactly matching those on my watch. The maid, Forbes, took our coats and hats, but Holmes retained his cane, explaining that his foot was a little sore and he needed its support. It was the first I had heard of it.

Lady Louise and Maybridge joined us, exiting the study together. Maybridge's features were set in curiosity, but the Baroness was composed and unreadable.

"Well, Mr. Holmes," said she, "you promised me a resolution this morning and I will hear it."

"I doubt I need to say much, your Ladyship. I consider it most likely you will have guessed my response."

She permitted herself a humourless smile. "Unfortunate."

"And so it is, Madam – for you and your co-conspirator here."

"I think not, Mr. Holmes." Maybridge produced a revolver with the air of a stage magician. "You chose unwisely."

"You think so?" Holmes's tight smile matched the Baroness's in coolness. "If you are referring to those letters in which you so clumsily attempted to impugn my friend Watson, then let me assure you they are worthless."

Maybridge frowned, his eyes flickering momentarily towards the longcase clock. In that second Holmes acted. Cobra-swift, his cane lashed across Maybridge's hand, knocking the revolver free.

"Watson, if you would oblige me."

I retrieved the gun and stood at my friend's side, aiming it at both Baroness and footman. Some of the *froideur* had drained from her face, while Maybridge was content to scowl, nursing his bruised hand.

"I am an indifferent shot, as Watson will no doubt testify, but with the single-stick, I admit to few superiors." Holmes flourished his cane, pointing it at the clock for a moment. "Last night I removed the six forged letters from that clock – wedged a little too tightly against the chiming mechanism so as to dampen them, just a little. I also took the liberty of searching elsewhere, in case you had the foresight to secret other copies, in those rooms I could gain access to without awakening the house. You wouldn't use the servants' quarters since they aren't involved, and you dared not risk curious eyes. I found none – although I accept there may be some placed where I couldn't search. Her Ladyship's bedroom, for example. I also saw fit to oil the study door hinges."

"Last night?" said the Baroness.

"When I had completed yesterday's examination of the study window, I took the precaution of wedging an empty matchbox under the sash. The minute gap was small enough to escape all but the keenest glance, while allowing me enough purchase to lever it up from outside. If you care to examine the ground below that window, you will see it now bears the footmarks which were so conspicuous by their absence before."

"The fire!" I exclaimed.

"Quite, Watson. Those letters were poor forgeries, but excellent for lighting my pipe."

"So you now add burglary to your many accomplishments?" Maybridge was sneering.

"Ha! And not for the first time – although such a petty crime pales beside the false imprisonment of a peer of the realm."

Maybridge straightened. "Indeed, Mr. Holmes. The Baron is still missing – "

"Hardly, as you know all too well. My peregrinations about this house last night weren't limited to the removal of litter and lubricating hinges. There was the small matter of an old longcase clock – the beating heart of the household – abruptly acting in a most uncharacteristic manner. Losing time, actually stopping on occasion."

"It is an old clock. It requires servicing."

"I don't doubt both statements are, in essence, true. But factor in the sudden disappearance of a member of this household, in a building which dates, in part, back to a regrettable period of English history when becoming invisible was literally a matter of living or dying."

"Elizabethan or older," I said, remembering the innkeeper's words. I snapped my fingers. "Priest holes!"

"Excellent, Watson. Now, consider an ancient timepiece which, due to that very age and its delicate mechanism, is ill-disposed to being moved. It would most likely stop – become unreliable at the very least. Would you not say so, Maybridge?"

The man remained silent, although his surly expression spoke volumes.

"I didn't simply spend my time here last night searching for lamentable forgeries," continued Holmes. "Primed with the knowledge of this building's age and considering how this clock – " He strode up to the clock and rapped it sharply with his cane. " – has only recently become haphazard and unreliable in its timekeeping, there was only one likely hypothesis – one I tested last night." He faced the Baroness and her servant. "I will not ask you to soil your hands, your Ladyship – I don't doubt you have avoided it so far – so, if you would, Maybridge."

The man stood defiantly, refusing to budge. The Baroness glared arrogantly at my friend, who simply shrugged.

"As you wish. Watson, don't take your eyes off our friends while I demonstrate what they already know to be true."

So saying, Holmes placed both hands against the clock and carefully pushed. It slid easily, although there was a muted clang from the pendulum as its equilibrium was disturbed. After Holmes had moved the clock by around a yard to the left, he stepped up to the dark panelling which had been behind it and pressed against an otherwise unremarkable wooden upright with an air of confidence. I may have heard a soft click, but an entire section of the panelling jerked back. Holmes pushed it further, swinging the hidden door open on a lightless void.

385

"It was in this ancient priest hole that the unfortunate Baron was hidden. This venerable timepiece took it ill, and promptly stopped – much as it did every time this access was used. Preparing the lamentable cell to receive Sir Lenham weeks in advance, placing him inside, feeding him – unless his wife and servant are even more inhumane than I take them to be. Maybridge – or whatever rogue he employed to care for the Baron – didn't think to restart the clock at the correct time. Perhaps they dared not tarry. More likely it didn't occur to them. This entire case has been a litany of inadequate reasoning and unwarranted assumptions."

"About time, Mr. Holmes," came a familiar voice from the inky darkness. "I was beginning to believe I'd been abandoned in this hell hole."

Maybridge and the Baroness exchanged looks. Lady Louise's composed features grew pale.

Holmes laughed for a second. "Ah, yes. I apologise. I quite neglected to mention that once I discovered your hiding place, I took the liberty of removing your prisoner and awaiting the arrival of Scotland Yard outside the Grange. I had earlier telegraphed my colleague, Inspector Lestrade, and he and his men came as swiftly as they could. By special train, I believe."

"Quite right, Mr. Holmes." A lean, cobwebbed figure stepped into the hall, brushing at his overcoat and hat. "And even though your sense of drama is catching," he added with a wry smile on his pinched face, "I would have much preferred a cleaner spot to while away the night." He addressed Lady Louise. "Have no fear for your husband, your Ladyship. He is presently enjoying the hospitality of one of London's best hotels. And he has already had much to say about the events of the last couple of days."

The Baroness considered his words. Then, pushing Maybridge aside, she rushed towards the front entrance.

"It will do you no good," said Lestrade calmly, enjoying the moment. "My men have your home surrounded. No one will be permitted to leave unless I say so."

As he spoke, two uniformed officers stepped through the portico and into the hallway. The Baroness hesitated in her flight.

"If you would be so good as to follow these gentlemen . . ." Lestrade said with the briefest of bows and smiling at Maybridge.

Both were led outside and, I imagine, an awaiting police carriage.

Once the hall was empty but for us three, Lestrade turned to Holmes and me. "Well, what are we to make of the woman?" he asked. "Kidnapping her own husband. Attempting to ensure your silence with clumsy blackmail . . . ?"

"The estate is losing money," said Holmes. He reached for the clock face, swinging open its glass plate, and moved the hands to the correct time. The pendulum, once again settled, was swinging with a gentle beat. "The innkeeper confirmed the local population is increasingly moving elsewhere for work. Thus, what had been a guaranteed income was gradually drying up. You saw how little furniture there is, Watson."

"Sold?" I said.

"I have no doubt. The books which undoubtedly once stood in Sir Lenham's study, too – discreetly, and hard to trace. Women such as Lady Louise would rather die than admit to financial difficulties." He glanced towards the portraits ascending alongside the stairs. "The only reason those dreadful paintings are still hanging is because I can conceive of no dealer who would take them. I cannot believe such a minor thing as sentiment would stand in her way."

"But why kidnap her own husband and attempt to keep you helpless?" said Lestrade.

"She and Maybridge – you will find his true name is rather more Scandinavian – are supporters of Estrup, Denmark's tyrannical Prime Minister, while Sir Lenham is more in favour of political reform. Reform which is calculated to bolster King Christian's failing popularity at the expense of the Prime Minister's. It is unlikely you will be able to prove Estrup's hand is on these particular reins, but I can guarantee his agents offered Lady Louise a princely sum to have Sir Lenham fall into their hands. Maybridge is most likely to be one of those agents. Don't be surprised, my dear Lestrade, if subtle pressure isn't brought upon Scotland Yard to have the man returned to Denmark without charge."

"We'll do our best to see him face Her Majesty's justice," said the inspector.

"Capital." Holmes lit a cigarette. "Money, and the removal of one she had come to regard as a political enemy, both in one tidy package. And too tempting to resist. Once sufficient time had elapsed – too long a period for my belated intervention – certain fraudulent letters would find their way to Baker Street, their usefulness expired, and she would begin restoring Hollingbourne Grange to its former glory."

"Regarding which," said Lestrade, "while not doubting the thoroughness of your search last night, if any more such documents should come to light as my men do their duty and comb this house from top to bottom – ?"

"You may do as you see fit," said Holmes.

"Ah," said the inspector with a lop-sided smile. "I expect we will uncover many official papers secreted about this house of the sort that require discretion and careful filing."

"Thank you, Inspector," I said warmly.

"It's a small enough token, Doctor. Now let's say no more about it." A group of uniformed men joined him and Lestrade turned away from us, directing them as to where they should begin their search of the premises.

"Well then, Watson," said Holmes, crushing out his cigarette on the hall floor, "once Forbes returns with our garments – if she hasn't simply discarded them now, she, like so many of the parish, is without a job – let's to London, post-haste. This country air is proving too refined for my palate, and the city's criminal fraternity grows quite ebullient if I am away for too long. It is careless of me to indulge them more than necessary."

The Professor's Assistant
by Chris Chan

There seems to be an inescapable rule in life that no sooner have you convinced yourself that one of your troubles has been permanently resolved that it returns with a vengeance. It was a beautiful day in May 1895, and I had assured myself that the shadow that Professor Moriarty had cast upon the world was now forever dissipated.

But as I am far from the first to note, life has a way of surprising us, and that afternoon, I discovered that the Moriarty legacy continued. Shortly after tea-time, a man knocked on our door, and from the expression on his face, it was obvious that he was in a state of considerable distress. He was a fairly young man, not far from thirty, but his hair was streaked with silver. His gaunt physique and well-worn suit indicated that his financial situation was strained, and that he hadn't enjoyed many square meals lately.

"Do you know who I am, Mr. Holmes?" our guest asked us.

It was impossible to read Holmes's face. At first, I thought I detected a trace of hostility in his eyes, but a moment afterwards I wondered if it was actually wariness. "I do. You are Eóghan Finucan."

"Have you met before?" I asked Holmes.

"I observed him from a distance over the course of multiple investigations several years ago, but we were never formally introduced."

"To which investigations are you referring?" I asked.

"Mr. Finucan is an academic specializing in advanced mathematics, Watson. For years, he was an assistant to then-Professor Moriarty at the small university where Moriarty taught."

My stomach clenched, and I now saw this seemingly harmless man as a potential source of danger. My fears that Mr. Finucan would attack us with a revolver or a dagger were unfounded, however, as the young man simply sagged backwards into his chair.

"That is true, Mr. Holmes. But for the benefit of Doctor Watson, could you please assure him that I was only his assistant in teaching and research?"

I looked at Holmes, who seemed to be choosing his words very carefully. "I subjected Mr. Finucan to considerable scrutiny, and I never found the slightest bit of evidence that he was involved in any of the Professor's illegal activities."

"Thank you, Mr. Holmes." Mr. Finucan seemed not to notice that Holmes had stopped short of actually declaring him an innocent man. "May I please tell you my story?"

"Proceed."

"When I began my studies in mathematics, I thought that the mentorship of such an eminent academician would assure me a comfortable position and a brilliant career. Unfortunately – for me, at least – soon after I received my degree, your investigation led to Professor Moriarty's downfall. For years, I graded examination papers for the Professor, copied notes for him, and performed all of the research he requested. I was his right-hand man, but only in terms of the university. I had nothing to do with the Professor's secret activities and I was ignorant of his true nature until after Doctor Watson published his account that I believe he titled 'The Final Problem'. That story had a devastating effect upon my life. The Professor was my primary reference, and my working relationship with him was common knowledge in academic circles – partly, I admit, because I publicized this at every opportunity, thinking it would help my career.

"Alas, my connection with him has doomed my job prospects. Even after he resigned his chair, I believed that the rumors about him were false and that he'd be restored to his position soon, so as I was completing my studies for my degree, I did a bit of additional research for the Professor when he was an army coach in London. With the revelations of Professor Moriarty's illegal enterprises, a job offer at a prestigious university was withdrawn the week before my employment was to begin. Part of me understands this, as the reputation of the institution demands that its faculty have absolutely unimpeachable credentials. Still, I consider it a terrible unfairness that my own name has been smeared because my mentor was not the man I believed him to be. I am a mathematician, not a criminal. But I have had no luck convincing prospective employers of my honesty and integrity.

"Ever since the revelations of the Professor's crimes, the doors of every institution of higher learning have been closed to me. None of my applications for employment have produced so much as an interview, and only a handful of colleges to which I've applied for work have bothered to send me even a short letter informing me that my services will not be needed. On several occasions, my attempts to visit these universities to plead my case have been rebuffed. No official or professor will meet with me, and invariably, I am informed that if I do not leave immediately, they will call the police and demand that I be arrested for trespassing.

"I haven't been able to find any sort of teaching position, not even in the smallest and most disreputable schools. On numerous occasions, I have attempted to find positions as a schoolteacher all over the country, but as soon as they look into my background, I am informed that I am no longer under consideration for the job. Even private tutoring employment has been difficult to come by, as I have managed to be hired a few times by wealthy families looking for someone to educate their children at home, but none of these positions lasted more than a week before I was summoned to meet the head of the family, informed that my services would no longer be required, and then handed a small envelope with a month's wages and told that I had one hour to vacate the premises, or otherwise the police would be called. None of my requests for a letter of reference were met with anything more than a scornful refusal. I've been making ends meet by working in shops and as a common labourer on odd jobs."

"Are you asking Holmes to clear your name?" I wondered.

"Yes, but for a specific more-recent accusation." Our guest sighed and leaned forward. "Please understand that I do not blame you for any of this, Mr. Holmes. You were trying to save this country from a terrible criminal, and I truly appreciate your efforts and sacrifices. For years, I thought Professor Moriarty was a genius, albeit a stern and severe man with no tolerance for incompetence or failure. When I learned the truth about my mentor, I was blindsided, but upon further thought and reflection, I was compelled to admit that there were signs that I missed.

"Over the years, I often saw individuals who clearly had no business at the university going into or out of the Professor's office at odd times, or the Professor disappearing for long stretches of time without explanation. He had several outbursts of temper, and once I saw him drinking from a bottle of port that looked too expensive for his salary. I think that pretty much everybody I knew from the later years of my education has been wondering how they missed all of the little signs suggesting the Professor had hidden secrets, though they have all concluded that I am guilty."

Mr. Finucan seemed utterly sincere, but I have been deceived innumerable times by talented actors, so I was reluctant to accept his claims to innocence, at least until I heard Holmes's thoughts on the matter. Mr. Finucan continued, staring at us with wide, pleading eyes.

"I had several friends in the mathematics department as I was earning my degree, and all of them received excellent jobs upon their graduation. None of them want anything to do with me. My attempts to talk to them to beg for help have all been rebuffed. Just today, I visited Adelard College, where two of my once-closest friends – Mackan "Mack" Butchart and Kenn Gorwydd – are currently enjoying brilliant careers. I had hoped that one or both of them might be willing to testify to my character and help me find some sort of position, and I approached the two of them when

391

I saw them walking along the pathway towards their offices. Both of them cut me dead, and refused to even glance in my direction when I pleaded with them to listen to me.

"I followed them inside the building, beseeching them for two minutes of their time. I realized a bit late that my pleading had gotten rather loud, but fortunately for what little remained of my dignity, the campus was nearly deserted, and throughout my time there I saw no one aside from the three of us. There was some sort of festival in a nearby village, I understood. In any case, the two of them refused to say a word or make eye contact, and locked themselves in their offices. Utterly crushed, I turned around and made my way to a local pub for a simple lunch of bread and cheese.

"Just as I was finishing my meal, a policeman came up to me and demanded that I follow him to the station immediately. When I asked why, he told me that I was a suspect in a theft, and that if I didn't come along quietly, he'd make a great big scene of arresting me, embarrassing me in front of all of the other pub patrons. Everybody was already looking at me suspiciously, but I figured I had nothing to gain by standing up for myself, so I quietly followed Constable Sallow a quarter-of-a-mile down the road to the station.

"There, I met my former friends Mack and Kenn, who were seated on a bench and staring at me suspiciously. I protested my innocence, but I was told to step into a room where I would be searched. Constable Sallow found nothing, and after a lot of questions on my part, I was informed that I was the prime suspect in the theft of a valuable bejeweled gold astrolabe."

"An astrolabe?" I asked.

"A device, first crafted in antiquity, used to measure and analyse the night sky," Holmes explained. "They have been used by astronomers across the world for millennia, and skilled craftsmen have occasionally made them out of precious metals and gems. Please, continue, Mr. Finucan."

"Thank you. Apparently, the item had been in the university's collection for some time, and had been placed in a glass case in the atrium near Mack and Kenn's offices in preparation for a group of prominent personages who were coming for a visit. The university hoped that the item on display would prove impressive to potential donors. Constable Sallow was in the midst of a routine check of the university property, and he discovered the glass case had been smashed and the astrolabe was missing. When he alerted Mack and Kenn of this fact, they stated that I must have stolen it.

"I was deeply wounded by the false accusation, but Mack and Kenn were unrepentant, claiming I must have hidden the astrolabe somewhere before my arrest. They kept explaining that I was Professor Moriarty's protégé, and that I was a criminal. Still, without any evidence, Constable Sallow couldn't arrest me, so I was released, though I was told that I'd be carefully watched. I figured that the police would follow me, but I tried to lose them as I hurried towards the train station. Then, as I bought my ticket with nearly all of my remaining money, I announced very loudly that I needed to get to London to see Sherlock Holmes, hoping that anybody tracking me would overhear and realize that I was seeking exoneration, not escape.

"Mr. Holmes, I swear to you that I am an honest man. I had nothing to do with the theft of the astrolabe. Will you help me to clear my name, please?"

Holmes said nothing for several moments. He tented his fingers and stared off into the distance for a few moments. "Mr. Finucan, I will investigate this case. I will make no promises regarding your exoneration. I will only attempt to determine the truth of the matter."

"That's the best – " He was interrupted by a knock at the door, and I opened it to greet an unfamiliar face from Scotland Yard. As we all expected, he was looking for Finucan, and once we had explained his reasons for coming here, the new-to-me inspector politely but firmly suggested that Finucan return to Adelard College to answer a few more questions. Finucan looked at us with severe embarrassment and murmured that he didn't have sufficient funds to pay for his train ticket back to the college. It was at this moment that I realized that this case was unlikely to be financially remunerative for Holmes.

We booked our seats on the train, and I wondered to myself if we could really call Finucan a client if we were paying for all of his expenses. The inspector, whose name I later learned was Havirmill, joined us in the second-class carriage, saying little but staring at Mr. Finucan as if he expected the man to jump out the window at any moment and make his escape. He needn't have worried. Finucan looked as if he didn't have the energy to walk down the length of the train, let alone run to freedom.

Eventually, Finucan dozed off and, after confirming that Inspector Havirmill would remain watchful, Holmes led me out down the corridor to an empty carriage for a private conversation.

"What are your thoughts on Mr. Finucan?" Holmes asked.

"He seems like a decent sort of chap, but you never know."

"Yes, that's what I thought about him when I was investigating him, trying to decide if he was a part of Moriarty's inner criminal circle." Holmes pulled a thin bundle of papers out of his pocket. "This is my dossier on him from several years ago. I don't believe I ever explained my ranking system to you."

"No. What do you mean?"

"While I was devoting myself to tearing Moriarty's web apart, we ranked people in Moriarty's orbit on a scale of one to four." He showed me a short list:

1. *The individual in question has only a passing acquaintance with Moriarty and has no connection to his criminal enterprise.*

2. *The individual in question has a substantial relationship with Moriarty, but the connection is strictly with his legitimate business in academia.*

3. *The individual in question is closely connected to Moriarty's criminal enterprises, but while the individual is aware of the illegality of the work, that person is being compelled to assist Moriarty through threats or blackmail, and therefore is morally innocent of wrongdoing.*

4. *The individual in question is closely connected to Moriarty's criminal enterprises, is aware of the illegality of the work, and is acting out of pure free will, making that person an accomplice to Moriarty's crimes.*"

Holmes sighed. "A neat little system if I do say so myself, Watson."

"Indeed. And what number did you assign Mr. Finucan?"

"Eóghan Finucan was one of Professor's Moriarty's closest associates at the college and, as his assistant, I was very suspicious of him. Finucan was Moriarty's right-hand man in the department, so I thought that it was quite likely that he might have been involved in the Professor's sinister extracurricular activities, though I warned myself not to jump to conclusions. My allies spent months quietly observing him and surreptitiously digging into his personal life. By the time of the destruction of Moriarty's gang, we had compiled quite the dossier on Finucan, but he was one of the numerous individuals to whom we had difficulty assigning a definite number.

"We knew that Finucan wasn't a Number One due to his close work with the Professor. However, we never found any definite proof that he was involved in Moriarty's criminal enterprises. Officially, we ranked Finucan as a Number Two, as the only provable connection was with Moriarty's academic career. However, we also thought it possible that Finucan was really a Number Three, as it was possible that Finucan was a purely innocent man who was being exploited by a terrible villain. Alternatively, Finucan may have been pressured to assist Moriarty, or he could have made a simple deliberate choice to allow himself to be drawn into the criminal web out of greed, making him a Number Four. But I doubt that the last one is true, though I freely admit that I cannot be certain.

"In short, we still simply don't know how involved Finucan was in the Moriarty gang. He certainly had the brains to be a valued member of the group, but Moriarty had a nose for detecting people of inflexible moral virtue, so it's certainly possible that the Professor decided that his assistant in the classroom would be of no use to him in the field of criminality. I regret that I cannot be more definite, but I just don't know. One point in Finucan's favor is that we never found any evidence of his receiving any money beyond his very modest teaching stipend. It's certainly possible that he could have tucked away some ill-gotten gains in a Swiss bank account, but as he appears to have been living hand-to-mouth lately, that seems rather unlikely.

"I should add that in my agents' casual interviews with Finucan's academic colleagues, most of them found Finucan to be an upright and decent young man, perhaps a bit full of himself and overly ambitious, but not the sort who would turn to crime for easy wealth. He has a brilliant mathematical mind, and it was hard to believe that the Professor wouldn't try to exploit it in some way. The worst that anybody had to say about him was that he was always convinced that he was far and away the cleverest man in the room, and his confidence in his own superlative cleverness was off-putting. He definitely had the arrogance of youth, and seemed to see a brilliant career at a top university as his due, but an inflated opinion of oneself isn't a crime. Otherwise, the prison cells would be so full no one would be able to sit.

"My instincts would rate Finucan as a two on the aforementioned scale, but you know how much I distrust intuition. Based on the evidence, there's nothing to justify a rating of three or higher, and yet . . . if he's as intelligent as we've been given to believe he is, he could be playing some long-range game. It's certainly possible that he worked hand-in-glove with Moriarty in his criminal enterprises. Moriarty could certainly have used a fellow with that level of intelligence in his organization, but I just don't see Finucan as a criminal."

"I must say, I'm reassured," I noted. "But then, who stole the astrolabe?"

"It's possible that Moriarty picked another criminal protegé from of his students. I'm not nearly so convinced that Mack Butchart and Kenn Gorwydd are honest men. I've always been certain that Moriarty had at least one young mathematics student working for him in his criminal organization, someone who could exploit an extensive skill for numbers for illegal yet highly profitable ends, yet stay sufficiently distanced from the dishonest activity so that we weren't able to find any solid evidence of complicity over the course of our investigation. Finucan is almost certainly not that man (though I admit my judgment isn't infallible), but I could easily see Mack Butchart or Kenn Gorwydd as master criminals in training.

"As I haven't had the opportunity to investigate Butchart or Gorwydd for several years, I hasten to add that my information may be out of date. However, when I last dug into Butchart's background, I learned that he was a compulsive gambler. He was absolutely addicted to playing cards, and would often go without sleep at least four nights a week so he could stay up and gamble. By all accounts, he wasn't very lucky at cards, and seemed to be poorer than most young scholars.

"Gorwydd, in contrast, comes from a very wealthy and prominent family. Given his personal affluence, he could pursue his interest in mathematics without worry. I never found any evidence of suspicious income, nor was there ever any proof that he had any more than minimal contact with Moriarty. And yet . . . I interviewed several of their colleagues, and all of them mentioned something odd. Frequently, Gorwydd would make odd comments about how he was so clever, he was wasting his time in academia, and he could make a fortune putting his mind to illegal enterprises, believing himself to be so intelligent he'd never be caught."

"Both of them seem like possible recruits for Moriarty," I commented.

Holmes nodded. "I think it's far more likely that either Gorwydd or Butchart was Moriarty's accomplice, but I have absolutely no proof to confirm my suspicions."

We returned to our original carriage and reached our destination a few minutes later. As we stepped off the train, we were greeted by a man who I soon learned was Constable Sallow. Using as few words as possible, he arrested Finucan for the theft of the astrolabe and hustled him away to the police station.

We were informed we'd be allowed to speak to Finucan in about an hour, so in the meantime we booked a pair of rooms for ourselves at a local inn. When we returned to the station, we had a word with Finucan in his tiny, dark cell. "I suppose it could be worse," he informed us. "It's more comfortable than it looks, and I've only seen three mice so far."

"Couldn't you have seen the same mouse three times?" I asked reflexively. From the expression on Finucan's face, it was clear that the possibility I had suggested had never crossed his mind.

"You're going to quite some lengths and expense to help me," Finucan muttered. "I don't know how I'll ever manage to pay you back, let alone pay your fees."

"That isn't worth worrying about at the moment," Holmes replied.

Finucan sighed. "You've made it clear that while you are willing to help me, you aren't yet convinced of my innocence, and that is fine with me. Just the possibility that you are willing to consider that I didn't steal that astrolabe means more than I can possibly express. You are probably the first person since Professor Moriarty's criminal activities were revealed to give me the benefit of the doubt, and given the pivotal role you played in bringing him down, I think it's rather remarkable that you're being so decent to me."

Holmes waved away the compliments, and then began questioning Finucan about his thoughts regarding the potential culpability of his former classmates. The prospect of their guilt didn't seem to shock Finucan in the slightest.

"If you'd asked me several years ago if Mack and Kenn were potential accessories in a criminal conspiracy, I would have vehemently denied that either of my friends was capable of such iniquity. Perhaps it's bitterness on my part over my own career disappointments, but if Professor Moriarty were to recruit someone from the general class of advanced mathematics students, Mack and Kenn would probably be at the top of his list. They both have first-rate mathematical minds. They are both highly ambitious. But are they criminals?

"Come to think of it, Kenn was always saying what a brilliant criminal he'd make, given the opportunity. He would often remark how a really clever mathematician could set up a system to skim millions of pounds a year from the accounts of any major corporation or bank. At the time, we were all thinking the Kenn was just full of hot air. He never did go into specifics. It seemed as if that was all simply his bloviating over his own cleverness. I simply have no evidence against Kenn.

"As for Mack, he's always struck me an essentially good person, and I wouldn't suspect him of committing a serious crime. He's a fairly quiet fellow, and I've never known him to express any interest in criminality. The only vaguely suspicious point that I know of him was that Mack was mildly obsessed with devising a mathematical formula for winning at various card games. Given the modest losses he generally suffered when I played with him, I don't think that he ever came up with a winning strategy.

"It raises an unsettling question, though: Why didn't Professor Moriarty ever try to recruit *me* for his organization? As you know, I was his assistant, and while I couldn't say that he was ever particularly warm or friendly towards me, I believe that I earned his respect. Only once, early in my association with him, did he ever find a mistake in my calculations, and I can assure you that I never made another error again after the tongue-lashing he gave me. The students were all quite approving of my lectures, and Professor Moriarty told me that I was the only person who he trusted to assist him with the calculations he needed for a revised and expanded version of his book *The Dynamics of an Asteroid*, which for obvious reasons was never published. It required a great deal of analysis of geometric angles, and he specifically asked for my opinion on his theories of pure mathematics.

"I have to say, working on *The Dynamics of an Asteroid* was quite possibly the most intellectually thrilling experience of my life. I spent hours calculating the effects of gravity on large masses, the damage caused when two bodies of equal size collide, the speeds and angles of falling objects, the study of angles of refraction . . . I'd work on the Professor's notes for over eighteen hours straight and then collapse, utterly exhausted and truly blissful. He was working on a follow-up book, and I was editing that manuscript for him. That was my major project in the weeks leading up to the Professor's arrest." He sighed. "I haven't had the chance to work on any really challenging mathematical problems in a very long time."

Holmes nodded slightly, and I couldn't tell for certain whether I saw a flicker of sympathy dance in his eyes or not.

"How are you doing now?" I asked.

After shrugging his shoulders, Finucan sighed. "Frankly, I'm feeling rather demoralized. The police are completely convinced that I'm guilty, and I can understand that. Have you heard the latest?"

"We have not."

"I'll fill you in, then. The astrolabe, as you know, was encrusted with jewels, nearly all of them quite valuable. When I came to town in search of work, the only place that I could find to stay that I could afford was a tiny little room at the local tavern. It's really more of a refurbished closet, just enough room for a narrow and lumpy bed, a few hooks on the wall for clothing, and a little table with a water jug on it, though I wouldn't drink the water in it if I were dying of thirst. It isn't clean at all, and it's opaque with rust.

"While I was meeting with you in London, the local authorities searched my room. Constable Sallow and one of his associates went through the few clothes I had and nearly pulled out all the feathers in the mattress. From what his associate told me, they were about to storm away when Sallow poured out all the water in the jug and discovered a garnet the size of the nail on my little finger at the bottom, hidden by the rusty water.

"And that garnet was from the astrolabe?"

"Yes. It was immediately identifiable from how it's roughly cut. I've no idea how it got there. I tried to protest my innocence, but it did no good. Someone could have slipped into my room and left the garnet to incriminate me, or perhaps someone dropped the garnet into the water *before* it came into my room, though who did it is a mystery to me."

There were tiny tears in Finucan's eyes as he turned towards Holmes. "Please, Mr. Holmes, I'm depending on you. Help me out of this horrible situation."

Holmes rose to his feet. "You're no fool, Mr. Finucan. You could derive no benefit from hiding a semiprecious stone in a pitcher of dirty water in your room. I'm now quite certain that someone is trying to incriminate you, but I shall have to do further investigating to find the identity of the guilty party. Please try to make yourself as comfortable as possible. I'll return as soon as I'm able to prove the true culprit's identity."

Two days passed. Holmes spent much of that time investigating on his own, while I stayed at the inn catching up on my correspondence. He met with a handful of individuals who had worked with him when he was trying to bring down the Moriarty gang, but I saw very little of him until dinnertime two nights after our arrival, when Holmes approached my table at the inn's restaurant and immediately helped himself to bread and butter without a word to me. After he had consumed a couple of slices, I asked him about the progress he'd made in his investigation.

"I've worked with a couple of long-time allies in order to look into the backgrounds of Gorwydd and Butchart."

"Have you found anything incriminating?'

"No. Not one tiny scrap of evidence against either of them. Every penny of Kenn Gorwydd's income of the last decade either comes from his educational stipend or from his family's substantial coffers. Aside from Moriarty himself, we have not found a single person in his circle of acquaintance who can be definitively traced back to the Moriarty criminal empire.

"Comparatively, Mack Butchart's record is spotless, aside from his one vice: Gambling. He devotes four to six nights a week to playing cards, and he wins nine times out of ten. When he loses, his wallet is never lightened by more than a pound or two. Of his wins, most are substantial. His salary at the college is quite modest, but when paired with his gambling winnings, I'd say that there are peers of the realm who would look at his annual income with envy. Perhaps I'm exaggerating a bit, but not by very much.

"The people he plays with come from all walks of life. There are doctors, lawyers, a mayor from a neighbouring town, the barmaid at the

Orange Trout, policemen, shopkeepers, other professors . . . All of them have lost a great deal of money to him over the past year. I could certainly see him being the *victim* of a crime, as one of his fellow players might be prepared to turn to murder to avoid having to pay off a substantial debt. I suspect that he's devised a clever mathematical strategy for winning at cards. I certainly wouldn't mind knowing what it is."

The waiter arrived with a plate of stew for Holmes, who consumed half of it quickly, then ate the rest more slowly in-between sentences as he spoke to me.

"In any event, my agents have delved as deeply as possible into his finances, and we cannot find any evidence of Butchart receiving a penny of income that didn't come from his teaching stipend or from his gambling winnings. During the years of Moriarty's reign of terror, Butchart never spent or bet any money that couldn't be accounted for by his legitimate income. Indeed, Butchart started to make a considerable amount of money from gambling only well after Moriarty's fall, after he'd had a few additional years to refine whatever mathematical calculations he uses to win at cards. Prior to Moriarty's defeat and, for a few years afterwards, he was living precariously close to the bone, and had to sell a few personal items such as his grandfather's pocket watch, and a tie-pin belonging to his late brother."

"Then you've made no progress in the case?" I asked.

"Quite the contrary. As for the astrolabe, I have a fair idea of what happened to it. Do you remember Father Ribchester of St. Drogo's Church? He was instrumental in helping me find the evidence that brought down the branch of Moriarty's gang that was making a killing by skimming off hundreds of thousands of pounds from charitable organizations across the country. The Reverend Ribchester noticed something fishy, and his investigation led directly to the arrest and conviction of forty of Moriarty's cleverest criminal minds. You never met him, but you may have read about this incident in the newspapers – he was the priest who was nearly killed when a two-hundred-pound gargoyle fell off the roof of the church and came within four inches of striking his head, though his right foot was badly injured. That happened less than a week before we brought down Moriarty's entire organization.

"Father Ribchester got in touch with me the other day to warn me about a new gang of criminals who work in fencing stolen goods, mostly antiquities and jewels. They specialize in finding unscrupulous wealthy buyers for priceless items, as well as fixing up damaged antiques and selling them at an enormous profit. A little effort put into repair can reap great dividends. Apparently, a parishioner of his was very upset because her brother had pinched a neighbour's silverware and sold it to this organization. Being a public-spirited citizen, and since this information wasn't brought to him under the seal of the confessional, Father Ribchester is now trying to seek out some people who might be able to break up this syndicate of fencers. The group has been operating in this area for only a couple of months, and though the police are aware of its existence, my sources tell me that no one seems to know any specific figures who are involved, nor do they know just how large the organization is.

"There's one other interesting bit of information: That one garnet that was found in Finucan's water pitcher? It was indeed from the astrolabe, but not originally. It seems that the red jewels on the astrolabe were all rubies initially, but somewhere along the line one of them fell out and was lost . . . At least, that's the official story. Perhaps the ruby was stolen a while back, I don't know. But in any case, they couldn't find a proper ruby to replace the lost stone, so they simply replaced it with a far less-expensive garnet. The emeralds, diamonds, and sapphires on the astrolabe were all genuine, as far as I know."

"But you still don't know the identity of the thief?"

"I have a suspicion, nothing provable. After we've finished eating, I intend to return to the police station to test a hypothesis, although I don't know if my fishing expedition will be successful."

An hour later, we were sitting in the sergeant's office at the station. Finucan was seated in a wobbly wooden chair, Butchart and Gorwydd were resting on a bench on the side of the room, and Constable Sallow was leaning against the wall in the far corner of the room. The two academics were grumbling about being summoned, but Holmes ignored their surliness.

"Professors Butchart and Gorwydd, your presence is appreciated, but you deserve to know that I don't currently suspect you of wrongdoing. I admit that for a while I thought that one or both of you might have been criminal associates of the late Professor, but I'm now certain that neither of you was involved in these crimes. Moriarty did rely on a young student to help him with his work, and I'm quite sure I know who it was. You see, my dear Finucan, the brilliant mathematical mind who assisted Moriarty in his crimes was *you*."

"No!" Finucan howled.

"Oh, yes, it was!" Holmes nodded. "Doubtless this comes as a shock to you. I can assure you that as long as you behave yourself, you're in no danger of being thrown back into a dark and dingy cell. Perhaps you're doubting your own sanity at the moment, wondering if you have had some sort of mental break, with one aspect of your psyche committing shady deeds while your regular mindset is utterly unaware of the horrible things the other half of your mind has done. You can relax on this point, as you are most certainly not a character straight out of Robert Louis Stevenson. You aren't a criminal, and morally, you are just as blameless as Butchart and Gorwydd.

"Recently, I explained to Watson how I once devised a ratings system for people who were connected to Moriarty." Holmes related his four-point system, and after finishing, he paused for a length of time that might well have been for dramatic effect.

"For years, I was able to categorize everyone in Moriarty's orbit into one of these four categories. Recently, however, I realized that there's a fifth category that I never needed to use before now: *The individual in question contributed to Moriarty's criminal enterprises, but this person had absolutely no idea that he was carrying out illegal acts, and therefore is morally innocent of wrongdoing.*"

Holmes smiled at Finucan and nodded. "And now, the penny drops. Suddenly you are looking at your years working with the Professor in a very different light. Your conscience was always clear, because you had no idea that your laborious calculations were being put to nefarious ends. I will go through all the different ways that your work was exploited later, but I will begin by referencing one major example in your work with the mathematics behind *The Dynamics of an Asteroid*. You mentioned how you toiled on some numbers connected to the angles and forces behind a large falling object.

"It is my belief that Moriarty was using you to either do his work for him or to confirm his own calculations that were being used to target a brave priest, Father Ribchester, who was doing his part to bring down Moriarty's gang. Not wanting to cause a scandal or draw unwanted attention by murdering a prominent man of the cloth, Moriarty decided to have him killed, but to make it look like an accident. An enormous gargoyle was dislodged from the top of his church and sent hurtling down towards him. Your calculations were used to determine the precise place Father Ribchester was supposed to stand, how long the gargoyle would take to fall, and the precise angle at which the gargoyle should be pushed. Perhaps it was an error in the math, maybe it was the hand of Providence, or possibly it was simply pure luck, but Father Ribchester survived (though just barely), and the Moriarty gang was broken up before they could try again.

"Incidentally, the reason for Moriarty using such a dramatic means of attempting murder is because he wanted access to Father Ribchester's church. The falling gargoyle was meant to lead to the hiring of an engineering crew to check the structural integrity of the building. The team would have been filled with Moriarty's men, who would have replaced many of the church's artistic treasures with forgeries before submitting their report.

"I have no doubt that you're responding with shock and horror at the realization that your work, which you thought was done purely for the sake of bringing knowledge to the world, was instead used with the intent of harming people and stealing from them. I'm fairly certain that many of your other calculations were also used for nefarious purposes. Other examples of your work being corrupted probably include your research on angles and other factors being utilized by Colonel Sebastian Moran for some of the more difficult shots he had to take with his air rifle.

"As you have a functioning conscience, I believe that you're feeling a wave of guilt over this realization. This is unfair to you. You had no idea that this was happening, and you bear no moral or legal responsibility for the way that Moriarty abused your trust and your work. Incidentally, I wouldn't be surprised if Moriarty also appropriated some of Butchart and Gorwydd's work for his own sinister purposes, though they were just as unaware of his true intentions as you were.

"You may be wondering how I've been able to clear Butchart and Gorwydd's names, especially since you found it so impossible to prove the negative that you yourself were not Moriarty's accomplice. Indeed, there is no definitive evidence that could clear their names beyond a shadow of a doubt, but there are a few telling points that convince me they had nothing to do with the Moriarty gang.

"First of all, my agents could find no evidence that Butchart had received any inexplicable money from any outside source. He had just barely been making ends meet, and there was no evidence of his receiving any money from outside means. Had he been working with Moriarty, he would have received substantial compensation, and he wouldn't have had to sell – not just pawn, but sell – items belonging to beloved family members. His luck at the gambling table was due to mathematical cleverness, and his fortunes only changed for the better long after Moriarty was no more. Butchart, therefore, wasn't a suspicious figure to me.

"Gorwydd, in comparison, was always talking about how his brilliance could make him the ultimate criminal. This is an eyebrow-raising comment to make, but when one thinks about it for a while, it actually works in his favour. Had Gorwydd truly been a member of Moriarty's crew, the Professor would have made absolutely certain that Gorwydd never said anything that might lead people to suspect he was involved in criminal activity.

"In any event, it was far safer and more profitable for Moriarty to exploit innocent people's work. Not only was he spared a security risk with one less-dangerous tongue to wag, but he also didn't have to pay these unwitting helpers anything. This is why he never recruited you. Aside from your character not being suited for a life of crime, the risks and costs of bringing mathematical students into his fold overwhelmingly outweighed the potential benefits.

"Having addressed the matter of whether or not Moriarty had a student mathematician in his employ, you are now probably wondering, if neither you nor your former colleagues are criminals, then who stole the astrolabe? Aside from the three of you, there was one person who was known to be present at the time of the crime: That person was Constable Sallow."

Sallow made a sudden movement, but Holmes had warned me to be ready, and I grabbed him before he could either run or attack. Holmes gave me a satisfied nod and continued.

"There was hardly anyone else on campus just then, so the list of suspects was small. It was Sallow who saw the astrolabe in the glass case and decided to seize an opportunity. With no one else around, he smashed the case, pocketed the astrolabe, and then raised the alarm, pretending to have discovered the theft that he committed himself. Sallow gave himself away by planting the garnet. Not only was he was the only person who couldn't have stolen the astrolabe, but who also had the opportunity to plant it in your room. Your former colleagues could have stolen the astrolabe, but they couldn't have planted the garnet.

"Sallow bore you no ill will, Finucan – you were simply a convenient scapegoat. Your supposed friends' false accusations simply played into his hands. But why did he violate the trust placed upon him by the community? Financial gain is the obvious reason, and though a man can have many reasons for being in debt, I made a very shrewd deduction that Mr. Butchart was responsible for Sallow's need to risk everything in order to make a little extra money. My investigator told me that Butchart was taking large sums of money from a very diverse group of card players – including members of law enforcement. My suspicion that Sallow was one of those fleeced individuals proved prescient.

"Sallow took the astrolabe to a criminal syndicate specializing in fencing rare and valuable stolen goods. As a member of law enforcement, he knew of their existence and how to reach out to them. They were quite interested in the astrolabe, but they had contempt for the nearly worthless garnet in the setting, which replaced a valuable ruby that was lost or stolen at some point in the past. They removed the garnet and handed it back to Sallow along with his payment. Doubtless they planned to reset the astrolabe with a genuine ruby in order to increase its value when they sold the refurbished astrolabe on the black market. In the meantime, they jettisoned the barely-precious stone, which was only worth a shilling or two at most.

"Sallow considered simply throwing away the garnet, as it was of little value to him and could serve only to incriminate him. But then he hatched the idea of using the garnet to clinch the case against you. When he pretended to search your room, he slipped the garnet into the water pitcher and 'discovered' it. Again, he didn't bear you any personal ill will, but he wanted to close the case, and you were simply an easy means of redirecting suspicion away from him. Incidentally, I wondered if the chambermaid might have planted the garnet, but I dismissed this idea, as I soon learned that was working at the time of the robbery, and it would have been foolish for a culprit to put himself in her power by involving her in a frame-up, and putting her into position as a potential blackmailer."

Some of Sallow's colleagues led him away to the cells. Butchart and Gorwydd hurried away without a word or even a glance at their former friend. I wondered if they felt the slightest bit of guilt for attempting to fasten the blame upon him. Upon reflection, I realized that part of their desperate attempt to incriminate Finucan was based on an attempt to protect themselves from suspicion of being involved in Moriarty's web by pointing the finger towards their colleague. In any case, Finucan was too relieved to take offense. Soon, we were back at the inn, enjoying restoratives. Finucan looked as if he was in desperate need of something to bolster his strength."

After finishing the last of his pint of bitter, Holmes turned to Finucan. "Now that you know what happened, there remains the issue of your future. Unfortunately, institutions of higher learning are obsessed with their own reputations, often at the expense of innocent people whose lives are shattered by unjust suspicions and cruel innuendoes with no basis in truth. My inquiries have confirmed that as frustrating as it may be and, to the best of my knowledge, no college or university in the United Kingdom is willing to provide you with an opportunity to make a living. Employers are simply too frightened by your close association to Moriarty.

"Therefore, if you seek a career outside of manual labour that will allow you to use your undoubtedly impressive mathematical skills, I suggest that you need to pursue unconventional employment. Thankfully, I've managed to find a man who is in need of an individual with your skills, and he has no fears about hiring a man with your unfortunate connection. My brother Mycroft's work for the British Government requires a team of skillful mathematicians to help him determine economic policies, rates of risk versus reward, and various issues connected to national security – although due to its nature, the work is quite secretive, and you won't be allowed the same level of recognition in intellectual circles that an academic job provides. We can discuss the matter in depth in the coming days, but if you accept this well-paying position, I can assure you that the work will be fascinating, and absolutely essential to the good of the country."

There were tears in Finucan's eyes. "That sounds wonderful."

I smiled at the young man. The last several years had been difficult for him, but now it finally looked as if his luck had turned.

The Mysterious Death
of the Russian Anarchist
by Jonathan Schneer

Many years have passed since Sherlock Holmes and I looked into the mysterious death of the Russian anarchist, Mikhailovich Kravchinski, or "Stepniak" as he was better known. Even today, neither one of us can recall that miserable affair without a shake of the head and sigh of regret. As my friend rapidly and brilliantly understood, M. Stepniak's passing was not merely cruel and unnecessary, which most premature and unexpected deaths are. It was also the result of a third party's matchless cynicism, whose ramifications we could not then measure, but which continue to reverberate even now – albeit, with consequences yet to be apprehended and, as I suspect, much to be feared.

I can fix the date of the poor man's death precisely, for Holmes noticed it on Christmas Eve morning, 1895, a Tuesday, and Stepniak had perished the previous day. I had no rounds at Barts Hospital on Christmas Eve, and Holmes was in a fallow period, but not yet chafing, and in fact rather enjoying the lull accompanying the holiday season. I still can see him as he was then, at our breakfast table sipping his morning coffee, and beyond, through the window, grey Baker Street, for at that time of year the early morning sun reached it only indirectly. Holmes suddenly raised his eyebrows, his gaze focused, although not on the newspaper he held before him.

"A curious conjuncture, Watson, I think."

I looked at him enquiringly.

"See here," he said rustling the newssheet. "The Grand Duchess, Xenia Alexandra, daughter of the Russian Tsar Alexander II, is in Denmark with her husband, the Grand Duke Alexander Mikhailovich. The couple propose extending their European tour with a visit to this country. The Duchess is, after all, our Queen's niece by marriage."

"And?" I asked him.

He turned the page of the newspaper to find the entry that interested him. "'*Death of a Russian Anarchist*'," he read to me, and put his finger to the line of print as he read. "'*A shocking accident occurred yesterday on the North and South-Western Railway, Chiswick, by which the well-known Russian exile and author, M. Stepniak was killed.*'" His finger slid downwards as he continued. "'*M. Stepniak was noticed walking down the road, absorbed in thought or reading. A moment later the whistle of an approaching train was heard, and it was seen that at the level crossing the unfortunate man had been caught by the engine, which had knocked him down, and the whole train passed over his body, which was terribly mutilated.*'" Holmes looked up at me, over the newspaper.

"Awful," I murmured. I paused for a moment pondering. "But I fail to see the connection between the poor man's accidental death and the possibility that a Russian Duchess and Grand Duke may call upon our Queen."

"Ah, Watson," said he, sighing, still regarding me steadily. "Because the connection is not visible to your eye hardly means it does not exist. I fancy – "

But he interrupted himself. "A cab has stopped, and a man has stepped from it." Then, a moment later, "It is Brother Mycroft. His gout has eased. He has not yet breakfasted."

"Holmes – " I began, for the window was behind him. He could have seen nothing, and the latter two observations confounded me. But before I could complete the sentence, Mrs. Hudson had knocked at our door and appeared in our sitting room with Mycroft Holmes only a step behind. Belatedly, I realized that he couldn't have kept up with her climbing the stairs if gout was troubling him and, of course, Holmes had recognized his brother's heavy tread the moment he set foot outside the vehicle that had conveyed him to our premises.

"Good morning, Sherlock," the big man greeted him. He nodded in my direction. "Dr. Watson." And then in his deep, rumbling, voice, "Mrs. Hudson, would you be so kind as to give me a boiled egg and pot of coffee?" And to us both: "You will have realized already that my man spends Christmas Eve with his family, and that consequently I have had nothing to eat this day."

"But you enjoyed last night's curry," Holmes observed dryly, and Mycroft glanced at the faint spot on his sleeve.

"Ahmed was born in Delhi," Mycroft conceded – which I belatedly remembered, and I understood how Holmes knew his relative had dined on curry and not a chop the night before. "And you both know he married an English girl," which I also belatedly remembered, from which I understood why, despite being a Mohammedan, Ahmed was with his family and unable to cook for his master that day or the next. As usual, my friend had been far ahead of me.

"But of course you were expecting me," Mycroft continued, gesturing at the newspaper.

"Russian aristocrats and anarchists," Holmes observed almost dreamily.

"Naturally," said Mycroft, "the War Office keeps an eye on both."

"And you keep an eye on the War Office."

His brother made a dismissive sound. "In light of the royal pair's pending visit, my colleagues are particularly interested in Russian anarchists at the moment." He paused to add, "Although I readily admit they have caused us little trouble of late."

"The Fenians too, appear to have gone silent," Holmes agreed. "It was a Frenchman who carried out the bombing last year in Greenwich."

"We are watching them all," Mycroft said. "The Irish are merely hibernating, I think. But when any anarchist residing here comes to a sticky end, we must look into it, whatever the nationality."

"There is more to it than that, I fancy," said Holmes. He was gazing shrewdly at his brother.

Mycroft nodded. "Of course, or I would not have come to you. M. Stepniak dead – of all people. His most recent book appeared only two days ago, less than twenty-four hours before he met his end."

"I'm aware of that," said Holmes. "I glance often at his newspaper, *Free Russia.*"

"Then," said Mycroft, "you must know that he has traveled a long distance – I don't mean only in miles – since the day in 1878 when he stabbed to death the state chief of police, General Mezentsov, in St. Petersburg."

"He has been rather wandering from the pure anarchist doctrine in recent publications," Holmes agreed dryly, "but I haven't read his latest effort. As you say, it has only just come out."

"I have read it in proof," said Mycroft. "It is an important statement. In it, M. Stepniak renounces '*propaganda of the deed*'. But I would not yet call him a meliorist. He still advocates violent methods as a last resort."

"Do you think some anarchist madman considered that a betrayal and pushed him to his death?" I broke in. "Do you want your brother to find out which of them it was?"

"The Russians have been quiet of late," Holmes reminded me, "and, in any event, no witness to the incident reported anything untoward."

"What then?" I asked. "If there was no foul play, it must be as the newspaper says. M. Stepniak was absorbed in his book, or in his thoughts, and did not hear the approaching train."

"M. Stepniak was preternaturally alert, Doctor," Mycroft explained. "He had to be, or would not have lived so long. He survived guerrilla warfare in Bosnia and the anarchist uprising in Benevento. He managed a successful escape from Petersburg after stabbing Mezentsov. No doubt, he has been looking over his shoulder ever since – even while living here in

London. It is nearly inconceivable that he walked inadvertently before a locomotive."

"Do you believe the Russian royals had something to do with his death?" I asked. "Surely, that is inconceivable."

"I do not know," Mycroft stated. "But they plan to visit here, and the man stepped in front of a train. The question is: Why did he?"

"If there is a connection, we need to find it," Holmes spoke up, and drew a happy breath. "The game's afoot, Watson. I thought it was, as soon as I saw the morning paper. Grab your cloak and hat. We're off to Chiswick."

We left Mycroft sitting contentedly before not one but two boiled eggs, a rasher of bacon, a rack of toast, small pots of marmalade and butter, and a large jug of steaming black coffee. A short railway journey brought us from Baker Street to Turnham Green, from which it was rather a pleasant walk to Woodstock Road, in the salubrious neighborhood called Bedford Park. Holmes consulted the newspaper carrying the account of M. Stepniak's death.

"He lived at Number 48," he reported. "Let us take just a peek."

It proved to be a large house, semi-detached, three stories tall, with a well-tended garden at the front and sides – not the sort of place in which I imagined a Russian anarchist might reside. That morning it was the destination of a steady stream of visitors, many of them obviously foreign, most bearing wreaths and flowers, all come to pay their respects to the unhappy widow. We saw her framed in the doorway more than once as she greeted the mourners, or bade them farewell. She was a pretty woman, but very pale. We could not fail to recognize several prominent British personages among her well-wishers – literary people, leading trade unionists, a Labour M.P.

"Holmes," said I, greatly surprised, "that man just leaving is Dr. Spence Watson, a Liberal Party *eminence gris*."

"Confirming what I have long surmised," Holmes replied. "There was more to M. Stepniak than you might imagine." He turned away. "I have seen enough here. Let us examine the fatal crossing. The event occurred only yesterday. The police have had no reason to inspect it, and we still may find something of interest there."

We turned from the house to walk north along Woodstock Road which, in those days, ended in a field and continued as a footpath until it reached the railway crossing, ten minutes from the house. The crossing was entirely unprotected. No bridge spanned the rails. On either side were two low wooden fences running parallel to them, risible as barriers. On our side, the footpath led to a stile for climbing the fence. Next to it was a notice board with the words *"Beware of Trains"* printed in large black letters. Holmes mounted the stile, scanning in both directions. The railway stretched half-a-mile either way, straight as an arrow might fly. It seemed inconceivable that Stepniak could have climbed over the stile and stepped before a passing train inadvertently.

Holmes slid down the other side of the stile and crouched low. "Ah." He pointed to a boot-heel impression dug into the dirt between stile and rail. Then, he crawled the remaining few yards to the track on hands and knees, his face no more than six inches from the ground. Whatever he saw seemed to please him. When he rose, he examined his immediate surroundings with the same intensity and spotted something a few feet up the railway line. "Look!" He picked up a cigar, half smoked. "Jamaican," he said. "Not inexpensive." He smiled slightly and muttered, "I would wager that M. Stepniak was right-handed."

As so often, I watched and waited, and tried to reason as my friend was doing, and could not. What did it matter that a cigar, which could have belonged to anyone, and not necessarily to M. Stepniak, lay two paces distant from the stile? What could be the import of a heel-print that likewise, as I judged, could have been left between stile and rail by any passing stranger? And why ever could it be significant that the dead man had been right-handed?

But Holmes was not finished. He was tramping purposefully along the rail, scanning eagerly in both directions. I remembered that the train had dragged the body of the unfortunate Stepniak some thirty yards.

"They mentioned he was reading a book, but never gave a title," Holmes said. "Perhaps they never found it." Suddenly, perhaps ten yards along, he stooped to pick up a *Lett's Pocket Diary* from among the weeds parallel to the track. He brandished it before me. "Ha! As I suspected: The man was not reading during his final moments. He was *writing*."

Holmes began thumbing through its pages. "Here is the final entry." He showed me a single word, written in Russian, under the date, December 23rd. The word was: *"Достаточно!"* I peered at my friend, mystified. *"Enough!"* Holmes translated.

We attended the inquest on Friday, the day after Boxing Day. A dozen witnesses testified. I paid little attention to the equal number of attending reporters, but examined Stepniak's friends and colleagues with interest, and listened carefully not only to them but also to the railwaymen and passersby who had witnessed the tragedy.

Members of the Russian émigré community were easy to identify, not only by their thick accents, but by their appearance as well. Their dress betrayed them. All wore shabby, heavy overcoats, trousers that had gone shiny at the knee, and scuffed footwear. To a man, they had long hair. Most had long beards as well. Quite obviously, they had not prospered as Sergei Stepniak had done. One called Lazar Goldenburg, a short thin bespectacled man, claimed to have been the first to discover the body, and to have rushed to tell Stepniak's wife what had happened. Another, George Lazerov, also short, but in his case stout, explained that he and Goldenburg had been walking together, intending to join Stepniak at the home of yet a fourth anarchist, Felix Volkovsky, to discuss founding a new political journal of which Stepniak was to be the editor. He mentioned that the "line" the new journal would take was in dispute, and divided them to a degree. I thought that might be important, a falling-out among men for whom violence was a way of life, and glanced at Holmes. He was watching keenly, but said nothing, and his face remained inscrutable.

Was it possible that Stepniak had neither seen nor heard the approaching train? The engine driver thought not. He had seen the deceased getting over the stile when the engine was thirty or forty yards from the crossing and immediately had opened the whistle. "The deceased appeared to hesitate a moment and then rushed across the line and was knocked down."

But George Lazerov thought it likely. "His friend had a great deal of work on hand which was urgent and important, and when that was the case, he was frequently lost in deep thought and very absent-minded." It occurred to me that Mr. Lazerov intended to minimize such disagreements as had divided the little anarchist circle. I stole another glance in Holmes's direction. As before, his face revealed nothing.

But then another of Stepniak's associates, obviously neither émigré nor anarchist, supported Mr. Lazerov: York Powell, Regius Professor of History at Oxford, a tall man who was, by his own proud admission, "a friend to all who long for liberty". He knew Stepniak through an organization called the "Friends of Russian Freedom", which the latter had founded, and he, Powell, had supported. Professor Powell was elegantly dressed. His black top hat rested on his razor-pressed trousers at his knees. His white shirt-cuffs, fastened by black onyx cufflinks, each with a facing gold eagle, peeped from the sleeves of his well-cut frock coat. Professor Powell said that Stepniak had dined as his guest at his club, the Reform, the evening before his death. They had drunk brandy. Stepniak had smoked a cigar. He had been in the best of spirits. The terrible event the next day could only have been an accident. "There was nothing to lead anyone to think he would take his life."

And then, Mr. Tchaycovsky, yet another of Stepniak's Russian anarchist friends, said the same thing: "He would never have taken his own life. There was no reason for it. He had exceptionally brilliant prospects and was particularly respected and loved by his friends."

Holmes rose, his face grim. "There is nothing more to be learned here."

And we left.

The next morning, Saturday, December 28th, was grey and threatening rain. We made our way to Waterloo Station to attend a memorial service in the dead man's honor. It was an impressive demonstration, attended not only by many who were entirely new to me, but by those I had seen at the inquest the previous day, the Regius Professor prominent among them, not least because he stood a full head taller than they, and also, by those who had paid their respects at Woodford Road the day before that. Once again, I saw the Labour M.P., the Liberal Party *eminence gris*, the playwrights and poets. Holmes identified additional notables I didn't recognize.

"There is the daughter of Karl Marx and her paramour. That is the radical artist and poet, William Morris. That's Bernstein, a leader of the German Socialist Party, and that's the Italian anarchist, Malatesta." I hadn't suspected my friend possessed such knowledge.

A band playing "The Dead March" arrived, preceding the open hearse which bore a white coffin garlanded with flowers. Then the grieving widow, who fell upon the coffin, kissing it and weeping. One after another the dignitaries spoke briefly from a parapet before the station, extolling the dead man, lamenting all that had been lost with him, insisting that his cause had not died with him – and indeed would never die until all men were free. They spoke in German, Russian, Polish, French, Yiddish, none of which I understood. But perhaps the Regius Professor said it best, and in the Queen's English: "Sergei had the heart of a lion, the nature of a child. He had much to live for. His mission, a free Russia, still called to him, as it calls to us, even now."

An hour and it was done. The coffin was brought into the station and loaded onto a train whose destination was the crematorium at Woking. The crowd began to disperse. Holmes took my arm in a grip of iron and we hurried to the front of the station. I was about to question him, but, "Hush!" he commanded, and signaled for a two-wheeler. "Hold," he said to the cabbie, and we watched as Professor York Powell, his top hat marking him out from the rest, hailed a cab himself. "Ten to one, it's the Reform Club," Holmes told our driver, "But follow at first to make sure." By the time the hansom cab in front of us had reached Trafalgar Square, Holmes knew its destination. He knocked at the roof and our driver pulled up. "We'll walk from here," Holmes told him, paying him off. To me he said, "We want him comfortable when we confront him."

"Confront him?" I could not help asking. "For goodness' sake, what for?"

"I have seen much to appall me in my time," Holmes said grimly, "but this is cold-blooded evil such as I never have encountered." He sighed. "I fear there is little that I, myself, can do about it — except to ensure it does not happen again." That was all he would tell me, as we made our way along Cockspur Street to the eastern end of Pall Mall, past the Atheneum. The broad avenue stretched before us. Besides the Army and Navy, I knew many of the other Pall Mall clubs by reputation: the Travellers, the Oxford and Cambridge, the Diogenes, the Carlton, the Jockey Club, the Guards, and several more. We stopped before the heavy double portals of the Reform Club, seat of British Liberalism.

"It is not my brand of politics," Holmes said, "but I once did the head porter a great favor." Moments later, that man having told us where to find Professor Powell, we were inside the imposing building and climbing a grand dark staircase. Aristocrats, and their dogs and horses, stared down at us from ornate gilt frames. Enormous statues with sightless eyes loomed blindly, recalling Roman emperors. We walked swiftly through one vast chamber, in which men sat on scattered couches and armchairs, reading or chatting quietly, and into another. Professor York Powell was sitting in an overstuffed chair in an alcove at its far end, with a whisky-and-soda on the side table next to him. He was reaching for a copy of that day's *Times*. He looked up as we approached, but did not recognize us, and was therefore startled when Holmes drew up a chair to sit by his side. I took another, and sat opposite Holmes. I had no idea what would happen next.

"*Достаточно*," Holmes breathed. He pronounced it in the Russian manner: "*Destatichna*." York Powell did not so much as move.

"Do not tell me," Holmes nearly growled, "that you fail to understand."

The professor regarded Holmes calmly. I hadn't seen him before at close quarters. Now, I noted the set jaw, masked by a full dark beard, his strong, yellow teeth, his beak of a nose, his glinting grey eyes. For all the hours that its owner must have spent in libraries and archives, it was a formidable visage, set atop a square, strong torso. The frock coat was gone. Now, a white handkerchief peeped from the breast pocket of the black suit jacket he'd worn to Stepniak's funeral. The professor removed a pair of reading spectacles to examine my friend carefully.

"Who are you, and what do you want?" He was not the least bit rattled.

414

Holmes reached into his pocket and withdrew Stepniak's diary, but he held it just out of reach, so that Professor Powell had to stretch for it. As he did so, Holmes grabbed the man's wrist. "As I thought," he said, and let the wrist go, and drew back the diary. "Mark the cufflinks, Watson. Facing gold eagles on a black background." I was mystified.

"Tell me what you know," the professor commanded. "Tell me who you are." That was all.

Holmes regarded him steadily. "I am Sherlock Holmes. And you, Englishman though you may be, Professor York Powell, are the colleague of the Russian blackguard, Pyotr Rachkovsky, who is based in Paris, and directs *Okhrana* operations throughout Europe. You are no sympathizer of subject peoples struggling to be free. That is merely your affectation and pose. You wear your true affiliation on your sleeve. It is an unpardonable demonstration of vanity and arrogance – and indeed, it is what first gave you away. You would have been safer had you not attended the inquest and memorial service, but I suppose you thought his friends expected that you would."

"Mr. Sherlock Holmes," said York Powell thoughtfully. "I see you do know who I am, and I congratulate you on being the first of your countrymen to recognize the design on my cufflinks. I wear them on special occasions only. They seemed appropriate to wear these last few days."

"*Okhrana*," said I, the first glimmerings of understanding coming to me. "The Tsar's secret police."

York Powell seemed to notice me for the first time. "You must be Dr. Watson. I have read your stories in *The Strand*. They are most amusing. I never thought to meet you. I am pleased to make your acquaintance."

"Sergei Stepniak threw himself in front of that locomotive to escape from you," Holmes said. "He stood on the stile waiting for the train. He was smoking a cigar, as was his habit, as you yourself testified at the inquest." Holmes pulled an envelope from his pocket and extracted the remnants of the cigar. "A Jamaican," he said, holding it before York Powell. "They cost three shillings each. No man throws one away half-smoked – unless he is very rich, which Stepniak was not, or because he has just come to a supremely important decision and decided to act upon it."

York Powell said nothing. Holmes continued. "M. Stepniak saw the train. He heard the whistle. He did act. He threw the cigar away to his right, where I found it, sprang from the stile onto soft earth, landing on one heel. He stepped once more on the ground before the rails, lightly, with his toes. The marks were nearly gone, but I saw them. Then he launched himself into the path of the oncoming train, still clutching the little Lett's

415

diary, in which he had just been writing. The great wheel wrenched it from his hand and sent it spinning just past the cinders onto the verge, where I came upon it as well."

Still York Powell remained silent.

"When I read the diary entry for December 23rd," Holmes explained, "I knew what I already suspected: The poor man had decided to end his life. '*Enough!*' he wrote, minutes before he died. And, when I saw your cufflinks at the inquest, I knew the *Okhrana* was involved."

"Clever," said the Regius Professor.

"It is obvious you forced him to it," Holmes went on.

Finally, York Powell permitted himself a gesture. It was a smile of triumph. He thought, as I was just beginning to realize, that however guilty Holmes deemed him, indeed however guilty he was, Sherlock Holmes could not bring him to justice. There had been murder, but there was no murder weapon, except a train. Moreover, no doubt he, the man responsible for Stepniak's death, had been far from the scene when Stepniak died.

"*Достаточно*," he repeated, and he was no longer smiling. "M. Stepniak had had enough of living a double life."

Holmes steepled his fingers and said nothing. His gaze at York Powell was hard and unrelenting.

"He has belonged to us for twenty years," said the professor who was also a foreign agent, "but then he tried to forget it."

"The police caught him after he stabbed General Mezentsov in Petersburg nearly two decades ago," Holmes explained. "He escaped shortly thereafter – because you let him."

I felt like a man furiously pedaling a low-geared bicycle trying to keep up with a faster man on a better vehicle.

"You broke him first," Holmes went on, "in Petersburg in '78. You made him your creature. He would not have escaped, had you not allowed it."

"Well," said Powell, "not I personally."

"He thought he had left you behind forever when he fled to England. Over time, he moderated his views. He wrote books. He lectured. He grew successful. He took a wife."

"He had become practically a meliorist," I put in, "an advocate of peaceful methods." I was beginning to understand the dimensions of the tragedy. A man haunted by disclosures he made under unspeakable duress had flown to London, and mistakenly thought he had found safe harbor. He had mistakenly thought he could be a force for good, and had taken his own life when he realized he could not be.

416

"Almost a meliorist, yes," Powell assented. "Most unfortunately for us and, in the end, for him as well."

"The *Okhrana* needs its anarchists to be wild men, absolute nihilists," said Holmes, "or it has no reason for being, no one to persecute. Moreover, it needs bogeymen with whom to frighten the Russian public. It needs an easily discredited opposition. M. Stepniak's recent work must have annoyed you considerably."

York Powell nodded. "It did. We had to put a stop to it. We had to remind him that he belonged to us."

"So you went to him when you learned," Holmes continued, "several days before the press did – that the Grand Duchess, Xenia Alexandra, and her husband, the Grand Duke Alexander Mikhailovich, were planning to come to this country. You told him to organize a terrorist act when they arrived."

Powell shrugged. "He didn't want to do it. He could be most stubborn. I threatened to unmask him before all the friends who so respected him, before the wife who loved him." He shrugged again. "I thought that would be sufficient. But Sergei Stepniak had had 'enough'."

"You are a fool," said Holmes. "Your policy of encouraging terrorism will not save your master, the Tsar. Rather, it will doom him."

"It is working so far." Powell replied.

"*Достаточно*," said Holmes in disgust. "I, too, have had enough."

The Diogenes Club was five minutes' walk down Pall Mall. A driving rain had begun, accompanied by a cold wind. "I have no doubt we shall find Mycroft there," Holmes told me, and we did. A quarter-hour after leaving the Reform, we were seated with my friend's brother in a room no less grand than the one we had just exited, and equally uncrowded, but this time with little puddles of rainwater pooling at our feet. Mycroft sat before the crackling fireplace, Holmes and I sat to either side, warming.

Mycroft thrust his hands before the fire. "To destroy the Tsar's enemies," he explained, "they encourage the Tsar's enemies to commit atrocities. It is, as you say, Sherlock, a most shortsighted program. And, moreover, in this instance, it was for naught." He pulled a paper from his breast pocket, a copy of a telegram from the Foreign Office, and read to us aloud: "'*Owing to an unexpected illness, the Grand Duke Alexander Mikhailovich begs to inform Her Majesty that the planned excursion with the Grand Duchess to Windsor must be postponed.*'" Mycroft added: "Sergei Stepniak died too soon."

That brought me up sharp. "How so? Did you sympathize with him?"

Holmes's brother shook his head. "Not for a minute, meliorist or no. We are not socialists. But we were pleased by the evolution in his viewpoint. We thought that in time we might turn him to our advantage. Unfortunately, Professor Powell put paid to that."

"Surely so great a villain cannot be allowed to go scot-free!" I protested. "He is a murderer!"

"Do not worry on that score," Holmes assured me. "The good professor's days as a British agent of the *Okhrana* are over. I cannot put him in jail, but I have no doubt my brother's people will find a way to make his life a misery."

Mycroft nodded. "We can do that. Oxford nearly belongs to us. We will put out the word. Henceforth, the professor lives in Purdah. No decent man or woman will receive him, or study or work with, or for, him. He will be a marked man. Moreover, now we know him, we will dog his steps. We will ensure he makes no more mischief. He will go on living, but he will not enjoy it. Effectively, his life is over."

Mycroft turned to his brother. "You have done it, Sherlock, as I knew you would, unmasking a dangerous and conscienceless foreign agent in the process. Her Majesty's Government is indebted to you once again."

"Even so," responded Sherlock Holmes, "this little case leaves a bad taste." He waved away a servant offering to take our orders for drink. "Thank you, but I feel need of my violin." He faced his brother. "This will not surprise you, Mycroft. Vitali's "Chaconne in G Minor" is the piece I shall play. It is dreadful, soaring, sad, and mysterious – as I expect Russia's future will be."

He stood. "Come, Watson. Baker Street calls."

And so we passed out into the dreary day.

Sergey Mikhaylovich Stepnyak-Kravchinsky
aka Sergius Stepniak
13 July, 1851 – 23 December, 1895

A Matter of ABC
by Susan Knight

"I have to say, Watson, this really isn't good enough. Wherever has the dratted woman gotten to now?"

Holmes drummed impatient fingers on the breakfast table, the cause of his irritation being our landlady, Mrs. Hudson. She, who was usually so prompt, was late on this dismal February morning in bringing us our boiled eggs and toast. I should add that there was often a diverting element to this daily ritual: While I happily settled for whatever was placed in front of me, Holmes was most particular regarding his eggs. Five-minutes-and-fifteen-seconds for a just-set white and a soft yolk. Any less, he claimed, and the albumen would be disgustingly runny. Any longer and the yolk would be too set for the soldiers of toast. If he complained, which he did frequently, Mrs. Hudson would reply sharply, "Mr. Holmes, I have better things to do than stand over a hot stove counting seconds. If you don't like the way I make your egg, why don't you cook it yourself, over that Bunsen burner of yours?"

"Do you not think that I might have better things to do?" was Holmes's customary riposte.

At which, Mrs. Hudson would sniff and swish off out of the room with our cleared plates, only pretending to be offended. The pair of them relished their verbal duals.

On this particular morning, however, the ordinarily punctual lady was nowhere to be seen. We waited a little longer, Holmes becoming ever more testy, until he flung down the morning paper, leapt to his feet, and expressed the startling notion that he was going to find out exactly what was going on "down there".

To venture into the kingdom below stairs where Mrs. Hudson reigned supreme! I had to be part of this epic confrontation and followed him down to the kitchen.

An astonishing sight met our eyes as we burst through the door. Even Holmes was taken aback. An unknown woman, in the throes of a violent hysterical fit, was clinging desperately to our landlady who, in turn, was trying without success to calm her, while Phoebe, the little scullery maid, stood awkwardly in the corner, looking on with big eyes.

"Oh, Dr. Watson!" exclaimed Mrs. Hudson. "Thank goodness you're here. Please try and pacify Nelly, will you, for I cannot."

Holmes, never at ease in the presence of powerful female emotions, rather shrank into the shadows with Phoebe while I tended to the distressed woman.

"Now Nelly," I said, for I did not know what else to call her, "take some deep breaths."

I tested the pulse in her wrist and then laid firm fingers upon her burning forehead, encouraging her in her breathing. Gradually she calmed down.

"Now, please tell us what is troubling you,"

The fit looked about to start up again.

"It's her son, Ralph," Mrs. Hudson explained quickly. "My nephew."

Suddenly everything fell into place. This Nelly had to be Mrs. Hudson's widowed sister, with whom she had journeyed to Paris a year or so earlier, as I remembered, in order to extract the same young blade from a pickle. * Now, it seemed, he was causing trouble again.

"I'm sorry about your breakfasts, gentlemen," Mrs. Hudson remarked, "but Nelly was in such a state. I couldn't leave her."

I assumed that she would not trust Phoebe, ever accident-prone, to negotiate the stairs safely with a laden tray.

"Are these our eggs?" Holmes asked grimly, indicating a pot bubbling on the stove.

"Oh dear!" Mrs. Hudson exclaimed. "They must be well and truly done by now . . . Never mind," she continued, "I can add them to a kedgeree for supper, and boil up two fresh ones for you now."

"Make a good strong pot of tea as well, Mrs. Hudson, if you please," I said. "I think we could all do with a cup. And then, perhaps, your sister . . . Mrs. . . . er . . . ."

"Morris."

"Yes, thank you. Perhaps Mrs. Morris can then explain exactly what is troubling her."

I ignored the dark look shot my way by Holmes. My concern had to be with the lady. Her colour was unnaturally high and her pulse was racing. I quite feared for her heart. Sharing her problem might help to ease her mind.

So, while Mrs. Hudson busied herself making tea, and Holmes, refusing to sit with me at the kitchen table, leaned against the Welsh dresser tapping an impatient foot, Mrs. Morris relayed her tale. It seemed that after returning home from Paris with his mother to the northern city of Liverpool, the young man could not settle.

"You see, Doctor, Ralph had so wanted to succeed as an artist in Paris that the thought of getting an ordinary job in an office or bank, as his late father had done, appealed not at all . . . And Ralph could have been an artist, Martha, couldn't he? He possesses a natural talent."

"Mmm." Mrs. Hudson's back was non-committal.

"I suggested he take up his brushes again, but he refused. Or only, he said, as a house painter. Of course, he was joking."

Being on the estuary of a large river that emptied into the Irish Sea, Liverpool bustled with ocean-going vessels as well as smaller craft. Ralph soon found employment as a clerk in a shipping office, the which, according to his mother, engendered in the restless young man a yearning to travel – to seek his fortune, as he told her, in the colonies.

Was this then the source of her anguish, that her only son might leave her for distant parts? No, not at all. That she would not have minded. (A muffled snort from Mrs. Hudson.) The problem was that, all too soon, Ralph had found himself in bad company, with fellows who led him astray.

"Of course, he's not paid nearly enough by the company for all the work that he does. He is so very very conscientious, you see." (Mrs. Hudson's back twitched.) "So poor Ralph is always short of money. Running up debts all over the place, Doctor, which I've often had to settle for him."

"Money you can ill afford." Mrs. Hudson, turning at last, placed a big teapot on the table.

"Yes, but Martha," her sister continued, "Ralph has assured me there would be severe reprisals if the debts were to remain unpaid. Nasty people might come looking for him. He might even be shipped abroad against his will at Her Majesty's pleasure." She stared at us through wide open and slightly foolish eyes. "That means as a prisoner, doesn't it? Oh, I've been so afraid for him!"

Mrs. Hudson's pursed lips, as she poured tea into cups for us all, while stirring a heaped spoonful of sugar into Nelly's, seemed to say that such a fate might not be a bad thing, and might even put manners on the boy. Ralph was clearly no favourite of hers.

"So then, as I said," her sister continued, "he met these fellows, Ken and Bill. They came to the house one time, and one time only. Two bad lots and no mistake. I told Ralph to have nothing more to do with them. But did he listen to his mother?" Her look challenged us. "Of course not!" She wrung her hands. "Oh, if only dear George were still around to tell him what's what!"

"Nelly's late husband," Mrs. Hudson explained.

"He was my rock . . . ." She gave a little sob. A tear ran down her cheek.

"What about Ken and Bill?" I asked, to stem any further sentimental reminiscences.

"They told him," she continued, pulling herself together somewhat, "that there was good money to be made elsewhere by an enterprising fellow like himself."

"Good money, is it?" Mrs. Hudson exclaimed. "Bad money more like."

She took a judgmental sip of tea.

"Make money how?" I asked.

"He wouldn't say. When I asked if it was dishonestly to be got, he laughed and said 'Of course not!' But could I believe him, gentlemen? Dear Ralph is so easily led, you see."

"All no doubt very distressing for you, Madam," Holmes interrupted, "but I'm afraid Dr. Watson and I have pressing business to attend to."

I could not imagine what he meant, unless it was to feast on our delayed breakfast, and assumed he simply wished to hear no more of what seemed to him a banal-enough domestic saga. He beckoned to me.

"I trust properly cooked eggs will follow us shortly," he added.

"Oh no, Mr. Holmes. Please stay a while longer," Mrs. Hudson begged. "I was hoping you could give some assistance to my poor sister."

Holmes raised eyebrows that nearly disappeared into his hairline.

"Did you, indeed?"

"There is an element to her story which may intrigue you."

Holmes's expression clearly implied, if that was the case, that Nelly should get on with it. With a resigned sigh, he slumped into a chair.

"Ralph has disappeared," Nelly said. "And I am afraid something terrible has happened to him."

She started to shake again. I took hold of her hand and held it firmly until the tremor ceased. She then removed a letter from her reticule and held it out to us. Holmes took it, scanned the contents, and passed it over to me. Written in a wobbly, uneducated hand, it read as follows:

Dear Madam,

Your son is in grave danger. If you wish to know where he is and what he been doing, consult ABC. But take care. One false step and all is over.

A Well-wisher

"What the devil does that signify?" I asked. "Consult the *ABC Railway Guide*, perhaps."

Mrs. Morris shook her head.

"I have no idea what it means, Doctor, but it terrifies me. How will I know if I've made a false step or not?"

She looked from Holmes to me and back again, a pleading expression on her face.

"Tell your tale from the beginning, Mrs. Morris." Holmes said, kindly enough. I think the letter had indeed piqued his interest. "When did you last see Ralph?"

"Well," she replied, "he failed to return home from work on Friday, although . . ." becoming a little embarrassed, "that is not altogether out of the ordinary, Mr. Holmes. He's young, do you see, and likes to go on the town with friends, sometimes forgetting to tell me first."

"Out all night?" Holmes asked.

Nelly nodded.

"Tsk," from Mrs. Hudson.

Holmes held up a finger to forestall interruptions.

"The first time he didn't come home, I got so very anxious. But Ralph hates it if I make a fuss, so, on this occasion, I tried not to be too much concerned. But when he didn't come home all weekend, then I really started to worry. And yesterday evening I received this frightful missive. I couldn't think what else to do, so I took the first train down this morning to see if Martha could help."

"You mean, if Martha's *lodger* could help," Holmes replied. "Well, perhaps he can."

He studied the envelope in which the letter had come. Now, while you and I might see nothing out of the ordinary, what Holmes can glean from a seemingly plain piece of stationery frequently amazes me.

"Posted in London," he said. "Which is presumably why you travelled down."

The lady looked flustered.

"No, no, it was to see Martha . . . and yourself . . . Was it really posted here, then?"

Holmes sighed.

"You can clearly observe the mark over the stamp. It was applied at a post office in Bow at 3:30 p.m. on the day before yesterday, the letter subsequently transferred by night train to your home city – as evidenced by that countermark here – thus enabling it to be delivered to you the following day."

Mrs. Hudson smiled. She was used, as I was, to witnessing Holmes's powers at work. Her sister, however, looked at Holmes as if he had just performed a magic trick.

"Furthermore," he continued, taking up the letter from the table where I had placed it, "we can see from the handwriting that a woman has penned it. Do you have any well-wishers in London, Mrs. Morris?"

She shook her head.

"Only Martha."

"Well, I didn't write it," exclaimed that lady.

"Of course not, my dear," her sister said. "But there is no one else I can think of."

"I guessed not," Holmes continued. "In any case, such anonymous persons, in my experience, are usually far from wishing anyone well. Quite the opposite, in fact. The script suggesting a person of limited education."

He held the paper up to the light.

"Cheap stuff, no watermark, purchased in any stationer's shop."

He sniffed it. "No perfume . . . Yet a faint whiff of . . . What is that, Watson?"

He passed it to me. I could smell nothing, and gave it back.

"Almost imperceptible, and yet . . . *Bow!*" he exclaimed loudly, smacking the table, making the rest of us jump, and the china cups rattle on their saucers. "What does that say to you, Watson?"

I gave him a blank look.

"Bow bells," Mrs. Hudson suggested. "Oranges and lemons. Dick Whittington."

Holmes shook his head.

"Nothing so harmless," he said. "The proximity to Limehouse, plus the faint whiff of ammonia from this letter, give rise to certain conclusions. Watson, you are familiar with such, I think."

I nodded, knowing now what he meant and yet was reluctant to speak the word aloud to the ladies: *Opium.* The opium dens of Limehouse. If Ralph had fallen victim to the people who prey on human misery in those establishments, then God help him.

"Mrs. Morris," Holmes said. "I shall do my best to find your son and restore him to you."

Her gratitude was overwhelming. If he had not dodged out of the way in time, I think she would have embraced him.

"Of course, you can stay here, Nelly," Mrs. Hudson said, "while the gentlemen look into the matter."

Her sister smiled gratefully and hugged her instead.

"Ken and Bill . . ." Holmes asked. "I don't suppose you know their last names?"

Mrs. Morris shook her head.

"Perhaps they work in the same office as your son."

"I didn't get that impression. His office is a most respectable establishment."

"Nevertheless, perhaps someone there knows them. Please to write down the address for us and we will check it out."

He had quite forgotten breakfast in his eagerness to get started on the search. I, however, had no intention of embarking on a new adventure on an empty stomach, and said as much. Whereupon Mrs. Hudson sprang into action, and soon Holmes was dipping a soldier of toast into a perfectly boiled egg.

It proved gratifyingly simple to discover the full names of the two men implicated by Mrs. Morris in the disappearance of her son. Holmes, off on another mission, had delegated to me the task of contacting by telephonic means the office where Ralph was working. The helpful clerk was only too happy to give me the information required.

"Ken Bourne and Bill Ward, the laziest pair of good-for-nothings we've ever had working for us, Dr. Watson. Good riddance to them if they've gone for good."

So, despite Mrs. Morris's protestations, the two men had indeed worked in that most respectable of establishments. Not in the office, however, but as casual labourers in the docks.

The clerk was further able to provide their last address, a boarding house in what he described in supercilious tones as "a most unsavoury part of the city." Interestingly, however, the men hadn't been seen since the previous Friday, the day Ralph failed to return home.

"I hope young Morris will recover soon," he added. "His mother told us he is ill."

Cunning Nelly, covering her son's absence from work with a little fib.

"Nothing too serious I hope, Doctor," he added.

I mumbled something non-committal, thanked him, and bade him goodbye.

It would be too much to hope that the boarding house indicated would also be contactable by telephone, and such proved to be the case. Instead, I sent a telegram enquiring if Bourne and Ward were still in residence, hardly expecting a response. However, a reply came back almost immediately. It seemed the two had left on the previous Friday without paying their bill and the aggrieved landlady, a Mrs. Bridget O'Faherty, broadly hinted that I might pay off what was owed!

I did not need Holmes to tell me that the disappearances of both Ralph and his cronies at precisely the same time was hardly a coincidence. But where were they? Had they come to London, from where the anonymous letter had been posted? For what reason? What, indeed, was the purpose of that mysterious letter and who had written it?

I returned to Baker Street to find Holmes already back from his own expedition.

"Well," said he, lighting his pipe, "you've had better luck than me at least."

He had travelled to the East End of the city to enquire among his various, mostly disreputable, connections there regarding *ABC*, but no one was able or willing to enlighten him. He agreed with me, however, that Bourne and Ward were key to the search.

Once more we descended into that part of the house occupied by Mrs. Hudson to get a description of the two men from Mrs. Morris.

"Oh dear," she said, all flustered, "I can hardly tell you. I only saw them briefly, not wanting to linger in their company . . . ." Her voice dropped to a whisper. "They had been drinking, you know."

"Well now, Mrs. Morris," Holmes said, "I am sure you can do better than that. What ages were they, for instance?"

"Oh, young, I suppose. Well, not that young. Not as young as Ralph."

"In their twenties? Thirties . . . ?"

"Yes."

He tried to suppress a sigh.

"Were they dark or fair?"

"Neither particularly."

"Hmm."

"One was quite fat. I noticed that, because his jacket was too small to button across . . . across his stomach. Bourne, I think, that was. Or Ward."

"Probably," Holmes replied drily.

"Now Nelly," Mrs. Hudson broke in. "Think. Didn't you tell me they had Cockney accents?"

"Oh yes," her sister replied, "they sounded most rough."

"That's a help," I said encouragingly. I think Holmes rather intimidated her.

"The fair-haired one was quite tall," she continued, "compared to the other one."

Holmes threw up his hands in exasperation. "Mrs. Morris, you just said neither was particularly fair or dark."

"Sorry," she said timidly, "but now I come to think of it, one was fairer than the other. Not white-haired, you understand, just . . . fairer."

"How were they dressed?" I asked.

"Oh . . . Yes, I can tell you that. Flashy. That's how I'd describe it. Cheap and flashy. Big checks on the fat one's jacket. A striped waistcoat on the other."

"Blood out of a stone," I said a while later, back in our sitting room, shaking my head.

"Not quite," Holmes replied. "While blood cannot under any circumstances be extracted from a stone, squeeze Mrs. Morris hard enough and at last something emerges. Not much, admittedly. However, I think that if I put the Irregulars on the case, we might be able to track down the fellows."

"You think they are in London, then?"

"Most probably. In or around Limehouse."

No sooner said than done. But once Wiggins and the other band of street urchins who made up the Baker Street Irregulars were on the hunt in the East End, there was little we could do in the meantime. Holmes was inclined to pack Mrs. Morris off back to Liverpool, although the lady was most disinclined to go, until he suggested that perhaps Ralph had returned in the meantime and was as worried by her absence, as she had been by his.

"If that, sadly, is not the case," he said, "perhaps further letters have arrived from your well-wisher regarding his whereabouts."

She was persuaded at last after our assurances that we would most certainly inform her of any developments this end. Mrs. Hudson, having seen her safely on her way, subsequently confessed to me that, much as she loved her sister, it had been something of a trial to have her under her feet all day and night.

"So difficult to get anything done," she said, looking around herself as if critically, whereas to me everything seemed as neat and tidy as ever. "Phoebe, of course, is no use at all."

She often complained about her maid, who truly seemed more of a hindrance than a help, forever breaking things, burning things, and generally creating more work for her employer. However, when I once asked why she didn't dismiss her, Mrs. Hudson's face softened.

"I wouldn't have the heart, and anyway, she's better than she used to be." (I rather doubted that from my own observations.) "Her poor mother has it hard, you know, Doctor, with so many children, another on the way, and the husband a useless piece of work if ever there was one. No, I could never dismiss little Phoebe."

Mrs. Hudson was able to give us a more objective view of young Ralph than we had received from his mother. Or perhaps "objective" is the wrong word, since I had been correct in my surmise that she had a pre-existing low opinion of him. Selfish, lazy, and self-indulgent, with a deep-seated sense of grievance against a world that would not properly recognise his merits, summed him up in her eyes.

"Merits, by the way, that exist only in the minds of himself and his doting mother. None of it being entirely his fault," she conceded. "Ralph has always been his mother's pet, spoilt rotten by her, especially after George died and she had no one else at home to cosset."

"What age is the young man now?" I asked.

She thought for a moment. "Twenty-three in years, but adolescent in behaviour."

No, Ralph was certainly not a favourite.

"Of course," she went on, "I pray nothing bad has happened to him. Perhaps he has just decided to escape his mother's clutches for a while."

"To sow his wild oats," I suggested.

She pursed her lips. "He did quite enough of that in Paris," she said.

While awaiting developments in the case, Holmes and I pursued our separate interests, my friend employing a lean time in the detection world to throw himself into a study of cuneiform script, myself attending to my medical duties, sadly neglected of late.

Three days passed before we heard again from Wiggins, shown up to our rooms by Mrs. Hudson with more enthusiasm than she usually displayed at the advent of the little ragamuffin. He entered with a broad grin that revealed a missing incisor.

"You have good news for me," Holmes surmised.

"I 'ave that, Guv'nor," Wiggins replied, expanding a meagre chest proudly. "Bobs found 'em." He grinned further. "Bobs yer uncle, so ter speak."

This mysterious discourse was elucidated by Holmes.

"Bobs being one of Wiggins's trusted lieutenants," he explained

"Yus," Wiggins confirmed. "And a bloody good leftynent, 'e is, too."

"Tsk," from Mrs. Hudson, who had remained to hear what the boy had to say.

"Pardnin' my French, Mrs. H.," Wiggins said apologetically. "I forgot you wuz there."

"Get on with it, will you," Holmes urged.

"Yeah, well, Mr. H, they be 'oled up in Bow, like what you said. Mornin'side Road. Number 23. Big 'ouse belongin' to a dame name of Ada Clyde. And what goes on in that there 'ouse, I'd blush to repeat in front of a lady."

He nodded respectfully towards Mrs. Hudson.

"You are sure it's Bourne and Ward."

"Oh, yus. Them all right. Well, one all the time. The other visitin', like."

"Is Ralph there, too?" Mrs. Hudson broke in.

429

Wiggins shook his head, "That fact, Mrs. H., I am unable to confirm nor deny." The pompous phrase sounded most comical coming from a street urchin. "But," he continued, "no sign of 'im. O' course, that there Clyde woman has several 'ouses . . . and when I say 'ouses, I means . . . ."

He gave a knowing wink.

"Yes, yes," Holmes said. "We understand. Can you tell us where they are all located?"

"All in doo course, Mr. H. Be assured my leftynents are on the job. Day and night." Wiggins fell silent, and stood looking expectant.

Holmes fished a sovereign out of his pocket and tossed it to the boy, who caught it expertly.

"Excellent work, Wiggins. I hope to hear from you again very soon."

"Perhaps," I said to Mrs. Hudson, "you can find some buns or biscuits for this most deserving young man."

"I'm sure I can," she replied, at which point the two of them left the room, Wiggins grinning broadly.

"What now?" I asked Holmes.

"Simple as *ABC*," he replied, "assuming Ada Clyde's middle name is Betsy or Bernardine or some such."

I clapped my hands together. "Of course. *ABC*. How slow I am! I presume, from Wiggins's broad hints, the woman in question runs a bawdy house or two."

"That is the inevitable conclusion," he replied, and frowned. "But how Ralph would fit into her scheme is unclear."

"Heaven forbid," I said, shaking my head at the thought, "he has become a procurer . . . ."

"Let us not speculate yet," he interrupted me. "However, I shall have to visit the house at Morningside Road."

"Alone?"

"Unless you wish to enjoy the pleasures on offer there yourself."

"Good Lord, Holmes! Surely you do not intend going there as a client!"

"The easiest way, my friend. If Bourne and Ward are on the premises, their function is to discourage unwelcome visitors." He laughed. "Fear not. I shall maintain my virtue, despite any temptations to the contrary."

I had no fears on that score. Nevertheless, I spent some uneasy hours awaiting his return that night, and must confess I had recourse to the brandy bottle on several occasions to keep up my spirits, the latest issue of *The Lancet* failing to enthrall. I eventually sat, light dimmed, at the window, looking out over Baker Street in the hope of discerning the familiar tall and lanky returning figure of my friend.

430

I must have glanced away for a moment for, without having observed anyone approach, I heard the front door open and close, followed by steps on the stair. Seconds later, Holmes had joined me in the room.

"In darkness, Watson?" he asked,

"I was dozing," I lied.

"Hmm." He stood over the lamp and lit it, heavy shadows emphasising the gauntness of his face. He had donned one of his many disguises for the enterprise, and it was a sea-faring man I saw before me, reeking of strong spirits, he having splashed abundant quantities of rum over his pea-jacket.

"This coat will need cleaning," he remarked, casting the thing from himself.

"Well?" I asked. "How did you get on?"

He slumped into his chair and gratefully accepted the glass of brandy I offered him.

"I sometimes despair of the human race, Watson. How certain people use the power they have to inflict suffering on the weaker and more helpless. Those poor unfortunate girls . . . ."

Having entered the house at Morningside Road, and, after paying the required amount to a person who had to be Bourne or Ward – a fat and greasy individual in a checked jacket that did not button up properly – he was shown into a seedy-enough salon, where a number of half-clad girls lounged, looking tired and bored.

"Cheer up, trollops," Ward (or Bourne) had urged in sharp tones. "'Ere's Midshipman Smiff, come to sail away with one 'o youse to Paradise."

"Smith?"

"It is the usual appellation, is it not, Watson, for someone wishing to maintain their anonymity?" Holmes explained. "I took my time choosing a girl, rejecting anyone pert or brazen, or else cowed and broken. Sarah, a little older than the others, seemed the best of a bad lot, and we duly ascended the stairs to a musty-smelling bedroom, stained sheets on the bed. Even if I were as drunk as I pretended to be, I doubt I could have brought myself to lie down upon them."

He went on to explain how he had, with difficulty, stopped the girl from disrobing completely.

"I had to gain her trust, and give a convincing reason why I did not wish to avail of her services. I told her that I had been away at sea for longer than expected and was now looking for my daughter, whom I feared had fallen on hard times in my absence, adding that I suspected she might have entered such a place as this to earn her keep."

"Did she believe you?"

431

"I don't know, but she became more friendly when I produced a sovereign. No, there was no Antoinette in this house, she said, but might be in one of the many others."

"The last letter I received from her, I said, posted to me in Bilbao – (*I might as well have mentioned Timbuctoo, Watson, for all the girl knew of such places!*) – mentioned having met a woman called Mrs. Clyde . . . Well, no sooner had I uttered that name than Sarah shuddered. "If she's met Ada," she said, "God 'elp 'er, sir!" I urged her to tell me more. She was reluctant at first, but when I produced another sovereign, her greed or need overcame her fears."

Ada Clyde, it seemed, owned a string of "houses" across East London. When asked how she managed to stay out of public notice, Sarah gave Holmes a "queer look". But, at last, she revealed that the woman had protection.

"'Igh-ups look after 'er, sir. 'Igh-ups with strange tastes. Cruel tastes." Holmes related her words as he remembered them. "This 'ere 'ouse ain't much, Mister, but it suits me. Ken ain't bad, treats us fair most times. 'E don't expect us to do nothing except the usual. There's another 'ouse I've heard tell of . . . Well, all I know, sir, is that some girls go in and don't come out again. Boys, too. That's what I meant, sir. God 'elp your daughter if she's in there!"

I looked at Holmes in horror. "Boys! Could Ralph be in such a place?"

"I hope not, Watson, but that's as much as Sarah was able or dared to tell me. I left her there, reluctantly, because she seemed a nice-enough girl, not utterly corrupted, and in other circumstances might have led a respectable and happy life."

It was very late, the sky beginning to pale into dawn. We agreed to sleep for a few hours and then plan our next move. Perhaps Wiggins would come up with more useful information in the meantime.

I found it difficult to settle, the probable effect of too much brandy, which set my heart and mind racing. Could Ralph really have entered one of those terrible houses? Yet, the young man was surely able to extricate himself if he so wished. He was no wretched indigent, but had a loving mother to support him.

The following morning had Holmes and me glumly in our sitting room, the mood not lightened by the lowering skies hanging over Baker Street. My head was throbbing so badly, despite the nostrum of feverfew I had taken, that I could not settle even to read the newspaper, while Holmes, smoking an evil pipe over pages of cuneiform script, annoyed me greatly by exclaiming, "Fascinating!" or "Most interesting!" from time to time. All the same, I felt that his absorption in those strange wedge shapes was feigned, and that his ears, as much as mine, were pricked to listen out for a visitor.

At last, the doorbell rang and we both perked up. It was not Wiggins, however, who appeared, but Mrs. Hudson, bearing a telegram in her trembling hand.

"From Nelly," she said. "I am sure of it."

Holmes ripped it open. He scowled.

"Nothing," he said. "No sign of the boy. No new letter from the well-wisher."

He screwed up the yellow paper and tossed it on the floor.

"Your sister might have spared herself six-pence."

Mrs. Hudson picked up the scrap and hurried out before Holmes could see her tears.

"That was harsh," I said.

"It's this accursed inactivity," he replied. "Damn the Sumerians!" He swept the cuneiform scripts off the table.

"Well," I said, rising to my feet and stepping carefully over the scattered sheets. "I am going for a walk in the park to clear my head. Will you join me?"

Holmes looked out of the window. "It is raining," he said, "and in any case, Watson, one of us has to stay here in case Wiggins turns up."

I didn't mind the rain for, after all, it was only a light drizzle. Moreover, I was anxious to escape the oppressive effects of Holmes's bad temper, as well as the thick plumes emitting from his pipe. Once outside the house, I immediately felt a lightening in my spirits, despite the cloud still hanging over young Ralph. There is something reassuring about crowds of people all busy with their own concerns. A matter of perspective, I suppose.

Briskly directing myself towards the park, I nearly collided with a girl hurrying, head down, in the other direction. Something about her caused me to turn and look after her. It wasn't at all that she was pretty, and her plain dress hardly revealed an enticing figure – she dragged a leg behind her and had the suggestion of a humped back – and yet something about her intensity of purpose compelled my curiosity. This turned to surprise when I saw her pause outside 221b Baker Street before limping away, turning, lingering and finally knocking on the door. I hastily retraced my steps, hoping that her business was with Holmes, and not some domestic trifle to do with our landlady.

It seemed that the latter was, after all, the case. Holmes was alone when I re-entered. He looked up, a smug smirk on his face.

"That was quick," he observed. "I knew the rain would discourage you."

"Not at all," I said. "It is most refreshing out, but I thought I saw a visitor arrive."

He leaned back and sighed. "As you can see, you were mistaken."

At that moment, however, the sound of footsteps on the stairs gave the lie to his remark. Mrs. Hudson entered, followed by the same young person I had observed in the street, painfully thin, bent under the hump on her back, her wizened face prematurely aged.

"This is Delia," our landlady informed us, veritably sparkling with excitement. And when the newcomer shrank into a timid silence, added, "Go on, dear. Tell the gentlemen what you told me."

"Oh, ma'am!" the girl said at last, in a rush. "Can't you say what I said?"

"It would be better coming from you," Mrs. Hudson replied.

"Why don't you sit down," I said in gentle tones, since the girl looked terrified. "Mrs. Hudson can bring us up some tea.

"Oh no!" Delia replied. "Don't go, ma'am, if you please."

Was it we who frightened her so much? Why? Because we were men? I had a horrible suspicion that this young person had good reason for her fears. And yet, as her story emerged – in fits and starts, it must be said – it seemed that she had suffered at the hands of both sexes.

"If she finds out what I done, she'll kill me. Bill, too. I shouldn't never 'ave come."

She looked around wildly at the door, as if about to bolt out of it.

"What is it that you have done, Delia?" Holmes asked.

She stared at him.

"Come 'ere, o' course," she replied at last. "If she finds out . . . Oh, Lord!"

She covered her face with her hands as if that would make her disappear.

Holmes looked helplessly at Mrs. Hudson.

"Delia knows where Ralph is," she said.

Apparently, this astounding statement broke the ice as far as the girl was concerned. Suddenly, she started talking in a rush.

"See, 'e don't know yet what she's really like. But I do. I know."

It took time and patience to follow her thread but, to summarise, Ralph had arrived the previous week at the house where Delia was working, in the company of Bill – her brother, as it turned out.

"Such a nice-looking young man," she said. "Nice and polite to me. Not like the others . . . I could see 'e was different from them. Not cut out for . . . for . . . the life."

She hesitated, and glanced at Mrs. Hudson.

"What is this 'house'?" Holmes asked. "Somewhere for men to visit?"

Delia almost laughed, then.

"Oh no, Mister. Not in that 'ouse. No men visitors there."

"Not women, surely?"

"Ladies, more like. 'Oity-toity ladies . . . ." She looked at Mrs. Hudson again, as to apologise for her words. "You should see 'em with their stays off, ma'am. Not quite so uppity then."

Holmes was aghast, as was I. Of course there were, sadly, plenty of brothels in London where men went to have relations with women. Places too, I am afraid, where men went to meet with boys. But a house for rich women to pleasure themselves with young men – that was new to us both.

Delia, she told us, was the slavey, the cleaner and cook, and the butt, too, of any discontent on the part of the visitors or, indeed, of the lady of the house herself.

"Ada Clyde?" Holmes asked.

Delia shrank at the name.

"She's a devil," she whispered, as if the woman herself were within earshot. "If she finds that I've come 'ere . . . ."

"You are the 'well-wisher' who wrote to Ralph's mother, aren't you?" Holmes suddenly exclaimed.

Oh, that all-too-familiar expression of disbelief at the detective's seemingly supernatural sagacity! Finally, the girl nodded.

So there was no malicious intent there, after all.

"It was well-written, Delia," I said.

Too well-written for the likes of her, perhaps.

"I copied some of it from a book, sir." That explained it.

"How did you know where to send it?" This from Holmes.

"I asked the young man about where 'e come from. Liverpool. 'E also told me 'e 'ad an aunt 'ere in Lunnon. Living along a famous 'tective."

So Ralph boasted of the connection. Holmes smiled. "Why should you concern yourself with Ralph in particular?" he asked.

"'E don't know what she's like." Delia shivered. "Oh Lord!"

"What danger is Ralph in, exactly?"

Delia, glancing again at Mrs. Hudson, coughed and then resumed her account.

"There's another 'ouse . . . That's where she sends 'em when she gets tired of 'em."

"Another house?"

"An 'orrid place, as I've 'eard tell. Ada wanted to send me there . . . See, some of 'em visitors would like freaks like me. That's what she said."

435

The girl gave us a timid look. "But Bill said, 'Not my sister, Bea! Not Dee!' I can thank him for that, at least."

Holmes shook his head. "You must try to be clearer, Delia. Who is Bea?"

"Oh, sorry, sir. That's what Bill calls Ada. Beatrice being 'er middle name, see. I wouldn't dare. She's 'Madam' to me."

"Ah." Holmes sat back, making a steeple of his fingers. "As we thought. *ABC*."

The girl smiled properly for the first time, and almost became pretty.

"Yes, sir. *ABC*. That's what the girls call 'er behind 'er back."

"So what about this other house, then?"

"Awful, the things that go on there, sir. So Bill says. Won't tell me what . . . 'Yer hair would stand on end, Dee,' 'e says . . . And see, I'd be afraid that Ada plans to send the young man there."

"But surely he can leave whenever he wants," I said.

She looked at me sorrowfully.

"Not now she's got 'im 'ooked. Poor chap don't know which way is up no more."

Mrs. Hudson gasped in horror.

Delia explained further how Ada Clyde sent Bill and Ken around the country from time to time, to find pretty boys and girls and lure them to London with promises of wealth. This appalling woman would then choose a few favourites, and feed them drugs to make helpless addicts of them.

"Then she sends them to that there 'ouse. Or sells 'em."

"What!"

"There's people, Bill says, what likes to buy slaves."

In England! In the eighteen-nineties! Surely not.

The girl gave us the address of the house where Ralph was located. Mrs. Hudson urged her not to go back, most kindly offering for her to stay in Baker Street until a suitable new position could be found for her. Delia demurred, however.

"Oh, I have to go back, ma'am. For 'is sake, God bless 'im."

Had she fallen in love with Ralph simply because he had said a few kind words to her? My heart went out to the poor creature.

"Anyways, if I don't go back, they'll surely find me, and it'll be all the worse for me then."

Mrs. Hudson insisted on feeding her some nourishing soup before she departed. Delia left our room with our kindly landlady. Holmes and I then discussed our best means of proceeding.

"We should alert Lestrade," I said.

Holmes shook his head. "Not yet. We have no proof that any criminal activities have actually taken place."

"Running brothels isn't criminal?"

"Well, of course, we could urge Lestrade and his men to go in and clear the swamp. But I suspect this Ada Clyde, from what Delia has told us, is protected by influential friends. High-ups, she said." He shook his head. "When I say 'criminal', I mean regarding Ralph."

"Then perhaps we could simply buy Ralph back," I said. "Supposing that money talks to this Ada Clyde."

"He might not wish to be rescued, Watson. After all, he's become dependent on the Clyde woman for his drugs. He may even like the life. Remember what happened at Aldershot."

I did indeed. When the National Vigilance Association planned to close the brothels there, offering the women the chance to reform, they were met with a protest march of ninety prostitutes and had to give up.

"All the same," Holmes continued. "I think an interview with *ABC* should definitely be our next move. I am most curious to meet the devil who inspires so much fear."

Easier said than done. We had no notion in which of her many houses Ada Clyde could be found at any particular time, having omitted to enquire this of Delia. Luckily, later that day Wiggins finally turned up with a scrawny little cross-eyed fellow in tow. This was Bobs. Something about the lad caused me to make sure to keep a firm grip on my wallet and fob watch.

"Well, Bobs," Holmes said, "what have you to tell us?"

Bobs looked sideways at Wiggins. At least, I think he did. It was hard to tell where his eyes were directed.

"That's all right, Bobs," Wiggins said. "I'll do it . . . Bobs can't talk," he explained.

I regarded the lad with more compassion then. I still would not have trusted him near my valuables.

What followed was an astonishing mute conversation of flapping hands. Holmes watched intently, for I knew he had studied this mode of communication. However, it seemed the boys had developed their own version, which was as foreign to him as cuneiform script to me.

Much of what Wiggins translated confirmed what Delia had told us regarding the various houses, their addresses, the sort of clients catered for in each. Bobs had no knowledge of the house of horrors, but was able to inform us, through Wiggins, that, every morning, Ada Clyde attended the one serving ladies.

"That's when they go. See, it's s'posed to be a dress shop," Wiggins said. "Though no one ever buys nothing. Well, not dresses, anyways." He scowled disapprovingly.

"Is Ralph there?" I asked.

Bobs shrugged his shoulders and twisted his hands into a maybe-or-maybe not shape.

"Bobs wouldn't know Ralph from Adam, Watson." Holmes regarded me reprovingly, as if I should have known better than to ask. "But young men are there, aren't they, Bobs?"

The boy nodded vigorously. He swept grubby fingers across his face in a curl and preened himself, as if to express handsome. Something he most definitely was not.

"We will hope to accost Madam Clyde tomorrow morning," Holmes said, reaching for his money pouch. "Good work, boys."

Bobs grinned broadly, while Wiggins said coolly, "Fanks, Guv'nor. Anytime." And adding hopefully, "Will Mrs. H. 'ave any spare biscuits today, d'you fink?"

"I'm sure she has," Holmes replied, and the two lads scampered off down the stairs, the front door slamming after them fifteen minutes later. Not just biscuits, then, but tea or maybe table beer, and some of our landlady's most excellent scones.

The next morning, we duly set out for Bow, where Ada Clyde's "dress shop" was situated. It was hardly the most salubrious part of the city for ladies to visit, though the house looked to have pretensions above its neighbourhood, with a brass sign on the wall reading *Exclusive Paris Fashions*, stones steps leading up to a front door painted white, and surmounted by a stained-glass panel featuring swirling pink flora. Headless mannequins stood in the bay windows, clad in gowns of silk, and a little faded and dusty when one looked closely.

Following our knock, the door was opened by a maid who clearly expected someone quite different, for she became quite flustered. Before we could introduce ourselves, a man pushed past her, presumably Bill or Ken, a tow-headed individual with the flushed and coarse complexion of a heavy-drinker. The man was sporting the red silk waistcoat with yellow stripes described by Mrs. Morris that distinguished his otherwise unexceptional slovenly dress. Challenging us to know our business, he looked ready to slam the door in our faces. However, Holmes politely enquired if Madam Clyde was within and presented his card. Without a word the fellow stalked off, presumably to search out his employer, leaving us standing on the threshold by the open door, the little maid trembling uncertainly, not knowing whether to go or stay. We might as well enter, so we did and stood in a hallway decorated to reflect feminine taste of an extreme variety. Dimly lit, it was all very pink, not to say rosy. Frills and flounces adorned every part of the furniture, coyly covering even the legs of the side table and chairs. A pair of large gilt mirrors, considerably foxed, faced each other across the hallway, our reflections within them disappearing off into infinity. A crudely executed painting of a reclining nymph hung over the side table, her ample breasts bared, a wispy scrap of diaphanous material covering her lower regions. Over this simpering maiden, a lustful satyr crouched, as if about to pounce.

"Intriguing, is it not?" A low voice tinged with amusement caused me to spin around.

The woman had approached quite soundlessly and now stood regarding us with a quizzical expression, Bill or Ken at her shoulder.

I cannot speak for Holmes, but Ada Clyde was not at all as I had imagined her to be. Not some sly old crone, immensely fat, like a spider at the centre of a web, but instead a slim and elegant woman of uncertain age. Indeed, she looked quite the part of the *couturiere* she pretended to be in her neatly tailored dark grey suit, a pink silk scarf at her neck. With skin of an extraordinary whiteness and hair to match, and eyes so pale as to be colourless, I wondered could she be an albino.

I muttered an embarrassed reply, but she had no further interest in me. All her focus was on Holmes.

"Follow me," she told him. I stumbled on behind as she led the way into a small parlour, rather less frivolously accoutred than the hall. To maintain the pretence, a tailor's dummy, pigeon-breasted, stood in one corner.

"So," she said, after dismissing her bodyguard and seating herself in an armchair, gesturing for us to do likewise, "to what do I owe the honour of a visit from Mr. Sherlock Holmes. I rather suspect you do not wish to purchase a gown."

"We represent the concerned parent of a young man," Holmes replied. "I believe he is living here."

"Living here! In a dress shop? Whatever gave you that notion?" She smiled. Against her pale lips, her teeth showed yellow, with little gaps between them. It was unaccountably horrible and I shivered.

"Let us not play games, Ada," Holmes said. "Ralph Morris. Brought here from Liverpool by Ken Bourne and Bill Ward. The foolish lad thought to make his fortune. I doubt he knew what was awaiting him."

The woman stretched back, crossing one slim leg over the other, and studied the detective. Then she leaned forward.

"Oh, but he did. It was all made quite clear to him." She laughed, a gurgling chuckle. "Since you seem to know so much, I won't beat about the bush . . . You see, what we do here, gentlemen, could almost be called *charitable* work, bringing pleasure to ladies whose husbands, if they have any, have failed abysmally in that regard. You are not married yourselves?" Neither of us deigned to respond.

She laughed again and then pulled a bell rope. After a while, Delia entered, clearly aghast to see us. Holmes discreetly pressed a warning finger to his lips, having already instructed me, quite unnecessarily – I am not that foolish – to express no recognition, should we encounter the girl.

"See if dear Ralph is free at the moment, Delia, and if so, ask him to join us."

The girl bobbed awkwardly and limped out, casting a last terrified look back at us.

"Another charity case," Ada Clyde remarked. "I am all heart, as you see." She slowly tapped slim fingers on that swelling part of her anatomy. "But I am remiss," she added, starting to rise. "A glass of champagne for my esteemed visitors."

We both demurred.

"A pity," she said, subsiding again into her chair. "I find it so much more amicable, under trying circumstances, to share a drink."

A light tap on the door was followed by the entry of Delia with Ralph. I suppose some might call the boy good-looking. He was almost as tall as Holmes, gingery curls forming a halo on his head. Indeed, in the loose white shift he was wearing, he could have served as a model for one of those rather too-pretty boys seen in the paintings of Signor Caravaggio. However, unfocussed eyes rather spoilt the overall impression.

"Thank you, Delia," her mistress said, dismissing the girl, who scurried out. "Now, come over to me, darling," she addressed Ralph. "I see we've disturbed your nap. So sorry."

He approached her, a foolish smile on his face, and stood by her chair. She took his hand.

"These gentlemen have come from your mama."

Ralph regarded us blankly.

"They want to take you home."

I could see how she caressed his hand.

"Home?" he said peevishly. "No, I don't wish to leave. This is my home now. Please tell my mother that."

Ada Clyde smiled, that same fearsome smile.

"You see? His mother has no need to worry. Her little boy is happy here with us."

"But this life, Ralph – " I started to say.

Holmes cut me short.

"No, Watson. Ralph has answered." He stood to leave. "He has made his bed here and must sleep in it. Come."

I was astounded. Why would Holmes give up so easily? However, there was nothing for it but to follow him out. As we went down the steps in front of the establishment, a veiled woman was ascending them. She gave an involuntary squeak of shock at the sight of us and hurried past, into the house.

Holmes emitted a low chuckle.

"The Duchess of -----," he said, "if I'm not very much mistaken."

I had no interest in Duchesses.

"What was that about, Holmes?" I asked. "Are you really planning to leave Ralph to his fate? You know what Delia told us. He will end up in The House of Horrors."

"My friend, there was no point in continuing the discussion with that woman present and Ralph in the state he was in. Anyone could tell he'd been smoking opium."

"Yes, but what are we to do now?" I paused. "I suppose you're going to tell me we must kidnap him." My laugh was cut short by the expression on Holmes's grim face.

"If it comes to that," he said.

He strode ahead of me, veritably trembling with rage. It seemed he intended to walk back to Baker Street, all of six miles, to work off his suppressed energy. As for me, I had no such impulse, especially given the dank chill of that wintry morning, so I called to Holmes that I would take a cab. Without turning, he raised his arm and made a dismissive gesture.

Once home, I warmed myself with a glass of Mrs. Hudson's Smoking Bishop and awaited the arrival of my companion. The drink, the heat from a blazing fire, and the excitement of the morning caused me to doze off, and I was only awakened by someone bursting into the room. It wasn't Holmes, however, but the boy Bobs, in a highly agitated state, Mrs. Hudson behind him.

"I couldn't stop him, Doctor," she said, apologetically.

"That's all right," I answered, rising up. "What's the matter, Bobs?"

I could make no sense of his waving hands, only their urgency and the fact that he wished for me to follow him. Disregarding my previous suspicions of the lad, I threw on my coat and followed him out. It seemed walking would not do it. We must take the cab that was waiting for us.

Back we journeyed all the way to the East End, Bobs hopping up and down on his seat with impatience. I couldn't imagine what we might find when we arrived, though was filled with a sense of foreboding. The driver seemed to know where to stop, at the entrance to a dark alleyway. Bobs jumped out and ran into it, I following more circumspectly. Was it a trap after all? However, I soon discerned a figure slumped against the slimy wall of the place. It was Holmes!

I rushed up to see what had happened, and was shocked at his appearance. An ugly gash was on the side of his head, and blood all over his coat. He looked up at me, a despairing expression on his face.

"They killed her, Watson!" he said. "*They killed her!*"

My eyes followed his gaze. What I had taken for a heap of rags beside him was in fact the broken body of poor little Delia, beaten to death.

"I tried to stop them," he continued, "but I was too late. They would have killed me too, but I got the better of them."

"Ward and Bourne?"

"The same. That she-devil must have guessed it was Delia who had alerted us."

While he spoke, I examined his head. The cut was much less severe than I had at first thought. In fact, the blood on his coat didn't come from any wound that I could see, and I surmised it belonged to one or both of his would-be assailants.

"I don't understand," I said, "how you came upon the scene in the first place."

"It was Bobs," Holmes replied. "He's been keeping an eye on the place and must have seen them drag little Delia out. He came chasing after me, and brought me back here, where the two *thuggees* were setting about the girl . . . I was too late to save her, Watson."

He held his head in his hands.

"But one of them was her brother!" I exclaimed.

"I know. Can you imagine the evil there? But, Watson, I am responsible."

"No, you are not." I spoke in a firm voice, although inwardly I was much less certain. We should have insisted the girl stay with Mrs. Hudson.

"You sent for me," I continued, "but this is surely a matter for Scotland Yard?"

"Bobs has alerted a constable. He should be on his way . . . However, I doubt he'll find anyone at the House. Ada Clyde and her gang will be long gone by now – although they might have to carry Ward. I think I broke his back."

I shall not linger over the details of the arrival of Scotland Yard in the formidable person of Inspector Lestrade. And Holmes was almost right: A search of Ada Clyde's known houses proved fruitless as far as tracking down the woman and her two officers. However, the houses were by no means empty: *ABC* had abandoned her boys and girls and their visitors without a warning. I can only imagine the consternation of the Duchess of ----- and others when burly constables burst in upon them.

One other person was missing: *Ralph.*

"There is apparently another house, the whereabouts of which we are ignorant," Holmes informed Lestrade. "I have heard it called 'The House of Horrors'. Perhaps you know of it."

Lestrade shook his head. "I'll ask the local men, but I think word of such a place would have reached the Yard before now. We knew of this particular house, of course, and the one in Morningside Road, as well as a couple of others, but were instructed to turn a blind eye." He sniffed. "Went against the grain, of course, but the order came from high up . . . The very top, in fact, if you get my meaning."

Surely not a Royal Edict! However, I couldn't help but recall how whispers had gone around about the involvement of Prince Albert Victor, Duke of Clarence, in the Cleveland Street Scandal, with some people even claiming that the Duke was Jack the Ripper himself! I myself had never believed a word of it, but now started to wonder.

Lestrade refused to say more on the subject. Just now, in any case, our priority was to track down Delia's murderers, and find Ralph, if it wasn't already too late.

"There is no alternative," Holmes said. "I shall have to consult with Mycroft. At least I always know where to find him."

Holmes's older brother seldom went anywhere except to walk from his rooms in Pall Mall across the road to the Diogenes Club, or else to his office in Whitehall. Even so, he seemed to know everything that was going on everywhere in the kingdom and beyond.

Holmes consulted his fob watch. "Just now he should be at his desk. We will go there instantly, Watson."

I was taken aback. "Surely you wish to change and clean yourself first," I said, regarding his filthy, blood-stained coat, the cut on his head crusting over now into an ugly scab.

"There is no time to be lost in trivialities," he replied. "Anyway, Mycroft will think it is one of my disguises."

But will the doorman even let us in, I wondered?

There was no need for me to worry. The man in question never raised an eyebrow, clearly recognising Holmes. He even gave a little bow on admitting us.

I had met Mycroft on many previous occasions, and was always struck by the absence of a physical resemblance between the brothers, Holmes so long and lean and lithe, while the older man was obese from inactivity and too much rich food. With a head buried in his fat neck, Mycroft always reminded me of some huge toad. No, they were totally dissimilar – until, that is, one caught their eyes, with the same steely grey, the same penetrating stare.

Mycroft greeted us with a fat smile.

"Good Heavens, Sherlock. Whom have you killed now?"

Holmes was in no mood for levity and set out in brief harsh terms what had transpired. His brother's wide face contracted into a deep frown.

"Ada Clyde!" he said. "Our hands have been tied regarding that virago. Someone – " He raised his eyes to the ceiling, or perhaps to Heaven. " – wants her left alone. I surmise she must be in possession of some incriminating material which certain people of influence wish to keep hidden."

"Blackmail!" I exclaimed.

Mycroft shrugged enormous shoulders.

"That would fit," Holmes remarked.

"As to 'The House of Horrors'," Mycroft continued, "rumours have come to me, but its location – even if it exists outside the realm of fairy-tales – remains unknown. I am sorry not to be able to help you further."

Could not, or would not? At any rate, we were dismissed and had no alternative but to thank him for his time and leave, sorely disappointed.

Sometimes, however, lucky chance lends a hand. We were hardly back in Baker Street when word came from Lestrade for us to return immediately to Limehouse. A cab stood waiting to convey us thither. At least Holmes had the chance to put on a clean coat, passing the soiled one to a shocked Mrs. Hudson, with instructions to "See to it, please."

We then proceeded on a route across the city that was becoming all-too-familiar. This time our destination was a local police station where we found Lestrade, together with a very sorry, bedraggled specimen of sub-humanity lying flat on a trestle table, his check-patterned jacket sodden. This, we finally established, was Bill Ward.

He eyed Holmes venomously. "That's the blighter what broke me back," he spat. (In truth, using a much more offensive word to designate the author of his ills. I have refrained from reproducing it, to avoid offending the susceptibilities of my readers.)

"You killed your own sister," Holmes countered.

"I did not!" Bill shouted, trying to rise up, but subsiding in agony. "That was Ken, that was. Dee weren't meant to die. Just get roughed up a bit. Teach her a lesson, like. But Ken got carried away."

"I didn't see you trying to stop him."

"No . . . Well you didn't see everything, Mister. Anyways, Bea was furious after. Yelled at Ken 'ow 'e spoiled everything, specially after she 'eard you was there and we didn't finish you off, too."

"Tell the gentlemen how you come to be here," Lestrade said. "It'll amuse them."

Bill evidently did not wish to share the joke.

"After all I done for 'er, and all," was as much as he would say.

"He was found half-drowned off Limehouse Dock," Lestrade said.

"Bea said I weren't no use no more. Told Ken to get rid of me, so he tipped me into the water. Some mate, eh!" He shook his head with difficulty. "After all I done."

"So where are they now?"

"Planning a bunk, I reckon. That was always the idea, if things got too 'ot."

"A bunk? How, and where to?" Lestrade asked, and, when the man remained stubbornly silent, he added, "It'll go better for you, if you talk, Bill. We mightn't pursue the murder charge."

"I'd be better off dead anyways," came the reply. But then he reconsidered. "Plan was to take the cruise ship from Lime'ouse to Liverpool, and then over to Amerikay. Bea reckoned no one would look for us on a pleasure steamer. That's probably what they done."

"Did they take Ralph with them?" Holmes asked.

"Reckon they did. Bea said 'e was their insurance."

That sounded ominous, but at least, if Bill was right, Ralph was still alive.

He closed his eyes, wincing in agony. Rotten as he was, I could not but pity him. Lestrade must have read my thoughts, for he said, "We'll be taking you to hospital now, Bill. See what they can do for you there."

The ruffian made a slight nod. Perhaps he knew there was not much to be done.

Holmes, wasting no sympathy, addressed the local constable who was standing by.

"What about this cruise ship, then?"

"Goes around the coast, sir, stopping at Plymouth and Falmouth. Takes four days . . . I wouldn't fancy it in this high wind, though."

"Plymouth! That's good. We can pick them up there."

"It should arrive tomorrow, sir."

"Excellent!"

Thus it was that we were waiting at the quayside by Plymouth Sound – Holmes, Lestrade and his men, an over-excited Mrs. Morris, whom we had notified, and myself – when the cruise ship *Pride of Kent* docked the following afternoon. Lestrade boarded first, instructing the Captain not to let anyone disembark under any circumstances. He then enquired of the steward about our quarries. Of course, they weren't using their real names, but a description soon elicited a nod of recognition.

"That there woman. She's an odd one. Only comes out after dark," the steward said.

"Just like a vampire," I mused aloud, thinking of Mr. Bram Stoker's recent novel.

Holmes gave me a hard look. This was no time for flippancy. However, the bloodsucking propensities of Dracula seemed to me not so very far distant from the activities of Ada Clyde.

The steward led us to the lady's cabin. Low moans could be heard from within, and, fearing the worst, Holmes, with Lestrade, broke through the door.

An extraordinary sight met our eyes. The moans were coming from a man, bent over in apparent agony, Ada Clyde standing beside him.

"The fool can't get it into his head that we've docked," she said. "No cause to be seasick now."

It was all turning into something of a farce, especially when Mrs. Morris pushed past me and exclaimed, "That's Bill or Ken! I'd know him anywhere."

Ada Clyde turned tired eyes upon us. "Who in Heaven's name is this person?" she asked.

"I'm Ralph's mother, Nelly Morris. Ralph's my son. What have you done with him?"

"Ralph?" Ada looked as if she had no idea what Mrs. Morris was talking about. Had she taken drugs too? Or was she simply acting? "Who are you all?" She looked at Holmes. "Oh, I know. The insulting detective . . . I mean *consulting*." She gave a little laugh.

Lestrade coughed, then became official, informing Ken Bourne that he stood accused of the wilful murder of Delia Ward, and Ada Clyde, no high-ups able to protect her now, of instigating the said act.

"Rubbish!" she snapped. "I loved that girl like she was my own daughter!"

"Bill done it," Ken said, raising his head. "If 'e said t'was me, 'e's lying in 'is teeth."

"Ken!" The warning shot out of her like a bullet.

"Why not say it, Bea? Bill must'a turned nark on us for them to be 'ere."

She slapped his face hard, fury overcoming her prudence. "You told me you dealt with Bill."

The man gave Lestrade a cunning look and continued in wheedling tones. "Yus, you said to finish 'im orf, Bea, but, see, Bill were my friend. Couldn't do it."

"No," Lestrade said, "you just pushed him off the dock, and left him to drown."

"Fool!" She was about to strike him again when Holmes intervened and held her back.

"Where is Ralph?" he hissed in her ear.

"Who?"

"You know very well who."

The steward stepped forward.

"There's another cabin," he said.

"You go, Watson," Holmes told me. "I want to keep this slippery snake where I can see her."

The steward led Mrs. Morris and me to the adjoining cabin. It proved to be empty, however.

"Oh, Lord!" Mrs. Morris exclaimed. "What has she done with him?"

I was wondering the same thing. Had he been dumped at sea, too, as an inconvenient appendage?

Just then a crewman joined us.

"Bit of a row on deck, sir" he said to the steward.

We followed him up, and found a familiar slim young man struggling between two muscular sailors, a few passengers looking on with the usual fascination evinced by witnesses to a fracas.

"They won't let me go!" he shouted. "I demand to be let off the ship!"

"Ralph!" Mrs. Morris cried.

"Mother!" He stopped fighting and curled into a ball, a pitiful expression on his face. "Oh, Mother dear! You've come."

The sailors released him into her embrace.

"Take me away from this horrible place, Mother!" Ralph begged her.

"Of course, my darling boy." She made towards the gangplank.

"Not yet, ma'am," the steward told her. "Everyone's to stay on board. Captain's orders."

She looked pleadingly at me. I shook my head.

"Nothing I can do. The inspector will wish to interview Ralph."

The young man burst into tears. I regarded him with disgust.

"Why did you leave like that, without a word?" his mother asked.

"Bill and Ken promised I'd get rich, and quickly." He frowned sulkily. "But I didn't. She took the money. Told me it was to pay for my keep. Still, you know, it was quite fun at first. All those old women making a fuss of me." I shuddered. The lad had a strange idea of fun! "Then it got horrible, Mother. Bea got horrible! Told me I was becoming a nuisance and that she'd send me to . . . to a horrible place. And she wouldn't give me any more of the . . . the . . . ."

"Medicine?" I suggested.

447

"Yes. *Medicine*. Really mean of her! Then she dragged me onto this horrible ship."

"My poor boy!" Mrs. Morris stroked his hair, while he nestled into her embrace.

To think poor Delia had paid with her life trying to protect this worthless individual.

At that moment, Lestrade arrived on deck, followed by the prisoners.

Ada Clyde looked disdainfully at Ralph.

"The cause of all my troubles," she said. "Your mummy is welcome to you."

It was while they were leaving the ship that it happened. Because the gangplank was so narrow, we all had to descend in a single file. Somehow Ada managed to slip through the guard ropes and plunged into the water. Mrs. Morris screamed, while the rest of us looked on in horror. Then an enterprising sailor jumped in after her, but Ada's heavy dress must have caused her to sink straight to the bottom. The sailor emerged some seconds later from the filthy water, shaking his head. Another lad pulled him out.

"Well," Lestrade said, "I suppose that's one way of dealing with the problem."

Ken emitted a harsh laugh. "More fool you lot," he remarked with satisfaction, "if you think she's gorn. Bea can slip out of any sittiation, she can. You can bet ya life, she'll be back some day to plague yous all."

It was true that her body was never recovered, but that was explained by the tides, or by the debris at the bottom of the dock. If she had got entangled in that, she would stay there forever. Ken made a less lucky escape and – the jury disbelieving his account – was duly sentenced to be hanged for Delia's murder, as well as implicated in the disappearances of many others. Lestrade kept his promise to save Bill from the gallows. Instead, the rogue received a sentence of life imprisonment, and languishes yet in Wandsworth Prison, a pitiful wreck. Mrs. Morris took Ralph back to Liverpool by train, eschewing the chance to continue their journey on the cruise ship. Mrs. Hudson informed us later that Nelly never lets the boy out of her sight. How long, I wondered, will he put up with that?

As for The House of Horrors: Try how he might, Holmes was unable to track it down.

"Perhaps it only existed as a threat," I said.

"Maybe," Holmes replied darkly. "But maybe not."

He neatly cut the top off his boiled egg and sighed deeply.

"Mrs. Hudson!" he shouted. "This egg is too hard!"

NOTE

*   More about Mrs. Hudson and Nelly's 1895 trip to Paris to find Ralph can be found in *Mrs. Hudson Goes to Paris* (2022)

The Taverne Emerald
by Alan Dimes

$\mathbf{M}$r. Sherlock Holmes, the consulting detective of 221b Baker Street, seldom took a holiday. He was wont to say, not without a little vanity, but also with some justification, that during his absence the London criminal classes would become more active, and take more liberties, than they would when he was in his proper place in the metropolis. Moreover, there was also the possibility that while he was away, crimes would be committed whose urgent solution was beyond the abilities of Scotland Yard.

Nevertheless, in the late summer of 189-, I accompanied him on a short cruise to Portugal, Spain, and the western Mediterranean. Why this was necessary, and what befell during that brief period at sea, I shall now relate.

The early months of that year were marked by repeated absences on Holmes's part. He did not neglect those cases which came to him in the usual manner, but took every opportunity to be off on some mysterious business of his own which kept him away from our lodgings for increasingly longer and more frequent periods.

My feelings regarding the situation were mixed. Whatever he was involved in, it was clearly absorbing his attention, making it less likely that he would experience that stifling *ennui* which, after all these years, might still lead him back to the use of cocaine. On the other hand, I was a little piqued by the fact that he hadn't chosen to take me into his confidence. I was no stranger to his habit of squirreling away some vital fact or deduction until the right dramatic moment presented itself, but this was the longest he had kept me in the dark – at least while we were occupying the same apartments.

One evening in April, alone in our rooms, I was looking up at the clock and wondering whether to have an early night or spend an hour or two reading the latest issue of *The Lancet*, when I heard Mrs. Hudson's voice raised in protest and the clump of heavy footfalls on the stairs. The door to our sitting room was then flung open and a sinister figure stood on the threshold. Clad in threadbare dark clothes, he was tall and bulky, but his back was somewhat bowed. He had a head of thick wavy red hair, a set of yellowed teeth, and a scar along the length of his left cheek. He came into the centre of the room with a shambling gait.

"Are you Holmes?" he asked in a distinct Irish accent.

"I am Dr. Watson," I replied, standing up from my chair. "Can I be of help?"

"Nah, it's Holmes I need to see. When will he be here?"

"I couldn't say."

"Now that's a pity, so it is."

So intimidating was the fellow's manner and aspect that my sight stole over to the nearest object I might use as a weapon – a fire iron standing next to the grate, a couple of feet from where I stood.

The fellow must have followed my glance, for he said:

"Sure now, there's no need for that. I've come here to help Holmes. Got some information for him. Patrick O'Flynn's the name."

"Mr. Holmes isn't here and, as I said, I have no idea when he'll be back."

"He's back now," the man said in a familiar tone, and piece by piece, the elements of the disguise – the red wig, the false scar, the padding used to bulk out his wiry frame – were removed, to reveal the face and form of my fellow-lodger. With a quick movement, he pulled a handkerchief from his pocket before doffing the shabby topcoat and then rubbed the yellow tincture from his teeth, and the transformation was complete. While my features no doubt registered my surprise, any comment I might have made regarding the imposture seemed superfluous, so I remained silent as Holmes reached for his Persian slipper and his old clay pipe and sat down with a sigh of pleasure. "Ah, the comforts of home! You are aware, of course," he said, filling the bowl, "that the late unlamented Professor Moriarty had two brothers, one a Colonel and the other a station master in the West Country."

"Of course," I replied, resuming my chair. "It was in response to Colonel Moriarty's letters in *The Times* that I felt compelled to set down the true story of our dealings with the Professor."

"Well, I received word from Shinwell Johnson that a Moriarty was attempting to revive his brother's criminal organization. I thought it unlikely that it was the station master, but I investigated him thoroughly to be on the safe side. He is actually a half-brother to the other two, some twenty years younger than the Professor and sixteen years younger than the Colonel. Since both of those gentlemen left home when he was still a young boy, it is unlikely that they had any malign influence on him. There is no evidence that he is other than what he seems, a law-abiding citizen with a responsible job who has remained in his immediate environs for some years."

"And the Colonel?"

"He served in India alongside Sebastian Moran, and it may well have been he who brought Moran to the Professor's attention. While he did nothing criminal on his return to England, he displayed two dangerous traits: He idolized his older brother, and, unlike the Professor, he is reckless and hot-tempered. Consider, for example, how injudicious those letters to *The Times* were. He should have realised that the investigation and the subsequent trials left no doubt as to the Professor's criminality."

"But you completely destroyed Moriarty's organization."

"Yes, I did, with, you must concede, more than a little assistance from Scotland Yard – and you, Watson."

"Then how can his brother revive it?"

"My dear Doctor, all of the criminals in London didn't belong to the organization. Parker, the garrotter, for example, did not, but upon my return he was very quickly recruited by Moran. And, sad to say, a fresh generation of criminals has arisen since our friend the Professor went over the Reichenbach Falls."

"What will you do, then?"

"I shall continue to gather information, both with Johnson's help and in my guise as Patrick O'Flynn, the cracksman from the Emerald Isle. The Colonel is, of course, nowhere near as gifted or as astute as his late brother, and so the whole affair provides none of the intellectual challenges presented by the older Moriarty. It is simply hard work. If I have kept my recent doings from you, it isn't out of secretiveness, but because they contained little of interest, and certainly not anything that you could spin into one of your compact little narratives."

"But why that particular disguise?"

"I considered it vital that I present myself as a complete outsider. Had I adopted the persona of a London criminal, there might have been those who were suspicious of the fact that I was unknown to them and had never been heard of in the metropolis. So I concocted a story in which I had fled Dublin in haste because the police were finally closing in on me. Hence the poor condition of my clothes. I also dropped fairly obvious hints that 'Patrick O'Flynn' might not be my real name, just in case anyone made enquiries in Ireland. You will recall that I keep several rooms around the city where I can change my appearance, and since the majority of the recruitment is taking place in the East End, it is to my foxhole in Bethnal Green that I have had most frequent recourse."

By the beginning of July, Holmes had accumulated enough evidence to prosecute Colonel Moriarty on several counts of criminal conspiracy, which also implicated the members of the higher echelons of his organization, to say nothing of being responsible for the arrest of many lesser felons, some of whom had been reckless enough to boast of their criminal exploits to "Patrick O'Flynn". But all this came at a great personal cost to Holmes. On the evening on which he informed me that his labours in this matter were now at an *end*, I called his attention to the physical toll the case had taken on him. He was pale-faced and more gaunt than ever. There were dark circles below his eyes, and, although he said nothing of it, I recognized the symptoms of someone suffering from occipital headaches and nervous spasmodic cramps.

"You have perhaps the strongest constitution of any man I have ever known," I began, "but there are limits to even your powers of endurance. I speak as both your friend and your medical advisor when I say that you must take a holiday. If you do not, there may be serious consequences – to your health, your sanity, and even your life."

"I am afraid you exaggerate, Watson."

"You don't trust my judgment, then, or my medical skill?"

"On the contrary. I have the highest regard for both – except where I am concerned."

"And what do you mean by that?" I said with some asperity.

"A husband should never treat a wife, a parent, a child, nor a friend. Your friendship with me compromises your diagnosis."

"I see. Well then, if you will not accept my opinion, will you consent to see a specialist? Penrose Fisher or Sir Jasper Meek? Or Charles MacNaughtan?"

Holmes agreed to see Meek. I accompanied him to the consultation, and though I was not, of course, privy to their conversation, I deduced from Holmes's unaccustomed air of contrition when he emerged from the surgery that the well-known expert had confirmed my conclusions.

And so it was that less than a week later we found ourselves in adjoining cabins on the *S.S. Amphitrite*, calling at Lisbon, Cadiz, Tangier, Gibraltar, Alicante, and Algiers. I had taken the precaution of booking us on board under assumed names, to prevent any problems that might arise from Holmes's celebrity. I embarked as Dr. James Wilson, while my friend was to be known as Simon Holland, thus ensuring that the initials on our luggage didn't betray us. Our only confidant was the captain, one Hamish Robertson, a strongly built man of middle height with a black, spade-shaped beard and a light Edinburgh accent.

On the first Saturday evening aboard the *Amphitrite* a dinner and dance was scheduled to take place in the ship's great hall. Holmes and I were invited to dine at the captain's table. There were ten of us in all, and when everyone was seated Captain Robertson, clad in an immaculate white dress uniform, made the introductions. On his immediate left were Emily Audley and her husband, Ronald Audley, Liberal M.P. for Ceredigion. Audley was known as a fast-rising member of his party, and expected to achieve high office when the Liberals returned to power. A tall, well-built man who held himself as upright as a guardsman, he exuded self-confidence, while his wife, the younger daughter of the celebrated society portraitist Edmund Lowery, seemed quite a frail creature. Her hair was mousy, her face pale, and her manner ill-at-ease. One had the impression that she couldn't easily keep up with her ambitious, energetic spouse.

Next to the Audleys was Lady Caroline Porter, a woman of unusual and striking beauty who was also an advocate of women's suffrage. Once known for the luxuriance of her chestnut hair, she now wore it in a short bob. She was outspoken in her views, and many young women were already adopting her distinctive style of dress, which was predicated on comfort and ease of movement rather than elegance. Sitting beside her was John Cardew, and beside him, opposite the captain, was Cardew's aunt, Lady Taverne.

The first thing that struck one about John Cardew was his remarkable good looks. He appeared to be as flawless as a Greek god: His hair was thick, black, and wavy. His skin was clear and without the slightest hint of a wrinkle, his eyebrows described two perfect narrow arches above his startlingly blue eyes, and below his straight nose, his regular teeth shone white behind his well-shaped lips. His manner was easy, and he spoke in an attractive light baritone.

Cardew's aunt, on the other hand, was remarkably plain. True, she must have been in her seventies, and thus well past the age by which most good looks have faded, but it was clear that even in her heyday she wouldn't have been pretty, let alone beautiful. Now her hair, well arranged though it might be, was clearly grey and wispy, her face and form almost painfully thin. A complex net of wrinkles had gathered around her eyes, which were the same colour as her nephew's, but lacked any trace of their clarity and sparkle. And yet, whatever she looked like now, or had looked like in her youth, at least one man had seen beyond the transient, superficial envelope of flesh to the good, kind heart that lay beneath, and had loved her. Sadly, he had died early, leaving her alone and childless, and it was obvious to the most casual observer that she now lavished all her affection on her favourite nephew.

I was sitting on Lady Taverne's left, next to the Dowager Duchess of Swanley. The Duchess must have been widowed early, as she appeared to be in her mid-forties. She was short, trim, and blonde, and wearing a pale green dress discreetly decorated with pearls. Next came Holmes, and sitting between him and the captain was Isobel Dewey, an American heiress and a veritable Gibson Girl: Tall, green-eyed, and full bosomed, with her thick blonde hair piled high upon her head.

454

"Excuse me, Lady Taverne," said Ronald Audley when the waiter had finished serving us all aperitifs, "but is that the famous Taverne Emerald you're wearing?"

Everyone else at the table looked over at the old lady and the great stone in its elaborate silver filigree setting that hung from a chain about her neck. "Why yes, Mr. Audley."

"I'm a little surprised," said the M.P. "I rather thought you'd keep in a safe or a strongbox somewhere."

"Well, I hope you'll forgive an old woman's vanity, but I enjoy wearing it, and I like having everyone else see it. Besides, I doubt very much if anyone here's going to try and steal it, if that's what you were thinking. And if they do," she concluded with a little laugh. "don't you know there's a curse on it?"

"A curse?" said the Duchess of Swanley.

"Yes."

"Oh, do tell us about it!"

Lady Taverne laid an affectionate hand upon the dark sleeve of her nephew's dress jacket.

"John can tell the story much better than I can. He knows all about it, don't you dear?"

"Is that all right with you, sir?" Cardew asked the captain.

"Oh, you go right ahead, laddie," said Robertson. "We've still got a few minutes before they serve dinner, and I'd like to hear the tale, too."

Cardew took out a silver case, lifted out a cigarette with an immaculately manicured finger and thumb, put it between his lips and, striking a vesta, applied the flame of the match to the end. He expelled a thin stream of smoke, blew out the match, and then, picking up his aperitif glass, he drained its contents and signalled to the waiter for a refill.

"Well then," he began, "according to the legend, there was a great temple in northern India, dedicated to the Hindu goddess, Parvati. On display in this temple, but closely guarded, was a small figurine of the goddess, carved from what was said to be the largest emerald ever mined in India at that point, sometime in the fourteenth century. For over two-hundred years, the statuette was safe. Then, in the middle of the sixteenth century, the temple was sacked by Pathan tribesmen who took the image as part of the loot."

"Ferocious warriors, the Pathans," I said. "I encountered them when I was serving in Afghanistan."

"Quite. Anyway, as Parvati's high priest lay dying from horrendous wounds, he put a curse on the Pathans and on any not of the Hindu faith who so much as touched the holy statue. The figurine was broken into four pieces."

"How did that happen?" asked Audley.

"That part isn't clear."

Cardew paused as the waiter refilled his glass.

"Thank you."

He took a sip of wine.

"As fanatical Muslims, the Pathans had no respect for anything the Hindus held sacred. Apart from despising what they saw as polytheism, they also believed that one shouldn't try to make pictures or statues of the divine. So perhaps they were simply destroying it as an image, or perhaps they were dividing it so that four deserving leaders could each have a piece. Whichever it was, those stones were eventually polished and recut and faceted so that no one might see the true nature of their origin, but the curse remained. The pieces went to four different destinations, and in time brought death and misfortune on whosoever had possession of them. I have to say, they must have passed through quite a few hands, but we only know about what happened to the famous ones."

He flicked the ash from his cigarette into the glass ashtray at the centre of the table.

"One found its way to the Ottoman emperor, Osman II, who was strangled at the age of eighteen in 1622 by one of his own Janissaries. It next turned up in Russia, where it is supposed to have caused the death of Czar Alexander II. Another piece was presented to the Mughal emperor, Dara Shukoh, who was assassinated by his younger brother Aurangzeb in 1659. The third piece wound up in Ethiopia. It fell into the hands of the Emperor Iyasu, who was murdered in 1706 at the order of his own son, Tekle Haymanot, who was apparently known as *Irgum*, which means '*the accursed*'. He outlived his father by less than two years, because he himself was killed by a rebel group of courtiers. What happened to those three pieces after that, no one seems to know."

"You see?" Lady Taverne said proudly. "He knows all about it. He even remembers the dates."

"As to the fourth piece," Cardew continued, "well, if you believe the story, that's what my aunt is wearing around her neck. Somehow, it reached England, where it caused the deposition and execution of Charles I. After the Restoration, James II inherited it and he was deposed too, in the Glorious Revolution, though he managed to escape to France."

"So how did it come to be in your family?" asked Lady Caroline.

"Lord Taverne's ancestor was a devout Catholic, and one of James's most ardent followers. The stone was given to him in recognition of his devotion to the King's cause, and ever since then it's been known as the Taverne Emerald."

"You're very quiet, Mr. Holland," observed Lady Caroline.

"I've never had much time for such fairy tales," said Holmes. "There are much better explanations for murder and assassination. Greed and ambition are more common, and likelier, than curses."

"Ah," said the captain, dispelling the momentary mood induced by Holmes's somewhat dour pronouncement, "here comes the first course."

All discussion of the jewel was suspended while we all turned our attention to the Brown Windsor soup. This was followed by fried Dover sole, accompanied by boiled new potatoes, garden peas, and tomato compote. The meal concluded with chocolate mousse and fresh fruit salad. All was washed down with a couple of bottles of Muscadet from the captain's own stock. When everyone had finished eating, another bottle was brought. Lady Caroline was the only smoker amongst the women. She produced a small bag of tobacco and a packet of papers, rolled a cigarette, and took a light from Audley, who then lit a Sullivan's for himself.

Holmes accepted a panatela from Captain Robertson and Cardew offered me a cigarette from his silver case. As plumes of smoke rose into the air, the table split into smaller conversational groups. The captain turned to Emily Audley, who was sitting on his left, and with his calm and reassuring air coaxed her a little out of the shy silence she had displayed for most of the meal. Next to her, the lady's husband was speaking across the table and applying his considerable charm to the Duchess of Swanley, who was smiling rather coquettishly amid little bursts of laughter.

I turned my attention to Lady Taverne and her nephew.

"Mr. Cardew – " I began.

"Oh, call me John, please."

"Well then, John, I wanted to ask you a little more about the Taverne Emerald, if you don't mind."

"Not at all. Please do."

"You said about the other three pieces that only the stories about the famous people who were affected by it have survived. But the Taverne Emerald – there must be more known about it, surely. Is there any more evidence for the curse?"

"You don't believe in it?"

"No, of course not. I'm just wondering if there any events in the Taverne history that might encourage others to. Any mysterious deaths, murders, anything of that sort? I like a good story, and this has me intrigued."

"The Tavernes have always been a military family, so one would expect a certain number of early deaths in the ranks. One of them, Ernest I think, was killed in the Crimea in 1854 in the Charge of the Light Brigade, at the age of twenty-six or so. Oh, and before that, a Taverne died in the Black Hole of Calcutta, 1756. Then there was the terrible scandal of 1867 – "

"Do you have to bring that up, John?"

"Come on, Aunt Jane, don't be squeamish. I'm just trying to answer Dr. Wilson's question."

"Oh, very well."

"Charlotte Taverne was the sister of the then-current title holder, and in possession of the emerald. She was swept off her feet by a dashing young officer in the Buffs called Reginald Tremayne. After a short engagement, they married and went to live in Canterbury, where the Buffs were garrisoned. But it seems the old adage, 'Marry in haste, repent at leisure', applies here, because it wasn't too long before Charlotte discovered that Tremayne was a wastrel, an utter cad. He gambled, and womanised, and quickly got through even the generous dowry the Tavernes had handed over. When Charlotte reproached him, he was violent towards her. She had to start wearing dresses with long sleeves and high collars, even in summer, to cover her bruises. She could only take this for so long. Finally the inevitable happened. She found someone else, an Italian music teacher. One evening Tremayne came home from a regimental dinner unexpectedly early and found them *in flagrante*. He took out a pocket pistol he always carried and shot them both. They died instantly. A maid who had heard the shots burst into the room and found Tremayne standing over the bodies with the gun still in his hand."

"Tragic," I said in a low voice.

"Well, yes," said Cardew. "Tragic enough, even though in some ways it's an old, old story. Charlotte's mother died not long after, and her brother, the fifteenth Lord Taverne, was a broken man for the rest of his days. I suppose some would attribute that to the curse. Oh, the orchestra's starting up! Excuse me – I promised the first dance to Miss Dewey."

The Audleys also got up and went onto the floor.

"Lady Taverne, would you care to dance with me?"

"Kind of you to ask, Captain Robertson, but my dancing days are long over. I'm sure the Duchess of Swanley would be pleased to accept your offer. And everyone – don't stay here on my account. Go off and enjoy yourselves."

"Are you sure you'll be all right on your own?" I asked.

"My dear boy, I'm used to being on my own. Now off you go."

Lady Caroline had stood and was waving to a friend at another table before going over to speak to her. Neither Holmes nor I had any taste for dancing, so we made our way over to the well-stocked bar just as the lights were being dimmed a little to provide a suitably romantic atmosphere.

"What do you make of John Cardew?" asked Holmes when we were both seated with a drink in hand.

"Well, he's a very handsome young man, well-mannered, and a fair storyteller."

"Ah, I should have known that that aspect of his personality would appeal to you."

"And he seems to be devoted to his aunt."

"She is unquestionably devoted to him, but I wonder how far that devotion is reciprocated. My suspicion is that he's taking advantage of her."

"You seem to know a lot about them."

"I know a little. She is in receipt of an allowance from her brother-in-law, which he isn't obliged to continue after he is married. And she can only use the title of Lady Taverne until then."

"Will she have to give up the emerald?"

"Yes, I believe so, and the probability is that he will marry soon. In the meantime, she appears to be lavishing most of her allowance on her nephew rather than herself. Her dress, for example, is quite old. It's been mended and redyed. Excellently done, but not well enough to fool a trained eye. You realize that Cardew has no blood connection to the Tavernes?"

"Really? He seems to know a lot about their family history."

"His mother was Lady Taverne's younger sister. She and her husband were killed in a train crash when Cardew was about thirteen. Lady Taverne was already a widow by then, and she took him in. When she dies, he'll be virtually penniless."

"What about Audley and his wife? They strike me as an ill-matched pair."

Holmes was about to reply when from the other side of the hall there arose an ear-piercing scream.

The orchestra fell silent.

"Oh my God! The curse of the emerald! Lady Taverne's dead!"

It was the Duchess of Swanley who spoke.

Then Captain Robertson cried, in a loud, commanding tone: "Please remain where you are, everyone. Stewards: Close the doors and windows. Lieutenant McAvoy, turn the lights up."

"Aye, aye, sir."

A tall young officer, clad in a similar white-dress uniform, left his table and hurried to comply with his captain's command. When the lights were up, Robertson went over to Lady Taverne and, kneeling down beside her where she lay, gave her a quick examination. Like all his officers, he had been trained in first aid.

459

"She isn't dead," he pronounced in a loud voice, and there was an immediate relaxation of the tension which had instantly pervaded the room.

"She seems to have fainted. McAvoy, fetch the nurse."

"Look! Look!"

It was the Duchess again.

"The Taverne Emerald! It's gone!"

"Everyone remain still. No cause for panic."

Robertson pushed Lady Taverne's chair, which had turned over, to one side and made a quick examination of the floor immediately around the fallen woman. There was no sign of the emerald. The only thing he found was her reticule, which he placed on the table. McAvoy returned with the nurse, who bent down and waved a small bottle of smelling salts under the old lady's nose. She came round quickly.

"It's gone! It's gone!" she cried in a shrill voice. The nurse, a brisk, efficient-looking woman in her early thirties, helped Lady Taverne to her feet, saying, in a lilting voice tinged with a Welsh accent, "Come with me, Lady Taverne. We'll keep you in the infirmary overnight, where we can take care of you. You've had a nasty shock. We'll see how you feel in the morning."

"Thank you," Lady Taverne said weakly, "but let me go to my cabin first. I want to get my nightdress, and some other things."

"All right, I'll take you there. How about that?"

"Don't forget this," said the captain, holding out the little purse. The old lady took it with a thin smile and then shuffled out of the room, the nurse's arm around her stooping shoulders, through a door held open by one of the stewards.

"I am afraid this isn't going to be very pleasant," the captain told us all. "The Taverne Emerald appears to have been stolen, and everyone will have to be thoroughly searched. Lieutenant McAvoy and I will search the gentlemen, and our two assistant nurses will deal with the ladies."

He looked over at another of the stewards.

"Tomlinson, fetch Miss Grierson and Mrs. Fitch."

"Aye, aye, sir."

Robertson came over to where Holmes and I were sitting and said, *sotto voce*, "It looks as if we may need your assistance, Mr. Holmes."

"Certainly not," I replied softly. "Mr. Holmes is on holiday, recovering from a long and exhausting investigation."

"I can speak for myself, Watson. Have everyone searched, and if there is no sign of the stone, I will give you what help I can. But on no account are you to reveal our identities."

460

I opened my mouth to protest, but then closed it without speaking. Holmes had set out his terms, and I knew from long experience that his resolve couldn't be shaken. The best I could do was to keep watch, and respond to any sign I might see that his health was endangered.

"I don't see John Cardew," said Holmes, looking around the room after the captain had gone about his business.

"Nor do I. Do you suspect him? After what you have told me, he seems a likely culprit."

Holmes glanced around once more.

"I don't see Isobel Dewey either. That settles it, I think."

In an hour or so, the long and somewhat embarrassing business of searching and being searched was concluded, without the emerald being discovered, and we were all permitted to go to our cabins for the night.

"Holmes," I said as we parted for our separate rooms, "you are still recuperating, and I am still your medical advisor. Don't stay up contemplating the solution to this case. Get a good night's sleep. Whoever the thief is, he or she cannot escape from a ship at sea. The mystery will still be there in the morning."

"As you wish. Goodnight, Watson."

When morning came, I was awakened by movement in my cabin, and opened my eyes to see Holmes standing before me.

"Good morning," I said, stretching a little. "You're up already."

My companion appeared to in a rather cheerier mood that he had been of late.

"I'm not just 'up'. I've already been for a little walk. You know – to stretch my legs, work up an appetite for breakfast, that sort of thing. And to confirm a suspicion I had. And would you credit it, I was right! Look!"

He reached into the pocket of his canvas jacket and pulled out a heavy object which dangled on the end of a silver chain. I jerked upright in bed.

"My God! The emerald! You've found it! The Taverne Emerald!"

"I didn't so much find it as steal it."

"Steal it? What are on earth do you mean?"

"Well, not last night. This morning. Technically it was theft, because I picked the lock and broke into the temporary dwelling of the person it belongs to, and took it from there without their knowledge or permission."

"The person it belongs to? You mean Lady Taverne? How could it possibly be in her cabin? It was stolen."

Holmes gave an enigmatic smile.

"Now, get up and get dressed, please, as we have something to do before breakfast, which is at eight. It is now a quarter-past-seven."

461

Five minutes later, we were strolling along the deserted decks under a brilliant, cloudless blue sky.

"You still haven't told me where we're going," I said.

"The infirmary, to speak to Lady Taverne."

"Are you sure that's wise? She had a terrible shock last night."

"Oh, don't trouble yourself on that account."

As we turned the corner to the infirmary, we found Captain Robertson waiting for us at the door, dressed in his dark blue peaked cap and working uniform.

"I got your note, Mr. Holmes," he said. "You'd better be right about this, is all I can say."

"If I'm not, then there will be a blot on my reputation, but no disgrace to the Attic Line, or to the captain of the *S.S. Amphitrite*. In any event, I've recovered the jewel, which is surely the most important thing. Shall we?"

The head nurse greeted us as we entered the hushed, slightly darkened rooms.

"Good morning, Mrs. Davies," said the captain. "We've come to see Lady Taverne. Is she awake?"

"Yes, sir, and she seems well enough to get up and have breakfast in the dining hall."

"Is anyone else here at the moment?" asked Holmes.

"No, sir."

"Good. Let us proceed."

Lady Taverne, who was sitting up in bed, looked rather surprised to see three people enter her room, but before she could speak, Captain Robertson said, "Excellent news, my Lady. The best possible. The jewel is recovered."

Holmes once more pulled the Taverne Emerald from his jacket pocket, but instead of the old lady's face suffusing with joy, it turned deathly pale.

"Lady Taverne," said the detective gently, "you would have made a fine actress, but a very poor criminal. I know you acted out of love, but having deduced your intentions, I'm afraid my conscience will not allow you to carry out your plan."

Lady Taverne broke into racking sobs. I instantly sat in the chair beside the bed and took her pulse. It was regular. Her hands were perhaps a little cold, which might well be attributable to her advanced age. At the same time, I doubted that she should be subjected to an interrogation, and shot a warning glance at Holmes.

He moved closer and said in a still gentler tone, "No true criminal would have tried to steal so conspicuous an object in such a crowded space, however dim the lights. Who is the only person who is never searched when such a crime takes place? The victim, of course. Your scream, your fainting fit, they were performed to make sure that everyone present was convinced that that was what you were. You were very lucky that no one saw you undo the clasp and slip the emerald into your reticule."

"How do you know that?" said Lady Taverne, the tears streaming down her wrinkled cheeks.

"Because that's where I found it when I went into your cabin, less than an hour ago. You insisted on returning there last night – not because you wanted to pick up your nightdress, but because you wanted to leave the reticule there, behind a locked door where there was no chance that its contents might somehow be revealed. And you did all this, you broke a lifetime's habit of honesty, all for your nephew, John."

"Yes, yes, for my lovely Johnny. When I die, he will have nothing. What could I do?"

"So the jewel was 'stolen' in front of a huge number of witnesses, and couldn't be found. You had it heavily insured, I think, and would put in your claim when you returned to England. In the meantime, you could sell the jewel at one of the ports we are calling at in the course of the cruise. There are plenty of places where no questions would be asked. The emerald could be broken up into smaller stones and those sold, and no one would be the wiser. That was it, wasn't it?"

"Yes, it was."

"Is John Cardew really worthy of such love as yours?" I asked.

"I know what he's like – what he is – if that's what you mean. Have you ever loved, Dr. Wilson?"

"Yes, yes I have."

"Then perhaps you will agree that if love was only given to those who are worthy of it, then very few of us would be loved. And now, could all three of you please leave me in peace?"

The cruise liner *S.S. Amphitrite* continued to make its leisurely way round the western Mediterranean, stopping at Tangier, Gibraltar, Alicante, and Algiers. The next Saturday there was a dinner and dance, and John Cardew danced each dance with Isobel Dewey. Lady Taverne had her meals brought to her cabin, which she never left for the rest of the cruise. As for Holmes, to my great relief he relaxed and seemed to enjoy the remainder of the holiday. One afternoon, we were standing at the ship's rail in the bright sunshine and gazing out over the blue-green ocean.

"There's one thing I don't understand," I began.

"What's that?"

"On the night of the 'theft', when you couldn't see either Cardew or Isobel Dewey, you said, 'That settles it.' What did it settle?"

463

"Well, like you, I at first considered Cardew the likeliest culprit. But he and Isobel Dewey were clearly taken with each other. I was sitting next to her, you may recall, and she never took her eyes from him. They had danced together, and then left the hall, no doubt for a little privacy. When, then, had he a chance to steal the emerald, even assuming he could somehow have lifted it from his aunt's neck without her knowledge? And however strong the attraction between them, Miss Dewey's complicity on such short acquaintance was unlikely."

A few weeks after the end of the cruise, Holmes and I were having breakfast in Baker Street when Mrs. Hudson came up with the morning papers. I selected *The Daily Telegraph* and, having already finished my boiled egg and toast, turned the pages, taking occasional sips from my cup of coffee.

"Dear me," I exclaimed.

"What's that?" asked Holmes, looking up from the Clarion.

"Lady Taverne's dead. Died in her sleep. They found her yesterday morning."

"It's on this page too," Holmes replied. "Births, marriages, and deaths. But listen to this: '*The engagement is announced today of Mr. John Cardew of 34 Tranmere Square, London S.W., to Miss Isobel Dewey of Baltimore, Maryland.*'"

"The American heiress. So 'lovely Johnny' has actually fallen on his feet . . . ."

"Quite so, but I haven't finished. '*On Saturday, 24th August, the marriage of Michael, Lord Taverne, to Gwendolyn Ruddick will be solemnized at St. Stephen's Chapel Westminster.*'"

"It's rare to find life being neater than fiction," I noted. "All the ends tied up in one day."

"Poor Lady Taverne. You know, sometimes I wonder if that curse isn't still at work, only in less obvious ways."

"Come, Holmes, you don't believe in curses any more than I do."

"A good woman very nearly became a bad one," observed Holmes. "A subtler horror than mere death."

"The key words in that sentence are 'very nearly'. That didn't happen, because you were there to stop it happening. And you wouldn't have been if I hadn't forced you into taking that cruise."

"*Touché*, Watson. No, it was love that created the situation. Love. The greatest curse of them all."

"For some. For others, the greatest blessing."

"As so often, old friend, we must agree to disagree."

About the Contributors

The following contributors appear in this volume:
The MX Book of New Sherlock Holmes Stories
Part XLIV – 2024 Annual (1889-1897)

Brian Belanger, PSI, is a publisher, illustrator, graphic designer, editor, and author. In 2015, he co-founded Belanger Books publishing company along with his brother, author Derrick Belanger. His illustrations have appeared in *The Essential Sherlock Holmes* and *Sherlock Holmes: A Three-Pipe Christmas*, and in children's books such as *The MacDougall Twins with Sherlock Holmes* series, *Dragonella*, and *Scones and Bones on Baker Street*. Brian has published a number of Sherlock Holmes anthologies and novels through Belanger Books, as well as new editions of August Derleth's classic Solar Pons mysteries. Brian continues to design all of the covers for Belanger Books, and since 2016 he has designed the majority of book covers for MX Publishing. In 2019, Brian received his investiture in the PSI as "Sir Ronald Duveen." More recently, he illustrated a comic book featuring the band The Moonlight Initiative, created the logo for the Arthur Conan Doyle Society and designed *The Great Game of Sherlock Holmes* card game. Find him online at:
www.belangerbooks.com and
www.redbubble.com/people/zhahadun and
zhahadun.wixsite.com/221b

Chris Chan is a writer, educator, and historian. He works as a researcher and "International Goodwill Ambassador" for Agatha Christie Ltd. His true crime articles, reviews, and short fiction have appeared (or will soon appear) in *The Strand*, *The Wisconsin Magazine of History*, *Mystery Weekly*, *Gilbert!*, *Nerd HQ*, Akashic Books' *Mondays are Murder* web series, *The Baker Street Journal*, *The MX Book of New Sherlock Holmes Stories*, *Masthead: The Best New England Crime Stories*, *Sherlock Holmes Mystery Magazine*, and multiple Belanger Books anthologies. He is the creator of the Funderburke mysteries, a series featuring a private investigator who works for a school and helps students during times of crisis. The Funderburke short story "The Six-Year-Old Serial Killer" was nominated for a Derringer Award. His books include *Sherlock & Irene: The Secret Truth Behind "A Scandal in Bohemia"*, *Murder Most Grotesque: The Comedic Crime Fiction of Joyce Porter*, *Sherlock's Secretary*, *Of Course He Pushed Him*, *Nessie's Nemesis*, *Ghosting My Friend*, She *Ruined Our Lives*, and *The Autistic Sleuth*.

Mike Chinn's first-ever Sherlock Holmes fiction was a steampunk mashup of *The Valley of Fear*, entitled *Vallis Timoris* (Fringeworks 2015). Since then he has written about Holmes's archenemy in *The Mammoth Book of the Adventures of Moriarty* (Robinson 2015), appeared in several volumes of *The MX Book of New Sherlock Holmes Stories*, and faced the retired detective with cross-dimensional magic in the second volume of *Sherlock Holmes and the Occult Detectives* (Belanger Books 2020).

Alan Dimes was born in Northwest London and graduated from Sussex University with a BA in English Literature. He has spent most of his working life teaching English. Living in the Czech Republic since 2003, he is now semi-retired and divides his time between Prague and his country cottage. He has also written some fifty stories of horror and fantasy and thirty stories about his husband-and-wife detectives, Peter and Deirdre Creighton, set in the 1930's.

Sir Arthur Conan Doyle (1859-1930) *Holmes Chronicler Emeritus*. If not for him, this anthology would not exist. Author, physician, patriot, sportsman, spiritualist, husband and father, and advocate for the oppressed. He is remembered and honored for the purposes of this collection by being the man who introduced Sherlock Holmes to the world. Through fifty-six Holmes short stories, four novels, and additional Apocryphal entries, Doyle revolutionized mystery stories and also greatly influenced and improved police forensic methods and techniques for the betterment of all. *Steel True Blade Straight.*

Steve Emecz's main field is technology, in which he has been working for about twenty-five years. Steve is a regular speaker at trade shows and his tech career has taken him to more than fifty countries – so he's no stranger to planes and airports. In 2008, MX published its first Sherlock Holmes book, and MX has gone on to become the largest specialist Holmes publisher in the world with over 500 books. MX is a social enterprise and supports three main causes. The first is Happy Life, a children's rescue project in Nairobi, Kenya, where he and his wife, Sharon, spend every Christmas at the rescue centre in Kasarani. They have written two editions of a short book about the project, *The Happy Life Story*. The second is Undershaw, Sir Arthur Conan Doyle's former home, which is a school for children with learning disabilities for which Steve is a patron. Steve has been a mentor for the World Food Programme for several years, and was part of the Nobel Peace Prize winning team in 2020.

Paul A. Freeman is an English language teacher. He is the author of *Rumours of Ophir*, a crime novel which was taught at 'O' level in Zimbabwean high schools and has been translated into German. In addition to having two novels, a children's book and an 18,000-word narrative poem (*Robin Hood and Friar Tuck: Zombie Killers!*) commercially published, Paul is the author of scores of published short stories, poems and articles. He is a member of the *Society of Authors* and of the *Crime Writers' Association*. He lives and works in Mauritania.

Mark A. Gagen BSI is co-founder of Wessex Press, sponsor of the popular *From Gillette to Brett* conferences, and publisher of *The Sherlock Holmes Reference Library* and many other fine Sherlockian titles. A life-long Holmes enthusiast, he is a member of *The Baker Street Irregulars* and *The Illustrious Clients of Indianapolis*. A graphic artist by profession, his work is often seen on the covers of *The Baker Street Journal* and various BSI books.

John Atkinson Grimshaw (1836-1893) was born in Leeds, England. His amazing paintings, usually featuring twilight or night scenes illuminated by gas-lamps or moonlight, are easily recognizable, and are often used on the covers of books about The Great Detective to set the mood, as shadowy figures move in the distance through misty mysterious settings and over rain-slicked streets.

Arthur Hall was born in Aston, Birmingham, UK, in 1944. He discovered his interest in writing during his schooldays, along with a love of fictional adventure and suspense. His first novel, *Sole Contact*, was an espionage story about an ultra-secret government department known as "Sector Three", and was followed, to date, by three sequels. Other works include seven Sherlock Holmes novels, *The Demon of the Dusk*, *The One Hundred Percent Society*, *The Secret Assassin*, *The Phantom Killer*, *In Pursuit of the Dead*, *The Justice Master*, and *The Experience Club* as well as three collections of Holmes *Further Little-Known Cases of Sherlock* Holmes, *Tales from the Annals of Sherlock* Holmes, and

468

The Additional Investigations of Sherlock Holmes. He has also written other short stories and a modern detective novel. He lives in the West Midlands, United Kingdom.

Paula Hammond has written over sixty fiction and non-fiction books, as well as short stories, comics, poetry, and scripts for educational DVD's. In 2024, her first Holmes collection, *Sherlock Holmes: Eliminate the Impossible*, was published. When not glued to the keyboard, she can usually be found prowling round second-hand books shops or hunkered down in a hide, soaking up the joys of the natural world.

Stephen Herczeg is an IT Geek, writer, actor, and film-maker based in Canberra Australia. He has been writing for over twenty years and has completed a couple of dodgy novels, sixteen feature-length screenplays, and numerous short stories and scripts. Stephen was very successful in 2017's International Horror Hotel screenplay competition, with his scripts *TITAN* winning the Sci-Fi category and *Dark are the Woods* placing second in the horror category. His three-volume short story collection, *The Curious Cases of Sherlock Holmes*, will be published in 2021. His work has featured in *Sproutlings – A Compendium of Little Fictions* from Hunter Anthologies, the *Hells Bells* Christmas horror anthology published by the Australasian Horror Writers Association, and the *Below the Stairs*, *Trickster's Treats*, *Shades of Santa*, *Behind the Mask*, and *Beyond the Infinite* anthologies from *OzHorror.Con*, *The Body Horror Book*, *Anemone Enemy*, and *Petrified Punks* from Oscillate Wildly Press, and *Sherlock Holmes In the Realms of H.G. Wells* and *Sherlock Holmes: Adventures Beyond the Canon* from Belanger Books.

Roger Johnson, BSI, ASH, PSI, etc, is a member of more Holmesian societies than he can remember, thanks to his (so far) 16 years as editor of *The Sherlock Holmes Journal*, and thirty-two years as editor of *The District Messenger*. The latter, the newsletter of *The Sherlock Holmes Society of London*, is now in the safe hands of Jean Upton, with whom he collaborated on the well-received book, *The Sherlock Holmes Miscellany*. Roger is resigned to the fact that he will never match the Duke of Holdernesse, whose name was followed by "*half the alphabet*".

Naching T. Kassa is a wife, mother, and writer. She's created short stories, novellas, poems, and co-created three children. She resides in Eastern Washington State with her husband, Dan Kassa. Naching is a member of *The Horror Writers Association, Mystery Writers of America, The Sound of the Baskervilles, The ACD Society, The Crew of the Barque Lone Star*, and *The Sherlock Holmes Society of London*. She works in Talent Relations at Crystal Lake Publishing and was a recipient of the 2022 HWA Diversity Grant. You can find her work on Amazon.
https://www.amazon.com/Naching-T-Kassa/e/B005ZGHTI0

Susan Knight's newest novel, *Mrs. Hudson Goes to Paris* (2022) from MX publishing, is the latest in a series which began with her collection of stories, *Mrs. Hudson Investigates* (2019), the novel *Mrs. Hudson goes to Ireland* (2020), and *Mrs. Hudson Goes to Paris* (2022), and *Death in the Garden of England* (2023) She has contributed to many recent MX anthologies of new Sherlock Holmes short stories and enjoys writing as Dr. Watson as much as she does Mrs. Hudson. Nine of these stories comprised *The Strange Case of the Pale Boy and Other Mysteries* (2023). Susan is the author of two other non-Sherlockian story collections, as well as three novels, a book of non-fiction, and several plays, and has won several prizes for her writing. Susan lives in Dublin.

Daniel Lenois graduated with a Bachelor of Arts in English Literature from Central Connecticut State University in 2023. A lifelong appreciator of Sherlock Holmes since reading the original stories as a child with his father, Daniel currently moonlights as a graduate student while also pursuing his real passion in the area of literary achievement. Prior and forthcoming publications include *The Helix*, *Blue Muse*, *Unleash Lit*, *Savage Planets*, and *Shacklebound Books*.

David MacGregor is a playwright, screenwriter, novelist, and nonfiction writer. He is a resident artist at The Purple Rose Theatre in Michigan, where a number of his plays have been produced. His plays have been performed from New York to Tasmania, and his work has been published by Dramatic Publishing, Playscripts, Smith & Kraus, Applause, Heuer Publishing, and Theatrical Rights Worldwide (TRW). He adapted his dark comedy, *Vino Veritas*, for the silver screen, and it stars Carrie Preston (Emmy-winner for *The Good Wife*). Several of his short plays have also been adapted into films. He is the author of three Sherlock Holmes plays: *Sherlock Holmes and the Adventure of the Elusive Ear*, *Sherlock Holmes and the Adventure of the Fallen Soufflé*, and *Sherlock Holmes and the Adventure of the Ghost Machine*. He adapted all three plays into novels for Orange Pip Books, and also wrote the two-volume nonfiction *Sherlock Holmes: The Hero with a Thousand Faces* for MX Publishing. He teaches writing at Wayne State University in Detroit and is inordinately fond of cheese and terriers.

David Marcum plays *The Game* with deadly seriousness. He first discovered Sherlock Holmes in 1975 at the age of ten, and since that time, he has collected, read, and chronologicized literally thousands of traditional Holmes pastiches in the form of novels, short stories, radio and television episodes, movies and scripts, comics, fan-fiction, and unpublished manuscripts. He is the author of over one-hundred-twenty Sherlockian pastiches, some published in anthologies and magazines such as *The Best Mystery Stories of the Year 2021* and *The Strand*, and others collected in his own books, *The Papers of Sherlock Holmes*, *Sherlock Holmes and A Quantity of Debt*, *Sherlock Holmes – Tangled Skeins*, *Sherlock Holmes and The Eye of Heka*, and *The Collected Papers of Sherlock Holmes* – six volumes and more to come. He has won back-to-back first place fiction awards from *The Arthur Conan Doyle Society* (2023 and 2024) and the Nero Wolfe *Wolfe Pack*. He has edited over 1,100 Holmes adventures and eighty books, including dozens of traditional Sherlockian anthologies, such as the ongoing series *The MX Book of New Sherlock Holmes Stories*, which he created in 2015 to promote traditional Canonical Holmes. This collection is now at forty-five volumes, with more in preparation. He was responsible for bringing back August Derleth's Solar Pons for a new generation with his collections of authorized Pons stories, *The Papers of Solar Pons* and *The Further Papers of Solar Pons*. Pons's return was further assisted by his editing of the reissued authorized versions of the original Pons books, and then several volumes of new Pons adventures. He has done the same for the adventures of Dr. Thorndyke, and has plans for similar projects in the future. He has contributed numerous essays to various publications, and is a member of a number of Sherlockian groups and Scions, as well as *The Mystery Writers of America*. His irregular Sherlockian blog, *A Seventeen Step Program*, addresses various topics related to his favorite book friends (as his son used to call them when he was small), and can be found at *http://17stepprogram.blogspot.com/* He is a licensed Civil Engineer, living in Tennessee with his wife and son. Since the age of nineteen, he has worn a deerstalker as his regular-and-only hat. In 2013, he and his deerstalker were finally able make his first trip-of-a-lifetime Holmes Pilgrimage to England, with return Pilgrimages in 2015 and 2016, where you may have spotted him. Another is planned in mid-2024. If you ever run into him and his deerstalker out and about, feel free to say hello!

Kevin Patrick McCann has published eight collections of poems for adults, one for children (*Diary of a Shapeshifter*, Beul Aithris), a book of ghost stories (*It's Gone Dark*, The Otherside Books), *Teach Yourself Self-Publishing* (Hodder) co-written with the playwright Tom Green, and *Ov* (Beul Aithris Publications) a fantasy novel for children.

Sidney Paget (1860-1908), a few of whose illustrations are used within this anthology, was born in London, and like his two older brothers, became a famed illustrator and painter. He completed over three-hundred-and-fifty drawings for the Sherlock Holmes stories that were first published in *The Strand* magazine, defining Holmes's image forever after in the public mind.

Tracy J. Revels, BSI, a Sherlockian from the age of eleven, is a professor of history at Wofford College in Spartanburg, South Carolina. She is a member of *The Survivors of the Gloria Scott* and *The Studious Scarlets Society*, and is a past recipient of the Beacon Society Award. Almost every semester, she teaches a class that covers The Canon, either to college students or to senior citizens. She is also the author of three supernatural Sherlockian pastiches with MX (*Shadowfall*, *Shadowblood*, and *Shadowwraith*), and a regular contributor to her scion's newsletter. She also has some notoriety as an author of very silly skits: For proof, see "The Adventure of the Adversarial Adventuress" and "Occupy Baker Street" on YouTube. When not studying Sherlock, she can be found researching the history of her native state, and has written books on Florida in the Civil War and on the development of Florida's tourism industry.

Jonathan Schneer is an *emeritus* professor at the Georgia Institute of Technology, where he taught modern British history for thirty years. He has written nine history books published by university and commercial presses. His work has been translated into Russian, Chinese, Turkish, Estonian, French, and German. He has held many visiting fellowships at Oxford and Cambridge Universities, and elsewhere, has spoken about his books on radio, television, and podcasts, at seminars, conferences, meetings, book fairs, community centers, museums, libraries, book stores, etc. Now that he is retired, he divides his time between Williamstown, MA, and Decatur, GA. He certainly enjoys writing about Sherlock Holmes.

Hailing from Bedford in the South East of England, **Matthew Simmonds** has been a confirmed devotee of Sir Arthur Conan Doyle's most famous creation since first watching Jeremy Brett's incomparable portrayal of the world's first consulting detective, on a Tuesday evening in April 1984, while curled up on the sofa with his father. He has written numerous short stories and his first novel, *Sherlock Holmes: The Adventure of The Pigtail Twist* was published in 2018. A sequel, *Sherlock Holmes: The Adventure of The Found Note* was published in November 2023. Matthew currently co-owns Harrison & Simmonds, the fifth-generation family business, a renowned County tobacconist, pipe and gift shop on Bedford High Street.

Shane Simmons is the author of the occult detective novels *necropolis* and *Epitaph*, and the crime collection *Raw and Other Stories*. An award-winning screenwriter and graphic novelist, his work has appeared in international film festivals, museums, and lectures about design and structure. He was born in Lachine, a suburb of Montreal best known for being massacred in 1689 and having a joke name. Visit Shane's homepage at *eyestrainproductions.com* for more information.

Daniel Stashower, BSI, is an acclaimed biographer and narrative historian and winner of the Edgar, Agatha, and Anthony awards, as well as the Raymond Chandler Fulbright Fellowship in Detective Fiction. His work has appeared in *The New York Times*, *The Washington Post*, *Smithsonian Magazine*, *AARP: The Magazine*, *National Geographic Traveler*, and *American History*, as well as other publications. His books include *The Ectoplasmic Man*, *The Hour of Peril*, *Teller of Tales*, and *The Beautiful Cigar Girl*.

Thomas A. (Tom) Turley has been "hooked on Holmes" since finishing *The Hound of the Baskervilles* at about the age of twelve. However, his interest in Sherlockian pastiches didn't take off until he wrote one. *Sherlock Holmes and the Adventure of the Tainted Canister* (2014) is available as an e-book and an audiobook from MX Publishing. It also appeared in *The Art of Sherlock Holmes – USA Edition 1*. In 2017, two of Tom's stories, "A Scandal in Serbia" and "A Ghost from Christmas Past" were published in Parts VI and VII of this anthology. "Ghost" was also included in *The Art of Sherlock Holmes – West Palm Beach Edition*. Meanwhile, Tom published two collection of historical pastiches entitled *Sherlock Holmes and the Crowned Heads of Europe* (2021) and *Watson's Wives and Other Tales of Sherlock Holmes* (2024). Although he has a Ph.D. in British history, Tom spent most of his professional career as an archivist with the State of Alabama. He and his wife Paula (an aspiring science fiction novelist) live in Montgomery, Alabama. Interested readers may contact Tom through MX Publishing or his Goodreads author's page.

DJ Tyrer is the person behind Atlantean Publishing and has had fiction featuring Sherlock Holmes published in volumes from MX Publishing and Belanger Books, and an issue of *Awesome Tales*, and has a forthcoming story in *Sherlock Holmes Mystery Magazine*. DJ's non-Sherlockian mysteries can be found in anthologies such as *Mardi Gras Mysteries* (Mystery and Horror LLC) and *The Trench Coat Chronicles* (Celestial Echo Press), and on *Mystery Tribune*.

DJ Tyrer's website is at *https://djtyrer.blogspot.co.uk/*
DJ's Facebook page is at *https://www.facebook.com/DJTyrerwriter/*
The Atlantean Publishing website is at *https://atlanteanpublishing.wordpress.com/*

I.A. Watson's first professional publishing credit was with a Sherlock Holmes story. The tale in this book will be his 50th (counting his novel *Holmes and Houdini*, and one or two short stories in publishers' queues). He is constantly surprised at how many ways there are to tell Sherlock Holmes adventures, which he holds to be a sign of Sir Arthur Conan Doyle's genius in developing so flexible and resilient a format for such a compelling cast of characters. A full list of I.A. Watson's 100+ published works including twenty or so novels is available at:

http://www.chillwater.org.uk/writing/iawatsonhome.htm

Emma West joined Undershaw in April 2021 as the Director of Education with a brief to ensure that qualifications formed the bedrock of our provision, whilst facilitating a positive balance between academia, pastoral care, and well-being. She quickly took on the role of Acting Headteacher from early summer 2021. Under her leadership, Undershaw has embraced its new name, new vision, and consequently we have seen an exponential increase in demand for places. There is a buzz in the air as we invite prospective students and families through the doors. Emma has overseen a strategic review, re-cemented relationships with Local Authorities, and positioned Undershaw at the helm of SEND education in Surrey and beyond. Undershaw has a wide appeal: Our students present to us with mild to moderate learning needs and therefore may have some very recent memories of poor experiences in their previous schools. Emma's background as a senior leader within the independent school sector has meant she is well-versed in brokering relationships between the key stakeholders, our many interdependences, local businesses, families, and staff, and all this while ensuring Undershaw remains relentlessly child-centric in its approach. Emma's energetic smile and boundless enthusiasm for Undershaw is inspiring.

Marcia Wilson is a freelance researcher and illustrator who likes to work in a style compatible for the color blind and visually impaired. She is Canon-centric, and her first MX offering, *You Buy Bones*, uses the point-of-view of Scotland Yard to show the unique talents of Dr. Watson. This continued with the publication of *Test of the Professionals: The Adventure of the Flying Blue Pidgeon* and *The Peaceful Night Poisonings*. She can be contacted at: *gravelgirty.deviantart.com*

The following contributors appear in these companion volumes:
Part XLIII– 2024 Annual (1874-1888)
Part XLV – 2024 Annual (1898-1917)

Ian Ableson is an ecologist by training and a writer by choice. When not reading or writing, he can reliably be found scowling at a clipboard while ankle-deep in a marsh somewhere in Michigan. His love for the stories of Arthur Conan Doyle started when his grandfather gave him a copy of *The Original Illustrated Sherlock Holmes* when he was in high school, and he's proud to have been able to contribute to the continuation of the tales of Sherlock Holmes and Dr. Watson.

Mike Adamson holds a Doctoral degree from Flinders University of South Australia. After early aspirations in art and writing, Mike secured qualifications in both marine biology and archaeology. Mike has been a university educator since 2006, has worked in the replication of convincing ancient fossils, is a passionate photographer, master-level hobbyist, and journalist for international magazines. Short fiction sales include to *Metastellar*, *Strand Magazine*, *Little Blue Marble*, *Abyss*, and *Apex*, *Daily Science Fiction*, *Compelling Science Fiction*, and *Nature Futures*. Mike has placed some two-hundred stories to date, totaling over a million words. Mike has completed his first Sherlock Holmes novel with Belanger Books, and will be appearing in translation in European magazines. You can catch up with his journey at his blog "The View From the Keyboard"
http://mike-adamson.blogspot.com

Gretchen Altabef has authored five Sherlock Holmes novels. Her stories, though murder mysteries, are full of hope and the bonhomie of friendship. Her fictional journeys grow out of her historical research. She shares with her main character a half-humorous perspective on the world and the creative application of imagination, and intuition. She is a member of *The Sherlock Holmes Society of London*, *The Adventuresses of Sherlock Holmes*, *The ACD Society*, *The John H. Watson Society*, and *The Sherlock Holmes Society of India.*

Tim Newton Anderson is a former senior daily newspaper journalist and PR manager who has recently started writing fiction. In the past six months, he has placed fourteen stories in publications including *Parsec Magazine*, *Tales of the Shadowmen*, *SF Writers Guild*, *Zoetic Press*, *Dark Lane Books*, *Dark Horses Magazine*, *Emanations*, and *Planet Bizarro.*

Donald I. Baxter has practiced medicine for over forty years. He resides in Erie Pennsylvania with his wife and their dog. His family and his friends are for the most part lawyers who have given him the ability to make stuff up just as they do.

Craig Stephen Copland confesses that he discovered Sherlock Holmes when, sometime in the muddled early 1960's, he pinched his older brother's copy of the immortal stories and was forever afterward thoroughly hooked. He is very grateful to his high school English teachers in Toronto who inculcated in him a love of literature and writing, and even inspired him to be an English major at the University of Toronto. There he was blessed to sit at the feet of both Northrup Frye and Marshall McLuhan, and other great literary professors, who led him to believe that he was called to be a high school English teacher. It was his good fortune to come to his pecuniary senses, abandon that goal, and pursue a varied professional career that took him to over one-hundred countries and endless adventures. He considers himself to have been and to continue to be one of the luckiest men on God's good earth. A few years back he took a step in the direction of Sherlockian studies and joined *The Sherlock Holmes Society of Canada* – also known as *The Toronto Bootmakers*. In May of 2014, this esteemed group of scholars announced a contest for the writing of a new Sherlock Holmes mystery. Although he had never tried his hand at fiction before, Craig entered and was pleasantly surprised to be selected as one of the winners. Having enjoyed the experience, he decided to write more of the same, and he has now written new Sherlock Holmes mysteries related to and inspired by each of the sixty stories in the original Canon, along with a number of others.

Martin Daley was born in Carlisle, Cumbria in 1964. His thirty-year writing career has seen over twenty books and numerous short stories published. Inevitably, Holmes and Watson remain his favourite literary characters, and they continue to inspire his own detective writing. In 2010, Martin created Inspector Cornelius Armstrong, who carries out his police work against the backdrop of Edwardian Carlisle. With the publication of the first *Inspector Armstrong Casebook* (published by MX Publishing), Martin became a member of the Crime Writers' Association. Most recently, he published *The Selected Cases of Sherlock Holmes*. He lives with his wife Wendy, in Kirkcudbrightshire, in Southwest.

Alan Dimes also has stories in Parts XLIII and XLV

Brett Fawcett is a humanities and Latin teacher at the Chesterton Academy of St. Isidore in Sherwood Park, Alberta. He lives with his wife and son in Edmonton, where he is a member of The Wisteria Lodgers (The Sherlock Holmes Society of Edmonton). He vividly remembers the first time he finished reading the Sherlock Holmes stories in Grade 6, and has been a student of Holmesian literature and scholarship since then. He is also a frequent author of columns and articles on topics like theology, education, and mental health, as well as the occasional mystery story.

Arthur Hall also has stories in Parts XLIII and XLV

Paula Hammond also has a story in Part XLIII

Paul Hiscock is an author of crime, fantasy, horror, and science fiction tales. His short stories have appeared in a variety of anthologies, and include a seventeenth-century whodunnit, a science fiction western, a clockpunk fairytale, and numerous Sherlock Holmes pastiches. He lives with his family in Kent (England) and spends his days taking care of his two children. You can find out more about Paul's writing at: *www.detectivesanddragons.uk.*

Kelvin I. Jones is the author of six books about Sherlock Holmes and the definitive biography of Conan Doyle as a spiritualist, *Conan Doyle and The Spirits*. A member of *The Sherlock Holmes Society of London*, he has published numerous short occult and ghost stories in British anthologies over the last thirty years. His work has appeared on BBC Radio, and in 1984 he won the Mason Hall Literary Award for his poem cycle about the survivors of Hiroshima and Nagasaki, recently reprinted as "Omega". (Oakmagic Publications) A one-time teacher of creative writing at the University of East Anglia, he is also the author of four crime novels featuring his ex-met sleuth John Bottrell, who first appeared in *Stone Dead*. He has over fifty titles on Kindle, and is also the author of several novellas and short story collections featuring a Norwich based detective, DCI Ketch, an intrepid sleuth who investigates East Anglian murder cases. He also published a series of short stories about an Edwardian psychic detective, Dr. John Carter (*Carter's Occult Casebook*). Ramsey Campbell, the British horror writer, and Francis King, the renowned novelist, have both compared his supernatural stories to those of M. R. James. He has also published children's fiction, namely *Odin's Eye*, and, in collaboration with his wife Debbie, *The Dark Entry*. Since 1995, he has been the proprietor of Oakmagic Publications, publishers of British folklore and of his fiction titles.

Daniel Lenois also has stories in Parts XLIII and XLV

Jeffrey Lockwood spent youthful afternoons darkly enchanted by feeding grasshoppers to black widows in his New Mexican backyard, which accounts for his scientific and literary affinities. He earned a doctorate in entomology, and worked as an ecologist at the University of Wyoming before metamorphosing into a Professor of Natural Sciences & Humanities in the departments of philosophy and creative writing. He considers Sherlock Holmes a model of scientific prowess, integrating exquisite observational skills with incisive abductive (not deductive) reasoning.

David Marcum also has stories in Parts XLIII and XLV

Mark Mower is a long-standing member of the *Crime Writers' Association*, *The Sherlock Holmes Society of London*, and *The Solar Pons Society of London*. His pastiche collections include *Sherlock Holmes: The Baker Street Case-Files*, *Sherlock Holmes: The Baker Street Legacy*, *Sherlock Holmes: The Baker Street Epilogue*, and *Sherlock Holmes: The Baker Street Archive* (all with MX Publishing). His non-fiction works include the bestselling book *Zeppelin Over Suffolk: The Final Raid of the L48* (Pen & Sword Books). Alongside his writing, Mark maintains a sizeable collection of pastiches, and never tires of discovering new stories about Sherlock Holmes and Dr. Watson.

Will Murray is the author of some 75 novels, including some 20 posthumous Doc Savage collaborations with Lester Dent, and 40 books in the long-running Destroyer series. Other Murray novels star the Executioner, Tarzan of the Apes, The Spider, Pat Savage and the Mars Attacks characters. His book, *Nick Fury, Agent of S.H.I.E.L.D.: Empyre* (2000) foreshadowed the 9/11 terrorist attacks. Murray has penned more than 45 Sherlock Holmes short stories. Twenty of Murray's Holmes short stories have been collected as *The Wild Adventures of Sherlock Holmes*, Vols 1 and 2. His novelette, "The Adventure of the Vengeful Viscount", in which Tarzan of the Apes, otherwise Lord Greystoke, hires Sherlock Holmes to solve a mystery, was approved by both the Estate of Sir Arthur Conan Doyle and Edgar Rice Burroughs, Inc. Murray is the author of the non-fiction book, *Master of Mystery: The Rise of The Shadow*, which is an exploration of the famous radio and magazine character, and a sequel, *Dark Avenger: The Strange Saga of The Shadow. The*

Wild Adventures of Cthulhu Vols 1 & 2 collect Murray's Lovecraftan short stories. For Marvel Comics, Murray created the Unbeatable Squirrel Girl with legendary artist Steve Ditko. Website:
www.adventuresinbronze.com

Ember Pepper was born and raised in San Diego, CA. She has an M.F.A. degree in Creative Fiction Writing. She has been a fan of The Great Detective since she was a pre-teen and her greatest artistic enjoyment is challenging herself to write quality pastiches of Sherlock Holmes and his stalwart biographer and friend, John Watson.

Tracy J. Revels also has stories in Parts XLIII and XLV

Roger Riccard's family history has Scottish roots, which trace his lineage back to Highland Scotland. This British Isles ancestry encouraged his interest in the writings of Sir Arthur Conan Doyle at an early age. He has authored the novels, *Sherlock Holmes & The Case of the Poisoned Lilly*, and *Sherlock Holmes & The Case of the Twain Papers*. In addition he has produced several short stories in *Sherlock Holmes Adventures for the Twelve Days of Christmas* and the series *A Sherlock Holmes Alphabet of Cases*. A new series will begin publishing in the Autumn of 2022, and his has another novel in the works. All of his books have been published by Baker Street Studios. His Bachelor of Arts Degrees in both Journalism and History from California State University, Northridge, have proven valuable to his writing historical fiction, as well as the encouragement of his wife/editor/inspiration and Sherlock Holmes fan, Rosilyn. She passed in 2021, and it is in her memory that he continues to contribute to the legacy of the "*man who never lived and will never die*".

Dan Rowley practiced law for over forty years in private practice and with a large international corporation. He is retired and lives in Erie, Pennsylvania, with his wife Judy, who puts her artistic eye to his transcription of Watson's manuscripts. He inherited his writing ability and creativity from his children, Jim and Katy, and his love of mysteries from his parents, Jim and Ruth.

Jane Rubino is the author of *A Jersey Shore* mystery series, featuring a Jane Austen-loving amateur sleuth and a Sherlock Holmes-quoting detective, *Knight Errant, Lady Vernon and Her Daughter*, (a novel-length adaptation of Jane Austen's novella *Lady Susan*, co-authored with her daughter Caitlen Rubino-Bradway, *What Would Austen Do?*, also co-authored with her daughter, a short story in the anthology *Jane Austen Made Me Do It, The Rucastles' Pawn, The Copper Beeches from Violet Turner's POV*, and, of course, there's the Sherlockian novel in the drawer – who doesn't have one? Jane lives on a barrier island at the New Jersey shore.

Jonathan Schneer also has a story in Part XLIII

Fifteen of **Brenda Seabrooke**'s Sherlock Holmes pastiches have been anthologized in MX Publishing and Belanger Books, six in *Best Crime Stories of New England*, one in *Destination: Mystery* and *Mystery Tribune*, and twelve in literary reviews such as *Yemassee, Confrontation*, and one in *Redbook*. Twenty-two of her books for young readers have been published at Penguin, Clarion, etc., and won awards such as a Notable from the National Council of Social Studies, Junior Literary Guild, Hornbook Honor, an Edgar finalist, etc. She received a grant from the National Endowment for the Arts, and The Robie

Macauley Award from Emerson College. In 2022, MX published her collection, *Sherlock Holmes: The Persian Slipper and Other Stories*.

Alisha Shea has resided near Saint Louis, Missouri for over thirty years. The eldest of six children, she found reading to be a genuine escape from the chaotic drudgery of life. She grew to love not only Sherlock Holmes, but the time period from which he emerged. In her spare time, she indulges in creating music via piano, violin, and Native American flute. Sometimes she thinks she might even be getting good at it. She also produces a wide variety of fiber arts which are typically given away or auctioned off for various fundraisers.

Peter Shumway is a retired computer professional residing in Pennsylvania with his wife, Patty. They have been married forty-one years and have two daughters and four grandchildren. In the early 1970's, Peter performed magic with Bill Baker's World of Magic, John Bundy's Magic Concert, and traded secrets with David Copperfield when they were teenagers. Peter read the original Sherlock Holmes stories while in college in 1979, and has enjoyed rereading them many times since. He published his pastiche *Sherlock Holmes and The Kiss of Death in* 2005 and *Gullible's Journey* in 2023. When he was offered the opportunity to write a short story for the MX Series, he picked up his pen one more time.

Hailing from Bedford in the South East of England, **Matthew Simmonds** has been a confirmed devotee of Sir Arthur Conan Doyle's most famous creation since first watching Jeremy Brett's incomparable portrayal of the world's first consulting detective, on a Tuesday evening in April 1984, while curled up on the sofa with his father. He has written numerous short stories and his first novel, *Sherlock Holmes: The Adventure of The Pigtail Twist* was published in 2018. A sequel, *Sherlock Holmes: The Adventure of The Found Note* was published in November 2023. Matthew currently co-owns Harrison & Simmonds, the fifth-generation family business, a renowned County tobacconist, pipe and gift shop on Bedford High Street.

Denis O. Smith's first published story of Sherlock Holmes and Doctor Watson, "The Adventure of The Purple Hand", appeared in 1982. Since then, numerous other such accounts have been published in magazines and anthologies both in the U.K. and the U.S. In the 1990's, four volumes of his stories were published under the general title of *The Chronicles of Sherlock Holmes*, and, more recently his stories have been collected as *The Lost Chronicles of Sherlock Holmes* (2014), *The Lost Chronicles of Sherlock Holmes Volume II* (2016), *The Further Chronicles of Sherlock Holmes* (2018). He also wrote a Holmes novel, *The Riddle of Foxwood Grange* (2017). Born in Yorkshire, in the north of England, Denis Smith has lived and worked in various parts of the country, including London, and has now been resident in Norfolk for many years. His interests range widely, but apart from his dedication to the career of Sherlock Holmes, he has a passion for historical mysteries of all kinds, the railways of Britain and the history of London.

Robert V. Stapleton was born and brought up in Leeds, Yorkshire, England, and studied at Durham University. After working in various parts of the country as an Anglican parish priest, he is now retired and lives with his wife in North Yorkshire. As a member of his local writing group, he now has time to develop his other life as a writer of adventure stories. He has published a number of short stories, and he is hoping to have a couple of completed novels published at some time in the future.

Kevin P. Thornton has had a varied career. He has been a soldier, a military contractor, a logistics consultant and, at various times, a forklift driver and a barman. It was not a well-thought-out path. He has played rugby, cricket, and other games of violence with virtually no success but plenty of gusto, and has the aches and scars to prove so. He has also had a varied writing career. In his time, he has written for *The New York Times* on the wildfires in Alberta, as well as a long running column in the *Fort McMurray Today*. He has had poetry published in more than a dozen collections, some of which have even sold commercially. He has also edited a journal on a military base in Afghanistan, and is currently the chief and only writer of a magazine for a Dene and Cree First Nation in Canada. He has written about half-a-dozen books, all of which were shortlisted in the *Crime Writers of Canada* unpublished awards, all of which are still unpublished. He has had rather more success with short stories, with somewhere around thirty anthologized. Many of these involve Sherlock Holmes and, while he would hesitate to call himself a Sherlockian – just as he hesitates over such titles as author, poet, journalist, columnist, editor – he is quite fond of the gentlemen of 221b. "They allow me to write crime stories succinctly, and if I were to title myself, I would take that as a starting point; if forced to take a stand I would describe myself as a storyteller." Kevin is one of the founding members of the *Northwords Literary Mag*azine of Fort McMurray, Alta. and a current or former member of the CWG, WGA, CWC, CWA, MWA, ITW, S-in-C, MofM, and the IACW. Decoding available on request. In 2015, he was accepted as a member of *The Keys*, the London based organization of writers founded by G.K. Chesterton and Ronald Knox. He has two sons of whom he is enormously proud, and a wife he adores, and who in turn seems to love and tolerate him, depending on the mood and the moment.

Daniel D. Victor is a retired high school English teacher who lives with his wife in his native Los Angeles, California. His doctoral dissertation on the assassinated American writer David Graham Phillips led to Victor's first Sherlock Holmes pastiche, *The Seventh Bullet* (St. Martin's Press) and ultimately to his ongoing series, *Sherlock Holmes and the American Literati*. Each novel in the series introduces Holmes to an American author who was writing during the period Holmes was detecting. Victor has also recently published *Cruel September*, a novel based on his many years of teaching in Los Angeles.

Marcia Wilson also has stories in Parts XLIII and XLV.

478

The MX Book of New Sherlock Holmes Stories

Edited by David Marcum

(MX Publishing, 2015-   )

"This is the finest volume of Sherlockian fiction I have ever read, and I have read, literally, thousands." – Philip K. Jones

"Beyond Impressive . . . This is a splendid venture for a great cause!"
– Roger Johnson, Editor, *The Sherlock Holmes Journal*,
The Sherlock Holmes Society of London

Part I: 1881-1889; Part II: 1890-1895; Part III: 1896-1929

Part IV: 2016 Annual

Part V: Christmas Adventures

Part VI: 2017 Annual

Eliminate the Impossible
Part VII: (1880-1891); Part VIII: (1892-1905)

2018 Annual
Part IX: (1879-1895); Part X: (1896-1916)

Some Untold Cases
Part XI: (1880-1891); Part XII: (1894-1902)

2019 Annual
Part XIII: (1881-1890); Part XIV: (1891-1897); Part XV: (1898-1917)

Whatever Remains . . . Must be the Truth
Part XVI: (1881-1890); Part XVII: (1891-1898); Part XVIII: (1898-1925)

2020 Annual
Part XIX: (1882-1890); Part XX: (1891-1897); Part XXI: (1898-1923)·

Some More Untold Cases
Part XXII: (1877-1887); Part XXIII: (1888-1894); Part XXIV: (1895-1903)

2021 Annual
Part XXV: (1881-1888); Part XXVI: (1889-1897); Part XXVII: (1898-1928)

More Christmas Adventures
Part XXVIII: (1869-1888); Part XXIX: (1889-1896); Part XXX: (1897-1928)

2022 Annual
Part XXXI: (1875-1887); Part XXXII: (1888-1895); Part XXXIII: (1896-1919)

"However Improbable . . . ."
Part XXXIV: (1878-1888); Part XXXV: (1889-1896); Part XXXVI: (1897-1919)

2023 Annual
Parts XXXVII (1875-1889), XXXVIII (1889-1896), and XXXIX (1897-1923)

Further Untold Cases
Part XL: (1879-1886), Part XLI: (1887-1892) and Part XLII: (1894-1922)

2024 Annual
Parts XLIII (1874-1888), XLIV (1889-1897), and XLV (1898-1917)

In Preparation *. . . Part XLVI (and XLVII and XLVIII as well?)*
and more to come!

The MX Book of New Sherlock Holmes Stories
Edited by David Marcum
(MX Publishing, 2015-   )

Part VI: *The traditional pastiche is alive and well . . . .*

Part VII: *Sherlockians eager for faithful-to-the-canon plots and characters will be delighted.*

Part VIII: *The imagination of the contributors in coming up with variations on the volume's theme is matched by their ingenious resolutions.*

Part IX: *The 18 stories . . . will satisfy fans of Conan Doyle's originals. Sherlockians will rejoice that more volumes are on the way.*

Part X: *. . . new Sherlock Holmes adventures of consistently high quality.*

Part XI: *. . . an essential volume for Sherlock Holmes fans.*

Part XII: *. . . continues to amaze with the number of high-quality pastiches.*

Part XIII: *. . . Amazingly, Marcum has found 22 superb pastiches . . . his is more catnip for fans of stories faithful to Conan Doyle's original*

Part XIV: *. . . this standout anthology of 21 short stories written in the spirit of Conan Doyle's originals.*

Part XV: *Stories pitting Sherlock Holmes against seemingly supernatural phenomena highlight Marcum's 15th anthology of superior short pastiches.*

Part XVI: *Marcum has once again done fans of Conan Doyle's originals a service.*

Part XVII: *This is yet another impressive array of new but traditional Holmes stories.*

Part XVIII: *Sherlockians will again be grateful to Marcum and MX for high-quality new Holmes tales.*

Part XIX: *Inventive plots and intriguing explorations of aspects of Dr. Watson's life and beliefs lift the 24 pastiches in Marcum's impressive 19th Sherlock Holmes anthology*

Part XX: *Marcum's reserve of high-quality new Holmes exploits seems endless.*

Part XXI: *This is another must-have for Sherlockians.*

Part XXII: *Marcum's superlative 22nd Sherlock Holmes pastiche anthology features 21 short stories that successfully emulate the spirit of Conan Doyle's originals while expanding on the canon's tantalizing references to mysteries Dr. Watson never got around to chronicling.*

Part XXIII: *Marcum's well of talented authors able to mimic the feel of The Canon seems bottomless.*

Part XXIV: *Marcum's expertise at selecting high-quality pastiches remains impressive.*

Part XXVIII: *All entries adhere to the spirit, language, and characterizations of Conan Doyle's originals, evincing the deep pool of talent Marcum has access to. Against the odds, this series remains strong, hundreds of stories in.*

Part XXXI: *. . . yet another stellar anthology of 21 short pastiches that effectively mimic the originals . . . Marcum's diligent searches for high-quality stories has again paid off for Sherlockians.*

Part XXXIV: *Mind-bending puzzles are the highlight of Marcum's fully satisfying 34th anthology, which again demonstrates that multiple authors are capable of giving Sherlock Holmes and Watson innovative mysteries to tackle while staying in character. Marcum's inventory of canonical pastiches shows no signs of being exhausted any time soon.*

The MX Book of New Sherlock Holmes Stories
Edited by David Marcum
(MX Publishing, 2015-   )

482

An Investees' Anthology

Edited by David Marcum

(MX Publishing, 2022)

Selected Contributions to
The MX Book of New Sherlock Holmes Stories
by Members of
The Baker Street Irregulars

*All royalties from this collection are being donated
for the benefit of the preservation of Undershaw,
a school for special needs students located at
one of the former homes of Sir Arthur Conan Doyle*

Stories, Forewords, and Poems in this volume
have previously appeared in Parts I – XXXVI of
The MX Book of New Sherlock Holmes Stories

Featuring Contributions by:

Mark Alberstat, Marino C. Alvarez, Peter Calamai, Catherine Cooke, Carla Coupe, David Stuart Davies, John Farrell, Lyndsay Faye, Sonia Fetherston, Jayantika Ganguly, Jeffrey Hatcher, Roger Johnson, Leslie S. Klinger, Ann Margaret Lewis, Bonnie MacBird, Stephen Mason, Julie McKuras Nicholas Meyer, Jacquelynn Morris, Otto Penzler, Christopher Redmond, Tracy J. Revels, Steven Rothman, Nancy Holder, Mark Levy (and Arlene Mantin Levy), Nicholas Utechin, and Sean M. Wright (and DeForeest B. Wright, III)

MX Publishing

MX Publishing is the world's largest specialist Sherlock Holmes publisher, with over five-hundred titles and over two-hundred authors creating the latest in Sherlock Holmes fiction and non-fiction

The catalogue includes several award winning books, and over two-hundred-and-fifty have been converted into audio.

MX Publishing also has one of the largest communities of Holmes fans on Facebook, with regular contributions from dozens of authors.

www.mxpublishing.com

@mxpublishing on Facebook, Twitter, and Instagram